# A
# *Crown*
# *of*
# *Life*

BRIAN PATRICK MITCHELL

# A
# *Crown*
## of
# *Life*

A NOVEL OF
THE GREAT
PERSECUTION

ALEXANDRIA, VIRGINIA

A Crown of Life

Pontic Press
P.O. Box 1
Alexandria, Virginia 22313

ISBN 978-0-9910169-0-7

First Edition January 2014

Book design: John Mitchell

# Geographical Glossary
## of Ancient and Modern Names

*Abus*—Hull River, England

*Aelian Bridge (Pons Aelius)*—Newcastle upon Tyne, England

*Amasia*—Amasya, Turkey

*Amisos*—Samsun, Turkey

*Lamb River (Amnias)*—Gök River, Turkey

*Ankyra*—Ankara, Turkey

*Arelate*—Arles, France

*Augusta Taurinorum*—Turin, Italy

*Augustodunum*—Autun, France

*Basilia*—Basel, Switzerland

*Bodotria*—Firth of Forth, Scotland

*Bonna*—Bonn, Germany

*Bononia (Gesoriacum)*—Boulogne, France

*Brigantio*—Briançon, France

*Brixia*—Brescia, Italy

*Byzantium*—Istanbul (Constantinople), Turkey

*Caesarea (in Cappadocia)*—Kayseri, Turkey

*Camulodunum*—Colchester, England

*Cantii*—Kent

*Carnuntum*—halfway between Vienna, Austria, and Bratislava, Slovakia

*Carrhae*—Harran, Turkey

*Castamon*—Kastamonu, Turkey

*Cherson (Chersonesus)*—Sevastopol, Ukraine

*Claudiopolis*—Iskilip, Turkey

*Clavenna*—Chiavenna, Italy

*Colonia (Augusta Colonia)*—Köln (Cologne), Germany

*Comum*—Como, Italy

*Corduba*—Cordova, Spain

*Crococalana*—Brough, Nottinghamshire, England

*Danuvius*—Danube River

*Dubris*—Dover, England

*Eboracum (Eburacum)*—York, England

*Elvira*—Granada, Spain

*Euxine Sea (Pontos Euxeinos, "Hospitable Sea")*—Black Sea

*Temple of Fortune (Fanum Fortunae)*—Fano, Italy

*Gallic Strait*—English Channel

*Gangra*—Çankırı, Turkey

*Genua*—Genoa, Italy

*Golden Wedge (Cuneus Aureus)*—Splügen Pass

*Chain (Halys)*—Kızılırmak (Red River)

*Herakleia Pontica*—Ereğli, Turkey

*Herakleia Propontis*—Marmara Ereğlisi, Turkey

*Ionopolis (Abonitichos)*—Inebolu, Turkey

*Iris (Rainbow)*—Yeşil River

*Kerasos*—Giresun, Turkey

*Lake Larius*—Lake Como

*Londinium*—London, England

*Lugudunum*—Lyon, France

*Manduessedum*—Mancetter, Warwickshire, England

*Massilia*—Marseilles, France

*Mediolanum*—Milan, Italy

*Mogontiacum*—Mainz, Germany

*Mosella River*—Moselle (Mosel) River

*Narbo Martius*—Narbonne, France

*Neocaesarea*—Niksar, Turkey

*Nicomedia*—Izmit, Turkey

*Padus*—Po River, Italy

*Paduva*—Padova (Padua), Italy

*Phazemon*—Merzifon, Turkey

*Propontis*—Sea of Marmara, Turkey

*Rhenus*—Rhine River

*Rhodanus*—Rhone River, France

*Savus*—Sava River, Serbia

*Segusio*—Susa, Italy

*Sinope*—Sinop, Turkey

*Sirmium*—Sremska Mitrovica, Serbia

*Tamesis*—Thames River, England

*Tinus*—Tyne River, England

*Trapezus (Trebizond)*—Trabzon, Turkey

*Trinovantes*—Essex and Suffolk, England

*Treveris (Augusta Treverorum)*—Trier (Treves), Germany

*Valentia*—Valencia, Spain

*Verona* —Verona, Italy

*Verulamium*—St. Albans (Verulam), England

WESTERN
E M P I R E

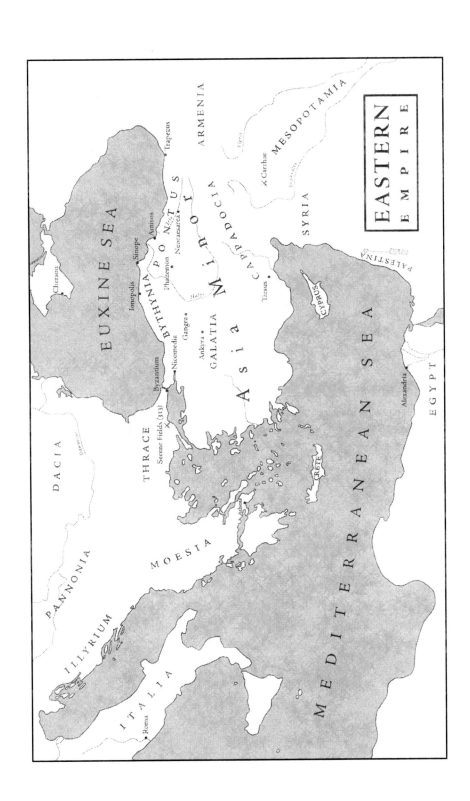

# A
# Crown
## of
# Life

*Blessed is the man that endureth temptation:*
*for when he is tried, he shall receive the crown of life,*
*which the Lord hath promised to them that love him.*

James 1:12

# I

*Ides of February*
*Nineteenth Year of the Reign of the Princeps Caesar*
*Gaius Aurelius Valerius Diocletianus*
*Pius Felix Invictus Augustus*
*Pontifex Maximus*
*Imperator*

Blood pooled upon the marble, overflowing the altar's edges and spilling onto the stone pavement in the central court of the imperial palace. Half a dozen white-robed priests labored over the altar like women in the kitchen, heads covered respectfully by their cloaks, bloody hands busy with knives and cleavers, hacking away at the flesh of sixteen geese offered in sacrifice to Jupiter, the Optimus and Maximus.

The chief priest stood with his head covered and his arms raised in prayer, entreating the god's favor. His words were obscured by the tangled melodies of a band of panpipes. Any harmony between the melodies was accidental. A pounding drum provided accompaniment, along with a jangling tambourine in the clutch of a wan young virgin swaying restlessly in rhythm, as if entranced. Smoke curled from two smaller altars flanking the main one, each attended by a single priest whose only duty was to heave a handful of incense onto the smoldering coals, for a fresh burst of smoke and odor.

The emperors Diocletian and Galerius sat side by side under a tasseled awning at the top of the steps, awaiting the results of the augury. Galerius surveyed the officers in attendance, then leaned toward Diocletian, so as not to be overheard. "Gorgonios," he said, in a low voice.

Diocletian glanced at Galerius. "What about Gorgonios?" he asked.

"He's one of them," said Galerius.

"Gorgonios? No. He can't be," said Diocletian.

"He is. I have it on the best authority."

Diocletian grunted dismissively. Still a bull of a man at sixty, he was finely attired in a long white robe, richly embroidered with gold and silver thread. A purple mantle, likewise embroidered, hung from his shoulders. Red silk slippers studded with amethyst adorned his feet. A diadem of pearls encircled his bulging cranium, Persian-style. "Whom else would you accuse?" he wondered aloud.

Galerius scanned the faces before him, then nodded to his left. "Dorotheos," he said.

"Dorotheos? No-o-o-o-o," said Diocletian, the augustus.

"Ye-e-e-e-s," said Galerius, his caesar.

"I've known Dorotheos for forty years, since we were both lowly legionaries. He couldn't possibly."

"He is. I swear it, by our divine patron. And then, of course, there's Petros."

"The eunuch?"

"Your very own chamberlain. See how close they've crept, worming their way into our very bedrooms? No wonder our wives have started listening to them. They are everywhere."

The elder emperor grunted again, shifting impatiently in his chair and adjusting his mantle. "What's taking them so long?" he groused.

Galerius shrugged.

To better rule the far-flung empire, Diocletian had promoted three fellow generals to the imperial dignity, to serve alongside him as co-emperors. Two ruled the eastern half of the empire, and two ruled the western half, with the senior emperor east and west bearing the title of *augustus* and the junior emperor east and west bearing the title of *caesar*.

Diocletian himself was the augustus of the East, and Galerius was his caesar. He was a brutish man of middle age, with narrow shoulders, a pigeon chest, and a swelling belly. His capital was in Sirmium on the Savus River, 600 miles away, but he was often at Diocletian's court in Nicomedia in western Asia Minor to confer on matters of state—and advance his own interests.

"Here comes Hierocles now," said Diocletian.

Sossianos Hierocles, governor of Bithynia and Pontus, knelt at the bottom of the steps and bowed before the emperors, touching his forehead to the pavement in an act of adoration, a Persian practice lately introduced at the Roman court.

"Lords," said Hierocles, rising to his feet. He spoke in Latin, but his form of address was also Persian. Only under Diocletian had Romans been obliged to address an emperor as *domine*—lord. "The augurs report some confusion in the reading. The signs are mixed. There is something amiss."

"Well, what is it, or don't they know?" asked the augustus.

"The sacrifice has been profaned," said Hierocles. He glanced left and right and then added ominously, "By the presence of the atheists."

The augustus rose from his chair and waved Hierocles to the top of the steps. Galerius rose also. Diocletian put his hand on Hierocles's shoulder and whispered to him, "I suppose you mean the Christians."

"Yes, my lord," answered Hierocles.

"Bastards!" said Diocletian, dropping his hand.

"See what I mean?" said Galerius. "They're a plague upon us."

"I mean the priests!" snapped Diocletian. "Now which one of you put them up to this?"

"My lord," pleaded Hierocles, "we have seen them making the Christian cross in our very midst, on the breast and on the forehead even. The priests can't help but notice, and the gods likewise. It can only displease them."

"This isn't the first time, you know. It happened twice last week," Galerius added.

"So I've heard," said Diocletian.

"They despise all gods but their own," said Hierocles. "They spoil the sacred amity among us, condemning people for living as they please, sowing the seeds of intolerance and division, inspiring hatred of their fellow man. It is an offense against our shared values as Roman citizens."

"I've read your book, Hierocles. You don't need to recite it."

"But you know he's right," said Galerius. "No god but their own. Always out for converts. Damning the rest of us as sinners. They're troublemakers, all of them."

"I know what trouble they've been as well as anyone, but why this? Why now?" said Diocletian, pointing toward the altar.

"My lord," said Hierocles, "they have used their presence here at court to increase their numbers. The treasurer, the keeper of the privy purse, the master of the wardrobe, and the grand chamberlain himself—all these are Christians. The people have begun to wonder whether the empire will desert the gods before the gods desert the empire."

"They're getting far too close to the throne," said Galerius. "Everyone's talking, wondering when we'll all fall into the thrall of this womanish superstition."

Diocletian groaned and rolled his eyes. The pounding and jangling quickened, driving the scurrying melodies into a frenzy. Galerius pressed his case.

"We've put up with them long enough," he said. "They breed dissension. They dishonor the gods. They deny the very basis of our authority. They oppose everything we do, all our reforms, all the progress we've made. It's not enough to ban them from the palace. They keep creeping back in! We must root them out once and for all."

"We have cause for concern," Diocletian said firmly. "But how do we get out of our present predicament? What will satisfy the priests?"

"Consult the gods directly, my lord," said Hierocles. "Send a delegation to the Oracle of Apollo at Didyma, near Miletus. The words of the Oracle will satisfy them, as well as provide a guide for future action."

"A guide or an excuse?" said Diocletian. "Never mind. We will send a delegation."

"I'll go myself," said Galerius.

"You'll stay right here," said Diocletian. "We'll send the boys instead, Constantine and Maxentius—and talk this out between us while they're gone."

# II

Farther east, 300 miles along the northern coast of Asia Minor, in the city of Sinope, a young woman leaned over the railing of her balcony to see the new ship in the harbor. She was not yet twenty and still unmarried, healthy but thin—thinner than most girls her age, which puzzled and worried her mother. Her face was round and somewhat flat like the people of the north, across the sea, with plump pink cheeks, full lips, olive-green eyes, and a little nub of a nose, reddened by the winter chill. It was not the prevailing standard of beauty, but it held an attraction all its own for many men. The sculptor working below in her father's shipyard had used her often—without her knowledge—as a model for the divine images he carved to fit her father's ships. For this one, she was Demeter; for that one, Artemis; for another, Athena.

Today she was worried.

"KREE-na-a-a!" cried a young voice from far inside the house.

Makrina left the balcony, closing its doors behind her.

"I saw him! I saw him!" cried her sister Eugenia, twelve years old, skipping gayly into the balcony room. Sunlight shone through the oiled lambskin stretched across the carved balcony doors, bathing the small salon in a golden glow.

"Saw who?" asked Makrina.

"*Who?* Marcus, silly! We had to wait for such a long time while they brought the boat in, but then there it was and there he was. He was the first off."

"Was he well?"

"I think so. Two arms, two legs. So far as I could tell, he had all his fingers, too. Not a scratch on him. Some soldier he is! Not like the other one," said Eugenia, alighting upon a cushioned seat near the balcony doors, "the one with the broken nose and a great scar across his cheek—*krrrrek!* Now *he's* a soldier!" She giggled.

Makrina sat down next to her. "But Marcus, how did he look?"

"As handsome as ever," Eugenia answered. "The handsomest of all. He's the man of my dreams. If you die, can I marry him?"

"Don't be silly. Now tell me seriously, was he in good spirits?"

"I guess so," said Eugenia. "Maybe a little tired, but happy to see Kimon."

"Kimon was there? Oh, no!"

"Yes, unfortunately. I'd have gotten to say hello if Kimon hadn't seen me first and sent me home. But I did see him greet Marcus. Marcus looked happy then."

Makrina stood and paced the room. "Oh, Kimon! He'll spoil every-thing. What am I going to do? What am I going to do, Eugenia?"

"Huh?"

"Oh, never mind," said Makrina, turning to her sister. "Go find Kimon and tell him I must see him at once! And without Marcus. Now go!"

"Oh, all right," said Eugenia before hurrying off. Makrina returned to the balcony, parting the doors for another peek at the harbor.

It wasn't long before she heard her brother's voice and went to meet him.

The family house in town was built around a court, partly paved and partly planted. On the ground-floor, around the court, were many rooms: a sparsely furnished atrium for receiving visitors; a tablinum with sofas, chairs, and side tables for relaxing; a triclinium for dining; a kitchen and pantry; a private bath in the back, overlooking the bay; a row of cubicles for the men of the house to sleep in; and directly below the balcony room, a study for Makrina's father. The women's rooms were upstairs: sleeping cubicles, dressing rooms, and the balcony room or ladies' tablinum.

From the gallery outside the balcony room, Makrina looked down and called for her brother: "Kimon!"

Kimon appeared below at the far side of the court. He was tall and thin and several years her senior, with dark eyes and hair and a black beard cut close. His deep green cloak was swept to one side, revealing his loose-fitting Dalmatian tunic underneath. Fine laced boots with soft soles protected his feet. Only his knees were bare.

"Yes, Makrina?" he answered, looking up at her with a wide, teasing grin revealing a full set of long white teeth.

"May I speak with you for a moment, up here?"

Kimon made his way idly up the stairs, torturing his sister with every slow step. He found Makrina once again in the balcony room. "Yes? What is it?" he asked.

"You saw Marcus?"

"I did."

"And he is well?"

"He is. Very well, I should say. Anxious to return to Rome, though."

"Did he speak of me?"

"Not a word."

"Liar," said Makrina. "You're as foolish as Eugenia. She gets it from you, you should know."

"Certainly not from you, my saintly sister," said Kimon. "Of course, he spoke of you, Makrina. He can't stop speaking of you."

"What did he say about me?" she asked.

"Well," began Kimon, "he said he's madly in love with you and can't wait to marry you and beget a brood of little Marcuses and Makrinas, or some such nonsense."

"What did he really say about me, Kimon?"

"I can't remember his exact words, Makrina. I wasn't collecting his deposition."

"Then how did he say it?"

"What do you mean, how did he say it? He said it as if he had lost his senses. How would you expect?"

"Did he say anything else? About me, I mean."

"No, I couldn't bear it any longer and made him stop," said Kimon.

"Oh, you've had too much wine. Now what did you tell him?"

"I told him we lost three ships in last month's storm."

"About *me*, you fool—what did you tell him?"

"I told him nothing."

"I don't believe you."

"I told him that you are purer than Athena and that he doesn't deserve anyone so virtuous."

"Be serious, Kimon. What did you tell him?"

"I told him just that. I swear, by Athena," said Kimon.

"Did you tell him anything else?"

"No, Makrina. I have kept your secret."

"As you kept it from Nonna?!"

"I learned my lesson, Makrina. I swear, by Athena," said Kimon.

"Not by Athena!"

"Whatever you say, Makrina."

"You told him nothing?"

"Did you want me to tell him?"

"No!"

"Then all is well."

"All is not well!" cried Makrina, sinking onto the couch by the balcony. "All is wrong! Marcus must still be told! And then Mamma and Pappa. Oh, Kimon, what am I going to do?"

"You must tell him, Makrina," he said, sitting down next to her. "And you must not wait long. He deserves to know."

"Maybe you can tell him first, Kimon. At least he will be forewarned and I won't have to pretend when I first see him."

"I won't have time, Makrina. He'll be here within the hour."

"Within the hour?! But I'm not ready! I can't face him yet!"

"Makrina, he's been away five months. The Furies couldn't keep him away longer," said Kimon. "You'll have to face him, but you can wait until after dinner to tell him."

Makrina dropped her head upon Kimon's shoulder and took hold of his arm with both hands. "Oh, Kimon, what am I going to do?" she moaned. "I can't face him yet. I'm not ready."

"Well," said Kimon, thinking aloud, "you don't have to be here when he arrives. If you need more time, go out for a while. Go for a walk."

She lifted her head. "Decent women don't stroll around town alone at this hour. You know that."

"Go see a friend, then. Go see Chione."

"Chione's no help," moaned Makrina.

"Why not? She got you into this."

"It wasn't just her."

"Then go see whoever it was. The least they could do is help you figure a way out."

"There is no way out," Makrina whined.

"Then say your prayers, Makrina. He'll be here soon."

Makrina arose abruptly. "That's it," she announced. She turned to face him. "Tell them I've gone to see Chione and will be back soon."

Kimon nodded. "You've gone to Chione's and will be back soon."

"And don't say anything else."

"I won't say anything else."

"Thank you, Kimon! I love you," she said, kissing him on the lips before hurrying off.

Makrina did not return for some time. "Where is she anyway?" her father Aristoboulos asked. "She should have been home by now."

Kimon shrugged. "I've sent for her at Chione's, but neither she nor Chione were there. She should be home soon, though," he said.

Aristoboulos frowned and grunted in acknowledgment.

They were standing in the court with Philodemos, the mayor of Sinope, and a young Italian tribune, Marcus Aemilius Canio. The sky overhead was still blue, but the winter sun had already begun to set, leaving the house in cool shadows.

"So, Canio, what does your father think of the reforms coming out of the capital these days?" asked Philodemos. "Canio?"

Marcus turned to the mayor suddenly. "I'm sorry, sir. What did you say?" He was wearing a short, trim, blue uniform tunic, quite unlike the loose and droopy dalmatics of the others, although it did have long sleeves. Even more unusual were his trousers, which only soldiers wore and only then when it was cold. A scarlet chlamys with a narrow purple border hung from his shoulders, regulation dress for a tribune second class. The rectangular cloak was pinned upon his right shoulder with a golden eagle of his own choosing. Around his waist he wore an officer's cingulum—a red leather belt with a silver buckle. Buff boots covered his feet and shins. His hands were square and strong. His hair was curly brown and neatly clipped. His face was freshly shaven and even-featured, with soft brown eyes, a slightly Roman nose, thin lips, and a straight chin. Altogether, his face achieved a certain balance of manliness and grace—neither too refined for a soldier, nor too brutish for a patrician.

The mayor smiled. "I asked your father's opinion of the latest reforms. I would expect he'd have very strong opinions about them, especially about the edict on prices."

"He hasn't mentioned them in his letters. He keeps them brief and personal," said Marcus.

"It's just as well nowadays," said Aristoboulos. "You never know who's reading them."

"Well, what about you, Canio? What do you think of the latest rumors?" asked Philodemos. As mayor, he held little real authority since the emperors appointed curators in every city to keep order and collect taxes. It was an honorary post that rotated among the city's leading men. Aristoboulos himself had served as mayor for many years before stepping aside to let his younger colleague assume the dignity.

Marcus shrugged. "I've been with the legions too long," he answered. "The only rumors I've heard are about troop movements."

"Troop movements? To where?" asked Aristoboulos.

"There's talk of moving a few legions in Syria to other fronts, the Danuvius most likely. The West can always use them."

There were nods of agreement all around, then the sudden slamming of the front door. The men looked toward the atrium, which in the winter was closed off from the court by heavy curtains. From beyond the curtains came the sound of excited female voices, not quite loud enough to be understood.

Presently the curtains parted and Hilaria, the wife of Aristoboulos, appeared, smiling politely. She was the epitome of feminine grace appropriate to her age and station, with the beauty of her youth artfully preserved, as much as a woman might hope, in both face and figure.

"Please excuse the interruption, but your daughter Makrina has just returned and will join you shortly, as soon as she has had a moment to refresh herself," she reported.

Aristoboulos smiled and stretched out his hand to take his wife's. "Thank you, dear," he replied. "Did she say what kept her?"

"The affairs of friends, I'm afraid," said Hilaria.

"Friends? Oh. Friends," said Aristoboulos, with a frown.

Hilaria excused herself and left.

The mayor turned to Marcus and said, "Your first day back is obviously too dear to waste on me. I'll see that your man has everything you need. What's his name?"

"Alexander," answered Marcus.

"That's right," said the mayor. "How could I forget? Only every other man in Asia is named Alexander. Good night."

"I'll see you out," said Aristoboulos. They exited through the atrium, leaving the younger men alone in the court.

Kimon turned to Marcus. "Another moment and your wait will be over," he said.

"Another moment is an eternity," said Marcus.

Kimon groaned. "Listen to you," he said. "Does that sound like the pious Marcus Aurelius? Where's the stiff and stuffy stoic I used to know so well?"

"He's in love," said Marcus, "in a way the pious Marcus Aurelius never was."

Kimon rolled his eyes. "O Thrice Great Hermes!" he exclaimed.

"You should try it sometime, Kimon. It does wonders for one's outlook."

"Yes, well, maybe someday—when I'm old and addled and have lost half my mind, maybe then," said Kimon. "At the moment, I'm still looking for something else."

"If the Fates ordain that I be happy, who am I to cross them?"

"The Fates can change, dear brother. About that, the divine Aurelius was right." A moving curtain caught Kimon's eye. "Your eternity is up," he said. "Here she is."

Makrina was standing at the edge of the court, in a rose-colored dalmatic of soft Ankyra wool, with wide sleeves cut at a slant from the elbow, baring the long, tight sleeves of a creamy cotton under subtunic. The subtunic was visible also beneath the hem of her dalmatic, leaving just the toes of her red-leather slippers exposed. A crimson sash was tied around her waist, and a sea-green wrap or *palla* hung from her shoulders, reaching nearly to her knees.

She looked strangely serene to Kimon, and when Marcus held out a hand to welcome her to him, she smiled broadly and rushed to greet him. "Marcus, welcome," she said, wrapping her arms around his neck and kissing him fondly on the lips. "I'm sorry I wasn't here when you arrived. I hope you didn't have to wait too long."

"You are worth any wait," said Marcus, "though of course I'm glad it's over."

They kissed again, longer this time, while Kimon looked on in silence, amazed and amused. When their lips parted, Makrina rested her head against Marcus's chest. "Kimon?" she said.

"Yes, Makrina?" Kimon answered.

"Go away."

Kimon exchanges glances with Marcus. "As you wish, my lady," he said with a bow, before walking off.

"You are so cruel to him, Makrina," teased Marcus when he was gone.

"He deserves it," said Makrina.

"You know in Athens we called him 'Timon.'"

"Timon?"

"After Timon of Athens, the legendary misanthrope," said Marcus. "He was such a sophist. Whatever someone was defending, he was attacking. Whatever someone was attacking, he was defending. He was quite good at it, actually. The professors dreaded him."

"I'm not surprised."

"Do you remember Athens?"

"Of course, I remember Athens, but not much of you then, I'm afraid. You were just one of Kimon's friends."

"One of many, and every one of us remembered your visit. You were about Eugenia's age and such an imperious little princess that we all forgave Kimon for his habitual antagonism, guessing that it was the only way he could put up with you."

"Well!" Makrina huffed in mock protest. "Did it ever occur to you that I was the way I was *because* of his incessant teasing?"

"It did," said Marcus, "but he was already our friend, and not one of us had yet fallen in love with you. Now, I must admit, I see things differently."

Her eyes held his for a moment before she lowered them. "I can hear that your accent has gotten no better since you left," she said.

"Blame the army," said Marcus. "The soldiers are all Pannonians and speak only Latin, and not very good Latin. You'll have to perfect my Greek yourself. Of course, once we settle in Rome, I'll have to perfect your Latin, which, I would bet, has gotten no better since I left?"

"No, it has not," Makrina confessed.

"Then repeat after me: *Te semper.*"

"*Te semper.*"

"*Amabo.*"

Makrina hesitated, then looked down at the eagle pinned to his cloak. "*Amabo,*" she said without looking up. "I will love you always."

Just then, Eugenia bounced in from the triclinium. "Health to you, Marcus," she said excitedly.

"Health to you, Eugenia," he said, leaning over to kiss her forehead.

"I've been sent to lead you into dinner," she announced. "You are staying, aren't you? Mamma said you were."

"Yes, I am—if you don't mind," said Marcus.

"Of course I don't mind. I'd be delighted," said Eugenia. "But I should warn you about our new cook. He's from Alexandria, in Egypt, and he makes the strangest dishes. Last night he just *ruined* a perfectly good goose by smothering it in this sickening mustard sauce. *Yuck!* I couldn't eat it. Tonight it's fried veal. Who knows how it will turn out?"

"Eugenia?" called her mother, appearing from the triclinium.

"Yes, Mamma?" answered Eugenia.

"You can show them the way now," said Hilaria.

"Yes, Mamma," said Eugenia, then she grabbed Marcus's hand. "This way, Marcus—oh, but you already know the way, unless you're very forgetful."

"I remember," said Marcus.

The triclinium was a large room off the court and garden, furnished with three wide dining couches arranged around a low serving table. Makrina's father and mother took the center couch, leaving the left couch for Marcus and Makrina and the right couch for Kimon and Eugenia. Resting their elbows on the long bolsters at the head of each couch, they ate from the table between them, tended by servants.

The first course was a stew of apricots in a sweet, thick white-wine sauce called *passum*, flavored with mint and honey. Marcus and Aristoboulos raved about it; Eugenia suffered silently, moving the golden glumps around in her dish with her spoon until the serving girl Vassa came to take it away. The veal was more to Eugenia's liking—fried in olive oil, then simmered in a sauce of raisins, honey, wine, oil, salt, and a thick fig syrup. For dessert, there were boiled dumplings made with milk, eggs, crushed walnuts and pine kernels, passum, and minced rue, a bitter herb. They were topped with honey and pepper. Passable, thought Eugenia as she chewed her way through one, though she preferred the dried dates stuffed with pine kernels and dripping with a syrup of honey and red wine.

For everyone but Eugenia, the menu hardly mattered. The occasion itself was a feast. Marcus did most of the talking during the meal, though for this he could not be blamed. Hilaria plied him gently with questions about his home and family, and about his plans and ambitions, without appearing too inquisitive. Aristoboulos wanted to hear more about the campaign against the Persians. Eugenia kept quiet, having been warned beforehand by her mother not to intrude into the conversation. Kimon kept quiet also, but only because he was more interested in watching Marcus and Makrina for signs of stress. Makrina said little and hardly ate at all, but gave Marcus her full attention, listening with apparent interest to everything he said. Still, it seemed to Kimon that neither of them was fully present during the meal.

The winter sun had set by the end of their dinner. The lampstands in the four corners of the room were lit, and the brazier against the far wall was supplied with fresh coals and chips of apple wood, which gave the room a pleasant odor. The diners relaxed for awhile with their last cups of wine, except for Eugenia, who had been sent to bed already. Then, when Aristoboulos took an interest again in the campaign, his wife suggested it was time to retire.

"Oh, very well," he said. They all rose from their couches. Aristoboulos clasped Marcus by the shoulders and kissed his cheek. "Goodnight, Marcus. It's good to have you back."

"Good night, Marcus," said Hilaria, delivering a kiss of her own. "Thank you again for the pleasure of your company."

Custom required that Kimon stay behind as chaperon, but her parents were hardly out of sight before Makrina asked Kimon if she could speak to Marcus alone. Kimon obliged her with uncharacteristic courtesy, telling Marcus he'd see him in the morning.

# III

The next day, Kimon found Marcus still in bed at mid-morning, in the house of Philodemos, the mayor of Sinope, with whom Marcus was staying. "Didn't you get my message?" he asked, pulling open the curtain in the doorway to let a little light into the small sleeping cubicle.

Marcus sat up and swung his legs out of bed. A mat of coarse wool protected his feet from the cold tile floor, but the short-sleeved, cotton subtunic in which he had slept was no match for the room's chill. "Yes, I got your message," he answered, pulling the down-filled coverlet over his shoulders.

"We have to talk," said Kimon, clearing the heap of discarded clothes off a small stool. "You should have heard things after you left! I have never seen my mother so hysterical, and of course Father was furious. They were almost as angry to find out that she's been fasting. I kept that secret, but Eugenia didn't."

"Didn't they know Makrina had become a Christian?"

"They knew she had become a Christian. They just didn't know it would stand in the way of her marrying you. None of us expected that. I don't think Makrina herself made up her mind until yesterday. I was still hoping she would give in and marry you. Most other girls would have, but Makrina can be very stubborn."

"Yes, I know," said Marcus. "What can your parents do?"

Kimon shrugged and loosened his cloak around his neck. "Not much, I'm afraid. They can keep her from seeing her Christian friends. She's already confined to the house and barred from receiving visitors, except you, of course. They're on your side, Marcus. They wanted me to tell you that. They've asked me to beg you to be patient."

"I have to be in Nicomedia next week," said Marcus.

"But after Nicomedia, couldn't you come back here?"

"For what?" said Marcus. "To sit around waiting for Makrina to change her mind? I'd feel foolish and humiliated, pining away like a love-sick suitor. I can't woo her all over again. Everything has changed."

"But she still loves you, Marcus. She could change her mind, although it might take time. Stay as long as you can, at least long enough for us to find out if she's right about not marrying outside the Assembly. Father insists she's not, but I'm not sure how much he knows. We all know Christians who are married to others, but I don't know that any of them were Christians before they were married. Makrina says they weren't."

"Who would know for sure?"

"I have an educated Christian friend who's the town clerk. His name is

Theodoros. I'm sure he would know, and we're likely to find him at his office at this hour, if you'd like to meet him."

"What else can I do?"

They found the clerk Theodoros at the city basilica in the town's small forum, as Kimon expected. He was a little man with more hair on his chin than on his pate. He greeted them cheerfully and offered them some refreshment, which they declined. Then he settled onto the stool beside an angled writing desk in his office. The window behind him was fitted with small round panes of amber glass. A covered brazier beneath the desk warmed his feet and filled the room with the ever-present smell of burning charcoal. On one wall was a wooden rack of square pigeonholes, variously stuffed with rolls of paper.

The clerk listened patiently while Kimon explained their business. "She is quite right," he said to Marcus, as soon as Kimon had finished. "A Christian cannot marry a 'Greek,' an unbeliever. It's unthinkable for a number of reasons." He spoke softly, with a slightly effeminate intonation that hardly fit the bluntness of his words. "First there's the question of rites. Which god would be called upon to bless the marriage? For a Christian, it can only be the Christian God. A Christian cannot participate in other such rites. They shouldn't even attend the weddings of Greeks, much less be married in one. I'm sorry to say that such rules are not always observed. People are weak and cannot separate themselves as they sometimes should."

"But some Christians are married to Greeks, aren't they?" countered Kimon.

"The Assembly honors marriages of Christians to Greeks provided such marriages occurred before the believers were called," said Theodoros. "Our hope is always that the unbelieving husband or wife will be saved through the believing spouse. But it is very difficult for a Christian to live in such a union, and if the unbelieving spouse wishes to separate, the Assembly does not insist that they remain married."

"But what if a Christian did marry a Greek?" asked Marcus. "What would happen?"

"He—or she in this case—would be separated from the Assembly. She would have separated herself from the Assembly by entering into an intimate union with someone outside the Assembly," said Theodoros.

"But what would that mean, practically speaking?"

"She could not participate in our holy Mysteries, our sacred rites. She would still be welcomed to our public worship, but only as a penitent. We wouldn't shun her, of course, or revile her publicly. That is not our way. But we couldn't pretend that she has done nothing wrong, and she couldn't partake of the true life of the Assembly."

"Forever?" asked Kimon.

"Perhaps not forever," said Theodoros. "She might be readmitted to the Assembly after a period of repentance, but that could last two or three years, and it must be genuine. She must sincerely regret her choice to marry outside the Assembly. It might even be required that the marriage be ended before she were readmitted, or that the husband believe and accept baptism. That would be up to the local *episkopos*—'supervisor,' you might say in Latin, or perhaps 'overseer.' It would depend upon the persons involved and the facts of the case."

"What if she married an unbeliever, a 'Greek,' secretly?" asked Marcus.

Theodoros's eyes widened. "That would be a plain denial of Christ," he said. "Christ is the Truth. He says so himself. The Gospel is all about truth—truth and love, but you can't love someone with lies. Without truth, you can't even know what love is. If she were to marry you secretly and continue partaking of the Mysteries, she would be putting herself and you in grave danger. 'He who eats and drinks unworthily, eats and drinks damnation unto himself.'"

"What's that?" asked Marcus.

Theodoros shook his head. "I'm afraid I can't say more on that point. Some things are too hard to explain, even to those who believe."

"Are there no exceptions to the rule?" asked Kimon. "My father swears he knows men who have married women who were Christians well before their wedding."

"I cannot speak for every congregation everywhere," said Theodoros. "There are those we call 'choosers' because they choose to believe only parts of the Gospel. Some choosers might permit such marriages. Some forbid marriage entirely, even for Christians. But what both choose is not the true faith. Makrina should know that." Turning to Marcus, he said, "You must understand that we take the conjugal union very seriously. When a man unites with a woman, the two become one flesh. We do not allow them to be separated, except for the extreme cause of adultery, and not always even then."

"But why should it be so scandalous to marry an unbeliever? What is the harm, as long as the unbelieving husband is not hostile to your Assembly?" asked Marcus.

"The Assembly is the Body of Christ," said Theodoros. "Everyone who is part of the Assembly is part of the Body. As our bodies have different parts, so the Assembly has different parts. There are overseers, whom I mentioned. Also *presbyteroi*, or elders, and *diakonoi*, which in Latin would be ministers or servers, and many others: prophets, teachers, readers, singers, right down to each believer, even the lowliest of them. All together, they make up the continued presence of Christ's divine humanity. Not that any one of us is another Christ. We are all still sinners. But we all struggle as Christians to be like Christ, and inasmuch as we struggle together as parts of the Body, we are Christ to the world. It is a very intimate connection, a mystical connection in fact. I can't explain it fully. No one can. But it means that we cannot be intimately connected to those who do not believe in Christ and struggle to be like him, and so we are told, 'Be not unequally yoked together with unbelievers, for what part has righteousness with unrighteousness, and what communion has light with darkness?'"

"But are only Christians righteous?" asked Marcus. "Surely there are righteous men who happen not to be Christian. Would you consider them a part of the 'communion of darkness'?"

"Whom did you have in mind?" asked Theodoros.

"Apollonios of Tyana," said Marcus. "He had all of the Christ's wisdom and virtue, without his unmanly humility. He worked wonders like Christ. He raised the dead, he healed the sick. And he did not allow himself to be abused and humiliated by fools."

A broad grin spread across Theodoros's face. "I'm sorry, Canio," he said, "but you see, with us, humility is a great virtue and absolutely necessary for the truly righteous. Without humility, one cannot know the truth, and therefore without humility one cannot truly love others."

"But if love is so important, and if Makrina loves me and I love her, why should our marriage be forbidden—by people who are expected to love everyone?"

"There is something else, Canio," said Theodoros. "Actually there is much else, but you are not ready to hear it. There are things we reserve for those who truly want to believe, those who want to know the whole truth, not just how they can have what they want. To know the whole truth, you must be open to it, and that means humbling yourself and accepting the truth, even when it won't give you what you want."

"Is there no hope for us then?"

"There is always hope, Canio, but as Christians our hope is always that others will believe. I hope you will, but it's up to you."

Kimon thanked Theodoros for his time, and they said their farewells.

Afterwards, Kimon led Marcus to a tavern nearby. As they entered, he drew Marcus's attention to the outline of a fish carved into the wooden lintel above the tavern door. "A Christian tavern?" said Marcus. Kimon shrugged. "Well," said Marcus, "if it's supposed to keep me away, it won't."

The tavern was dark and nearly empty. Three old men were huddled in the back, well away from the drafty shuttered windows. The air was thick with the smell of burning wood and mulled wine. The stone floor was spread with stale sawdust. It was the kind of place that could seem cozy or gloomy depending upon one's mood. Marcus's mood dictated the latter.

"Dio!" called Kimon stepping up to the tiled counter. A young man of about twenty emerged through a door in the back and greeted Kimon cheerfully from across the counter. "Strong hot wine for my friend and me," ordered Kimon.

Dio lifted the lid on a pot set into the counter and gently stirred its dark, steamy contents so as not to disturb the sediment of spices at the bottom. Then he carefully ladled the wine into two earthen cups and handed them to Kimon, wishing them health as he did so. Lastly, he drew two scratches on a slate behind him with a piece of chalk. From the number of the scratches, Marcus concluded that Kimon came here often.

"So who's the Christian?" he asked Kimon, as they settled onto low stools in a corner of room.

"Don't know," said Kimon. "Maybe the owner. Maybe a previous owner. Maybe Dio."

"I thought you knew everyone in Sinope?" asked Marcus.

"I do," said Kimon. "I just don't know everyone's god. I don't even know my own god."

"Careful there. Whoever it is, your fortune may depend on him," said Marcus smiling morosely.

Kimon chuckled. "I'm as pious as the next man," he said. "I make my sacrifices according to custom. Every September, during the festival of Serapis, you'll find me in his temple over there, doing my public duty to the great and terrible god of my ancestors. Even the philosophers tell us to honor the gods. Too bad they can't tell us more about them."

"For that there are seers," said Marcus.

"Sure, there are plenty of seers, and oracles, and prophets," said Kimon. "Down the coast a ways is the village of Ionopolis. Have you been there? Of course not. It used to be called Abonitichos—A-bo-ni-ti-chos—but the locals thought that name too provincial, so they gave themselves a new one. There's only one reason anybody goes to Ionopolis, and that's to visit the local deity. You see, they have their very own god there, a snake-god named Glykon, with a prophet and a temple and a cult following throughout much of Asia. People travel for hundreds of miles to honor this god and hear its prophecies, and not just peasants, either, but people from Ankyra and Laodikea and Pergamum. I've been there, too, and I've seen this snake-god and heard its prophecies. I swear I've never seen a plainer fraud than the snake-god Glykon. And yet, people believe in it, people who should know better. There's no accounting for it. Demosthenes was right: People believe whatever they want to believe. Some people want their god to be a snake. I don't."

"But there are other oracles and other gods," said Marcus.

"And I don't deny them all," said Kimon. "I just can't say for certain which are true and which are false. Some I know are false, and the ones I like, I can't say for sure are true. I'd like to think they are, but maybe they're just better frauds than Glykon. They're ancient enough, but for all their years there's not much to them." Kimon swallowed a gulp of wine, now cool enough to drink quickly. Then he added, "That's one thing you can say for the Christians: There's a lot to learn about their god. They have books and books about him. If you like to read and study, you'd feel right at home."

"With your friend the city clerk," said Marcus.

"That's right," said Kimon.

"No thanks."

Kimon laughed. "So Theodoros isn't the best salesman for their faith, at least for a strong, tough soldier like yourself. I don't know who would be. But while you're pondering dark alternatives to life at the present, you might at least look at the cult that has stolen Makrina's heart. It's not all reading and study. They have a rather respectable ritual, if you don't mind the company."

"You've seen it?"

"Well, yes, I have, two or three times, at least the parts that are open to outsiders. Not everything is, of course. They meet every Sunday, actually every Saturday after sundown by Roman reckoning. That's tonight, Marcus."

"So it is," said Marcus.

"They have a basilica not far outside the city walls, east up the hill a little. They call it their 'Lord's house.' *Kyriakon* in Greek, shortened to *kirk* in some dialects. I can show it to you if you like."

"Why the sudden enthusiasm for what you know is impossible? Is it the wine or are you mad?"

"Not mad, Marcus, just desperate. As desperate as you are not to lose Makrina. I can't think of anything else that will take me to Rome, or any reason for you to return east if you don't marry her. If you lose Makrina, I lose you, which, believe it or not, would pain me greatly." Kimon held his hand to his heart to dramatize his hurt.

"It's the wine," said Marcus. But suddenly the tavern seemed to Marcus a shade less gloomy. Tired as he was from a sleepless night, it had to be the wine, he thought. "Do you think this Serapis of Sinope cares for jilted suitors?" he asked.

Kimon leaned his head to one side and said, "If it were your foot instead of your heart that ached, you could buy a little silver foot to offer as a sacrifice and then spend the night in the temple. Maybe even lie with one of the holy whores who work the place. Then sometime during the night a cure would come to you in a dream, supposedly. But I doubt that the 'God of the Dead' knows of a cure for heartache. You would do better to visit the temple of the Great Mother in Ankyra—or the 'kirk' of the Christians, right here in town. You know what they teach, don't you, Marcus: 'God is love'?"

Marcus slept the rest of the morning, having not slept at all the night before. Afterwards, he tried writing a letter to a friend in Rome, but couldn't think of what to say. Then he went for a walk, east up the hill and around the flattened crown of the old volcanic mount, rising out of the sea, connected to the mainland by the narrow isthmus occupied by the crowded city. It was the quickest escape from the city, less than a mile from Philodemos's house. Along the way, the houses thinned and gave way to empty hillside. The trees that had once covered the slope had long since fallen to the builder's ax. Nothing now covered the hill but green grass, green year-round on account of the moist winds sweeping down off the sea all winter long.

At the crest of the hill, Marcus looked back upon the town. It was all there before him, very nearly surrounded by water and squeezed at both ends by the ancient hills of Hephaestos. Sinope seemed impossibly small for a man of his ambitions, a tiny place compared to his native Rome. Yet in it lived the love of his life, perhaps happily until yesterday. He lingered there longer than he intended, recalling one by one the times he had spent with Makrina—evening strolls by the harbor, days in the country at the family villa, picnics on the hill where he now stood. At the end of a perfect September day, they had sat just there on that very spot, looking down on the city and the sea, watching the sun set in the west. Now the cold wind made him shiver, and he couldn't help but think also of the Christians' house of worship somewhere below him.

Later, at about the ninth hour, he met Kimon at the city baths.

"I spoke to Makrina," said Kimon, climbing down into the steaming water.

"How is she?"

"Sad but resolute," said Kimon. "She has spent most of the day in her room, praying. We've all tried to talk to her, but without much success."

Marcus said nothing.

"You don't look much better," said Kimon.

Marcus frowned and looked away.

"Is there anything else I can do?" asked Kimon.

Marcus did not respond.

"Maybe I could get her to see you again."

"What good would it do?" asked Marcus.

"You could plead your case. You could give her another chance. At the very least, you could force her to turn you away again. Maybe she wouldn't have the strength to do so."

"I will not grovel at her feet," said Marcus.

"You don't have to grovel," said Kimon. "You can just ask her if she has changed her mind. Perhaps ask her to explain herself."

Marcus said nothing.

"I'll ask her," said Kimon. He waited a moment for an objection that didn't come, and then said, "Father has asked me to ask you to be patient. He thinks he can wear her down. Stay a while in Nicomedia, or visit Athens before going home. Maybe in a month or so, she'll be ready then."

"I don't know, Kimon. The longer I wait, the more foolish it seems."

"But try and wait, for all our sakes, Marcus."

They sat silently in the pool for a long while. Then suddenly Marcus asked, "How does she pray, Kimon? Have you seen her?"

"She won't pray around me, but Eugenia has prayed with her," said Kimon. "She lights a lamp and then reads from a little codex of verses, no bigger than your palm. She also has a shingle of wood painted with a scene of Jesus and his Apostles. She painted it herself. She's actually quite skilled. She usually stands when she prays, but Eugenia says lately she's been on her knees."

"What does she say when she prays?"

"I don't know. Eugenia isn't very clear about that."

Marcus was silent.

"If you want to know how Christians pray, you should visit their worship," said Kimon. "Tonight's the night. You're safe if you go. Makrina won't be there. Father has forbidden her to leave the house."

"I'll think about it," said Marcus.

Marcus thought about it the rest of the afternoon. Then, as the sun was just beginning to set, he set off on foot to find the building Kimon had spoken of. The route was simple: follow the main street of Sinope out the east gate in the city walls, then on up the hill for about two stadia before turning right down the lane that led to the new city cisterns. Barely a hundred paces down the lane, Marcus came upon a simple basilica set back by itself to the left. Little windows under the upper eaves glowed with candlelight, hinting at the life inside. Suddenly a great chorus of male and female voices burst forth from the building through the open doors. Marcus listened from the lane long enough to hear the chorus die and then revive again and again, in a continuous cycle of singing.

An intermittent stream of late arrivals entered through the open doors. Marcus was encouraged to think he could slip in unnoticed, as one of the many, while everyone inside was busy singing. He adjusted his cloak to hide his military garb, then walked straight for the doors and on inside.

To his relief, he found himself in a dimly lit narthex, separated from the nave of the basilica by a wooden screen. There were many others in the narthex as well, men and women and quite a few children fidgeting about at their parents' feet, but the lack of light made him at least feel less conspicuous. An elderly man waved him up to the wooden screen for a better view.

The nave was filled with people, all standing, men on the right and women on the left. It was impossible not to tell them apart. The men were all bare-headed, and the women were all covered. In the center of the nave was a lectern set upon a podium. Gathered on the podium were several men in white robes. Some were barely old enough for whiskers, while one or two were of middle age. The men took turns singing verses from several scrolls spread across a lectern. The rest sang the responses, accompanied by the entire congregation in unison.

At the far end of the nave was an apse, barely visible from the narthex. There, it seemed, was a large table draped in white linen. Two large candelabra adorned the table, candles ablaze. That much Marcus could see. All else at the table was obscured by a bearded man in a white dalmatic who stood before the table swinging a censer from a chain. With each swing, a puff of smoke rose from the censer and ascended toward the rafters, where a great gray cloud hung in stillness. The odor, even in the narthex, was sweet and pleasing.

Marcus looked about the nave for a familiar face, half hoping, half dreading to see Makrina, but he did not see her. Nor did he see anyone else he knew.

Without warning the singing stopped, and the bearded man at the table turned and sang out in a booming voice, "Wisdom! Let us attend!" From the platform, one of the men announced a reading from an epistle of the apostle Paul to the Corinthians. Then the same man began the reading, but instead of merely reading it aloud, he chanted it slowly and clearly. There were no responses to this reading, which went on for many verses. When at last he had finished, the reader bowed and received a blessing of peace from someone in the apse. A chorus of alleluias followed, interspersed with verses sung by others at the platform.

Next the bearded fellow lifted a large codex from the table and raised it above his head before carrying it out to the podium and setting it down upon the lectern. As he did so, the people nearer the front turned to face him. There among them Marcus saw Eugenia, standing in the far left corner in a group of girls her own age. She was smiling and sometimes giggling with the others, apparently paying more attention to the teen-age boys helping out up front than to the proceedings. From that point on, Marcus couldn't help but pay more attention to her. She looked so young and yet so much like Makrina. Would she someday break a heart the way her sister had, he wondered. Then another question occurred to him: Had she come alone? Or had she come with Makrina?

Marcus spent the rest of his visit in utter misery, desperate to see Makrina but sick with dread, regret, and finally disappointment. He could hardly pay attention to the service, which continued through a long lecture by an elderly man, whom Marcus had not noticed sitting in a large chair in the apse, behind the table. Then there was a long prayer for those under instruction, and before he knew it, the bearded fellow up front was calling for everyone but the faithful to depart. Eugenia and many others started toward the doors. It was time to go: the rest of the service was clearly for the baptized only.

Determined not to be seen, Marcus hurried out the door and into the fresh air. He fled as fast as he could so as not to meet Eugenia. How embarrassing that would be! How hard to explain! How cruel to Makrina if it gave her false hope, to hear that he had actually been there!

Before long, his fear and dread gave way to a feeling of foolishness. How foolish it was for him to sneak off to see how Christians worshipped, to allow himself to be intrigued by their pomp, and then to be tortured with the hope and dread of seeing Makrina. Was he not a man, a Roman officer, the son of a senator, educated in the philosophies of the ancients? How then could he submit to this un-Roman religion? *Enough of this!* he thought to himself as he hurried into the night. *Enough of these Christians! Enough of Makrina! Enough of this little town!*

Kimon was surprised and disappointed when Marcus informed him the next morning that he had decided to leave Sinope for Nicomedia as soon as possible.

"Are you sure you want to do this, Marcus? Have you given up all hope?" Kimon pleaded.

"I don't know what else I can honorably do, Kimon. Right now I don't know if I'd marry Makrina if she gave in this instant. I don't know how I could. She has changed. She's not the woman I fell in love with. Even if she were to give in now, what kind of start would that be to a life together? Too much has happened."

"What if she changes her mind after you're gone?"

"Write and tell me about it."

"In Rome?"

"I don't know. Maybe I'll stay in Nicomedia for a while, or visit Athens. I'll let you know."

As it happened, there was a boat leaving for Byzantium late that afternoon. Kimon and Eugenia met Marcus at the docks. From where they stood, the house of Aristoboulos was easily visible a short distance away, and more than once Marcus looked up at the second-storey balcony overlooking the harbor, but there was no one there. The doors stayed shut.

"She hasn't left her room since hearing of your departure," said Kimon. "Your leaving is the end of her hopes, too."

"She asked me to give this to you," said Eugenia, holding out a small, flat object tied up in one of Makrina's perfumed scarves. "She told me to tell you it is very dear to her."

Marcus accepted the gift without unwrapping it. "Tell her . . . I wish her well," he said. Then, as an afterthought, he removed a gold signet ring from his finger and gave it to Eugenia to give to Makrina. Eugenia kissed his cheek, and he kissed her forehead twice, once for her and once for Makrina, he said. Kimon and Marcus embraced and said their farewells.

When they had gone, Marcus first thought to toss Makrina's gift into his field desk unopened. But the silk scarf he recognized, and its scent stirred his memories. Carefully he untied the knot, to reveal a wooden plaque painted with the scene of a group of men gathered around for what seemed like a ceremonial meal. About the head of the man in the middle was a nimbus of glittering gold. The rest of the scene was executed in deep blues, reds, and black.

Marcus studied the image for a moment, holding her scarf to his lips while savoring her scent. Then without thinking, he fixed his eyes on the image's central figure and muttered, "God or not, have mercy on us both."

Marcus was both heartbroken and seasick all the way to Byzantium, but as the boat docked the nausea left him and his spirits rose. He began deliberately rebuilding his dreams on the new foundation the Fates had laid for him, concentrating his thoughts on Rome and the prospects it offered, as he and his aide Alexander went ashore to spend the night, before crossing over to Nicomedia on the morrow.

At the best inn in Byzantium, reserved for official travelers, Marcus chanced upon a boyhood acquaintance, now in the service of the governor of Bithynia and Pontus. Marcus recognized him immediately by his refined appearance and noble bearing.

"I know you," said Marcus. "You're Valerius Marcellinus."

"Yes, indeed. Gaius Valerius Marcellinus," said the man, with mild surprise. "And you are . . . ?"

"Aemilius Canio. We were boys together in Rome."

"Ah, yes—Marcus. How could I forget, the son of the senator," said the fellow, smiling politely. "You're in the army now," he noted, glancing at Marcus's military dress.

"Not for long, though. I'm taking leave of the army after a stop in Nicomedia. Then it's back to Rome."

"Lucky you," said Marcellinus.

"Where are you headed?" asked Marcus.

"East, on a tour of Pontus. You must have just come from there?"

"Yes, in fact. From Armenia, really, but back by way of Sinope in Pontus."

"Perhaps you can fill me in on the place. Let's have a drink together."

They settled by the fire in the inn and talked amiably about their positions and adventures. Then Marcellinus inquired about Marcus's travels in Pontus. They were on their third cup of wine by the time Marcus's account of his itinerary reached Sinope, about which Marcus was careful, for his own sake, to say no more than he had said about Trapezos, Amisos, or Neocaesarea. But Marcellinus was especially curious about Sinope. "Tell me," he said, "are there many Christians in Sinope?"

Marcus felt a sudden pain in his heart but was determined to ignore it. "Quite a few, in fact."

"Is that so? They have a temple, I suppose, a 'Lord's house,' as they call it?"

"Yes, not far east of town. A modest basilica, nothing special."

"You've seen it?"

"Once, yes."

"How long did you say you were in Sinope?"

"Several weeks, off and on, in the past year," said Marcus.

"Really? Why so much time there?"

Marcus smiled with embarrassment. "Well, Gaius, there was a girl there I was supposed to marry."

"Marry? What happened?"

Marcus sighed. "When I returned last week, she told me she had become a Christian and couldn't marry me because I was not one."

"Truly?" said Marcellinus. "I'm sorry to hear it—for your sake, of course."

Marcus smiled sadly and nodded.

"Had you known her long?"

"Years," said Marcus. "She was the sister of a friend of mine from before the army. Still, I didn't see it coming. No one in her family is Christian, and she never talked about it to me."

"What a blow!" said Marcellinus. "You must be heart-broken."

Marcus just shrugged.

"What was her name?" asked Marcellinus.

"Makrina, the daughter of Aristoboulos the shipbuilder," said Marcus, staring into the fire.

"Makrina. Beautiful name."

"Beautiful girl," said Marcus, still staring at the fire.

"I'm sure she was," said Marcellinus. "I'm sorry to have pulled it out of you. My apologies. Perhaps I should leave you be."

When Marcus did not respond, Marcellinus rose to retire.

"Goodnight, Canio," he said, clapping a hand on Marcus's shoulder, "and good luck in Rome. I'm sure the world awaits you there."

Marcus responded absently, still staring at the fire.

Marcellinus lit a taper before leaving, to light the lamp in his room. Once there, he took a leather-bound sheaf of papers from his travel chest, along with a quill pen and a jar of ink. He readied the pen and the ink before taking out a small blank sheet of paper. Then on the paper, he wrote:

*IV before the Kalends of March—tribune M. Aemilius Canio, lately arrived from Sinope, names one Macrina, daughter of Aristoboulos the shipbuilder of said Sinope, as a Christian.*

# IV

Nicomedia had been a pleasant provincial town until Diocletian made it his capital. A boom in growth followed. The harbor was crowded with warships, merchant ships, and sumptuous yachts. The streets were bustling with people, and everywhere there was building, building to consume the countryside, building to enlarge or replace the old with the new.

After a day's sail from Byzantium, Marcus left Alexander to unload their baggage at the docks while he went alone to the garrison, which was housed within a spacious walled compound encompassing the imperial palace and other government buildings. The soldier Diocletian had constructed the compound in the manner of a Roman camp—a regular rectangle divided neatly into quadrants by intersecting avenues. At their intersection stood an octagonal temple dedicated to Jupiter, the emperor's patron among the gods.

The garrison occupied the north end of the compound. Outside its gate was a large public forum, pierced by two main thoroughfares, the way to the harbor and the road east. Entering the forum from the harbor, Marcus noticed a large building apparently in the process of demolition. Piles of shattered roof tiles lay about its perimeter. The roof beams themselves had been dragged down from their posts. Presently the demolition crew was hitching up two large teams of oxen to pull down the building's facade.

Demolition was a common sight in the growing capital, but from previous visits Marcus remembered the forum itself as relatively new. Its structures could hardly have been old enough to require demolition already.

At the gate to the compound, Marcus handed his papers to the orderly. "What was that?" he asked in Latin, pointing to the half-demolished building.

"Temple of the Christians," said the orderly, in a Dalmatian accent. "A sacrifice to the old god Terminus, you might say. The emperors wanted it torched for the god's festival, but the city prefect was afraid it would burn down the whole city. It's taken longer to pull down than they expected. Wait here, sir."

The orderly disappeared inside, leaving Marcus to watch the ruination of the building. It was then that he noticed a gruesome sight. From a post in the center of the square hung the headless body of a man, dangling upside down, its unbound arms reaching toward the ground. Ravens were squabbling over its flesh, though there was still plenty left.

A moment later, a centurion of the guard appeared to escort Marcus to the prefect of the Guard. "We weren't expecting you for some days, Canio, but it's just as well you're here now," he said. "Follow me."

Marcus followed the centurion through the gate and down the main avenue toward the temple of Jupiter. "What's this about the Christian temple?" he asked.

"Imperial edict," said the centurion. "All Christian houses of worship are to be dismantled or destroyed, all Christian books and paraphernalia are to be confiscated, and all public Christian worship is to be forbidden. And anyone accused of resisting the edict is to be tried for treason. The poor wretch hanging in the square tore up a copy of the edict as soon as it was posted. For that, he lost his head."

Marcus could scarcely conceal his surprise. Not in his lifetime, not since the reign of Valerian some 40 years earlier, had the state moved against the Christians, although they had not been welcomed in the army in recent years.

"When did this happen?" he asked.

"Two days ago," said the centurion. "The edict has just gone out. I think that's what they want you for."

*What they want me for?* Marcus wondered. He almost asked, but it seemed he'd know soon enough. They skirted the temple of Jupiter to the left and entered the first building they came to. In the central entrance hall, the centurion informed an orderly of the arrival of the tribune Aemilius Canio. The orderly left the hall through the double doors to one side and returned a moment later. "The prefect will see you now," he said.

The centurion waved Marcus through the doors and into a large room with arched openings leading out into a walled garden. The room was nearly empty and could easily have accommodated all of a legion's officers. Against one wall was a long table, heaped with large, rolled maps. Also on the table was a blackened leather canister, about two feet long and four inches in diameter. The cap of the canister was secured with a leather cord wound around the canister and kept in place with not one but two seals of purple wax. The prefect entered through a door at the other end of the room.

"Welcome, Canio," the prefect said in a loud voice that filled the empty chamber. He was younger than Marcus expected, a man in his thirties with a receding hairline but a thin, straight face without the fleshy fullness of age. To be the praetorian prefect in Nicomedia, he would have been a personal friend of Diocletian. Marcus had never met him before, nor did he ever expect to meet him again.

"Health to you, sir," said Marcus with a respectful bow. The gaps grow greater between the ranks with each step up. As a tribune second class, standing before the prefect, Marcus felt like a lowly legionary.

The prefect nodded and said, "I understand you are leaving our service and returning to Rome. We have one last mission for you." He took the leather canister from the table and handed it to Marcus. "You will take this dispatch with you to Rome and deliver it personally to the City Prefect. The case contains the imperial edict, bearing the personal seals of the Augustus Diocletian and the Caesar Galerius, setting forth the new policy regarding those of the Christian cult."

Marcus took the case and held it reverently.

"This should have left two days ago," said the prefect, "but the first courier met with a mishap down the coast, so we're sending it with you. That means you'll have to leave immediately. There's a ship waiting for you in the harbor. It will sail as soon as you are on board. Stop by the officers' mess before you leave. With that in hand, they'll give you anything."

"Yes, sir."

"Any questions?"

"No, sir."

"Good, then. Give my regards to the City Prefect. He's an old friend. Tell him Gaius Valerius Veturius wishes him the favor of the Unconquered Sun."

"I will, sir," said Marcus.

"That's all."

Marcus touched his right fist to his left shoulder, then extended his arm forward, fingers straight and palm down.

The prefect responded casually. "Farewell, tribune," he said on his way out.

For a brief moment, Marcus examined the purple seals securing the cord to the canister. Then he left the room in haste.

On his way back to the harbor, Marcus wondered what this would mean for Makrina. His first impulse was to send warning, but there wasn't time. Neither was there any question now of returning to Sinope. He had a mission to accomplish that would take him all the way home. *Maybe this is what they need*, he thought. *Maybe this will bring her around.* But what did it matter? Sinope was a long way from Rome, and Marcus, it seemed, was already a longer way from Makrina.

He found Alexander waiting for him on the pier with their baggage.

"What's that?" Alexander asked, pointing to the canister.

"An imperial edict. I'm to take it to the City Prefect in Rome. There should be a boat here somewhere waiting for us."

"We're not leaving now, are we? We've just arrived."

"Orders," said Marcus, handing Alexander a basket of bread, cheese, sausages, and wine from the officers' mess. "I'll ask the harbor master."

The harbor master identified the boat, and Marcus identified himself to the boat's captain. Alexander arranged for the stevedores to transfer their baggage from the pier to the boat. While this was done, he and Marcus sat down on some crates on the pier and silently ate the food Marcus had brought. When all was ready, they boarded the ship and cast off, with just enough time to clear the harbor of Nicomedia before sunset.

☩    ☩    ☩

"Tell me you don't miss him," said Chione, sitting with Makrina in the tablinum, five days after Marcus's departure. She was about Makrina's age, with wavy black hair, dark eyes, and very pale skin, hence her name—"Snow." Makrina was still not allowed to leave the house or receive visitors, but Chione was an exception, on account of her parents' close friendship with Makrina's parents.

"Of course I miss him," said Makrina. "What I said was that Kimon misses him more, or seems to. He acts as if he's lost his only friend in the world. He's been brooding about it for days."

"And you haven't been?" said Chione.

"I said I miss him," replied Makrina. "It's just that . . ." She turned her gaze toward the bright, visible rays of sunlight illuminating the peristyle. The weather had turned suddenly warmer, and the curtains that had closed off the tablinum were tied back to let the light in. "It's just that I expect Marcus will come back someday. I can't say why I believe he will, but I do."

"What if he doesn't come back?" Chione asked.

Makrina turned back toward her friend. "If he doesn't," she said, "then it wasn't God's will."

Eugenia entered the tablinum from the atrium and stood before them. "What is it, Eugenia?" Makrina inquired. Her impatience caught the younger sister by surprise. "Well?"

"Mamma's going through our summer wardrobe and wants you to help," Eugenia reported.

Makrina stared at her sister defiantly, then turned back to Chione. "Anyway," she said, "the real reason Kimon's upset is that he's lost his excuse to travel. He was so looking forward to going to Rome. Now he's afraid Pappa won't let him go anywhere. Of course, he blames me. You should have heard him when I told him that Marcus would come back. He was livid."

The great bronze knocker on the front door clanked three times. "I wonder who that is," said Makrina. They waited where they were until Vassa appeared from the atrium. "It's the mayor, my lady, here to see your father," she said to Makrina.

"He's in his study," said Makrina. Vassa hurried off across the peristyle to fetch Aristoboulos, while Makrina arose and went to greet Philodemos in the atrium. "Health to you," she said with a smile.

"Is your father at home? I must see him at once," said Philodemos.

"I've sent for him. He'll be here shortly. Can I bring you some refreshment?"

"No thank you."

Makrina knew Philodemos to be a self-important man, but this time she thought his seriousness greatly exaggerated. "Wonderful weather we're having, isn't it?" she said to test his mood.

Philodemos grunted in acknowledgment and then ignored her. Makrina, Chione, and Eugenia stood by uncomfortably, until Aristoboulos arrived. "I must have a word with you alone," said Philodemos. "Affairs of state," he added.

Without a word to the girls, the two men left the atrium and crossed the peristyle to Aristoboulos's study.

"That Philodemos is so pompous," said Chione.

"I wonder what he wants," said Makrina. "Wait here." Makrina hurried alone across the peristyle to the study, leaving her friend with her sister.

"She doesn't seem to me to miss Marcus that much," said Chione.

"She misses him," said Eugenia, "just not as much as she should. Not as much as I do."

"You? Why would you miss him?"

Eugenia smiled impishly. "Because I was in love with him, too," she answered. "*Really* in love with him."

Chione laughed. "And I thought Makrina was foolish for falling in love with him," she said. "He's nearly twice your age. Besides, you couldn't have married him either, and still joined the Assembly."

"Given the choice, I might have married Marcus."

"Eugenia! How can you say that?" said Chione. "I hope you are not serious. Your sister was right not to marry him."

"Only because she never really loved him."

"Don't be silly. They were nearly betrothed."

"She liked him well enough," said Eugenia, "enough to marry him I suppose, but she wasn't in love, not like I was."

"This is nonsense," said Chione. "Is everyone in your family crazy?"

Eugenia just giggled.

Aristoboulos and Philodemos emerged from the study and started back across the peristyle, with eyes on the ground and a worried look on their faces. They passed through the atrium with barely a glance at Chione and Eugenia.

"Thanks for the word," said Aristoboulos at the front door.

"It's all I could do," Philodemos replied. They said their farewells and parted. Aristoboulos looked at the girls. "Where is Makrina?" he asked. Eugenia shrugged and Chione shook her head. Aristoboulos frowned and started back to his study.

A moment later, Makrina appeared in the atrium. Her eyes were wide with alarm. "Is he gone now? Is the mayor gone?" she whispered excitedly.

"He's gone. What's wrong?" said Chione.

Makrina checked the tablinum, then the peristyle, then turned to Chione. "We must warn the Assembly!" she whispered. "They're sending soldiers to confiscate the holy scriptures! They'll be there within the hour!"

"What? What are you saying?"

"The emperors have issued a new edict banning Christian worship! The scriptures are to be confiscated and destroyed, and all their temples are to be pulled down!"

"You can't be serious. Are you sure?" asked Chione.

"Of course I'm sure! I heard Philodemos tell Pappa! We must warn the overseer!"

Makrina headed for the door, followed by Chione and Eugenia.

They were in the vestibule hurriedly donning their cloaks when Hilaria found them. "Makrina! Where are you going?" she demanded.

Makrina was startled. "Oh, um, out, Mamma. On an errand, just a short one," she answered.

"I've been waiting for you for some time. Did you not hear that I needed you?"

"I did, Mamma. I'm sorry. I forgot."

"Then come now."

"But, Mamma, I can't! There's something important I must do!"

"You are not leaving the house. Now put your cloak away and come with me."

"But Mamma—"

"Come with me, Makrina," said her mother, turning to go.

Makrina's face flashed red with anger. "I am not a child!" she declared.

Hilaria wheeled about and glared at her. "When you are older, Makrina, and wiser and *married*, you may do as you please, but until then, you are still my daughter and you will do as I say! Now put away your cloak and come with me!"

Chione touched Makrina shoulder to get her attention. "I'll go," she said. Makrina scowled at her, then threw her cloak onto the rack in the vestibule and marched off after her mother.

"Come!" said Chione, pulling Eugenia out the door.

In the mood she was in, Makrina was not of much use to her mother. Before long, Hilaria had sent her to her room. "She's completely impossible, Aristo," Hilaria complained to her husband. "It's as if she's lost her senses. I don't know what to do with her."

Makrina paced the floor in her room for half an hour, alternately praying that Chione would reach the Lord's house in time and arguing in her mind against her mother and father. *Why can't they listen? Why don't they understand?*

She was still fuming when she heard the front door slam shut. She emerged from her room to find Eugenia struggling up the stairs with a heavy bundle in her arms. "What's this?" Makrina asked.

"Gospel books. Two of them," Eugenia answered, panting heavily. "So the soldiers won't get them."

"Here. Let me have them."

"I want one! I did all the work!"

"*Shhhh!*"

Eugenia lowered her voice. "I did all the work," she repeated.

"Very well then," said Makrina, guiding Eugenia into her room. Eugenia dropped the bundle onto Makrina's bed and let her sister untie the knotted cloth in which they were wrapped.

Inside Makrina found the Gospels of Mark and John—large, handsome codices with ornate wooden covers, inlaid with turquoise, with bronze hinges. She stared in amazement at the covers, with Eugenia looking over her shoulder. They had often heard the Gospels read in the worship, but they had never seen the books up close, never lifted the covers, never read the divine words just as they were written, right there on the page.

Makrina knelt beside her bed and reverently lifted the cover of the smaller codex. "This is Markos," she said in awe. "See: *TO KATA MARKON HAGION EVANGELION.*"

"I can read," said Eugenia with annoyance.

She settled next to her sister, as Makrina began to read aloud: "The beginning of the Gospel of Jesus Christ, the Son of God; as it is written in the prophets, Behold, I send my messenger before thy face, which shall prepare the way before thee."

Somewhere outside, they heard their mother's voice. Makrina jumped up and peeked out from behind her curtain.

"Is she coming?" Eugenia asked.

"No. I think she's gone now," said Makrina. Returning to the bed, she closed the codex and handed it to Eugenia. "Here," she said. "Hide it well and don't let anyone see it. And don't tell anyone you have it."

Eugenia nodded and exited the room cautiously, heading for her own room next door.

Makrina picked up the remaining codex and started to put it away in her clothes chest, but the temptation to open it overpowered her. She set it back down on the bed and settled again on her knees before it. Then she lifted the cover.

She was there a long while reading through the book, shifting about from place to place, marveling at actually reading the stories she had only heard read until then. She was so engrossed, she didn't notice her mother looking in on her.

"What is this?" Hilaria asked.

Makrina turned and gasped. "It's—It's just a book, Mamma, borrowed from the Assembly. Since I can't go out, I have to read it here. Just for a while. It will give me something to do."

"What kind of book?" Hilaria entered the room and stood by the bed.

"A Gospel book, Mamma. It tells the story of the Lord Jesus Christ. This one was written by the Apostle John," she said. "The Apostle John knew Jesus and walked with him. This is what he saw and heard."

Hilaria knelt gracefully beside her daughter and examined the careful, hand-printed text.

"Listen," said Makrina. Picking a place at random, she began to read:

> *Amen I say unto you, he who believes in me has everlasting life. I am the bread of life. Your fathers ate the manna in the wilderness and are dead. This is the bread which comes down from heaven, that one may eat of it and not die. I am the living bread which came down from heaven. If anyone eats of this bread, he will live forever. And the bread that I will give is my—*

Makrina stopped suddenly and read ahead with her eyes. "Let's go back to the beginning," she said, carefully closing the codex and opening it again at the beginning. Then she read:

> *In the beginning was the Word, and the Word was with God and the Word was God. He was in the beginning with God. All things were made through him, and without him nothing was made that was made. In him was life, and the life was the light of men. And the light shines in the darkness, and the darkness comprehended it not.*

She paused and looked at her mother. "It's beyond me, Makrina," said her mother, shaking her head.

"Wait," urged Makrina, and she closed the codex again and opened it near the end. "Let me read you about the resurrection."

"Some other time, Makrina," said her mother, standing up.

"No, wait, Mamma. Please. I can explain it to you."

"Some other time," said Hilaria, looking down at her daughter and seeing the disappointment in her face. Hilaria sighed with exasperation. She smiled and touched her daughter's hair with her hand. "I just don't know what has happened to you," she said. "You are so beautiful, Makrina, more beautiful than I was at your age. Don't spoil it by taking the wrong things too seriously. You're still young and full of enthusiasm. In a few years, you may look back on things differently. Be careful now, and think of your future."

"But I am thinking of the future, Mamma," said Makrina.

"Think of your life, think of whom you will marry and how you will live. These things matter and they don't happen on their own. You must plan for them. You must think of your life."

"But I am, Mamma. I am."

# V

Eugenia and Chione reported later what had happened at the basilica. The soldiers cordoned off the building from the gathering crowd and then began hauling away nearly everything inside—tables, lecterns, the overseer's and elders' chairs, lamp-stands, candelabra, candles, censers, serving plates, chalices, the collection box, vestments, even the clothes collected for the poor, and books, of course, which were mostly scrolls. They made a great heap of everything in the lane outside the building, then loaded it all onto a cart to be hauled away. No one knew where.

A fight broke out between some boys, including Chione's younger brother Euplios. The soldiers put a stop to it, but not before Euplios received a bloody nose. When it was all over, the soldiers nailed the doors shut, posted a guard, and dispersed the crowd.

The next day, the mayor, Philodemos, called again to see Aristoboulos, to ask if he could come by the mayor's office in the town hall that afternoon to meet the new inspector general of Pontus. "About the ninth hour, if that's all right with you. And can you bring Makrina?"

"Makrina? Why Makrina?"

"Well, you see, this young fellow from Nicomedia is charged with enforcing the new edict against the Christians. He's heard about Makrina being one, and he'd like to ask her a few questions. She's in no danger, of course. He has assured me of that, but he thinks she might be able to help him. His name is Valerius Marcellinus, an Italian, from Rome, in fact."

Aristoboulos kept the appointment, appearing with Makrina at the ninth hour outside the mayor's office. They were received immediately and graciously by the young Italian. "It is an honor to meet you, sir," said Marcellinus. "Philodemos has told me so much about you. And what a pleasure to meet your daughter. I had heard that she was beautiful. Still, I'm surprised at just how beautiful."

He spoke Greek with great precision, though with a slight Italian accent that reminded Makrina of Marcus. In looks, too, there was some resemblance, in part because Marcellinus was also in uniform, as an officer of the civil service. He wore a long-sleeve, light-blue tunic with two wide yellow stripes descending from each shoulder. His cloak also was yellow, trimmed with silver and gathered at his right shoulder with a large official silver brooch, bearing the images of the emperors of the East. He was clean-shaven like Marcus, but his face was more refined and perfectly balanced, with straight, clean features. His curly brown hair was expertly cut and combed.

One striking difference was the color of his eyes. They were sparkling blue, bluer than Makrina had ever seen, and quite alert and attentive.

"Makrina," he said with a warm smile, "My name is Gaius Valerius Marcellinus. I'm a friend of the tribune Aemilius Canio."

A look of surprise appeared on Makrina's face.

"We grew up together in Rome," he continued. "I happened upon him in Byzantium on my way here, and he said he knew you."

"Yes, indeed," said Makrina. "How was he, when you saw him in Byzantium?"

"In good health," said Marcellinus, "but sad to have left you, I'm afraid. He must have been quite fond of you, but then I can see why. He mentioned that you were a Christian. Is that so?"

"Yes. I am," she answered.

"May I ask how long you have been one?"

"Two months," she said.

"Not long at all. But you must have studied the Christian religion for much longer."

"I was under instruction for almost a year."

The surprise this time was on her father's face.

"How did you first learn about the Christian religion?" Marcellinus asked.

"Excuse me?" asked Makrina.

"Who first introduced you to it?"

"My friend Chione."

"Who were your teachers?" he asked.

Makrina hesitated, feigning distraction. She was, in fact, still thinking of Marcus. "I'm sorry. What did you say?" she asked.

"Who were your Christian teachers?"

"The elders of the Assembly. Why do you ask?"

"My apologies, Makrina. I should have explained. I'm here to accomplish certain duties with regard to the recent imperial edict. As a Christian, you might be able to help me. You're in no trouble yourself, of course."

"How can I help you?" she asked.

"We'd like to know more about the Assembly here—its leaders, its people."

"I can't help you. I'm too new to the Assembly," she said.

"Specifically," said Marcellinus, "we'd like to know what has happened to certain scriptures not found at the Christian basilica. We have, of course, recovered many books—some Jewish scriptures, some works by various Christians—but no Gospels. I know that there are four Christian Gospels, and I would expect that a congregation as large and as wealthy as the one here in Sinope would have all four, perhaps even more than one copy of each. We've found none. Have you any idea what has become of them?"

Makrina shook her head slowly, thoughtfully. "No," she answered.
"Would you have any idea who might know?"

Makrina paused for time to think. "No, I wouldn't," she said.

Marcellinus bowed his head to hide a spreading smile. Moving around
to the other side of the mayor's desk, he said, "You might still be of some
help to us, Makrina. Whoever has the Gospels must turn them in. The penalty for defying an imperial edict of this kind is severe. If the Gospels are
not surrendered and the persons responsible are not identified, the penalty
may be applied to the entire congregation. You could prevent that, Makrina,
first by warning the congregation of the dangers of holding out and urging
them to submit, and second by informing us of anything you might learn
regarding the whereabouts of the Gospels. We would be very grateful for
your assistance."

Makrina looked at the handsome young Italian and for a moment
imagined Marcus in his place.

"I have nothing further," said Marcellinus. "It has indeed been a pleasure
to meet you, Makrina. I do hope that we shall see each other again. Thank
you, Aristoboulos. May the gods be with you, and all your household."

Makrina bowed respectfully and hurried out of the room, not waiting
for her father.

There were others brought in that day for questioning, including Theodoros,
the town clerk; Posidonios, who was Chione's father, like Aristoboulos a
provincial decurion, responsible for public works and revenue; and the elderly overseer Archelaos, who was held for further questioning when he
refused to say where the Gospels were.

In the days that followed, many more Christians were questioned by the
charming official, who became the delight of Sinopean society, Christians
excepted. Soldiers began to dismantle the Christians' basilica, but no other
Christians were charged or arrested before Marcellinus left on a inspection
tour of the surrounding villages.

Then, shortly after his return, the town received another edict from the
court in Nicomedia, this one ordering the arrest of the heads of all congre-
gations. Archelaos was already in jail, but Marcellinus took the opportunity
to arrest the rest of the clergy because the Gospels were still missing. In less
than an hour, eight Christian men, including the elder Theogenes and the
readers Philippos and Andreas, were arrested and jailed. Within a week, six
more elders were added from the surrounding villages.

The edict also required the dismissal of Christians from public office
and the demotion of Christians from the ranks of the nobility. Theodoros
lost his position as town clerk, Posidonios was removed from the town
council and demoted from the rank of decurion, and Bardas the trader

and Hermogenes the baker lost their concessions as suppliers to the army. Everyone then knew how effective Marcellinus's interrogations had been. There was hardly a soul in the local Assembly who was not now known to the authorities. Among the clergy, only Philippos the elder remained at large, on account of being confused with Philippos the reader, and everyone thought it was only a matter of time before that mistake was noticed.

The day after Theodoros was dismissed from his post, Philodemos the mayor got Aristoboulos to ask Kimon if he would take Theodoros's place, at least until another qualified candidate could be hired. Much as Aristoboulos expected, Kimon at first refused, saying he didn't need the job, didn't want the job, and wouldn't take the job away from a friend.

"How could I hold my head high through the streets of town with everyone knowing I had benefitted from a friend's misfortune?" Kimon protested, but his wily father already had the answer.

"Hire Theodoros as your private secretary and pay him whatever you like to do the job for you," suggested Aristoboulos. "Philodemos will overlook it as long as appearances are maintained, which means that the very worst of it for you, Kimon, is that you'd have to get out of bed at a decent hour and go to work like the rest of us. You'd do that, of course, to save a friend from penury, wouldn't you?"

Kimon took the job and did as his father suggested, paying Theodoros exactly what the city paid him as the new town clerk.

With all known Christian clergy in custody, Marcellinus proceeded to press his case for the surrender of the missing Gospels. Through Posidonios he informed the Assembly that he wanted the Gospels in hand before the governor arrived in April for his annual assizes. He was reluctant to use torture in his interrogations, but he was prepared to make an example of the clergymen if the Gospels were not surrendered. He would begin by flogging one clergyman a day as long as the Assembly resisted.

The next morning at about the third hour, the whole town heard the first crack of the whip, coming from the garrison. Word spread quickly that the soldiers were flogging one of the Christians. A crowd soon gathered at the garrison gate, which was open for viewing as usual but blocked by guards.

Peering over shoulders, the widow Euphemia gasped when she recognized Andreas the reader. "Go tell Theodoulia!" she shouted to a neighbor.

Eleven lashes later, a young woman in her last month with child struggled to the fore, helped by her mother and sister. "Andreas!" she shrieked suddenly, seeing her husband dangling at the post, his back already striped with lesions. "Andreas!" She reached forward desperately, but the guards held her back, not without difficulty. "No! No! Stop! Stop!" she wailed, bursting forth with tears. "Please stop!"

The guards looked at each other uncertainly. "Can't you see she's with child!" shouted Theodoulia's mother at the guards. "Tell them to stop!"

An officer of the guard walked over and eyed the wailing woman. "Take her away," he said to the mother.

"Have mercy!" her mother demanded. "Her life's in danger, and the life of her child. You'll kill them both if you don't kill him!"

"Take her away," said the officer again.

"She's almost in labor already," said her mother. "What good would it do?"

The officer looked at Theodoulia, who was wailing in terror and pain. Then he turned and said, "Enough for now." The soldier coiled his whip and handed it to another. "Twenty-six," he said. "Your turn tomorrow."

Theodoulia sobbed as they cut her husband down and carried him away face down on a litter. He could barely raise his head to see his wife still straining to get past the guards.

"Come along, Doulia. It's over now. He'll be well again," said her mother, easing her sobbing daughter away from the gate. As they passed, Euphemia reached forward and touched Doulia on the shoulder. Her mother looked at her grimly. "God save us," she said.

That afternoon, Aristoboulos summoned Makrina to the tablinum, where she met her mother and Chione's father, Posidonios. "Posidonios says you have the missing books," said Aristoboulos. "If that's so, you must give them up."

"It's for the best, Makrina," said Posidonios. "If they are not turned over, there may be more beatings and perhaps more arrests. We can't allow that to happen."

"But they are Gospels. How can we give them up? They may be destroyed," said Makrina.

"We have no choice," said Posidonios. "The law requires it. As Christians we must obey the laws of the caesars. They are, after all, appointed by God."

"Has Archelaos said this?"

"Archelaos speaks as a true champion of Christ," said Posidonios. "We would not expect anything else from such a noble soul. But we must think of what is good for all. The arrest and beating of the clergy is only the first step. There could be widespread confiscations of property, perhaps the dispossession of the entire Assembly, if the edict is not obeyed. We must show the Caesars we are true Romans, loyal citizens of the empire, and that we are not a source of discord and division."

"But the Gospels are not Caesar's to demand."

"That's enough, Makrina," said her father. "If you have the books, go and get them. Eugenia's, too, if she has any."

Makrina gritted her teeth and did as she was told, returning soon with both Gospels, her own and Eugenia's. Posidonios thanked Aristoboulos, who provided a servant to carry them. Makrina left quickly without waiting to be dismissed and returned to her room, where she remained a long time.

The next morning Posidonios delivered all four Gospels to Marcellinus at the town hall, in the presence of Philodemos the mayor and Kimon, the new town clerk. They had been hidden away by zealous youths, explained Posidonios, who gave assurance that the imperial edicts would be obeyed. Marcellinus thanked him profusely and promised that the cooperation of the Assembly would not go unrewarded.

When he had left, Marcellinus inspected the codices to his satisfaction. "At last all is in hand," he said, with a smile of delight. "Our job, Philodemos, is nearly finished, and just in time, too. The governor will be here the week after next."

"Why not wait until then and destroy the books in his presence?" said Kimon. "I would expect that the illustrious Hierocles would enjoy such an event."

"An excellent idea," said Marcellinus.

"Yes, indeed, an excellent idea," said Philodemos.

"Very well, then, Kimon," said Marcellinus. "See that the books are secured until then. You might also give some thought to a fitting ceremony to attend their burning."

"Certainly, sir," said Kimon.

Marcellinus and the mayor left to resume their hearings, and Kimon himself locked the Gospels in the city vault, to which only he and the mayor had access.

In a back room of the city building, out of the sight of Marcellinus, Theodoros was at work as usual when Kimon came to see him. "We have the Gospels," Kimon announced. Theodoros looked at him with alarm. "Posidonios turned them in this morning to Marcellinus and the mayor."

"All four?" asked Theodoros.

"Yes," answered Kimon. "Marcellinus inspected them himself and was quite satisfied."

"How could Posidonios do this? Did he say who had them?"

"He didn't volunteer any names, and Marcellinus didn't ask."

"Where are they now?" asked Theodoros.

"In the vault."

"What's to be done with them?"

"They are to be held for the governor's arrival and destroyed in his presence, in a sort of welcome ceremony," said Kimon.

"What an evil idea!" exclaimed Theodoros, rising from his chair. "To think of that vile enemy of Christ Hierocles reveling in the destruction of the Gospels of our Lord! Whose idea was this?"

Kimon shrugged.

"Give them to me, Kimon. We can put other manuscripts in their place. They'll never know."

"They would know, Theodoros. Marcellinus would know. He knows your books. He would recognize the substitution at a glance. I can't take that chance."

"Then let me make copies."

"Copies? You can't make copies in a couple of weeks, and I couldn't get away with letting you try unless I locked you in the vault with them."

"Please, Kimon. We must preserve them somehow."

"I don't know how. I can't risk a conspiracy against the caesars just to save a few books."

"They're not just any books, Kimon. They are the Word of God, the Holy Gospel! Nothing means more to us!"

Kimon shook his head. "Theodoros, surely there is more to your religion than a collection of texts. From what you've told me, there is much more, and I would expect that your faith would survive the loss of a few books."

The usually calm little man was now quite animated. "This is a vile evil and a great sin for those who gave them up! They have all made themselves agents of the Antichrist, the children of Satan! A few years of prosperity and they're all willing to surrender everything to keep the few luxuries they've accumulated! Lord have mercy!"

With that, Theodoros stormed out of the room and left the building. Kimon threw up his hands and returned to work, with even less enthusiasm than before.

In the week that followed, the Assembly in Sinope was split between those who approved of the surrender of the Gospels and those who condemned it. The former favored cooperating with the authorities in the hope that the persecution would soon pass if the authorities were not provoked. The latter sought resistance and confrontation to make the most of their witness.

From his cell, the overseer Archelaos urged reconciliation, not approving the surrender of the Gospels but forgiving it. Others among the clergy were less forgiving, and the split widened when Marcellinus released all of the clergy except Archelaos and the chief elders of the surrounding villages, whom the second edict required him to imprison. Some of the servers and readers who were released professed their willingness to suffer for the cause of Christ and condemned the quick surrender of the Gospels, which they regarded as cowardly and foolish, or premature at the very least.

Marcellinus concluded his investigations and spent his final days before the governor's arrival preparing for the event and again making the rounds of Sinopean society. The recovery of the Gospels had added to his prestige. Once again all of Sinope was again talking about the young, handsome, exceptionally competent official whose future appeared so bright. Even some Christians, besides Posidonios, spoke well of him, though they, he knew, would have their own reasons for doing so.

"We mean them no harm," Marcellinus once confided to Kimon. "But the good of all must come first. If Christians would only at least outwardly honor the other gods once in a while, no one would care what they did in private. But they insist upon denying all other gods, condemning everyone else for not believing in theirs, and dividing the empire between us and them. Very un-Roman."

Kimon saw him most during those final days, being responsible for many of the details of the governor's visit. This year as every year, the governor would stay at the country villa of Aristoboulos, the senior decurion in Sinope, and this year as every year, his visit would begin with a gala reception at the villa, hosted by the town council and attended by all of Sinope's leading citizens.

Kimon had been involved in the preparation of the event in previous years, but never before had those preparations been so extensive. Marcellinus thought of everything. His dedication was admirable, and his understanding of people and protocol and politics was amazing. He was obviously very intelligent, in a way Kimon knew he himself was not. Even compared to Marcus, whose practicality Kimon admired, Marcellinus came out ahead. Marcus was handsome, well-bred, and earnest. Marcellinus was all that and more. He knew the ways of the world. He knew how to make his way upward without appearing overly ambitious. And he knew how to win the confidence of educated provincials like Kimon.

The reception for the governor was held shortly after his arrival during the first spell of especially pleasant spring weather—long, warm days followed by cool, crisp, pest-less nights. The only thing Marcellinus could not control had turned out perfectly anyway. (The gods did seem to favor him, thought Kimon.)

The entire event was held out of doors in the villa's expansive terrace. Everyone who was still someone in Sinope was there. Posidonios and his wife Kallista were not, nor were any other known Christians, except Makrina, whom nobody minded. The governor, attended by his military aide, greeted everyone upon arrival, after which there was an extended period of mingling before the gathering was called to order by Aristoboulos, who wasted no words in introducing the mayor, who wasted many words in introducing the governor, who then gave a long, sententious address on the restoration of Roman values that went right over the heads of everyone present except Kimon, who wasn't in the least interested, and Marcellinus, who was busy the entire evening behind the scenes, ensuring the event's success.

The climax of the evening came after the sun had set and the air had turned cool. The guests had not prepared for the change in temperature, but Marcellinus had. A pyre was prepared in one corner of the garden, and before it was set a table on which were displayed the four codices confiscated from the Christians. The mayor made some remarks about his city's faithfulness to the emperors and the empire. Then the governor, accompanied by the mayor and Admiral Ammonius, commander of the Euxine Sea fleet, took a closer look at the codices, lifting the cover of one and flipping casually through the pages, examining the carved covers of the others more carefully, and then pronouncing them all fit for burning. The books were placed on top of the pyre, and the pyre was kindled. The audience showed little interest until the small pyre suddenly burst into a billowing bonfire, with the aid of a certain well-placed incendiary material. The crowd gasped and jumped backward and then cheered the spectacle.

Makrina watched the ceremony from the edge of gathering, shivering under her summer mantle. When the flames of the fire engulfed the Gospels, she raised her right hand to make the sign of the cross, but before it reach her forehead, another hand intercepted it. She turned and found the smiling face of Marcellinus.

"Careful," he said, clutching her hand gently. "Someone might be watching."

Slowly he lowered her hand back down to her side, without letting go of it. Makrina glanced around nervously while Marcellinus gazed at the fire.

"They are only books," he said.

"You don't understand," said Makrina.

"I think I do," he replied.

Makrina shivered uncontrollably.

"Cold?" he asked. She nodded, and he removed his cloak and draped it over her shoulders. Her hands now clutched his cloak around her, but his arm drew her even closer.

"I'm leaving tomorrow for Amisos, but I'll be back in a few months. I would like to see you then," he said.

"You are an enemy of my people. You persecute my God. Why should I want to see you?"

"These are perilous times, Makrina. You may need someone to protect you."

"From whom would I need protection?" she asked.

Marcellinus laughed. "You have less to fear from me than you think," he said. "I'm only doing my duty, enforcing the laws of the empire, preserving and defending the Roman way. Even Christians believe in obeying the rulers of this world. Are rulers not ordained by God to punish evildoers?"

"Sometimes the rulers are wrong and their laws are evil."

"The worst is over. As long as Christians keep their cult to themselves, they will be left in peace. The emperors will overlook them, as I will overlook you. Farewell, Makrina. May your god be with you, until we meet again."

He left before she could speak, but it was just as well. She didn't know what to say.

She stood there staring at the fire, thinking over his words and wondering about his intent. Then she remember his cloak, still around her shoulders.

# VI

Marcus slept too long after a long night out with friends. He had dreamed he was battling Isaurian bandits in the mountains of Cilicia when reality came to his rescue. He was never so happy to be home as in that waking moment, and he thanked his stars for the room he had been so anxious to leave a few years before.

After a sickening sea journey from Nicomedia to Ostia, he had quickly discharged his duty to the emperor with the delivery of the imperial dispatch, and now he was a civilian again. Laying aside his tribune's cloak and belt had not been easy, but he knew he would not miss the demands and deprivations of service. Freedom for all ex-soldiers is very sweet, for a while.

His first two weeks in Rome had been a whirlwind of obligations and diversions. He had honored his mother Racilia at her mausoleum on the Appian Way, paid his respect to family friends, greeted family clients, and even offered a sacrifice to the goddess Roma to inaugurate his return. He had joined friends at the baths and the theaters, dined with them in their homes and apartments, and watched the progress of their lawsuits in the courts—a popular attraction when there were no games or races scheduled. He had enjoyed most the many little things that civilians took for granted— sleeping late, daily shaves, leisurely baths, walks through the public squares and gardens, reclining at meals.

The previous night, Marcus's former schoolmate Quintus Ennius Felix had hosted a dinner party in his honor, a proper Roman cena that began early and ended late, after many courses and much wine. Even so, it was a tame affair—Felix's new wife Calvina saw to that. Her motive seemed to be Marcus's introduction to her cousin Vera, who had recently arrived in Rome from Carthage. For Marcus, it could only have been better if more of Marcus's friends had been there, but so many were now somewhere else. Titus Quintillianus was now in Egypt as deputy quaestor of Alexandria, Gaius Aerecius and Spellius Longinus were both at the court of the augustus Maximianus in Mediolanum, and Martius Condianus had just left Mediolanum to take over as governor of Corsica. Rome, it seemed, was just not the place to be for young ambitious patricians anymore.

The weather had just turned warm in Rome, so Marcus had Alexander give him his morning shave in the garden. Before leaving the army, Marcus had offered to buy out Alexander's term of enlistment if he would remain as Marcus's personal secretary. Alexander jumped at the opportunity. An educated Syrian from Antioch, he was always more comfortable in the imperium's major cities than on its frontiers, but he had been a good soldier and servant through Marcus's last campaign, and Marcus valued the company of a fellow veteran who understood the habits of a former soldier.

The domus Canio was a spacious residence on the Janiculum Hill, a suburban neighborhood on the west bank of the Tiber River, where many wealthy Romans retreated to escape the crowded and confused confines of the old city. Its garden offered a panoramic view of Rome. From it, Marcus could have seen all seven hills of Rome, had they not been buried beneath many layers of construction and debris. The capital of the world was a whirlpool that sucked everything to it. For centuries it grew both outwards and up, limited only by the ingenuity of its architects. The emperors had tried repeatedly to reign in construction and enforce building codes, but they were never successful.

Recently Rome's growth had stalled. Her emperors held court in other cities, her privileged status was all but abolished, and her wealth began to ebb away. Decay outpaced repair. Tenements rose and fell with equal frequency. Demolition rivaled construction for the engineers' attention. Fire was an expedient. From the Janiculum, Marcus could see columns of smoke rising from every quarter. Rome in those days was always burning. Day and night in one precinct or another the fire alarms sounded.

Sitting for his shave in the warm April sun, amid the comfort and beauty of his father's townhouse, Marcus wasn't thinking of Rome's decline. He was thinking instead of the hardships of army life. "Do you miss the camp, Alexander?" he asked, between strokes of the razor.

"Not in the least," answered Alexander, without stopping.

"Neither do I," said Marcus.

"It's too soon, sir. You're still making up for all you've missed. Give it a month or two and you'll have had enough of soft civilian life."

"You just want me to laugh so you can cut my throat and go back to Antioch."

"Not at all, sir. Alexandria, maybe, but not Antioch." Alexander was a rakishly handsome fellow, with the broken nose and scarred cheek that had so impressed the young Eugenia on the quay in Sinope.

"Why not Antioch?"

"Well, sir, there is a certain very wealthy, very powerful man in Antioch who has promised to relieve me of my manhood if I return there," said Alexander.

"Great gods! What did you do to him?"

"Made him a cuckold. In gratitude he vowed to make me either a soldier or a eunuch."

"He gave you a choice?"

"It was only fair," said Alexander. "After all, it was she who seduced me."

"So you gave up your freedom to save your manhood."

"You could say that. That's what I told myself then. For a long time I wasn't so sure."

"Was she worth it?"

"Worth three years of servitude and suffering? No woman is worth that, not if you can't keep her."

Marcus grunted his agreement.

"So now Antioch is out of question for me," said Alexander, "but Rome is more than enough to take her place. I heard yesterday in the forum that Diocletianus is coming next month for his very first visit as emperor. Is that true?"

"Could be. I don't recall that he's ever been here," said Marcus.

"It is true," said an elderly voice.

"Good morning, Father," said Marcus.

"Good morning, Marcus," said the elder Canio with a nod to Alexander. "Diocletianus has never been to Rome since taking the purple. If he was ever here before that, no one ever noticed." A thin smile stretched across the old man's face. Age had reduced his stature and dried up his features, accentuating the size of his half-bald head, but his eyes were still lively and piercing.

Marcus Aemilius Canio Senior was the oldest member of the Senate, scion of a distinguished clan of Roman patricians, the gens Aemilius. Family legend counted them among the early supporters of the first Caesar Augustus in his bid for imperial power, but their present fortune had been made under the Antonine caesars—the last of the truly great Roman emperors. Since the death of Marcus Aurelius more than a century before, the imperial dignity had been claimed by many lesser lights and some thoroughgoing scoundrels before finally falling into the hands of a new breed of professional soldiers, who included the two reigning augusti and their two subordinate caesars.

With few exceptions, this new breed was of common stock and barely more than barbarians. Diocletian was the son of a Dalmatian freedman, Maximian had been a common soldier from beyond the Danuvius, and Galerius had been a drover in the Carpathians. Constantius Chlorus, who alone could claim noble birth, had a modest upbringing in the Illyrian countryside. Their distinction was that they were indeed good soldiers and generals, sometimes good sovereigns, and always dedicated Romans, though not the kind of Romans that die-hards like M. Aemilius Canio would have preferred.

"Would you rather the emperor stay away now, Father?" asked Marcus.

"We've seen enough of the emperors. We see the augustus Maximianus more than we should. Oh, the people love to see them because they expect to be showered with favors and entertained at the circus and amphitheater while they are here. Diocletian is coming to celebrate his vicennalia. They'll be expecting quite a show for that."

"So it takes two decades for a Roman emperor to visit Rome?"

"He hates the Senate, Marcus, and for the same reason he hates the City," said the old man, looking out over the eternal Urbs. "The joke is that most senators haven't been here either."

"Most, Father?"

"You won't find five here now, though I expect a few more will show up for the emperor."

Alexander finished his work and handed Marcus a warm, wet towel before taking his leave. Marcus rose to his feet and wiped his face carefully, looking for traces of blood on the towel while listening to his father.

"The Senate has never been more representative, not of Rome but of the imperium," said the elder Canio. "Virtually everyone within the bounds of imperium is a citizen now, and so the Senate has Gauls, Syrians, Iberians, Illyrians, and Africans, as well as Italians. No Egyptians at the moment. Diocletianus hates Egypt more than Rome, but with better reason. Every senator is lord of his own locale, with local interests and local gods, but they are all now Romans. Rome is the imperium now, Marcus, not the City. This you see here, this is not Rome. This is merely Rome's cradle—old, empty, and unneeded."

Marcus had never heard his father speak this way. In his youth, his father had spoken so often, so inspiringly of the glory of Rome, the City as well as the imperium.

His father continued: "It had always been the dream of your mother and mine that you would follow my path and one day enter the Senate yourself. Everything we gave you—your education, your discipline, your training—was meant to guide you along that way. Now, however, I'm afraid that my path will not lead you to the Senate, and that perhaps the Senate is not where you ought to go."

"What do you mean?"

"I mean, Marcus, that the Senate doesn't much matter nowadays. A senatorship is now more a reward than an office, a reward for services rendered to the imperium, or rather to the emperors. All power lies in the hands of the emperors, so it is them whom you must please, and Rome isn't the place from which to do it. There is very little here for you if you want to make something of your life. Oh, you could live here quite a long time if you aspired to being nothing more than comfortable. An older man than you, a man of another mind might be content to busy himself here with commerce or the law, but these alone will get you nowhere. If you want the dignified ease of our ancestors—the *otium* of a Cicero or a Pliny—there are better places in which to find it. On the other hand, if you want to count in this world, if you would be a man of moment, Marcus, other places matter more."

"Other places?"

"You are a soldier, Marcus, in a world ruled by soldiers. You belong in Nicomedia or Mediolanum or Treveris. The last is the best. The caesar Constantius is at least a man of honor and education. He would value the same in you. Besides, Treveris would keep you closer to your mother's estates in Aquitania. Weigh that in your mind, Marcus. Enjoy your stay, but do not let fortune find you napping, for someday the emperors will turn on this city and take it by force, and woe to him who would defy them in its defense."

The old man excused himself to take his rest, leaving Marcus in the garden staring pensively at what was left of Rome.

Later that afternoon Marcus met Felix for a vigorous game of handball at the new baths being built by Diocletian. Marcus lost. Lack of practice, said Felix. *Lack of concentration,* thought Marcus. Afterwards they sweated out the wine of the previous evening in the steam room before immersing themselves in the luscious warmth of the caldarium.

"So, what did you think of Vera?" said Felix, sliding down into the steaming water.

Marcus thought for a moment. "Oh, Vera. Pleasant, pretty. Is that why Calvina insisted that you meet me here today?"

"I suppose so. She's not usually so generous with my time," said Felix. "I've taken to staying late at the courts just to have some time to myself. Just pleasant and pretty? Well, don't worry. Calvina has many more cousins and friends."

"I'm honored that she's so anxious for me to marry."

"I think she's more concerned for her cousins and friends. She hardly knows you, although you did impress her last night. Serious, capable, upright, ambitious. Women love that in a man. It says money, glamor, and security to them."

Marcus shrugged. "Do you know, Felix, I've not been home two weeks and already people are telling me that I should be someplace else."

"Who would be so foolish?"

"My father, for one."

"Well, he's an old man, Marcus. He's bitter because the emperors all but ignore the Senate and he's ashamed that the City isn't home to the court anymore. So what? Rome's still the capital, still the greatest city on earth. Who would want to live anywhere else? All those petty provincial patricians—they all want to come here. So why would you want to leave? Where else are you going to find a wife? Rome's the best market for women in the world. You obviously didn't find one in Asia, at least not one worth bringing back."

"I did, Felix."

"You did? Well, where is she? What happened?"

Marcus hesitated. He ached to tell someone, but he would rather that Felix not be the first. "Let's move to the tepidarium," he said, climbing out of the water and heading off without looking back.

Felix followed Marcus to the tepidarium, a larger, less private pool, much cooler than the caldarium but still warm. "So who was she?" Felix asked, once in the water.

Marcus took a deep breath and sighed. "She was the daughter of an eminent man, a decurion in Sinope. She was very beautiful and very charming, but she wouldn't come with me to Rome to be my wife."

"Why not?"

"She was a Christian and she said she could only marry another Christian."

"Oh, really? When was this?"

"Just this spring, on my way home."

"So you're still trying to forget her, or are you?"

"I am."

"You know it's better that you didn't marry her. It would hardly help your career to marry a Christian, especially with this new edict."

"You know, Felix, I almost didn't come home. I had almost decided to wait in Nicomedia to see if she would change her mind, but when I got there they handed me a dispatch case with the edict in it and told me to deliver it to the City Prefect here in Rome. It was my last official duty before leaving the army."

"So you've paid her back. Good for you. Serves them right."

Marcus said nothing.

"You wouldn't want to marry a Christian anyway, even if they weren't outlawed. She'd be after you all your life to become one, wanting you to attend their services, having you meet their 'elders.' And if you didn't become one, she'd start telling your children how evil you were because you wouldn't obey their god. Of course, she'd insist upon having them baptized."

"Yes, you're probably right."

"Of course I am. Look, there are plenty of women in Rome you can marry instead. Rome is full of young, rich virgins, and any one of them would marry a senator's son. Once we sort out those among them who also happen to be Christians, you'll still have plenty to pick from. With luck, you'll find one with family and friends here who simply can't leave the City. Then you'll be here forever. It shouldn't take any time at all, though there's no need to rush. In the meantime, you might consider taking a mistress, or maybe just someone to sleep with. That would help you forget her."

"It's not that easy," said Marcus.

"Sure it is. Everybody who's not married has one or the other. Why be so hard on yourself, Marcus? Your father took in someone after your mother died. If you don't marry immediately or take a mistress or concubine, everyone will think you're just a profligate who prefers prostitutes, or worse."

"Think of something else, Felix."

"I'm just trying to help," said Felix. "Cheer up, Marcus. You've got a lot to look forward to." He paused to await a response from Marcus, but when none was forthcoming, he floated away and submerged himself in the middle of the pool. A moment later he was back beside Marcus. "Sulpicia's in town," he said.

"Aelia Sulpicia? But she married Ulpius Florianus?"

"Yes, she did, and he's older than ever. Spends all his time in the countryside writing poetry and gardening. She's here most of the time, in a very nice apartment on the Aventine. I'm sure she'd love to see you. Why, with any luck, he'll be dead and out of your way before too long. Not that you'd want to marry her."

"No, I wouldn't," said Marcus, climbing out of the pool.

"Where are you going now?"

"Where else? To the frigidarium, to cool off."

For several weeks, Marcus tried as best as he could to find a place for himself in Rome. He visited friends and relatives in their offices, secretly observing the life they led, comparing it to others and to the army. He spent many hours at the law courts listening to the advocates and the judges, and wondering all the while if he could bear to lead such a life. The law had once attracted him and many other ambitious young Romans, who saw it as a path to prominence, but this was less so since the emperors had moved their courts elsewhere. Now he saw the best advocates as wasting their greatness on mundane matters—adulteries, breeches of contract, boundary disputes. Such cases interested him for an afternoon, but not much more.

Nothing he witnessed in the law courts impressed him as much as the sights and sounds of battle. One incident in particular stuck in his mind. It was toward the end of the debacle at Carrhae in upper Mesopotamia. As the Roman army was trying to disengage from the Persian host, a cavalry trooper, already ahead of Marcus in the retreat, suddenly turned about and galloped alone back into the fray, to rescue another trooper whose horse was down. The inexplicable nobility of the act surpassed everything he ever saw in Rome. He tried to tell Felix about it, but Felix didn't seem impressed. Perhaps only a soldier would be.

When he was not looking in on the lives of friends of friends, Marcus was revisiting Rome. At first there was too much to see and not enough time to spend in each place, but before long he had run out of things to see, and nothing seemed worth visiting twice.

His restlessness increased as the days grew warmer. Spring was the season for new campaigns. In the City, it only lengthened the days he was trying to kill. He could only spend so long in the libraries of Trajan's Forum, catching up on his reading. Then he would stroll aimlessly through the streets and alleys of the city, following a fleeting hope that something or someone he would meet along the way would rescue him from his memory of Makrina.

He spent an entire afternoon sitting on the steps of Tiber Island, staring into the flowing water, recalling everything he had ever known about her, examining every episode of their courtship, savoring every touch, every kiss, every joy he had known. When the sun set, he packed each memory away in his mind, where he found them again the next day, and the next.

All the while he felt the nagging demand of the flesh. It had haunted his life unremittingly for years, confounding his attempts to follow a philosophic life. Try as he might to rise above it, through contemplation, through study, through exercise, through diversion, his body pulled him down into abject surrender. It had been easier to resist while in camp, though he could not claim that his time in the army was without defeat. Every furlough had prompted the same demand, which had to be met.

In his first month in Rome, he had yielded to it only once, with a girl who approached him one evening near the basilica of Diocletian. Having thus once appeased the dark gods in the blood, he was relieved of the threat for awhile. But the tension grew again with time, and its assault upon him redoubled when he remembered Sulpicia.

Barely a week after dinner with Felix and Calvina, Marcus received a note from Sulpicia welcoming him home and inviting him to call. He did not respond.

Then, late in May, the emperor Diocletian and all his court arrived in Rome amid much fanfare and public celebration. The guards could barely hold back the crowds for the emperor's procession to wend down the Sacred Way through the Great Forum to the Imperial Rostrum, where the emperor was greeted by the City Prefect and the Senate. From there they climbed the Capitoline Hill to the Temple of Jupiter Optimus Maximus Capitolinus, where the emperor, in his role as pontifex maximus, offered sacrifice on behalf of himself, the City, and the empire. Marcus and other members of the senatorial and equestrian classes waited below in the plaza of the Comitia outside the Senate house.

Sulpicia was among them. Marcus eyed her at a distance. She looked as alluring as ever, though modestly dressed for the state occasion. A yellow silk palla covered her head and shoulders. Beneath it was a sea-blue stola with deep folds that discreetly hid her figure, the figure of Venus, as he remembered. The hair of her head was dressed in braided loops about her ears, and a simple diadem made, it seemed, of crystal rested upon her forehead. That was all Marcus could see from where he was, and he would not move closer and risk being seen by her. Instead he slipped away unnoticed, and was quite pleased with himself for doing so.

He was not so lucky the next day at the opening of the games, when the crowd was just settling into their seats at the circus and she saw him first.

"Marcus!" she shouted. "Dear Marcus! What a joy to see you!" She rushed up to him, clasped his head in her hands, and kissed him hard on the lips. No sooner had she done so, than she suddenly pushed him away. "Where have you been?" she demanded. "I've been worried sick that you wouldn't come see me!"

Marcus saw her pouting face and decided he had better make the most of it. "I've been away," he said, "at the Port of Augustus. I'm sorry, I should have called."

In an instant she was back in his arms with her cheek on his chest. "Oh, Marcus, Marcus, I've missed you so much," she said. Then she was free again. "Look, Mucia, it's Marcus. Publius, I want you to meet Marcus Aemilius Canio, the too handsome son of the too great Senator Aemilius Canio. Marcus, this is Publius—" The rest of the name, Marcus didn't catch, but it didn't seem to matter. As soon as the poor fellow's name was out, Sulpicia turned her back to him, latched onto Marcus's arm. "Come sit with me," she commanded.

They settled together in the section reserved for them near the imperial *pulvinar*, at the west end of the Circus Maximus. The silent Publius sat on Sulpicia's other side, and beside him sat Mucia Porenia, who seemed to be with a fellow named Tiberius, whom Marcus did not know. Before long they were joined by more friends, who sat just behind and below them, and then by Felix and his bride Calvina.

"Marcus!" said Felix, with a knowing grin, "Well, what a surprise. Look, dear, it's Marcus Aemilius—and Sulpicia."

Calvina's eyes widened momentarily and then narrowed when she saw Sulpicia. "Health, Marcus," she said. "Health, Sulpicia."

"How are you, Calvina?" said Sulpicia sweetly. "It's been so long since I've seen you."

"Since our wedding, I think," said Calvina.

"Was that the last time? Well, I hope you'll join us here so we can catch up," said Sulpicia.

"Thank you, Sulpicia. We'd love to," said Felix, feeling a sudden twinge of pain in his lower back, where Calvina had secretly pinched him sharply.

"So, Marcus," said Sulpicia, "Felix said you've left the army and are home for good."

There was another pinch in Felix's back, sharper than before, saying clearly, *When was the last time* you *saw Sulpicia?*

"I've left the army. I think I'm home for good," replied Marcus, covering his uncertainty with a confident grin.

"But what will you do?" asked Mucia from down the line.

"Find an eligible woman to marry," Calvina volunteered. This time it was Felix who pinched Calvina.

"Well, actually," said Marcus, "I'm thinking of becoming an obsessive gambler who spends his life at the circus and the amphitheater."

"Sounds good to me," said a hefty fellow named Rebonius, whom Marcus had just met.

"But, Marcus, you don't gamble. Felix said so," said Calvina.

"Well, anyone can start," said Marcus.

"Here's a start. Ten denarii on the Greens in the first race," said Rebonius.

"You're on," said Felix.

"Felix!"

"Ten denarii on the Blues in the first," said Felix.

"What about you, Marcus?" asked Rebonius.

"Ten on the Blues," answered Marcus.

"I'll take ten on the Blues, too," said Sulpicia. "Publius?"

"Ten on the Greens," said Publius grimly.

"Doesn't anyone want the Whites or the Reds?" asked Mucia.

"That's what I like to see at the circus: someone who'll lay down their money just to make sure the field is covered," said Rebonius.

"Go ahead, Mucia. Waste your money on the Whites if you feel sorry for them," said Felix.

"Well then, ten on the Whites," she said.

"Whose keeping the tally today?"

"Not Felix. He's a lawyer."

"Marcus?"

"No thanks."

"Publius?"

"No."

"Please, no amateurs. I'll keep the tallies," said Rebonius.

"Of course," said Felix. "Let a professional handle it."

One by one the men in the group and a few of the women registered their bets with Rebonius, who recorded everything on a folding wax tablet.

The circus was nearly filled to capacity by then, making it difficult to hear all but the loudest voices.

Sulpicia slipped her hand into Marcus's and leaned close. "Come to dinner with us tonight, Marcus. We're having a cozy little cena at my apartment across the way. It won't be any fun without you, not for me anyway," she said. Her eyes, her lips, her rich perfume, the warmth of her arm against his gave him pause. The dark gods began to stir. "You owe me, Marcus, for all the years you've been away breaking my heart."—Not quite what he remembered, but just then it didn't matter. He nodded his head in acceptance.

Suddenly the crowd surged with excitement. A chorus of trumpets announced the arrival of the emperor. Everyone stood and strained to see him appear upon the pulvinar, a high marble platform jutting out to the edge of the track from the old imperial palaces on the Palatine Hill. There he was, arms upraised to greet the people, who responded by cheering ecstatically and waving their handkerchiefs high in the air. He was a big man, solidly built, with a thick neck and a massive jaw. Beneath his purple cloak, he wore a heavy gold dalmatic over a long white robe with full-length sleeves. A wide, white diadem of pearls—a most un-Roman affectation—adorned his forehead. His gray hair was sprinkled with gold dust, which gleamed divinely in the sunlight. To some, he looked like an oriental god. To Marcus, he looked like an aging centurion masquerading as a Persian prince.

They cheered him nevertheless for as long as he stood there, which was at least a quarter of an hour. When he finally took his seat, the master of the races signaled for quiet with the sounding of a large gong. Then an assemblage of priests and augurs proceeded with the sacrifices at an altar at the middle of the *spina* or spine running the length of the circus, between the tracks. Towering above the altar was the obelisk of Rameses II, taken from Heliopolis by the very first Caesar Augustus. Seven giant bronze eggs and seven bronze dolphins flanked the obelisk on the spina. The eggs were nearly five hundred years old; the dolphins were over three hundred.

The crowd went back to its betting and chatter, waiting patiently until the religious preliminaries were over, but then a disturbance arose. It started, it seemed, with a few boisterous voices shouting demands in the direction of the pulvinar. The curious crowd listened carefully, and when it was sure of what it heard, other voices picked up the demand and began shouting it in unison: *"Christiani tollantur, Christiani non sint!"*—Out with the Christians, let there be no Christians!

"What started this?" asked Sulpicia. Her friends looked at each other. Rebonius shrugged his shoulders.

Before long the whole circus, it seemed, had picked up the chant, to which was added the rhythmic clapping of hands. Over and over again it sounded:

*Christiani tollantur, Christiani non sint!*
*Christiani tollantur, Christiani non sint!*
*Christiani tollantur, Christiani non sint!*

"Look!" shouted Sulpicia, pointing to a young man in the stands not far away who had been set upon by those around him. A bald man with short arms punched at the back of his head repeatedly. Another beat his back with his rolled mat meant for sitting. The young man cowered and covered his head with the arms and started to flee, but when he stumbled under a passing blow, his bald assailant seized him by the collar of his tunic and threw him toward the exit. The man's head struck a stone step and he fell dazed and bloodied upon the pavement. Several bystanders kicked him where he lay, until others stepped in to stop them. They were on the verge of blows when the guards arrived and restored order. Two soldiers carried the senseless victim out of the circus, to the applause of many, while four other soldiers stayed behind to keep the peace.

Similar scenes were acted out in many parts of the circus, as hapless Christians were kicked and punched and pelted with missiles in the crowd's efforts to drive them from its midst. After half an hour, the storm subsided, with the help of more troops. The emperor was not yet ready to risk a riot to encourage support for his policies against the Christians.

The little party of patricians gathered around Sulpicia eased its way back to the event. "It's just as well, leaves more room for gamblers," said Rebonius. "Their leaders rail against the games all the time, so they shouldn't be here anyway," said the one named Tiberius. "Poor fellow," said Mucia. "I hope he's well."

Presently the gates of the stables at the west end opened and four char-iots, each drawn by four restless horses, made their way slowly into position. The crowd sprang to life with cheers of approval and support. "Look, there's Scarpa!" said Mucia.

"Really?" said the young Ponia, squinting to make out the driver of the Blues' chariot as it rounded the opposite end of the spina. "Yes it is!" Scarpa was an ape of a man, short but thick with muscles bronzed by the sun and barely covered by the brief blue tunic of his team, emblazoned with a golden lion's head, his personal insignia. His thick black hair was streaked with gray and flowed behind him like a horse's mane. The reins of his four-horse *quadriga* were wrapped around his waist. A hooked knife was tucked into his belt, should he need to cut himself free in an emergency.

"So the old man's still racing," said Marcus.

"And still winning," said Felix.

"Not today," said Rebonius.

"Ten denarii on Scarpa!" cried Mucia.

"Too late, Mucia," said Tiberius.

"I don't understand women, swooning so over a charioteer," said the gloomy Publius. "The man's an animal."

"I understand them perfectly," said Felix. "The man's an animal." Tiberius and Rebonius laughed. Ponia blushed and Mucia poked Tiberius in the ribs.

"Yes, but he's such a virile animal," said Sulpicia, "unlike some men."

The horses snorted and stamped the sand at the starting line in front of their stables. The breathless crowd hummed with excitement. From a platform atop the stables, the master of the races raised a white kerchief above his head and suddenly threw it out over the track. A trumpet shrieked, whips cracked, the horses sprang to life, and the crowd leaped to its feet and shouted its desire. *Go Blue! Go Green! Go Scarpa!*

Out of the first turn, the Green chariot was already in the lead with the Blue directly behind him. With each lap another bronze dolphin on the spina was tipped forward, nose down as if diving into the dirt. The crowd roar incessantly. The Green held his lead for five full laps before Scarpa made his move on the second leg of the sixth lap. Out of the turn he swung wide just far enough to pull alongside his rival. Partisans of the Blues roared encouragement. "Go Scarpa!" shouted Mucia. "Go Blues!" shouted Sulpicia, jumping up and down in her seat with the use of Marcus's shoulders as lifts.

But the Green driver was able to swing wide in the stretch and force Scarpa wide into the next turn. "Go Green!" shouted Publius and Rebonius.

A less experienced driver would have lost more than his position, but Scarpa backed off just in time and deftly cut his course sharply coming out of the turn, thus managing to hold on to the tail of the leader for the first leg of the seventh and last lap. In the final turn, the Green driver himself swung wide to prevent Scarpa from overtaking him again on his right, but the sly Scarpa this time cut left and forced the leader out of his way. "Go Blues!" shouted Marcus, with sudden ferocity. In the home stretch, both drivers whipped their horses furiously, but the Blue horses were faster and crossed the finish line in front of the imperial pulvinar a head sooner than the Green.

"We won! We won!" shouted Sulpicia still jumping though now with her arms around Marcus's neck. "Write that down, Rebo—we won!"

"Yes, yes. Well, that's what makes it interesting," Rebonius lamented.

# VII

They met again hours later at Sulpicia's apartment, after many more races and a quick trip to the baths to wash away the sun and sweat. Sulpicia greeted Marcus in the atrium with the same unconcealed delight. "What a treat to have you here!" she said, pressing herself against him. She had traded the day's attire for a crimson stola of flowing silk, loose about the legs for comfort in dining, breathtaking for Marcus because of how much of her back it left bare.

Sulpicia's apartment covered the entire ground floor of the Insula Felicita, with the exception of the shops on the outer walls that opened only to the street. Ground-floor apartments in Rome were always the best because they were the only apartments likely to have access to the garden or to running water. Sulpicia's had both.

For the occasion, she had hired extra servants, including a trio of musicians. Three large dining couches were brought into the triclinium, off the center court of the building. There Marcus found Mucia, Tiberius, Ponia, and, to his surprise, Felix and Calvina. "How did you get her to come?" he asked Felix when it was safe. "I told her someone had to keep an eye on you," answered Felix. "And she didn't trust me alone."

Rebonius and Publius had stayed for the rest of the races and were expected later. Ponia insisted that they not wait for her husband Rebonius. "If he hasn't lost it all at the circus, he will have wagered on when the sun will set," she said.

But Rebonius did arrive before the sun set, just as they were finishing the hors d'oeuvres—black and white olives and sticks of celery filled with pomegranate seeds. "Where's Publius?" asked Sulpicia. Rebonius shrugged. "Isn't he here?" he asked.

Sulpicia shook her head. "I hope he isn't staying away out of jealousy," she said, more amused than remorseful.

"Now why would he do that?" said Calvina. Sulpicia just smiled at her.

"Maybe he'll show up later," said Rebonius, taking the place reserved for him on the couch next to Mucia.

"Oh, Rebonius, go wash up first," said Ponia. While her guests sipped warmed honeyed wine, Sulpicia's chambermaid showed the unembarrassed Rebonius to Sulpicia's private bath and brought him a clean tunic and dalmatic. He returned refreshed just as the first entree was being served, snails sautéed in mushrooms and covered with melted Trebulian cheese.

"My, my, Sulpicia: that dalmatic looks familiar," said Mucia.

"Too big to be mine," said Felix. Calvina's eyes flashed him a warning from across the table. Sulpicia had divided the three couples between two couches on opposite sides of the serving table. She and Marcus reclined on the third couch between the two, with Sulpicia in the center and Marcus on her right, in the place of honor. The place on her left awaited the absent Publius.

"It belongs to Ulpius, of course," said Sulpicia.

"And how is your husband, Sulpicia?" asked Calvina.

"Happy not to be here—in the City, I mean. He loves the country. He's quite a farmer and is more at home in his vegetable garden with his radishes and cabbages than in any city."

"Why, with your love of agriculture, you should be with him," Tiberius teased. "Think of it, Sulpicia. What could be better than spending your days stooped over like an old peasant woman, pulling weeds until your hands are raw and cracked?"

"Spare me, Tiberius. Ulpius knew when he married me that I wouldn't leave the City. He's here often enough. I think I saw him—last January?" She tittered.

When they had finished the snails, Sulpicia ordered the lamps lit and called for the second entree, three broiled capons stuffed with buttered oysters and raisins. The diners opened up the capons with their knives and then pulled them apart with their fingers, eating the oysters and raisins with their spoons. Servants supplied them with hot white rolls and filled their drinking bowls with a fine wine from Tiburtina, as good as any Falernian, chilled with Alpine snow. A third entree soon followed the second—four whole boiled lobsters. Her guests were delighted, and even Calvina seemed impressed, and the roasts had not yet been served. They came after the jugglers.

While the other guests were entranced by the cycle of objects through the air, Marcus leaned close to Sulpicia and said privately, "A cozy little cena, you said. With jugglers and musicians?"

Sulpicia feigned embarrassment. "I made a few changes to the program, just for you," she said. "Enjoy yourself, Marcus. There's more."

There was more: a leg of roast lamb, which the diners consumed with noisy pleasure. The wine and food were having their effect. Ponia and Rebonius traded loving jibes across the table for the benefit of others. "Rebo, stop making such a pig of yourself. Mucia, take that away from him. He's had enough." "Tiberius, see what you can do to get Ponia to eat more. At least when her mouth's full we won't have to listen to her."

Tiberius and Felix discussed the law and the trials in progress, who was winning and who was losing, who had delivered speeches worthy of Cicero and who had just made a jackass of himself. Mucia quizzed Marcus on events in Asia. Calvina and Sulpicia at least discovered they patronized the same dressmaker, an Egyptian named Nemos from Alexandria whom Rebonius mocked for his effeminate ways.

After the lamb came a brown-skinned, scantily clad Iberian maiden who twirled lasciviously around the room to the clatter of castanets, while Rebonius improvised the role of a lustful clown. The dance set the mood for the cena's climax—the wanton devouring of a second roast, a succulent piglet still steaming hot. The pig took some time, and when it was nearly finished the guests were ready for a rest. They settled into quiet contentment, nibbling on figs, dates, and damascene plums while listening to harp and flute.

Marcus looked around the room at his present company. The scene was pleasantly familiar, though a few of the names and faces were new. It had been a fitting end to a fine day, filled with the nostalgic thrills of the circus and the convivial company of friends, spiced with the suspense of serious flirtation, which raised in him one desire still wanting satisfaction.

"Marcus? Marcus?"

Marcus turned to Sulpicia, who laughed and said, "Welcome back. Where have you been?"

"In the clouds," said Tiberius.

"Communing with the higher powers," said Felix. "Don't worry, Sulpicia. He does that often. Just punch him a few times and he'll come to his senses."

Sulpicia poked Marcus in the cheek playfully with her fist and giggled.

"I'm sorry," said Marcus. "You were saying?"

"I had asked if you saw Valerius Marcellinus while you were in Asia," she said, with exaggerated annoyance. "Do try to pay attention now, dear."

"I did see him, but just once, by chance. I ran into him in Byzantium on my way home."

"Really? How was he?"

"Well, I suppose," said Marcus. "He was just beginning a tour of Pontus in the service of the provincial governor."

"I always knew he'd do well," said Felix.

"He was so smart and so handsome," said Ponia.

"You wouldn't have liked him, Rebonius. He wasn't much fun," said Sulpicia. "Too serious, too ambitious. Not like Marcus here." She bumped him with her shoulder.

"You think so? What a shame. He seemed so adorable," said Mucia.

"Did you know his uncle is the leader of the Christians in Rome?" said Felix.

"No! That can't be," said Sulpicia.

"He is. I swear it."

"I don't believe you."

"By the gods, I swear it. I was in court the day his uncle and several

Christian elders presented a petition protesting the destruction of their basilicas. He is their president, their 'episcopus.'"

"Well, that would explain why Marcellinus was such a stiff," said Sulpicia. Mucia laughed.

"Surely he's not a Christian, too," said Ponia. "Is he?"

Felix shrugged.

"What do you think, Marcus? You knew him," said Sulpicia.

"Not well," said Marcus, "but if he ever was a Christian, I doubt that he is now. He could not have kept his office if he were one, not after the recent edicts."

"There's your answer," said Sulpicia. "Marcellinus is too ambitious to be a Christian."

"That was so frightful today at the circus—the chanting and the beating," said Mucia.

"What was so frightful about it? They were only Christians. They deserved it," said Tiberius.

"Oh, Tiberius, you're a beast," said Ponia.

"Not at all. They deserved it. They weren't supposed to be there. Their own leaders preach against it, and on that I agree with them. If they don't go to the temple, they shouldn't go to the circus."

"He's right, by Jove!" declared Rebonius. "The circus should be only for the pious!"

Everyone laughed except Tiberius.

"Imagine that: the Vestal Virgins and the eunuchs of Isis, sitting there alone in the stands! What a fun lot!" laughed Sulpicia.

Tiberius waited for the laughter to subside before insisting, "If they don't honor our gods, they don't belong among us."

"What does it matter whose god they honor?" said Ponia. "We all honor the gods that suit us. What difference does it make?"

"Quite a lot to them. They aren't so tolerant," said Tiberius.

"So what do you propose we do about them, Tiberius?" asked Felix. "We've torn down their temples and forbidden them to worship publicly. We've removed them from public office and from the army. We've even now thrown them out of the circus. What more can we do to them without injury to the state? We can't throw them all in jail; the jails are already full of their priests. We can't send them all to the salt mines; there aren't enough mines to hold them. There are just too many of them."

"Are there really that many? I don't know anyone who's a Christian, except Marcellinus's uncle," said Sulpicia.

"Neither do I," said Mucia.

"Yes, you do," said Calvina. "Placidia Dolabella is a Christian. She told me so herself."

"Really?" said Sulpicia.

"Well, I'm not surprised. She's such a prude," said Mucia.

"And her husband, too, and nearly all their household," said Calvina.

"Prudes?"

"No. Christians, silly."

"Really?"

"I asked her if there were any others of our rank, and she said yes, quite a few," said Calvina.

"She's lying, of course. They all say that, just as they all pretend to be so upstanding," said Tiberius.

"How do you know they're not, Tiberius?" said Rebonius. "How many Christian virgins have you deflowered?"

"I've heard what they say about themselves to each other," said Tiberius. "All kinds of scandals! What else would you expect: they welcome the lowest sort of people—fools, simpletons, wretches."

"And there are none who are truly pious?" said Calvina.

"Oh, perhaps a few idiotic, hysterical women," answered Tiberius.

"The ones he can't seduce he calls idiotic and hysterical," said Rebonius to Felix.

"How can you make light of their danger?" demanded Tiberius. "They're always out for converts. They're always looking for ways to influence policy. They are not loyal Romans. They can't be trusted. They have their own agenda. They would close down the circus and the amphitheater and the theater if we let them."

"Poor Rebo, what would you do then?" said Ponia. "You'd have to spend all your time at home—with me."

"May the Fates spare us both!" laughed Rebonius.

"I've known some good soldiers who were Christians," said Marcus. "There was an officer in Asia by the name of Georgios who was relieved of his command when they discovered he was a Christian. He was a good man and a good soldier, but when they found out that he was a Christian, they sent him to Nicomedia to be court-martialed for disloyalty. I don't know what happened after that."

"Have you heard about the tribune Callistratus, Marcus?" asked Felix. "Last summer, this fellow Callistratus arrived here from Africa where he apparently earned quite a name for himself in the legions. When they found out he was a Christian, they brought him before Persentius, who was then the Praetorian Prefect. Persentius demanded that he sacrifice or else, but the man refused to sacrifice, even after scourging. So they stripped him of his rank and took him to the Port of Augustus, where they tied his hands and weighted his feet with ballast blocks and threw him over the side of a boat in the harbor. But hear this: Instead of sinking, he was taken up by two dolphins who carried him safely to shore."

"Bah!" said Tiberius.

"It's well attested," said Felix. "Dolphins have been known to save sailors. Anyway, they took him farther out off the coast and dropped him in the water again, but again the dolphins rescued him. This time the soldiers just hacked him to pieces with their swords, right there in the surf."

"The Christians have many stories about those of their kind being saved by their god. A lot of them still died under Decius and Valerian. Their god apparently can't save them all," chuckled Tiberius.

"What could possess them to die instead of sacrifice? It isn't as if they've been asked to curse their god," said Calvina.

"They just delight in defying authority," said Tiberius.

"They have their own authorities," said Marcus.

"Yes, and their authorities aren't our authorities," said Tiberius. "They are enemies of the Republic. They set the gods against us. Is it any wonder we have other enemies pressing constantly against our frontiers, threatening to overrun the civilized world?"

"Oh, Tiberius, drink some wine and relax. You're too serious. You're not running for office," Sulpicia scolded. Then she rolled over onto her back and rested her head on the cushion. "You, too, Marcus. Drink up," she cooed.

"Marcus, tell us your ghost story," said Felix.

"Ghost story?" said Sulpicia, sitting up. "Wait." She clapped her hands loudly. "That's enough music, you can go now," she told the musicians. "Now what about this ghost story?"

"It's not really *my* ghost story. It's a story told in Athens that goes back some time. I don't know how far, but it's also well attested." He glanced at Tiberius.

"Tell us the story," said Mucia.

Marcus took a sip of wine and set his bowl down.

"There was this house in Athens, a rather fine house with many rooms. It had had many tenants, but none would stay on account of strange noises heard in the night, like the sound of chains clattering. Some tenants claimed to have seen the ghost of an old man with shaggy hair and a long beard, walking from room to room, shaking his chains as he went. Then the philosopher Athenodorus came to Athens and heard about the house and immediately decided to buy the place for his academy. The price was right, I suppose. His first night in the house he lit a lamp and sent out his servants and settled down on the ground floor to do some writing in his notebook. Before long, he heard the clatter of chains. He looked up from his notebook and peered into the darkness. Suddenly there was a loud crash, as if someone had kicked over a bronze brazier in the next room. Then there was another crash, this time in the room with Athenodorus. He looked toward the door and saw the old ghost standing there, beckoning with its finger. Then the ghost turned to leave. Athenodorus got up and followed it with his lamp. The ghost moved slowly through the house to a far room. Then it vanished, leaving Athenodorus alone in the empty room. The house was quiet the rest of the night. The next morning, Athenodorus ordered his servants to tear up the floor tiles in the room where the ghost had vanished and dig beneath them. Just a foot or two down they found the bones of a man bound in chains. They buried the bones elsewhere, and the ghost was neither seen nor heard again."

"Oooooh," said Mucia.

"True story?" asked Felix.

"Well attested," said Marcus.

The rest looked at each other in the lamplight. Then Sulpicia asked, "Who's next? Who has another?"

"I have," said Felix.

"Wait, wait," said Ponia, hurrying over to Rebonius. "Trade places with me, Mucia."

Mucia joined Tiberius on the right, as Ponia curled up with Rebonius on the left. Then Felix told his story about a werewolf that attacked a party of soldiers on the road at night. Then it was Calvina's turn, and then Tiberius's, then Rebonius's. Between each story, one or two of the diners left the room to relieve themselves after so much wine and water, and after a while, the conversation turned to other things.

Ponia was still curled up next to Rebonius, her head on the cushion, asleep it seemed. Rebonius and Felix were talking about the circus, with Calvina trying repeatedly to interrupt. "Felix, it's late," she said several times, but he kept putting her off. Then Marcus noticed that both Mucia and Tiberius were missing.

"Where are Tiberius and Mucia?" he asked Sulpicia.

Sulpicia nearly laughed aloud. "That's the difference between you and Valerius Marcellinus. You are so charmingly naive, so unsuspecting," she said.

Feeling suddenly foolish, Marcus looked around the house at the several darkened doorways in view. Then he looked back at Sulpicia. With Calvina in mind, Sulpicia had been careful to keep her distance during the dinner, but now she was much closer, gazing back at him and gently running her fingers through the hair at the nape of his neck.

Then suddenly there was a banging at the front door and a loud voice demanding to be let in. "It's Publius!" she said, rising quickly and hurrying to the front door.

"Open up!" the voice demanded.

"Sounds drunk," said Rebonius.

Ponia stirred and sat up. Calvina nudged Felix and said, "Go see. She may need help." Marcus and Rebonius followed him.

"Where have you been? We've been worried that something fearful had happened to you," said Sulpicia closing the front door.

Publius looked with surprise at Felix and Rebonius, but he didn't see Marcus, whose instincts had told him to keep out of sight. "I see I'm not too late," said Publius loudly. "Let's have a commissatio! You pick the drink and the order, Sulpicia."

"Publius, you've had enough, and it's too late for drinking games," said Sulpicia.

"No! It's never too late for drinking games. Let's have a commissatio!"

"It's time to go home," said Sulpicia.

"Not until after the commissatio."

"Go home, Publius," said Sulpicia.

"Come, Publius, I'll take you home," said Felix, firmly escorting Publius back to the door.

"It's early! We have time."

"You're drunk, man. It's time for bed," said Rebonius. "I'll give you a hand," he said to Felix. Rebonius then turned to Marcus, who had just then emerged from the shadows. "Good to meet to you, Marcus," he said. "See you around town, I suppose. Ponia?"

Marcus moved toward the door, but just as he hoped, Sulpicia stopped him with her hand firmly on his chest. "Stay," she said. Not wanting to face Calvina, Marcus withdrew again into the shadows.

"Goodnight, Sulpicia. Thank you for a wonderful evening," said Calvina, giving her hostess a polite embrace. She looked briefly around the room for Marcus but did not see him. She looked for him also in the street.

"Goodnight, and thanks for everything," said Ponia, hugging Sulpicia tightly.

"Take care of Publius for me," said Sulpicia.

"We will." Ponia and Sulpicia talked for moment about future plans, while Marcus ambled back to the triclinium and waited. The door closed and all was quiet.

Marcus waited a while longer in the triclinium, then walked slowly back to the atrium in search of Sulpicia, but she was not there. Slowly again he started back for the triclinium.

"There you are," he heard her say. He turned to see her striding gracefully toward him, not stopping until she stood hard against him, her arms around his neck. "At last, at last, you're mine again!" she purred. She kissed him warmly on the lips, but when he tried to put his arms around her, she broke away and disappeared in the direction of the triclinium.

He found her on her back, lying diagonally across the center couch, eating a plum. He stood there watching her for a moment, then a broad grin stretched across his face and he chuckled. *This is Sulpicia*, he thought.

"Hungry?" he asked.

"Yes, very," she answered.

Marcus watched her a while longer, realizing that everything he could think to say sounded stupid. At an earlier age, he would have felt compelled to speak, but he had learned something of women, and of Sulpicia, over the years. *This is not the time to talk*, he told himself.

He started to sit down on the open corner of the couch, but she quickly swung her legs around to block him. She was obviously in control, and all he could do was wait.

"Would you like one?" she asked.

"No thank you. I've had enough," he answered.

"So have I," she said, tossing the unfinished plum over her head and onto the table. Extending her arms above her head, she stretched her body before him and gently rocked from side to side. "Oh, Marcus, Marcus. How long has it been? Two years, ten years?"

"Five years."

"Too long!" she said. "But now you're back and we're together, just you and me, once again."

She slithered closer on the couch, without rising, then reached up to grasp the hem of his tunic. "I shall miss you in your tribune's uniform," she said, tugging at his tunic. "You looked so handsome as a soldier, so strong and manly, even in your army trousers. Like a god."

She ran her hand playfully up the back of his thigh.

"But not in trousers, of course," she said. "The gods don't wear trousers, do they, Marcus? Mostly they wear nothing at all. . . . You look like a god then, too."

She smiled at him seductively, then giggled and rolled suddenly off the other side of the couch. Before he could move, she had disappeared through the darkened doorway of a nearby room.

Marcus looked around. The house was silent and dim in the lamplight. *Take your time*, he told himself. *Show some control.* He picked up his drinking bowl and took one last, leisurely sip. Then he set it down and followed after her.

No sooner had he crossed the darkened threshold than her arms were around his neck. She pressed her naked body hard against his loins and whispered, "Where you are Mars, I am Venus."

Sulpicia waited until he was asleep before slipping away to her own room, but somehow he was aware of her leaving. The room grew cold and still. Its darkness deepened; she had extinguished the lamps in the court before retiring. In time, his body recovered. Blood flowed freely again, clearing his head and waking his conscience to the familiar irony of overwhelming passion spent so completely and quickly, leaving him drained and diminished.

He tried to sleep, but the curse of Mars disturbed his rest. All that had gone before—the hope, the desire, the play, the passion—seemed pointless and purposeless now. Her profane parody of the Roman wedding vow haunted him: *Ubi tu Gaius, ego Gaia*—Where you are Gaius, I am Gaia. She had spoken rightly. He was the fool Mars and she, the strumpet Venus. To each other, they could never be anything more. Marriage was out of the question. That hope of an earlier age had been in vain, and his new hope for her had been the violation of her marriage bed.

Not that he cared for her cuckold Ulpius, but he knew he had accomplices. How many others had joined him in this sordid crime, made petty by repetition? How many others had she entrapped in her loins for the pleasure of seeing them unmanned and debased? How many others had she cruelly cut off as she had cut off the pathetic Publius that very day, in Marcus's own honor? How he did enjoy that snub of Publius! Yet he knew there was a time when he, like Publius, had clung to her too long and felt the pain and humiliation of being sent away to make room for someone else. He had been naive and inexperienced then; now he knew better.

What, he thought—what if she should conceive by him? She had applied none of the usual defenses—old olive oil, honey, cedar or balsam sap, mixed with white lead—neither had she stuffed herself with wool. If she did conceive, he did not doubt that she would do away with the child before it was born—by over exertion; a bath of linseed, wormwood, marsh mallows, and Greek hay; or a deadly suppository of myrtle, snowdrop seeds, and bitter lupines—as she must have done many times before. Her only concern would be her own safety. He meant that much to her, and nothing more. The thought revolted him, and he begged the gods, known and unknown, to keep her from conceiving. He determined then to leave before first light. He could not face her in the morning, not in the presence of Tiberius and Mucia, not as just the latest of her many paramours. Tired from sleeplessness, sick from indulgence and disgust, he left her house when the first cock crew and was home before dawn.

At midday she sent him a message saying she was disappointed that he had left and expressing sweetly her desire to see him again. He wanted to believe that he had been wrong, that she could still be his, but reason and experience told him that the only way to salvage his self-respect was to ignore her and go on. On to what? He did not know.

That afternoon he was again in Trajan's libraries hoping to purge himself of his worldliness by immersing his thoughts in the mind of the philosophers. In the Latin library, he sat down with a familiar volume of the pious emperor Marcus Aurelius, to re-acquaint himself with an old rule. It was there that Marcus had first sought relief from the pains of life— from the wound inflicted upon a young boy when his mother died, from the alienation the boy had felt among his peers on account of his father's unpopularity, and from the humiliation of a disastrous romance between the young Marcus and the more mature Sulpicia.

The philosophers advised Marcus to ease life's sorrows by suppressing the passions, cultivating a dignified apathy and a deliberate indifference to misfortune. In this dismal discipline, Marcus had achieved some measure of gloomy success, until he was lured away from it by the joy of his love for Makrina. He gave up philosophy in the belief that happiness was his. Now, with his loss, he needed it again.

In the weeks that followed, Marcus labored to regain his lost equilibrium. He spent long hours in study, re-reading the works of Cicero, Seneca, Epictetus, and Aurelius. All of Rome celebrated with the emperor at the circus and the amphitheater, but Marcus avoided them completely because of the passions they inflamed, and because he would not risk seeing Sulpicia. He declined Calvina's invitations to dinner, thinking it best also to avoid all women for a while, until he was again in control of himself. He fasted rigorously, eating only in the evening and taking little wine or meat. He let his beard grow without trimming, affecting the look of a philosopher, but giving his father the opportunity to remark pointedly that beards suited soldiers as well as philosophers.

Yet for all his efforts, he found little comfort. The dark gods of the blood still demanded their occasional sacrifice, and Marcus was still unable to refuse them for long. He could not escape his memory of Makrina and was haunted by fantasies of what life in Rome would have been like with Makrina as his wife. He had yet to find a compelling reason to stay in the City, and by September he had stopped trying. He shaved his beard and announced that he would be going north to join the army of Constantius. His father received the news without emotion, nodding his head and saying simply, "Go soon."

Alexander first declined an invitation to accompany him, then changed his mind. He had heard good things about the caesar Constantius, and he missed the camp, he said. Felix and Calvina were surprised and disappointed, for different reasons. Marcus sensed Calvina's disapproval in her reticence. He left them with the task of saying his farewells to others.

The morning of his departure, Marcus found his father in his senatorial toga, his head covered piously, standing before the family lararium burning incense as a sacrifice to the household gods. This Marcus had seen him do many times in his youth. Always his father had seemed grand and dignified. Now he seemed quaint and pathetic.

Marcus himself was dressed for traveling, with a coarse barbarian cloak over a woolen shirt and trousers. His father glanced at him and smiled. The contrast in their attire was not missed. "*O tempora! O mores!*" said his father, quoting Cicero. The times, the customs.

"I don't know when I'll be back," said Marcus.

His father shook his head. "It does not matter," he said. "Your fate is elsewhere, Marcus. Do not shrink from it."

They embraced briefly and said farewell. The father returned to his sacrifice, and the son began his journey.

# VIII

The office was quiet by noon. The clerks and servants had been let off early to attend the public games that accompanied the festival of Serapis, Sinope's divine patron. Throughout the summer, there had been few moments in town as peaceful as this one. All summer long, Sinope was filled as usual with sailors, merchants, and travelers. Its streets were always crowded. Its inns and taverns and brothels thrived. The families of the well-to-do retired to the countryside for peace and decency, but business kept the men in town most days, except during the festival.

For the festival, everyone adjourned to the fairground west of town, near the beach, for five days of boxing, wrestling, dancing, racing, and combats. Sinopeans were not especially fond of blood sports, but the last day of the program was reserved for the slaughter of wild beasts, pitted in the temporary arena against each other and against armed men. The slaughter of armed men was not intended, but it was always anticipated.

Kimon himself had planned to attend at least the races—it was expected of him as town clerk—but it wasn't often that he had time alone in the town hall. A cool September breeze poured in from the open window above his desk as Kimon pored over a large, bound manuscript laid out on his desk:

> *And Jesus answered them, saying, "The hour is come that the son of man should be glorified. Amen, Amen, I say unto you, except a corn of wheat fall into the ground and die, it lives alone. But if it dies, it brings forth much fruit. He that loves his life shall lose it, and he that hates his life in this world shall keep it unto life eternal. . . . "*

By coincidence, he had saved the very same Gospel Makrina had cherished so much before their surrender. The other three had gone to the fire, along with the wooden cover and first page of the Gospel of John. Kimon had split Matthew's Gospel in two and covered one half with the cover and first page of John's. Both Gospels had been made by the same copyist, and Kimon had counted on the governor not knowing enough of the Gospels to notice the substitution. He had held his breath in fear as the governor perused the first page of John before turning past it to second half of Matthew, but when the great Sossianos Hierocles closed the book and approved the sacrifice, Kimon had smiled and relaxed.

Since then he had delved into the forbidden book on several occasions,

though he could not complete a thorough study of it, for lack of both time
and interest. It defied comprehension and he was tempted often to consult
Theodoros on its interpretation, but he didn't dare reveal his possession of
it. His secret was too dangerous to entrust to anyone.

The day before he had gone to the temple of Serapis to present his annual sacrifice, had remembered his conversation with Marcus and Theodoros
in that very room, and had turned again to the book for answers:

> "I am the light of the world, that whosoever believes in me
> should not abide in darkness. And if any man hear my
> words and believe not, I judge him not, for I came not to
> judge the world, but to save the world."

Kimon shook his head and sighed. "Another riddle," he said to himself.

Hearing someone in the hall, he quickly closed the book and returned
it to the cupboard beside his desk. A moment later, Theodoros appeared
at the door. As a pious Christian, Theodoros neither attended the games
nor took part in the festival. "Did you ask him? Has he given an answer?"
Theodoros asked.

"He said no," answered Kimon. "He doesn't feel he has the authority,
and he's afraid of crossing the governor."

"Just as I expected," said Theodoros, taking a seat opposite the desk that
had been his own until the spring.

"He's cautious," said Kimon. "And he's right. He doesn't have the authority, though he could probably get away with letting them go during
the festival."

Days before, a new edict had been published permitting the release
of Christian clergy, on the condition that they offer sacrifice to the gods
on behalf of the emperors and the imperium. The Christians in Sinope
proposed to offer their own sacrifice—a "bloodless sacrifice," they called
it, a "sacrifice of praise"—with prayers for the emperors and the imperium,
to earn the release of those held. Posidonios had presented their proposal
to Philodemos the mayor, who had demurred. Kimon had been asked to
remind Philodemos that custom recommended amnesty for those charged
with minor offenses on the day of the city festival.

"He said you'll have to ask Marcellinus himself when he returns," said
Kimon. "You can submit a petition."

"A petition would have to be signed, and no one would want to draw
attention to themselves," said Theodoros. "Besides, Marcellinus is not likely
to show us mercy."

"What makes you say that? He's a reasonable man. He will listen
to reason."

"There is nothing reasonable in any of the edicts against us, Kimon. There is only malice toward God."

"Marcellinus doesn't seem to me to be a man of malice," said Kimon. "He is not your friend, but neither is he your enemy. He's just doing his duty."

"Marcellinus is a man of the world, serving the powers of this world, and they are our enemies. I have no doubt he will do anything they tell him to do, however unreasonable."

Kimon shrugged and said, "What Marcellinus might do if ordered is one thing. What he will do on his own is another. On his own, I think he is open to persuasion, and there is someone who might be able to persuade him to approve the release, someone even he has reason to please, however unreasonable she may be."

"She?"

"Makrina."

"Makrina?"

"He asked about her when he was here. He might want to see her when he returns. Certainly we can arrange that. It may take some time for her to soften his heart, but perhaps by the end of the month she can ask him."

"We have our own feast this month, on the ninth before the Kalends of October, in honor of the overseer Phokas who won his crown in the reign of Trajan," said Theodoros.

"His crown?"

"His crown of life, for those who die bearing witness to the Gospel. We commemorate his victory with a feast each year beside his grave."

"Yes, I know. That has to be the strangest of all your customs," said Kimon.

"We do not fear death, Kimon, nor do we despise the dead," said Theodoros. "To us, they are merely sleeping."

"Well this year you had better let them sleep alone. Settle for the release of the living," said Kimon.

"When is Marcellinus due back?"

"Day after tomorrow. I'll ask Makrina today, if you like, after the games. With a little tutoring, I'm sure she'll get all the arguments right. But then, she might not need them."

"He's an evil man and an enemy of God, and I won't have anything to do with him," said Makrina, when Kimon spoke to her late that afternoon at their father's villa.

Her reaction surprised him a little. Marcellinus, it seemed, was either loved or hated in Sinope. "What do you really know of him? He's just doing his job and doing it well. Besides, you don't have to marry him, Makrina.

Just treat him kindly, give him some attention, flatter him a little, and then ask him to please you with this favor," he argued.

"But what if he wants more? What else can I give him? I won't marry him and can't make him think I will. I don't dare. Sooner or later he'd know the truth. I'd have to refuse him and he'd be angered and offended."

"Yes, we know how that works," said Kimon bitterly.

Makrina's eyes flashed with pain and anger. Kimon decided to change the subject.

"Honestly, I don't know why I'm even concerned with this," he said. "It's not my faith. I'm only trying to do some friends a favor. If you don't want to do as much, there's nothing I can do."

Makrina held her peace, waiting for Kimon to continue, as she knew he would.

"You're going to have to face him anyway, Makrina. If you treat him coldly from the start, he'll have no reason at all to show mercy upon the Christians. If you show him a little kindness, a little 'Christian love,' things would only be easier. . . . And even if he does take an interest, it's not all that certain that you'd have to offend him to end things. He could lose interest. He could meet someone else. He travels a lot, he meets other women. He might realize on his own that he can't involve himself with a Christian. . . . He might know that already, and still it might flatter him just to know he has pleased a beautiful woman. Men are like that, you know. Always flirting with some woman they find attractive even if she's much too young or already married. They won't have any intention of going any further, but still it pleases them to please a lady. Haven't you noticed how Chione's father treats you? Of course he doesn't mean anything improper, but—"

"Oh, Kimon, give up."

"Think about it, Makrina. You may have nothing to worry about, and it may be your only chance."

"You should have been a lawyer."

Makrina thought about it, and was still thinking about it with Marcellinus reclining across the table from her at the villa. The past several months had not been easy for her. She missed the weekly worship and the constant company of her fellow Christians. They had taken to meeting in secret in small groups at various locations in town and in the countryside, but since moving to the villa for the summer, Makrina had been unable to attend more than two such meetings.

Once a week she joined Chione and others in visiting Archelaos and the rest in jail. The news from other parts was frightening. In Nicomedia, the overseer Anthimos was rumored to have been beheaded and several Christians holding offices in the imperial palace were said to have been tortured and killed. Elsewhere in the province, outside the imperial capital, the persecution had been less severe, though there had been many more Christians arrested and tortured in Amisos and Amastris.

And now here was one of their tormentors, smiling, laughing, charming her mother with compliments and her father with talk about business. He had been welcomed upon his return as the town's honored guest, there being no doubt now about his social standing. Protocol required him to dine in turn with the town's leading families, but it was obvious from his arrival at the villa of Aristoboulos that protocol was not his only reason for coming. He brought gifts for the women: emerald earrings for Hilaria, silver bracelets for Eugenia, and a pearl necklace for Makrina. It hung now around her neck like a sign saying, "The *traditor* Makrina, who surrendered the Holy Gospels for a string of pearls." That's what Latins called Christians who handed over the sacred books: *traditores*—traitors.

They dined before sunset on the terrace looking out toward the mount of Sinope, some twelve miles distant. Marcellinus was gracious and gallant as ever, sparing Makrina any special attention that might have made her uncomfortable. Makrina was polite and reserved, until Marcellinus happened to mention that he had already seen Pompeiopolis on his tour of duty, and she blurted out, "How many innocent men did you arrest there?"

"Makrina!" said her mother.

Kimon closed his eyes and dropped his head. Her father smiled.

Marcellinus smiled, too. "Not a one," he said to Makrina. "They had already gone into hiding."

Makrina looked him in the eye and said coolly, "Why should innocent men need to hide?"

"That's enough, Makrina," said Hilaria.

"Emperors have very generously offered all Christian leaders their freedom if they will but sacrifice," said Marcellinus. "I can't see why that should be so difficult, but obviously there's more to the matter. Perhaps someday you should explain it to me, Makrina."

"Perhaps someday I shall," said Makrina.

The next morning Makrina made an unexpected appearance at the games, where she was warmly welcomed by Marcellinus to sit with him on the podium reserved for dignitaries. It had taken Kimon most of the evening after dinner to persuade her to go. She did not approve of the games, especially the hunting sports, but Kimon insisted that it was the only way she could show Marcellinus she did not despise him.

The day's program included wrestling, boxing, and bear-baiting, giving Makrina good reason to leave early. She stayed for less than an hour, during which she tried unsuccessfully to draw Marcellinus's attention away from the games. He talked freely but kept his eyes fixed on the fights. When the first bloodied boxer was carried unconscious from the arena and Marcellinus stood with the crowd to applaud the victor, Makrina made known her annoyance. "Which are you applauding, the victory or the beating?" she asked, nearly shouting to be heard.

"Neither," he answered, still watching the arena. "I'm applauding the occasion."

"The occasion?"

The applause subsided and Marcellinus sat down with the crowd.

"What occasion?" asked Makrina.

"The games," said Marcellinus. "They are the true religion of the people. To show no interest in the games is to dishonor their gods—a very grave offense. Gaius Julius Caesar offended all of Rome by catching up on his correspondence during the games. Since Caesar Augustus, every petty official in the imperium has known better."

"So you're only here because it's expected of you, and you really have no interest in the games themselves?"

"That's correct, but don't tell anyone I said so."

"I don't believe you," said Makrina.

Marcellinus laughed. "What was it the philosopher Demosthenes said, 'We believe whatever we want to believe'? What do you want to believe about me, Makrina? That I'm evil embodied because I've enforced an edict against your Assembly? But Christ died for me, too, did he not?"

Makrina peered at him warily.

"Aren't I worth a little time, a little patience, a little Christian charity? Perhaps a prayer or two?"

Makrina sat silently during the next match, and when it was over she announced abruptly that it was time for her to go. "When might I see you again?" asked Marcellinus.

"Whenever you like," she answered. "The soldiers know where I live. You can arrest me at any time." She smiled at him, then turned with a snicker and walked away.

That afternoon, Marcellinus asked Aristoboulos for permission to call on his daughter, and with Makrina's consent, a time was arranged for the following afternoon at the villa. "The gods have given you a second chance," Hilaria told Makrina. "Wear the necklace he gave you. He'll want to see it on you. Nothing flatters a man more than letting him think he's picked the right gift for a woman."

Kimon had other instructions for her, relayed in private. Don't ask about releasing the clergy—save that for later. Don't talk about Marcus (men hate that). Try to avoid talking about religion and, above all, don't argue about the edicts. Remember that he can help or hurt, depending upon how well he is treated.

Moments before Marcellinus arrived at the villa, Makrina was in her room, dressed and ready, but kneeling before her nightstand, her arms extended in supplication. She prayed often for Marcus, whose ring still lay beside her little book of psalms. Should she not also pray for Marcellinus? When her mother called for her, Makrina made the sign of the cross, bowed and touched her forehead to the floor, then she stood erect, straightened her stola, and went to meet him.

Marcellinus was waiting with Hilaria in the tablinum when Makrina appeared. The look on his face reminded her of the moment she walked into the mayor's office months before for her interview with him. He had seemed then simply stunned by her beauty, and so he seemed again.

Hilaria suggested they go for a walk in the garden, where she would have refreshments sent out for them. They strolled out across the terrace toward the garden. It was indeed a beautiful day, pleasantly warm with just a slight breeze. Leaving the house, Makrina instinctively started to cover her head with her palla. No, she thought, that would insult him. She played at adjusting it on her shoulders for a moment and then left it alone. "I still have the cloak you left with me last spring," she said.

"I haven't missed it," he replied. "Actually I've thought of it often, but only because I've thought so often of you. Thank you for keeping it for me. . . . It had occurred to me that you might have had it torn into rags for the servants to use."

Whatever Kimon said, there was no use pretending there weren't differences between them. "That's a thought," she said, with a coy smile.

He chuckled and shook his head. "You seemed so sad that evening," he said.

"It was a sad occasion for me. But, as you said, they were only books." *What am I saying? What's he supposed to make of that?*

"I'm sorry, Makrina," he said, pausing at the edge of the terrace. "I know now how deeply you felt about them. I didn't know that then."

Makrina scrutinized his face expecting to see at least a trace of insincerity, but there was none. "I can forgive your words much easier than you deeds," she said.

He nodded. "My words are my own. My deeds often belong to those who have sent me. I am, after all, a man under authority."

His words sounded strangely familiar. Had she not heard them in the Assembly? "How is it you know so much about our faith?" she asked.

They stepped off the terrace and started slowly down one of the garden paths, pebbles crunching beneath their feet as they walked. "I have known

Christians all my life. There are some among my family. A favorite uncle of mine is active in the Assembly at Rome."

"And yet you are not one?"

"No."

"And have never been one?"

"No."

"Why not?"

Marcellinus shrugged and said, "I might have been had I stayed in Rome. My uncle tried his best to make me one while I was there. But I went on to other things, and time passed, and there has been no one as persistent or as persuasive as my uncle to talk me into it."

"It's never too late," said Makrina.

"There is much to admire in the Christian faith," said Marcellinus. "Its rites are beautiful and decent. Its promise of salvation is the most appealing of all the cults I know of that make such promises. The devotion of its adherents is to be admired. The Christians I've known have all been good, honest people, and their works of mercy put the rest of us to shame. Perhaps someday by their example, the rest of us will learn to be as merciful, as concerned for the welfare of others, as giving toward the good of all."

"So why are we persecuted?"

"Because Christians present the imperium with a difficult problem. They wish to make everyone Christian, and to bring the entire world under the reign of Christ. They are intolerant of others, they despise other faiths, and they actively encourage people to abandon the religion of their race. Now, where would the world be if the people gave up believing in their gods? If they gave up their sacrifices, in their hope of help from beyond? The world would go mad. People would lose heart. They'd be lost. They wouldn't know how to live. They wouldn't know what to live for. No *emperor*, no *king* could rule them. Everything would be chaos."

"But they can believe in *our* God, the one true living God."

"But they won't believe in your God because of what that would mean. Imagine if your overseers and elders ran the imperium, made its laws, and pronounced its edicts. What would that mean? In practical terms, it would be the end of the games, the end of the theater, the end of many pleasures that many people live for. I meant what I said yesterday about the people's religion. They have their gods, their desires, which they cannot deny, but that is just what the Christian faith demands."

"But people *can* deny their lusts and live in purity," Makrina protested.

"*Some* people can, but not everyone. Here's where I think Christians err. Some thoughtful, disciplined, enlightened souls can ascend to a higher level, but most people can't. So we must make allowance for them. Expecting everyone to live as Christians live would be disastrous. The people would rebel. They want their games. They want their diversions, their fashions, their fantasies. They want to satisfy themselves. It's only natural. They can't all be consecrated virgins."

"No, they can't," said Makrina, "but they can live chaste lives as faithful husbands and wives."

Marcellinus stopped suddenly and turned to her. "I worried for months that when I returned you would have been consecrated a virgin. I glad you weren't," he said.

"How do you know I wasn't?" Makrina asked.

"I know," said Marcellinus. "I know."

He turned and resumed their walk. "Kimon would have told me. And if he hadn't, I'm sure someone else would have," he said.

"I see," said Makrina. "But not everyone has been called to be consecrated in that way, and for the others there is marriage."

"Yes, but can they all live content without their other amusements? Without the races, the combats, the games of chance, the comedies and pantomimes? Without the clothes, the jewelry, the hairstyles? The gossip? Very few could live so plainly, so piously—praying unceasingly, fasting on Wednesdays and Fridays, worshipping every Sunday."

"Yes, we Christians are such bores and prudes that I'm surprised you'd want to spend any time with me at all," said Makrina.

Marcellinus opened his mouth to respond, but for once his wit failed him, and seeing this made Makrina laugh. "I'm relieved to see you're not simply angry with me," he then confessed.

"No, not angry," said Makrina. "More amused, and a little intrigued."

"But you see what I mean? Most people cannot live as Christians and would rebel if forced to. But Christians nevertheless aim to make the whole imperium Christian."

"But sir, no one I—"

Marcellinus laughed. "Please, call me Gaius," he said.

"Gaius," repeated Makrina, "no Christian I know expects to convert the entire imperium. True, we call all to salvation, but we know that few will come. We are even told that by our Lord Himself. So we cannot present the great danger you say we do."

"But you might convert enough to change the way the imperium lives, to change its laws and its customs. You have already converted quite a few decurions and other officials, even a few senators in the past. Who knows? You might someday convert an *emperor*, and what would that mean? A Christian empire?"

"Our kingdom is not of this world."

"It is a very real political possibility, and it would be disastrous," said Marcellinus.

"It is almost too much to even pray for," said Makrina.

"I'm only thinking of the good of others, Makrina. Personally I'm not much bothered by the Assembly. I'm much less bothered by Christian beliefs than by Christian ambitions. If Christians were more private about their religion, less aggressive in seeking converts, less exclusive of others, more tolerant of other cults, they would present no problem at all. And they might even win more converts. They might even win me."

"Oh? Is that a real possibility?" Makrina asked.

"I don't know, Makrina, but you give me one very beautiful reason to consider it," said Marcellinus. He turned suddenly and looked about. "The gardens are beautiful, as beautiful as any I've seen. Who keeps them for you?"

"His name is Phokas," said Makrina. "He's lived here all my life."

"You must know him well."

"Actually, no," said Makrina. "He's a queer old man. He has no family and keeps mostly to himself. He rarely speaks. When I was very young, I was afraid of him and wouldn't go near the gardens. Then one day he surprised me on the terrace with a garland of pretty white flowers. I was so scared I grabbed it and ran into the house without saying a word."

"Shame on you. Did you ever thank him?"

"No, not for that first one, but he gave me many more after that, and in time I got over my fear of him. He still makes them for me occasionally. . . . This way."

She led him through a vine-covered trellis to a small patio in the midst of the garden. There a table awaited them with a tray of candied fruits and a pitcher of lemonade. They settled onto a marble bench and talked of lighter matters while sampling the refreshments. Makrina was especially interested in hearing about Marcellinus's family in Rome, though she avoided asking specifically about the Christians he knew. She did not want to argue or accentuate their differences.

When it was time to go, they started back by a different route, which led them through a court of hedgerows six feet high. "How do you know Marcus?" Makrina asked.

"Who?" said Marcellinus.

"Aemilius Canio."

"Oh, Marcus. We grew up together in Rome. We had the same tutors. Our families were close."

"When was the last time you saw him, before seeing him in Byzantium?"

"Many years ago. He left to study in Athens, and I went to Alexandria. After that he went straight into the army. That always surprised me. It's not the normal course. Sometimes a father will discover that his son has wasted all his time and money in Athens and then send him off with the barbarians—make him join the army, in other words. I don't know what happened with Marcus, but I understand he served well in the ranks."

"You said he was well in Byzantium?"

"I believe so, though obviously disappointed you turned him away. But I wouldn't worry about him. Marcus was never one to brood for long over something lost. I'm sure he's happy now in Rome."

"Oh."

"Who is that?" asked Marcellinus.

Makrina looked up just in time to see an old man with a long gray beard and a broad-brimmed hat turn about and disappear into a gap in the hedge up ahead. "That's Phokas," she said, hastening forward. "Phokas! Phokas, come back!"

The old man reappeared with his hat in his hands and was greeted by Makrina with a playful tug on his whiskers. Though now stooped with age, he was still unusually tall, taller than the hedges even. An aged Achilles who might have given quite a fright to any little girl, thought Marcellinus. His bare feet were the largest, the widest Marcellinus had ever seen. His workman's tunic hung loosely from his broad, bony shoulders. A leather apron girded his waist. "Forgive me for intruding, my lady. I thought I saw you with Master Kimon," said the old gardener to Makrina in a deep but weak voice.

"This is Valerius Marcellinus, Phokas. He's an official from Nicomedia," said Makrina.

Phokas stooped a little lower than usual and introduced himself, saying, "Your servant."

"I was just admiring your work, Phokas. These gardens rival any I've seen in the empire," said Marcellinus.

"Thank you, my lord, but you are too kind."

"I've told him about you, Phokas, and about the garlands you used to give me."

"Oh? Yes, well, I made this for you just now." From behind his big, flimsy hat, the gardener pulled a plaited ring of deep red posies.

"Oh, look, Gaius. How lovely!"

Phokas held the garland out to Makrina, then suddenly shifted it to Marcellinus instead. "For her," he said.

"I thank you for the honor," said Marcellinus. Facing Makrina, Marcellinus set the flaming garland gently down on the crown of her head. "It becomes you perfectly," he said.

Makrina turned quickly to Phokas to thank him. "You're so sweet," she said.

Phokas smiled and bowed once more. "I'll be going now. Good day, sir," he said. He disappeared again through the gap in the hedge.

Makrina and Marcellinus returned to the house and met her mother in the atrium. "How was it?" asked Hilaria.

"Very nice, Mamma. See what Phokas made me?"

The three of them chatted for a moment about the gardens and the weather. Then Marcellinus said his farewells and took his leave.

"He seemed pleased," said her mother, after he had left.

"Yes, he did, didn't he?" said Makrina.

When Kimon returned from town later that evening, Makrina reported that the visit had gone well. "You didn't argue?" asked Kimon.

"No, we didn't argue. But we didn't pretend to be of one mind either."

"What do you mean? What did you say?"

"We had a brief, friendly discussion of our differences and then left it at that. I was careful not to provoke him. He was tactful and charming. He even apologized for things he said last spring."

Kimon thought for a moment, trying to decide whether to believe her. "What do you think of him?" he asked.

"Oh, I don't know, Kimon," said Makrina. "What should I think of him? He knows the Gospel and yet rejects it. Did you know that? He has Christians in his family in Rome."

"Really?"

"An uncle, at least. I didn't probe, so I don't know anything more," said Makrina. "Even so, he persecutes the Assembly of Christ."

"So he's a monster."

"Not a monster, but . . . "

"A charming monster."

Makrina smiled and tilted her head to one side and then to the other. "Yes. A charming monster."

# IX

The next day, as planned, Makrina sent an invitation to Marcellinus asking him to meet her at the gardens north of town the following day at the ninth hour. Near the end of the same day, at Kimon's cue, the elders of the Assembly presented Philodemos with their petition requesting release of the overseer Archelaos and the others upon the condition that the Assembly, publicly or privately, would offer a Christian "sacrifice of prayer" for the emperors and the empire. Marcellinus had already left for the day, so Philodemos waited until the next morning before forwarding the petition to Marcellinus. As expected, Marcellinus took the petition under consideration, deferring a decision until later so as not to appear peremptory.

Later that morning, Makrina, her mother, and Eugenia took a carriage into town, accompanied by several maidservants under the direction of Nonna. At their house in town, they began preparations for Makrina's afternoon rendezvous. Hours later Makrina emerged from the house in an altered state. Her face and arms were painted with white lead. Her cheeks were reddened with the lees of wine. Her eyebrows and the outlines of her eyes were drawn with ash. Perfumed oils scented her neck and underarms. Her long hair was tied up in a neat coif, decorated with an intricate net of golden treads from which dangled little jade fish. Pearl eardrops hung from her lobes, complementing the necklace Marcellinus had given her. Her arms were banded in gold and silver, and her fingers were adorned with gems. Her pale green gown was pulled tight around her midsection by an embroidered Persian corset, which accentuated the curves of her figure. Jeweled slippers covered her feet, and tiny bells tinkled from her anklets.

Hilaria and Nonna were very pleased with their work. At last Makrina looked like the rich young maiden she was. Eugenia was in awe, but hid her awe by teasing Makrina about her appearance. "What would the elders say? And the widows and virgins?" giggled Eugenia.

Makrina was annoyed with Eugenia and displeased with herself. She had agreed to everything, knowing full well that this was the accustomed way of courting, but her Christian scruples pained her. "This is not how we dress!" she whispered to her mother in a moment alone.

"Oh, Makrina, I've allowed you enough dowdiness," said her mother. "A lady must learn to use her charms discreetly for her own good."

Makrina was actually relieved when her mother decided that she would ride to her rendezvous in her mother's canopied litter. The litter had curtains to shield her from the sight of others. Makrina kept them tightly drawn, to the dismay of her chaperon Nonna, who would have liked to show her off.

There were two public gardens in Sinope. The larger and more popular was on the bay, between the harbor and the admiral's house, but to escape the smell of fish, which pervaded Sinope in August and September, Makrina had chosen the garden on the opposite side of the narrow peninsula, which offered the shelter of a pine grove refreshed by a gentle sea breeze. Marcellinus was waiting with one of his aides when she arrived. Upon seeing her emerge unveiled from her litter, he raised his arms in amazement and then bowed low before her. "Surely you are the most beautiful woman in all of Pontus," he said.

Makrina forgot her embarrassment and smiled. "Why not all of Asia?" she teased.

"Dear lady, forgive me," he pleaded. "I have seen only all of Pontus, but I will swear to Asia, also."

He offered his arm and she took it, and together they began their stroll through the grove, away from their attendants.

"It's been just two days and yet I find myself missing you, Makrina."

"So soon? Am I really that charming?"

"Why yes. And I'm really that fond of you. When does your family move back to town? That would make it easier for us to see each other."

"Not until early October, a few weeks from now."

"Hmmm—I'd have to extend my stay in Sinope," said Marcellinus.

"You had planned to leave before then? But what will you do when you leave if you've missed me after just two days?"

"I will pine away, no doubt. Perhaps I can find a few official matters to keep me here a while longer." He patted her hand and took a deep breath. "I have just received a petition from the leaders of your Assembly, asking for the release of your overseer on the condition that the Assembly offer their own kind of sacrifice to their own god."

Makrina glanced at him nervously. She had not expected him to broach the subject. "Is that not permissible according to the new edict?" she asked.

"Perhaps," he said. "One might argue that granting their request has been left to the discretion of local authorities, in the absence of the governor or his representative. But a safer argument would be that only the governor or his representative may grant it. I could order the overseer and the others released myself. Would that please you?"

"Yes, of course, it would," she answered.

"Of course," he said.

"I would be most pleased."

"I thought you might."

"It's a terrible hardship for the families of the men in prison. They have been forced to depend upon others for support and deprived of the guidance and love of husbands and fathers. They are not dangerous men and will do no harm if released. Common decency would recommend their release."

"Would they obey the edict banning public worship and the possession of Christian scriptures?" asked Marcellinus, his smile widening knowingly.

"Well, they—I'm—you have the scriptures, or had them. I'm sure they would obey the Caesars and their edicts," she stuttered.

"That is my concern, Makrina: that they obey the edicts—*all* of the edicts. If I can be assured of that, well, then this petition is well worth considering. But you see the position I'm in? I have a job to do, and I must do it—with, of course, the proper respect for common decency."

"I understand, but really there's no danger to you by letting a few old men go, and it would make me very happy." She brought them both to a halt and took hold of his arm with both hands. "It would certainly make me feel better about you, about seeing you," she said. "I mean—I want to see you, Gaius, but still I think I shouldn't. I'm running a terrible risk, a risk of—embarrassment, and censure. This would show me that you're not my enemy, that I'm not endangering myself or others by seeing you."

"So I should prove my good will through some act of mercy," he said.

"Yes, yes," said Makrina.

"I shall consider it."

"Do, please do."

They resumed their walk toward the end of the grove, where a low wall separated them from the rocky edge of the sea. The afternoon sun shone brightly on the cliffs to their right. For many moments Makrina's mind was occupied with her plea and his consideration, but Marcellinus found a way of distracting her by picking out a family of seagulls wandering among the rocks, giving them names, and then interpreting their dialogue. It was a silly game, but his confidence and lightheartedness made her laugh and she was soon again in his company. An hour passed as they sat upon the wall talking of the places they had visited. Marcellinus, it seemed, had been everywhere, except Cherson across the Euxine Sea, "but I've been there and it's a wonderful place, just wonderful," boasted Makrina, exaggerating her praise for the full effect of the tease. The walk back was quick and pleasant, and they parted with a kiss upon Makrina's painted cheek. By then her mission had been almost forgotten.

The next day Marcellinus summoned Posidonios to the city hall and gave his response to the Christians' petition. He had been remiss, he said, in not respecting the local custom of granting a general amnesty during the feast of Serapis. To avoid offense to either the god or the people of Sinope, he offered to release the Christian leaders, provided they gave solemn assurance they would obey the laws of the imperium and honor the emperors in all worldly matters. The "bloodless sacrifice" was not required. Whatever Christians did in their own homes was not his concern, he said, but no general meeting of the Christian Assembly was permitted and all public observance of the Christian cult was still prohibited.

Posidonios accepted Marcellinus's offer on the spot, thanking him profusely for his generosity and promising on behalf of the whole Assembly that his conditions would be met. Afterward he went immediately to the garrison to inform the prisoners, then returned straightway to Marcellinus to report that all was in order.

The prisoners were released within the hour, before some of their families were even informed. They gathered for a while at the house of Posidonios for refreshments and a brief prayer of thanksgiving. Then the elders from the countryside departed for their homes, while the overseer Archeloas went to live with Hermogenes the baker.

Makrina heard the news from Kimon, while preparing for another visit from Marcellinus later in the day. "See, I told you, he's a reasonable man. What do you have to fear?" said Kimon.

Makrina just smiled. "Go back to work, Kimon. I'm still dressing," she said, shooing him out of her apartment.

The drill would be the same: hair, face, dress, jewelry, perfume, and then face again. It was already beginning to seem routine, as it was for so many women. Marcus certainly had not expected it of her, but Makrina assumed Marcellinus did, and today of all days she would not disappoint him.

She was pleased with him and made sure he knew it when he arrived, greeting him with a casual touch on the arm and a kiss upon the cheek. They had a pleasant visit, without the tension of their previous visits. Makrina even ventured to ask another favor of him, though she had little hope that he would grant it, and indeed, when she asked, he shook his head doubtfully. She was not dismayed and quickly eased the conversation on to something else.

"You asked him about the feast day?!" exclaimed Kimon, when she told him about it later.

"Yes, I did. Should I not have?"

"There is only so much he can do, Makrina."

"But I can't let him off too easily. He wants to please me, and I want him to please me, too," she said smiling. "Besides, it wasn't as you think. I didn't pressure him. I didn't pout. I just mentioned that it would be nice if he could let us celebrate the feast the way we always do. Hardly a bother. When he said he couldn't, with regrets, I said I understood and we went on. No harm done. No tears shed."

Two days before the Christians' feast in memory of their departed

ancestor, Marcellinus left town unexpectedly on a six-day tour of the countryside. Six days, he said. He would be back on the 26th of September. "See,"
Makrina said to Kimon, "he does want to please me."

On the 22nd of September at about the fourth hour, over a hundred
Christians gathered where their basilica had once stood and moved in procession to the "sleeping places" of their venerable ancestors in faith, singing
a solemn hymn of praise for the departed saint. There they prayed and sang
a single hymn before sitting down among the tombstones and sarcophagi
to begin their picnic. Normally the celebration would have included the
great Thanksgiving, but the overseer Archelaos and the elders were mindful of their promise to obey the edict against public worship and wished to
allow themselves some line of defense if accused of violating the edict with
the procession.

Kimon, who knew and disapproved of the planned procession and
feast, stayed close to the city hall all day, waiting to see if anyone took note
of the event. Around noon Philodemos the mayor stopped by with a few
nervous words about an unrelated matter, but nothing was said about the
Christians. Later in the day, Kimon encountered Quartillius the local curator, who was no less cordial than usual and gave no indication that he had
heard of the Christians' feast.

It was quite plausible that he hadn't. The necropolis was east of town,
and the ruined basilica was not in sight of the city walls. If either Quartillius
or Philodemos had heard of the feast, they might have heard too late. At
least, that is what they could have claimed if Marcellinus had asked them
about it upon his return, but he didn't. Officially nothing had happened.
Kimon was surprised and relieved. Makrina was pleased and encouraged.
Marcellinus was uninquisitive and patient.

Not long after, Marcellinus invited Kimon to lunch at the admiral's house.
He was leaving Sinope soon, he said, and had a few things to discuss with
Kimon before he left. They had talked often in recent weeks, not only
about official business but about shared personal interests. This sounded to
Kimon like something in between.

The winter residence of the admiral was also the temporary residence
of visiting officials like Marcellinus. The admiral was not often at home. In
the summer, he deployed with the fleet to forward bases in Kotyora and
Trapezos. In the winter, while the fleet was idle in Sinope, the admiral and
his family were often elsewhere. At the moment, the admiral was absent,
and Marcellinus and Kimon could be assured complete privacy.

Their lunch was light—a snack really: flatbread, olives, a chickpea paste
flavored with garlic and olive oil, wine and water to wash it down. Reclining
on a teal-green couch cushion, Marcellinus wasted no time in getting to

the point. "Have you ever considered imperial service, Kimon?" he asked, dipping a piece of bread into the chickpea paste.

Kimon froze while reaching for an olive. "No. Never," he answered emphatically.

Marcellinus chuckled. "Relax, Kimon. I'm not asking if you'd ever considered becoming a palace eunuch," he said.

"Is there any difference? Aren't all public servants eunuchs?"

"I should hope not, or else we've both been un-manned," said Marcellinus.

"We have, in a way," said Kimon. "We've both lost some of our potency to our office."

"Well if that's so, then please, for my sake, don't tell Makrina," said Marcellinus.

"But she knows, Marcellinus. She knows you're not a free man. And it's good for you that she knows, otherwise she'd blame you more for what you've done."

"Yes, you're probably right about that. But, seriously, other than the loss of one's manhood, what keeps you from considering imperial service?"

Kimon chuckled and sighed. "Public work has never interested me," he said. "The affairs of government really amount to records, rules, routines— responsibility for many very petty matters, and a few extremely unpleasant ones."

"There are rewards and honors as well," said Marcellinus.

"But I don't need the rewards and I'm not impressed by the honors," said Kimon.

"Well," said Marcellinus, reaching for his drinking bowl, "I admit that the rewards and honors aren't all that important to someone as thoughtful as you. And, I admit, there are many things about public service that may seem boring or petty or unpleasant, but that's life, of course. There are things we do daily because we have to do them, and so we resign ourselves to do them without complaint and go on."

"You sound like my father," said Kimon.

"I sound like *my* father," said Marcellinus. "Believe me, Kimon, I know how you feel, but I also know that it's really not all that bad. Now, you've been in your present office for several months. Can you honestly say you've been living in the tortured underworld, struggling like Sisyphus at a futile, frustrating task everyday?"

"No," answered Kimon, "but I can't really say it has made me want more of the same."

"Imperial service wouldn't mean more of the same, not in today's world," said Marcellinus. "There are many different positions you could fill, and some you might find quite enjoyable. The palace is always looking for educated, thoughtful, high-minded young men to which to entrust some important policy or program. The Caesars, though not themselves espe-cially well-educated, nevertheless value erudition. They understand the im-portance of philosophy and art to the imperium. Diocletianus himself is especially sensitive to this, and he has assembled a court of the best and brightest minds from all over the imperium. You'd love Nicomedia. At the moment, it rivals Athens as the philosophical capital of the Roman world."

"But what do all the young philosophers do?" asked Kimon, just barely betraying his incredulity.

Marcellinus shrugged. "Anything that needs doing, and, Kimon, there is much to be done. Diocletianus has embarked upon an ambitious pro-gram of reform intended to secure prosperity for the imperium by strength-ening the hand of justice and advancing Roman values and education. My own superior, the governor Hierocles, is in the center of it. Indeed, much of it derives from his own ideas and his influence at court. He's an amazing man, Kimon. I'm sure you'd like him. I wouldn't want to serve any other. And his star is still ascendant. He won't end as governor of Bithynia and Pontus. I guarantee it."

"But what would be my part with this?"

"You're just the kind of men we need—bright, well-bred, well-educat-ed, well-versed in the philosophers, respectful of religion, and keenly aware of the world in which we live. Your father is a well-known and respected decurion. He might someday soon be asked to join the Senate. And, as if you needed anything else, you have me to speak for you. All you need is a little experience, and a little coaching in political ways, but we can provide you with that. The governor will see that you are well cared for. With our patronage, you could go very far, Kimon. Very far indeed."

"But it's still just politics."

"But what is politics? Politics is everything. Politics is life—how we live, how we work, what we value, whom we fight, whom we worship. Everything is political. There is nothing that does not concern the state. And there is no more exciting time to be in politics than now. We are living now at the beginning of a glorious revival of the Roman world, the start of a new age that may in time surpass even the Peace of Augustus. There is so much to do, so many important tasks to accomplish. And you can be a part of it, Kimon. Thank your stars. Thank your daemons. Thank your genius. Thank the gods who have shown you this great favor. So many people will live out their wretched lives and not even notice the glory around them, but men like you and me will bask in the glory of having accomplished great things, for our empire and for the world."

Marcellinus paused and smiled confidently, and finally drank from the bowl he had been holding so firmly during his appeal. Kimon smiled in re-turn and then looked away as if in thought. This surge of passion from one usually so cool and careful unnerved him. He dared not resist any longer. He stared for a moment at the table between them, poking pensively with his finger at an arrangement of olives while thinking of how to respond.

"This is all very interesting," he said, at last. "Certainly something I should consider. You must tell me more."

Marcellinus's smile widened into a grin as he relaxed on his couch. "I knew you'd take interest. You're a Greek. You're one of us," he said. "And I haven't even gotten to the things that attract most men."

"And what things are those?"

"Oh, nothing but a few worldly trifles, to which I'm sure a serious intellectual like yourself is utterly indifferent."

"Such as?"

"Such as travel to the major cities of the imperium—Rome, Alexandria, Antioch, where you would see everything worth seeing, taste every delight known to man, move among the most famous, most important people in the imperium, and of course, meet more beautiful young women than you could possibly remember."

"How vulgar."

"Yes, I thought you'd think so. And I'm sure you wouldn't care at all that someday, when the time came, you could no doubt settle down with some beautiful senator's daughter."

"Wouldn't care at all."

"No, of course not," said Marcellinus. "Think about it, Kimon. Dream about it. . . . I do."

# X

The crack in the balcony doors let in cold air but also bright light, without which Makrina would not have been able to read Marcellinus's letter at all.

"Let me try," said Chione, taking the letter from Makrina's hand. She read aloud:

*Mea Macrina cara, dies numero dum ad Sinopem reddo*
*ut carmen vocis tui, luminem oculorum tuorum, et saporem*
*saviolorum tuorum denuo sciam. . . .*

"My dear Makrina, I count the days until I return to Sinope so that—again I may know—the song of your voice, the light of your eyes, and the savor of your *saviolorum?*"

"Kisses, of course," said Makrina.

"But I thought *bascii* was kisses?"

"Not these kinds of kisses. Give me that. Your Latin's worse than mine."

"I've just had less practice," said Chione, "I haven't made a habit of falling in love with—*infideles Italiani.*"

"I'm not in love with him," said Makrina. Chione looked at her incredulously. "I'm not!" Makrina insisted.

"Why does he write in Latin?" Chione asked, again taking the letter from Makrina.

"He doesn't usually, but I wrote him last month in Latin just to amuse him. He sent it back corrected."

"What a show-off!"

"No, it's not like that at all. He's just playing. Some of his 'corrections' were as funny as my mistakes. He's a lot like Marcus in that way. I guess that's one reason I'm attracted to him. Anyway, I suppose he's writing now in Latin to amuse me. I'd be more amused if I wasn't waiting for him to respond to my last letter. I wrote him a long letter about the faith, and now I'm afraid I've offended him."

"What did you write?" asked Chione.

Makrina sighed. "I wrote what's in my heart. I wrote of why I became a Christian. I wish I hadn't now. I don't know what he'll think. It won't surprise him, but it might disappoint him."

"You didn't tell him you wouldn't marry him, did you?"

"No, I didn't. He knows our ways. He knows one of us has got to give in. Of course, he's probably hoping I will. When he reads my letter, he may wonder why he even bothers with me. I don't know. Maybe he shouldn't have bothered with me. When he was here last fall, it seemed so unlikely we would fall in love that I didn't worry about the future. Then when he left and we began exchanging letters, it seemed so easy to believe that things would work out—that I could continue as a member of the Assembly and that he might some day believe and be baptized, and then—and then everything would be well."

"So why did you write what you did?"

"I wanted to avoid what happened with Marcus. I never told Marcus. I didn't warn him in advance because I was afraid to. Now I've bared my heart to Marcellinus and I'm afraid I may have ruined things."

"Well it certainly doesn't sound like you've ruined things here," said Chione, glancing over Marcellinus's letter.

"But he doesn't even mention my last letter, so he might not have received it when he wrote this. Or maybe he has received it and he's ignoring it, which is worse. I shouldn't have sent it."

"It's a shame Marcus didn't take things better. I liked Marcus," said Chione.

"What do you think of Marcellinus?" asked Makrina.

"I hardly know him," said Chione. "Pappa speaks well of him, says he's very intelligent, very reasonable. But I've only seen him once and that wasn't a pleasant occasion. Oh Makrina, this past year has been so painful for us. You don't know how hard it's been. Your life has hardly changed at all. Instead of Marcus, it's Marcellinus, but otherwise everything's the same for you."

"What do you mean?" asked Makrina.

"Your family is still welcomed around town. You still go to dinner parties and festivals. You still receive important visitors. Your property's safe."

"And yours isn't?"

"We've already lost our estate near Amisos because of a lawsuit Pappa couldn't contest because, as Christians, we have no standing in court. Pappa said they had an altar set up in the courtroom and that everyone was required to sacrifice to the Caesars before pleading his case. He didn't have a chance."

"Is there nothing that can be done? Maybe Marcellinus can intervene."

"Makrina, he is our persecutor! He could have set the altar up himself; it's within his area." Chione sighed and turned away. "It pains me to hear you speak of him so fondly," she said, staring at the crack of light between the doors, "after all he's done, after what we've suffered. It hurts more than you know, Makrina, to be shunned like lepers. Everyone in town keeps their distance from us. Even some of the believers keep their distance, either because we're too well-known as Christians or because they fault Pappa for cooperating with Marcellinus. That's what Mamma says."

"I'm so sorry," said Makrina, putting her arm around her friend. "I didn't know it was so difficult." Chione nodded silently and Makrina tightened her embrace. "What must the others think of me, for seeing Marcellinus?" she wondered aloud.

"They don't hear how you speak of him. Only I do," said Chione. She handed Makrina the letter. "I've got to go. Are you coming tonight?"

"I can't," said Makrina. "We're having visitors."

Chione frowned and dropped her eyes. Then she stood and prepared to leave. "I will pray for you during the liturgy," she said, glancing down at Makrina.

"Thank you," said Makrina weakly. Rising to her feet, she said, "I will pray for you, too, Chione."

The women embraced and parted wishing each other the blessings of God.

Throughout the fall of the first year of persecution—"the days of surrender," as they were later called—the Christians of Sinope met regularly in private to continue their life of worship. Emboldened by having escaped punishment, they were sometimes careless of their secrecy and became a source of increasing worry to the mayor, Philodemos. In January, when he could stand it no longer, Philodemos summoned Posidonios and the overseer Archelaos and informed them that their meetings had to stop, or else they would both be jailed. Archelaos insisted that Posidonios bore no responsibility for the meetings, but would not promise to stop them. And indeed the meetings continued, though with some efforts to make them less noticeable.

The night after seeing Makrina, Chione slipped away from home to meet with twenty or so believers in the home of Hermogenes the baker. "Does your father know you are here?" asked the elder Theogenes. Chione bowed her covered head in shame. "I should send you home," he said.

"No, please," Chione pleaded. "Not this time. It's been too long since my last Thanksgiving."

The elder relented and let her stay.

The overseer Archelaos himself presided over the service, assisted by Theogenes, the server Eustratios, and the reader Philippos. Outside, the world was dark and cold. Inside, the house was bright with candles and warm with songs of praise. Before long, Chione forgot about her transgression.

In the midst of a very long prayer by the overseer, Chione thought of Makrina and began to pray for her silently.

Then came a knock at the door. Archelaos paused and everyone looked toward the door. There was a second knock and a voice outside ordered, "Open up in there."

"It's Quartillius!" whispered one of the believers.

Chione gasped and instinctively covered her face with her palla. Several others started toward a back door, but the voice outside said, "It's no use. The house is surrounded."

Archelaos nodded to Hermogenes, who then opened the door. Quartillius entered unbidden, followed by soldiers. He stopped in the middle of the room and, looking over the gathering, announced, "In Caesar's name, you are all under arrest."

More soldiers entered the house and began rounding up those who had tried to flee. "Who is in charge here?" Quartillius asked.

"I am," answered Archelaos from one end of the room.

Quartillius made his way to Archelaos, passing right by Chione, and laid a hand on the overseer's shoulder. "I arrest you for defying the emperors' edict banning public worship by Christians," he said.

"But this is a private home," said Archelaos.

"You have made it a public place," said Quartillius.

The soldiers began escorting believers toward the door, where an orderly was taking names and scratching them into a wax tablet with a wooden pen. Chione watched and listened fearfully as the others were questioned and taken away. She saw Quartillius lead Archelaos from the room. Then a soldier took her by the arm and led her to the door.

"Name?" asked the orderly. Chione hesitated.

The orderly looked up from his tablet to see only her eyes not covered by her palla. Using the end of his pen, he gently pulled back the fold of her palla to see her fearful young face. Her snow-white skin was now flushed red. *Did he recognize her?* she wondered.

"Your name and parentage?" he asked.

Chione took a deep breath. "My name is Christian," she declared, "and I am a child of God."

A fortnight later, the curator Quartillius was standing in front of Marcellinus in the office of the mayor, where Makrina herself had stood for a more cordial interview nearly a year before. "Read it!" said Marcellinus handing Quartillius a small scroll. "Aloud!"

Quartillius read:

> *Quartillius Damianus, Curator, Sinope salutes Valerius Marcellinus, Inspector General of Pontus: Hail Caesar! This is to inform you of the recent arrest of a company of*

*Christians who were surprised while engaged in public
worship in a private home—*

"Stop!" commanded Marcellinus. "Whose home?!" he demanded.
"Hermogenes the baker," answered the perplexed Quartillius.
"Continue!"
Quartillius read on:

> *. . . in violation of the imperial edict banning such assemblies.
> The accused have been interrogated and jailed and await
> your examination. They number 21 adults: 13 men and 8
> women, including a decurion's daughter—*

"Stop!" commanded Marcellinus. "Whose daughter?!"
"Posidonios's," answered Quartillius.
"Posidonios is no longer a decurion, and the girl Chione is no longer
a decurion's daughter!" said Marcellinus. "They both lost that distinction
last spring on account of the second edict against the Christians, which you
appear to have forgotten. Had you arrested a real decurion's daughter, my
immediate departure from Nicomedia and haste in getting here would have
been justified. Had you mentioned her name, I would have seen your error
and not come. Instead, my duties have been needlessly interrupted by your
inexcusable carelessness!"
"But they do require your attention—"
"They could have waited until I arrived next month! I'm sure it would
have done them good!" said Marcellinus. "In the future, you will remember
to be more accurate *and* more explicit in your dispatches. Is that understood?"
"Yes, sir," said Quartillius.
"Very well, then. Bring in the mayor. We'll settle this now."

Makrina had heard of Marcellinus's return and was waiting impatiently in
the tablinum of their townhouse when he arrived. Hearing Nonna's greet-
ing, she rushed into the atrium and threw her arms around him, kissing
him quickly on the cheek and then resting her head on his shoulder. "Gaius!
Thank God you're here!" she said.
"Is your mother or father home?" asked Marcellinus.
"Well, no, not at the moment," she answered.
"We have to talk, and I'd rather we weren't disturbed," he said.
"Certainly," said Makrina. "We'll be in father's study, Nonna."
"Yes, my lady. Would you like me to bring some refreshments?"
asked Nonna.
"Yes."

"No," said Marcellinus, abruptly. Seeing the concern on Makrina's face, he smiled at last and said, "Perhaps later. Let's talk first."

Makrina led him through the courtyard to a large room with a balcony of its own, directly below the upstairs balcony.

"You arrived so soon. Did you get my letter?" she asked, closing the doors behind them.

"Which letter?" asked Marcellinus, collapsing onto a sofa on the far side of the room.

"The one about the arrests," said Makrina, following him across the room to open the doors to the balcony for fresh air and sunlight.

"No. I left as soon as I received Quartillius's dispatch. The idiot said he had arrested a decurion's daughter. I thought it was you," he said, looking up at her longingly.

Makrina had never seen him this strained. She sat down close to him and stroked his forehead with her hand. "Poor dear," she said. "You must have had a miserable journey."

"I did. But seeing you again is more than enough consolation," he said with a weary smile. "I suppose I should thank the idiot now for bringing us together ahead of schedule."

"He must have meant my friend Chione," said Makrina.

"He did."

"Can you help her?"

"I've released her to her father pending trial. She should be home by now."

"I'll have to go see her later. What about the others?"

"They'll have to remain in custody. They're all at risk of flight."

"I see," said Makrina. "What will happen to them?"

Marcellinus sighed. "They have committed a serious crime, and the punishments could be severe. But the governor's practice has been to excuse such violations if the accused will sacrifice to the gods."

"But they can't do that."

"It's their only hope," said Marcellinus.

"But that would mean denying Christ."

"They don't have to deny Christ. They can confess whatever they want about Christ—within the limits of the edicts, of course. But they must offer sacrifice to save themselves."

He looked up at the ceiling and said, "Great gods! I should never have been so generous. It only emboldened them."

"You did so to please me," said Makrina.

"Yes, yes. I would do many things to please you, Makrina, but there are some things I can't do and some I shouldn't do for our own good."

Makrina withdrew her hand and turned away. "It could have been me who was arrested. I would have gone that evening, had I not been expected here."

"It must never be you, Makrina," he said firmly. "You must stay away from their worship. Their worship has got to stop anyway."

Marcellinus sat up and drew his arm around her. "I know how you feel, Makrina. I know what you believe. I've read your letter," he said. "But you must understand. Things have changed. The mood at court has changed. Life for Christians who defy the Caesars could get very difficult soon. I'm not sure how. No decisions have been made. But what is certain is that things won't get easier."

"Then what are we to do?"

"We must submit. We must go along—publicly at least. Believe whatever you want in private, worship Christ or whomever you like in your room or in your home, but not in public, not among others, not outside your family. That is what we all must do. Publicly we must all show our loyalty to the empire and our commitment to the common good, at least for a time, at least for now. It's the only way."

Makrina stood and stepped toward the balcony doors. "Our faith is not like that, Marcellinus," she said with quavering voice. "It cannot be hidden. It cannot be confined to a closet or to the home. To confine it is to kill it, just as to hide the truth is to deny the truth. Christ demands all of us, all of our lives. Everything—every thing, every thought, every moment—must be sanctified with prayer and offered back to Him. Whatever we withhold from Him will only bind us to this world."

Marcellinus rose and went to her, grasping her about the shoulders from behind and speaking softly into her ear. "Just for a while, Makrina, for a little while, until we can see the way clear. For our sake, for us, for me."

Tears formed in her eyes and her body trembled.

"For me!" Marcellinus whispered. She turned and looked up at him, and he held her tightly to him. With a sigh their lips joined in a kiss of passion and desire, as the tears rolled from her eyes.

Marcellinus did not stay long in Sinope before starting back for Nicomedia, but the day before he left he pulled Kimon aside in the nave of the city basilica to tell him of his inquiries into the possibilities of imperial service.

"There are two positions I think you should consider. One is in the office of the quartermaster of the army. It's a prestigious post. Nothing receives more attention from the Caesars than the care of the legions. Of course, you'd have to deal often with the soldiers at court, which could be good or bad. Good if they like you, and disastrous if they don't. Some of these military men resent having to depend on civilians for anything. On the other hand, if you can show them how to keep more troops in the field, you'll never find more loyal allies."

"I see," said Kimon warily. "What's the other position?"

"The other is personal secretary to our very own governor, Sossianus Hierocles. It's not nearly as prestigious and certainly not something you'd want to do for very long, but it could lead very quickly to greater things. The work might actually be more interesting. It's normally filled by someone younger than you, but you're not too old yet. If I were entering service for the first time at your age, I wouldn't be at all ashamed to take it. The risk of failure is less, and the opportunities for advancement may actually be greater. Of course, I'd be able to help you more in the governor's office than if you were with the quartermaster in the palace."

"So that's what you'd recommend?"

"At the moment," said Marcellinus, "but think on it a while. When I get back, I'll find out more about both and let you know by letter what I find. After that, it's up to you. Once you've decided, it shouldn't take any time at all for me to arrange things."

Kimon smiled knowingly. "Is there anything you can't arrange?" he asked.

Marcellinus chuckled and set his hand on Kimon's shoulder. "I can't arrange your accession to the purple, so don't expect to occupy the palace when you arrive in Nicomedia," he said, turning with Kimon to begin moving back toward their offices. "I *can* advise you on where else you might stay. I know all the right neighborhoods—and the best wrong ones, too."

"Of course," said Kimon. "That reminds me: Makrina said you'd said there has been some change in Nicomedia with regard to Christians?"

Marcellinus nodded his head slowly as he walked. "Since the augustus Diocletian left for Rome last May, the caesar Galerius has been chiefly responsible for most matters and, well, they say he's impatient with the pace of the reforms. It's strange: he's a soldier through and through, but about some civil matters he's extraordinarily enthusiastic. Anyway, Diocletian is still in Dalmatia, taking his time with his return. The palace has exhausted its stables keeping up with the flurry of dispatches between the caesar and the augustus. My guess is that we should see some new edict in a month or so."

"Good or bad?"

Marcellinus paused. "The rumors say both, but I would say bad, though not too bad, I hope. No details. If you don't hear about it from me first, wait until you receive my instructions before acting. I'm sure the governor will have something to say about how it's implemented."

He resumed his walk with sigh. "Once you've been in Nicomedia awhile, Kimon, you'll see that there are many who think that all they have to do is give the command and everyone will fall in line. I myself tend to favor a slower course, to give people time to adjust to each new step. You'd be amazed at how much you can accomplish that way. To paraphrase a centurion I once knew: if you want an ass to climb a mountain, you'd be ill-advised to beat his hindquarters while commanding him to jump. With a little patience, you can lead him up the trail step by step without his objection. It's the same with people. If you introduce things slowly enough, you can make them do anything you like, Kimon. Anything at all."

In the spring of the twentieth year of the reign of Diocletian, the emperors issued an edict requiring every man, woman, and child to offer sacrifice to the gods. Any means were authorized to compel obedience to the edict. No mention was made of the Christians in the edict, but the only exception granted was for the Jews.

Official notification of the edict arrived in Sinope accompanied by instructions from the provincial governor concerning its enforcement. No action was to be taken until the publication of a list of known or suspected Christians, to be provided by Marcellinus upon his return. Following publication of the list, the population was to be allowed a fortnight to comply. The town clerk was responsible for supervising compliance and recording the names of all who sacrificed. After the fortnight, everyone on the list who had not yet sacrificed was to be arrested and compelled to sacrifice or face trial before the governor.

The dispatch containing the edict and the instructions also contained two brief personal letters from Marcellinus. One letter was for Kimon, and in it Marcellinus reported that all that remained before Kimon could be brought on as personal secretary to the governor was an interview with the governor and the present secretary, which would take place when the governor arrived in Sinope the following month for assizes. The other letter was for Makrina, and in her letter Marcellinus urged that she take no precipitous action on account of the new edict, for her safety would be secured. At first opportunity, Makrina showed her letter to Kimon, who read it without comment.

"Do you know what this means?" she asked.

Kimon shrugged. "It means he loves you," he said.

"It means I'm his prisoner—his personal prisoner," said Makrina, snatching back the letter. "It means I'm dependent upon his protection and so I dare not cross him."

"So don't cross him," asked Kimon.

"But very soon he will ask me to marry him," said Makrina.

"So marry him," said Kimon.

"*Marry* him? What are you saying? You know I can't marry him."

"Why not?"

"Why *not*? You know why as well as anyone!"

"Makrina, times have changed, the law has changed, your 'Assembly' has changed. There's no one to punish you for marrying outside it. You can't be kept from joining the Thanksgiving, because there won't be any Thanksgivings for a while, perhaps for quite a long while. So what harm can come from marrying Marcellinus?"

"Great harm," said Makrina. "Great harm!" she repeated. "Marrying him would only separate me farther from the Body, from Christ himself."

"There are many believers who are married to nonbelievers, are there not? Then it is possible to be a Christian and marry someone who is not. And nowadays it hardly seems to matter. Everyone of your fellow believers has had to adjust in some way to get by under the present edicts. You could do a lot worse than marrying an unbeliever, especially one who'll guarantee your safety—and not force you to sacrifice."

"How do you know he won't force me to sacrifice? Where does he say that?" countered Makrina, waving the letter in Kimon's face.

"He said to do nothing. He said that you are safe. He could have urged you to sacrifice, Makrina. He could have spent the last several months trying to win you away from your beliefs, but he hasn't, has he?"

"No, he hasn't."

"Of course not, because he loves you. He loves you enough to stick his neck out to protect you. He's taken a terrible risk just writing you that letter. You're not the only one in danger, Makrina. He risks his own safety to protect you."

Makrina froze with sudden recognition, as Kimon moved closer for the kill.

"He loves you, Makrina," he said again. "He loves you enough to let you remain a Christian. So marry him."

She glanced at him out of the corner of her eye and then moved away from him quickly. "You talked me into seeing him with assurances I wouldn't have to marry him, and now when your assurances have proven worthless, you try to talk me into marrying him!"

Kimon laughed and said, "But *you* gave *me* assurances you wouldn't fall in love with him, and now *your* assurances have proven worthless as well."

Makrina blushed and scowled at once, as Kimon circled about her, grinning cruelly.

"Times have changed, Makrina, and you have changed, too," he said. "If you don't want to marry him, you can still escape having to sacrifice by running away and hiding in the mountains, as I expect many Christians will do. But that will mean never seeing Marcellinus again. Can you do that, Makrina? Can you?"

# XI

Many Christians did just as Kimon expected, without even waiting for their names to appear on the list of suspects. Theodoros, Kimon's principal support in his capacity as town clerk, was the first to leave, the day after the edict was officially announced. He was followed soon by other well-known Christians who could expect to be listed as suspects, including the reader Andreas, whose whole family went with him.

When Marcellinus arrived a few days later, Quartillius complained that many principal suspects had already fled, but Marcellinus was unconcerned. "We have enough in custody to use as examples," he said. "When they have been persuaded to sacrifice, others will sacrifice more willingly. The governor wants loyal, obedient citizens, not defiant 'witnesses.'"

When the list was published, Marcellinus's intentions with regard to Makrina became clearer. Her name was not on it. Chione's name was, as were the names of her father and mother and also her younger brother Euplios, none of whom had yet fled, for fleeing while Chione was awaiting trial would have meant the loss of everything they owned. Posidonios preferred to wait and see if it were not possible to find some way around the requirement, just as he hoped to free Chione from her legal jeopardy.

Very soon after his return, Marcellinus, accompanied by his aide Libanius, paid a call on the family at their house in town. Chione watched from a distance as the ever gracious official greeted her father and her mother Kallista, whom he was meeting for the first time. Then the official and her father repaired to another room to talk privately. Before long, the pair returned and the official said farewell to her mother and father as if he had come about the lightest matter. Chione emerged immediately after he had left. Her mother started to send her away, but her father said, "No, she should stay. It concerns her." Then he turned to Chione. "You must be taken again into custody in preparation for your trial," he said.

Kallista gasped. Posidonios continued: "The governor will be here early next month, and the trial will begin shortly thereafter. You won't be long in the prison, and Marcellinus assures me you will well cared for. He will take you there himself, day after tomorrow. He said he thought you would need time to prepare."

Chione sighed sadly.

"He wants us all to sacrifice," said Posidonios. "He said he could promise the governor's mercy if we did so."

"What did you tell him?" asked Kallista.

"I told him we would consider what he said. He doesn't expect an answer, just that the records show we have sacrificed," said Posidonios.

"Lord have mercy!" said Kallista.

That evening Posidonios went to see Kimon and explained the situation privately, hinting that he was willing to offer a bribe to whomever necessary to avoid having to sacrifice. "Whatever it takes is not too much," he said.

"I'm afraid that with Marcellinus, too much would not be enough," said Kimon. "He's not that kind of man, Posidonios. I wouldn't think of taking your money, of course, but it would be too dangerous for me to simply falsify the records. You're too well known. There may be some other way around this, but I'll have to give it some thought."

In the next few days, the citizens of Sinope who were not Christians began lining up outside the temple of Serapis to fulfill their obligation. Some brought offerings of wine to be poured out on the altar or on the ground as a libation to the gods. Others brought animals of all kinds to be slaughtered on the altar and then cooked and eaten. The fire upon the altar burned continuously through the day, filling the sanctuary with a dense cloud of smoke.

The handful of men of the city whose turn it was to serve as priests at the temple were at first delighted to accept the sacrifices, but they soon tired of the constant attention the sacrifices required, and people began to grumble about having to wait too long for their turn.

Then there was the requirement to record each sacrifice, which meant stationing a municipal scribe at the temple all day long, to do nothing more than take names and write out receipts. When the scribes complained of the tedium of the task, Kimon, always one in search of escapes from the tedium of work, thought of an alternative, which actually solved several problems. Outside the town hall, he placed a small altar of the Divine Sun and there during regular hours he stationed a scribe. During those hours, for a small fee, the people could purchase a pinch of incense and burn it in honor of the sun god.

Marcellinus was impressed. Implementation of the edict of sacrifice was greatly simplified and accelerated. The administrative expenses of implementation were defrayed by the charge on incense. And the people were encouraged to fulfill their obligation by the ease and convenience of the requirement.

Unbeknownst to Marcellinus, the arrangement also provided Christians like Posidonios a means of being counted as having sacrificed without actually having done so. "I have a new scribe from Ionopolis who doesn't know you or anyone else in Sinope," Kimon told Posidonios one evening. "When it's his turn at the altar, send one of your slaves to sacrifice in your name. The scribe won't know the difference."

The trick worked easily, so easily that by the end of the official fortnight many other Christians in Sinope had found others to sacrifice for them, though some were pierced by guilt at even having a sacrifice recorded in their name.

Marcellinus again was pleased, this time with the apparent compliance of so many Christians. When Quartillius reported that everyone on the list had either sacrificed or fled, Marcellinus expressed his complete satisfaction and praised Kimon for his part in making compliance so convenient.

There were still the trials for the purpose of obtaining the public submission of the Christian Assembly. They began the following week, once the governor, Sossianos Hierocles, was again comfortably lodged in the villa of Aristoboulos.

The first day of the trials was like the opening of a festival. Spectators gathered early at the basilica to lay claim to the best spots from which to view the proceedings. Many more lined the main street and forum to witness the governor's arrival. About the fourth hour, the city shook with the sound of the governor's cavalcade clip-clopping down the paved thoroughfare toward the forum. A troop of cavalry led the way, followed by three fine carriages for the governor and his staff. All were sumptuously attired.

The people along the route gawked and cheered. Persians would have held their tongues and bowed their heads before a lord so lofty, but Romans—especially Greek Romans—still needed to be taught such respect. The governor ignored them, sitting motionless in his carriage, his eyes fixed forward, his face expressionless, as if his very presence was a distasteful condescension. His face was gaunt and grave from long study and light eating. His beard was full but neatly clipped. His fern-green mantle of office covered the simple white robe of a philosopher, though this robe was made of fine Indian cotton instead of a philosopher's coarse wool.

The parade came to an anticlimactic end outside the city basilica, where the governor descended from his carriage and went inside without ceremony.

The prisoners waited out of view of the governor, under guard around the back side of the basilica. A crowd of free Christians had gathered to comfort and encourage them. Makrina and Eugenia were among them. Someone had brought water in jugs, so the women joined in filling cups and passing them among the prisoners. "Are you hungry? Shall I fetch bread?" Makrina asked. The elders declined, with thanks. "We have prepared ourselves with fasting," said the overseer Archelaos. "Just provide us your prayers, child," said Theogenes.

When the cheers of the crowd in the forum signaled the arrival of the governor, the family and friends present exchanged kisses and embraces.

Chione, who had stood silently for some time, her slender wrists bound with twine because the shackles were too big, turned suddenly to Makrina and said, "Come with me, Krina. Hear my witness."

Makrina folded her arms around Chione and held her tight. "Be strong," she said. "The Lord is with you."

The pair walked together arm in arm around the building, through the crowd, and up the steps of the basilica. Then, on the crowded porch, just outside the door of the basilica, two firm hands took hold of Makrina's arms from behind and guided her to the side. Chione looked back to see Makrina being led away by Libanius, Marcellinus's aide. "Keep moving," ordered a guard at the door, prodding Chione gently forward, alone.

"My lord has asked me to escort you home," Libanius explained to Makrina.

"What? Where is he?" said Makrina.

"He is at his post, and he wishes that you not be present for the trial," said Libanius. "Please come." He led her down the steps and through the forum, not letting go of her until they had reached her house, whereupon he bade her good-day and waited until she had gone inside. Makrina slammed the door between them. "His prisoner, indeed!" she huffed.

Inside the basilica, now a courtroom, the prisoners were led to the center of the nave and made to stand in three ranks bounded by guards. Chione was tethered to one end of the second rank. She looked around the building for her father and mother but found first her brother Euplios, a boy in his early teens, standing conspicuously on the base of a column on the far side of the room. He saw her, too, and waved, then pointed her out to her parents, who were standing below him.

At the apse end of the basilica, upon a dais draped with crimson cloth, sat the governor, Sossianos Hierocles, in the curule chair. The chairs beside him were taken by two assessors, who would provide him with legal advice during the trials. The lictor and other members of the staff, including Marcellinus, stood behind them. Banners hanging overhead displayed the images of all four emperors—the augusti Diocletian and Maximian and the caesars Galerius and Constantius.

More spectators filed noisily into the building after the prisoners, sorting themselves to the aisles on both sides of the nave where there was still standing room. The lictor pounded the dais with the governor's rod of office and called for silence. "Let the charges be read," the lictor ordered.

The curator Quartillius came forward, saluted and bowed, and then addressed the governor. "Your Excellency, the accused—" he then read the list of names, identifying each of the prisoners with the name of his father "—were arrested on the eighth day before the Kalends of February while engaged in Christian worship in the house of Hermogenes the baker, in violation of the imperial edict banning such meetings. None of the accused has denied the charge under interrogation. All have confessed to being Christians and have heretofore refused to offer sacrifice to the gods as required by the recent edict of the Caesars."

The governor nodded in acknowledgment. "Who presided over the meeting?" he asked.

"Archelaos, the son of Archippos," answered Quartillius.

"Bring him forth."

Quartillius motioned for the turnkey to free Archelaos from the front rank of prisoners.

"Are you the accused Archelaos?" asked the governor.

"I am," answered Archelaos.

"Do you deny the charge?"

"I do not."

"You confess to having presided over an illegal gathering of Christians for the purpose of worship?"

"I do."

"Did you not know that such gatherings are forbidden by imperial edict, and that the penalties for violating such edicts are severe?"

"I knew."

"Why then did you hold the meeting?"

"I must obey God before man."

"Your god commands you to oppose the emperors?"

"Our God commands us to worship him in spirit and in truth."

"Who is your overseer?" asked the governor, taking a roll of paper from one of his assessors.

"Christ is my overseer," said Archelaos.

"In this world, in this city, who is your overseer?"

"I told you—our Lord Jesus Christ."

"I take it that you yourself are the overseer of the Christians here."

"I am."

"Very well then," said the governor. "You are charged with a very serious crime, for which you could be put to death, but as you know the pious Diocletianus Augustus and all the Caesars have issued an edict requiring all loyal Roman citizens to offer sacrifice to the gods. I can assure you, as I have some personal knowledge of the emperors and their aims, that they have no desire to see their citizens punished or put to death needlessly. They wish only that all Roman citizens demonstrate their loyalty by offering sacrifice, to secure the continued prosperity of the empire with the gods' favor. With that wish in mind, I offer you the opportunity to free yourself of this charge of illegal gathering by sacrificing to the gods. Even more, because you are their leader, I will dismiss the charge of illegal assembly against everyone, if you alone will but sacrifice. What do you say?"

"I cannot sacrifice to your gods," answered Archelaos.

"Perhaps you didn't hear me. I'm offering to release everyone on the condition that you alone give sacrifice. It's a most generous offer. Will you not sacrifice to save your people from judgment?"

"I cannot sacrifice," answered Archelaos.

"That's it? That's all you have to say? Many other of your Christians have already sacrificed," said the governor, holding up the roll of paper. "I have here a list of every Christian in Sinope who has chosen to obey the Caesars and honor the gods of the empire with sacrifice. It is a very long list. Shall I read it to you?"

"It would make no difference," said Archelaos.

"But they have sacrificed," said the governor.

"What they have done, they have done," said Archelaos.

"Why will you not sacrifice?"

"I do not know how," answered Archelaos.

"How can you not know how? In all your years, you have never learned to sacrifice to the gods?"

"It is not our custom."

"Well it's very simple," said the governor. "You take a pinch of incense and you cast it upon the altar."

Nervous laughter rolled through the crowded hall. The lictor pounded on the dais for silence.

"I will not sacrifice, for God does not wish such immolations. He will not be satisfied with whole-burnt offerings of lambs or bulls, or offerings of incense or flour."

An assessor leaned forward in his chair. "Is this a question of flour?" he said. "You are treating for your life. Be careful what you say."

"What kind of sacrifices does your God like?" asked the governor.

"Purity of heart, sincere faith, and truth."

"Well then, with purity of heart, sincere faith, and truth, sacrifice." The governor waved his hand toward a dish of coals, supported by an iron tripod with legs in the form of satyrs, standing to the left of the dais.

"I will not sacrifice."

"Paul sacrificed."

"He did not."

"He denied Jesus Christ, didn't he?"

"No."

"But he was a persecutor and put many Christians to death."

"By the grace of God, he was redeemed and became our steadfast defender, who himself was persecuted."

"But he was an uneducated Syrian who spoke only his native tongue."

"He was a Hebrew who spoke Greek and knew the law. He was the wisest of men."

"You will soon be saying that he was wiser than Plato."

"Not only wiser than Plato but than all the philosophers. In fact, he argued with and convinced many very wise men."

"Was Paul God?"

Archelaos smiled. "No, of course not," he said.

"Who was he then?"

"A man like you and me. But the Spirit of God was in him and by this Spirit he gained knowledge and wisdom and did wonders and miracles. If you like, I will explain his teaching to you."

"The gods forbid. Sacrifice!"

"I will not sacrifice."

"Moses sacrificed!"

"The Jews were commanded to sacrifice to one God, and only in Jerusalem. They sin now if they sacrifice in other places."

"Enough of this useless discourse. Sacrifice, I say."

"I will not stain my soul by so doing."

"I can force you to do so."

"You cannot force me to worship idols."

"Take his hand and make him sacrifice!"

The guard standing next to Archelaos grabbed his arm and pulled him up to the smoldering altar, then forced incense into Archelaos's hand and shook it over the altar. Instantly a puff of smoke arose from the coals.

"See there. You have sacrificed," said the governor.

"I have not sacrificed," said Archelaos.

"We have all seen you."

"You have seen the guard sacrifice using my hand, which I must wash at first opportunity."

The audience laughed, but not for long. "Strike his mouth!" commanded the governor. The guard hit Archeloas with his fist and nearly knocked him to the floor.

"Sacrifice or I will have you flogged," said the governor.

Archelaos straightened up and rubbed his jaw. "Do what you must—I will not sacrifice," he said.

"Flog him," ordered the governor. "And then bring him back," he added as Archelaos was led toward the door. "We will see yet if he won't sacrifice."

The movement of spectators outside to witness the flogging caused quite a commotion in the hall, while the governor conferred privately with his assessors. When the commotion settled, the lictor pounded the dais with his rod, and the governor called for Hermogenes the baker. "Why did you allow that man to hold a secret meeting in your house?" asked the governor.

"He is my overseer, and we gathered to celebrate the Thanksgiving, without which we cannot live," said Hermogenes.

"But you know the law. Should you not have preferred the edict of the Caesars to the will of your overseer?"

"God is greater than the Caesars," answered Hermogenes. Heads turned as the first crack of whip sounded in the forum.

"I will offer you the same mercy as your overseer. If you will but sacrifice, I will free you this instant."

"I cannot sacrifice, your Excellency," said Hermogenes.

"Your overseer has set a dangerous example. One might expect that from a leader, but you are a baker and not a elder or overseer. Why should you hazard your life and your fortune for something so simple?"

"I am a Christian," said Hermogenes almost apologetically. "I cannot sacrifice."

"You have a family?"

"Yes, your Excellency."

"Were they with you when you were arrested?"

"No, your Excellency. My wife is not a Christian."

"Is she here today?"

"Yes, your Excellency," said Hermogenes, glancing toward the side aisle.

"Stand forth, woman, and plead for you husband," commanded the governor. "Your name?"

"Klaria . . . your Excellency."

"How is it that you have not been able to turn your husband from his superstitious ways?"

Klaria shook her head helplessly. "He is my husband, he does what he wills," she said.

"But you are his wife and you can bend his will."

"Does your wife bend your will?" countered Klaria. The audience snickered.

Sossianos Hierocles, who was not married, ignored the remark. "Have you sacrificed in accordance with the edict?" he asked.

"No, your Excellency," answered Klaria.

"Why not?" asked the governor.

Klaria shrugged. "I will do so now," she offered.

"Then do so," said the governor.

Klaria stepped toward the altar and quickly tossed a pinch of incense from the serving tray onto the coals.

"See there, baker? That wasn't so difficult. A very small thing really.

And if you do likewise, you may go freely home with your wife this instant," said the governor.

Hermogenes and Klaria looked at each other. "I cannot sacrifice," he said.

"Not even for your wife's sake?"

Hermogenes shook his head.

"Sacrifice or join your overseer at the post!"

"I will not sacrifice," said Hermogenes.

"Away! Away with him!" ordered the governor, raising his voice in frustration. A guard led Hermogenes toward the door with Klaria hurrying after them. "Please, please, sacrifice," she pleaded, but her husband kept shaking his head.

"You have seen what happens to obstinate people," said the governor to the remaining prisoners. "If you do not obey, you will be treated in the same way. If anyone wants to save himself, let him speak up."

"We are Christians," shouted a young man from the last rank.

"Who said that?" demanded the governor.

"I did," answered Dio the taverner.

"Then you belong at the post, too!" shouted the governor, and Dio was led away to be flogged. The chamber rumbled with voices and motion. On the dais, the governor conferred again with his assessors. Then Marcellinus stepped forward and spoke into the governor's ear. The governor nodded and signaled to the lictor, who pounded the dais with his rod once more. "Bring the maiden Chione forth," ordered the governor.

Chione shook with sudden alarm and stared forward with wide eyes and gaping mouth. Her heart raced as a guard cut the cord connecting her to her fellow prisoners and then led her before the dais. Without a covering for her head, she felt shamefully exposed before the crowd of onlookers. "You are Chione, the daughter of Posidonios?" asked the governor.

"I am," she peeped.

"Speak up, child."

"I am," she repeated.

"You were with the rest when you were arrested for worshipping together as Christians?"

"I was."

"Speak up," said Quartillius.

Chione glanced at him fearfully and then turned back to the governor. "I was," she said.

"Young woman, I will give you the same choice I gave the others. If you will but sacrifice, you shall be cleared of all charges and may return to your home a free woman. Will you sacrifice?"

Chione trembled as she spoke: "I am a Christian. I cannot sacrifice."

"Speak up!" ordered Quartillius.

Chione took a deep breath and said louder than ever, "I cannot sacrifice for I am a Christian."

The chamber fell suddenly silent. The governor leaned forward in his chair and spoke in a conciliatory tone: "Consider, dear girl, what you are saying. You have seen what has happened to the others who defied the Caesars by refusing to sacrifice. I would be pained to subject a creature as young and as fair as you to the same torment, but if you persist in this disobedience, you will give me no choice."

Before she could answer, Marcellinus handed the governor a sheet of paper and spoke again into his ear. The crowd murmured while they waited. Then the governor nodded and signaled again to the lictor to call for silence.

With order restored, the governor held the paper up for all to see and said, "I have here a petition protesting that the girl Chione is incompetent to stand trial on account of her age and her infirmity of mind. The petition is submitted by the city clerk, Kimon, son of Aristoboulos the decurion. Is the clerk present to speak for his petition?"

"Yes, your Excellency," said Kimon stepping down from one end of the dais.

"Well then?" said the governor.

"I have known the maiden Chione for many years, and also the former clerk Theodoros, a Christian who is now a fugitive from the law. Some time ago this young girl fell under the spell of this Theodoros and conceived a mad, childish love for him, which accounts for her present irrational behavior. As the child is neither of legal age nor of sound mind, I submit that she cannot, according to the laws of the empire, be held accountable for her actions."

"Is this so, girl?" asked the governor.

"No, it is not!" said Chione, staring at Kimon in amazement. "I hardly know Theodoros and I'm not in love with him!"

"Your Excellency," said Kimon, without looking at Chione, "I have observed the progress of their affair over the past many months. I swear the child is quite smitten with this older man and therefore should not be held accountable for her present foolishness, given the frailty of her age and sex."

"No! No!" protested Chione, her face now flushed with embarrassment. "Tell them it's not true. Tell them, Kimon!"

"The man is trying to save your life," said the governor. "Why do you deny him?"

Chione shook her head bewildered. "What he says is not true. I hardly know Theodoros, and he is not why I will not sacrifice. I have been a Christian all my life. I was born of Christian parents and raised in a Christian home. I was baptized as a babe and have been obedient to my father in all matters of faith ever since. I cannot sacrifice because I am a Christian, not because I'm in love with Theodoros!"

"Your father is the former decurion Posidonios?" asked the governor.

"Yes, he is," said Chione.

"Is Posidonios here?"

"I am, your Excellency," answered Posidonios, stepping forward not far from Kimon.

"What do you know of your daughter's, er, relationship with this Theodoros?" asked the governor.

"I have no knowledge of it, your Excellency," answered Posidonios.

"Is what this man says about your daughter then not true?"

"I cannot say, your Excellency," said Posidonios. "If it is true, it has been hidden from me."

The governor looked in turn at the witnesses before him. "Is there anyone else here today with knowledge of this matter who can swear that the allegation of an affair is true or not?" he asked. Murmurs filled the chamber, but no one came forth. The governor conferred once again with his assessors and with Marcellinus and then announced his decision.

"It seems reasonable to me to err on the side of doubt in this case," he said. "Whatever the truth of the matter, the girl Chione is young and still very impressionable, having yet shown no independence from others. I am inclined to entrust her again to her guardian. I see from this list that you, Posidonios, have already offered sacrifice in accordance with the edict. If you will now sacrifice again before us, I will accept your sacrifice on behalf of your daughter and clear all charges against her."

Kimon looked at Posidonios and saw his face pale in an instant. For a long moment, Posidonios did not move, not even to breathe.

"Go on, Posidonios," said the governor. "The sooner done, the sooner you and your daughter may go home."

Posidonios hesitated a moment further, then lurched forward toward the altar where he swiftly lifted a pinch of incense from the tray and dropped it onto the coals. Some in the audience gasped in astonishment while others groaned with dismay.

"You may go now," said the governor.

Quickly, very quickly, and without looking at anyone, Posidonios took Chione by the arm and led her out of the chamber, as people began to murmur.

Makrina heard the news of Chione's release and Posidonios's failing from Eugenia and set out immediately to Chione's house, with Eugenia following. They were just outside the door when they heard the sound of voices raised in anger. The shrillest was barely intelligible—loud but indistinct and coming it seemed from well inside the house. They knocked and were let in by the servant girl Petra, whose fearful greeting added to their concern.

Then suddenly Chione's brother Euplios came storming in from the garden, moving through the tablinum like a tempest, kicking at over tables and chairs and crying, "You didn't have to do it! You didn't have to do it!" Eugenia and Petra fled in fear to another part of the house, as Makrina shrank back into the atrium and up against the wall in the corner.

"Come back here!" ordered Posidonios following his son through the tablinum. Euplios saw Makrina and reeled away from the door in embarrassment and shame, only to be caught by his father in the tablinum. "Listen to me!" shouted Posidonios, seizing his son by the shoulders. "Listen to me!"

"You didn't have to do it!" cried Euplios, his words twisted in anguish almost beyond recognition. He was now bawling uncontrollably and looking, for all his fourteen years, like a very frightened little boy.

"I did it for Chione! I did it for you and for your mother! If I hadn't done it, we'd have lost everything—our land, our freedom, *our lives!*"

"I don't care! I don't care! You didn't have to do it!"

"I had to do it for your sake, for Chione's sake!"

"*She* didn't sacrifice! *She* would have earned her crown if you hadn't sacrificed for her!"

"Is that what you wanted?! For your sister to suffer?!"

"What should I have wanted?! That you should deny Christ?! That's not what you taught me! That's not what I believe because of you!"

"I didn't want to do it! I wish I hadn't had to, but I did it for your sake, for all our sakes, because I'm your father!"

"*You are not my father! I don't have a father!*" screamed Euplios, breaking free and bolting toward the door.

"Don't say that!"

"*It's true! It's true! I don't have a father!*"

"*Don't say that!*"

Euplios flung open the door and ran into the alley, screaming again and again, "*I don't have a father! I don't have a father!*"

"*Euplios!*" cried Posidonios, standing in the doorway. "*Come back here!*"

But Euplios was gone, and the house and alley were suddenly silent. Posidonios stood in the doorway for a moment catching his breath and trying to calm himself. Then he turned and saw Makrina cowering in the corner. He looked at her with sad, watering eyes, then just shook his head and walked away.

Makrina found Eugenia with Chione, huddled against the wall in Chione's room. "He's gone now. Euplios, I mean," said Makrina, but neither girl moved. From the redness of Chione's eyes, Makrina could tell she had been crying. Makrina sat down on the floor next to Chione and put her arm around her. Chione laid her head on Makrina's shoulder and began again to cry.

She had only just dried her eyes a while later when the girls heard a man's voice downstairs in the atrium. Makrina left the room to see who it was and found Petra looking for her master. "He's wanted by the governor," said Petra. "Euplios has been arrested!"

When the girls reached the basilica with Posidonios and Kallista, Euplios was standing under guard to one side of the nave while the governor interrogated Archelaos for the second time. The boy's rage had gone. His head was bowed, his hair was tousled, and his tunic was torn and dirty. Blood showed through the cloth on his back. He had already been flogged. His mother and sister rushed to his side, but the guards kept them back.

When informed of Posidonios's arrival, the governor broke off his interrogation and ordered Archelaos returned to prison. As Archelaos was led away, Posidonios approached the dais and bowed before the governor, who nodded in acknowledgment. "Bring the boy forth," he ordered. The guards led Euplios before the dais.

The battered boy looked up at the governor and said, "What do you want, devil?"

The governor looked at him in amazement. "Strike his mouth," ordered Quartillius. One of the guards holding Euplios slapped his face with the back of his hand. "Have you learned nothing from the lash?" asked the governor.

"I have learned that you hate God," said Euplios.

"Hit him again!" ordered Quartillius. The guard punched Euplios in the jaw so hard that the boy fell against the other guard and collapsed at his feet. The guards picked him up.

"I should cut out your tongue for your insolence, boy," said the governor. "If your father were not here I would."

"This man is not my father," said Euplios. "God in heaven is my Father. I have no other."

"You would renounce your own father—and the protection he offers?"

"I do renounce him, I have renounced him," answered Euplios.

"Euplios, no!" pleaded Posidonios. "You don't know what you're doing!"

"I know who my father is and I know where to find him," said Euplios.

"Who is your father?" asked the governor.

"God is my father," said Euplios, "the God of Abraham, Isaac, and Jacob, the God of the Apostles, whom I long to see."

"Euplios!"

"Very well then," said the governor. "Posidonios's pleas will no longer be heard, and you, boy, will be sent to your father."

"Your Excellency, hear me please!" begged Posidonios, drawing nearer the dais. In the aisle, Kallista wailed aloud and dropped to her knees.

"This court has heard enough," said the governor, addressing the chamber. "We have seen nothing but disrespect and disobedience today, a most amazing resistance to the justice and mercy of Roman law. I have never seen anything like it. I have been patient. I have tried to reason with these people. I have shown them the lash as a corrective, but I have spared their lives in hopes that they would rejoin our good society. I had hoped not to make 'witnesses' of these people, but now this insolent youth volunteers to be the first. So be it! By the sword, before the sun sets, you shall see your father!"

Kallista screamed and fell prostrate on the floor. "Excellency!" shouted Posidonios, but the governor had risen and left his chair. The lictor pounded the dais three solemn times with his rod, raised it high, then lowered it again, signifying the end of the proceedings. The governor's assessors and staff repaired along with the governor, and the people in the aisles began to disperse.

Euplios, his hands bound with twine behind his back, said quietly, "Thank you, your Excellency." The guards then led him away.

From the courtroom, Euplios was taken to the garrison and held in seclusion while preparations were made for his execution. Outside the gates of the garrison, Kallista, Chione, and several other women of the Assembly gathered to plead and weep and console one another. About the eleventh hour, a squad of soldiers formed in the garrison yard, now shadowed by the sinking sun. Euplios, looking tired and sad, was brought forth and secured with ropes between two files of soldiers. His hands were still bound with twine, and a wooden placard was hung about his neck, bearing the words:

*EUPLIOS THE CHRISTIAN*
*ENEMY OF THE GODS*
*AND THE CAESARS*

"Clear the gates!" the guards ordered, pushing away the women with careful sweeps of their spears. On order, the column of soldiers started forward through the gates and into the street, turning left toward the mainland. In the lead was a herald proclaiming every five paces, "Euplios the Christian, enemy of the gods and the Caesars." Each time he did so, Euplios replied, smiling, "Thanks be to Christ my God." At the end of the procession came a helmet-less soldier with a dun-colored cloak drawn about him. The bare, rounded tip of a very long sword showed beneath the hem of his cloak.

Makrina caught up with the procession at the city gates and followed it the rest of the way, helping Chione comfort her distraught mother. Eugenia had been there from the beginning. Many more people joined the procession as it passed by, most just to see the spectacle.

The procession stopped at the sandy field west of town where at other times the games were held. Kallista was at last allowed to approach her condemned son. "My son, my child, my baby!" she cried, enclosing him in her arms and holding him tight. She wiped his face with her palla moistened with her tears and kissed his cheeks, then knelt before him and hugged his legs. "Forgive us, Euplios. Have mercy and forgive us," she pleaded.

Euplios, who had appeared strangely serene, suddenly burst forth with tears of his own. "I do, Mamma. I forgive you!" he said.

Then the sergeant signaled for Chione and Makrina to take her away. Makrina led Kallista aside while Chione hugged and kissed her young brother. "Remember us, Euplios, when you come into the Kingdom," she said, with tears flowing afresh from her eyes. "I will," he said.

Chione straightened his hair and forced herself to smile, then traced a cross upon his forehead and left to join her mother. The guards moved forward to clear room for the work at hand, pushing back the spectators with their spears held parallel to the ground. Before they could stop her, Eugenia slipped between them and ran up to Euplios. Bussing him on the cheek, she said, "Remember me to God, Euplios." He looked at her curiously and then smiled. She ran away before the guards could catch her.

When the area was cleared, the executioner stepped forward and removed his cloak. Beneath it, he wore a loose workman's tunic, the kind that left the arms free and the right shoulder bare. He stretched his arms and shook his shoulders, then drew and examined his sword. Eugenia gasped and shrieked with sudden horror and then started to cry. Euplios was made to kneel in the sand. The herald read the sentence:

> By the laws of the Roman imperium, justly given with respect
> for the gods by the pious Augustus Diocletianus, et cetera:
> I, Sossianos Hierocles, Governor of Bithynia and Pontus,
> sentence Euplios, the Christian atheist, son of Posidonios, to
> die by the sword this day before sunset.

The executioner stepped up to his victim, looking impassively upon the boy for the first time. Euplios looked skyward and mouthed a prayer heard only by the angels, then bowed his head.

Makrina wrapped her arms tightly around Eugenia. "Don't look," said Makrina, turning her own head aside.

The executioner raised his sword slowly, then swiftly brought it down on the nape of the young neck. Head and body dropped separately to the ground. Kallista screamed and fainted. Chione screamed. Eugenia screamed.

Makrina looked upon the bloody boy and trembled violently, then burst forth with an anguished cry of her own.

# XII

"Cut that one off right about—there." From atop his horse, the legate Sergius Gratianus threw a stone and struck the trunk of a pine at a point just below his horse's head, but forty feet from the tree's base.

"Got it," replied an aide, acknowledging the mark. The aide then guided a pair of sappers up the trunk of the pine to the designated spot, where one used a hatchet to weaken the trunk on the side they wanted the tree to fall, before passing the hatchet to his partner to start the bite for the saw in the bark on the opposite side. A short time later the upper half of the tree toppled down the steep slope of the hill, opening a deep vista of blue sky, green hills, and yellow meadows on the far side of the bend in the river.

"Perfect," said Gratianus, admiring the view, but not for its beauty.

"Hail, Caesar," announced a guard, drawing his general's attention to the imperial party trotting up the trail on horseback, the caesar himself in the lead. Gratianus turned his mount and rendered his own salute. "Hail, Caesar," he said.

"Health, Gratianus. How goes it?" The caesar Flavius Valerius Constantius was in his early 50's but already gray and paler than when they dubbed him *Chlorus*—"the Pale-faced." His time-worn cheeks were covered with a thin, gray soldier's beard, beneath a hooked nose flanked by large grey eyes, sunken now in the shadow of his wrinkled brow. Cloaked in purple and encased in a steel-blue breastplate adorned with gold medallions awarded to him for past victories, he was an awesome sight, the very image of the man every soldier would want to call father.

"You're just in time to see us roll up the last of the renegade Franks," said Gratianus, motioning toward the clearing in the trees. "They're already on the move down in that valley there in the distance. We let them cross the river before hitting them with the hammer. Down there to the left, just inside the tree line, is the anvil, the First and Third Cohorts under Victorinus. Favonius is waiting with the Second Cohort beyond the meadow there to seal the trap. When the rebels reach the meadow at the bend in the river, they'll have no place to go. The nearest ford is two miles down stream. If they swim, the banks on this side are too steep to let them to get away before they're rounded up."

"Who's driving the hammer?" asked Constantius.

"The senator's son, Aemilius Canio."

"Oh? How has he fared?"

"Very well in the field. Somewhat less well in garrison. The routine can't seem to hold his attention. Gets on well enough with the other officers, although some consider him too pensive. They suspect he has—how should I say?—philosophic pretensions."

The emperor allowed himself a rare chuckle in the presence of a subordinate. "Does he really?" he asked.

"Perhaps, my lord," said Gratianus. "In spite of which, the young Canio is a good soldier. He's a gifted tactician, and he's energetic and fearless in battle—just the man to light a fire under the Franks."

"Then Veturius's loss is our gain."

"It seems so." Gratianus turned suddenly to his caesar. "You don't want him back, do you?" he asked.

"Not at the moment, Gratianus," said Constantius, smiling. "Let's watch him a little while longer."

Aemilius Canio's petition to join the army of Constantius had been received with some suspicion. Centurions often transferred from one unit to another, but a young senatorial tribune would normally have attached himself to some senior commander, in whose footsteps he would follow. Leaving the army on one front and then seeking to rejoin the army on another front raised the suspicion that he was running from failure. Marcus would have to prove himself all over again to fiercely judgmental men who would assume the worst, in the absence of some other explanation. It was an almost impossible task unless they were given some assurance that this was not the case.

Before offering Marcus a commission, Constantius's adjutant requested a report on his service from the army of the East. The request went first to the imperial court at Nicomedia, then mistakenly to Armenia, then back to Nicomedia and on to the province of Dacia where his old legion, XV Apollinaris, was now stationed. It took four months for the reply to reach Constantius's headquarters at Treveris on the Mosella River in the province of Belgica. There was nothing in it to explain his transfer, only commendations for services rendered. The adjutant forwarded Marcus's request and the report on his service to the caesar himself for a decision.

"I can't explain it. His record is excellent. Perhaps he's just young and foolish," said the adjutant.

"Perhaps he's a spy," said Constantius. "He wouldn't be the first. . . . But as long as he's a good soldier, it doesn't matter, does it? I have nothing to hide. Extend to him my personal welcome and find a place for him with the legions."

Marcus waited for word from Treveris at his mother's estates in Aquitania through most of the fall. The lands had not been well tended in the absence of their owner, and there was much to do to put them in order, everything from reorganizing the staff, to negotiating boundaries and right-of-ways with neighbors, to mending fences and aqueducts. Much of it was back-breaking work that Marcus could have left for the slaves, but he joined right in, working as hard or harder than they did, to Alexander's surprise and dismay.

Why all this exertion? he asked his master, resting one day while restoring a well. Marcus was sitting in the sun sweating and panting heavily, naked except for a pair of leather breeches cut off below the knees. Gray clay coated his legs and his forearms like paint. His forehead was streaked with gray from his attempts to wipe the sweat from his brow. "At least," said Marcus, "at least this can be fixed. This I can set right." Besides, he said another time, the work would toughen them for the camp.

The work had eased by November, and Marcus was just beginning to relax and enjoy the leisurely life of a country gentleman when the offer of a commission arrived from Treveris. At first, he wasn't sure that he would take it, but upon reflection he convinced himself that he had no choice. He could not stay in the country anymore than he could stay in Rome. These were not the times to take one's ease.

"There they are, coming around the low ridge on the far side of valley," said Gratianus.

"You eyes are better than mine," said Constantius.

"Their trains are at the head. We must have thrown them into complete disorder. . . . A few horsemen taking the lead."

"I see them now."

The first frantic cries of alarm and distress reached their ears from across the valley, the faint fury of a far-off panic, somewhat out of sync with the sight seen by the caesar and his general. Whips cracked, wagons rumbled, and worried warriors shouted desperately to take control of the fleeing Franks, trampling over the yellow meadows.

The first horsemen had just about reached the tree line on the far side when a flight of arrows cut them down. At once, a trumpet sounded and the soldiers entrenched inside the treeline roared to reveal their presence. The lead elements of the Franks drew up short so suddenly that they were rammed from behind by the next in the train. Collisions continued as horses and wagons poured into the meadow from the valley beyond the ridge. There was an aborted attempt to lead the column up the low bare ridge away from the river, but this move was blocked by Favonius's cohort. Others who tried the river found the water too deep and the far bank guarded by archers. There was no way out and little time to circle the wagons before the Alemanni cavalry arrived at the head of Canio's hammer, overtaking the remnants of the rebels' rear guard and dispatching them with the sword and the lance. It appeared at first that the Alemanni would flood the meadow and slaughter the hapless Franks, but they were soon called to regroup else-where and Roman regulars took their place.

"A good show, Gratianus," said Constantius, when the Alemanni had left.

"Better than any in the arena," said Gratianus. "Now all they have to do is surrender." They talked over the operation for less than an hour during negotiations with the rebels. All the while the vari-ous Roman units down below took turns beating their shields with their spears and chanting threats to the Franks, each unit trying to out-do the others with its performance. The rumor was that Caesar was watching.

The terms were generous. Rebels, twice conquered, were often pun-ished with death. This time the Romans offered the Franks slavery, and they accepted. When the surrender was announced, a cheer arose along the whole line of legionaries, which was then picked up by their detachment on the heights above the river. Constantius turned to Gratianus and said, "I think it's time to congratulate the victors." They left their stand in the trees and crossed over to the other side at the ford downstream.

Marcus arrived last that afternoon on the ridge where Favonius's co-hort had blocked the rebels' escape. Still flushed with the thrill of vic-tory, he rode right up to the command tent and saluted Gratianus before seeing Constantius standing with him. "Hail Caesar!" he quickly added, with obvious embarrassment. The victors were in an indulgent mood and let this breech of military courtesy go with a good laugh.

"Hail Aemilius," Constantius replied. "Well done, Canio. You've saved the rest of us a great deal of work."

"Thank you, my lord," replied Marcus. His eyes and mouth alone were visible beneath his heavy, silver-plated iron helmet, with its hinged cheek pieces and long nose guard. Sitting low over the wearer's eyes, the helmet needed neither visor nor peak. Its high crown was reinforced with a ridge stretching from the nose guard to the nape of the neck.

Constantius turned to Gratianus. "I'll be returning to Treveris tonight and I'd like you to join me. Good day, commanders, and good work." The officers saluted and Constantius left, along with several aides. Gratianus issued final instructions on the disposition of the Franks to Victorinus, his second-in-command, and then went to join Constantius.

"Come on down, Canio, and let's have a drink," said Favonius, when the imperial party had left. "It's not every day that we clear the forests of rebels."

Marcus climbed down from his horse and let an attendant lead it away for watering, then untied the strap to his helmet and lifted it carefully from his head. His hair was matted and sweaty, and his beard had been let to grow for more than a week. His upper body was protected by a solid bronze breastplate, shaped to resemble the naked torso and decorated with cult figures and battle scenes. His shoulders and loins were covered with a double layer of *pteruges*—long strips of hardened leather, dyed red and studded with decorative brass. Beneath his armor, he wore a long-sleeve tunic and trousers, both of blue wool. His scarlet tribune's cloak was held about his neck by a silver pin. He used the hem of his cloak to wipe his face before accepting a cup of wine and water from a servant's tray, just before Victorinus offered a toast to their caesar.

"So, Marcus, how does war taste on the northern frontier, compared to Asia?" asked Victorinus, while a servant refilled his empty cup.

"It tastes greener," said Marcus.

"That's true. Not as dry here. I suppose that's why the woods are teeming with barbarians."

"Not like Asia, if it's as desolate as it used to be," said Favonius, a senior centurion, many years older than Marcus.

"You served in Asia?" asked Marcus.

"Five years under Galerius."

"What brought you here?" asked Marcus.

"I followed Gratianus, who followed Chlorus," said Favonius. "But what about you, Marcus? What brought you here?"

Marcus shrugged. "I missed the trees? I don't know. I left the army to return to Rome. I left Rome to return to the army."

"Why not to your old unit?" asked Victorinus.

Marcus thought for moment. "The army of the north is different from the army in Asia," he said. "There, it seems, everyone is angling for advancement, for the eye of the emperor."

"You think so?" said Favonius.

"I was there to serve, and after serving I went home. Too many others were there to succeed to command. It's as if every man wants to be caesar."

"And it's not like that here?"

Marcus looked Favonius in the eye and returned his smile. "No. It's not," he said.

"Hah!" exclaimed Favonius slapping Marcus on the shoulder. "By Jove, the youngster's right, Victorinus. They do raise 'em different in the East. We're all from the same stock, nearly all—except you, Canio—but the army of the East takes the same men and makes them strangers and rivals to one another, enemies even. If this were the East and Constantius were Galerius, instead of congratulating each other on bagging the Franks, we'd be complaining about your handling of the Alemanni."

"You handled them perfectly," said Victorinus.

"That's what I mean. But if this were the East, we wouldn't have admitted it. And if Constantius were Galerius, he wouldn't have noticed it."

"So why is it different, Favonius?" asked Marcus.

"It's different because Constantius is different," said Victorinus. "He's a better caesar, a better general, and a better man. So much better that every flat-footed legionary doesn't dream of taking his place. They know they never could. It's quite enough for all of us just to serve under him."

"Whereas in the East," continued Favonius, "Galerius is such a brute and a clod that every man thinks the opposite—'If he can be caesar, then so can I.' So they all spend their careers angling for the purple. They're all a lot of get-alongs and geldings. I have friends in the East, but still they're only half the men they could be, for fear of falling out of favor. Galerius swears by Jupiter, so every one of them swears by Jupiter."

"This new edict against the Christians is a perfect example," asked Victorinus. "Nowhere but in the East would the emperors expect everyone in the imperium to worship the same gods. They're gotten so used to groveling from army officers that they expect it now from civilians. It's as if everyone is in the army. Everyone must do as they're told. To get along, go along."

"What has Constantius done with the edict?" asked Marcus.

"Hasn't published it and doesn't plan to, from what I hear," answered Victorinus.

"He has too much sense," said Favonius.

"And too many other things to worry about," added Victorinus.

"What did he do with the first edict against the Christians?" asked Marcus.

"Pulled down a building or two in the bigger cities, confiscated a few books. Nothing to brag about if he'd wanted to. Just enough to say he did something. That's why I can't imagine him putting someone to death for not sacrificing to the gods."

"Death? Is that the punishment for not sacrificing?" asked Marcus.

"In the extreme, but that could mean anything: banishment, imprisonment, scourging, forfeiture most likely, who knows?"

"I have friends in Asia who are Christians," said Marcus.

"I wouldn't worry too much about them, Marcus. Bribery is always an option. And if worse comes to worse, they can always sacrifice. There's the irony: What have the emperors accomplished by forcing the Christians to roast a bit of meat and eat it? Theirs is a forgiving god. They can sacrifice today and still be Christians tomorrow."

"I'm not sure my friends would see it that way."

"Hail Caesar!" called a junior officer, trotting up on horseback, followed by a brightly colored, covered barbarian cart.

"Hail Terentius. What's this?" asked Victorinus.

"The spoils of war, sir," said the grinning young subaltern, halting the cart in front of the officers. "A gift from King Gennaboudes himself."

With a showman's flourish, the subaltern threw back the rear flap of the canvas cover and presented the cart's contents to the officers. Inside sat three young maidens, richly adorned and quite attractive, for barbarian women. Their blonde hair was braided into two long tails framing their faces. Their cheeks and lips were painted red, too red by civilized standards, but then their eyes were just a little too blue too, compared to more civilized eyes. The eldest was not more than twenty, by Marcus's estimate, and the youngest could not have been more than fifteen. Huddled together in the cart, they appeared as frightened as the officers were intrigued.

"Who are they that Gennaboudes would send them as gifts?" asked Victorinus.

"They're his daughters, sir. Gennaboudes is dead," said Terentius.

"Well, how nice of him to leave them to us," said Favonius. "And how convenient that there's three of them and three of us. Go ahead, Marcus. Take your pick." Marcus looked perplexed. "Don't tell me you've never had your pick of prisoners?"

"In fact, I haven't," said Marcus.

"Well lucky you. My first prize captive was a British bowman with no front teeth."

Marcus looked quizzically at the women. "But—what would I do with one?" he said.

They all laughed loudly, except Marcus, until finally Victorinus said, "Well, Marcus, one of them just might be able to cook, and if she can't do that, I'm sure she can do other things."

They laughed again. Marcus laughed a little, too, then wondered aloud, "How does one choose?"

Terentius, still on horseback, said, "Check their teeth, sir."

"Good idea," said Favonius. Moving to the rear of the cart, Favonius bared his teeth and, pointing to them, said slowly in Latin, "Show us your teeth." The girls just looked at him in amazement. "*Dentes*," he repeated, clicking his own together, "*Den-tes*." Turning back around, he said, "By Jove, Marcus, I'm afraid they're all deaf."

"Mute would be better in a woman," Terentius added.

"Let's settle this by age," said Victorinus. "Oldest to the oldest and youngest to the youngest. Fair enough?"

Favonius and Marcus took a last look at the girls. There was no question who Marcus would receive, but Favonius wasn't sure. Victorinus was impatient. "Come on, Favonius. You know Hortensia won't let you near her after today anyway," he said. Favonius shrugged, and Victorinus called for an interpreter. "Ask them who was born first," he said.

The interpreter, a soldier himself, spoke to them in German. At first it seemed the girls did not understand, but then slowly, unwillingly, they gave up an answer.

"Deal?" asked Victorinus.

"Deal," answered Favonius.

"Very well then. Tell them they won't be harmed. Tell them they'll be better treated than our own soldiers."

The interpreter spoke again, but the girls appeared unmoved.

"Ask them their names," said Marcus.

One by one the girls volunteered their names. Marcus remembered only the last, the youngest's. It sounded like *Bovina*, but he wasn't sure. An unfortunate name in Latin, he thought, which will have to be changed.

Victorinus excused himself and took Terentius with him just as Alexander, still dressed for battle, rode up with a message for Marcus. He saluted and handed Marcus a folded sheet of bark, a cheap substitute for papyrus. Alexander peered inside the cart and asked, "Who are they?"

Marcus scanned the message quickly and said, "The young one there is—our new cook."

"Cook? But we have a cook."

Favonius laughed and walked away. Marcus stuck the folded bark into his sword belt. "Find a cart or a horse for her to ride. Better a cart. And then don't leave her side. Her name is—Dovina."

Dovina spent the night alone in a separate tent next to Marcus's. Alexander made sure she was treated well, providing her the few material comforts the camp could muster and keeping the other soldiers at a distance. An orphan and a slave now, Dovina was nevertheless a barbarian princess and behaved as such, bearing her misfortune despite her age without tears or hysterics. For two days on the road, she neither wept, nor spoke, nor smiled, nor turned away in shame when beheld by others. She was quite a sight for the soldiers heading back to the headquarters of the XXII Primigenia at Mogontiacum on the Rhenus River, and many managed a chance for a closer look at her. Few, though, could stand her retaliatory stare, and many were unsettled by her stony gaze. Was it hatred in her eyes or merely contempt? Were her nerves made of steel or had the weight of misfortune squeezed all feeling out of her, leaving her hardened and numb?

Alexander puzzled over her for many miles. What *would* they do with her? he wondered. "She's not likely to add a cheery light to the old house, is she, sir?" he remarked once to Marcus, trying to draw him out on the matter, but Marcus wasn't speaking. Some changes would have to be made if she was to stay in the household. Theretofore, the house had accommodated only men: Marcus and Alexander, the steward Crescens, Faustus the cook,

Sextus the groom, and the orphan-boy Pudens. It was a skeleton crew, but sufficient for a bachelor who was rarely home and didn't require much when he was. Dovina just wouldn't fit, unless something were done.

Marcus had the answer. Immediately upon arrival in Mogontiacum, he hired a widowed freewoman named Pollentia to join his household as Dovina's guardian, with a few additional responsibilities for the maintenance of the house. Pollentia spoke both Latin and a dialect of German similar to Dovina's, and she came on the recommendation of Hortensia, the wife of Favonius. She moved in immediately and just as soon set about putting the house in proper order, as only a woman can do. Shooing the men from the roost for most of each day for a week, she led Dovina inch by inch over every surface in the house, clearing, sweeping, scrubbing, mending, washing, cooking, and decorating as they went. In this exercise, Pollentia accomplished two tasks: the overhaul of the house and the domestication of Dovina.

Dovina showed Pollentia no more warmth than she showed the soldiers. She spoke when spoken to and did as she was told, but without much care for pleasing anyone. Though obedient at first, she sometimes responded wildly to correction, once tearing a tunic in half when told to rip out her careless stitches and begin the mend again. For such times, there was the rod, which Pollentia did not spare. Stern and exacting in her standards, she was determined to tame the young rebel, and so she did.

At the end of the week, the men were amazed at the change in both the house and the girl. The house was much improved. The garden had been weeded and primped. There were fresh flowers in vases in the atrium and tablinum. An embroidered tapestry that Pollentia discovered in storage now graced a wall in the tablinum, and curtains everywhere had been cleaned and mended.

Dovina, on the other hand, never looked so plain. No trace remained of the rouge on her lips and cheeks, and her gaudy Burgundian gown had been replaced by a simple Saxon tunic and apron. Her long blonde braids were now tied behind her back to keep them out of the way of work. Her rings, bracelets, armbands, and earrings were all absent, stored now out of view in a small casket in her room. Such adornments, said Pollentia, befitted only the mistress of the house, not the housekeeper and certainly not the housekeeper's girl.

The change in behavior was less dramatic. She accepted Pollentia's rule but refused to have anything to do with the male servants, Alexander excepted. Perhaps as a soldier he rated higher in her esteem. Perhaps she was grateful for his protection and kindness. He himself was never quite sure. She never spoke to him, but she would obey his commands and attend willingly to his needs. Once he heard her singing sadly to herself in the kitchen when she must have known he was present, but when he showed that he was listening, she stopped, and when he begged her to continue, she ignored him.

Around Marcus, she was even less at ease, though it was easy for all to believe that he had given her cause. He didn't mean to be unkind, but he did mean to keep her at a distance. His motives were unclear, but his coldness toward her was palpable. He was always on his guard around her, and the result was a most unnatural way for a young man to behave around a young woman, even considering the differences in their station.

Fortunately for both him and her, he was frequently away from the house. Mogontiacum, named after the Celtic sun-god Mogon, was the headquarters of both the XXII Legion and the Roman army of Germania Superior. From it Marcus journeyed many times to inspect the fortifications along the *Limes*, a chain of forts and fences stretching from the province of Raetia in the mountains to the banks of the Rhenus just south of the towns of Bonna and Colonia, then following the Rhenus all the way to the northern sea. Everywhere along the Limes, soldiers were at work on roads, bridges, aqueducts, temples, and other public buildings. Much of the countryside thereabouts was laid waste decades earlier by civil war. Upon restoring order, the emperors Diocletian and Maximian began extensive repairs, which would take years to complete. Marcus's contribution was more official than functional. The building crews were in the hands of engineers and hardly needed his attention. The garrisons gave him a little more to do, but after the thrill of defeating and capturing the Franks, the chore of minding the readiness of a peacetime army bored him. Better men, better soldiers, would not have let their boredom affect their performance of duty, but Marcus was not that disciplined. He was not able to keep his boredom from affecting his work, and his awareness of this failing only aggravated his uneasiness.

He had a close call during preparations for the cavalry sports held near Mogontiacum in July. This five-day spectacle drew cavalry units from up and down the frontier for purpose of boosting morale, rewarding achievement, encouraging the military arts, and impressing the local barbarian chieftains with the technical superiority of the Roman military. Men and horses, both bedecked in ornate sporting armor, paraded and charged and wheeled and rallied amid a festive flutter of colorful dragon-headed streamers.

Marcus had been charged with seeing to the quartering of the visiting formations, an awesome logistical responsibility which he did not relish. On the eve of their arrival, he was standing outside his tent near the parade ground with Alexander and the centurions Mumius Lolianus and Lucretius Celer, going over a terrain model of the various cantonment areas draw before them in the ground. In the midst of the review, Marcus stopped suddenly and looked up. "Hay," he said to himself. "There is no hay for the Companions."

The other officers looked at him anxiously. The Companions consisted of three mounted regiments making up the emperor's personal guard and tactical reserve. The lack of hay for the horses of the imperial guard would be a major embarrassment. It was too late to have the vast amount of hay needed delivered to the cantonment of the Companions, and without it either the Companions or several other cavalry regiments would have to be quartered elsewhere, probably miles from the parade ground, an inconvenience that would redound with disgrace upon those responsible. "Are you sure?" asked Mumius.

Marcus hardly moved but answered, "I requested fodder for the legionary squadrons but not for the Companions."

"You did, lord. I remember it," said Alexander.

"I did?" said Marcus uncertainly.

"You did. I'm sure of it. I wrote out the requisition myself. The hay is there, and all is well," insisted Alexander.

Marcus saw the look on Alexander's face and then he understood. The hay was there. All was well. He had indeed forgotten, but Alexander hadn't.

The one benefit of Marcus's military duties was that they kept him away from Dovina. The few days he had been home, off and on, had been manageable, from his point of view. Perhaps it wasn't so dangerous having her there, he thought.

Then one warm evening in August, in a moment of idleness after supper, he found himself watching her work. She was unpacking a crate of glassware and stowing the contents in a cupboard some distance from the couch where he had been lost in thought until she drew his attention. He watched her for quite a while unnoticed. There was nothing remarkable in her appearance that day, for she was modestly attired and unadorned. Still she held his eye. She seemed almost happy. Her face was cloudless, her movements smooth and free. Once or twice she stopped to admire a piece of glassware before putting it away. He was fascinated, and then suddenly concerned that she would see him.

She did, of course. She held a goblet up to light and there he was. She froze for a moment and stared back at him with the wide eyes of a wary animal. He looked away, and so did she. She went about her business but not as before, and he turned again to watch her. She was obviously agitated. Her head was down, her lips were pursed, her movements were hurried and tense. Sawdust flew as she hastily wiped the pieces clean. Glasses clinked as they collided in the cupboard. Every few moments, she would glance over at him to see him still staring. He didn't mind now that she knew. He was as fascinated by her unease as he had been by her cheerfulness.

Dovina worked faster and faster until Pollentia appeared. The women exchanged a few quick words in German. Pollentia glanced over at Marcus, who turned away embarrassed. A moment later Dovina was gone and Pollentia had taken over her chore. Marcus made his own escape to the garden.

He lingered in the garden for a while, recalling the sight of her working, of her seeing him, of her agitation. He was flattered and thrilled by his effect on her and craved more of it. The sudden end of their encounter left him restless and unsatisfied. He wandered about the house and grounds in hopes of running into her again, but she was nowhere to be seen. Frustrated and annoyed, with himself in part, he left the house for a walk. He didn't really want to give up the possibility of seeing Dovina again that evening, but walking allowed him every option. It could always take him either home or away. It was the perfect activity for temporizing, for acting without consequence, biding time in the face of temptation without ruling out temptation altogether. He had done it before on many occasions, steering like Ulysses in range of the Sirens yet refusing to surrender until circumstances overwhelmed him one way or the other, drawing him in or pulling him out. Either way, he suffered—regret if he succumbed, disappointment if he didn't.

He held out until the sun began to set and then at last turned his steps toward home. *What if she's still up and about when I return?* he wondered. His pace quickened. He wanted to return before it was too late, before she had gone to bed. But he had misjudged his distance, and by the time he returned, the house was quiet and dark. Everyone seemed asleep. He felt a twinge of anguish when it seemed he had missed his chance. There was nothing for him to do but go to bed. He went to his room disappointed, reluctantly consoling himself with reasons why his desire could not and should not have been satisfied. Age and status argued against it. She was too young and she was his slave. *But she was a woman, and she was his slave— what he did with her was his business.* He could not submit to the baser instincts and still live up to his philosophic ideals. *But he was a young man, a man of vigor and passion, and more a man than a philosopher.* Alas, it hardly mattered. The house was still. He had missed his chance.

The night was warmer than usual, too warm for the tunic he usually wore to bed. He took it off and lay down in just his loincloth, but his nakedness only aroused him more. His heart pounded and his blood rose. Before long, he had thought up a reason to get up and venture out into the darkness. The water in the pitcher in his room was warm. It would be cooler from the barrel in the kitchen. He left his room undressed and without a lamp, padding like a werewolf down the airy walkway past Dovina's door. *Don't stop,* he told himself, *Keep walking.* Her door was half open for ventilation, and his shadow fell across her floor as he passed. *Don't think of it. Get your water and go to bed.*

In the kitchen in the dark, he drew himself a cup of water and drank it down, then drew another. *You are stalling—go to bed.* He turned to leave but got no farther than the doorway of the kitchen before he stopped to give his desire one last chance. He could not now simply lie down and go to sleep. He was too close. He was too aroused. With a heavy, trembling sigh, he made his decision. He left the kitchen having resolved to go to her. Satyrs danced delighted in his heart as he trod the path to her door. He paused only briefly before crossing its threshold.

To his surprise, he found her sitting on her bed with her legs drawn up before her, her arms wrapped around her ankles, the hem of her tunic reaching to mid-calf. He could not see the expression on her face, but nothing about her indicated surprise on her part. He stood before her as a shadow in the pale light of the doorway, silent except for his pounding heart, naked except for the cloth pulled tightly about his loins. She could have screamed, she could have sent him away. Instead, she did not move. Marcus moved closer and stood beside her bed. Slowly lifting his hand to her face, he touched her cheek and caressed her chin. *You can still leave now,* his defeated conscience counseled, *You can still spare her and save yourself.* But the satyrs would have none of it.

Marcus sat down beside her on the edge of her bed and savored the sweet and salty smell of her sudden sweat mixing with the day's perfume. With one hand he gently stroked her bare calves, raising the hem of her tunic over her knees. With the other he grasped the nape of her neck beneath her golden braids. She trembled at his touch. A solitary tear crept slowly down her burning cheek. Marcus wiped it away tenderly with the tip of his finger, then kissed her moistened skin, her parted lips, and her pulsing neck. The barbarian princess released her hold on her fearful young body and folded herself into her captor's arms.

# XIII

That night, Marcus played the bestial Jupiter carrying off the helpless virgin princess Europa, and for the first time in his life, his pleasure survived his passion. Regret dawned on him slowly, and for a while he wasn't even sure it was regret. He was not proud of his carnality. He felt sorry for any shame she might have felt. Most of all he feared the embarrassment they might suffer once their relations became known to the household. Then there was the uncomfortable question of how they would behave toward each other in the future. They were still not quite on speaking terms. Neither had said a word through the course of the night.

Still, with all this, he did not truly regret their union. He had enjoyed her too much. The memory of that night filled his thoughts for days. He was more distracted than usual when going about his official duties. At home, at first, he was uneasy in her presence, until it became apparent that they could go on as before, pretending for the sake of appearances that nothing had happened. In truth, they did change in their behavior toward each other. He was still formal but less cold toward her, and she was impassive and unsmiling as always, but less apprehensive and more submissive toward him. This seemed to suit them both, and he was encouraged to think that their secret could be easily kept between them.

The change between them was noticed, however, by Pollentia, when she saw how attentively Dovina waited on Marcus, and by Alexander, when he noticed that Marcus no longer went out of his way to ignore her and seemed instead to relish her sight.

Marcus held off for more than a week before going to her again at night. He would have liked to have repeated that first night, but he soon realized it wasn't possible. They were not who they had been to each other. He was not now her fearsome conqueror, and she was not his virgin prize. He could never appear to her so strong and lordly, and she could never appear to him so enticingly innocent and helpless. Their second night was a disappointment, as much as he did not want to admit it. The next day he was actually glad to leave town on an inspection tour.

Nevertheless, when he returned the following week, he could not help himself and went to her again, this time with humbler expectations. It was easier that time, so easy that it was not long before he was back, and soon it happened that he could not stay away. The pull of her body was so strong that it enslaved him to her. Her proud captor was reduced in time to a pitiful paramour drawn panting to her door under the cover of night. Once she even turned him away, showing him the bloody rags to prove her time had come. He had gone back to his room that night frustrated, humiliated, and ashamed, and shocked by her reminder of the inerotic reality of mortal flesh.

Of course, their secret could not be kept forever. Marcus never knew if anyone else knew, but he always suspected. He scrutinized Pollentia's words and actions for indications of awareness, and he took great pains to throw Alexander off track. He was worried for his reputation. He could not allow it to be publicly acknowledged that Dovina was his concubine. Though many men kept concubines, Marcus knew that he would suffer the penalty of his own pretensions. Claudius Agricola, his fellow tribune, could take a concubine openly and nobody would think twice, because Claudius Agricola had no pretensions and concubinage suited him. But Marcus Aemilius Canio was high-born and proud, and a student of philosophy, and people would expect better of him. He expected better of himself as well, and so could not even admit to himself that she was his concubine. Legally, she was still his slave.

Yet the public revelation of their relationship was an almost certain eventuality, as she was likely sooner or later to conceive. Their secret would then be out. He would have to admit his paternity. Things would have to change. The mother could not possibly become the wife of the father in this instance, but neither could she remain his slave. Marcus would have to set her free, and then the only question would be whether, after setting her free, he would send her away or keep her openly as his concubine. Either way his reputation would be remade, and both his public and his private life would be greatly complicated. Regret dawned slowly, but in time it blazed like the midday sun.

Marcus wanted to confide in someone, but there was no one at his new post with whom he could share a matter so humiliating. In the whole world there were only two friends to whom he could confess his foolishness. Not two, but one he could trust with this matter. He could not have told Felix even if he were there, for Felix would just have laughed. Where was Kimon when he needed him? In Sinope? In Athens? How ashamed Makrina would be of her handsome tribune now! The thought struck Marcus like a dagger.

He was on the road with Alexander, under a gloomy October sky that suited his mood perfectly. The pain in his heart was accompanied by the first few drops of a cold rain. Gradually it began to rain harder, and then suddenly it poured. Marcus and Alexander kicked their horses toward a roadside shrine up ahead where they could find shelter. They were nearly there when Marcus's mount slipped and fell in the fresh mud, throwing its rider onto the wet ground. Marcus was furious. Before his horse could stand again, he kicked at its flanks and cursed it to the heavens. He drew his sword as if to slay it, but Alexander intervened in time to spare the beast, which was not injured. Instead, Marcus threw his sword into the sodden earth, where it stuck easily, and stormed off to the shrine, limping slightly with his left leg.

Alexander retrieved the sword and gathered their kits from their horses, then joined Marcus in the shrine's small sanctuary. "Are you all right?" he asked.

"NO I AM NOT ALL RIGHT!" Marcus yelled, his voice reverberating in the hollow chamber. He moved outside onto the covered porch and removed his helmet, dropping it carelessly to stone floor. It hit with a dull bang. He then took off his cloak and shook it vigorously three times to free it of mud and water.

Alexander unpacked his kit and handed Marcus a dry towel to wipe his face. "Are you injured?" he asked.

"No!" said Marcus, snatching the towel. He wiped the mud from his face and beard, handed the towel back to Alexander, and reentered the sanctuary. Alexander followed him at a safe distance. Inside he found Marcus still fuming, standing in the center of the chamber, arms akimbo, glaring at the shrine's idols. "Even Gallic gods keep consorts!" declared Marcus, pointing to the crude figures of a nude male and a clothed female, brightly painted as realistically as possible. Back by the door, Alexander wiped the discarded sword with his cloak and handed it back to Marcus, who shoved it back into its scabbard. "If only I could keep it sheathed!" he said, turning his back on the gods.

Marcus loosened the cinches of his breastplate, wrapped himself in his cloak, and sat down by the doorway of the sanctuary, facing out. Alexander removed his helmet and set it down on the porch, then loosened the binding of his lamellar corselet, constructed of row upon row of thin metal plates laced together with rawhide.

"How do you do it, Alexander?" said Marcus, staring out at the rain. "How do you live without women? You're older than I am. How is it you've never married?"

"I'm a soldier, sir. It's difficult for a soldier to keep a wife. The legion is a jealous mistress," said Alexander, sitting down next to Marcus.

"But how can you stand not having someone around, a wife or mistress, without spending a fortune on prostitutes? Oh, never mind. I shouldn't ask."

"Is that what's been troubling you?" asked Alexander. "Doing without women?"

Marcus kicked at his helmet on the porch and watched it wobble. "Not quite," he said. "I haven't been 'doing without women.' I've been seeing someone all too often, and I'm afraid I can't stop seeing her."

"Why should you worry about wanting to see her? As long as she wants to see you, you've a perfect arrangement."

Marcus gritted his teeth and growled. "It's Dovina, Alexander," he said.

Alexander's eyes widened, but his master was too ashamed to witness his surprise. "I see," he said.

Marcus groaned and shook his head, and then offered his apology. "What can I say? There she was, living under my roof. I avoided her for months, and then it seemed I couldn't take my eyes off her. Now everything's all wrong. Sooner or later everyone will know, and I'll look like a fool, a lecherous fool. What can I do? I can't marry her. I can't make her my mistress or keep her as a concubine. And yet I can't resist her when she's around."

"Send her away then," said Alexander. "Send her to Aquitania."

"I'd have to put her in a cage to get her there, and they wouldn't know what to do with her when she arrived. Pollentia's the only one who can handle her."

"Send Pollentia with her."

"I can't send Pollentia unless she's willing to go, and I doubt that she would be. She's lived her whole life in Mogontiacum. She has family and friends there. I can't ask her to leave everything because of my—my incontinence."

"I guess not," said Alexander.

"The only thing I can see to do is free Dovina and send her off on her own. The trouble is, I don't know if I can, knowing what I'll face without her, knowing that she might be still just across town."

"Are you in love with her?" Alexander asked.

"No, no, of course not," said Marcus. "I'm not in love—I'm in heat. I'm as much an animal as she is. I just can't deny my body what it demands. I've tried. Again and again I've tried. I just can't, not forever. There is not the power in me to do it. Can you do it, or any man you know? Do you know of anyone who is free of this curse and not also free of his manhood?"

"Well," said Alexander hesitantly, "there are some, I know, who are eunuchs in a sense, although not in body. They are holy men, sir."

"What kind of holy men?" asked Marcus skeptically.

"Christian holy men, sir," said Alexander, "at least the ones I know."

"Lot of good that does me," said Marcus. "Maybe I just need a wife."

"Maybe so," said Alexander. "Why trouble yourself so much? There should be hundreds of rich, beautiful women who would marry you. Just pick one and be done with it. No one would blame you for that."

"I don't know if I can, Alexander," said Marcus mournfully. "Any good wife would expect me to love her, and I don't think I'm ready for that yet. I still think of Makrina. I'm still in love with her."

"But, it's been over a year—"

"I know, I know," said Marcus, "but I can't help myself. I . . . " He shook his head and didn't finish.

"You need to find someone else," said Alexander. "Look around. You never know. You might find someone just like her, or someone even better suited for you. Believe me. I've surprised myself, finding someone in Mogontiacum, of all places."

"What?" asked his surprised master. "You've found a wife in Mogontiacum?"

Alexander grinned. "I found a woman there whom I would like to make my wife, though nothing is decided yet."

"What's her name?" asked Marcus.

"Lucia," answered Alexander. "She's a good woman, quite chaste, quite pure, purer than—"

"Athena?"

"I was going to say purer than I deserve," laughed Alexander.

Marcus dreaded going home. He dreaded seeing Dovina again. He dreaded sending her away. He dreaded finding out that she was pregnant, but he didn't have that chance. Waiting for him at home was news of his father's death and a summons for him to appear in Rome to settle the family estate. Gratianus had already given him leave, and arrangements had been made for Marcus to join a detachment in transit to the court at Mediolanum. Alexander had barely enough time to pack before they were off again, now with many more things to think about through the long days ahead.

The detachment followed the Rhenus south to Basilia and crossed the Alps to the east through the Golden Wedge, a pass through the highest mountain range. Then it skirted Lake Larius to Comum and finally Mediolanum. On their own, Marcus and Alexander continued south by the Via Aemilia to the Temple of Fortuna on the Adriatic coast. From there the Via Flaminia took them all the way to Rome. The journey took three weeks.

The first person Marcus saw outside his father's household was Felix, who had left word for Marcus to send for him as soon as he arrived in Rome. Within an hour of Marcus's arrival at the domus Canio Felix was there. "I thought you ought to be given some idea of what to expect from your father's will," he explained.

"You've seen it?" Marcus asked.

"No, but your father's executor, Manlius Augustinus, is a colleague of mine, and with all the rumors flying about I was able to persuade him to brief me on your behalf. All of Rome has been wondering what will become of your father's estate. I didn't want you to be the last to know."

"Know what?"

"Again, I haven't seen the will, so I cannot speak of its precise terms. Manlius has advised me only of its main points."

"Which are?"

"Your father has left you everything, except a small monetary bequest to the City for public works. No surprise there," said Felix, "but the reason for the rumors is that there is not much of your father's estate left, not nearly as much as you might expect."

"But how can that be?"

"Marcus, your father, as you know, had certain interests, certain political interests, and he invested much of his wealth in those causes, but he did not prevail. His opponents did, time and time again. Some of his fortune went to finance electoral campaigns. Some went to advance candidates for appointed offices. A lot went to litigate against his rivals, and even more went to defend himself against retaliatory litigation. It ruined him, Marcus. It ate up almost everything he owned, according to Manlius."

"Almost everything?"

Felix nodded and placed his hand on Marcus's shoulder. "You're not penniless," he said. "But what you have lost may pain you greatly. Most of your father's properties in Italy have already passed out of the estate, including this house."

"This house?"

"It has already been sold and then leased back to the estate. Your father knew he was dying, and he knew he had accounts to settle. He sold many of his properties to pay his debts, so that what he did leave you would be free and clear."

"But what's left if everything in Italy is gone?"

"I don't know the details. He owned estates in Aquitania and in Africa, didn't he? Manlius assures me that something somewhere remains. I just don't know what or where."

"But why would my father sell everything in Italy, in Rome especially, and leave me a few farms in faraway places? This house has been in the family since the time of the Antonines. How could he sell it, knowing how much it would mean to me? Wouldn't it be the very last thing he would sell?"

"I don't know for certain, Marcus. He apparently doesn't declare his motives in his will. It may simply have been easier to sell what was closer at hand, or it may have been a matter of how much money he needed and could get for the properties he sold. Or," said Felix, "he may have wanted you to stay in the army, so he left you nothing to come back here to."

"No," Marcus whispered to himself.

Felix sighed and said, "Manlius says he had his reasons. He didn't want you to be tempted by affairs here in Rome. He didn't want you to waste your life here with people like me, I suppose. That, too, has been the source of rumors."

The will was read the next afternoon by the executor Manlius Augustinus in the presence of Marcus, Felix, and Alexander. There were no surprises, except for a paltry sum left to the City for the building of a public latrine, "for the benefit of the Senate and the Roman people," said the will.

To Marcus went the estates in Aquitania formerly belonging to Marcus's mother, Racilia. There were three estates in all, of varying sizes and amounting to about 50,000 acres. They were barely profitable, having suffered for many years from neglect, despite Marcus's attentions of the previous autumn.

Everything else was already gone, the villas at Praeneste and Centumcellae, the vineyards in Campania, the wheat plantation outside Leptis Minor in Africa, and the domus Canio with all of its slaves and furnishings, which now belonged to an investor identified only as P. Lateranus. The lease on the house was set to expire a fortnight after settlement of the will.

Throughout the proceedings, Marcus sat in stunned silence. Manlius was respectful and considerate. "Your father and I were good friends for a long time," he said to Marcus when it was over. "You are welcome in my house whenever you are in Rome, Marcus. I'd be honored if you would dine with us tonight. I'm sure Claudia would enjoy seeing you again, and my boys would enjoy meeting a real military man."

Marcus accepted as a courtesy, suppressing his true desire. It was a pleasant dinner, however. Manlius's wife Claudia was a charming hostess, and his two young sons did indeed enjoy meeting a real soldier. Marcus even learned a few things about his father from the stories Manlius told, although they both avoided the subject of his father's ruination.

Marcus spent the following day gathering together his few personal belongings in his father's house and preparing them for shipping, either to Mogontiacum or Aquitania. It occurred to him to try to buy the domus Canio, but he wasn't at all sure he could afford it. The upkeep alone would have strained his known resources.

That night Marcus dined with Felix and Calvina, who was nursing their newborn girl named Priscilla. They seemed so happy that Marcus envied them. Calvina still talked of matching Marcus with one of her friends or cousins, but Marcus knew that it could never be. *She still thinks I'm rich and highly placed, but I'm not anymore,* he thought. *Everything has changed, and now I'm just a professional soldier, a simple "military man."*

On his last full day in Rome, Marcus saw off his shipments and said farewell to the house staff, some of whom he had known since his childhood. He paid a last brief visit to Felix and Calvina before the November sun set, then took an early supper with Alexander back at the house.

The next morning, they were up and ready before dawn. Marcus lingered a while at the family lararium, where he had said farewell to his father the previous year. Now as then he was dressed for travel, but this time he was in uniform. The contents of the altar had already been shipped: Marcus's schoolboy's bulla, his grandfather's signet ring, and a miniature portrait of his mother and grandmother. Their absence left a great void for Marcus. He tried to think of one of his father's prayers, but the only words that came to his mind were Felix's explanation of his father's intentions, that he should have "nothing to come back to."

A deep sadness filled him. He could barely utter the words to depart. They left well before dawn to avoid the throngs of people that would later fill the streets. The streets were bustling already with carts and wagons, which were banned from the City during the day. In the dark, the silent pair of soldiers led their horses unnoticed down from the Janiculum, across the Tiber, and through the Campus Martius to the Via Flaminia. At every turn, Marcus imagined his past slipping away from him. At first light, he paused upon the Milvian Bridge, just north of Rome, and looked back at the waking city. *Its life will go on,* he thought, *but never again with me.*

It had all happened so quickly. Marcus had entered Rome a week earlier as a rich man of senatorial rank. He was leaving now as a man of modest means, perhaps barely able to maintain equestrian rank. He wouldn't know until he could conduct a thorough audit of his estate. How Rome would talk when he was gone! How cruel the fates had been to him! What had he done to offend them? The answers multiplied in his mind as he journeyed. He had dishonored the gods. He had neglected their worship. He had refused the wisdom of the philosophers. He had failed in discipline and shrunk from virtue. He wanted to protest his treatment, but his feeling of failure justified his fate. His successes were far from mind, his momentary, tactical achievements, which he knew were largely dependent upon luck—the right terrain, the right weather, the right moves, the right mistakes. He had always feared his luck would run out. Now it seemed it had.

One night while on the road, Marcus dreamed of Dovina mocking him bitterly for his fallen fortune and offering herself to Alexander instead! He could not put the dream out of his mind for more than a day, and while it persisted, he could not help but compare himself unfavorably to his servant. Their relationship had changed so much in recent years. Once Marcus had been so haughty toward the ranks, so jealous of his privileges and prerogatives, so careful to keep Alexander in his place. But over time, Alexander had shown his own nobility. Marcus knew him now as a brave and able soldier, a trusted assistant and advisor, and a discreet confidant. Marcus, on the other hand, had felt himself sinking a little in his own esteem since leaving Asia, in fact since leaving Sinope. Humbled now by staggering blows, he saw little distance between himself and his servant. He had already given up many of the pretensions of rank, and possibly compromised his leadership by revealing to Alexander too much of himself. The thought only added to his dejection. On the long road to Mediolanum, Marcus was too dispirited to maintain his military bearing and made little attempt to conceal his sadness.

In Mediolanum, they joined a small caravan escorted by a squad of soldiers for the crossing of the Alps. They stopped the night first in Comum, the next in Clavenna, the last town south of the Golden Wedge. From Clavenna the road rose steeply to the pass in the mountains. It was not an otherwise difficult stretch, except that it was snowing the morning they left. Several miles north of Clavenna, a cart in the caravan slid sideways into the curb of the road and popped a wheel off its hub, dumping its contents into the ditch between the road and the hillside. The wagonmaster reported it would take several hours to fix. Marcus looked up the snow-covered road. "How far is the garrison?" he asked from atop his horse.

"Ten miles, maybe less," replied the wagonmaster.

Marcus looked at Alexander inquiringly. Alexander shrugged. "We'll meet you at the pass," said Marcus to the wagonmaster.

Marcus and Alexander continued slowly up the road on horseback, as the snow continued to fall. Before long the caravan was out of sight. There was little wind and not a sound from anything other than their plodding, snorting mounts. Marcus was again lost in thought, his head bent low to avoid the snow, his eyes lightly closed at times, at other times starring absently at the road before him. Alexander, however, was intrigued by the quiet and keenly aware of the passing world. Some miles after leaving the caravan, he noticed a wooden shack with a high-pitched roof perched high upon a hilltop overlooking the road for miles. Smoke trailed from the vent in its roof. *Who could live there?* he wondered. He started to tell Marcus, but hesitated and then decided to let him be.

A little farther the shoulder of the road dropped off sharply to the right. Rounding a bend, they found the road blocked by a pine that had fallen from its place on the left bank. A few feet of clearance remained on the far side of the road. Marcus's horse angled unguided toward the gap, followed at a length by Alexander's. Marcus was almost at the gap when he heard Alexander call out in his native Greek: "*Kyrie!*" Lord! That's odd, thought Marcus, turning in his saddle.

The sudden flurry of arrows caught him by surprise. His horse jumped and brayed and then crumpled to the pavement, its neck pierced twice. A third arrow had pinned Marcus's calf to the horse's belly. He screamed with pain when the fall of his horse ripped the arrow through his flesh. "Bandits!" yelled Alexander, kicking his horse toward Marcus. Marcus reached up and grabbed Alexander's outstretched arm. Alexander's horse wheeled about and started away, dragging Marcus from one side, but then a second flurry of arrows caught it in the neck and flank. Marcus let go and the beast staggered to the side of the road and collapsed. A fearsome cry arose from unseen assailants as Alexander struggled to free himself from his cloak, caught beneath his horse.

Marcus tried to stand but his left leg was useless. He drew his sword and braced himself against the horse's hindquarters. *"Look out!"* cried Marcus, seeing two cloaked figures rush at Alexander with spears. Suddenly free, Alexander drew his sword and swung it furiously at his attackers. His first swing caught the foremost spear and drove it into the stone pavement. His second swing hacked the hand off the second attacker, whose spear had glanced off Alexander's corselet. His third swing nearly severed the man's arm, but even as it did so, the first attacker drove his spear into Alexander's neck. Marcus watched in horror as his servant, his aide, *his friend* fell to his knees, blood gurgling in his throat.

"Kill him!" commanded a voice from behind. A blow to the back of Marcus's head sent him sprawling unconscious on the road.

They stripped the bodies of rings, boots, weapons, and armor. They plundered the baggage and left what they didn't want scattered in the road. They took the horses' tack and cut out their arrows for future use. Then they disappeared.

# XIV

A shroud of snow gently covered the bloody scene where Marcus lay near death, until kinder hands bore him up and bound his wounds, wrapped him warmly and carried him to a place of rest. For three days he lay unconscious, cared for and prayed over by he knew not whom. He first became conscious of his throbbing head, then his parched throat. When he opened his eyes he could barely see. The darkness frightened him. He reached out in panic and found his bed closed off by heavy woolen curtains. The light of a lamp shone reassuringly through a crack in the curtains. So he was not dead and this was not his grave.

Marcus lay there for some time struggling for control of his faculties, until the sounds of someone stirring in the room gave him the courage to sit up and peer beyond the parted bed-curtains. At the other end of a small room, he saw a young man—a boy really—in a short brown tunic and trousers, stoking the fire in the hearth. Beside the hearth was a wooden straight chair. A small scroll lay in its seat, which glowed with the playful light from the hearth.

Presently the boy straightened up to return to his reading, only to be startled by the sudden sight of the pallid Marcus, head bandaged as if for burial, staring out of his gaping tomb like one risen from the dead. The lad stumbled backwards over his chair, then scrambled to his feet and ran for the door, which slammed behind him. Marcus sank back onto his bed, closed his eyes, and waited.

Some time later—he wasn't sure how long—Marcus heard footsteps on wooden steps outside, then inside on the wooden floor. The bed-curtains were parted, and a shaft of bright light struck Marcus in the face, causing him to wince. Then the light faded and Marcus opened his eyes. A shadowy figure surrounded by an aura of white light was bending over him.

Marcus was startled. The figure withdrew and stood erect. Bright light from an open window fell again on Marcus's face. Squinting, he saw an old man with a long white beard, clad in a heavy winter robe, one hand resting on a short walking stick.

"Good afternoon," said the man in an aged voice. "My name is Arcadius. Welcome to my home."

The old man waved his free hand at the sparsely furnished room. The boy Marcus had seen earlier was standing at a distance.

"You have been asleep now for three days," said the man. "You will sleep again soon, but first you should eat, for your strength, no?"

He turned to the boy and ordered water and soup. Then he pulled up a stool and sat down by the bed. Marcus opened his mouth to speak but no sound came out. "No, no. Don't speak," said the old man, putting a hand to Marcus' shoulder. "There will be time for talk later. You are staying the night, no? Perhaps even longer," he said with a smile.

The old man's voice held traces of an accent uncommon in the area, which Marcus, in his daze, could not recognize.

The boy brought Marcus a cup of water and raised his head to drink.

"Careful. Not too quickly," said the old man, as Marcus slowly emptied the cup. The water was cool and clean, giving instant relief to Marcus's parched throat.

"Where am I?" he asked. His words reverberated unexpectedly in his head.

"Not far from where we found you," answered his host.

"Who are you?" asked Marcus.

"A friend," said Arcadius. "Eat first. Then we'll talk."

The boy brought a pillow and helped Marcus sit up. Then he returned with a bowl of steaming broth, testing its temperature with a touch of a wooden spoon to his tongue. The broth smelled and tasted of chicken, and Marcus ate it eagerly, fed by the boy at a cautious pace.

"Better?" asked the old man, when the bowl was empty.

"Yes. Thank you," said Marcus. "What did you say your name was?"

"Arcadius, and this is Lucas," said the old man, pointing to the boy, who nodded respectfully. "You are a soldier, no? A tribune even. Your name is . . . ?"

Marcus opened his mouth to say Aemilius Canio, but instead said simply, "Marcus."

"And your friend's name was . . . ?" asked Arcadius.

"My friend?" said Marcus, stunned by sudden recollection. "His name was Alexander."

Arcadius turned to Lucas and said, "The servant of God Alexander."

Marcus saw the boy nod and make the sign of the cross, touching his forehead, then his chest, then his shoulders with his right hand. Arcadius did so also, then said, "Your friend has received a fitting burial, in accordance with our custom."

Marcus looked puzzled. "What do you mean?" he said. "He wasn't a Christian."

"No?" said Arcadius. "We found this with his things left by the thieves."

From a table, hidden from Marcus's view by the bed-curtains, Arcadius took the painted plaque Makrina had given Marcus before he left Sinope. Marcus hadn't seen it since.

"That's mine," he said. "He . . . He must have packed it with my things."

"It belongs to you?" asked Arcadius, handing the painting to Marcus.

"Yes. Yes," said Marcus, looking down at the painting in his hands, "but it was just a gift. I mean I'm not a Christian. Just a gift, from a friend. . . . I didn't know he packed it."

"But we also found this around his neck," said Arcadius. He held up a simple wooden cross, hanging by a leather cord.

"It can't be," said Marcus in disbelief. "It just can't be."

"If he was not a Christian, he had Christian friends," said Arcadius. "The cross is inscribed."

Marcus took the cross into his hand to examine it. Both the cross and its cord were stained with blood. On one side of the cross, at the intersection of the bars, was the Christian Chi-Rho symbol, which Marcus recognized. On the other side were the words VIVAS IN DEO and the name LUCIA.

Marcus stared at the name. "There was a girl named Lucia he hoped to marry," he said, " . . . in Mogontiacum." Tears welled in his eyes and he turned his head.

Arcadius sent Lucas away with a wave of his hand, and Arcadius rose to go as well.

"Your friend Alexander lies now asleep in the Lord, where there is neither sickness nor sorrow nor sighing, but life everlasting," said Arcadius before leaving. "Rest now. We can talk more later."

Left alone to himself, Marcus clutched the cross and wept for the loss of Alexander, and for his own part in Alexander's end. Had he not decided to leave the caravan? Had he not ventured carelessly into the trap? Had Alexander not been killed coming to his aide? Was he not at least in part responsible for Alexander's death, as he was responsible for his humiliation in Mogontiacum? Had not the fates cursed him, too, with the loss of his fortune? Now here he was, laid low in a mountain shack, lost to the world. Alexander was dead, but a pious young woman named Lucia was still awaiting his return. His head pounded fiercely. *Rest,* he told himself. *Sleep . . . Rest . . .*

When Marcus awoke, Arcadius was settled upon the stool by the hearth, stirring an iron pot over the fire. The room was dark except for the firelight, and Marcus sensed that the sun had set. He started to sit up and found the cross still in his hand. Its edges had left deep red furrows in his palm.

"Good evening, Marcus," said Arcadius, looking over his shoulder. "You slept well, no?"

"I did," said Marcus, propping himself up on one elbow.

"Some water, perhaps, before supper?" asked Arcadius.

"Yes, please," answered Marcus.

His host rose slowly and filled a cup with water from a pitcher on the table by the bed, then handed it to Marcus. "Thank you," said Marcus.

"We have a special treat for supper," said Arcadius, returning to his pot. "Rabbit stew, and even some wine to wash it down."

The old man ladled the stew into a bowl and brought it to Marcus, then took his place on the stool beside the bed. His head was bald on top, but the sides and back were decked with the white locks. His face showed the hollowness of age, though this was masked somewhat by his long, full beard. His hands resting upon his walking stick were thin and boney.

"Where is the boy?" Marcus asked, between spoonfuls of meat and carrots.

"Home were he belongs," said Arcadius. "He comes every day to read my books. How can I turn him away? At least he works for the privilege."

"You live here alone?"

"Yes, of course, for many years now. How many I do not know. It does not matter."

"But your accent—you're not native to this region, are you?"

Arcadius chuckled. "We are always what God has made us, no?" he said. "I was born and raised in Hispania, at Valentia on the coast, where my father was a local official. When I was about your age I moved to Mediolanum, where I lived for many years, although not long enough to learn the language, it appears."

Marcus smiled with embarrassment. Arcadius was joking. Latin was his native tongue, but his regional accent gave him away. "You speak it expertly," said Marcus.

Arcadius nodded his thanks and then said, "What about you, Marcus? For a soldier, I'd say your Latin is too good, too polished."

"I was born and raised in Rome," said Marcus, "where my father was also an official. After studying in Athens I joined the army. Since then, well, I haven't had a home."

"No wife and family?"

"No," answered Marcus.

"No relatives still in Rome?"

"No."

"I see," said Arcadius, studying the young man's face. "More stew?" he asked.

Marcus shook his head and felt it throb. "No, thank you," he said.

"Wine, then?"

"Yes, please," said Marcus.

Arcadius mixed a cup of wine and water and handed it to Marcus, who could not remember tasting wine that seemed so good. After a few sips, he lay back on the pillow to settle his head. "What do you do here in the mountains?" he asked.

"Pray, mostly," said Arcadius, "when not bothered by visitors. They come sometimes all the way from Comum, even Mediolanum. The farther they come, the longer they stay, no? But I shouldn't mind."

"Why do they come?" asked Marcus.

"For counsel, for advice. Sometimes for correction, sometimes just to talk," said Arcadius. "The persecution has scattered the faithful in all directions. Many overseers and elders are in hiding. Some have gone north where it is safer, so the people left behind come to me."

"Are you some kind of a priest?"

"Oh, no, no. Neither an elder nor an overseer nor even a simple reader. For that, I thank God. I am just an old man who has struggled with his own sins for many years. By the grace of God, I am sometimes able to help others avoid the same pitfalls."

Arcadius paused and then added, "I also tend the road for a league or so, clearing it of debris when necessary, keeping watch for the garrison, assisting travelers like yourself."

"Don't the soldiers at the garrison know you are a Christian?"

"Yes, of course, but what harm is an old man who lives alone in the mountains? In town, it's another matter. In Mediolanum, it's another matter still. Up here, we need each other to survive, against the cold and snow, against the wolves and bears, against the bandits, no?"

Arcadius rose wearily and said, "Time to rest again. Please excuse me."

Marcus watched as Arcadius secured the house for the night, removing the stew from the hearth and adding a log to the fire. Then he spread several thick blankets on the floor by the fire and rolled another into a pillow. Lastly, he knelt beside the blankets and made the sign of the cross. For some time he prayed quietly to himself, his lips moving but his voice barely heard. At times, he bowed his head toward the floor, but mostly he looked heavenward with his arms raised, like a child wanting to be picked up by a parent.

When he had finished, he crossed himself again, bade Marcus a good night, and laid himself down to sleep.

Arcadius was gone when Marcus awoke the next morning. The house was quiet except for the crackling of the fire and the whirr of the wind through the vent in the ceiling for the smoke. Marcus lifted the bedcovers and examined his bandaged leg in the dim firelight. Then he felt the wrappings around his still aching head. He couldn't tell much except that the bandages were clean and fairly fresh. His only pressing need was for a chamber pot, which he found without difficulty under the bed. Before lying down again, he poured himself a cup of water from a wide-mouth pitcher on the table next to the bed. Then he noticed Makrina's plaque, propped up on the table, leaning against a wooden candlestick.

Half an hour later, when Arcadius returned, the plaque was in

Marcus's lap. "Good morning," said Arcadius, throwing off the hood of his cloak. "How are you feeling today?"

"Much better, thank you," said Marcus. "Tell me, Arcadius, what do these letters mean?"

The old man sat down beside the bed and leaned close to the plaque Marcus was holding in his lap. Over the head of the central figure in the scene were the letters IC and XC.

"They stand for Jesus Christ," said Arcadius. "Iota and sigma for *Iesous*. Chi and sigma for *Christos*." Pointing a boney finger at the image, he said, "This scene we call the Last Supper of our Lord. Do you know the story?"

"I've heard it," said Marcus. He studied the plaque a moment longer, then returned the plaque to the table. When he did so, Arcadius noticed Alexander's cross dangling from Marcus's wrist.

"I've sent word of you to the garrison," said Arcadius. "The commander will be coming this afternoon to see you. He has asked for your full name. All I could tell them was Marcus."

"Aemilius Canio," said Marcus.

Arcadius's face lit up. "Aemilius Canio? Then you are Canio the younger, son of the late senator. Well, well, that explains your Latin. I am honored to be your host—but I am sorry for the loss of your father. He was very well respected, I know. The Augustus Maximianus declared three days of mourning throughout all of Italy. Were you in Rome when he died?"

"No," answered Marcus. "I was with the legions on the Rhenus. I returned to Rome to pay my respects and settle the estate. I'm on my way back to Mogontiacum now."

"Oh?" said Arcadius. "I would have thought there would be much more for you to do in Rome in your father's absence."

"Actually, no," said Marcus. "There's nothing for me in Rome right now."

"I saw your father once, at a festival in Mediolanum years ago," said Arcadius. "I shall never forget it—the gravity in your father's visage. It was the very face of Rome. We were both much younger then. He probably looked much like you. My eyes fail me now, so I cannot tell."

"I'm afraid I was always said to favor my mother," said Marcus with a smile. "What did you do in Mediolanum in those days? You haven't said."

"At that time, I taught at the municipal academy."

"As a Christian?" asked Marcus.

"I wasn't then a Christian," said Arcadius. "I was raised a Christian, but when I came to Mediolanum as a young man I fell into other ways. My professors at the academy seemed so wise, so knowledgeable, so intelligent, and so cultured. I was ashamed of both my provincial upbringing and my Christian faith. So I adopted the beliefs fashionable at the time. I became a Platonist. I even dabbled a little in the various eastern mysteries, but my philosophical tutors discouraged such things. There was never much in the mysteries to hold a rational mind anyway. Their rituals can be quite entrancing, but when the trance has ended, what is left?"

Marcus nodded. "I know what you mean," he said.

"After a few years I realized that the professors I thought so wise and knowledgeable were not so wise or knowledgeable after all. Intelligent, yes. They were intelligent. Many were more intelligent than I. But the more I learned, the more I saw the holes not only in my own knowledge, but in theirs. And the more I served under them, the more I came to know how afraid they were of those holes and how determined they were to ignore them. That's what they used their intelligence for—avoiding the holes in their philosophies, contriving elaborate covers for the questions they could not answer. They cared less to be wise than to be thought wise. A life such as this, in a small shack in the country, would have driven most of them to despair, and yet this is how half the human race lives, no? What good then is their philosophy?"

"But how could you give up the academy and the city for this?"

Arcadius shrugged and said, "It was not so hard. As a young man, I thought my professors' wisdom was the source of their haughtiness. Once relieved of that illusion, I no longer cared for their approval or their company. I did not immediately move here, nor did I immediately return to the Assembly. For a while, I was lost. I lived the routine of life, lecturing at the academy and tutoring on the side to make ends meet, without the satisfaction of living for a purpose. Then my father died, at home in Valentia. I had not visited him in years, and it pained me greatly that he died disappointed in me because I had abandoned the Gospel. I grieved for him, and I realized that my professors and all the philosophers could not give me comfort. Only then in my grief did I turn back to Christ and His Assembly. There in Mediolanum I met a elder of the Assembly who understood my emptiness and my grief, and he showed me the way back. That is the only way it happens—person leading person. Indeed, that is one reason the Son of God himself became incarnate, to lead us all back to the Father."

Arcadius paused for a breath before finishing. "And then, after rejoining the Assembly, I felt a growing need to mend my soul through prayer. I quit the academy and tutored a while on my own, but I eventually gave that up and left the temptations of the city for the countryside, and then from the countryside I came here. Still I haven't been able to get away, from either temptations or people, but I am at least needed here."

"You never married?" asked Marcus.

Arcadius shook his head. "I don't know why, except that I never really determined to marry and no one forced me into it. As a young man, there was one young lady from a good family, but I believe she tired of waiting for me. After my return to the Assembly, it was easier to resist the demands of the body and so I lost much of the desire for marriage."

"How is it possible?" asked Marcus. "To resist the demands, I mean."

"It is easier than you might think, Marcus. Prayer and fasting help, but for me it would be impossible outside the Assembly, without the grace of God. Someday perhaps you will have an occasion to find out. I'm afraid now you wouldn't understand. As you may know, we have our own mysteries, which we reserve for hearts prepared to hear them."

Marcus nodded.

"What about you, Marcus?" asked Arcadius. "Have you a philosophy?"

"I have always taken counsel from the Stoics," said Marcus.

"Like your father, no?"

"Like my father," said Marcus.

"The Stoa is at least a manly attempt at wisdom," said Arcadius. "But it is hardly a cheerful one. Does not the esteemed Epictetus himself counsel self-destruction when the smoke becomes too thick?"

Marcus nodded. "'The door is always open,' he says."

A moment passed without a word from either man. Then Arcadius rose and made his way to a large chest that sat against the wall. "I have some things that might interest you, here among my books," he said, lifting the lid. "Let's see." He searched the chest's contents, checking the titles on a dozen or so scrolls, before returning to his stool with two.

"This one is an old favorite, which I'm sure you've read, but with time on your hands it might be worth re-reading," he said, handing Marcus a scroll labeled *On Friendship* by Marcus Tullius Cicero. "And here's a Christian author better known in the East. Lucas has been struggling to read it in Greek but must have given up." The work was entitled *Peri Archôn* ("About First Things") by one Origenes Adamantius. A curious name, thought Marcus. What did it mean? Origen the Hard-headed?

"Of course, I've no way of knowing what might really interest you," said Arcadius. "You are welcome to anything else you can find. Lucas will be by later and can help you look."

The old man excused himself and left the cabin. Marcus settled into reading, naturally turning to the one book he had not already read.

An hour later, the boy Lucas appeared, shyly begging Marcus's pardon for the interruption. Then he went about his chores in silence, sweeping the floor, emptying the bedpan, washing out the dishes, bringing in firewood, and fetching fresh water for the pitcher beside the bed. He was a thin lad with a round, boyish face and bright red cheeks too young for even the earliest whiskers. His head was covered with a thick mop of light brown hair that reached nearly to his eyebrows and almost covered his ears.

Marcus watched him from behind a scroll. When the boy seemed about to settle into his chair to read, Marcus asked him the hour.

Lucas stood up straight with a look of surprise. "Almost the seventh hour, my lord—I think. I'm not sure," he said, with the accent of northern Italy.

"Is it?" said Marcus, thinking aloud for the boy's sake. "I seem to have slept late. Your name is Lucas?"

"Yes, my lord."

"How old are you?" asked Marcus.

"Fifteen, my lord."

"And you come here everyday to read?"

"Almost everyday, my lord. Every day I'm not needed at home. Since we moved from Mediolanum, it's the only way I can keep up my studies."

"You're from Mediolanum? Then what brought you up here?"

Lucas answered uncertainly. "The edicts, my lord. It's safer up here for us."

Marcus nodded. "You miss Mediolanum?" he asked.

"Oh, yes, my lord. I'd lived there all my life. It's a beautiful city, and I left behind all my friends."

"No friends up here?"

"None my age," said Lucas. "At least none to take the place of my friends in the city, one in particular."

Marcus puzzled a moment over his answer. "Boy or girl?" he asked.

Lucas blushed and grinned. "Girl, my lord," he answered.

Marcus chuckled. "Sit down, Lucas, and tell me about her," he said.

Lucas sat down on the edge of his seat by the fire, fidgeting nervously with an unread scroll in his hands. "She's beautiful, my lord," he said. "She has dark brown hair and green eyes and the prettiest smile. And a dimple right in the middle of her chin. Her name is Irene. It means 'peace' in Greek."

Marcus smiled and nodded.

"She's sweet and modest, too, not loud and showy like some girls."

"How long has it been since you've seen her?"

"Almost a year!" said Lucas. "We write, though, so she hasn't forgotten me."

"She's still in Mediolanum?"

"Oh yes, my lord."

"But why hasn't her family also fled since the edicts?"

Lucas looked suddenly sad. "Her father isn't a believer, only her mother, and he made them all offer sacrifice."

"I see," said Marcus. "How many of your Christian friends offered sacrifice to escape punishment?"

"Most," said Lucas.

"Really?" said Marcus.

Lucas nodded. "A few families fled, but the parents of most of them found some way to justify it."

"Not yours, though," said Marcus.

"No, of course not. My father would never allow that. I don't know about my mother. Sometimes I think she would."

"What about you, Lucas? Would you sacrifice to stay in Mediolanum?"

"No," said Lucas.

"Even if it was the only way to see Irene again?"

"No. Never. I couldn't," said Lucas. "I couldn't betray my father and give up all that we believe in."

"I see," said Marcus, searching Lucas's face for any sign of uncertainty. Finding none, Marcus changed the subject. "Tell me more about this girl. How did you meet her?"

A smile returned to Lucas's face, and for a quarter of hour he talked of his sweetheart.

Their conversation ended with the arrival of the commander of the garrison at the pass, a centurion named Rutilius. A rough-looking man, he nevertheless treated Arcadius with kindness and respect. Arcadius welcomed him as a guest and offered him a cup of wine, which he declined. "I won't be long," he said.

He asked about the attack and the attackers, and then about Alexander. Was there anyone he should notify of the death besides the legion in Mogontiacum? No, said Marcus.

"How long before he's able to travel?" the centurion asked Arcadius.

"A week at least," said Arcadius. "I wouldn't risk it before then."

Turning to Marcus, the centurion said, "The road through the mountains is blocked by an early snow. I can get word of you through to Mogontiacum by imperial post, in a roundabout way, but you had better postpone your return until the roads clear."

"How long will that be?" asked Marcus.

"Four months."

"Four months!"

"March at the earliest," said the centurion. Arcadius nodded in agreement.

"Great gods! I can't stay here until March!"

"You don't have to stay here," said Arcadius. "The road south is still clear. When you're well enough, you can move to Clavenna, or return to Mediolanum."

The thought was small consolation to Marcus. There were so many things that required his attention in his changed situation. The one that came first to his mind was the task of telling a young woman named Lucia that her Alexander was dead. How could he make her wait so long for such bad news? How could he break the news to her sooner, knowing nothing more about her than her first name?

"Can you get a letter to Mogontiacum for me?" he asked the centurion.

"It will take longer than usual, but it can be done."

"I will have it ready tomorrow, if you will send someone to pick it up."

"As you wish, sir," replied the centurion.

He took his leave, and Arcadius saw him off.

Marcus wrote his letter to Favonius, commander of the Second Cohort, asking him to look after his household in Mogontiacum and to locate the woman Lucia and deliver the news. He knew he could trust Favonius to be discreet.

The next day a soldier arrived and took charge of the letter. For that day and the next, Marcus was too restless to read, however much he tried. Frustrated by his helplessness and tortured by his wait, he surrendered his thoughts to his failures and misfortunes. He lay all day in bed without reading, speaking, or eating. Lucas tried to talk to him, but Marcus would not even answer.

On the morning of the third day, however, Marcus had had enough. "I would like to see Alexander's grave," he announced impatiently when Arcadius had finished his prayers at the third hour.

"Very well," said Arcadius. The old man helped Marcus dress for the cold, then found a sturdy branch for Marcus to use as a crutch. Together they hobbled out the door. The hillside was covered with snow, which made it difficult for Marcus to see. The heavy hood of his cloak provided some shielding.

Arcadius led him slowly up the hillside along a lane partly sheltered by pines and matted with pine needles. In a small, snow-covered clearing, Marcus was shown the grave, marked by a large stone, on which was chiselled: HIC IACET ALEX MIL X. Arcadius provided the translation: "Here lies Alexander, Soldier of Christ."

"Lucas carved the marker," said Arcadius. "I hope it pleases you."

Marcus nodded. "Very much," he said.

"He only sleeps, Marcus, and will one day rise again," Arcadius added.

A rush of wind cast flakes of snow in Marcus's face as he stared at the humble marker. Behind him, Arcadius uncovered his head and made the sign of the cross. Raising his eyes and hands skyward, the old man whispered a brief prayer. When he had finished, he covered his head again with his hood and waited a while longer.

At last Marcus turned away, and the feeble pair hobbled in silence back to the cabin.

Once again in the cabin's warmth, Marcus committed himself to biding his time as best he could. Before long he was reading again, sometimes for hours on end without food or drink or sleep. He was favorably impressed by the work in Greek on "first things" by Origen of Alexandria. This fellow wrote like a philosopher, although from Christian suppositions. But before Marcus had finished it, Lucas recommended a Latin work entitled *On the Soul* by one Quintus Septimius Florens Tertullianus, who made quite a different impression. Tertullian wrote like a lawyer, mocking in beautifully merciless Latin the teachings of the greatest philosophers the world had ever known. The tone surprised Marcus, and at first he did not take the author seriously, but the more he read the more troubled he was by the contrast between Christian belief about the soul and the philosophers' wide-ranging speculations.

One point hammered home by the lawyer hit Marcus hard: The great philosophers could not agree among themselves on anything. "Wide are men's inquiries into uncertainties," wrote Tertullian. "Wider still are their disagreements about conjectures. However great the difficulty of adducing proofs, the labor of producing conviction is not one whit less!" In contrast, Christians seemed utterly sure and satisfied with their own doctrine, which made at least as much sense as the philosophers', and some were so sure and satisfied that they were willing to die for it.

Arcadius seemed surprised to find him reading Tertullian. "Does he not offend you?" he asked with a smile.

"A little perhaps," said Marcus. "He has a genius for rhetoric, and many of his criticisms make sense, but he seems to see nothing good in any other man of genius—in Plato, in Aristotle. It's a little much for an educated man to swallow."

"Which is why I gave you the Alexandrian instead," said Arcadius. "But Lucas in his youthful ignorance and enthusiasm has ushered you straight into the arena to face his champion."

"I hope you won't punish him for it."

Arcadius chuckled. "No, of course not," he said. "The great Tertullian is my champion, too, and who can know what will move a man to salvation? We try not to offend unbelievers unnecessarily of course, but often people need a line in the sand—a clear, honest choice of truth or error. Faith cannot be administered like medicine—mixed with so much honey that the sick child cannot taste it. Faith must be founded on truth, and the truth is what it is. It cannot be imparted in disguise. People can no more be tricked into truth than they can be fooled into wisdom. They must be shown wisdom and encouraged to choose it."

"Wouldn't everyone choose wisdom when shown it in the right way?"

Arcadius shook his head. "No, Marcus. No," he said. "They will not choose it because it is not cheap, because it will cost them dearly. Many would rather forsake wisdom and keep their friends or their status or merely the comfort of their accustomed ways. No better argument, no greater knowledge will dissuade them. They have what they want in life and they will not give it up, not for truth, not for wisdom, not to save their souls. Offered wisdom, they choose foolishness. Offered God, they choose not God. By their choice, they judge themselves. Ours is not a gnostic faith, Marcus. God will judge us not on what we know, but on what we desire in our hearts. Do we desire the good or no? Do we desire the truth or no? God himself gives us that choice in the clearest possible way, in the choice of a good man or a bad man—Jesus of Nazareth or Jesus Bar Abbas, an innocent healer and teacher or a convicted thief and murderer. Whom will we free and whom will we crucify?"

"But who would knowingly crucify an innocent man?"

"Men who hate his teaching because it is not their own, who fear that he has come to take their place, who care more for their careers than for the truth, or who are themselves thieves and murderers. Some would just to please their family and friends. Have you never read the Gospels, Marcus?"

"Never."

"Someday you must," said Arcadius. "God wants you for his own, Marcus. The Holy Spirit is pursuing you in earnest. Even before he delivered you into my care, he introduced you to other Christians, your servant Alexander and the friend who gave you that image."

Marcus looked over at Makrina's painting, leaning against the wall on the table. "She was the girl I was supposed to marry," he said, still gazing at the painting.

"Oh?" said Arcadius.

"But she refused me because I was not a Christian."

"It must have been very difficult for both of you," said Arcadius.

Marcus nodded. "It was. It certainly broke my heart. Hers, too, perhaps. I don't really know."

"She must have been a very beautiful soul to have loved the Lord so much."

"She was. She was indeed. Purer than—I deserved."

"Do you still love her?"

Marcus shrugged. "I suppose I do," he answered. "It was long ago and so far away. Things have changed since I last saw her. I have changed. But yes, I still love her, and think of her often."

"Never stop thinking of her, Marcus, but think also of God and turn your thoughts into prayers, for her—and for you."

A few short days later, Marcus was awaiting the arrival of a troop of soldiers from the garrison, who were to escort him back to Clavenna and on to Mediolanum. Lucas's family had provided him with two changes of clothes, not at all what Marcus was accustomed to wearing, but comfortable and suitable for traveling. They had also provided a leather satchel of food and drink, packed alongside Makrina's painted plaque. Marcus wore Alexander's cross around his neck for safekeeping.

When the soldiers arrived, Marcus was standing beside Alexander's grave, leaning on a sturdy wooden crutch Lucas had just finished for him. He limped back to the cabin in no hurry. The soldiers had brought a small wagon for him to ride in, on account of his head and leg injuries. Lucas loaded his satchel while Marcus thanked Arcadius for his hospitality.

"After all you've done for me, I have still one favor to ask," said Marcus.

"Which is?" said Arcadius.

"Pray for me, Arcadius. I can't say where I will end up, but please pray to your god for me."

"Of course I will, Marcus. I will pray for you as I would pray for my own son," said Arcadius. "Now, I have one last question for you: The girl who gave you the image, what was her name?"

"Makrina, the daughter of Aristoboulos," Marcus answered.

"I will pray for her, too—for Makrina, the daughter of Aristoboulos."

# XV

His excellency the governor, Sossianos Hierocles, beckoned to a servant to refill his drinking-bowl, then turned to his host and said, "Tell me, Aristoboulos, have you heard from your son Kimon since he arrived in Nicomedia? How does he like his new station?"

Six men reclined around a semi-circular table in the banquet hall of Aristoboulos's country villa, enjoying a leisurely after-dinner conversation in the cool of an early September evening. The governor was at one end in the place of honor; Aristoboulos was at the other. Between them were Philodemos the mayor; Hippolytus Pollio, Hierocles's lieutenant governor; Titus Statilius, an official of the court of the caesar Galerius; and Gaius Valerius Marcellinus.

"I have, your excellency," answered Aristoboulos. "He has written once and seems quite pleased with his duties and with the capital."

"He is a fine young man," said the governor, "a glory of the empire and credit to your house. You should be very proud."

"He has always been a fine example of Roman manhood, your excellency," said Philodemos, who had recently been elevated to the rank of provincial decurion. "I have watched him grow into it from an early age and can attest to his loyalty and service. I always knew he would make good."

Aristoboulos chuckled. "I myself had doubts. I thought he would never return from Athens, and when he did, I lived in constant fear that he would abandon us for the schools of Alexandria. His fascination with the philosophers had quite overwhelmed his interest in anything else."

"Hardly a fault in a bright young man," said the governor, "especially in the present day, when so many young minds are abandoning our shared values and accumulated wisdom for absurd superstitions. If more of them were like young Kimon, the emperors would not have needed to resort to unpleasant measures to preserve the peace and prosperity of our society."

"Well said, your excellency," said Hippolytus, the lieutenant governor.

"Well, indeed," said Philodemos.

Titus Statilius turned to Philodemos and said, "Is it true the edicts have met some resistance here in Sinope?"

Philodemos looked offended. "None to speak of," he answered. "Nearly everyone in the city and countryside has complied with the edict of sacrifice, and a great number of those not long after the edict was issued. It's true, a handful still refuse, but only on account of his excellency's patience."

"It has been my desire, Titus, to school as many as I can of these misguided Christian atheists back to the path of public virtue without resorting to the use of force," said the governor. "Many are merely in need of education, and once educated I have no doubt they will see the light of reason and rejoin the community of loyal Roman citizens."

"A noble ambition," said Statilius. "May the gods grant you every success in it."

The governor nodded his thanks, then turned to Marcellinus, whose eyes were on the floor. "Gaius, you seem unusually quiet this evening. Would you care to venture an opinion on the matter?" said the governor.

Marcellinus looked up at his superior and said, "I beg your pardon, your excellency, but I found no need to speak when all that I believe had already been said so well."

The governor smiled and saluted Marcellinus by raising his drinking bowl into air. "You are an example to us all, Valerius Marcellinus. I drink to your health," he said.

"I, too," said Philodemos, raising his bowl and drinking also. Marcellinus nodded in acknowledgment, as the others followed suit.

Servants entered silently to light the lamps, which soon filled the room with a warm yellow glow and the smell of scented oil. The governor sat up in his place and said, "Where are the women? What's keeping them? I wanted them to see this, too."

Aristoboulos signaled for a servant to send for the women, and before long the women entered in order of unofficial rank, chatting amicably among themselves. Clea came first, the governor's niece, a plump and pretty young woman who obviously knew how to enjoy herself; then Politta, the somewhat older wife of Hippolytus, finely dressed and meticulously made up, but showing the first thin lines of age in her face and neck, tradeoffs for her efforts to maintain the figure of her youth; next, the stately Hilaria, wife of Aristoboulos, and lastly Demetra, wife of Philodemos, not as pretty as Clea, not as stylish as Politta, not as graceful as Hilaria.

Two women were missing from this company of consorts: the wife of Statilius, who was at home in Nicomedia, and Makrina, unaccountably.

"Is it safe now, uncle?" Clea teased. "Have you finished your dull discourse?"

"Your untroubled minds were never safer, my dear," said the governor, rising from the couch.

"Then promise us not a word of philosophy or politics for the rest of the evening or we shall all leave immediately," declared Clea, receiving her promise from the smiling governor.

Chairs were brought for the women and arranged in front of the couch, but the governor quickly sent the chairs away and welcomed the women to the couch. With mock disgust, the women squeezed in next to their husbands, with Clea taking the governor's place. Marcellinus offered his place to Hilaria and quietly excused himself to his host and hostess.

"What's become of Gaius?" asked the governor when he had gone.

"Gone to retrieve his little lady falcon, no doubt," said Statilius. The others laughed.

Marcellinus found Makrina alone on the terrace, gazing up at a gibbous moon rising over of the gardens. A chorus of tiny creatures sang its greeting in the cool evening air. Only the faintest sounds of conversation strayed from the faraway banquet hall. Marcellinus approached her from behind and spoke her name.

Makrina was startled. "You frightened me," she said reproachfully.

Marcellinus thought at first to beg her pardon but suppressed the impulse. "Why were you not with the others?" he asked.

Makrina shook her head and turned back toward the moon.

"You'll catch cold in this air," he said. "Can I offer you my cloak?"

Makrina pulled her palla tighter about her shoulders. "No, thank you," she said without looking at him. "I am quite comfortable."

He stepped forward and stood beside her at the marble balustrade, just within range of her perfume. "Is it the company?" he asked.

"Yes, the company," she said.

"They're vain and foolish women. I'm sorry you have to put up with them."

"It's not just them, Gaius. It's—it's everything," said Makrina. "It's the women, the governor, that obsequious Philodemos. And it's you, Gaius." She turned at last to face him. "It's you most of all. I can't bear to face you. It hurts me too much. As fond as you are of me, as fond as I was of you, that's how much I now hurt. . . . I can't marry you, Gaius."

"I haven't asked you to."

"But I know it's what you want. Why else would you have indulged me and protected me all these many months? You've been patient. For a man in your position, you've been as patient as Penelope waiting for Odysseos. But you must know by now that I cannot be moved. I cannot marry you because of what it would mean."

"Makrina," he said plaintively, "We've talked this all out before. Has all that I've said, all that I've written in my letters not counted? You can keep your god, secretly for the time being. I will not hold that against you."

"It's too late, Gaius. Too much has happened. Things have changed," said Makrina. "There was a time when I thought I did love you and even dreamed that I could marry you. I wanted there to be a way. I allowed myself to believe there was a way. But now I can only believe that—you and I are enemies. Whatever we feel for each other, we are enemies. The world has made us so. There is blood to prove it—innocent blood. I am your enemy, Gaius, and I am afraid of you, and my fear has killed my fondness for you."

She turned away from him, but he moved closer, touching her arm tenderly. "What have you to fear from me?" he said into her ear. "I would never hurt you."

Makrina bowed her head. "You would. I know you would," she said.

"Never," said Marcellinus.

"Yes, yes. You would," she said, facing him. "You would because of who you are, because of what you believe, because of what you want. You will not give up your life—everything you've earned so far and all your future dreams—just to have me."

"Is that what it would take? Everything I am and could be?"

"Yes," she answered.

"Makrina," he pleaded softly.

"Everything, Gaius. Me or everything. Make your choice."

A chilling breeze blew between them. Marcellinus turned toward the house. "It's getting late. We will be missed," he said. "Would you at least spare me the embarrassment of returning without you?"

Makrina nodded and loosed a hand from her tightly wrapped palla to take his arm. They left the terrace and entered the moonless shadows of the house. As they neared the banquet hall, they heard voices, but not in conversation. Makrina stopped suddenly. "What is that?" she asked.

Marcellinus listened for a moment to the sound of someone solemnly intoning an incantation in a strange tongue. "His excellency," he answered.

Makrina glanced at him incredulously. She hurried onward and stopped again at entrance of the banquet hall. There she saw the diners standing in a semicircle, facing a familiar bronze figure of Hermes brought in from the reception hall and set upon a pedestal between two tripods of incense. His excellency, the governor, stood before the idol with his arms raised and his head covered in his cloak.

"Hail, O Thrice Great Hermes, dispenser of secret knowledge," the governor chanted. "Honor us with thy presence and glory!"

In an instant, fire burst forth from the tripods, producing a great cloud of smoke that obscured the idol. Then it seemed the idol spoke.

"Hail to thee, great Hierocles!" said a strange voice. "Thou hast excelled in wisdom and knowledge beyond all thy mortal kin. In all of Pontus, there is none that is greater. Yea, all of Asia!"

The spectators stared at the idol in amazement, except Marcellinus, whose eyes were on Makrina. He saw her gasp and shudder. She turned to him with horror in her eyes, her mouth agape, but his own expression showed only disappointment.

Makrina glanced again at the spectacle, then turned abruptly and ran away. Marcellinus watched her go, knowing she would not return. Then he turned his attention back to the room, waiting in the shadows without interest until the show was over before rejoining the group.

The next morning Aristoboulos wandered into his wife's dressing room as Nonna was pinning up her mistress's hair. Like most couples who could afford to, Aristoboulos and Hilaria slept apart and did not often see each other in the morning until both were up and about. This morning, however, he had sought her out.

"I dreamed I arrived home one afternoon to find the place deserted except for Philodemos. Everyone who actually lives here had disappeared," he explained, pacing the floor.

"Too much to eat and drink?" Hilaria asked.

"Too much nonsense," he muttered. "All that mumbo-jumbo last night. Who knows what demons that sorcerer conjured up?"

"Harmless, I'm sure, dear," said Hilaria. "I can't believe that the really fearsome ones would pay any attention to him. He's such a droll fellow."

Aristoboulos chuckled. "Yes, well, there's one benefit to Philodemos's elevation to decurion," he said. "Next time, happy fate, the governor will stay with *him*. They deserve each other."

An hour later, Aristoboulos accompanied his male house guests—the governor, Hippolytus, Statilius, and Marcellinus—into town for the governor's induction into the college of priests of Serapis, in preparation for the god's annual festival, which would commence the following day.

Afterwards Aristoboulos returned to his work, with Statilius tagging along. The governor repaired to the garrison to continue his examination of the handful of Christians who still refused to sacrifice. Of the twenty-one arrested, only four remained imprisoned with the overseer Archelaos. Most of those arrested had sacrificed to secure their safety immediately after the death of Euplios, fearing the worst for themselves or their families. Some had tired of their fight during the long summer in prison and given in to the edict in despair. They were the most defeated. The faithful four were the elder Theogenes, the reader Philippos, the widow Euphemia, and Dio, the taverner.

Patient though he was, the governor was nearing the end of his drive to persuade the holdouts to submit. If they could not be brought to obedience, they could at least be brought to account, and there was no better time than the festival to conclude the matter, one way or the other.

Makrina rose early that morning but did not leave her rooms until she was sure the men had gone. Near noon she was helping Eugenia with her Latin in the tablinum in the women's wing of the villa, when Clea and Politta trooped in cheerily and settled themselves on a nearby couch.

"Makrina, dear, how are you feeling today?" said Clea. "Gaius said you were ill and had gone to bed early. I do hope it's nothing serious."

"I'm fine, thank you," answered Makrina.

"It's a shame you weren't able to rejoin us," said Clea. "We had a marvelous time with the men afterwards. Didn't we, Politta?"

"Yes, indeed," said Politta, "though you should have seen poor Marcellinus, Makrina. He was lost without you. Hardly said a word all evening."

"Yes, what a shame, too," said Clea. "He's such a charming fellow, a joy to have around. I've begged Uncle to invite him along as often as possible."

"He's so handsome, too—trim and strong. I envy you, Makrina," said Politta.

"If he were not already so in love with you, I would fight you for him," said Clea.

"But what would 'Uncle' do then?" asked Makrina.

"What would he do?" wondered Clea. "The gods only know!"

Clea and Politta exchanged glances and giggled. "Oh, dear, what a thought!" Clea added, fanning her neck and bosom with an arrangement of baby peacock feathers.

"What a beautiful fan," said Eugenia. "Wherever did you get it?"

"Oh, this thing?" said Clea. "Uncle got it for me in Egypt. If it charms you so, I'll leave it with you later. Right now, though, I'm afraid I'd die without it. Who'd ever think it could be so hot in the day and so cold at night?"

"You look so nice today, Politta. Are you expecting someone?" asked Makrina.

"Me? Expecting someone? Now who would I be expecting in this little place? I wouldn't know anyone within a hundred miles."

"What a shame, then," said Makrina. "Your beauty will be wasted on us."

"Why, thank you, dear," said Politta, uncertainly.

Hilaria entered and asked if anyone would care for lunch.

"Not I, alas," said Politta. "I am starving myself for Hippolytus's sake. The things we women do for our husbands!"

"Clea?"

"Oh, no, thank you, dear," replied Clea. "I've risen so late it hardly seems time yet."

"Makrina?"

"No, Mamma. Suddenly I'm not feeling well again. I think I'll lie down for a while."

She rose to leave.

"Have a pleasant nap, dear. Hope you feel better," said Clea.

"Thank you—dear," said Makrina.

When she had gone, Politta also excused herself for a walk in the gardens.

"Won't you be uncomfortable in the sun?" asked Hilaria.

"I don't mind," said Politta. "I've a parasol, and besides, a little warmth will be good for my complexion."

As the sun reached its zenith, Hilaria and Clea were comparing Persian and Indian tapestries in a cupboarded corner of the banquet room. Eugenia was dining alone in the triclinium nearby. Makrina was lying listlessly on the bed in her room, trying to sleep in the heat.

Well out of sight of the house, Politta settled herself under her parasol on a marble bench in the garden.

She hadn't been there long before Phokas, the gardener, appeared before her. She gasped and cringed and almost screamed. He was a frightful sight for anyone who did not know him, big and bony in his soiled tunic and leather apron, with his broad brimmed hat overshadowing his overgrown beard. In his hand, he carried a sickle and at his side hung a hooked pruning knife.

He looked at her with eyes as wide and fearful as hers and said, "No, no, my lady. You mustn't stay. You must leave at once."

"What? Whatever do—do—do you mean?" Politta stammered.

Phokas shook his head forlornly. "The garden is not the place. It is not decent. You must leave at once. Please, please leave, before—before—" Phokas looked up to see Titus Statilius hurrying toward them. "Lord have mercy," he moaned.

"What is this?" demanded Statilius. "Who are you, and what are you doing?"

Phokas bowed abjectly before him. "I—I—"

Politta got up and hurried into Statilius's arms. "This *monster* jumped out of the bushes at me and *ordered* me out of the garden!" she declared. "I nearly fainted with fright!"

"How dare you!" said Statilius. "Who are you to even speak to a lady, much less order one about?"

"Forgive me, master. Forgive me, please," Phokas pleaded, without looking up.

"Who are you anyway? What is your name?"

"The gardener only. The name is Phokas. Just the gardener."

"Has your master made you *lord* over the gardens, to order people about in them?"

"No, master, I was only concerned for the lady's honor."

"My honor?" said Politta.

"What concern is that of yours?" said Statilius. "What kind of man are you, to worry about someone else's honor."

"I—I—"

"Answer me! What kind of man are you?"

"Well, if you must know, master, I am a Christian," said Phokas.

"A Christian! I might have guessed!"

"A Christian!" said Politta. "That explains it."

"Go on. Go away. I'll deal with you later," said Statilius. "Go!"

Phokas bowed low and hurried off into the bushes.

Statilius helped Politta back to the house, where they reported the offense to their hostess, Hilaria. Before long, the whole house was abuzz with the scandal. Makrina heard the news from Eugenia. "Phokas? A Christian?" she wondered. "How can this be? I never saw him in the Assembly. How can it be?"

"I never saw him either," said Eugenia, "but we'll know for sure soon enough, when Pappa and the governor return from town."

When the other men returned to the villa later that afternoon, Phokas was brought before the governor for an informal interview in the men's tablinum, with only Aristoboulos and Marcellinus present. Phokas had never ventured so far inside his master's house. He entered as an interloper, looking about in awe and apprehension at the painted walls and mosaic floors.

The governor was awed also, by Phokas himself. A monster, he seemed indeed—so big and crude against the delicate trappings of the tablinum. He stood among them somewhat stooped by age and humility, with his hat in his hands, clad only in his workmen's tunic, leather belt, and well-worn sandals, which seemed the size of camels' hooves.

Without a dais to sit on, the governor stood so as not to be overshadowed by the accused. Even so, he found himself looking up at the strange man in their midst. "Are you the gardener Phokas?" he asked.

"I am, excellency," answered Phokas meekly.

"The Lady Flavia Politta says that you entered her presence unbidden and frightened her, ordering her to leave the gardens immediately. Is that so?"

"Yes, excellency," said Phokas. "I did speak to her unbidden. I didn't mean to frighten her. I was only concerned for her honor. Mistress Politta is a woman of birth and breeding. I wished only to discourage her from soiling herself."

"What are you talking about?" asked the governor.

"Oh, excellency, I am ashamed to speak of it," said Phokas.

"Speak of what? Come on. Tell us what you mean."

"Twice, excellency, I have found Mistress Politta alone in the garden,

yesterday and today. Yesterday she was joined by Master Statilius, and together they withdrew to a far corner for some time. I dare not say what else
I saw. Seeing her again today, waiting for Master Statilius as before, I meant
to send her away. That is all. The gardens are not the place, not the place at
all, excellency."

"I see," said the governor, exchanging glances with Marcellinus and
Aristoboulos. "I suppose it's true you are a Christian. Have you sacrificed
as required by law?"

"I have never sacrificed in all my years, except with praise and repentance to our Father in heaven," answered Phokas.

"Oh? How is that?" the governor asked Marcellinus.

Marcellinus shook his head. "We have no record of him. No one has
identified him as a member of their Assembly," he answered.

The governor turned back to Phokas. "How is it that you have managed
to remain hidden until now and thus escaped having to sacrifice?"

Phokas shrugged his bony shoulders and said, "It must have pleased
God to have preserved me until this time. I was like a stone the builders
rejected, but now, after years of toil and exile, the Lord wants me for His
house. As He wishes me to be discovered, I am ready to suffer for His name."

"Then you know the penalty for refusing to sacrifice?"

"I do, excellency."

"And you are prepared to suffer the penalty rather than sacrifice?"

"I am, excellency."

The governor looked to Aristoboulos and Marcellinus. "Then so be it,"
he said.

Makrina begged her father to intercede for Phokas. "You can't let them do
this to the poor old man," she pleaded. "He's just a harmless old soul who
would never hurt anyone. Whatever he said or did to Politta, I'm sure she
deserved it, the old crow!"

Aristoboulos felt much the same way, but knew better than to encourage Makrina's ire. "This is not some local maiden who has stolen your boy-
friend," he told her. "This is the wife of the lieutenant governor, our superior
and our guest."

"But Phokas is our faithful servant and a dear friend! You can't just
stand by and see him destroyed!"

"There are laws, Makrina, and there is only so much we can do about
them. You can only make things worse by blaming Politta."

Desperate to save Phokas, Makrina then turned to Marcellinus, sum-
moning him to her private quarters, over the objection of Nonna.

"You can't let them harm Phokas," she told him when they were alone.

"He's just a harmless old man who has never bothered anyone except Politta, and no doubt she deserved it. You must beg the governor for mercy."

"Makrina, I can't," he said. "It's settled. The man's a Christian, he refuses to sacrifice, and he's caused a terrible embarrassment to some very vindictive people. He's doomed."

"For *me*! You must do it for *me*—in my name. You must beg the governor for mercy on my behalf."

Marcellinus threw up hands. "Why should I bother? Why should I risk it for your sake?"

"Save him and I'll marry you," Makrina said.

Marcellinus couldn't believe his ears. "What did you say?" he said.

"Save him and I will marry you."

"You'll marry me?"

"Yes," said Makrina, unflinching. "I will, I swear it."

"You would marry me to save some old servant?" said Marcellinus. "Not because you love me, not because you want to be my wife, but because you want to save your—*gardener*? I don't believe you, Makrina. You're just saying this in desperation."

"I mean it, Gaius," said Makrina firmly. "I can't stand it any longer. I can't stand this persecution. I can't stand to see a kind-hearted, innocent old man like Phokas suffer. He's been my friend all my life, since I was a little girl. He has been an angel to me, and now I know why. Save him and I'll marry you. I swear it."

"But it goes against all that you believe, all that you've been beating me with these past many months, about not forsaking Christ, about not defiling the Assembly. What about the great victory it is to die for Christ? Don't you want that victory for Phokas? *He* apparently wants it."

Makrina shook her head wearily as her eyes filled with tears. "God have mercy on my soul! I can't stand to see him die!" she cried. She threw herself at Marcellinus, wrapping her arms around his waist. "Please, Gaius, save him. Save him and I'm yours!"

Marcellinus shuddered with desire feeling her body against his. She had not stood so close to him in weeks. He drew a trembling breath that brought her scent inside of him. He knew it was hopeless, but he could try, and if he tried perhaps Makrina would marry him anyway. So she was not unmovable, as he had come to believe. She had already laid aside her objections, at least for Phokas's sake. How could she take them up again, after he had proven his love for her by attempting the impossible?

"I'll try," he said. "I'll try."

Makrina hugged him tightly, wiping her tears of shame upon his chest.

# XVI

On the morning of the first day of the festival of Serapis, the god's golden idol was being scrubbed and polished and anointed with oils by a crew of municipal slaves, in preparation for its annual afternoon procession through the town.

At the same time, Sossianos Hierocles, the god's newly installed high priest, was sitting in the study of Aristoboulos's country villa as his valet applied curlers of heated iron to his beard, in preparation for the high priest's role in leading the procession. Few men were permitted to approach the governor at such times, but Marcellinus was one who was.

"What's troubling you, Gaius?" asked the governor, seeing Marcellinus out of the corner of his eye, as his valet removed the last of the curlers.

Marcellinus smiled. "Do I look troubled, your excellency?" he said.

"Too troubled for the first day of a festival," said the governor. "Today we must wear our comic masks to play our parts for the people. You seem to have left yours in your trunk."

The valet examined the governor's beard critically, rearranging a curl or two and clipping stray whiskers away with a crude pair of iron scissors.

"I'm sorry, your excellency, but I have been thinking of the Lady Makrina. She's quite distraught over the gardener Phokas. She grew up in his gardens and is very fond of him. She is now quite distressed at his fate."

"And she has begged you to come and plead for his life," said the governor.

"Yes, indeed," said Marcellinus. "I've made inquiries and have found no evidence that he was ever a member of the Christian Assembly here in Sinope. No one recalls ever having seen him at worship. Even their overseer was surprised at his confession. By their own laws, he's not one of them."

"But he says he is, Gaius, and he refuses to sacrifice. He may not be a Christian by their laws, but he is a Christian by ours. He has defied our laws and made himself an enemy of the State."

"But he's a harmless old man, your excellency, without much time to live anyway. For all that he has meant to the family of Aristoboulos, for all his years of faithful service, without giving offense to anyone until yesterday, some less extreme punishment would seem enough."

The governor dismissed his valet and rose from his chair.

"Dear Gaius," he said, resting his hand on Marcellinus's shoulder. "Nothing would please me more than to help you please your lady. I am touched by your devotion to her, and also by your courage and respect for me, that you would come to me, as a son to a father, and earnestly request something you yourself know is impossible to grant."

Marcellinus started to speak but the governor raised his hand for silence.

"The unfortunate old gardener is certainly doomed," he continued. "I can tell you what I could not tell Aristoboulos when he was here awhile ago to make the same plea. Besides the embarrassing circumstances, of which you are quite aware, I am under pressure from above to take stronger measures against the Christians. Titus Statilius has urged the use of all due force against rebellious Christians. I cannot ignore the opinions of emperors' ministers. Then, too, my own patience is worn thin, and one way of avoiding rumors about the gardener is to handle him exactly as I am forced to handle the others. In normal circumstances as you know, I would myself loathe the shedding of blood, but it is they who seem to wish for it. They really give us no choice, do they? They oppose us with their very lives, laying down their lives in defiance of the laws upon which all order and security depends. What else can we do?"

Marcellinus shrugged and the governor went on.

"It is they who are responsible, who refuse to submit, who despise the freedoms we enjoy as Romans, who would force their ways upon us all. They will not keep their cult to themselves and insist upon proselytizing others, which sets them at odds with the founding principles of the Republic, our rights as Romans, our tolerance for all people who accept Roman rule and for all cults excepts those that hate and oppose all other cults. To preserve such freedoms, it is sometimes necessary to use extreme force to end a rebellion and make peace among the people. Considering all that is at stake, five lives to put things right in Sinope would seem a bargain. Don't you agree?"

"Yes, your excellency," said Marcellinus.

"I know you, Gaius, as I would know my own son," said the governor. "I am sure that were it not for the Lady Makrina, you yourself would have discerned this prudent course and advised me of it. Don't worry. I won't hold this against you, and I'm sure the Lady Makrina won't either. You've done all that you could. She could not have asked for a better advocate."

"Thank you, your excellency," said Marcellinus.

Marcellinus waited until the governor left for town, before seeking out Makrina to break the news to her. He found her sitting in the women's tablinum with her mother and Eugenia. They were all surprised to see him. "I thought you had gone with the others, Gaius," said Hilaria.

"I've a few things to straighten up here before the festival," said Marcellinus. "May I have a word with Makrina?"

"Certainly," said Hilaria. She started to rise but Makrina rose instead and welcomed her mother to remain seated, then hurried to join Marcellinus at the door.

"Let's talk on the terrace," said Makrina.

They walked silently out of the house and onto the terrace, stopping by the steps leading down to the gardens, where for the first time in thirty years, Phokas could not be found. Once sure that they were alone, Marcellinus turned to Makrina, trying to appear as sympathetic as possible.

"I tried," he said sadly. "Your father tried, too. It's no use. There are just too many reasons for the governor to do something and not enough reasons to show mercy. I'm sorry, Makrina. I tried."

Makrina just looked at him, the worry in her face turning slowly to sorrow. He waited for her to speak but she said nothing and finally turned away to gaze out over the gardens.

"He was my friend," she said at last. "He was my guardian. He rescued me from snakes, soothed my bee-stings, and carried me home when I skinned my knees. He was the kindly giant who watched over my little girl's world."

Her voice failed and she wiped her eyes with the edge of her palla. She breathed deeply and swallowed to clear the knot in her throat. "What's to be done with him?" she asked.

Marcellinus hesitated, knowing how hard she would take it. Then he put his arm around her and clasped her shoulders gently. "The arena," he said. "At the festival, tomorrow afternoon."

Makrina twisted herself free. "The arena?" she said. "How could they? How could they?"

Marcellinus shrugged. "Pressure from above," he said. "I know it's harsh. I'm sorry."

"The devils!" Makrina hissed. "And all because poor Phokas happened upon that lascivious witch lying in wait!"

"It's all an unfortunate accident, Makrina," said Marcellinus, trying to calm her down. "Had Phokas not claimed to be a Christian and refused to sacrifice, he would have been spared as just an old man who spoke out of turn. As it is, he has doomed himself to suffer the same penalty as the others."

"The others?" said Makrina.

Marcellinus had not intended to mention the rest, but it was too late now. "Archelaos, Theogenes, and the rest," he admitted.

"In the arena?" asked Makrina.

Marcellinus nodded.

"Even Euphemia? Poor old Euphemia?"

Marcellinus nodded again.

"The devils!" shouted Makrina, glaring at Marcellinus ferociously. "The devils!" she shrieked, striking at Marcellinus's chest with her raised fists.

"The devils!" she cried, as he laid hold of her forearms and struggled to control her.

Then suddenly they were both aware of another presence on the terrace. They turned and saw Clea and Politta standing near, with parasols in hand, watching them in amazement. "Pardon us," said Clea. "We were just going to go for a walk in the garden."

Makrina pulled herself free from Marcellinus and launched over at Politta, swiftly landing her hand flat against the woman's cheek with a resounding *smack!* that knocked her into Clea's arms. "*SLUT!!!*" shouted Makrina, loud enough to be heard throughout the house. "*BITCH! WHORE!*"

"Great gods," Marcellinus moaned, as Politta and Clea staggered and bumped and poked each other with their parasols. Before they could recover, Makrina was gone.

Marcellinus was obliged to render aid to the aggrieved party and to escort the women into the house, where Clea presented him as a material witness in her complaint to their hostess, Hilaria. Politta was in tears on account of yet another unforgettable insult in the house of Aristoboulos, and the whole party would be moving immediately to the villa of Philodemos for the remainder of their stay in Sinope. Afterwards the women insisted that Marcellinus accompany them on their way to town for the procession, leaving much earlier than necessary.

Marcellinus knew what to expect in town and began to prepare his mind for what his fortune would require. He had finally lost Makrina, but after all that he had done for her, there was still a certain danger to be avoided.

They found the governor and Hippolytus visiting with Philodemos at his townhouse and wasted no time in rousing everyone to hear their accusation. "She's arrogant, she's insolent, she's *crazy*," declared the irate Politta, once the facts had been established. "And she's dangerous. I won't spend another minute in her company. No sane woman should. The whole household fills me with unease. Some evil lurks there. Some awful magic. Nowhere have I felt more unwelcome than in that house! I wouldn't be surprised if every one of them were Christian."

The governor looked at Marcellinus inquisitively.

"No, of course not," said Marcellinus, feeling unexpectedly on the spot to explain Makrina's behavior. "Makrina is young and rash and sometimes, yes, insolent. She is upset about losing a favorite servant. There's no excusing what she did. She's deserves to be punished by her parents, but her anger is easily understandable."

"But she is a Christian, Gaius," said Clea. "I know she is. I heard her praying in her rooms, and afterwards I saw her little painting of her god by her bed, and her little book of psalms. I confess I snooped a little, Uncle, but I was curious." She smiled at the governor with guilty pride.

"There you have it! She's an evil, arrogant atheist with no respect for gods or men," said Politta.

"Is this so, Gaius?" asked the governor.

"She is a Christian, your excellency," answered Marcellinus. "I can't believe she is evil, just misguided."

"Not after what she did?!"

"Peace, Politta," said the governor, who then turned to Marcellinus. "I don't recall her name on any of the lists you showed me. I'm sure I would have noticed had it been there," he said.

Marcellinus shrugged to avoid appearing to have anticipated the question, though indeed he had while on his way to town. "Her brother kept the lists. He must have left her off," he said.

"Has she sacrificed?" asked the governor.

"Yes, of course," Marcellinus lied. "I saw to it myself."

"It seems to have done her no good," said Politta. "Make her sacrifice again, your excellency. Make them all sacrifice to prove their loyalty and teach them respect."

"Oh, not the whole family or household, Politta, but perhaps young Makrina," said Hippolytus. "There is certainly no reason why she could not be required to sacrifice again. Perhaps it will humble her."

"Rather light punishment, I'd say," said Clea, "after what she's done."

"Enough, enough," said the governor. "We owe it to her father to consult him before passing judgement. At the moment it would appear that a public sacrifice and renunciation of the Christian cult by the young Makrina would be in order, if that would satisfy you, Politta?"

"Yes, your excellency, if she will do it," said Politta.

"I have no doubt she will when shown the consequences of her refusal," said the governor. "These recent incidents only prove how necessary it is that this obnoxious superstition is rooted out. I am dismayed and appalled that yet another leading household here in Sinope has been tainted by its evil. The people must be shown the seriousness of the matter, and the young Makrina could serve as an example of obedience."

"Either obedience or defiance," said Titus Statilius. "She has that in her."

"Indeed she does," said the governor, "but if she shows it, then we shall make her an example of justice, for the people must know that the law will be obeyed."

Marcellinus returned to the villa alone and on horseback, meeting Hilaria and her daughter Eugenia headed toward town in a canopy-covered carriage about a mile from the villa.

"Where is Makrina?" he asked.

"She wouldn't come and it's just as well, after this morning," said her mother.

"She *must* come, Lady Hilaria. She's wanted in town," said Marcellinus. "If you could return to wait for her, I will see that she's ready."

Hilaria ordered the carriage turned about while Marcellinus hastened on ahead. Arriving at the villa, he left his over-heated horse unattended in the courtyard and went to look for Makrina. The house was cool, dark, and quiet when he entered the atrium, as most of the servants had been given their leave to attend the opening of the festival. He took a moment in the atrium to wipe the sweat from his brow and catch his breath. His hair was tossed by the wind, and his face with red with sun and exertion.

"Makrina!" he called aloud.

The porter's assistant hurried to greet him. "She's in her rooms, my lord," he said.

Marcellinus marched straight to Makrina's rooms, nearly colliding with her in the entrance to her apartment. She gasped and backed away.

"Get your wrap. You're going to town," he ordered. She started to protest but he ignored her. "The carriage will be back any minute to take you. You haven't much time. Put your things in this bag. You won't be coming back tonight." He cast an empty linen bag on her bed.

"What do you mean?" she asked.

"They know you are a Christian and they are demanding that you sacrifice as punishment for your impudence. If you won't sacrifice, they will hold you accountable. I wouldn't test their ill will if I were you. They are determined to prove a point, and you've given them a perfect excuse with your childish, arrogant behavior. Your choices are to flee now or die with the others tomorrow."

"But where would I go?"

"Posidonios will see to that. Your father has made arrangements. Your mother knows nothing and your father doesn't want her to. First you must be seen in town with the others. It will be easier to slip away during the procession. I will carry your bag to town and deliver it to Posidonios. If there's anything else you'll need, it can be sent later, after the governor and his party leave and things settle down."

"But this is so sudden!"

"You've no choice if you want to live. Now pack your things."

"I do want to live, but there are some things more important than life in this world. It would be better for me to stay and bear witness with the others."

"I'm not going to let you, Makrina. I have sworn that you have sacrificed once already, and I'm not taking any chances that they will find out you haven't. If they do, I'm ruined. I will not die with you."

"So that's it," said Makrina bitterly. "You're not doing this to save me. You're doing this to save yourself."

Marcellinus reached forward and grabbed Makrina's ear, pinching it painfully with his thumbnail. She shuddered and cringed and looked at him in fear.

"Listen to me, Makrina," he said menacingly. "You are a vain, spoiled, foolish little girl with no real concern for others and a lot of silly, little-girl ideas about life. I have put up with you long enough and right now would just as soon see you win your heart's desire in the arena tomorrow. But I will not sacrifice all I've worked for for that brief pleasure! You will go to town with your mother, and you will follow Posidonios or whomever else to wherever they lead you. Now pack your things and get out of here!"

From faraway in the house Hilaria called for Makrina. Marcellinus led her by the ear to her wardrobe chest, forcing her to her knees before releasing his hold on her. "Open it," he ordered. Makrina pressed one hand against her injured ear and opened the chest slowly with the other hand. She was trembling and on the verge of tears. Her mother called again.

Marcellinus peered outside into the hallway, then turned back to Makrina. "Put whatever you want to take on the bed. I'll get it later. And don't take too much time. I'll be waiting in the atrium with your mother," he said. Then he left.

A little while later, Makrina appeared obediently in the atrium, with her head and shoulders already covered her palla. Marcellinus's look was hard and grim, a threat to ensure that she did as she was told. With barely a word of parting, he ushered the women to their carriage and watched it drive off. Then he returned to Makrina's rooms to collect her things.

The drive to town was silent and tense. Hilaria stared angrily out at the countryside. Makrina, sitting opposite Hilaria, seemed in a daze, rarely moving or raising her eyes. Twice Eugenia saw her steal a fearful glance at their mother. Once Makrina caught Eugenia watching her, but neither sister looked away. *What's wrong?* Eugenia wanted to asked, but didn't dare. Makrina just stared at her sadly, as if for the last time.

Not a word was said until they reached the town. The main street was crowded with people streaming from the surrounding area for the festival. On one corner just outside the forum, a group of adolescent boys milled about in high spirits, on the look out for friends and foes.

"Eugenia! Eugenia!" one youth shouted above the buzz of the crowd.

Hilaria's eyes narrowed upon a handsome, grinning boy being goaded to the fore by the elbows of his friends, all rakishly dressed for boys their age, in loose-fitting, adult-looking dalmaticas.

"Who is that?" Hilaria asked her daughter.

"I don't know, Mamma," answered Eugenia, but she did.

The forum was already packed with people awaiting the start of the procession. On the rostrum in front of the temple, an earnest orator was still delivering an energetic panegyric to the emperors, oblivious to his large but inattentive audience. A gaggle of little girls adorned with garlands and carrying baskets of blossoms traipsed by at his feet on their way to the temple.

The pious and the proud stood about with their fatted calves and goats and cocks, waiting for the end of the procession when the sacrifices would begin. Vendors circulated among them selling cups of water or wine from large, leather bladders strapped to their backs, and sesame-flavored bread rings stacked three feet high around wooden poles.

The press of the crowd forced the women to leave their carriage at the forum's edge and make their way through the crowd to the steps of the temple, where the city's leading citizens were assembling. Aristoboulos was already there, standing with the other members of the town council on the opposite side of the steps. He waved discreetly to his wife and daughters, but was prevented from greeting them by guards, who were keeping the entrance to the temple's sanctuary cleared for the idol's exit.

From her place on the steps, Makrina looked about for familiar faces in the crowd, wondering who would lead her away. She felt a bitter pang of spite when she spotted Clea and Politta in the place of honor, on the top step of the temple nearest the entrance, gabbing gayly with Demetra and the smug wives of other councilmen. Hilaria was there normally, but her late arrival left her only the lower steps on which to stand.

There were other reasons Hilaria did not claim her usual place, which pained Makrina more when she saw how somber her mother looked, in contrast to the gaiety of the other ladies. Without thinking, Makrina wrapped her arm around her mother's and lowered her head to her mother's shoulder.

"Makrina! Stand up straight," her mother chided. She was always one to insist on proper decorum, especially in public.

Makrina did as she was told, freeing her arm and stepping back so that her mother wouldn't see her wiping a sudden tear from her eye with her palla. Eugenia moved up a step to take Makrina's place beside her mother. From the opposite side of the steps, another boy waved and shouted her name.

Eugenia gave a little wave in return. Her mother looked at her reproachfully. "And who is *that?*" Hilaria asked.

Eugenia smiled and shrugged. Then, without looking, Eugenia reached back and clasped Makrina's hand, squeezing it tightly.

The orator finished his panegyric with barely a nod from the crowd and was followed by nothing immediately. Aware of the unexpected pause in the program, the crowd fell suddenly quiet. Everyone looked to the temple where the attendants were still burning large doses of incense in the bronze dishes at each corner of the temple's porch. Boughs of evergreens adorned the temple's facade. Then, without announcement, the drums began a steady beat. The crowd gave a cheer. The procession was soon to begin.

A moment later the trumpets sounded, and the crowd responded with a loud cheer that lasted as long as the fanfare. The forum fell silent. Then the drums began again. From the darkened entrance of the temple's sanctuary there emerged a singer cradling his gilded lyre in his arms. Then three arm-lengths behind him came an astrologer carrying an evergreen bough and a graven chart of the horoscopes. Next came a scribe wearing a winged helmet and carrying a book and a rule, and then the temple stole-keeper carrying a cup for libations, and then the local prophet, a squalid man in a tattered robe with a scraggly beard, long dirty hair, and overgrown fingernails. Quite a contrast the louse-ridden seer presented for the man who came after him, the newest High Priest of Serapis, His Excellency the Governor Sossianos Hierocles, dressed all in white except for the rings on his fingers and the gilding on his sandals. His fellow priests walked together behind him, and behind them came the gold-plated idol of Serapis, the larger-than-life figure of a beefy man with long hair and beard, seated on a throne and holding a tablet in one arm and a spear in the other. Cerberus, the three-headed dog of Hades, lay at his feet.

The crowd cheered wildly as the idol emerged from the temple, borne upon a raft on the shoulders of twenty-four strong men, all in white. The sea of people parted as the procession made its way slowly through the forum to the sound of trumpets and drums. The city council fell in line behind the idol, and councilmen's families fell in line behind them.

Clea and Politta descended from their perch, passing right by Hilaria without a glance or a greeting. The other wives and daughters followed after them before Hilaria herself joined the procession, with Eugenia and Makrina on her heels.

They hadn't gone far when Makrina felt a gentle hand on her arm. She turned to find Petra, the servant girl of the house of Posidonios.

"Please follow me, lady. My lord is waiting," said Petra. Makrina hesitated. "Please, lady. They said to hurry," said Petra.

Makrina let go of Eugenia's hand and started away with Petra, then stopped suddenly and looked back. Eugenia was watching her leave. "Where are you going?" she called to Makrina.

Makrina shook her head and turned away. "Wait!" shouted Eugenia, following after her.

Hearing her daughter's voice, Hilaria turned to see Eugenia disappearing into the crowd. "Genia!" she called through the din, but it was too late. The girls were gone.

Two hours later that afternoon, Aristoboulos was sitting by the fountain in the courtyard of his house in town, waiting for Hilaria to answer his summons. The noise of the festival could be heard from inside the house, but the house itself was quiet, until Hilaria stormed through the door and the atrium, with Eugenia trailing silently behind her.

"She's gone!" fumed Hilaria, throwing her palla off her head. "She's gone! Your daughter has run away, only the gods know where! She slipped away from me at the start of the procession and no-one's seen her since. I thought she'd merely met up with friends and was with them, but when it was all over she was nowhere to be seen. I had the servants look everywhere. Then finally *this* one here shows up as if nothing happened. Now she won't say a word except that she would have gone too if Makrina had let her, and she hasn't shown the slightest concern for the worry she and her sister caused me. Did you hear me, Aristo? Makrina's gone! She has run away!"

Aristoboulos rose to his feet without a change of expression. "Makrina is safe," he said. "There is nothing to worry about."

"Safe? But she has run away! How can she be safe?" Hilaria protested.

Aristoboulos lifted a finger to his lips. "Not so loud," he said. "Someone will hear. Makrina has gone for her own good. She had no other choice. She has escaped."

"Escaped? From what?"

"From Politta's revenge," said Aristoboulos. "They found out she was a Christian and were prepared to make her sacrifice. Punishment for her insult to Politta. To avoid having to sacrifice, she has fled."

"How do you know all this? Where have you been for the last hour?"

Aristoboulos again put a finger to his lips. "Don't ask," he said. "And don't talk about it—to anyone, at home or elsewhere." He looked at Eugenia. "Is that understood?"

"Yes, Pappa," she answered.

"But where is she?" whispered Hilaria.

"I don't know, but I'm sure she is in good hands. They have places to hide, these Christians. They'll take care of her."

"When will we see her again?"

"Sometime soon, when things settle down. It won't be long, I promise."

Hilaria put a hand to her forehead. "Oh, dear," she said. "I've lost my daughter, my dear little Krina."

"She'll be all right," said her husband, putting his arm around her.

"It's not supposed to happen this way, Aristo. I'm supposed to lose her to some young man like Gaius or Marcus who will make her happy, not to some god who makes her run and hide in fear for her life. I may never see her again."

"Of course, you will," said Aristoboulos. "It's just a matter of time. We must all be patient. Someday you will lose her to Gaius or Marcus or someone like them, and then we'll all be happy. I'm sure of it."

# XVII

The main road south from Sinope was as smooth and straight as any Roman military road, but the covered ox cart in which Makrina rode was crude and cramped. After traveling a few miles atop a wooden crate, feeling every paving stone that passed beneath the cart's wheels, Makrina begin to search about for something softer to sit on.

With the flaps shut tight both front and rear, the cart was surprisingly dark in the middle of the afternoon, and unbearably hot. Makrina quickly shed both the heavy traveling cloak Chione had given her and her light linen palla, but still it was a steam bath. Her fine silk gown was soaked with sweat and clung immodestly to her body, but who was there to see her? Only Simon, her driver, the grown son of the trader Bardas. Since leaving Sinope, Simon had not bothered to look in on her. Then, after fumbling in the darkness for a mile or more looking for a softer seat, Makrina was overcome by frustration and let out a plaintive, girlish yelp that no man could ignore. Simon parted the flaps in front. "Are you well, miss?" he asked.

Makrina remembered herself and answered unconvincingly that she was. After pausing for a moment to settle herself, she decided that Simon posed no immediate threat to her modesty and peeked out between parted the flaps to beg that the flaps be opened now. Simon checked the road ahead before giving his approval, but all he could see was his father's cart leading the way. "Not much chance of being seen now," he said.

Makrina threw back the flaps up front, then stumbled to the rear to do the same. The fresh air brought immediate relief, and the daylight let her see what she could not have seen before. Lashed to the side of the cart, almost hidden behind a bundle of farm tools, was a bundle of animal skins imported from across the sea. She quickly pushed aside the tools, loosened the lashing around the skins, and stowed the bundle in a convenient corner to form a relatively comfortable recline. Then she lay back to watch the countryside drawing away from her out the back of the cart.

With her family, Makrina had sailed to every major port on the Euxine Sea, but she had never traveled farther overland than from Sinope to the family's villa. Seeing the turn off to their villa fading slowly into the distance, Makrina knew she was now venturing beyond the limits of her world, in more ways than one.

She had left so abruptly, without a word to her mother and barely an embrace from Eugenia and Chione. Her bags had already been loaded onto the ox cart, the one packed by Marcellinus and another donated by Chione. Chione also passed along from Makrina's father a small leather moneybag and, more importantly, a leather pouch containing a vellum letter guaranteeing compensation for any expenses incurred on Makrina's behalf and offering a generous ransom to captors if she were delivered unmolested to her family. The offer of ransom was necessary to raise her value as a hostage above her value as a slave. No sooner had Makrina tucked these away in her cloak than she was rolling down the alley under cover, wishing she had taken longer to say farewell.

Her last encounter with Marcellinus would not leave her mind. How cruelly confident he had seemed, like an indulgent parent whose patience had finally run out, coldly meting out punishment to a deserving child. She had pleased herself by turning him away, yet it hurt her now to be dismissed by him so surely. His confidence in his criticism of her made her doubt herself. She had enjoyed her slap at Politta, but her memory of her own anger troubled her conscience and raised an accusation she desperately wanted to deny—that she had earned her exile.

By late afternoon, they had seen the last of the fields and orchards of the coastal plain and entered the deepening shade of the evergreen foothills. The temperature dropped as the sun began to set and the altitude rose. While the sky was still light, Bardas halted the company for a rest. Weary and sad and smelling of dried perspiration, Makrina covered herself with her palla and climbed down onto the road when certain that there was no one in sight. Simon and Bardas watered and fed the oxen, then set out a modest meal of flat, round bread and a chickpea paste on a saddle blanket spread upon the pavement behind Simon's cart.

"Where are we going?" asked Makrina, standing by the side of the road, with one hand clutching her palla tightly about her.

The burly Bardas brought down a crate from Simon's cart and set it beside the blanket for Makrina to use as a seat. "There's a place a few days from here in the mountains where you should be safe," he said. "They have offered refuge to others fleeing the edicts. Last time I heard, they had still escaped the notice of the authorities. Let's pray that's still so."

Makrina nodded silently and sat down gingerly on the crate. Still standing, Bardas made the sign of the cross and said a quick prayer over the food, at the end of which Makrina crossed herself and mumbled an amen. Simon offered her a piece of bread and paste. It was not unfamiliar food, but to Makrina it tasted a little too much of garlic.

"We'll rest here until the sun goes down," said Bardas, squatting down by the blanket and dipping a piece of bread in the paste. "Then we'll move again. It's not safe to spend the night on the road, and we'll need to keep moving through the night to make the caravansary by tomorrow evening."

"But when will you sleep?" asked Makrina.

"We won't," said Simon, passing her a cup of water mixed with a little wine.

"We'll rest a little before dawn and catch up on sleep tomorrow night," said Bardas. "The caravansary's safe and comfortable. You'll see."

Before the sun set, Simon rearranged the cargo in his cart to make a bed for Makrina. Then as soon as it was dark, they rumbled off again. Makrina curled up in the back under a bearskin and tried to pray herself to sleep, without success. Sleep came but her prayers were repeatedly disturbed by anxious thoughts and dreadful dreams.

Sometime before dawn, Makrina sensed that the carts had come to a halt. For an hour the world was still and quiet, except for snores from the lead cart. Gradually, the faint gray light of dawn grew through the cracks in the flaps. How long would they sleep? Makrina wondered.

Before long she heard the sound of someone moving about in the brush outside. She sat up and peeked out just as Simon was stepping down from the bank by the side of the road. His hair was matted and messy, and his eyes looked tired and puffy. Still he smiled when he saw her and wished her a good morning. "We'll be leaving soon," he said, glancing back up the bank. "I've a basin and towel if you'd like to wash up."

Makrina borrowed his basin and towel and carried them both along with a skin of water up the bank and into the pines. How wild the world seemed to her then, and how strange she felt, wiping away her makeup with the towel and gazing at the reflection of her unadorned face in the water in the basin. It was the same face she had seen in her fine silver mirror every morning at home, yet now it seemed flat and plain, the face of a girl fallen into the rough.

Bardas wished her good morning when she returned to the road, but Makrina barely noticed. Once again in her cart, she stared out at the silent timbers trooping by, her thoughts turning again and again to the events of the past days. Tired from worry and regret and her restless night, she dozed off at mid-morning and napped for more than an hour. The air in the mountains was cool and soothing, perfect for sleeping. She awoke refreshed and unburdened, until she recalled the fate of Phokas and the others who would be committed to the arena that afternoon. Reproving herself for forgetting her friends, she vowed to keep a vigil of prayer through the afternoon, to be sure to be praying for the souls of the witnesses in their hour of glory.

She very nearly kept her vow, despite her recurring regrets and the distractions of the journey. She was awed by the rugged beauty of the mountains, which she had only seen from a distance, and amazed that the sea and the coast were still sometimes visible from so far inland. Then, near noon, the road crested abruptly and began a gradual descent into the valley of the Amnias River, a tributary of the great Halys River, the longest in Asia

Minor. The sea and coast were seen no more, and mountains now separated Makrina from everything she knew. Almost everything.

The sun faded prematurely from view as the road twisted its way into a sudden, shaded gorge. The deeper they descended the darker it grew, until at last the road bottomed out at a narrow stone bridge across the swift and rocky river. It was nearly the first hour of night when the carts crossed the bridge and came within sight of the gloomy fortress where they would stay the night. Simon called back for Makrina, who poked her head out and immediately asked, "What's that?"

"The caravansary," answered Simon.

"That's a caravansary? But it looks more like a prison."

"It is, in a way," said Simon. "Once the doors are closed at night, no one leaves until everyone is satisfied that he has what belongs to him. You were expecting a proper inn?"

"I've never seen one before," said Makrina, gazing in awe at the high, strong, windowless walls of the caravansary. It was not really a fort, for there were no towers or parapets or ports for sentries or archers, just a single double-doored gate in one wall. There was not even a tiny spy-hole for the gatekeeper, for even a tiny hole could be used to pass stolen goods to accomplices outside. When the carts reached the door, Bardas was obliged to dismount and bang the large iron knocker. The doors swung open without delay, revealing a torch-lit court inside, with the warden and his guards standing by to receive them. Bardas climbed back up into his cart and drove his oxen through the gate, stopping just far enough inside for Simon's cart to enter behind him.

The courtyard was half full of carts and wagons parked neatly in rows to both sides of the gate. Makrina could see shadowy figures moving about among them, and here and there lamps peaked out through cracks in their covers. A company of latecomers had built a small fire in the yard and had filled the court with the smell of roasted chicken. Makrina felt suddenly hungry and was amazed that something as plain as chicken could smell so good.

"You'll have to get out now, while they take account of our goods," said Simon, climbing back up to his seat to help her out. Makrina quickly wrapped herself in her cloak and took Simon's hand as she climbed out over the driver seat and stepped down from the cart. Bardas accompanied the warden and his clerk to the first cart, naming the items he wished to declare and pointing them out to the clerk, who wrote them down in a wax tablet while the warden stood by holding a torch.

Soon they moved to the second cart and did the same, until coming upon the two bags belonging to Makrina. Leaving the clerk and the warden at the back of the cart, Bardas left the cart and walked around to Makrina and Simon. "Have you anything to declare?" he asked Makrina.

She looked at Simon and then again at Bardas. "What should I declare?" she asked.

"Anything you don't want to lose and think might be stolen, you should declare," said Simon. "On the other hand, anything you don't want the warden and his clerk to see, you shouldn't mention."

"No, nothing," said Makrina to Bardas, who then reported her answer to the warden and continued their inventory without inspecting anything of Makrina's.

Waiting in the darkness, Simon said, "So you've never seen a caravansary."

"No, never," answered Makrina.

"You haven't missed much, especially here," he said. "We'll stay with the carts tonight, but you'll have a room if there's one available. There should be. It's not too crowded."

Makrina looked around the court at the darkened two-storey loggia lining the walls of the fortress on all four sides. Above the loggia the walls rose two more storeys without any way to the top. "Is it safe?" she asked.

"Safer than you father's villa. Everybody here has an interest in keeping it that way. They only let in those who can pay—no vagrants. If there's any trouble, all you have to do is cry out and somebody will come running. No one gets away with anything in here."

When the accounts were settled, Bardas and Simon moved the carts into place while the warden showed Makrina to a room on the ground floor. "It's the best I can do at this hour," he said, handing her a small oil lamp. "Just be sure to keep the door bolted."

Surveying the room in the lamplight, Makrina wondered if the other rooms were any better or worse. Hers was a small cell barely big enough for its two low, wooden beds with thin mattresses of woven straw. A coarse woolen rug lay between them. Beneath each bed was an earthen chamber pot. When Makrina reached for one, a small black insect scurried across the rug and under the opposite bed. Makrina jumped and gasped. The lamp's flame flickered wildly as shadows dance around the room.

Makrina froze, and before long the light grew still. She waited a while longer without moving, then set her bags on the bed the bug had just left and sat down beside them. She sat there a long while scanning the floor for more surprises, but when none appeared she relaxed and began to think how she might make herself more comfortable after two days on the road. If she could not bathe, she could at least change her clothes. She set the lamp on the floor between the beds, then began unpacking the bag Marcellinus had packed for her, wondering with embarrassment if he had thought to pack her underclothes. He had.

It comforted her a little in this strange, dreary place to see her fine, familiar things. In a rolled palla, she found her carved ivory jewelry box, in which she found her grandmother's favorite earrings, the brooch her father had brought from Cherson, and the string of pearls Marcellinus had given her the previous summer. She examined each piece carefully in the lamplight before returning them to their place. Then she unfolded every article of clothing and neatly refolded them before returning them to the bag, where they could be kept free of the little black things that wandered about in the night.

She was shaking out a light cotton undertunic when she heard a heavy thump upon the rug and then the sound of something skittering across the floor under the same bed as the bug she had seen. Moving the lamp to the floor, she knelt down beside the bed and peered underneath it. Rolls of dust and their shadows obscured her view, but there was the bug making off toward the door, and there in the corner, where the bug had been, was a golden ring—Marcus's ring. "My God," she whispered with surprise. For so long it had lain neglected in the clutter on the table by her bed. Marcellinus must have thrown it into the bag loose, along with her little codex of psalms, which was also there.

Makrina looked around for a stick or staff with which to knock the ring out from under the bed, but finding nothing she instead pulled the mattress away from the corner, climbed up on it, and reached down between the slats of the bed to retrieve the ring. With a puff of breath, she blew away the dust and rubbed the ring clean against her tunic. She stared at it for a while, remembering the handsome young man she nearly married, wondering where he was now and where she would be if she had indeed married him. Life could have been so easy with Marcus, easier as an unbeliever, easier even as a less insistent Christian. But others had died that day for insisting upon the truth, for refusing to compromise, for seeking their salvation rather than their ease.

The thought upbraided her for her discomfort and self-pity. She put away the rest of her things, adding to the ivory box the armbands, anklets, necklet, and earrings she had worn since leaving home. But not the ring, which she slipped onto her index finger of her right hand.

Simon knocked at the door, bringing her a bowl of chicken soup and half a loaf of bread. "How much farther?" she asked him.

"Two more days, but don't worry," he answered. "Tomorrow night we'll spend with friends, God willing, and the night after that you'll be in your new home."

Makrina was so hungry she forgot about changing clothes. She ate the soup and bread alone, sitting on the bed in the lamplight. When she had finished, she set the empty wooden bowl and spoon in the far corner of the room to draw scavenging bugs as far away from her bed as possible. Then she made her palla into a pillow and curled up on the straw mattress, making sure to cover every inch of herself securely with her heavy cloak. Only when she was all settled did she remember her prayers. She tried to say them from where she lay, but before long her mind escaped into sleep.

Makrina was awaken the next morning just before first light by the general commotion in the courtyard. Everyone, it seemed, was up and about but her. She dressed quickly, throwing on the same silk gown she had worn since leaving Sinope. Then she hurried out with her bag to find Bardas and Simon picking through their carts in the spare light of dawn, verifying the presence of everything inventoried the night before. One by one the caravans sent word to the warden that everything was accounted for, and when all had done so, the warden ordered the gates opened. The carts and wagons began their creep toward gates in reverse order—first in, last out.

From the valley of the Amnias, Bardas and company continued south along the main road for ten leagues, crossing several smaller tributaries of the Amnias and Halys and gradually ascending the second range of mountains that paralleled the coast of Pontus. On the other side of the range, the road descended rapidly, zig-zagging many times before reaching a small village called Kargamon at the intersection of the road from Sinope and the provincial highway, just above a marshy basin that bordered the Halys on the north. To the west, the highway stretched a hundred leagues to Nicomedia, the provincial capital. To the east, it crossed the Halys at a distance of 15 miles and met the coast at Amisos after another 75.

About the tenth hour, Bardas pulled off the road from Sinope just short of the village and stopped the carts outside a large timber house with smoke curling from its chimney. Bardas and Simon dismounted and were greeted at the door by a gray-haired man of grave demeanor. Peaking through the flaps, Makrina could see the man's look of concern when Bardas explained their need. The man glanced once or twice in her direction, then suggested that they talk inside. Simon returned to help her out of the cart and carry her bags.

Inside the house, Makrina was introduced to Gerasimos and his wife Charita, a middle-aged woman with a kind smile and a round figure, modestly dressed with her gray hair parted in the middle and rolled up at the back. Charita excused herself to fetch her visitors wine and water, while Makrina and the men sat down in the large central room, lighted by two small windows on the opposite side of the house, looking out over the town and the valley. The house was modest compared to Makrina's home, with a floor of polished wood and plain paneled walls. But it was clean and well-furnished, with an odd collection of fine and simple things—chairs inlaid with ivory and enamel, lamps of brass and clay, and a crude wooden side table. The room smelled faintly of a wood fire.

Charita soon returned with a maid carrying a wooden tray of glass goblets, just as Gerasimos was explaining that their intended destination was out of the question.

"They have all fled elsewhere since the new governor arrived in Ankyra," he said. "The whole province of Galatia is too dangerous now. We have only escaped arrest by bribing the local curator, a petty and vain man who has already reached the limits of his competence. He now takes a third of my pension, and I expect soon he'll come back for more."

His age showed most in the dark hollows under his eyes. He spoke with the blended accent of an imperial official who had served in several parts of the empire, distinct from both the Pontic intonations of Bardas and Simon and Makrina's tutored, aristocratic Greek.

"There must be someplace else," said Bardas. "What about higher up in the mountains?"

Gerasimos nodded slowly. "There is a place I know across the border in the province of Cappadocia," he said. "It is not far but difficult to reach. I'd have to take her there myself. It's a humble little village, not what I would guess the lady is accustomed to, but it's safe, at least for now."

Bardas turned to Makrina and said, "I don't know anywhere else to take you, Makrina, and it may be too dangerous to travel too far into Galatia. Will you go with Gerasimos to this village?"

She looked at him with wide, helpless eyes. "If I must," she answered.

"Very well, then," said Bardas. "We'll leave you here with Gerasimos."

Their host explained that it would be better if Bardas and Simon did not stay at the house but moved to an inn in the village, where they would not arouse the suspicion of the curator. Finally, when they had emptied their cups, the two Sinopeans rose to go. Sensing Makrina's unease, Simon said, "Don't worry, Makrina. You're in good hands."

"The hands of God," said Bardas. "We'll be back through here every month and will let Gerasimos know when things change in Sinope. God willing, you'll be home before too long."

Afterwards, Charita showed Makrina to her room, which was quite an improvement over the caravansary. The bed was soft, the linens were fresh, and the floor by the bed was covered by a clean mat of plush wool. Charita set one of her bags atop a wooden chest and helped her off with her cloak. "You need a bath, child!" she exclaimed kindly. "Make yourself comfortable while I draw the water."

Makrina unwrapped her palla and folded it neatly, noticing its wrinkles before placing it on the bed. Then she loosened the silver chain-link cincture from around her waist and laid it with Marcus's ring on the palla. She sat down on the bed to untie her sandals and paused a moment to feel the soft, thick wool between her toes. Then she ran her hand across the smooth cotton pillowcase and felt the pillow's downy plumpness. With a weary sigh, she curled up on the bed, laid her head on the pillow, and closed her eyes.

She was almost asleep when the servant-girl knocked on the door and entered lugging a large wooden tub with brass fittings. "Excuse me, mistress," said the girl, setting the tub down on the floor. It was wide enough to sit in but only two feet high. When the girl left, Makrina sat up drowsily and looked around the room. On the wall above the bed she noticed a hand-size portrait of a man. It was expertly executed, though in a style Makrina thought strange and childlike. The face was round and the eyes were large, dark ovals. In one hand, the man held an open book. His other hand was raised in blessing.

Presently Charita returned with the first pail of hot water for the tub. "Where did you get this?" asked Makrina, pointing to the image.

"In Egypt, a long time ago," answered the pleased Charita. "Do you like it?"

"It's rather strange-looking," said Makrina.

"Perhaps it's not the best likeness of our Lord, but it reminds me of his presence," said Charita. "Looking at it I feel as if I'm looking at Jesus himself."

"When were you in Egypt?"

"When I was a young newlywed," said Charita. "It was our first posting together. Gerasimos worked in the office of the quaestor of the port of Alexandria."

The servant-girl returned with a second pail of water, and Charita left with her for more. Makrina stood and removed her tunic, the same one she had first put on the morning she accosted the lawless Politta. It smelled of sweat and mildew and was horribly wrinkled. She let it fall to the floor in a crumpled heap, then sat back down on the bed in her undertunic.

A few more pails of steaming water and the tub was ready. Makrina untied her long dark hair and shook out the tresses, then removed the rest of her clothes and left them in a pile with her tunic. Clutching a sponge to her chest, she stepped carefully into the tub. The water was comfortably hot. She sank down slowly into the steamy bath with a sigh of relief. She would have liked to have immersed herself entirely in its warmth, but she was satisfied to cover herself with water from the sponge.

Makrina lingered in the tub for nearly a quarter of an hour, resting her head on her folded knees and squeezing out the heavy sponge on her back over and over again. Charita came by with a large, warmed towel and helped to rinse and oil her hair. Afterwards Makrina sat on the bed wrapped in the towel while Charita combed her hair out.

Charita was not so large that she did not notice the lump that had rolled beneath her when she sat down on the bed. "What's this?" she said, finding Marcus's ring. "A man's ring. Your father's?"

"No," said Makrina, taking the ring from Charita and slipping it again onto her index finger. She held her hand out to look at it, as Charita began combing her wet hair. "It belonged to a young man I almost married. He gave it to me when he left a long time ago. I've not heard from him since."

"I'm sorry to hear that," said Charita. "He must have broken your heart."

"Oh, no," said Makrina. "I broke his. We were nearly betrothed before I was baptized, and after that I couldn't marry him because he was not a Christian. So I sent him away."

"Then you must have broken your own heart," said Charita. "You must still love him to be wearing his ring."

Makrina sighed. "It was with my things," she said. "I found it again just last night. I haven't thought of him for many months."

"I see," said Charita. "Have you given up praying for him?"

"Yes," said Makrina.

"You should never give up praying for someone. No one is beyond hope, and your prayers can only help him."

"I know, I know," said Makrina, guiltily. "It just seemed so pointless, even foolish, to keep praying for him. I had to give him up. I had to admit to myself that he wasn't coming back. I had to abandon the hope that he would."

"I understand, Makrina," said Charita. "You had to go on with your life. You had to learn to live without him. But you can do that without abandoning hope, and I'd guess you haven't really abandoned hope, have you? You would still want him to believe, wouldn't you?"

"Yes," said Makrina. "I would still want that."

"And maybe even return to marry you?"

"Maybe," said Makrina.

"Then you should pray for that," said Charita.

"Even when it's foolish to expect to get what I want?"

"Then most of all, if it's your heart's desire," said Charita. "Are we ever more humble, more childlike before God than when we plead for things we know we can't expect from Him? Without arguments about why we deserve it, without feeling that He owes it to us? We just want it. Even when we see the vanity of our desires, we still want it, and all we can do is confess our wants in all humility, and we plead for His mercy, like a child who begs for a toy he dearly desires but knows he doesn't deserve. How much more will a father pity a child who knows he doesn't deserve what he asks for than one who comes insisting that he does?"

"But how can I pray for something just because I want it when there are so many more important things, when people I know and love are dying for their faith? When I left Sinope, five of my friends, one who was very dear to me, were condemned to the arena. It seems so selfish and vain of me to be asking God for things that really don't matter, when others are pleading for their lives and salvation. I can't pray for these silly things that I just want while they endure such pain and death."

"Pray for your friends, too," said Charita. "Pray for their strengthening and perfection. But don't hide your heart's desires from God because you're ashamed of them."

"But shouldn't we want only the important things? Shouldn't we as Christians be free of desire for the things of this world that enslave the unbelieving?"

"God made us to desire some things—food and shelter and safety—and companionship, too. We should not be enslaved to such desires and sin to satisfy them, but there is no shame in the desires themselves, only in not desiring better things more. Our Lord himself desired to be spared the cup, but he desired even more to please the Father and to save us. And when he prayed to the Father in the garden, before his betrayal, he didn't hide his desire to live from the Father, did he?"

"No."

"Neither should we hide our desires, our hearts, from God," said Charita. "What good can that do? My husband Gerasimos and I worked a long time to have this house. I want to continue living here with him in health and safety. I know I should be able to live happily in Christ without the house or my husband. Should I then not pray for either?"

"But of course you should pray for your husband, for his health and safety and comfort," said Makrina.

"But what about the house, Makrina? What about my comfort?" said Charita. "I don't want to live anywhere else, with or without Gerasimos, and I know I will be very sad if we ever have to leave this place. Should I pretend to be stronger than I am? There may come a time, child, when all that you desire is what really matters, the important things, as you say. But until that time, it is wrong for you hide everything else in your heart from God, for it is only by giving over every part of yourself in prayer to God that you can free yourself of the things that draw you elsewhere. Prayer is not a way to get what we want or need, Makrina. It is our life with God. We pray because not to pray is to turn away from God, to hide from God. The things we want or need and don't pray for, those things we hide from God. Sometimes we hide the things we love most from God. It's as if we say to

God, 'I don't need you for that. That will come on its own.' But nothing good really comes on its own, does it? Everything good comes from God. And so every blessing should be offered back to God in prayer. So pray for this young man, whoever he is. Pray all your life for him, and whatever happens, you will both be better for it."

Makrina sat silently while Charita finished braiding her hair.

"What about your parents? Do you pray for them?" asked Charita.

"Sometimes," said Makrina sheepishly, "but they don't seem any closer to the faith than he did."

"Pray for them anyway. They're probably closer than you think just because they have you for a daughter, so keep praying for them. There now," said Charita. "How does that look?" She handed Makrina a shiny brass mirror.

Makrina examined the neat and stylish buns on each side of her head, then nodded and smiled at Charita. She really did like looking pretty, though she knew looking pretty wasn't one of the important things.

"You're a beautiful girl, Makrina, and very courageous for what you've done. Just don't let your pride keep you from prayer," said Charita. "It's almost time for supper now. We're so happy to have you with us. I only wish you could stay longer."

The three of them—Makrina, Charita, and Gerasimos—reclined for supper in one corner of the central great room of the house. After her plain, meager rations on the road, Makrina was starved for nourishment and delighted with the changed fare. She ate more than she thought polite and felt a twinge of embarrassment and guilt.

Charita talked cheerfully with Makrina during the meal. Gerasimos was polite but quiet and serious. Toward the end of the meal, he mentioned that there would be a caravan leaving for Amisos on Thursday, which they would need to follow for safety's sake as far as the bridge over Halys before setting off into the mountains. Charita was not pleased. "She's only just arrived, dear. Let her stay a while and rest," she said.

"She will be noticed in the village. The curator may take an interest," said Gerasimos.

"Even so, she needs to rest," replied Charita. "It's not as if we'll be parading her around the marketplace. She'll stay right here with me. Only the servants will see her."

"The servants talk. Everyone in the marketplace will know anyway," said Gerasimos.

"It will take some time before the curator or anyone else of consequence finds out, and she needs the rest before starting out on a journey through the mountains."

Gerasimos exhaled and relented. "Very well then," he said. "We'll leave Friday, but no later."

Feeling suddenly unwelcome, Makrina felt a sharp pain deep in her heart that made her want to break out in tears, but Charita distracted her with kind conversation and by the end of the meal she felt better.

Before bed, Makrina began her evening prayers as usual, standing with her arms uplifted before the cross and childlike image of her Lord, but soon she was on her knees begging her Father in heaven for forgiveness. She prayed for Marcus and her parents, that they believe and be saved. She prayed for Charita, that she keep her house, and for Gerasimos, that he not suffer for harboring her. She prayed for the safety of Bardas and Simon and Chione and her parents. She asked Phokas and the others who now stood before the throne of God to intercede for her. She even prayed for Marcellinus, that he be corrected and redeemed. For herself, she requested strength and wisdom and comfort and safety, and a speedy return home.

# XVIII

The next morning Makrina ate some dried olives and bread with olive oil. She would have liked to have had cheese and goat's milk as well, but it was Wednesday, a day when Christians fasted from meat and milk, to remember Christ's betrayal. In the morning she visited with Charita while her hostess was at work weaving a large carpet to cover the floor of the great room. They could have bought one made in India or elsewhere in Asia, but Charita wanted a particular color and design and enjoyed doing it herself.

Gerasimos returned after lunch with a pair of heavy leather sandals, new and undyed from the local leather-worker, in a size for boys, thought Makrina. "You will need these where you are going," he told her. "Soak them in water and wear them wet as much as you can while you're here to break them in."

Charita had a servant douse the sandals with water in the garden and then return them to Makrina, who tried them on. They felt cold and stiff and strange, and they looked ridiculous on her little feet. She had never worn anything like them, wet or dry. Even boys in Sinope wore lighter sandals. The sole was as thick as her thumb and the wide straps over the instep and around the ankle were rough underneath. By comparison, the sandals she had worn from home looked flimsy and effete. Was life so hard where she was going that her own sandals would not survive?

The new sandals worried her and embarrassed her in front of the servants, who snickered at the sight of the fine mistress so humbly shod, but she wore them anyway, as instructed. After all of Thursday wearing them around the house, the sandals seemed stiff as ever, but her feet and ankles were red and blistered. She realized then that wearing the sandals around the house was intended more to toughen her skin than to soften the sandals.

Friday morning Gerasimos announced that the next caravan heading west for Amisos would leave early Saturday. They dare not wait any longer, he said. The whole village was talking of the pensioner's beautiful "niece" with the funny sandals. Makrina was not surprised but disappointed. Among other things, she had prayed that she be allowed to stay longer in the house.

That day Charita made sure that Makrina was ready for her early-morning departure, seeing that her clothes had been washed, dried, and packed; providing her with additional garments she would need on the road and at her destination; and preparing the victuals they would take with them.

Later in the day, Charita sent all of the servants out for the afternoon so that she and Makrina could spend some time alone. They sat in the great

room by an open window while Makrina read aloud to Charita from a codex of the Gospel according to the Apostle Matthew, which Charita kept
hidden in her room. When they had tired of reading, they sat and talked
quietly together for almost an hour.

"What is this place like where I'm going," asked Makrina.

"I don't know. I've never been there. You'll have to write and tell me,"
said Charita.

"You're not going there with us?" asked Makrina with surprise.

"I'm afraid not, dear. It's a difficult journey for an old woman like me,
and Gerasimos is so secretive about it, he never takes more than one or two
companions with him," said Charita. "But don't worry. It's so out of the way,
it's bound to be safe. And Gerasimos speaks quite well of the people there.
They are all Christian, every last one of them—an entire village that makes
an Assembly."

"That would be nice," said Makrina. "Imagine a Christian town or province. What if the whole empire were Christian?"

Charita smiled at Makrina's fancy. "There you have something else to
pray for," she said.

Early the next morning Charita woke Makrina in the midst of a dream that
wouldn't leave her—that Marcus instead of Gerasimos was leading her to
her new home in the mountains. She put it out of her mind as she dressed
by lamplight in the clothes Charita had provided her—a plain, undyed, ankle-length undertunic; a slightly shorter gray overtunic with long sleeves;
a simple wine-red cord tied around her waist; and a long, hooded cloak of
coarse charcoal-colored wool—but the dream returned again while she was
sitting half asleep on her bed waiting for a servant to carry her bags outside
to Gerasimos. It was a haunting hope, and its impossibility was painful.

The sky had just begun to lighten when Makrina stepped outside into
the brisk early-morning mountain air. She covered her head with the hood
of her cloak and watched while Gerasimos secured her bags to the saddle
of a mule, one of two standing mute and motionless in the dim light of
dawn, as if still asleep. The houseboy holding the reins yawned, and so did
the maid standing silently with Makrina and Charita. Only Gerasmios's
Cretan hound Rama seemed eager to be up at that hour, stretching and
scratching and nosing about curiously near the mules. Gerasimos shooed
him away with a grunt and a stamp of his foot.

At first, all that Makrina could see of Gerasimos was the whitish hair
on his head. Then, as the darkness ebbed before her eyes, she could tell that
he was wearing open-toed boots, britches, and a short hooded cloak over a
long-sleeve tunic. A large hunting knife was attached to one side of his belt,
and, to Makrina's surprise, a short, sheathed sword hung from the other

side. He seemed not so old now and hardly feeble as he went about rigging the packs of the mules with grim vigor. When all was ready, he turned to Makrina and said, without even a quick good-morning, "Can you ride?"

Makrina gaped and stuttered. "I guess so," she said. "I haven't ridden since I was a girl."

"The mules are tame and slow. You shouldn't have much trouble," he said. Then he turned to his wife and told her when to expect him back.

"Go with God," said Charita to her husband. They kissed and then Gerasimos went to wait by the mules for Makrina. Charita hugged Makrina tightly and kissed her lips and cheeks. "May God bless you, child. Never stop praying. Pray unceasingly," she said.

Makrina nodded and thanked her for her kindness and hospitality. Then Gerasimos showed her where to hold on and what to do as he boosted her up onto the saddle. Her nervousness atop her mount distracted her from the sickness she felt at leaving. She glanced over her shoulder for reassurance from Charita, but did not dare let go of the saddle to wave farewell. Charita smiled and waved as Gerasimos led both mules slowly down the road into the sleeping village. In no time at all, they had joined the small convoy of carts and wagons—Makrina counted seven—waiting in line on the provincial highway. Gerasimos left the mules with one of the drivers while he went to report their readiness to the wagonmaster. When he returned, he had good news for Makrina. "You can ride in the rug cart if you prefer," he said.

He helped her down from her precarious perch and then into the last cart in the line, in which lay of tightly rolled wool carpets. Makrina made herself comfortable as best as possible, and Gerasimos returned to the mules. They waited another quarter hour for no known reason before the caravan began to move. Gerasimos fell in line behind the rug cart, riding the lead mule. It was almost dawn. Out of the back of the rug cart, Makrina surveyed the little roadside village she had only seen from above. Once the sun had risen and the village had disappeared, Makrina succumbed to the monotony of the journey and fell asleep.

The caravan moved east along the provincial road, paralleling the river Halys for twenty miles before crossing the river when the river turned suddenly north. At the stone bridge across the Halys, the caravan stopped and the lowered buckets into the river to bring up water for the animals. Makrina leaned out of the cart to look around. Mountains rose in all directions around the river's narrow gorge. A strong, cool breeze flowed up the gorge from the north. It was a beautiful day.

Gerasimos brought back two buckets for the mules, but offered Makrina a drink first. Makrina balked at drinking straight from the bucket, and Gerasimos was obliged to fetch a tin cup from his kit for her to use.

"You'll have to ride the mule the rest of the way," he said. "We'll be leaving the caravan shortly."

When he went to water the mules, Makrina climbed down from the cart on her own, sparing him the bother. She was standing in the sunlight on the bridge when Gerasimos's hound Rama loped over for a sniff. "Where have you been?" she asked the beast, fending him off with her hand wrapped in her cloak. The dog nosed his way into the lead mule's bucket until the mule rebuffed him with a snap of its teeth. The dog backed off and went to try the other bucket, where he found no more welcome. Poor thing, thought Makrina. Then she saw Gerasimos take the nearly empty bucket away from one of the mules and give it to the dog. Soon the buckets were put away and Makrina was back on her saddle, rocking rhythmically across the bridge and up the bank on the other side, where the road followed the valley of a tributary into the province of Cappadocia, which under Diocletian stretched hundreds of miles across inland Asia Minor, from the Cilician Gates in the south to the Euxine Sea coast as far east as Trapezos and Athenae.

Not far from the Halys, Gerasimos overtook the cart they were trailing and signaled to the driver that they were leaving the caravan. Then he turned and led Makrina's mule off the road to the north and down a steep path that seemed to lead down toward the tributary. Once out of sight of the caravan, he stopped and dismounted. "We'll wait here until they're out of sight," he said to Makrina.

Seeing that he was in no hurry, Makrina slid down from her saddle and disappeared into the pines that lined the path. When she returned, Gerasimos, sitting on a rock, offered her some cheese and bread. She ate silently, while sitting on a another large rock by the path. Then he repacked his kit, helped her back onto her saddle, and turned the mules around to head back up to the road. Once sure that the road was clear, they crossed to the other side and descended another path leading down to the Halys. They followed the Halys south for a mile, with the bridge clearly visible. Coming to the mouth of another tributary, they turned east away from the Halys and followed the tributary upstream for several miles.

Before long, Makrina was out of sight of civilization. All around her was the rocky riverbed and the dry, thin Anatolian forest. The path before them was barely more than a way through the rocks, unimproved and unmarked except for the hoof-prints of a previous journey. On this leg of her travels, there was no time for napping or idle daydreams. Their crooked, uneven course required her constant attention, and there were many sights along the way to excite her fears—big, deep, clawed paw-prints in the earth, scatterings of animal bones, a dead fish washed up on the pebbles, and the desiccated, half-devoured carcass of some small, fur-covered creature. Rama the hound didn't miss a scent, while Gerasimos kept a close watch around them. On his saddle, within easy reach, were a whip, a bow, a quiver of arrows, and a hatchet. Makrina prayed for safety and kept watch also, dropping her hood to see and hear better.

Late in the afternoon, they reached a large, placid pool beneath what must have been a waterfall in the spring. There they camped for the night on the far edge of the pool, partially sheltered by the ledge of the dry falls. Gerasimos gathered wood for a fire while Makrina washed her hands and face in the pool. Their supper consisted of cheese, dried and salted venison, hard scraps of day-old bread, and soft, moist raisin cakes Charita had prepared especially for their trip. Nothing needed cooking, but the fire was needed anyway to ward off animals. They ate silently and waited while the sun set and the shadows closed in on them.

"It's now the Lord's day," said Makrina, sitting on her saddle blanket with her cloak draped over her bent knees.

Stretched out on his own saddle blanket, Gerasimos just grunted and stared at the fire. The nearby stream kept up its constant clatter, plunging over the ledge into the pool.

"How much farther?" Makrina asked.

"We'll be there tomorrow," said Gerasimos. "It's just over the ridge, in the next valley."

"That close? Charita said it was out of the way."

"It's a difficult climb over the ridge," said Gerasimos. "You'll have to do it on foot. And it's the only convenient way in and out of the valley. This ridge here forms a spur that diverts the Halys westward about thirty miles. The stream on the other side meets the Halys about sixty miles upstream from the provincial road and there isn't a decent bridge anywhere near it. It's out of the way, and it should stay that way."

With that, he rested his head on his bed roll and closed his eyes.

"Are there bears in these woods?" asked Makrina.

Gerasimos opened his eyes briefly and closed them again. "Of course," he said.

"Wolves?"

"Yes," answered Gerasimos. A moment of silence passed, and Gerasimos opened his eyes to see Makrina staring fearfully into the darkness. "You won't see any bears or wolves," he said, closing his eyes for the third time. "You won't see any mountain lions either, but they're the greater danger. That's what Rama's here for."

Makrina looked at the sleeping hound lying between them. *What can he do?* she wondered.

"He'll smell them before we see them," said Gerasimos, his eyes still closed. "And if one attacks, he'll die defending us. You'd better sleep now. It will be a difficult morning."

Makrina looked at Rama again, suddenly seeing the friendly beast in mortal battle in her mind. The sun was well down by then, and the darkness was complete except for their fire. Makrina stared at the flames for a while, and then, softly and uncertainly, she sang the ancient evening hymn, hesitating now and then to listen in the darkness:

> O gladsome Light of the holy glory,
> Of the immortal Father,
> Heavenly, holy, blessed Jesus Christ;
> Having come to the setting of the sun
> And beheld the light of evening,
> We praise the Father, Son, and Holy Spirit as God.
> At all times Thou art worthy of praise in song
> As Son of God, Giver of Life,
> Therefore the world glorifies Thee!

When the hymn was ended, she curled up under her cloak and closed her eyes, praying silently for a guard of angels to protect them from all harm through the night.

Makrina slept fitfully on the hard ground, waking repeatedly and dozing again when reassured that all was well. She resisted rising after first light until she realized that Gerasimos was gone. In her drowsiness, she had mistaken Rama's snores for Gerasimos's. Alarmed she sat and looked around. He was nowhere to be seen, but the fire had been rekindled and everything else was in place. When he did not appear immediately, she got up and went to the pool to wash the sleep from her eyes, then tripped off into the woods a short distance to relieve herself. She returned as quickly as possible and was greeted by Rama, now awake as ever. Then she sat down again on her saddle blanket and waited.

Before long, Gerasimos returned with two small fish dangling from a line. "Good morning," said Makrina, trying hard to smile. Gerasimos just grunted and then told her to stoke the fire while he cleaned the fish. Makrina did as she was told and then watched with fascination while Gerasimos finished scraping the scales from the fish with his knife, then cut off the heads against a flat rock and gutted the underbellies. It was not a pleasant sight for Makrina, and seeing Rama gobble down the guts nearly made her sick.

Lastly Gerasimos pierced each fish with a forked stick he had already prepared and handed one to Makrina. "Hold it close to the flame, but not too close," he said. "Always keep the stick pointed up and don't let it burn. And be careful that Rama doesn't get the fish before you do."

They roasted their fish from opposite sides of the fire until the smoke forced Makrina to move closer to Gerasimos. His repeated corrections of her hold on her fish discouraged her desire for conversation. Instead, remembering that it was Sunday, she turned her thoughts to the Sundays she had known in Sinope before the persecution began. "Your stick's on fire," warned Gerasimos, pulling her stick away from the fire and blowing out the flames. "Now watch what you're doing or you'll have no breakfast."

When the fish had cooked long enough, Gerasimos scraped them off onto a wooden plate. Makrina picked at her fish carefully, trying not to dirty her fingers, but it was unavoidable. Afterwards, she hastened to wash them in the pool. Gerasimos was already packing their things and saddling the mules.

The gray morning sky did not clear before they started moving upstream again. They traveled on foot, leading the mules, for half a mile before turning up a narrow hollow south of the main stream. The hollow rose gradually at first, where the banks of its brook were still wide enough to tread upon. Farther up the sides of the hollow steepened and the bed of the brook rose like a stone staircase, with just a trickle of water seeping through the clogs of pine needles and debris. It was difficult enough at first for Makrina, mounting each slippery step with her tunics pulled high above her knees. Then the mules began to lag and Gerasimos put Makrina up front where she could pull on the reins of the lead mule while he beat its hindquarters with his crop while pulling the trail mule up behind him. Twice she slipped and fell, once skinning her shin on a jagged rock. She cried out in pain and sat down where it was dry to examine her wound. Down below Gerasimos waited impatiently for her to recover, but when it appeared she would not move again without encouragement, he climbed up to her and pressed a rag against the scrape to stop the bleeding, then helped her to her feet again, trying not to sound too annoyed while assuring her that it was nothing to worry about.

After a long and difficult hour of struggling up the trench, they reached an impassable pocket where the ground rose too steeply to climb any farther, even on hands and knees. Makrina stood helplessly as before a wall, wondering how they could ever go any farther. Her face was streaked with mud from trying to wipe away sweat with her dirty hands. She was out of breath and panting heavily, unaccustomed to both the exertion and the altitude. Her head was light from the thin air, and her spirit was overwhelmed with a feeling of being trapped in a hole with no way out. "Lord have mercy," she moaned, on the verge of tears.

"This way," said Gerasimos, pushing past her onto a ledge to her right. Makrina turned and watched him lead her mule out of the pocket by tacking across the side of the trench in the opposite direction. The trail mule followed without leading, and Makrina fell in behind it. Quickly and easily they climbed out of the trench and ascended the spur by walking along the spur's slope instead of straight up it. Makrina's confinement anxiety ebbed away in the openness of the wooded slope, where the only obstacles were tangles of thickets that were easily avoided. A carpet of dry pine needles presented a slipping hazard, causing Makrina once to lose her footing and fall. She landed softly on the same needles, but tore her tunic and scratched her cheek on a fallen branch. This time she recovered quickly and caught up with Gerasimos at the crest of the spur. "Can we rest here?" she asked between breaths.

"Not yet," said Gerasimos. "We'll rest on the ridge." They started immediately up the back of the spur, with the ground sloping away on both sides. Makrina followed at a slower pace. It was another three hundred paces before they reached the ridge line, and by that time, Makrina had almost lost sight of Gerasimos among the trees. Rama kept her company, though.

When she reached the top, Gerasimos was sitting on a log, catching his breath while keeping an eye on her slow but steady progress. Exhausted, she sank down onto the ground, holding herself up with one hand. Gerasimos fetched a skin of water from one of the mules and offered her a drink. She drank straight from the spout without hesitation, eagerly and clumsily, spilling water down the front of her cloak and tunic. When she had had enough, she handed the skin back to Gerasimos, who poured some water out on the ground for Rama, then sat down on the log and took his own drink. Still panting, Makrina tugged at the straps of her sandals. Her feet were wet and dirty and rubbed raw in spots.

"Don't take them off," said Gerasimos. "Your feet would swell and you'd never get them back on." He watched her pick burs off her cloak and tunic for a moment, then said, "You held up well."

She looked up at him. His expression had not changed, but it was the first kind word Gerasimos had said to her since she had entered his house. "How much farther?" she asked

"The village is just down in that valley," he said. "There's a trail leading down to it. It will be easier from here."

"How do know so much about the woods?" she asked.

"I grew up in the woods," said Gerasimos. "My father was a hunter and a guide for nobles who came to these parts to hunt for sport."

"But you were in the imperial service," she said.

Gerasimos nodded wearily, his age suddenly showing in the sagging wrinkles of his face. "My mother's ambition for me," he said. He looked away into the woods. "I might have left the service for this at one time, but then I met Charita and the security of the imperial service won out over other desires. It took me twenty years to return."

"Do you regret not returning earlier?"

"Not really," said Gerasimos. "Now I have a pension that enables us to live fairly comfortably in these parts. At least it did before the bribes."

"You pay the local curator to avoid having to sacrifice?"

"I pay him to keep my wife from having to sacrifice," said Gerasimos. "I am not a Christian, never have been."

"You're not? I assumed you were," said Makrina.

Gerasimos shook his head and said, "Charita was not when we married, nor for many years afterward. I was consumed with my duties then, and we were unable to have children and in her loneliness she turned to Christian friends. I was so busy in my own world that I hardly noticed at the time."

"Did you mind her becoming a Christian?"

"Not until it was too late," said Gerasimos. "Oh, we had some fierce fights for sometime afterwards, but she never gave up on me and I could never give up on her. She was always a good and dutiful wife, although perhaps a little young and selfish when we were first married. Joining the Christian Assembly gave her a kind of hope and comfort I couldn't give her, but instead of drawing her away from me, I noticed she only became more dutiful and devoted as a wife. Maybe it was just a matter of maturity. I don't know. But it made me more yielding towards her, more accepting of her faith and her friends."

"But did you ever consider joining her in the Assembly?"

"I never cared for cults or clubs of any kind," said Gerasimos. "I worked for forty years within a very prestigious and demanding club, putting up with all manner of annoyances and abuses, from superiors and subordinates alike. I'm happy now to be done with such associations. Charita is my society now. I want no other."

"So you do this—helping other Christians—for her sake," said Makrina.

Gerasimos nodded. "Her happiness is mine," he said. "That's all that still matters to me anymore."

As promised, the walk down the mountain was quick and easy. It might even have been pleasant for Makrina, had not been for her aching feet, her tired legs, and her low spirits. With the sky still overcast, she had no idea what hour it was when she caught her first glimpse of the village below through the trees. It was not an encouraging sight: a crowded cluster of stone cottages with rough-hewn timber roofs covered with pine bark. No bricks, no stucco, no finished wood.

Seeing the look on her face, Gerasimos said, "The Christ was born in a village such as this, wasn't he? In a stable even." Makrina stared at the village a moment longer, then made the sign of the cross and continued on.

"The people here are very poor," explained Gerasimos. "Most are illiterate. They speak a dialect that mixes Greek and a barbarian tongue. You should be able to make yourself understood. The headman and elder of the village is named Gregorios. He can read, write, and speak Greek. His wife's name is Anna. You'll be staying in their house."

"What is the village called?" Makrina asked.

"They call it *Oeki*, which means simply 'Home.'"

Children met them at the edge of village—pathetic looking children with dusty hands and bare, dirty feet. The littlest ones were completely naked, and the rest were clad in tattered tunics crudely cut from cast-off adult clothes. They were the poorest children Makrina had ever seen, poorer even than the children of beggars in Sinope. They swarmed excitedly around their visitors, chattering incomprehensibly, curious but careful to keep a respectful distance.

"Wait here," said Gerasimos, leaving Makrina surrounded by children, holding the reins to the mules, while he went to speak with two women, one about Makrina's age and the other much older, who had appeared outside a nearby cottage. Makrina saw the women bow to Gerasimos and Gerasimos bow in return.

While Gerasimos and the older woman spoke, the younger one and Makrina exchanged stares. The girl's face was plain and unadorned, with thick, dark eyebrows that appeared never to have been plucked. Her dress was not much better than the children's. Her once colorful tunic had worn thin and pale, and the kerchief tied securely over her head was greatly frayed. Like the children, she was barefooted.

From elsewhere in the village, more children came running, scattering the chickens that pecked about in the dusty lanes between the cottages. Women appeared in other doorways to see about the commotion. Some stared, some called out others and then returned quickly to their work.

Before long, Gerasimos returned with the older woman, whom he introduced as the widow Ioanna, the daughter of Gregorios. The woman bowed respectfully but said nothing. "The men are out with the herds, but it makes no difference. I have told Ioanna of your need and she says you are welcome to stay as long as necessary," said Gerasimos.

"Your are most kind," said Makrina to Ioanna. The woman nodded, still without speaking.

"I'll get your things," said Gerasimos.

The woman looked about at the crowd of children. "Titos, Nicanor, help Master Gerasimos," she ordered. Two boys jumped to Gerasimos's side and waited eagerly for him to hand down Makrina's bags. Undaunted by their burden, they trudged off proudly toward the cottage with her bags weighing heavily upon their backs.

"I'll be back before too long, within a month I'm sure," said Gerasimos, taking the reins from Makrina.

Makrina glanced at Gerasimos's kit still packed on the back of the lead mule. "You're not staying the night?" she asked.

Gerasimos shook his head. "With the men away, no, and I must be getting back. If I leave now, I can be over the ridge before sunset," he said.

"So soon? But—but—"

"You are safe here. Ioanna will take care of you. I'll see you in a few weeks. You are in kind hands," said Gerasimos. Then he turned to Ioanna and said with a bow, "Thank you, dear woman. Farewell, Makrina."

He wasted not another moment before turning the mules around and heading out the way they had come, with Rama trotting dutifully behind. Makrina watched him leave in silence, standing there with Ioanna and the children until he disappeared among the trees at the edge of the wooded slope.

"Come, we eat," said Ioanna, guiding Makrina toward the cottage.

The ground floor of the cottage served as a pen for animals. The top floor was accessible two ways, by ladder inside the cottage and by stone stairs outside. Ioanna ushered Makrina up the stairs and inside. The cottage was dark and smelled of smoke and animals. To the right of the door was a ladder leading up to a low loft. To the left was an open hearth tended by an old woman, whom Makrina could barely see at first. "Mamma?" said Ioanna, speaking louder than necessary except for someone hard of hearing. "*Ea Makrina, efras Christe.*"

The old woman turned and peered at Makrina through the darkness, squinting greatly. "*Hanta, hanta azul,*" she said, with a wrinkled smile.

"She says you very beautiful," said Ioanna. "Please, sit." She pointed to a ring of mats on the wooden floor, arranged around the blackened stone hearth. There were no chairs or benches to be seen. Makrina knelt upon the nearest mat and sat back on her heels. In an instant, two young girls plopped down on either side of her. "*Hut! Hut!*" scolded Ioanna. The girls backed off and settled together an arm's length away. "These my daughters Mara and Betha," said Ioanna. The girls smiled shyly and giggled. "Salome?" called Ioanna, looking around the cottage. She went to the open door and yelled in broken Greek for Titos to find Salome.

A moment later the girl about Makrina's age reappeared at the door carrying three loaves of bread in her apron. "Here I am, Mamma," she said to Ioanna. "I brought bread."

"We *have* bread," said her mother. "Now we have *more* bread. Go, sit down."

Salome gave her mother the bread and went to take her place by the hearth, but found Makrina already there.

"Sit down, Salome," said Ioanna.

Salome pointed to her place and said, "She there."

Ioanna groaned with annoyance and pointed to a mat on the opposite side of the circle. "*Here*. Here now. Sit," she said to Salome.

Ioanna started passing out wooden bowls to everyone present, then noticed Makrina wiping tears from her eyes. "Oh no, no, child. No tears," she said, handing the bowls to Mara and rushing to comfort Makrina.

But she was too late. The tears for every day Makrina had been away suddenly broke forth in torrents. She collapsed into Ioanna's arms, sobbing uncontrollably. *How could he leave her like this? How could he abandon her here? Was there no place else? Was this what she deserved? Was she that much trouble? Who would ever find her here? When would all this end? When, Lord, when?*

Salome and her sisters stared at Makrina in amazement as their mother and grandmother did their best to stop her tears. When she could not be comforted, Ioanna led Makrina, still sobbing loudly, to the far corner of the cottage, where upon a woolen bedroll she held Makrina tightly for a very long time.

# XIX

A quiet settled over the palace in the hour the aged emperor Diocletian regularly took his rest. Outside a sudden spring shower had washed the tiled roofs and paved plazas of the imperial compound. Inside, the augustus lay upon a curtained couch in his study, going over a list of names with his caesar Galerius in a chair by his side.

"Let's deal with the boys first. Any reason to consider Maximian's son, Maxentius?" asked the elder emperor.

"None at all," said Galerius. "He's too young and inexperienced, besides being an arrogant little snot. No one likes him. I doubt if his own father does."

"Yes, well, so much for Maxentius. What about Constantine then, Chlorus's son? How old is he now? At least thirty. Able, experienced, respected here at court. I rather like him."

"Not worthy. Thinks too much of himself. If he is contemptuous of me now as a tribune, what will he do when he's a caesar?"

"He can be Chlorus's caesar. Chlorus would be glad to have him, and the two would get on well together."

"Too well, I'm afraid. We'd be creating a family dynasty to rival my own authority, and Maximian would then want his own son elevated, either now or in the future. Best to make the point right now that emperors are picked the way generals are—on merit and not relation."

"Oh, very well, then. Who's left?" said Diocletian.

"Severus," said Galerius.

"What—the dancer?" chuckled Diocletian. "That drunkard, who turns night into day and day into night?" His chuckle loosened the phlegm in his chest, provoking a brief spell of coughing.

"He's a good horse for the team," said Galerius. "He served with Chlorus years ago and has commanded a legion under me ably. He's my first pick for the purple."

"Very well. Send him to Maximian if you like. Chlorus will see that he behaves. Who else would you clothe with the purple?"

"This man," said Galerius, pointing to a name on the list.

"Maximinus Daia? Who is he? I've never heard of him."

"A relation of mine," said Galerius. "My sister's son. Very well qualified."

"What has he done? Has he commanded an army or a legion? Has he held public office?"

"He has served me well in many capacities, and he has my absolute confidence. He's quite a sharp fellow. I have no doubt he's the best candidate."

"Better than Constantine?"

"Much better than Constantine," said Galerius. "I can trust Daia. He's loyal and able. There's no one else I would want to rule with me in the East."

Diocletian sighed wearily. "Oh, do as you wish," he said. "Just remember, sharp or not, he'll be your worry and yours alone from now on. Don't expect me to come out of retirement and bail you out if you get into trouble. I've had enough of the empire and its problems, and I would just as soon see nothing but the cabbages in my garden until the day I die."

"He'll do fine. The empire will be secured," said Galerius.

"It had better be."

The parade started from the north gate of the palace and marched in solemn order with drums pounding to a low hill three miles outside Nicomedia. At the hill's summit stood a porphyry pillar topped by a statue of Jupiter and flanked by banners of purple and white billowing in the breeze like the sails of a festive fleet. On this hill thirteen years earlier, Diocletian had clothed Galerius in the purple, raising him to the rank of caesar and inaugurating the rule of Tetrarchs. Now, on the first of May in the twentieth year of his reign, Diocletian had assembled the army here again to raise Galerius to the rank of augustus and clothe another in the purple as Galerius's caesar, before retiring forever from command of the empire.

When all was ready, Diocletian mounted the base of the porphyry pillar and surveyed in silence the formations before him. The hill in three directions was covered with soldiers in gleaming parade armor. Red military streamers fluttered from the standards scattered throughout the host. The eastern empire's senior commanders and civil officials stood in a semicircle at his feet. Behind him, the imperial carriage waited to carry him off to retirement at his fortified villa at Spalatum on the Illyrian coast of the Adriatic Sea.

Age showed itself in his thin, gray figure. "Romans!" he cried, his once booming voice sounding strained and weak. "Soldiers and citizens! Comrades and sons." He paused to rally his strength before continuing. "For forty years, I have toiled for your welfare and fought for your safety. For twenty, I have ruled in your interest, that the empire may be strong and prosperous." Slowly and thoughtfully he recited a long list of campaigns, battles, and other achievements before returning to his present business: "Now the weight of the world has grown heavy, and I have grown old and slow. I am weary of the world and its affairs and desirous of rest and repose. Today I will take my leave of the affairs of state, lay down that power entrusted to me, and retire in private to my country estate."

There were loud shouts of protest from the ranks and a few spears and swords banged against shields as an expression of grief. Tears rolled from the eyes of the augustus, but he waved for silence and continued on, announcing the simultaneous retirement of his co-emperor in the West, the augustus Maximian, and the elevation of Galerius and Constantius to the rank of augustus in the East and West, respectively.

The assembled soldiers responded dutifully by beating their shields with their knees to signal their approval. This much they had expected, but who, they wondered, would succeed Galerius and Constantius as the caesars of east and west?

"To continue the present organization of government, which has served the empire so well since instituted by me so many years ago, we now name two new caesars: Flavius Valerius Severus to assist the rule of Constantius in the West, and Gaius Valerius Maximinus to assist the rule of the augustus Galerius in the East."

A murmur of surprise and consternation rumbled through the troops. Many had expected Constantius's son Constantine to be picked. Who was this Maximinus? Had Constantine taken a new name? Was he now to be called Maximinus?

Their questions were answered when the emperor Galerius strode forth into the ranks of the imperial entourage and brushed past Constantine to throw his arm around his nephew—a thin-faced and balding officer known by the name of Daia—and lead him up to the base of the pillar of Jupiter. Without another word, the retiring emperor descended the base of the pillar, removed his purple cloak, and flung it around the shoulders of the new caesar Maximinus Daia, whose own cloak was removed and discarded. At once, the augustus Galerius stood back and shouted, "Hail Caesar!" Instinctively the troops picked up the cheer and again beat their shields with their knees, as Diocletian climbed into his waiting carriage and rolled away on his long journey north and into obscurity.

✠   ✠   ✠

That same spring Marcus returned at last to Mogontiacum, after a roundabout journey from Mediolanum to Genua, then by ship to Narbo Martius and overland to his mother's estate in Aquitania, where he took charge of his inheritance before returning to duty. The death of his father left him much diminished in status and wealth, and for the first time in his life, he had to consider the cost of living, starting from the day he left Mediolanum with a loan of 10,000 denarii from Spellius Longinus, a cousin on his mother's side.

As the son of a senator, Marcus had never thought twice about spending as much as 100 denarii on dinner at the best roadside inns. While traveling to Aquitania, he took pains to keep the cost of dinner under 40. Instead of the best wine at 30d a pint, he drank good beer at 4d. (He would not drink wine selling as cheaply as 8d a pint.) Instead of ham at 20d per pound, he had beef at 8d. In this way, he managed to arrive at his estate in Aquitania with a safe share of the 10,000d left over, which he hoarded carefully until a review of the overseer's books reassured him that he was not quite ruined.

Even so, the cost of replacing the things stolen by bandits made him cringe: 150d for a pair of good shoes, 100d for a pair of soldier's boots without hobnails, 500d for a military saddle, another 500d for a set of pteruges, 1,500d for a military cloak, 2,500d for a tribune's chlamys, and 6,000d for an officer's helmet. A solid bronze cuirass would have cost not less than 10,000d, so Marcus settled instead for a lamellar corselet for half as much. Lamellar armor was made of small, overlapping plates of lacquered rawhide, sown together with leather. It was lighter, more comfortable, and just as strong as metal armor, according to some. Many more officers were wearing lamellar these days, so Marcus would not feel embarrassed to join them.

Harder choices lay ahead for him in Mogontiacum. Dovina was indeed pregnant, and he did not doubt that he was the father. She hid from his sight the day he returned to the house, and though she was much on his mind, he did not ask about her until several hours later, when he was with Pollentia in private. Pollentia answered discreetly. "She's resting, my lord. This is her seventh month with child," she said.

Marcus was not surprised and did not pretend to be. He said nothing and looked away. In one sense, he was relieved. Had Dovina not been pregnant, he might have been tempted to keep her on. Instead, he made up his mind to send her away. As attracted as he was to her, he could not bear the thought of setting up house with her as if she were his wife. Even if she were nothing more than a concubine, her presence would complicate matters, and quite possibly exclude the possibility of a proper marriage later. If she stayed, he might grow too fond of her to send her away later. There was also the danger that she would grow too fond of him, so that sending her away later would break her heart. Marcus would not take that chance. He, the senator's son, would not settle the rest of his life with a barbarian slave girl, even if she were a chieftain's daughter.

The next day, having seen Dovina only once from a safe distance, Marcus called Pollentia in and explained to her that he could no longer afford her services, but that he could offer her half pay in perpetuity if she would take Dovina into her own home and care for her. Pollentia readily agreed, knowing that Dovina would not object. The next day she moved her young ward into a tidy little house on the other side of town.

That July Dovina gave birth to a healthy baby girl, which she named Marcia. Hearing of the birth from his steward Crescens, Marcus thanked his stars that the baby was not a boy and told Crescens to send the mother an aureus—a gold coin at that time so valuable it was almost useless as currency and was better kept safe for emergencies.

The departure of Pollentia and Dovina saddened the rest of the servants in the household and made them uneasy about other uncertainties in their situation. Their apprehension increased when Marcus announced that the household would be moving from their comfortable home on a hill outside town to a modest apartment closer to the garrison, where the rent would be much less. The move was necessary, he explained, to accommodate the added expense of a new aide and a new personal secretary.

Alexander had been both, but Marcus's new responsibilities for the estate in Aquitania required a division of duties. That meant adding two unknown personalities who would stand closer to their master than anyone else, sufficient cause for worry among even the most optimistic and trusting servants. Alexander had been well liked and appreciated in part because he provided a cordial link between the household staff and their aloof, unhappy master. Without him, the staff felt defenseless, and their master felt estranged.

Marcus filled one of the two positions quickly and easily, accepting the recommendation of Victorinus, Gratianus's second-in-command, on the behalf of an eager young trooper named M. Vesunnius Vitalis, the son of a Gallic centurion and a British mother. Vitalis was literate in Latin and could converse in the major dialect of the Britons, a talent that might prove useful in the future. Victorinus swore that it was just a matter of time before Constantius ventured again to Britannia to tie down the defenses of the isle against the savage Picts in the north and the Saxon marauders along the coast.

The position of personal secretary was more problematic. An adequate secretary needed to be literate in Greek as well as Latin, and in legion fortresses of the north like Mogontiacum, potential candidates were few. Marcus had no success until he went to see Favonius, the cohort commander, to ask after the girl Alexander had left behind.

"Of course I found her," said Favonius. "Through the local Christian overseer. He's a veteran, you know."

"The overseer?"

Favonius nodded. "Seven campaigns against the barbarians, not to mention a few civil wars," he said. "Fought with him against the pretender Caurausius when I was a newly minted centurion and he was commanding the cohort. His name is Marcus Briccus. We called him 'the Hammer.' A humble pensioner now."

"How did he become a Christian?"

"You'll have to ask him. I'll take you to him, if you'd like."

Favonius led Marcus to a small, two-story house near the city walls.

"Look at this place," he said. "Twenty years of service and this is all he has." With his vine-stick, his rod of office, he delivered several sharp raps on the door of the house, shouting, "Open up, Christians. It's the police!"

A moment later the door swung open. "You don't scare me, Favonius," said the square-faced fellow in the doorway. "I'd know your bark anywhere."

Briccus was a little shorter than Marcus, but meatier, with thick, hairy forearms sticking out from the sleeves of his plain gray dalmatic. The hair on his head and a week's growth of beard were both a snarl of black and gray. His voice was deep and rough.

When Favonius introduced Marcus, Briccus turned suddenly serious and said, "My condolences for the loss of your aide. I have heard only good said of him."

"I'm ashamed to say I didn't know he was a Christian until after his death," said Marcus.

"He was a catechumen, having only recently come under instruction," said Briccus. "He was betrothed to a young woman in the Assembly."

"That's why I've come," said Marcus.

At that point, Favonius excused himself and left. Briccus welcomed Marcus inside and offered him a chair in the large, sparsely furnished entry room spanning the width of the house. Marcus declined the chair and explained that he was looking for the woman Lucia to settle Alexander's estate. "He didn't own much, but what he did own should go to her," he said.

Briccus nodded and then went to the foot of the stairs leading up to the second floor. "Titus?" he called. "Yes, sir?" a voice answered from above. "Run over to Drusilla's and see if Lucia's there," said Briccus. "If she is, bring her back with you. She has a visitor."

A thin young man with a short, black, curly beard and a large nose descended the stairs and bowed respectfully towards Marcus. "Health, sir," he said before leaving the house.

Briccus smiled at Marcus when he had gone. "Another former soldier," he said.

"Favonius said you served with I Minervia," said Marcus.

"Yes, indeed, a lifetime ago, it seems," said Briccus.

They talked for a while about Briccus's career, and then, just as Marcus was about to ask how he had become a Christian, Titus returned in the company of two women, one well on in years wearing a dark shawl over her head and shoulders, and a younger one wrapped from the head in a faded green palla.

"Peace be with you, sisters," said Briccus.

"And with you, master," said the elder of the two.

"This is the tribune Aemilius Canio, Alexander's lord," explained

Briccus. "This is the widow Drusilla and her daughter Lucia," he said to Marcus.

The women bowed humbly, and Marcus nodded in response. He began nervously to relate his praises of Alexander as a faithful servant and able soldier, his gaze shifting nervously between the old woman and Lucia. Then he produced a small purse of gold pieces and offered it to them as a token of his sympathy. Briccus passed the purse to Lucia.

"You are most kind," said the old woman.

"He left a few things I can have sent to you," said Marcus, "and also this, which was found on his body." In the palm of his hand, he held the wooden cross and leather string.

Lucia's eyes widened with recognition, and she reached forward and took the cross. With her head bowed, she looked at it for a moment and then turned to her mother. "Look, Mamma," she said softly. "His blood has colored it."

Her mother looked at the cross, then put her arm around her daughter and said, "His race is finished. He's resting now."

Lucia wiped her eyes with her palla and turned to Marcus. "Thank you, sir, for your kindness. Alexander always said you were a good man," said Lucia.

Marcus was suddenly at a loss for words, so Briccus spoke up. "If you send his things here, I'll see that they receive them," he said.

Marcus nodded to him. Briccus then dismissed the women, who bowed before departing. "May God be with you," said Lucia's mother.

"Is there anything else I can do for you?" asked Briccus when the women had gone.

Marcus managed a perfunctory no. Then his host welcomed him to call again. "I'm sure we'd have much to talk about," said Briccus.

Marcus thanked him and then started to leave. In the doorway, he stopped and turned and said, "I'm looking for a private secretary, someone who knows both Latin and Greek well. Could you recommend someone?"

"Perhaps," said Briccus. "Let me pray about it. Can I send you word at the garrison?"

"Certainly," said Marcus. "I will look forward to hearing from you."

Three days later, the thin, bearded fellow with the big nose delivered a short note from the overseer Marcus Briccus to Marcus at the garrison. Marcus's new aide Vitalis was there, sitting on the edge of his master's desk, sizing up the visitor while Marcus stood and read the note. "He's recommending the bearer of this letter," said Marcus looking up at the nervous young man before him. "Is your name Titus Stratonicus?"

"Yes, sir," answered the young man.

"You can speak and write both Greek and Latin?"

"Indeed, sir," answered Titus. "I am well-schooled in mathematics as well. My father was an engineer with the army. Both he and my mother were Greek."

"Really? You were a soldier yourself, weren't you? Also an engineer?"

"Yes, sir."

"No longer?" interjected Vitalis.

Titus glanced at the aide. "I am a Christian, sir, and cannot serve under the law."

Vitalis raised his eyebrows and looked at Marcus.

"What are you doing now?" asked Marcus.

"I was studying under Briccus to become a server or elder in our Assembly. I am already a reader, but Briccus thinks I'm too young to go further yet and should learn to serve others first."

"So he's sent you to me?" said Marcus. He folded the letter and touched it to his lips pensively. "Do you want this job, Titus?" he asked.

Titus hesitated. "No, sir," he said. "I'd rather continue my studies, but I want to please my overseer. If he thinks this is best, I am prepared to accept his guidance."

"You trust his judgment?"

"Oh, yes, sir. Of course, sir," said Titus.

"Very well then," said Marcus. "We'll give you a try, and see how it works out."

Through the summer, Titus gave Marcus no reason to complain. He was very bright and eager to please, and he worked so hard that Marcus wondered if he really missed his studies. Being sympathetic to Titus's academic interests, Marcus allowed him every Sunday off. He had offered him every Saturday, which many Romans kept as a sabbath of sorts, following the custom of the Jews, but Titus chose Sunday instead—the Lord's Day, he called it.

Vitalis did not know what to make of the strange, intense young man who seemed to lack all ambition, except for the duties of his religion. And he could not understand Marcus's interest in the fellow. More than once Vitalis and Marcus would be enjoying some soldierly jest when Titus would appear and Marcus would immediately engage him in some philosophical discussion, leaving Vitalis to find something else to do.

Killing time was the principal duty of soldiers stationed on the quiet, secure frontier. Private soldiers spent much of their time farming small plots of land up through the Rhenus valley. Officers like Marcus and Vitalis hunted and sported and gamed their days away.

On occasion, Marcus went to visit the man who had once commanded a cohort but now commanded only Christians. "How," he asked Briccus, "does a man go from being a cohort prefect to being a Christian overseer and, well, outlaw?"

Briccus laughed and said, "I could not have done it at your age, Canio, but when I was older, it was very easy. Believe it or not, there may come a time when all that you value, everything that you think glorious and great, everything worth boasting about won't matter at all. The trophies, the decorations, the rank —" he shook his head "— they mean nothing to me now."

"But what was it that drew you to the Christian Assembly?" asked Marcus. "What compelled you to accept this faith?"

"My wife," answered Briccus. "My dear departed Flavia."

"Your wife?" asked Marcus incredulously.

"Yes, indeed," said Briccus. "She was a saintly woman, Canio. She lived with me just eight years as a Christian, and though I loved her dearly, I never thought much about her faith until the day she died. And then—well—I have seen many men die, young and old, slowly and quickly. Many died courageously, some even peacefully, but none died joyfully, as Flavia did. I would never have thought it possible—to die joyfully. But for her, the end was victorious. She had finished her race, she had fought a good fight, she had kept the faith. She died a conqueror, Canio. How could a soldier argue with that?"

Many times since leaving the mountains, Marcus had ached with an urge to write to Makrina, to express to her in some way what he had seen and heard. And yet he felt he could not write as long as he did not yet believe. Two years had passed since their parting, and she was perhaps now married. Certainly she would have forgotten him. It was even possible that she had fallen away from the faith after her youthful zeal had cooled. There was no point in writing now, it seemed, and doing so could be embarrassing. If by odd chance she had not lost faith, nor married, nor forgotten him completely, he could not bear to raise in her false hopes for his conversion, which still seemed to him impossible.

News of the persecutions changed his mind about writing. He heard from Titus and Briccus and others of severe persecutions of Christians in the East, with many executions, tortures, and other punishments. Fear grew in him that Makrina was in danger or suffering or already dead. He had to write. He had to know what had become of her. For half of a hazy, humid day in late August, he stayed holed up in his study, laboring on a long letter. The next day he tore it up and started again. On the third day, he copied his final version, much shorter than the first, and hastily posted it to his friend Felix in Rome, with instructions for forwarding it to Sinope. It read:

*Marcus Aemilius Canio salutes Kimon, son of Aristoboulos of Sinope: Health and the favor of the gods to you and all your family, especially your dear sister Makrina. Forgive me, dear friend, for not writing sooner. So much has happened since I left Sinope. I joined the army of Constantius a year ago, and I am with the army still, with Legio XXII Primigenia at Mogontiacum on the Rhenus. What good I can do here I cannot see. The frontier is quiet and the legion has little to do. I thank the gods for peace, but I wonder if my father misread the stars in thinking that my fortune lay only in the army. Time will tell. He died last October, and then my aide Alexander, on whom I depended for so much, was murdered before my eyes by brigands in the Alps. I was sorely wounded and rescued from certain death by an educated Christian hiding in the mountains. I spent several weeks with him and learned much about his religion, too much to tell here. Since returning to Mogontiacum, I have heard of persecutions of Christians in the East. I have feared for Makrina, and I beg you, dear brother, to look after her, for her sake and mine. The augustus Constantius has left Christians unmolested in his domains. I offer you any assistance I might be able to provide in securing the safety of your sister. Please write with news. Greet your father and mother and little Eugenia. Kiss Makrina for me when you can. I, Marcus Aemilius Canio, write this with my own hand.*

# XX

Makrina wept again three weeks after her arrival in the village, when Gerasimos showed up with two trunks of clothes sent by her parents along with two letters, one from her father and mother and one from Eugenia. Her parents' letter told her of the stir her escape had caused and of their hope that she could return home in the spring. Her heart sank when she read it. In her corner of the loft in the cottage, she opened one trunk and looked at the fine, clean tunics and robes and other things that had been hers at home. She could not wear them in this primitive mountain village, among these poor, plain people. She dared not even touch them with her dirty hands and instead closed the lid of the trunk and buried her face in her arms on top of it.

After three weeks, the blisters on her hands and feet had turned to calluses. She had learned to milk goats, churn butter, and grind grain in a quern. She had grown accustomed to the smell of the cottage and the village and her own unwashed body. She knew the daily routine and had learned to communicate with her host family. Learning to communicate with others in the village had not been necessary. Since the day of her arrival she had been shunned by everyone except a few daring children and two or three old widows, who stopped by from time to time to gawk and gossip with Ioanna and the aged Anna.

It was a long time before Makrina came to understand why. The sudden arrival of a beautiful, nubile young maiden threatened the social order of the community. Parents began to fear for the betrothals of their sons and daughters. Young men kept their distance and hid their fascination. Young women watched her jealously for any sign of flirtation. They did not know how little attraction she felt toward their men. They could only see how much more open this city woman was with strangers. *What manners city folk have!* they marveled with each other. *And yet they say she's a Christian!*

The responsibility of safeguarding Makrina's honor and the social order fell naturally to her surrogate mother, Ioanna, who watched Makrina like a hawk. She would not send Makrina through the village on errands and would not allow her to go anywhere alone. At worship, she kept Makrina carefully shielded behind Salome and her sisters in the back of the large cottage that served as their "kirk."

When the whole village gathered in the marketplace on the night of the first good snowfall, Makrina was sequestered at home with Salome and her grandparents, Anna and Gregorios. On that night, according to local custom, the young men of the village built a large bonfire in the marketplace and then welcomed the young women to join them in singing and dancing in a great circle around the fire. With their elders looking on and singing also, the young men, one by one, would whisk away the young women to whom they were betrothed. Custom ruled that any unbetrothed female found in the marketplace could be claimed by any unbetrothed male, so Makrina's absence was for her own protection. The next morning, when the newly married couples gathered in the kirk to receive the prayerful blessing of the Assembly, Makrina was hidden in the back as usual.

The burden of minding Makrina much of the time fell unevenly on Salome, who quickly learned to resent her guest. Makrina worked slowly and tired easily. She was clumsy and inattentive to her duties, her mind ever elsewhere. Often it was Salome who was obliged to finish what Makrina had started and Salome who was blamed for Makrina's mistakes.

Once before the snow they were in the yard behind the cottage making candles, when Makrina accidently dropped Marcus's ring into a pot of hot candle-wax. She was standing over the pot daydreaming as usual and fiddling with the ring until it slipped from her fingers and disappeared with a plop into the bubbling ooze. Horrified, Makrina gasped and cried, "My ring! My ring fell into the pot! Get it out, quick!" Salome watched in amazement as Makrina searched hysterically for some way to retrieve the ring. When she started to dump the pot out, Salome leaped forward to stop her. "No!" shouted Salome, pulling away Makrina's hands. "Wait!" she commanded.

Salome marched off out of the yard looking back over her shoulder to see that Makrina didn't dump the pot while she was gone. She returned a moment later with a wooden spoon from the house. Feeling carefully with the spoon around the bottom of the pot, she located the ring and finally brought it to the surface. Makrina reached forward to take it, but Salome slapped her hand away. "It's hot!" she said. She dumped the waxy blob containing the ring into the dirt and scraped the excess wax off the spoon as best she could. "Let it cool," she ordered crossly, before taking the spoon back into the house. When she returned again, Makrina was kneeling beside the ring watching it cool, still quite distressed and oblivious to the work that remained.

That evening, Ioanna found her spoon coated with wax and scolded Salome for taking it. Loudly and angrily Salome blamed Makrina in words Makrina could not fully understand, but she heard her name and could not mistake the scowl on Salome's face. *I didn't take the spoon, I didn't get wax all over it,* Makrina told herself, cowering against her trunks in her corner of the loft. But when Salome shot her an angry glance, she looked away and stroked her precious ring. Afterward she put it away in one of her trunks for safekeeping.

Life slowed down for the men of the village during the winter months. With their fields under snow and their flocks in pens, their days left ample time for the few duties that remained—hunting, harvesting timber, chopping firewood, mending fences and tools, and the like. One snow-bound morning, Makrina came back to the cottage after feeding the pigs and found three boys in their early teens sitting with the elder Gregorios beneath an oiled-skin window of the cottage. Ioanna quickly recruited her to serve them each a hot drink made by boiling the roots of various mountain shrubs. Curious as to their purpose, Makrina took her time delivering their drinks, then hovered nearby to see what they were up to, until Ioanna shooed her away and sent her up into the loft, where Salome was waiting for her to comb out the lice in her hair. Makrina began without complaint combing out Salome's braids with a fine-tooth wooden comb. "What are *they* here for?" she whispered to Salome.

"They learn to read," said Salome.

"Really?" said Makrina. She left the comb in Salome's hair and peered over the edge of the loft. Gregorios was sitting with his back against the wall, directly under the window, with a large wax tablet in his lap. In the bright yellow light, Makrina could see the gray-haired elder carve out the last letters of the Greek alphabet. The boys watched him attentively, each holding in his lap a smaller tablet. From across the room, Ioanna snapped her fingers and waved Makrina away from the edge. Makrina retreated and Salome handed her the comb with a look of impatience.

"Does Gregorios teach everyone to read in the village?" Makrina whispered, again applying the comb to Salome's tresses.

Salome gave a humph to show how silly the question was. "He teach boys," she said. "Some boys. Only smart ones."

"Only a few? How come?" asked Makrina.

"So they be readers and servers someday, for Assembly," answered Salome.

"But why only a few?" asked Makrina.

"Not every boy be reader or server someday, lammy," said Salome. *Lammy* was Salome's word for lazy or stupid youngsters, and she applied it often to Makrina.

"But that's not the only reason to learn to read. Surely others would want to learn also," said Makrina.

"Why?" asked Salome.

Makrina was astonished by her question, which sounded more like a challenge. "Well—well—so they can write letters to each other and read the letters that others write them."

Salome gave another humph. "Nobody write letters here. Nobody need to," she said.

"Well, then, so they can read books, so they can read the Gospels and the Epistles and the Prophets and the Law."

"Shhhh!" said Salome to quiet Makrina, who had forgotten that they could be heard. "Only Gregorios has books in kirk, and not everybody can read them," she said softly.

"But wouldn't you want to?" whispered Makrina.

"What for? I hear them in kirk. Gregorios and others read to all of us," said Salome.

"But wouldn't you want to read them yourself? You could learn so much more," said Makrina.

"What for? I learn enough," said Salome.

Makrina sighed with frustration. She had never heard anyone speak like this, and didn't know how to answer. A moment later, she whispered to Salome, "I could teach you to read."

"You, lammy?"

"I know how to read. I can read and write Greek *and* Latin. How do you think I read the letters my parents send me?"

Makrina had a point. Salome knew she had received letters. "What for?" said Salome.

"I could teach you in no time at all," said Makrina, ignoring Salome's contentiousness. "I taught my little sister to read, or at least I helped. It was easy. You'd be reading before spring."

Salome gave another humph but said nothing.

"You would," said Makrina.

That afternoon, when her mother had settled down for a nap, Salome brought Makrina a tablet and a stylus like the ones Gregorios had sent home with the boys before lunch. Thrusting the tablet toward Makrina, she said, "You teach me to read."

Makrina was delighted and sat down immediately to write out the alphabet for their first lesson. It was fun at first, the first real fun Makrina had had since coming to the village. But after many lessons Makrina began to wonder whether her boast could be fulfilled. Salome learned slowly, and Makrina quickly realized that her pupil was not just learning to read Greek but to speak it also. Once in frustration, Makrina threw down the tablet and stylus and declared that she had had enough and would teach no more. Salome calmly picked up the tablet and stylus and held them out to Makrina. "You said you teach me by spring," she said.

Angrily impatient, Makrina knocked away the tablet and shouted, "That was before I learned how *stupid* you are!"

Her violence startled Salome and her words stung. Salome backed away and swallowed hard. "I not stupid," she said, choking back tears. "I—am—not—stupid!"

Frustrated and sad, and now suddenly ashamed of herself, Makrina broke into tears, and a second later they were both sobbing loudly in opposite corners of the loft. Mara and Betha came running, followed quickly by Ioanna, who demanded to know what had happened. Makrina and Salome heaved and wailed and tried to explain, but their anguished words were barely intelligible and before long Ioanna threw up her hands and left them to themselves.

For days afterward, Makrina and Salome did not speak to each other, but the longer their silence lasted, the worse Makrina felt. She knew she would have to make peace before the next Lord's Day, for she would not dare to share the cup in the Assembly with such an offense on her soul.

On Friday, she slipped away without permission and found Gregorios at the kirk rehearsing a hymn with one of the chanters. She begged his pardon, and he sent away the chanter. Then, standing with him before the table at the east end of the room, facing the wooden cross on top of the table and a crude painting of the Last Supper on the wall behind it, Makrina explained to Gregorios all that had happened.

The old man listened patiently and when she had finished, he said to her, "Dear, dear lost child, you know what you must do. You must confess your sin to Salome and ask her to forgive you. It is the only way."

Makrina nodded penitently.

"Need I say anything more?" said Gregorios. "Here now you have confessed your sin to Christ. Let us ask his forgiveness."

Makrina knelt before the cross with her head covered and bowed. Gregorios laid his hands upon her head and prayed to God that she be forgiven. When he was finished, she made the sign of the cross and rose to her feet. "Go now, child," said Gregorios. "Make peace with your sister in Christ, and know then that you are forgiven."

Makrina left the kirk feeling that a great weight had been lifted from her shoulders. As soon as she could, she found Salome, confessed her offense, and humbly begged Salome's forgiveness. Salome was at first surprised and then overwhelmed by the fervor of Makrina's plea. "I forgive you," said Salome. "Please forgive me."

The women embraced and kissed each other on the cheeks. Makrina offered to continue her lessons, and Salome happily thanked her for it.

Salome did learn to read by spring, and by May she was attempting to teach her young sisters what she had learned. By then, Makrina had lost interest in the endeavor. Spring had not brought her deliverance. In their letters, her parents expressed their hope of obtaining a pardon from the governor, which would allow Makrina to return without fear of prosecution. Better to wait for the pardon than to complicate matters by returning prematurely. Just a little while longer, they assured her.

Springtime did bring other relief to Makrina, however. When the men of the village left to take their flocks to graze higher in the mountains, the women of the village decided that she posed little threat to their marriages and betrothals. One by one they stopped by the house with the excuse of visiting Ioanna or Anna, but always staying until they had met and spoken to the beautiful girl from the city. And no matter how much they learned about her, there were always rumors that went much further: that she was really an imperial princess banished from the palace for her Christian belief; that she had hordes of treasure in her unopened trunks; even that she was an angel in disguise sent to watch over the village and spy out the pious as well as the impostors.

Some of the younger wives were especially interested in hearing about life in the city. One named Rakhel, an indolent young bride with a tooth missing from her silly smile, was especially adept at catching Makrina when Ioanna was not around and wasting the girl's time with endless questions about her former life. One usually hot morning in mid June, Makrina and Salome were beating rugs behind the cottage while Rakhel sat idly by watching. Dust flew with every stroke of their wooden wands and stuck to the sweat on their faces and arms. Stopping for a rest, Makrina wiped her forehead with the back of her wrist. "If only I could have one real bath," she moaned.

Rakhel perked up. "Bath? What bath like in city?" she asked.

Makrina accepted the excuse to sit down for a rest and answer the question. "In the city," she said between breaths, "there are large, beautiful baths for everyone's use. All you pay is a penny to spend as long as you like. The floors and walls are made of cool, smooth marble of many colors. There's a hot pool and a tepid pool and a cold pool, and each one is bigger than this house."

"Bigger than house?" wondered Rakhel.

"It has to be big for everyone to fit," said Makrina.

"People wash together, in same pool? Men and women?"

"No, no, Rakhel," said Makrina, shaking her head disdainfully. "The women bathe in the morning and the men in the afternoon. It's not like washing out of a basin or the stream as we do here. The pools are big enough and deep enough for many people to sink into, like a baptism."

Rakhel oohed with wonder while Salome beat harder at the rugs. "For one penny, I take bath every week!" said Rakhel.

Makrina laughed. "In the city, everybody takes a bath every day," she said.

"Every *day*? You take bath every day there?" asked Rakhel.

"Every day," answered Makrina, "but not at the public bath. We have our own at home. I've never actually bathed in the public bath, but I've seen it."

"You have own bath at home?"

Makrina nodded. "Not as big as the public bath, but big enough," she said.

Salome interrupted by handing Makrina her rug-beater and saying, "Excuse us, Rakhel. We have work," trying to sound as unwelcoming as possible.

Rakhel sighed and got up to go. "Bath every day. Lord of wonders!" she said before wandering off.

When Rakhel was well out of sight, Salome stopped work suddenly and said to Makrina in a low voice, "I know a pool big enough for a bath."

"Where?" asked Makrina, incredulously.

"In the stream over the ridge there," said Salome.

Makrina thought for a moment. "Over that ridge?" she asked. Salome nodded and smiled. "I know that pool," said Makrina. "We camped there on our way here. Lot of good it will do us. It's surrounded by bears and mountain lions."

"What? There are no bears or mountain lions around here. The men see to that," said Salome.

"But Gerasimos said there were."

"What he know? What *does* he know?" said Salome.

"What about wolves?" asked Makrina.

"No wolves," said Salome. "Maybe wild boars, but our dogs keep them away."

"You're not suggesting we go there, are you?"

"Yes, yes," said Salome. "It's not far."

"But your mother would never let us."

"She does not have to know," whispered Salome.

"But we'd be gone all day, and she would know that. What would we tell her?" asked Makrina.

"I don't know," said Salome, "but I will think of something." She started beating the rugs again, but now with more vigor.

Makrina started again too, but all she could think about was the pool with the waterfall and what a pleasure it would be to immerse herself in it, if for just a moment.

Before long, Salome stopped again. "I know," she said. "We tell her we pick blackberries on the ridge."

"She will believe that?" questioned Makrina.

"Yes, yes. We pick them every summer up on the ridge." Salome smiled slyly at Makrina and then resumed beating the rugs.

"When could we go?" asked Makrina.

Salome stopped. "Tomorrow!" she said. "Or the next day!"

Makrina grinned. "Tomorrow," she said.

That afternoon, while Ioanna was napping, Makrina and Salome began their preparations. From her trunks, Makrina took two clean cotton subtunics, a few other underclothes, two towels, and several toilet items: a wooden strigil for scrapping the skin, a small glass vial of perfume, an alabaster bottle of oil, an ivory comb, and a silver mirror, only slightly tarnished. All of this, they packed into a burlap sack, which Salome then hid in a tree not far away from the village.

They could scarcely conceal their delight later when Ioanna gave them permission to go, but later Makrina began to worry about their safety. Salome assured her they would be in no danger. Would Ioanna let them go if she thought they were? But she thought they were only going as far as the ridge; she didn't know they'd be going down the other side. Makrina told Salome of the difficult climb up the streambed on the other side, but Salome said there was another way that would be easier.

The next morning, Ioanna packed them a lunch of bread and cheese and a small skin of water in their otherwise empty baskets. They were just about to leave when Mara and Betha complained about being left behind, and Ioanna decided to let them go along. Salome protested strongly against their going, but Ioanna insisted. "What are we going to do now?" Makrina whispered to Salome as the four of them walked out of the gate of the village, followed by too large, bony sheepdogs that were too old for herding. "We're going to pick blackberries," said Salome, crossly.

But upon reaching the entrance to the trail leading up to the ridge, she told the others to wait and went to retrieve their hidden sack. "What that?" asked Mara when Salome returned. "Never you mind," snapped Salome. They walked on for more than an hour up the well-trod trail to the top of the ridge, then stopped to rest near the spot where Gerasimos and Makrina had rested the previous fall. The pines seemed greener now and the ground beneath their canopy was cluttered with bushes and thickets. Makrina wasn't sure where she and Gerasimos had come up from the other side, but it didn't matter. When the girls started walking again, Salome led them east along the ridge for a couple hundred paces.

"Here the berries," said Betha. "Where you going?"

"We are not going to pick berries today," said Salome without stopping. "We are going to have a bath, a city bath."

"What? There no city bath around here, lammy," laughed Mara.

"We are going to the pool in the stream down the other side," said Salome. "Mamma does not know and you are not going to tell her. Do you understand?"

"But I don't want bath," said Betha.

"Me neither," said Mara.

"You have no choice," said Salome, "unless you want to go home alone."

"I want to go home," said Betha.

"Go home then, but watch out for mountain lions," said Salome.

Makrina gasped. "But you said—"

"Shhhh," said Salome with a furtive nod toward the little ones.

"I want to have bath," said Mara.

"Me too," said Betha.

At last they turned north down a steep, narrow, winding trail that quickly brought them out below somewhere upstream from the waterfall Makrina remembered. At first she was not sure Salome was taking them to the same pool, or whether this was even the same stream. It looked much deeper and faster than the trickling brook it had been the previous fall. Then they passed a narrow hollow that looked somewhat familiar, though now it was choked with undergrowth. A little ways farther and Makrina was sure. "That's it," she cried, looking back over her shoulder. "That's the way we went up the ridge last fall. The pool's not far now."

They trooped along the narrow bank of the swollen stream for another quarter of a mile before noticing the growing roar of water over the falls farther down. Soon it was almost deafening, and then they could see it—a steady pouring of water over a jagged rock rim. From the bank above it, they could see the spreading pool below, strangely peaceful despite the rush of the waterfall. Giddy with delight and anticipation, the girls quickly found their way down to the pool's edge.

The pool was much larger now and certainly deeper. Makrina tried to imagine where she and Gerasimos had made their camp but could only believe that the spot was now underwater. They stared at the pool for a moment as if not knowing what to do, then Salome pointed to a large flat rock lying in the sun at the opposite end of the flowing pool. "Safer there," she shouted over the roar of the falls.

Farther away, the noise was not so great. Salome and Makrina set their things down on a natural ledge in the flat rock and unpacked Makrina's white subtunics. With Mara and Betha looking puzzled, Salome and Makrina disappeared behind the rock and returned a while later wearing only the knee-length subtunics and carrying their usual clothes and their sandals in their hands. "What do we wear?" asked Mara.

Salome paused for a moment, as if giving the question serious thought, then smiled and said, "Nothing." She giggled cruelly, and so did Makrina, after seeing the frown on Mara's face.

Picking her way carefully across the rocks, Makrina found a spot where the water was shallow enough to see the bottom. She studied the bottom for a while to be sure where she was stepping, and finding a patch of smooth pebbles in water ankle-deep, she stepped right in. "Oooh! Oooh!" she cried, jumping back out. "It's cold!"

"How cold?" asked Salome.

"Ice cold!" said Makrina.

Salome made her way to Makrina and held her hand as she dipped the toes of her right foot into the swirling pool. "It *is* cold," she said, taking them out. "Too cold."

They stood there on their stone platform, clutching each other's hand and staring down at the submerged pebbles. "What are we going to do?" moaned Makrina. "All this way for an ice bath? Why is it so cold?"

"Snow melting in the mountains," said Salome. "I should have known, but I thought by now it would be warm."

Makrina leaned her head against Salome's. "Lord have mercy," she said.

Slowly they made their way back to the big, flat rock where Mara was waiting with a spiteful grin on her face. Betha, however, was sadder than Makrina. "I want bath," she whined.

"It's too cold," said Salome, sitting down on the rock. "You would freeze as in winter."

"Let's eat," said Mara. They unpacked the bread and cheese and divided it among themselves. Salome said a brief prayer and then threw the dogs the bones she had brought just for them. Except for Mara, the girls ate without interest. It was not quite noon, and their disappointment was greater than their hunger.

Makrina nibbled slowly on a piece of bread while staring at the pool. "I can't go back without a bath," she said absently. "Or at least without washing." She stared a moment longer, then laid aside her bread, took a towel from their sack, and climbed over to where the rock sloped gradually down into the pool. There the water was deeper, but the rock provided enough room on which to squat or sit in arm's reach of the water. Wetting the towel with the water, she began to wash her face and neck and arms. Salome joined her with her own towel and began to wash likewise.

When they had washed all of their exposed parts, including their feet and ankles, Makrina reached up, removed the pin that held her hair in place at the back of her head, and shook out her tresses. "What are you going to do?" asked Salome.

"Wash my hair," said Makrina.

"It's too cold," said Salome.

"I am going to wash my hair. Now hold my hand," said Makrina. Salome held Makrina's hand while Makrina knelt as close as she could to the edge of the rock and then bowed low over the water. With her free hand she flung her long hair forward until it touched the water's surface, then carefully lowered its length into the pool.

"Careful," warned Salome.

"I'm all right. Just hold on," said Makrina, scooping water over the back of her head. "Just a little lower."

Salome held Makrina's arm with both hands while Makrina lowered her crown into the water. Billows of long brown hair floated all around her like a graceful sea creature.

"Hold tight," ordered Makrina.

"I am," said Salome.

"It's cold," said Makrina.

"I told you," said Salome.

"It's—*ohhh!*" In an instant, Makrina had lost her balance. Salome let go to save herself and Makrina tumbled forward into the pool with the great splash. "*Eeeiiiiyyyyyy!*" she screamed upon coming to the surface, in water up to her waist. "O Lord," muttered Salome, quickly making the sign of the cross. Mara and Betha and the dogs came running.

"Salome!" cried Makrina, folding her shivering arms up over her chest, her long wet hair hanging down over her face and shoulders. "Why did you let go?!"

"I'm sorry. I thought I would fall in, too. Take my hand," said Salome, extending one hand cautiously over the water.

Makrina took her hand and grasped it tightly, then gave a sudden tug that brought the unsuspecting Salome to the tips of her toes on the edge of the rock. Salome tottered for a brief moment, straining wildly against Makrina's pull, then fell face forward into the water with a fearful shriek.

"Makrina!" yelled Salome upon reaching the surface. "You—! You—!"

Makrina started out onto the rock, but Salome grabbed her hair and pulled her backwards into the pool. She landed on her bottom in water up to her chin. At the water's edge, Mara and Betha were laughing loudly until Salome forced them to retreat with a well-aimed splash of icy water that caught Mara in the face. "Mamma!" cried Mara. "Mamma can't hear you, lammy," laughed Betha.

Makrina waited until Salome was out and away before climbing out herself without assistance. They stood together in the sun on the rock, clutching their shoulders and shivering uncontrollably while water streamed from their tunics and limbs. Salome's hair had come partly undone, and Makrina's was a complete mess. Their arms were covered with goose-pimples, their teeth chattered, and their lips had turned a pale blue.

Each gave the other an accusatory glance, but neither said a word until one of the dogs came over and started licking the water off Salome's bare calf. "Away," she ordered, shaking her leg free.

Makrina pulled her hair away from her face and hazarded a less hostile look at Salome. "Well," she said, with trembling lips, "we had our bath."

Salome glanced at Makrina, then grudgingly turned her frown into a smile. "A proper city bath," she said, with a shivering giggle. Makrina giggled and shivered, too.

They dried their faces and arms with a towel from the sack and sat down together in the warm June sun. When at last they stopped shivering, Makrina unpacked her comb and mirror and other toiletries. "Let me have that," said Salome, taking the comb. "Now sit here while I get the knots out."

Makrina sat with her legs folded up and her arms on her knees, tilting her head back to show her closed eyes to the sun, while Salome oiled and then carefully combed through Makrina's mess of hair. "Someday, when I'm home, I'll have to show you a real bath," said Makrina.

"When will that be, lammy? How could I ever get to the city?" said Salome.

"You could come with me when I leave," said Makrina. "You could keep me company on the journey."

"I couldn't leave Mamma with Grandmamma and Grandpappa and the little ones to care for."

"Oh, the little ones are almost old enough to take care of themselves. Surely you could come for just a visit."

"But I am to be married to Tychikos soon and he will need me," said Salome.

"That won't be until winter. We have until then for you to visit."

"You are leaving that soon?"

"I don't know," Makrina sighed. "Maybe not. Maybe I'll be here to see you married. I pray to God to return home soon."

"I pray for you, too," said Salome.

"You do?"

"Yes," said Salome. "At first, I prayed that you would go soon because I did not like you. Now I would pray for you to stay, but I know you want to go. I will miss you when you do."

"Then you must come with me," said Makrina. "I have a friend at home, a Christian friend, who is our age. I'm sure you'd like her, and I would want you to meet her. She's my best friend."

Salome tugged on a knot of hair but said nothing.

"Her name is Chione, which means Snow," said Makrina.

"Silly name," said Salome. "Snow is cold."

"Snow is white and pure," said Makrina. "She is a Christian. Her parents are also Christians. Her young brother Euplios was a witness for Christ. I saw him executed the spring before last. It seems like ages ago."

"Is it safe in the city? Can you worship there?" asked Salome.

"It's not safe anywhere anymore," said Makrina, "except here at Home."

"Yes. We are safe at Home, thank God."

Mara and Betha played around the edge of pool, soaking their kerchiefs in the water and then slinging them at each other, while Salome and Makrina combed and braided each other's hair, then tied the braids up neatly in the back, to be covered by their kerchiefs.

Checking their work in the mirror, Makrina noticed the change in her face. Her complexion was clear and colorful, tanned by the sun and ruddy from exertion. Her eyebrows had resumed their natural fullness, after many months without plucking. She looked like a young girl again, not the mature, marriageable woman she had seemed in Sinope. She was dismayed at first, but then cheered by a feeling of freshness and youth. In youth there was hope. She was still young and healthy, and there was still time for her to resume her normal life, to marry and live happily for a good long time, as she had always imagined she would, God willing.

In another hour in the hot sun and mountain air, they were nearly dry and it was time to go. With clean underclothes and sun-dried subtunics, they hardly minded slipping again into their summer overtunics. A touch of perfume to their necks and hands made up for everything else their day had lacked, and they left the pool with bright eyes and broad smiles.

The hike back up to the ridge seemed shorter and easier than the trip down. At the top, they stopped for a while to pick berries, but only those that were barely ripe, so they could explain to Ioanna why they had not picked more. It was still not yet supper time when they descended the ridge toward the village, teaching each other hymns they had learned as Christians. Back at home, Makrina took the lead in assuring Ioanna that they had looked everywhere but found only half a basket of berries worth picking. The others quickly made themselves very busy helping out around the house. That alone was enough to make Ioanna wonder, but the girls seemed so contented that Ioanna did not question them.

✠   ✠   ✠

The sky was still light but the sun had set, dimming the narrow alleys of the low-rent district of Nicomedia. Kimon stood at the railing around the porch of his fourth-floor penthouse, staring pensively into the alley while slowly stroking the billows of his beard with a rolled parchment. The smell of grilled meat emanated from the tenement across the alley. Outside the door of the tenement, an old man squatted beside a brazier over which he was roasting chestnuts for sale to passers-by. "Roasted chestnuts! Hot and delicious. Food for gods. Won't you try a few, sir?"

Two gentlemen in government uniforms strode past the old man without acknowledging him and crossed the alley to Kimon's building.

Kimon stepped away from the railing and went inside. His apartment was dark and there wasn't time to light the lamps. He stashed the rolled parchment in a cabinet and then stepped back outside to wait. Before long he heard a knock at his door but waited until he heard a second knock before responding. "Coming!" he called from the roof. Hurrying in again, he unbolted the door and opened it wide. The hallway was even darker than the apartment, but Kimon was not mistaken. "Gaius!" he said. "What a surprise. Come in."

"Lucky for you we're not a pair of thieves come to rob you blind," said Marcellinus. "In a place like this, you should ask who it is before opening up."

"Oh, it's not as seedy as it looks," said Kimon. "Besides, there's not a soul in the neighborhood who doesn't know I've nothing of value, except a few old books. Hello, Libanius. Good to see you again." Marcellinus's aide nodded without a word as he followed his master into the apartment. "Sorry about the light," said Kimon. "I must have dozed off on the porch and didn't realize it was so late."

"I'm sorry to have disturbed you, but I've been so busy this is the only time I'll have to see you before I leave. Do you mind?"

"Not at all," said Kimon.

Marcellinus looked around in the darkness. "Let's talk outside," he said.

Libanius stayed behind in the shadows while Marcellinus and Kimon moved out into the lingering light of dusk. "I'm leaving for Alexandria the day after tomorrow," said Marcellinus, glancing over the railing into the alley. "Hierocles says he wants me in Egypt before the end of October. I suppose I should be flattered. He's put off many of his reforms until my arrival."

"So how does he like his new post as prefect of Egypt?" asked Kimon.

"He's on top of the world, though with this new caesar, Maximinus Daia, I sense that Hierocles sometimes feels like he has the world on his shoulders," said Marcellinus. "Daia's headstrong and rash. He has his own ideas about how to do things, and though they're not all bad, he does rather insist on doing things his way."

From down in the alley they heard the sounds of a scuffle and cries of alarm. Marcellinus instinctively put his hand on the pommel of the short civilian's sword hanging at his side. He rarely wore one, but it was not safe to be about after dark in some quarters unarmed and unaccompanied. That's why he had brought Libanius. "How can you stand living here in this slum?" he asked Kimon.

"Does it matter? I'm never at home. I'm always at the palace," said Kimon.

"Always at the baths, from what I hear," said Marcellinus.

"Only since moving over into the office of the Adjutant General. It's a debilitating job. My brain would die from disuse if I spent too long in the office."

"It's only for a while. You're not doing your career any good by slacking off. Before long, word will get around and then you'll be finished as far as advancement is concerned."

Kimon shrugged but said nothing in his own defense.

"You can still come with me if you want to," said Marcellinus. "Hierocles holds nothing against you. He had to move you aside for political reasons. In Egypt, he won't have to pacify Hippolytus Pollio or his whorish wife. Now's your chance to get back on track by joining us there."

Kimon leaned on the railing and stared down into the alley.

"What's stopping you?" Marcellinus asked. "Alexandria has bigger and better slums than this one. I'm sure you can find a place that suits you."

Kimon chuckled and shook his head. "What about my sister? She's still a fugitive. How can I help her from Alexandria?"

"Kimon, friend, how can you help her from here? Pollio's acting governor now. Who knows when Hierocles's successor will be named? It might even be Pollio. A pardon's out of the question for the foreseeable future. You're wasting your time trying."

"She's my sister, Gaius," said Kimon.

"Isn't she safe, wherever she is? What more could you ask under the present circumstances? If she's safe, then there's nothing else you need do at the moment."

"Don't you still care about her, even a little?" asked Kimon.

"Of course I do," said Marcellinus. "But what can I do to help her? I'm as helpless as you are. I wish things hadn't turned out the way they did, but what can I do about it now? Pollio's in charge. It's his province now, and I'm wanted off in Egypt. There's nothing either of us can do. She'll just have to wait until things change."

Kimon peered at Marcellinus through the dusk, weighing Marcellinus's words.

"No one, not even Makrina herself, could have wanted things to turn out differently more than I did," said Marcellinus. "This wasn't what I had planned for us. But she wouldn't have it any other way. She made her own choices. She acted on her own, rashly and recklessly. She's a dangerous girl, Kimon—dangerous to herself and anyone close to her. And to think I tried so hard to get her to marry me."

Kimon turned and leaned against the railing, staring down into the now dark alley. "If it's any comfort, you weren't the first," he said.

Marcellinus puzzled for a moment, then clapped a hand on Kimon's shoulder. "That's right," he said, suddenly cheerful. "There was the younger Canio before me. She broke his heart. She destroyed him. See what I mean?"

Kimon did not respond, and after a silent moment staring with him into the alley, Marcellinus straightened up and stepped away from the railing. "It's late. I've got to go," he said. "Are you coming to Egypt or staying here? I need to know."

"I can't go," said Kimon, "not right now."

"Suit yourself," said Marcellinus, a trace of impatience. "Look, Kimon, I'll do this for you: if you show up in Alexandria before the end of November, there will be a place for you. If you don't, I'll assume you've decided otherwise. Fair enough?"

"More than fair," said Kimon, turning toward Marcellinus. "Thanks for everything, Gaius."

"Not at all," said Marcellinus. "Now go to bed and tomorrow, try showing up at the office early for once."

He collected Libanius on his way through the apartment and then led the way down the dark stairwell and out into the night.

Kimon watched them go from the porch, then felt around in the dark for an unlit lamp and carried it across the hall to beg a light from his neighbor. Returning to his apartment with the lighted lamp, he lit two more lamps, then retrieved the rolled parchment from the cabinet and settled down at his desk. Once more he read through Marcus's letter from Mogontiacum, then laid it aside and took up his pen and parchment to write a few letters of his own.

# XXI

The white cliffs across the Gallic Strait were almost invisible in the flurry of snow, which also muffled the rhythmic rushing of the waves, the screech of seagulls, and the pounding of hammers. Along the broad white beach lay scores of longboats in varying stages of construction, visible in either direction as far as the fog permitted. In the dunes just beyond the beach, Marcus and Terentius huddled under their hooded cloaks beside a bonfire while Terentius delivered his report, reading from a wax tablet.

"Nineteen is being tarred. 20 is being tarred. 21 is awaiting fittings. 22, awaiting fittings. 24, awaiting fittings. 25, awaiting fittings. They all need fittings," said Terentius. "And oars, of course. We can't go anywhere without oars."

Marcus poked pensively at the glowing embers with a piece of scrap wood. In his dreams the night before, he had seen Makrina calling for him, but no matter how he tried he could not reach her. People kept calling him away—Felix, his father, his commander officer, even the emperor Constantius. What did it mean? Was it a message from God, or just an expression of his frustrations and fears? *What if she is in danger?* he wondered. *What if she's dead?*

"Of course, we could always drag the boats back to Mogontiacum to use as sleds in the snow," said Terentius.

"Sleds?" said Marcus, looking up.

Terentius smiled and shrugged. "Just kidding," he said.

Marcus nodded.

"I was saying they all need oars," said the young centurion.

"I'll see what's keeping them," replied Marcus, still poking at the embers. Just before leaving Mogontiacum with the legion, he had received a letter from Kimon, in reply to his own, telling of Makrina's flight into the mountains. Though she was safe, Kimon urged Marcus to write to Aristoboulos to see how he might help. Kimon himself had been unable to help her while serving with the imperial service in Nicomedia and was expected to leave soon for a new post in Alexandria. Kimon in the imperial service? Marcus marveled. Things had changed indeed since he had left Sinope. Kimon wrote that he was forwarding Marcus's letter to Aristoboulos with the suggestion that Aristoboulos send it on to Makrina.

Upon receiving Kimon's letter, Marcus had quickly sent off two letters to Aristoboulos, one of which was addressed to Makrina, wherever she was. Shortly thereafter, Marcus's legion, XXII Primigenia, was ordered to the coast at Bononia to prepare for deployment to Britain. At that time, an impulse within him had made Marcus consider requesting leave to return to Sinope, but he had been away from his post enough already that year and could not very well leave now when his unit was preparing for action. Better to await word from Aristoboulos; then Marcus would have a better idea of what needed doing. Yet now it was already January, and Marcus still had not heard from Aristoboulos.

"Hail Gratianus!" cried an orderly nearby. Marcus and Terentius rose to their feet and saluted the legate Gratianus, wrapped in his crimson general's cloak with the gold and purple border, walking up from the beach with an aide in tow.

"Good morning, Canio. How are things?" said Gratianus.

"Well enough, sir," said Marcus, "but for the lack of fittings and oars."

"Terentius can give me a report later. At the moment, I've something else to discuss with you. Excuse us, please, Terentius."

Terentius saluted and left the dunes for the beach. Gratianus turned to Marcus. "I have good news and bad news," he said, "good for you and bad for me. The bad news is I'm losing you. The good news is you're being reassigned to the Companions, effective immediately. The emperor's son, Flavius Constantinus, has popped up unexpectedly here in Bononia, after giving Galerius the slip in Nicomedia. The emperor has selected you as his aide. You'll also be promoted to tribune first class. Congratulations."

"Thank you, sir, but why me?" asked Marcus.

"Well," said Gratianus, "you're the perfect pick. Constantius wants to provide his son with suitable company, and there aren't many in the ranks with your education and upbringing plus your military record. He expects that since you and Constantine have served in the East you and he will get on well together."

"I hope he's right," said Marcus. "What do you know of him?"

"Not much. Good reputation. Commanding presence. He's a little older than you. Rather reserved, like his father." Gratianus rested his hand on Marcus's cloaked shoulder. "If he takes after his father, you should have no trouble. It's a golden opportunity, Marcus, which can only lead to greater things. You've served long enough with a legion. It's time you moved up. At the very least, it will mean a substantial increase in pay."

Marcus smiled to hide his uncertainty. "I couldn't turn that down, could I?" he said.

Gratianus slapped him firmly on the back. "Go see the commander of the Companions right away. He's expecting you."

The imperial headquarters at Bononia was three miles east of town, at a spacious villa set upon a treeless hilltop overlooking the sea. The Companions were encamped outside the estate, but Marcus was directed to the villa itself by an officer of the Imperial Lancers, one of the three elite units that made up the Companions. The other two were the Imperial Shieldmen and the Household Protectors. From the gates of the estate, a young officer of the Protectors walked Marcus up the pebble carriageway to the villa, leaving Marcus's aide Vitalis behind with the horses.

About the villa, Marcus saw many more Protectors, each one proudly wearing his white cloak with the purple border and the embroidered medallion of the divine Hercules on the right shoulder. (By convention established by Diocletian, the emperors of the West claimed Hercules as their divine patron, whereas the emperors of the East claimed Jove.) Marcus did not meet the Companions commander but instead was escorted directly to the commander of the Protectors, a gray-haired veteran named Clodius Rufinus, who owed his position to many years of faithful service to his friend Constantius Chlorus, now Constantius Augustus.

"Have you ever been an aide to anyone before?" asked Rufinus.

"No, sir," answered Marcus.

"No matter," said Rufinus. "You are what your lord wants you to be. And since none of us knows the emperor's son, none of us can tell you what he wants. You'll figure it out before long."

Rufinus led Marcus to a large, apsed receiving room with a tessellated floor and painted plaster walls depicting scenes of the hunt. The room was empty except for two simple camp stools drawn up to a long table in the center of the room. Across the table was spread a huge, chamois-skin map of Britain, covered with the symbols of ports, forts, walls, and signal stations as well as many named cities. "Wait here," said Rufinus, before leaving Marcus alone in the room.

Like most soldiers, Marcus could not resist a long look at a good map, but before long he heard footsteps, many footsteps, coming down the hallway outside. A voice in the hall was saying, "Long term, my lord, the Saxons pose the greatest difficulty, but at the moment it's the Picts who are the problem."

Marcus instinctively drew back from the map just as the Emperor Constantius entered the room in the company of more than twenty senior commanders and staff officers. Courtesy would have called for Marcus to salute, but Constantius gave him just a glance and no one else paid him the least attention as they gathered around the great map. Marcus was not about to interrupt their discussion.

"You can see here the improvements we've made to coastal defenses," said the voice from the hall, whose uniform identified him as the Duke of Britannia, the province's senior military commander. "Two more large forts along the coast of Cantii, both constructed according to your model, my lord, with stone walls fourteen feet thick, sixteen feet high."

"Two more are planned for the coast of Trinovantes, but I'll need time and money to complete them," said another officer, the Count of the Saxon Shore, second in command in Britain. "I've also constructed twelve smaller camps between the Tamesis and the Abus, for use as needed."

"We can safeguard the shore with the forces we have now," said the duke, "but it doesn't leave us much to take north against the Picts. They're raiders. They strike and then they retreat. When we strike back, they retreat farther north into the wilds. It's like chasing boars through a forest. We'd need ten times their number to round them all up."

"Why not set a trap?" said a third officer, taller and younger than the others. (*That's Constantine*, Marcus thought, *and this briefing is for him.*) "Take a legion north by sea and up this inlet here."

"The Bodotria," said the count. "It leads to the old Antonine Wall."

"Land near the Antonine Wall, and then invade with two legions from the south. They'll have nowhere to go," said Constantine.

"Interesting," said his father, the emperor. "What do you think, Canio?"

Marcus looked up from the map to see the emperor smiling at him. "Brilliant," he answered. "And we already have the boats, or will have soon. Enough for one whole legion at least."

"We can't risk a crossing of the strait until March anyway," said the Praetorian Prefect, Julius Asclepiodotus, the emperor's long-serving chief of staff, "so we have plenty of time to finish any preparations."

"I'm all for it," said Crocus, the Alemanni king, a German whose attire betrayed his barbarian nationality. "Can't wait to see the panic on their painted faces when they realize they're trapped."

The discussion continued for another half hour, with junior staff officers competing against each other to add relevant details. Marcus just watched and listened. When the meeting adjourned, he followed the others to the officers' mess.

For days thereafter, Marcus tagged along with the imperial party without much more to say or do. Constantine was always in the company of the emperor, inspecting the boats, visiting the troops, conferring with commanders, and conducting civic business affecting nearly a third of the empire. Marcus was always close at hand, but not as close as others who had fled with Constantine from Nicomedia. They treated Marcus respectfully on account of the favor shown him by the emperor, but neither he nor they knew how they were supposed to work together, and they secretly suspected him of being the emperor's spy.

Two weeks passed before Marcus exchanged his first words with Constantine. They were on the road with a small company of Protectors, on their way to a Mithraic initiation as the honored guests of the XXX Ulpian Legion, which was also awaiting deployment to Britain. The cult of Mithras had been popular among Roman soldiers since the time of Pompey the

Great. According to Persian myth, there was only one great god, the Sun, and Mithras was its avatar. His cult promised devotees victory in battle and life after death. Aspirants gained admission by performing demanding trials like walking barefoot over hot coals. Further trials were required to ascend the seven ranks of the cult: Crow, Bridegroom, Soldier, Lion, Persian, Sun-runner, and Father. Constantine was to be elevated to the rank of Lion.

The ceremony was to be held in a cave as always, somewhere away from the coast in the province of Belgica. After a long spell of silence, Constantine suddenly said, "Canio, my father tells me you were at Carrhae."

Marcus kicked his horse closer. "I was," he answered. "With the XV Apollinaris. Not something I'm inclined to boast about."

"Understandably," said Constantine. "Don't worry. Galerius took all the blame for that near disaster."

"Is it true that Diocletian made him run alongside his chariot while making his report?"

"It is true. Diocletian was a great soldier and commander, and I learned a lot from him. That day, however, he let his pride get the better of him, and the lesson I learned was: Never humiliate an officer in front of his men— that is, unless you intend to fire him on the spot. Galerius never forgave those of us who witnessed his humiliation that day. I suspect that's why I'm here and my son is still in Asia."

"How old is your son?"

"All of seven. Just the age to leave the company of women and join the company of men. Instead, he's Galerius's hostage, but with my mother at Drepanon in Bithynia. His own mother died at his birth."

"I'm sorry to hear that," said Marcus.

"She was lowborn—a sandal-maker's daughter—but both very beautiful and very dutiful, like my mother. I loved her dearly."

"What was her name?"

"Minervina."

"A good name for a soldier's mother," said Marcus.

"A good name for a soldier's wife," added Constantine. "Are we sure we're on the right road?"

"Yes, my lord," said the trooper in the lead. "The landmarks all match up."

"Let's ask this shepherd while we have the chance," said Constantine.

The lead trooper called out to the shepherd, who had left his flock to watch the soldiers pass, but the shepherd seemed not to understand the trooper's Latin. "Pardon me, my lords," said Vitalis as he rode past Marcus and Constantine on his way forward. After a few unintelligible words with the shepherd, Vitalis reported back that the caves were indeed just three miles down the lane and that other soldiers had passed by not an hour before.

Constantine was relieved. "What is your name?" he asked.

"Vesunnius Vitalis, my lord. I am Aemilius Canio's aide."

"Are you from around here?"

"No, my lord. My father was a centurion with II Augusta, and I grew up in Britain, along the Wall. My mother was a Briton, and the Belgae speak a language like that of many Britons."

"But aren't the Belgae Germans and the Britons Celts?"

Vitalis shrugged and said, "We're a mixed race, my lord."

"Most real Romans are these days. But not your Lord Canio," said Constantine, with a smile and a glance at Marcus. "He's a Roman's Roman."

They found the cave without difficulty, endured the secret rite, and then shared the ritual repast of bread and wine, symbolizing the meal that Mithras made of the flesh and blood of a bull he killed on orders from the Sun. Marcus had partaken of it many times, but this time he kept thinking of how childish it was and how foolish a man would be to take it seriously. For all he could tell, no one did. It was a purely social affair, without deeper meaning.

The rest of the winter passed slowly, but in early March the legions crossed the strait to the white cliffs of Dubris without serious accident. It took two weeks and two hundred boats to ferry five legions—30,000 men and 3,000 horse—four miles across the strait, with the boats each making three trips. But once on land, the legions regained their famous footing, marching all the way to Eboracum in just ten days.

Marcus saw the best and the worst the province had to offer, though only in passing: plain but pleasant cities like Londinium and Verulamium, with a few fair-sized buildings of finished stone; towns built entirely of wood with strange names like Crococalana and Manduessedum; and squalid, nameless villages that were little more than clusters of thatched huts. The countryside in between was dotted with villas small and large, but all were modest compared to the mansions on the mainland. Along the way, they passed scores of wooden shrines to unknown deities and occasionally a stone pillar or pedestal to spirits more familiar—Silvanus of the forests, the Romano-Gallic war-god Mars Lenus, and the ubiquitous Mother Fates. Closer to Eboracum the signs of civilization thinned and the province took on a wildness surpassing any Marcus had seen.

Vitalis was in high spirits the whole way. He was ten when he left Britain, old enough to remember his native land fondly if not clearly. Returning for the first time since childhood, he was struck by the rudeness of the land and its people. He was proud of his Roman citizenship and his status now as an Imperial Protector, and embarrassed when his fellow Protectors turned up their noses at his countrymen. Still, he was happy to be home.

The army paused at Eboracum only briefly before heading farther north to the Aelian Bridge at the eastern end of Hadrian's Wall, near the mouth of the river Tinus, where they met the boats they had left a fortnight earlier. Constantine, King Crocus, and the XXII Primigenia Legion boarded the boats for the seaborne assault deep into the enemy's rear, as Constantine had suggested, while three of the five new legions joined the VI Victrix and the II Augusta in the ready along the Wall. They crossed the Wall as soon as the boats returned to the Aelian Bridge to embark another legion, the XXX Ulpian, to reinforce the XXII by sea. The plan worked wonderfully, catching the Picts so off guard that after a few quick skirmishes there was nothing left but mopping up. By June, the emperor Constantius was back in Eboracum, with Constantine in command of the army and two thirds of the land between Hadrian's Wall and the old Antonine wall under Roman occupation.

By July, however, the emperor Constantius was seriously ill, and Constantine was racing south to be with him. The palace had already begun to fill with important persons coming to pay their last respects to the dying emperor, to be there at the hour of death, and to take part in the aftermath. King Crocus, the Duke of Britannia, and the legates of all eight legions then in Britain arrived shortly after Constantine. Later in the week, the Prefect of Britannia, the Duke's civilian counterpart, arrived from his capital at Camulodunum, accompanied by the Count of the Saxon Shore. Orders were issued to the garrison and the town suspending all festivities. Soldiers and servants were instructed to keep their voices down and avoid commotion while preparing for the expected.

Then, just before dawn on July 25, at the age of 55, the emperor Constantius passed away peacefully in his bed with Constantine by his side. A loud gong was struck 70 times to announce his death to the palace. Before the sun was up, servants had draped the palace in black bunting. All shops and markets were closed, and all wheeled vehicles on post and in the town were stilled, with exceptions only for the workmen and wagons needed to prepare the funeral pyre. Throughout the day, the palace bustled with hushed officials streaming through the entrance hall of the imperial residence to view the emperor lying in state, in full regalia, his arms and armor arrayed about him. Constantine withdrew to his quarters, while Marcus and the other aides, Bassianus and Ablabius, took turns screening visitors and waiting outside his door.

Early the next morning, the imperial hearse—a large, flatbed wagon draped in black and drawn by six black horses—was brought out and left in the yard outside the imperial residence. The funeral began at noon, when the body and all its trappings were carried outside and loaded onto the hearse. The Protectors, on foot and wearing black sashes over their white uniforms, led the hearse out of the yard. At the gates of the palace, the Lancers took the lead, followed by the Shieldmen and then a corps of drummers beating out a solemn tattoo and a choir of trumpeters periodically sounding calls of distress. Behind the hearse came a contingent of designated mourners, drawn from among the palace servants, who wailed unceasingly, tore their clothes, and beat their breasts. Then came Constantine, alone and on foot, followed by the Praetorian Prefect, the Duke, the Count, King Crocus, and other senior officers and officials. Marcus, Bassianus, Ablabius, and the imperial staff came next, followed by representative detachments of the three oldest legions based in Britain—II Augusta, VI Victrix, and XX Valeria Victrix.

Local legionaries and auxiliaries lined the route to a hilltop outside of town, where a three-storied pyre awaited. The first story was a six-foot-high rectangle filled with firewood, thatch, and kindling. The second story was a canopied bier adorned with flowers and surrounded with spices, incense, and sweet-smelling unguents. The third story, much smaller than the first two, was a gilded cage containing an eagle. Upon arrival of the procession, the eight legionary legates lifted the pallet on which Constantius's corpse lay and placed it on the bier.

Custom required an emperor's successor or praetorian prefect to deliver his eulogy, but no one begrudged Constantine the right to speak for his father. Standing upon the now empty hearse, Constantine spoke of his father's many victories, his many honors, his fair and wise administration of the provinces, his care for the soldiers under him, his generosity to those who served him, his mercy toward those who opposed him, his legendary faithfulness to his second wife, the Empress Theodora, and finally his love and concern for his sons and daughters. It was a modest eulogy by the standards of oratory, delivered from the heart and in part extemporaneous. Though he spoke for almost an hour, he was never at a loss for words and seemed to take naturally to the task without a trace of self-consciousness.

After the eulogy, the soldiers were paraded in a circle around the pyre. Then Constantine, again in the chief role he had assumed, took a torch and applied it to the tinder at the base of the pyre. Immediately, an honor guard of centurions did the same all around the pyre. As the flames grew, several of the centurions took off their decorations and threw them in the fire as an act of mourning and as a sacrifice to the soul of the departed. The pull of a lanyard opened the cage atop the canopy and freed the eagle, which flew away fast and far, symbolizing the apotheosis of the augustus.

All present—the officials, the soldiers, the people—stood in silence as flames engulfed the pyre. Constantine stood by himself, between the crowd and the pyre, close enough to feel its heat. Crocus waited a quarter of an hour before stepping forward to stand beside him. "He wanted you to succeed him," he said, facing the fire. "He said as much. We all heard him. You did, too."

"But he's dead now," said Constantine, "while Galerius and the others still live. They will want a say."

"Bah! What say should they have? They're a long way off and don't know the North or its legions."

"Diocletian's rules of succession exclude sons from inheriting the imperial dignity."

"The laws of nature trump the rules of men, and by the laws of nature sons succeed their fathers. Everyone knows that. Everyone accepts it."

"If we break the rules, so will Maxentius. There will be war."

"There will be war eventually for one reason or another. There always is. Your father put down his share of usurpers. You will do the same. Every emperor must. . . . You've proven yourself, Constantine. You've proven you are his son. No one who has served him will not serve you."

"In Britain, no doubt," said Constantine. "In Gaul, perhaps. In Spain, perhaps not."

With that he turned and started down the hill where a horse awaited him. Crocus watched him go, wondering what to do.

Standing in the front rank with the other generals, Gratianus, commander of Marcus's old legion, muttered to himself, "Hail him, Crocus." Then, seeing the opportunity about to pass, Gratianus himself shouted out, "Hail, Flavius Valerius Contantinus *Augustus!*"

The soldiers and people fell suddenly silent. Constantine glanced over at the rank of generals. Crocus then sounded off with a salute: "Hail, Flavius Valerius Contantinus Augustus!"

The generals then answered him: "Hail, Flavius Valerius Contantinus Augustus!" Then the junior officers, Marcus included, and then the soldiers:

> *Hail, Flavius Valerius Contantinus Augustus!*
> *Hail, Flavius Valerius Contantinus Augustus!*
> *Hail, Flavius Valerius Contantinus Augustus!*

Constantine seemed determined to ignore them as he readied his horse, but when he mounted up, someone gave the order to break ranks. Soldiers swarmed around the horse and rider instantly, taking hold of bridle and reins or beating their shields with their spears while chanting, "Hail, Flavius Valerius Contantinus Augustus!" Several knelt and offered their shields for Constantine to stand upon. He smiled and almost seemed to laugh, so the soldiers were emboldened. When he did not dismount immediately, they grabbed him by the arms and legs, lifted him off his horse, and set him on his feet upon a shield. A purple cloak appeared from nowhere and in an instant was around his shoulders. Then they lifted him shoulder-high upon the shield with loud shouts of "Augustus! Augustus!" Their generals congratulated each other on their success, while the soldiers paraded their new augustus around in circles before the pyre.

Moments later a lone trumpet sounded the call for order, and the cheering soon subsided. The soldiers lowered the shield and allowed Constantine to dismount, into the company of his generals. Asclepiodotus was the first to formally greet him, saying, "Hail to the Augustus Constantine, my lord and emperor."

"Hail! Hail!" said the rest.

"I thank you all," said Constantine, "for your faithfulness to my father and for the favor you have shown me this day. I shall never forget it, as long as the gods give me breath. Now all we need is some brave soldier to break the news to Nicomedia."

"You mean some fool to feed to the lions," said Crocus.

"He'd stand a better chance with lions," said Constantine.

"I'll go, my lord," said Marcus, standing behind Gratianus.

"You, Canio?" said Constantine.

"I'd be honored," said Marcus.

"Not a bad idea, my lord," said Gratianus. "Imagine: The son of the illustrious Augustus Flavius Constantius sends the son of the venerable Senator Aemilius Canio to announce his succession as Augustus of the West. It's perfect. Galerius will have a fit."

"He will indeed," said Constantine. "Very well then, Canio. Go you shall."

# XXII

The court of Galerius at Nicomedia was much given to pomp, in marked contrast to the courts of earlier emperors. Since the first Augustus, Roman emperors had stood to receive visitors and expected no more from them than a respectful salutation. With few exceptions, they styled themselves as princeps—first citizens of the empire—a lesser dignity than the claim of kings. But in the troubled decades before the accession of Diocletian, the imperial dignity had suffered a dangerous loss of prestige threatening the effectiveness of the imperial government.

To strengthen the government, Diocletian and his colleagues had deliberately sought to aggrandize the office and person of the emperor, importing from Persia many practices that elevated the emperors well above their previous status and pushed the people into abject submission. The soldier-caesars were the first to be addressed as "lord," the form of address used by servants and slaves for their masters. They restricted access to their person through elaborate palace protocol and ceremonies. They remained seated when receiving visitors and required others to perform the Persian *proskynesis*—to kneel and touch their foreheads to the ground—in their presence.

Marcus had patiently abided by all these requirements, waiting for hours in one receiving room after another, from early in the morning to late in the afternoon, before finally being admitted into the presence of the senior augustus. In the lonely midst of the porphyry-columned throne room, gleaming with gold illumined by a vast array of multi-colored candles and heavy with incense arising from the altars to the left and the right of the imperial dais, Marcus had knelt and bowed at a respectful distance, some forty feet before the throne, and saluted his imperial host using all of the official forms: the pious, lucky, best, greatest, unconquerable prince Caesar Galerius Augustus, Pontifex Maximus, Imperator, Consul, Proconsul, Father of the Fatherland, *et cetera*.

Still it did no good. As Marcus read aloud the official notification of Constantius's death and Constantine's succession, the Augustus Galerius smoldered silently on his Jovian throne, with golden eagles supporting the ivory armrests and bolts of golden lightening radiating from the center of the back, wearing a tent-like dalmatic heavily embroidered with golden thread and a diadem of pearls around his fat gray head.

At the naming of Constantine as Caesar Augustus, Galerius winced and reddened and interrupted. "Let me see that!" he demanded, pointing past Marcus to the gilded standard held by Vitalis, from which was suspended a large painted portrait of Constantine in profile, wearing the laurel crown and Herculian insignia of the augustus of the West. The portrait was encircled by a laurel wreath dusted with golden glitter.

Vitalis started forward with the standard but was intercepted by a guard, who wrested the standard from his hands and carried it the rest of the way, stopping short of the imperial dais beside the smoking altar to the right of the throne. The nearsighted emperor leaned forward in his seat for a better look at the likeness. His face reddened further and his eyes blazed with fury.

"Why that impudent little upstart! How dare he! How *dare* he!—Take it away!" he shouted. "No, bring it here!"

Jumping down off the dais, Galerius snatched the wreath from the standard and hurled it into the fire of the nearest altar, then ripped the canvas portrait from its place and tore it in two from top to bottom, giving a great beastly grunt as he did so. The startled guard lost his grip on the standard and let it clatter to the floor. The emperor, undistracted, grunted again as he quartered the halves and then cast the tattered pieces of painted canvas before him.

"There!" he shouted at Marcus. "*That's* what I think of your traitorous little lord! The nerve of him! The arrogance!"

The dried laurel wreath began to smolder on the altar, emitting an unpleasant odor. Galerius turned toward his attendants and shook his fist in the air. "Whom has he commanded? Whom has he conquered? What makes him think *he* deserves the purple? I should never have let him leave, that vain little brat! He used my good will against me and now shows me outright defiance!" He turned back to Marcus. "And whom does he send to declare his defiance but another spoiled young brat, from a whole family of spoiled brats!"

Thus enraged, the emperor took up the discarded standard and hurled it at Marcus, who collided with Vitalis trying to dodge it.

"I should have you arrested for treason!" shouted Galerius.

Then suddenly he pressed his hand against his bulging belly and reeled about in pain. "Gods!" he gasped. The court physician stepped forward, but Galerius waved him away. Slowly he mounted the dais, struggling for control, then he turned once more to Marcus and shouted, "Constantine is *not* the Augustus—is that clear? *Severus* is the Augustus of the West! Constantine is his *caesar*, and Daia *out-ranks* Constantine as Caesar of the East! Constantine is *last*, do you hear me?! *Last!*"

The pain struck again, harder than before. Galerius leaned back and gripped an eagle's head on his throne to steady himself. The court physician rushed forward, snapping his fingers to signal that a litter be brought. "Get out," said Galerius to Marcus. "Get out!"

Marcus and Vitalis bowed and retreated hastily from the room. The pained augustus watched them leave and then was carried away to his bed.

Marcus wasted no time in leaving Nicomedia for Byzantium, where he deposited Vitalis and their guards before sailing off alone to Sinope by the fastest boat he could hire. Their journey east had been so swift that he had not bothered to send word ahead of his return, and just two days after leaving Nicomedia he was pounding on the door of Aristoboulos's townhouse in Sinope, pleading privately with the Christian God for someone to answer soon.

It had been three and a half years since he had left Sinope, and the sights and smells of the little city filled him with an intoxicating nostalgia that excited his hopes as well as his desires. Could so little have changed? Could it all still be here, this little world—Makrina's world—where once he was so happy? He pounded harder, and at last the door opened.

"Good day, sir. Can I help you?" asked a servant whom Marcus did not recognize.

"Is the family at home?" he asked impatiently.

"I'm sorry, sir. They're in the country. Were they expecting you?"

"No, no," said Marcus. "So no one's here?"

"Just Master Kimon—"

"Kimon?" said Marcus, pushing open the door and brushing past the servant. He marched through both the atrium and the tablinum and stopped at the edge of the open peristyle. "Kimon!" he shouted up through the loggia of the house.

From a downstairs bedroom came a bump and a curse and then a half-naked Kimon, stumbling out in just his loincloth, with his hair disheveled and his beard misshapen. Though it was already noon, he had apparently just woken up. "Marcus!" he cried. "Almighty gods! Where the devil have you come from? I thought you were in Britannia."

"I was," laughed Marcus. "But now I'm here. For God's sake, put on some clothes! Is this any way to greet a friend?"

"Later!" said Kimon, throwing his arms around Marcus and kissing him repeatedly. "But why now here? You're a long way from Britannia."

"I was sent to Nicomedia to deliver the news of the death of the augustus Constantius and of the succession of his son. I'm a tribune of the Protectors now, a member of the new caesar's bodyguard."

"I see!" said Kimon, glancing at Marcus's uniform. He had learned enough in Nicomedia to recognize the golden medallion of Hercules on the breast of Marcus's tunic and the purple and gold border of his white chlamys.

"Actually I'm supposed to be his aide, but it hasn't worked out that way. What about you? You're supposed to be in Egypt."

"I left there in May," said Kimon shamefully. "I quit the service. I just couldn't stand working for a living. Oh, it was fun at first and there's the prestige that goes with access to the palace and to the high and mighty. But after a while, that all wears off. What's it worth, after all? So I came back here to see what I could do for Makrina."

"That's why I'm here," said Marcus. "How is she, Kimon? Where is she?"

"I don't know," said Kimon, his smile fading. "Nobody knows."

"What do you mean?" said Marcus.

"We haven't heard from her in months—many months. She's somewhere in the mountains, safe I hope, but our link with her has broken down. The Christians who kept us in touch have disappeared. They were so secretive about where she was hiding, so afraid of being caught. Now they're gone and we've lost touch with her."

Marcus's mouth fell open and he stepped back away from Kimon. "Great gods," he moaned, staring blankly at Kimon.

"Didn't you get a letter? Father said he wrote to tell you."

Marcus shook his head slowly and silently.

"I've asked around," said Kimon. "I've even nosed about a bit through the province. I haven't heard that anything bad has happened to her. I just haven't been able to find out where she is."

"Is there no one who knows?" asked Marcus.

"No one we know," said Kimon.

"But isn't anyone who helped her still here?"

"Well," said Kimon, "there's Posidonios, but he's not in town at the moment. Last March he received a letter from Bardas the trader saying he could not deliver our letters to Makrina on his way south but would try again on his return trip. Posidonios hasn't heard from him since. He hasn't written and he hasn't returned, and of course we've had no word from Makrina."

Marcus felt his throat tighten and his eyes begin to tear. He turned away, struggling to keep from crying. "All this time . . . all this way . . . and I'm no closer to her," he said, wiping his eyes with his cloak.

Kimon shifted uncomfortably on his feet, feeling suddenly ashamed of his appearance and condition. "Father can tell you everything," he said, laying a hand on Marcus's shoulder. "Let's go see him."

Marcus nodded, unable to speak.

Two hours later, Kimon was leaning with one shoulder against the wall of the tablinum in his father's villa, in a dun-colored dalmatica with two broad blue stripes running vertically from the shoulders. His mother Hilaria was sitting on the couch with Marcus while his father Aristoboulos paced the floor before them.

"One can't know how the wind will blow from one day to next," he fumed. "For a while it looked as if the edicts would be forgotten. Then suddenly there's a new round of prosecutions. Every new official wants to make a name himself by showing how zealous and effective he is. None of them really cares, but they all have to make a good appearance initially and it's easier to arrest a few Christians than to tackle any *real* problem facing us. Six months ago the news from Galatia was all arrests, imprisonments, and executions. Now it's Cappadocia we hear about. They've both gotten new governors, you see."

"What about here in Sinope?" Marcus asked.

"It had been quiet," said Aristoboulos, "but we've gotten a new curator to replace Quartillius, whom you might remember, and the new fellow has been asking about the local Christians. He's come straight from Nicomedia and it seems the augustus Galerius may be testing your new king Constantine by insisting that the edicts against the Christian be enforced. So suddenly it's an issue again here."

"Is there any chance your king Constantine will act against the Christians?" asked Hilaria.

"I can't imagine it," said Marcus. "For all that anyone can tell, he's intent upon continuing the policies of his father. He's a decent and honorable man, and smart enough to know to avoid unnecessary trouble, especially while he's trying to establish himself as king. I can say for sure there's no interest in enforcing the edicts among the highest members of his court. Quite to the contrary, they are determined to ignore the edicts. It was one of their reasons for choosing Constantine over anyone sent by Galerius."

Hilaria looked up at her husband. "Well, dear?" she said.

Aristoboulos had stopped his pacing and was looking down at Marcus. After a moment's thought, he asked, "How long can you stay?"

"Not long," answered Marcus. "If I knew where Makrina was, I would take the time to rescue her. As it is, I can't justify staying any more than overnight. I've already delayed my return by a week at least."

"This is very sudden," said Hilaria.

Aristoboulos frowned and sighed, then said, "Marcus, had my elder daughter left with you three years ago, she would no doubt now be safe and happy. Now I must ask you to take my younger daughter with you west, where she will at least be safe."

"Eugenia?" said Marcus.

Aristoboulos nodded.

"We have been thinking of this since hearing from you last winter," said Hilaria.

"Makrina's example and that of others who have been arrested and punished have had a dangerous effect on her, so that now she seems at times determined to suffer as they have," said Aristoboulos. "It's quite childish, of course, and she might grow out of it—if she lives that long."

"But with the new curator and the shifting policy, and that awful Hippolytus Pollio still as governor, we're afraid for her safety," said Hilaria.

"She'd be safe in the West, and your rank and position would guarantee her safe passage. That's more than I or anyone else here could do for her," said Aristoboulos.

"Certainly," said Marcus, "if you think it's best—and if she's willing to go. It's the least I can do for you. When can she leave?"

"Whenever you like," said Aristoboulos. "She's staying the night at a friend's, but we can have her at the harbor in town tomorrow."

"That soon? Are you sure?" said Marcus.

"We wouldn't want to hold you up," said Hilaria. "It will hurt no matter when she leaves, and we decided this long ago."

"Does Eugenia know?"

"She does, and she will go," said Aristoboulos.

"Then I suppose it's settled," said Marcus. "We'll leave tomorrow."

Aristoboulos loaned Marcus his yacht for the return voyage. "Take her as far as you like. For speed and safety, she's the best you'll find," he said.

They were standing with Kimon on her deck the next morning when Hilaria arrived accompanied by her maidservant Nonna and three other women, two of whom were very young. Marcus recognized one of the young women as a friend of Makrina's whose name he could not recall. She watched him with great interest but kept her distance and did not speak. She smiled politely but looked sad nevertheless. Hilaria introduced her as Chione and the older woman with her as her mother Kallista.

The other young woman was less reserved but still a little shy and visibly nervous. Her eyes were everywhere—on her mother, on the others, on the boat and on the shore. When she looked at Marcus, her face flashed a brief, toothy grin. "Hello, Marcus," she chirped.

Marcus looked at her in amazement. *No, it couldn't be,* he told himself, but Kimon confirmed it. "That's Eugenia," he said, obviously amused.

Marcus had seen her last at age twelve, and now she was fifteen, from all appearances a fully grown woman. She was a little taller than Makrina and favored her father more. Her cheeks were thinner, her mouth was wider, and her nose was less delicate. Her eyes were greenish brown, darker than Makrina's, yet the more Marcus looked at her, the more he saw Makrina in them.

In less than an hour, their trunks were loaded and they were ready to sail. Eugenia hugged and kissed everyone but Marcus and Nonna, who would be her chaperon for her journey. Tears came first to Chione, and then to all of the women at once, including Nonna. Aristoboulos wandered aft to speak to the pilot, while Marcus and Kimon turned their backs to the women to say their farewells.

"Find her for me, Kimon. Search until you find her," said Marcus. "And when you do, tell her I'll marry her. Whatever it takes, I will marry her. I swear I will."

Kimon looked at him gravely. "You know what you're saying, don't you?" he said.

"I do," said Marcus.

Kimon nodded. They embraced and then rejoined the women.

Eugenia had her arms around Chione. "Pray for me now, too," she said tearily.

"I will," said Chione.

They parted with kisses, and then Chione did something Marcus had never seen before, making the sign of the cross over Eugenia's head and body. He had seen Christians cross themselves but never one another.

"Christ is with you always," said Chione, "even unto the ends of the earth."

⁜    ⁜    ⁜

Makrina had been overjoyed the previous November upon receiving Marcus's letter to Kimon, relayed by Kimon to his father in Sinope and then sent along as suggested to Makrina. Gerasimos had just arrived and was warming himself by the hearth with Gregorios when they heard her squeal of delight. A second later Makrina burst through the door of the cottage clutching a clutter of letters to her breast. "I got a letter from Marcus!" she announced, waving one of the letters in her hand. "See, Ioanna? It's from Marcus. See, Gerasimos?"

Gerasimos barely glanced at the letter, so amazed was he at Makrina's reaction. Every other time he had brought her letters, she had read them privately and then moped around disappointed the rest of the day. What news was there from this Marcus that made her so happy, he wondered.

"It's from Marcus. See, Salome?"

"What Marcus?" Salome asked.

"My Marcus!" declared Makrina. "The man who gave me his ring! The man I almost married! After all this time, he has remembered me and wants to help! It's a wonder of God! Charita told me to pray for him and I did and now he has written and wants to help! Tell Charita, Gerasimos! Tell her God has heard my prayers and answered them—the man of the ring has remembered me!"

She dropped the rest of the letters on the floor by Gerasimos, then took the reluctant Salome by the hands and led her around the room in a dance. Afterwards she settled down to write out her response:

> *Makrina, daughter of Aristoboulos of Sinope, salutes Marcus Aemilius Canio: Peace and health and the love of our Lord Jesus Christ to you and your house. I was overjoyed to receive your letter after so long with no word, and I thank God that you are well and pray that He keeps you so. I am reminded of you often by the ring you left with me, which I have with me in my present refuge. . . .*

It was a joyous letter, open and incautious, which worried Makrina later, after the letter was sent. Had she presumed too much? Had she read his letter wrongly between the lines? He had hardly offered to marry her again. There was only his offer of assistance, his fond first mention of her name, and his requested kiss—no admission that he missed her or still loved her, and nothing definite on how he could help. There was even the possibility that he was already married to or otherwise involved with someone else. His words had not ruled that out.

She questioned everything, the way a woman does—why did he say this, and why did he write that—giving more thought to his words than the author himself had. Why hadn't he said more? Why hadn't he written her instead of Kimon? Why had he written at all, after two years of silence? Just to offer help? But why?

For several days, she was sunk in the deepest depression, sure that she had bared too much of her soul and afraid her foolishness would scare him off. But when the natural swing of moods leveled her off, she began again to see his letter as a source of hope. By the first snowfall of the season, Makrina was cautiously restructuring her dreams to include Marcus.

Salome's time to wed had come. Her wedding chest was packed weeks in advance with everything a young wife would need in their tiny village, including several tunics, scarves, and other items donated by Makrina. Salome checked it daily. The anticipation showed in her demeanor. Just as Makrina was leveling off, Salome was growing anxious and unstable, crying when the yarn she was spinning broke in two and flying off at her sisters for peeking into her wedding chest. Ioanna's patience with both Makrina and Salome was wearing thin, until the morning the snow began to fall, in big, heavy flakes that quickly covered the ground as custom required. Salome turned suddenly calm and quiet, and Ioanna turned sentimental.

Makrina helped Salome bathe and dress in the traditional plaid wedding tunic, then braided her friend's hair for the last time, for ever afterwards Salome's hair would be braided by her mother-in-law, in whose cottage she would live. It was a sad time for the two of them, who had lived like sisters for more than a year. And yet for Makrina it was also a day of hope, a day to believe that things would change, that the world would not stand still nor pass her by, that someday she too would leave the house to wed someone whom God had chosen.

Late that afternoon, while it was still light, the friends of the groom besieged the cottage for the customary robbery, when the wedding chest was forcibly "stolen" and carried off to the bride's new home. In the village square, a bonfire was prepared, and when the sun had set, the young men of the village gathered around the fire to sing a bawdy song calling the young women out to play—the signal for the brides to leave their houses and join the celebration.

Makrina, of course, could not attend. She kissed Salome farewell at the door and slipped her a small bag of silver coins as one last wedding present. Then she settled down by the hearth to spend the evening with Salome's grandmother Anna listening to her grandfather Gregorios read from the Prophet Isaiah. Gregorios and his predecessors as elders of the Assembly in the village had done their best to discourage certain local practices of ancient origin. So far, he was content to let the evening ritual continue, purged of its more pagan elements. On the morrow, he would have them all in the kirk for the dedication of their marriages with prayer.

The fire in the hearth crackled and popped in quiet sympathy with the muffled cheers from the village square. Anna's spindle and distaff moved constantly, spinning length after length of new wool yarn. Gregorios read on with only an occasional pause to ponder a verse or to wet his lips with melted snow. Makrina tried to listen but more than once found herself straying into a delicious dream of her own wedding day. After a while, she put down her own spinning and stared intently at the fire.

Gerasimos did not visit in December, which caused Makrina no concern. He was an old man and getting older, and the winter weather made the trip more difficult. When he arrived again in January, he brought with him not letters from home, but people—the reader Andreas, his wife Theodoulia, their young son Stephanos, who was born the day his father was beaten for refusing to hand over the Scriptures, and Theodoulia's mother Elena.

Makrina was delighted and begged Ioanna to make room for them. The first night they stayed up very late, reminiscing about Sinope and catching up on events. Theodoulia was a few years older than Makrina and of a lower social rank, but they had known each other from the Assembly in Sinope and felt a common bond as fugitives for the faith. They had not seen each other since the spring before last, when Andreas and Theodoulia fled Sinope to escape the edict of sacrifice. They had stayed for a while in

Castamon and then moved farther south to a village in Galatia near Gangra. But they had been forced to leave Galatia by new persecutions and were on their way to Armenia, an ancient kingdom beyond the eastern border of the Roman empire.

"In Galatia, there are patrols of soldiers called Flying Squads that search the countryside for Christians," said Andreas. "They have unlimited authority to coerce obedience to the edicts. No one is safe, not even those who sacrifice."

"Come with us, Makrina," pleaded Theodoulia. "It will be safer in Armenia. The Caesars do not rule there, and there are many Christians. The king himself is one."

"Armenia?" said Makrina. "But it's so far. How will you get there? The roads aren't safe."

"But there is a way. Isn't there, Gerasimos?" said Andreas.

Gerasimos nodded, gravely as usual. Makrina noticed that the dark hollows under his eyes had deepened in the past months. "There are friends along the way, but still it will be dangerous," he said.

"Then we are safer to stay here at Home?"

"God only knows, Makrina. This is not Galatia, but what is happening in Galatia can happen here at any time. You would be safer in Armenia, if you can get there."

Everyone looked at Makrina as if expecting an answer. "I can't leave now," she said, "not when—when my parents might call for me any day. How would they ever find me in Armenia?"

"You can send them word when you get there," said Theodoulia.

"But it's so far," said Makrina. "It would take months to get there, and it would be many more months before I could return. I can't go. Not now."

Makrina did not go with them when they left three days later, with a local man to guide them to the next safe haven east of Phazemon. The villagers supplied them with food for the journey.

"Be careful, Makrina," said Theodoulia before they left. "We are sojourners in this world and must not cling to what must be left behind someday."

Her words frightened Makrina, and she did not forget them.

Gerasimos was back a week later with more fugitives, fifteen in all, from another village in Galatia. They too were headed for Armenia and left after a brief stay. Gerasimos advised Makrina to go with them. "Go while you can," he said. "Before long, the authorities will find out and intervene. Travel will become much more dangerous. The borders may be closed."

"But what about the people here at Home?" said Makrina. "If it is so unsafe, should they not go also?"

"They will never leave this village," said Gerasimos. "They are too poor and know no other way of life. They would not survive elsewhere. They know the danger, Makrina, but they would rather die for Christ than leave Home. You have no roots here. You have the means to survive elsewhere. You have your parents to live for. You must therefore do what you can to survive."

Still Makrina resisted: "Maybe later, but not now, Gerasimos. I can't go now, not while my parents are still working for my return. And I do have roots here, Gerasimos. I have Ioanna and the girls and dear old Gregorios and Anna. With Salome out of the house, Ioanna needs me more. Maybe this spring, if the danger persists. Maybe then."

# XXIII

Gerasimos did not return for more than a month, long enough for Makrina to convince herself she had made the right decision. Life in the village proceeded peacefully as always. Makrina's fears subsided and her hopes grew. Surely spring will bring deliverance, she told herself. Surely Marcus will have had time to help by then.

Then one day in March, Gerasimos arrived unexpectedly, not around midday as usual but in the evening after sunset, just as Makrina and Ioanna and the rest of the family were settling down around the hearth for supper. His wife Charita and two of their maidservants were with him. Makrina knew instantly that something was wrong, though the greeting Charita gave her was no indication.

"Makrina, dear child!" cried Charita, throwing her arms around Makrina before even taking off her cloak. "Oh, let me look at you. Still as beautiful as I remember, though I see the city has worn off of you. I have prayed for you every day for more than a year, and I see now that God has kept you well. Alleluia."

She was the first woman wearing makeup Makrina had seen in a year and a half, and Makrina was surprised at how strange and unnatural it looked. "Thank you, Charita, but how have you been?" she asked.

Charita closed her eyes for a moment and smiled. "Oh, as well as one might expect for an old woman in these times," she said. "Over the last several months, we had to sell nearly everything to buy our safety. All that's left is on those mules outside. We left like thieves in the night. It was the only way to escape the police. What we couldn't sell or bring with us, we had to leave behind."

"Lord have mercy! You must be heart-broken," said Makrina.

"I was at first, watching it go piece by piece, like a house built upon the sand that has just begun to crumble. But you know, Makrina, now that it's all gone, I thank God for the freedom it has given me. I'm an old woman. I've nearly finished my race. Now I'm actually happier without everything I once thought I needed. Oh, if someone offered it all back to me, I'd probably take it. But I wouldn't ask God for it back. Right now, I pray that He keeps it away."

"Where are you going now?" asked Makrina.

"To Armenia, child, where you must come too," said Charita.

"But—but—"

"We'll talk about it later. Right now I'm famished!"

The rabbit stew Ioanna had fixed was augmented with extra loaves of bread borrowed from neighbors by Makrina. Gregorios poured what little wine he had left for his grateful guests, who thanked him with a detailed account of the events leading up to their sudden departure. They were still savoring the last of their wine after the meal when the conversation turned to Armenia. "We have many friends already there and apparently safe. They have been begging us to come for some time," said Charita.

"Why haven't you gone before now?" asked Makrina.

"At first, I wasn't ready to give up everything to leave. Later, when I was ready, we had to stay to help others—not just you, dear, but the many who passed through our home on their way to elsewhere. Now it's our turn, and yours, too, Makrina."

"To go with you?" said Makrina.

"You must, Makrina," said Gerasimos. "You are in greater danger now than ever before. The curator in Kargamon knew all about our efforts. As long as we paid him, he ignored us, but now that we can no longer pay, he will prosecute everyone who cooperated with us. I don't know what he knows of this village, but he or anyone else would not have to look hard to find it."

"But then shouldn't we all leave?"

"Yes, everyone who can," said Gerasimos. "You can, Makrina."

"Go, child," said Gregorios. "There is nothing to be ashamed of. Our Lord Himself fled to Egypt to escape Herod."

"But my family won't know where I've gone. I will have disappeared just when help was closest. Charita, the man I once told you about, the man named Marcus who gave me his ring, is now trying to help my parents help me. If I leave now, none of them will be able to help me. I will be lost forever."

"Not forever, Makrina, just for a while longer, as God wills," said Charita.

"Charita and I cannot stay, and it makes no sense for you to stay after we have gone," said Gerasimos. "You shall have lost your link to home anyway. You must come with us to where it is safe, and then contact your parents."

"But couldn't you deliver one last letter for me, letting my parents know where I've gone? Is there no one in Kargamon who would post a letter for you?"

"It's too dangerous," said Gerasimos. "We must leave for Armenia as soon as possible, tomorrow morning."

"Tomorrow?! But that's too soon! Please, Gerasimos. One last letter. I will go with you to Armenia if you can deliver one last letter for me, so my parents do not lose hope and Marcus does not give up. Please?"

Gerasimos looked into her pitiful, pleading eyes. "One last letter," he said.

"Are you sure, Gerasimos?" said Charita.

"I know a man in town I can trust. Getting to him safely will be risky but it can be done. I'll leave before dawn and be back sometime the day after tomorrow. We'll leave then."

Makrina thanked him profusely, giving him a sudden kiss on the cheek. "God bless you Gerasimos," she said before rushing off to write her letter by the lamplight in the loft.

At the hearth, Charita whispered to Gerasimos, "Is this wise, dear husband?"

Gerasimos spoke in a low, deep voice: "Makrina has borne up in the past year because of the strength of her hope. This will encourage her hope and sustain her for the journey ahead. She will cause us less trouble on the road if her mind is at ease."

Gerasimos left before dawn as planned, traveling quickly alone on a mule. Makrina set about packing her things for the journey. Over the months, her parents had sent her seven trunks of things from home, but she could take only one to Armenia. One she had already given to Salome to use as her wedding chest, leaving six to sort through for the things she needed most. All six were stored in the loft of the cottage, stacked one on top of another against the back wall. With Ioanna's help, Makrina unstacked them all, selecting the largest to take with her. Removing its contents to the top of another chest, she then started sorting through the small chest she kept by her sleeping rug, the chest with her most precious and necessary items.

One by one, with some deliberation, she picked the things she would take and laid them out on her rug in the bright light from the loft window—her best mirror, her best comb, her favorite brooches and pins, a few vials of her favorite perfumes and oils, a few earrings and bracelets, her reading lamp, and, of course, her book of Psalms. Something was missing. She searched among the remaining contents of the chest. "Where is it?" she muttered to herself.

Quickly she turned to a second chest, used only occasionally, and began a frantic search of its contents. Scarves and kerchiefs and ribbons for her hair spilled out of every corner of the box. Nothing was left undisturbed, and when she was through the box was a bright jumble of untidy colors. "It's not here!" she exclaimed, turning back to the first chest. This time everything came out, with scant regard for order or placement. Desperately she ejected its content until there was nothing before her but an empty box. "It's gone!" she cried. "It's gone! I've lost it!"

"Makrina? Lost what?" asked Charita from down below.

"My ring! Marcus's ring! I can't find it! It was here in this chest where I always kept it, and now it's gone! It's gone!"

In an instant, the tension, the fears, the regrets and disappointments had burst forth into a tearful, ballistic hysteria. Ioanna rushed up the ladder and found the loft a mess. Makrina was on her knees in the midst of it all, clutching large wads of silk scarves in her fists and shaking them furiously at her side while screaming, "I lost it! I lost it!"

Ioanna ran to her and took control of her arms, then pressed herself firmly against Makrina's breast. "Peace, child, peace," she cooed into Makrina's ear, rocking her gently back and forth.

Makrina calmed down quickly. "It's an omen, Ioanna, a terrible omen," she sobbed. "Marcus is not coming. He's given up and he's not coming."

"No, no, child. Not an omen. You find the ring," said Ioanna.

Charita watched helplessly from below while Mara and Betha scurried up the ladder for a better look. With a flick of her hand, Ioanna sent them away, then suddenly called them back. "You be all right," she said to Makrina, kissing her on the eyes and forehead. "Mara! Betha!"

The two girls stood attentively at the top of the ladder, their heads nearly touching the sloping roof of the cottage. "Did you take ring?" Ioanna demanded of Mara, the elder of the two.

"No, Mamma," said Mara.

Ioanna looked at Betha. "Did you?" she said crossly.

"No, Mamma," said Betha.

Ioanna made the sign of the cross and said, "Before Christ our Savior, did you take ring?"

"No, Mamma," said Betha, making the sign of the cross.

Mara hesitated, and then her wide eyes filled with tears.

"Where is ring?" said Ioanna.

Mara ran over to her sleeping rug and cleared away the scattered the scarves. From underneath her pillow, she produced Marcus's gold signet ring. Ioanna pointed to Makrina, and Mara approached her shamefully, holding out the ring. "I was just looking at it," she said.

Makrina snatched the ring from Mara's hand and shouted, "May you never marry, you miserable little mountain goat!"

"Makrina!" shouted Ioanna.

Mara jumped back and started again to cry, then scrambled from the loft and out of the cottage. Ioanna picked up a wad of scarves and threw it into Makrina's lap with an angry grunt, then kicked her way through the rest of the mess and left the loft. Makrina scowled at Betha through teary eyes, then turned away and collapsed onto her rug, curling up into a ball to cry herself asleep with her precious ring held close to her lips.

An hour later, Makrina was awakened by the creaking of the ladder to the loft. She lay still and listened as someone too heavy to be a child slowly ascended the ladder and crept to her side. A gentle hand stroked her hair. "Better now, child?" said Charita softly.

Makrina sniffled. "No," she said weakly, without lifting her head.

"You're not still angry, are you?" asked Charita.

"No."

"Then you are better, at least a little," said Charita.

Makrina swallowed hard and sniffled. "But now I'm so ashamed," she said. "I'm so sad and ashamed."

Charita nodded, still stroking Makrina's hair. "The shame you can dispel by asking forgiveness. You have wounded a little girl's heart, and you have spoken a curse against her and against her family. Not that your curse will come true. God will decide whether Mara marries, of course. But you, Makrina, have wished evil on someone and spoken it aloud, and that offends the angels if no one else."

"I'm sorry," said Makrina.

"I know you are, child," said Charita. "You must tell Mara and ask her forgiveness. And then you must tell Ioanna and ask her forgiveness also. You may have hurt her more."

A stream of tears rolled across the bridge of Makrina's nose and dropped onto the wool rug.

"Come, dear. I'll help you pack."

Makrina wiped her eyes and her nose on one of the many scarves at hand, then slipped Marcus's ring around her forefinger and sat up. "I'm still so sad, Charita—sad and afraid. It's an omen, I know it is—an evil omen."

"What if it is an omen, child? You have the ring back. It wasn't gone for long, and it was never gone far. What does that mean? Someone else had it all along, someone close to you, and now it's yours again. But whether the ring is with you or someone else, Marcus will come back to you as God wills, no sooner and no later. Losing the ring won't keep him away if God sends him to you, and keeping it won't bring Marcus back if God sends him elsewhere. Put you hope in the Lord, Makrina."

"But should I give up hoping for Marcus?"

"No, dear. Never give up hope for any good thing. But hope according to the promises God has made. For the things He has promised us matter most. Hope for those things, and seek them first, for without His love, His grace, His forgiveness, His salvation, we are lost, and all the treasures and comforts of this world shall not save us. Come now. We've a lot to do."

Together they cleaned up the mess in the loft and began again to sort Makrina's things for packing. At noon they broke for the midday meal. Makrina climbed down from the loft and went over to Mara, sitting quietly in her place. Kneeling beside her, Makrina said, "I am sorry, Mara, for what I said and the way I acted. Please forgive me."

Mara turned to her and smiled.

"Mara?" said Ioanna.

Mara frowned and bowed her head and said, looking at the floor, "I am sorry for taking the ring. Please forgive me for it."

"Yes, of course," said Makrina, pulling Mara to her and kissing her cheeks. "Here," she said, handing Mara the ring. "You hold this for me while I pack, so that it doesn't get lost in the packing. Then before I leave, you can give it back to me. You won't lose it, will you? It means a lot to me."

"Oh, no, lady. I won't lose it. I will guard it with my life," said Mara.

"Good," said Makrina. She kissed the girl once more on the forehead and then stood up and went over to Ioanna. Kneeling also by Ioanna's side, she took Ioanna's work-worn hand and bowed low to kiss it, then said, "Please, Ioanna, forgive me for what I said and did. I am so very sorry for having offended you, after all you've done for me for so long."

Ioanna's stern face softened somewhat and a slight smile appeared. "I forgive you, Makrina," she said, "and—I will be sad when you go."

They embraced briefly, and when they parted Makrina saw Ioanna wipe a tear from her eye. It was only the second time she had seen Ioanna cry. The first time was the day Salome left home.

The following day Makrina was packed and ready, waiting nervously for Gerasimos's return. Salome came by about noon and stayed the rest of the day, helping her mother with a chore or two, but mostly just sitting quietly with Makrina. Between the sad sighs and nervous fidgets, they talked of their time together. Though it was considered bad luck to talk of the future when saying farewell, Salome hazarded a reminder of Makrina's promise, made many months before, after their icy mountain-stream bath. "You won't forget me, will you, when you are home and safe?" she said.

"Of course not," said Makrina. "I will never forget you."

"I would like to see the city someday," said Salome.

"I will send for you as soon as it is safe. You shall be my guest and stay as long as you like," said Makrina.

"And know a real city bath?" said Salome.

"Many real city baths, God willing," said Makrina.

"God willing," said Salome.

Other women from their village stopped by to meet the charming Charita and say their farewells to Makrina. Gerasimos arrived late in the day, too late and too exhausted to leave again immediately. They would wait until morning and leave before dawn. At dusk, Makrina and Salome said their last farewells and parted in tears.

Makrina went to bed early but had trouble falling asleep. When she was awakened before dawn, she was groggy and tired. Charita had intended to let Gerasimos sleep later than he had planned, but he awoke anyway and insisted that they leave as soon as possible. Makrina could have used the extra sleep.

She dressed warmly in two of her heaviest woollen tunics over a long-sleeved cotton undertunic. She had fur half-boots for her feet, woollen mittens for her hands, and a scarf of the finest, softest Ankyra wool to protect her neck. A heavy, hooded cloak covered everything but her face. Sitting sleepily on her trunk outside the cottage, watching Gerasimos pack the mules, Makrina was reminded of her early-morning departure from Kargamon, September before last. The similarity sickened her. She closed her eyes and tried to sleep sitting up.

Gerasimos came for Makrina's trunk last, and once it was securely lashed to the back of a mule, it was time to go. The travelers bade hushed farewells to Ioanna and the rest, then mounted up and started off down the path leading out of the village to the east, in the direction of Phazemon.

Before long they were well into the surrounding forest. All the world was black about them and bitter cold in early March. Makrina pulled her scarf up over her nose to protect her face from the pre-dawn chill. She closed her eyes but tried not to sleep, for fear of falling off her mule. Random thoughts ran through her mind, until one thought chased them all away. *The ring!* Her eyes flew open, her heart stopped, and a low whine rose from her breast. "*Charita!*" she whispered as loudly as she dared.

"Halt," ordered a firm and unfamiliar voice ahead in the darkness. Makrina froze in sudden fear, her ring at once forgotten.

"Where are you going?" said the voice, when the mules all had come to a stop. Up ahead, Makrina heard Gerasimos explaining that they were going to Phazemon to see a doctor.

"You can't go there. You must pull aside and wait," said the voice.

"But my wife needs a doctor immediately or she may die," said Gerasimos.

"Pull aside and wait in silence," said the voice.

Makrina gasped with surprise when a shadowy figure suddenly wrested the reins from her hand and led her mule off the path with the others. All six mules were brought up side by side and tied together in a narrow patch of snow between the trees. "Who are they, mistress?" asked one of the young maidservants on the mule next to Makrina's.

"Quiet," ordered the unfriendly voice.

"Soldiers," whispered Gerasimos.

"Soldiers," whispered Makrina, relaying his answer. Despite her outward calm, her mind was in a panic. Over and over again she prayed: *Lord Jesus Christ, Son of God, have mercy on us sinners. O Lord Jesus Christ, Son of God, have mercy on us sinners. O Lord Jesus Christ, Son of God, have mercy on us sinners. O Lord Jesus Christ, Son of God, have mercy on us sinners...*

Nothing moved and no one talked for what seemed like hours in the darkness. Then the slowly growing light of dawn gradually revealed a long gray line of helmeted men huddled under cloaks at ten-foot intervals, watching the forest between themselves and the village. "What are they doing?" whispered one of the maidservants.

A guard nearby looked back to see who had spoken. He was wrapped like the others in a long gray cloak reaching all the way to the top of his mud-stained boots. On his head was a plain, peakless helmet made of bronze with hinged cheek-guards and a wide, rigid neck guard that stuck out over his back like a duck's tail. In the cool air, his breath streamed from his nostrils like smoke. The look on his face was enough to keep them quiet, and the maidservant's question went unanswered.

The more they waited, the more Makrina shivered uncontrollably from the cold and the fear. When it was finally light, a troop of horsemen, twenty or more, thundered down the path toward the village. The soldiers on the line got up and stamped their feet against the cold, murmuring among themselves as they did so. There was something strange in their voices that struck Makrina's ears. She knew what it was a while later, when the command was given to move out: It was given in Latin.

Slowly the line of troops moved forward through the forest toward the village, with intermittent shouts to maintain their intervals. Four guards on foot then led the six mules and their riders back up to the path, where they were met by two soldiers on horseback and escorted down the path to the village. "Who are they, Gerasimos? They are speaking Latin," asked Makrina, when they appeared free to talk.

"They are Dacians," answered Gerasimos. The land of the Dacians, north of the Danuvius, had once been a province of the empire, conquered by Trajan two hundred years earlier, but given up by his successors as too difficult to defend. The semi-barbarous Dacians had learned to speak Latin and were regularly recruited for the Roman army. Like many barbarian soldiers, they were believed to be fierce and ruthless.

"What are they doing here?" asked Makrina.

"They work for the provincial police."

"But how did they find the village?"

"God knows," said Gerasimos. "Maybe I was followed."

"What are they going to do to us?" asked a maidservant.

Gerasimos shrugged. "Wait and see," he said sadly.

The village was surrounded by a cordon of soldiers, with horsemen guarding the several gates. In the village square were more troops corralling all of the villagers—every man, woman, and child—into a tight cluster in the center of the square. The crowd gasped as Gerasimos and his company were led into the marketplace and told to dismount by a giant of a soldier, at least a head above the tallest man Makrina had ever known, carrying a wooden club half his height with iron bands around its fat end. His Greek was not good but good enough for them to understand that they were to join the others. Salome and Ioanna rushed through the murmuring crowd to meet them, with Mara and Betha following close behind. Looking back, Makrina saw their mules being led away by soldiers.

A moment later a helmeted rider in a great scarlet cloak trotted up to the edge of the square from the lane leading to the gate outside Ioanna's house. The soldier giant walked up and saluted him. They spoke for a short while, with the giant leaning casually on his club with both hands.

Then the rider dismounted, removed his helmet, and hung it on the side of his saddle. His hair was black and closely cropped. His face was clean-shaven. His eyes were small and dark. His nose was bent from having been once or twice broken. A scar creased the left side of his upper lip, and another interrupted the hairline of his left temple. He looked small next to the giant, but he must have been of at least average height. His tunic and trousers were the same as those of the other soldiers, but his helmet had a short peak riveted above the brow, and his hands were protected by leather gauntlets. In them, he held a centurion's vine-stick as long as his arm.

"Who is your headman?" he asked aloud in accented Greek.

"I am he," answered Gregorios, stepping to the fore. "My name is Gregorios."

"Come forward, headman."

Gregorios walked to within 20 paces of the centurion. "That's far enough," said the centurion. "Where is your temple?"

"We have no temple," said Gregorios.

"No temple? Then what is that?"

"A house of worship," answered Gregorios. "But not a temple. No idol, no temple."

"No altar?"

"No altar," said Gregorios. "We are all Christians. We have no altars. We offer no sacrifice, except a sacrifice of praise. For that, we use a simple table, on which rests the Word of God."

"I don't care what you use, headman," said the centurion. "By the laws of the empire, you must offer sacrifice to the gods of the Empire. If you have no altar, you must call upon the gods to save you. If you do not obey, the penalty is death."

"We cannot sacrifice nor call upon any god but the God of Heaven— the Father, Son, and Holy Spirit."

"I say again," said the centurion, "the penalty for refusing to obey the edict of sacrifice is death. If you do not obey, you forfeit your life."

The giant of a soldier walked over and positioned himself two-arms-length from Gregorios's left side and slightly behind him. Gregorios looked around at the giant and then turned back to the centurion. "I will call upon our Lord Jesus Christ and no one other to save us," he said.

"Call upon the gods or die, headman," said the centurion.

Gregorios made the sign of the cross and lifted his eye toward the heavens. "Lord Jesus Christ have mercy on me and save my soul," he said.

The centurion nodded to the giant, and with one swift swing of his mighty club to the back of Gregorios's head, the giant laid the old man out flat with his face against the frozen earth. The villagers screamed in horror, and the elderly Anna ran forward hysterically. A soldier fended her off with the staff of his spear, knocking her to ground between her husband and the crowd. "Gregorios!" she wailed. "My Gregorios!" To shut her up, the soldier struck her in the face with the end of his spear. She crumpled before him and continued to sob. Ioanna edged forward cautiously to retrieve her, with the help of Salome and Makrina.

The giant walked over to his victim and prodded the lifeless body with his club, smiling as he examined the clean, wide crack at the base of his victim's skull.

"You must all call upon the gods to save yourselves," the centurion shouted. "You have seen what will happen if you do not. Swear by the gods and save yourself."

The villagers clung to one another in silence. Some who could not be seen made the sign of the cross and whispered prayers to heaven.

The centurion watched and listened, hearing only Anna's sobs and the whimper of little children against their mothers' breasts. Surveying the crowd, he spotted Gerasimos by his gray beard and his unpeasant-like dress. "You there, step forward," he commanded, pointing at Gerasimos with his vine-stick.

Gerasimos stepped forward slowly, his eyes on the fallen Gregorios.

"What is your name?" asked the centurion.

"My name is Gerasimos."

"Gerasimos?" The centurion smiled, crookedly on account of his scarred lip. "Well, well, what a catch. Didn't get far, did you?"

Gerasimos did not answer.

"You're an educated man, aren't you, Gerasimos?" said the centurion. "Not an ignorant peasant like the rest here. Surely you should be able to persuade these poor people to save themselves. All you have to do is get them to swear by the gods. What do you say?"

"They will not do so," said Gerasimos.

"Ask them anyway."

"They will not do it."

"Ask them!" demanded the centurion.

Gerasimos stared impassively at the centurion for a moment, then

turned slowly and addressed the people: "The government requires that all
citizens prove their loyalty to the Empire by offering sacrifice or swearing
by the gods. These men have been sent to see that you do. Anyone who does
not swear by the gods may be punished severely, even put to death."

Gerasimos turned and faced the centurion.

"Is that all?" said the centurion. "Their lives are in your hands and that's
all you have to say?"

"It doesn't matter. They won't swear by the gods."

"Plead with them, Gerasimos. Plead with them or they will all die, and
you with them."

"Sir," said Gerasimos in a low voice. "These people are just humble peasants. They offend no one with their life here in the mountains, but they take
their faith very seriously. Forcing their compliance will require more pain
than it can be worth."

"The laws must be obeyed, and I have my orders."

"Surely your orders do not require you to use the most extreme measures to obtain compliance. Why not take a few leading men into custody
for trial before the governor? That would make your point and show the
people the fairness of the law."

"There have been enough trials, and these people only use them to
show off their defiance. The case is plain enough if they refuse here and
now to obey the law, and I am empowered to do everything necessary to
obtain compliance."

"But sir —"

"Enough of this," said the centurion. "You have it in your own power
to save these people if you will but show them the way. Let them hear you
swear by the gods and they will see how easy it is and how pointless it is
to refuse."

Gerasimos did not respond.

"Go on. Show them how it's done," said the centurion.

Still Gerasimos did not respond.

"Swear by the gods!"

"I will not do so," said Gerasimos.

"You what?"

"I will not do so," repeated Gerasimos. "I have sworn by all the gods
many times in my life for reasons small and great, but I will not now swear
by the gods of such a government that would harm innocent people."

"Do you realize what you are saying? Your own life is now at stake.
Swear by the gods or lose it."

"I will not do so."

The centurion backed away from Gerasimos, while the giant stepped
closer to him.

"Call upon the gods to save you, Gerasimos," the centurion said aloud.
"I will not," Gerasimos answered.

The centurion nodded to the giant, and Gerasimos bowed his head.

"*Wait!*" cried Makrina, rushing forward. The giant stopped his club and relaxed his arm. "Spare him!" she shouted. A soldier ran over and stopped her. "Spare us all and you will be rewarded! My father is very rich and can pay you handsomely. Spare us all and I will see that he does."

The villagers murmured among themselves, and the surprised centurion looked at her curiously. "Who are you?" he asked, taking a few steps closer.

"I am Makrina, the daughter of Aristoboulos of Sinope, a decurion of the province of Bithynia and Pontus."

"Then what are you doing here?" he asked.

"Hiding, of course," said Makrina.

"Who is your father?"

"Aristoboulos of Sinope, a landowner and shipbuilder."

"Never heard of him," said the centurion.

"But it's true! He is very rich, and he will pay handsomely to have me back and to save these kind people who have helped me."

"How can I know this?" asked the centurion.

"You have my things on those mules. There is a letter from my father promising to pay my ransom if I am returned safely to him."

"I don't believe you."

"I am who I say I am," said Makrina. "Do I sound like a peasant? My Greek is better than yours, and I speak Latin as well. *Velisne audire?*"

The centurion looked at her critically. "Come closer," he said. The soldier restraining her stood aside, and Makrina advanced as far as Gerasimos and stood beside him.

The centurion moved closer also, until he was within an arm's reach of her. He looked her up and down, noting her fur half-boots, her woolen mittens, and her fine wool scarf. Slowly, so as not to frighten her, he lifted the hood of her cloak off her head with his vine-stick. Her long, brown hair was neatly tied behind her head. Her nose and cheeks were red with cold and fear. Her breath flowed excitedly between her parted lips. Her pale olive-colored eyes pleaded with his for mercy.

"How long have you been here?" he asked.

"A year or more," she answered.

The centurion smiled. "I believe you," he said. "I believe you are who you say you are."

Then he turned and walked back to his horse.

"Unfortunately for this village, I cannot accept your ransom," he said, taking the reins from an attendant. "I am a soldier, not a bandit, and soldiers cannot accept money from those they are sent to arrest. Your ransom would be to me a bribe, and I would never get away with it."

He snapped his fingers twice, and two soldiers came running. "*Carpete, non nocete,*" he ordered.

The soldiers grabbed Makrina's arms and began leading her away. "No! Please! Wait!" she cried. "Wait! Please!"

The centurion mounted up and turned his horse around to leave.

"*Et alteri?*" the giant asked.

The centurion answered in Latin. "*Ad ecclesiam congrega, tum incende,*" he said. The giant nodded.

"NO!" screamed Makrina, struggling against her guards. "NO! HAVE MERCY! *DA VENIAM! DA VENIAM! DA VENIAM!*"

Ioanna and Salome held each other tight and watched from a distance as Makrina was carried kicking and screaming from the square. "What are they going to do to her, Mamma?" asked a terrified Betha.

"I don't know, child," answered Ioanna, pulling Betha closer to her and wiping her own tears on Salome's shoulder. "I don't know."

# XXIV

The Clerk of Public Records in Ankyra must have been at least sixty years old, judging by his wrinkled appearance, but the dainty curls of hair plastered against his forehead and temples were still jet black and presumably dyed. The rest of his hair was covered by a brimless cap of red felt, adorned with a silver border and tiny teal-green tassels around its rim. The cap was fully visible only when he sneezed and the sudden motion shook the woollen shawl off the back of his head.

"The air in this town is poisoned, I tell you—*poisoned*," he said with effeminate precision, wiping his sagging nose with a silk kerchief. He lifted his shawl back into place and said, "We live in a bowl, you know, surrounded by mountains. Every winter the bowl fills with soot—nasty brown soot from a thousand home fires. It hangs over us in a big brown cloud. Disgusting. Of course there's nothing one can do about it as long as one has the habit of breathing. I'm sorry, what did you say your slave's name was?"

"Parmenides," said Kimon, standing with the clerk by a high reading table with a sloped tabletop, on which rested two large scrolls. Kimon himself was better dressed than usual, looking every bit the rich young heir that he was. His hair and beard had been neatly trimmed, and his apparel proclaimed a man of stature, rich but not gaudy, with a discreet display of gold on one or two fingers of each hand, in addition to the gold clasp that held his fine wool cloak together at the shoulder. There would be no mistaking him for a philosopher, student, or starving poet. None of the three would have received much cooperation from most public officials.

"Ah, yes, Parmenides," said the clerk, dabbing his nose again with his kerchief. "I don't recall anyone by that name in the records, but then I can't remember everybody who's ever been tried before the governor, can I? No, of course not. You say he ran away two years ago?"

"That's correct," answered Kimon. "He was a Christian and fled to avoid having to sacrifice. If he's not mentioned in the records, they might still lead me to someone who knows of him."

"I see," said the clerk. He patted the scrolls gently with a manicured hand and said, "Here are the dockets of all cases brought before governor in the past two years. Each case is cross-referenced with the transcript of the trial, so if you should find a case that interests you, just tell one of the assistant clerks and they'll pull the file. Please understand that neither I nor my assistants are responsible for the accuracy or completeness of any of the files. We only file them. If the file is here, we will find it. If it is not here, it does not exist."

Kimon nodded.

"If it's Christians that interest you, you might try the police. They have files on everyone," said the clerk.

"I'd rather not," said Kimon. "He was a faithful servant, and I'd like him back untroubled. Involving the police would only complicate things."

"I understand completely," said the clerk. "Just let me know if there is anything else you need." The clerk departed, leaving Kimon to wonder whether the clerk's lack of facial hair indicated a lack of other components.

Seating himself upon a tall stool before the table, Kimon unrolled the docket for the previous year and began scanning the lines for familiar names. It had been several months since he left home to search the countryside south and west of Sinope. He took with him Eustratios, the former server who had been arrested with Chione and the others, and who had sacrificed to save himself after many months of interrogation and imprisonment. Eustratios's fall had cost him his office in the Assembly and removed him from communion for three years, during which he was required to humble himself in service to others. Helping Kimon fit that purpose. With papers certifying his sacrifice, he could travel more freely through the empire.

From Sinope, Kimon and Eustratios had traveled south along the main road, stopping first in Claudiopolis in Galatia, then moving on to Gangra, slowly working their way to Ankyra, the provincial capital. At each stop, Kimon checked their list of names taken from Makrina's letters against the local records, while Eustratios attempted to contact the local Christian Assembly through members who had lapsed and who might still be living in the area. Local records gave them plenty of leads on lapsed Christians, but finding them and persuading them to talk proved more difficult. It seemed there were very few Christians left in Galatia, and those who were left were suspicious of inquiring strangers.

In Ankyra, Kimon came to understand why. There the records contained complete accounts of cases against hundreds of Christians tried before the governor for defying the edicts of surrender and sacrifice, including in most cases actual transcripts of the trials. From them, Kimon learned of the horrendous torture Christians faced. Reeds were inserted under their fingernails, mustard and vinegar were crammed up their noses, and molten lead was poured over their exposed flesh. Many were beaten with whips, scourges, and clubs. Some were stretched upon racks to have their flesh torn with iron hooks, until their bones lay bare and their bowels were exposed. Women had their breasts ripped with hooks. Some were stripped naked and publicly whipped. Others were sentenced to the public brothels. Men were sent to work and die in the mines, a sentence that included the immediate maiming of one leg, and sometimes the blinding of an eye, to prevent escape. Both men and women were beheaded, burned alive, and drowned in rivers and lakes.

Most of the Christians brought to trial lapsed under torture and eventually sacrificed. But a surprising number resisted heroically unto death. Their bravery was preserved in the transcripts, scribbled down by court stenographers, bearing abbreviated testimony to their faith and witness.

At the trial of a noble matron named Crispina, the judge asked, "Do you know what is commanded by the sacred edict?"

"I do not know this edict," replied Crispina.

"It commands you to sacrifice to our gods for the safety of our rulers in obedience to the law given by the pious Augusti Diocletian, etc."

"I shall never offer this sacrifice. I offer sacrifice to one God only and his Son our Lord Jesus Christ who was born and suffered."

"Abandon this superstition and bow your head before our gods."

"I venerate my God every day and I know no other gods but Him."

"You are being very obstinate and difficult. You will soon find out to your cost the force of our laws."

"Whatever happens to me I will suffer it willingly for my faith."

"You will lose your head if you do not obey the orders of our lords the Caesars, to whom you owe obedience. They have power over all Asia and you know it."

There followed a lengthy debate on theological matters with Crispina quoting repeatedly from the Christian scriptures. Then the judge ordered that her hair be cut off. Crispina said, "Let your gods speak and then I will believe them. If I had sought my safety I would not be standing before your tribunal."

When the judge sentenced her to be beheaded, she rejoiced at the verdict.

Some Christians were more aggressive in their defiance. At one trial, a learned young man named Edesius, who wore the robe of a philosopher and whose brother Apphianus had already been put to death, was so incensed by the proceedings against others that he attacked the judge, landing many a solid blow and kick until he was pulled away and cast into the river to follow his brother. At another trial, a woman denounced the emperor as a tyrant and the judge as an idiot before being taken away to be flogged and torn with hooks. During the tortures, another woman stood up in court and declaimed, "How long are you going to torture my sister so cruelly?" Upon admitting that she, too, was a Christian, this second woman was dragged to the altar and forced to sacrifice, though she put up such a fight that she knocked over both the altar and a tripod with fire. Both women were sentenced to be burned alive.

A young overseer named Irenaeus, who was married with several young children, refused repeatedly to sacrifice during his trial before the governor. The governor was incensed and said, "Sacrifice or I will put you to the torture."

"I shall be happy if you do, for then I shall be able to share the sufferings of my Master," replied Irenaeus.

He was tortured and then asked by the governor, "What do you say now, Irenaeus?"

Irenaeus answered, "With my endurance I am even now offering sacrifice to my God to whom I have always sacrificed."

More torture followed, with many of the elder's friends and family—his parents, his wife, his little children hugging his knees—begging him to submit and sacrifice, but Irenaeus remained firm. The governor asked, "What do you say? By the tears of these people, turn away from your madness, look to your youth and sacrifice!"

Irenaeus answered, "I am looking to my eternal future if I do not sacrifice."

He was taken back to prison for more tortures, and his trial was resumed later that night. "Now will you sacrifice, Irenaeus, and save yourself further torture?" asked the governor.

"You are doing what you are told. Do not expect me to do the same," said Irenaeus.

The governor become angry and ordered him to be beaten. Irenaeus replied, "I have God whom I learned to adore from my childhood. I adore Him who comforts me in all things and to Him I sacrifice. I cannot adore manufactured gods."

"Why not escape death? Surely the torments you have already suffered are enough?" asked the governor.

"I am escaping death all the time by means of the punishments you think are hurting me but which I do not feel. Through them I receive from God eternal life."

"Have you a wife?"

"No."

"Have you children?"

"No."

"Have you parents?"

"No."

"Then who were all those people wailing at the last session?"

"There is a commandment of my Lord Jesus that says, 'He who loves his father or mother or wife or children, or brothers or relations more than Me, is not worthy of Me.'"

"Sacrifice at least for their good."

"My children have the same God as I have and He will save them. Do therefore as you have been commanded."

"Look to yourself, young man. Sacrifice or I will torture you again."

"Do as you wish. You will see now what patience the Lord Jesus Christ will give me before your wiles."

"I shall pronounce sentence against you."

"I shall be happy if you will."

"Irenaeus who has been disobedient to the imperial command is ordered to be flung into the river."

"I expected you to carry out your threats of much torment and to condemn me to the sword. You have done nothing. I beg of you to do something, so that you may learn how, by their faith in God, the Christians are accustomed to despise death."

The governor became very angry and added death by the sword to his original sentence. Irenaeus was taken to a bridge, beheaded, and thrown into the river.

Kimon spent many hours reading these transcripts—many more hours than was necessary for his purpose. He was stunned, fascinated, and perplexed by the devotion of these people to their God, devotion unto death. Who would die for Zeus or Apollo or Isis or the Unconquerable Sun— these names for gods people barely knew, whose images men made out of wood, stone, and metal, disguising their ignorance with colorful stories and outlandish claims?

There were some things for which men and women would die. Mothers would die to save their children. Men would die in hopeless battles, fighting shoulder to shoulder with their comrades. Great men like Socrates would face death surrounded by admirers. And among some barbarous tribes, Kimon knew, young men and maidens would offer themselves as victims for sacrifice with the encouragement of their people.

But these Christians so often died alone, opposed by their countrymen, abandoned even by their fellow Christians, and with their families and friends pleading for them to live. Yet they went to their deaths bravely and confidently, even happily, sometimes thanking their persecutors for their service. Some apparently believed they were not alone. "Can you hear them? Can you hear their voices?" cried a widow sentenced to death in Amorium. Whom had she heard? The transcript didn't say.

After the first long day at the record office, Kimon started back toward the apartment he had rented for his stay. His legs and back ached from sitting too long on the stool, and his head ached from staring too long at the pages, straining to decipher the handwriting of the various copyists. He would have wanted a bath to relax, but it was too late in the day. It seemed even later, so thick was the sky with the brown soot the clerk had complained of.

On his way, he met up with Eustratios near a street corner where a vendor was grilling slices of an unknown red meat on a stick. The smell awakened Kimon's senses, and he suggested they take their supper then and there rather than wait for a proper meal to be prepared for them in the apartment. They paid their pence and found a spot on the curb where they could eat at ease.

The meat was surprisingly tasty. "What do you suppose it is?" Eustratios asked between bites.

"I don't dare wonder," said Kimon. "Dog, cat, rat, monkey—who cares? They're all edible. Besides," he said, pointing to the small urban shrine across the street, "the gods have given their approval upon the altar."

Eustratios stopped in mid chew and stared at the meat remaining on his stick.

Kimon gave him a friendly elbow in the shoulder. "Just kidding," he said. "Eat up."

The meal resumed.

"Find anything?" asked Eustratios. He was a swarthy fellow with a large nose and dense black beard, cut short. Under torture he had acquired a slight limp and a mass of scars on his back. Kimon had seen them at the baths in Gangra.

"Lots of names of people who sacrificed," answered Kimon. "No mention of Makrina or Bardas or any other name on the list. What about you?"

"I found that fellow Monagrios we heard of, and he introduced me to a few others, but nobody had heard of Makrina or Bardas," said Eustratios. "It's a big city. There are a lot more people to see."

"We could be here all year and not find her," said Kimon. "Maybe she didn't come this way. Maybe she went east."

"Maybe," said Eustratios. "We should have a good idea after a week or two. Then we might as well go elsewhere."

"Might as well," said Kimon. "Tell me, Eustratios: why is it so difficult for Christians to sacrifice? I read account after account of good, decent, educated people, people with everything to live for throwing it all away to avoid sacrificing. Why? Why should it matter that much? It's not as if someone were asking them to curse their own god, just to honor some other god, *any* other god. But they won't do it."

Eustratios paused for a moment before answering. "There is only one God," he said. "To honor a false god is to deny the true one."

"But all that they've been asked to do in some cases is pitch a pinch of incense upon the fire, or eat a piece of meat from the altar," he said, holding up a morsel of meat between his thumb and index fingers. "Why is that so dangerous? What does it matter where the meat comes from or whose incense one burns?" He then popped the morsel into his mouth.

"In truth, sir, it would not matter," said Eustratios. "'It is not what goes into a man's mouth that makes him unclean, but what comes out of his mouth.' But what it means before men makes all the difference. Everyone knows what the pinch of incense or the bite of meat means. It means that Jesus Christ is not God. That, we cannot say."

"But why not?" asked Kimon.

Eustratios looked puzzled. "Because it's not true," he said.

"So what if it's not true," said Kimon. "It's not as if everyone would think you suddenly stopped believing in Christ. You could still go on believing, as long as you didn't make a public show of it."

"But they don't want us to go on believing," said Eustratios. "They want us to give up our beliefs."

"They would be more tolerant of your beliefs if you proved your loyalty by sacrificing, which seems to me a very small thing to ask. Now, pulling down buildings and confiscating books and banning public worship—that all seems excessive and unreasonable. But a pinch of incense now and then seems hardly worth the worry. It's such a small thing."

"A small thing—punishable by death," said Eustratios. "I seem to agree with the Caesars on this point. It is not a small thing. If it were, why would they demand it?"

"I don't know," said Kimon. "Because they're soldiers and they expect everyone to salute sharply and obey orders. Because they're the government and they expect everyone to go along with their programs. What does it matter? We're all citizens of the empire. We're all subjects of a power not our own, ruled against our will. We all must go along with a lot of things we don't like. Where's the harm in going along with some minor outward show to avoid disruption and death? It seems to me that a just and loving god would forgive you for what you are forced to do."

"He is just and loving, and he does forgive, but those who refuse to sacrifice do right. Our Lord himself says, 'Whosoever therefore shall confess me before men, him will I confess before my Father who is in Heaven, but whosoever shall deny me before men, him will I also deny before my father who is in heaven.'"

"But why is a *public* confession necessary? Why do you have to tell the world? Isn't it what's in the heart that matters, between you and your god? Isn't that what he'll judge you on? Isn't that what you truly believe?"

"I'm not so sure," said Eustratios. "Do we believe what we only think and feel, or what we are willing to act upon? When I was in prison, I reasoned as you do now. Now I wonder whether I truly believed the Lord's promise of eternal life then, and whether I truly believe it even now. If I don't truly believe and I sacrifice, I lie when I say I do believe, and if I do believe and sacrifice, I lie in sacrificing. Either way, my sacrifice makes me a liar."

"Better a liar than a dead man," said Kimon.

"But, sir, if men will not die for what they believe to be true, then the cynics are right—there are no honest men. Neither is there any real truth, for what men say is truth is then just a convenient notion, a saying that suits their purposes. When it suits them no longer, they change what they say. They lie to suit themselves."

"The cynics *are* right. Men say what suits them."

"But, sir, not all men. Some men at least would rather die than dissemble. Our martyrs, our 'witnesses,' prove that. You may not believe in their truth, but you must admit that they act honestly, according to their beliefs."

"Granted," said Kimon. "They act honestly, but still foolishly."

"Why foolishly? Because what they die for isn't true, or because it's foolish to die for truth?"

"Both," said Kimon.

"Sir, sir," said Eustratios, "you are arguing now for dishonesty, either as a cynic or a sophist. I can't tell which."

"I just don't see why so many people have to suffer and die," said Kimon. "Surely there's a way to avoid that. Surely life itself is more precious than public appearances or metaphysical speculations."

"Life is precious," said Eustratios, "but if preserving it is all that matters, then men are no better than—than dogs." He flicked his last bit of meat to a mangy, starving hound scavenging in the gutter nearby. "Dogs do what they must to survive. That is all that matters to them. Where would we be if our survival were all that mattered? Where would we be if we taught our children that survival is all that matters, that they may lie, cheat, steal, even murder to save themselves? Where would we be?"

Kimon looked at the dog, now hungrily but fearfully watching the men eat, licking its chops again and again. "I'll grant you that point," he said. "I cannot deny the nobility of telling the truth and suffering for what is good and true. My problem is with the basis of nobility. Why is it good? What makes it make sense?"

"For us," said Eustratios, "it is God himself, who is good and true, who makes it make sense. It is the prospect of our becoming more and more like God, more and more divine. And it is the hope of the resurrection, the promise that there is a life after death in which doing good and telling the truth will be rewarded greatly. That makes sense of our witness, plain rational sense."

"But you have to first believe in that promise for it to make sense of the witness," said Kimon.

"Yes, you do," said Eustratios, "and that's another reason for our witness—that others may believe, that they may see our faith, our assurance of the resurrection, our readiness to give up this life in expectation of the next, and that from our example they might take heart and believe in the promise."

From Ankyra, they traveled east along the Royal Road, a well-maintained highway stretching across Asia Minor from the Aegean coast to Mesopotamia. Three days out of Ankyra, they passed through a narrow gorge called the Halys Gates and then across the Great Halys Bridge, a majestic stone structure rising hundreds of feet above the great river. A week later, they stopped for several days at a small village at the intersection of the Royal Road and the road to Sinope, which they had left at Claudiopolis two months earlier. Finding nothing, they continued east to Zela, where they stayed for several days before leaving the Royal Road and heading north to Amasia on the Iris or "Rainbow" river.

There at last in the local records Kimon found the names of Christians he recognized—not anyone Makrina had mentioned in her letters, but a family who had fled Sinope three years ago—the reader Andreas, his wife Theodoulia, and her mother Elena. According the records, the family had been arrested the previous spring shortly after the governor's annual visit. Instead of detaining them until the governor's next visit, the authorities had sent them on after him to stand trial in Neocaesarea.

It was the first hard lead on any of the Christians who had fled Sinope, and Kimon could not wait to follow up on it. Instead of continuing north from Amasia through Phazemon to Amisos on the coast and then returning home to Sinope by boat as he had planned, they headed east some 70 miles to Neocaesarea, a city on the banks of the Lykos or "Wolf" river.

When they arrived in Neocaesarea several days later, they were quickly disappointed. The records there made no mention of Andreas, Theodoulia, Helena, or anyone else sent from Amasia in the last year, and no one they interviewed admitted to having seen or heard of the family. The only lead came from a landlord named Encolpius who had defended himself against the accusation of being a Christian by readily swearing by the gods and offering sacrifice. Questioned by Kimon, Encolpius denied any knowledge of the Christians in Neocaesarea, maintaining that he had been falsely accused by a rival landlord. He had never heard of Andreas, Theodoulia, and Helena, but the mention of Makrina's name gave him pause.

"I'm not sure—I don't know really, but I think there was a young girl named Makrina among the Christians here. You'd have to ask someone else to be sure," he told Kimon. "Try the widow Optatia. She befriended many of them when the trials first began." He lowered his voice as if someone were listening. "She's suspected of being more than just their friend."

Kimon and Eustratios found Optatia in a grand old home near the center of town. At the mere mention of Encolpius's name, the aged dame spat upon her own fine floor and cursed him in the name of Zeus. "That gutless upstart!" she fumed. "Yesterday he's their proudest benefactor, and today he swears he never knew them. Of course he'd remember the girl Makrina. What man wouldn't? He probably couldn't keep his covetous little eyes off her—never mind her husband! She was such a pretty thing, and pure as mountain snow."

"She had a husband?"

"Yes, yes, a fine young man named Gregory. I've forgotten their daughter's name—Amalia, Amelia, Emilia—something such."

"A daughter? Were they from here or from elsewhere?"

"I wouldn't know," said Optatia. "I first met them when they came to me in the middle of the night, with their little baby tightly bundled to keep from her from crying and alerting the watch. It's a wonder they got away."

"They got away? To where?"

"To the mountains, of course. They're all in the mountains," answered Optatia.

"How can we find her?"

"Go see the miller east of town. Tell him I sent you. He'll get you started."

There was only a slim chance that this Makrina was his sister, but Kimon had to be sure. With little trouble, they found the miller, who directed them to a small village outside town. The next day the headman of the village led them up into the mountains, where they came upon a small cabin well hidden among the trees. Outside the cabin, a man was tilling a small patch of level soil. The headman addressed him as Gregory.

Gregory welcomed them warmly, calling for his wife to bring the visitors something to eat while they rested outside upon the ground. Very soon his wife appeared with two half-loaves of dry bread and a small pot of cold stew to use as a sop for the bread. She was covered completely except for her hands and face, which was pleasant but plain—its only adornment, a shy smile. In a low submissive voice, she begged their pardon for the meager fare, explaining that supper was not yet ready and inviting them to stay for it, but Kimon had satisfied his reason for coming and declined politely.

The woman returned to the cabin, and the men talked for awhile about the persecution. "We live among wild animals but we fear only wild men," said Gregory. The headman told of bands of soldiers given extraordinary powers to hunt out Christians in the countryside. "In the wilderness, they can do things they wouldn't dare do in the cities," he said. There were rumors of the massacre of whole villages of Christians, but these were still only rumors, said Gregory. "Lord help us if they are true," he said.

Now and then the little girl, Emmilia, would poke her head out of the door of the cabin and stare at the visitors until she was seen. Her appearances stirred Kimon's imagination. What future lay in store for this tender young soul, already an outlaw in the eyes of the world? Would she survive childhood to perish for her faith, as so many of her Christian sisters already had? Or would she marry another of her kind and bear little Christians of her own? What would their world be like many years hence, long after this present persecution had passed into history?

Emmilia's mother, the other Makrina, appeared to pour them more water, and in his mind's eye, Kimon saw her as his sister—a humble peasant wife hiding out with her husband and her own little girl in the wilds of Pontus. If only he could be sure that she had not suffered something worse!

They left after about an hour, returning in silence to the village to stay the night. Kimon thanked the headman with a gift of silver and entrusted him with a like gift for Gregory.

They arrived back in Neocaesarea about noon. Kimon went ahead to their apartment to rest while Eustratios returned their mules to the stable. He was reclining on a couch with his eyes closed when he heard a knock at the door.

"It's unlocked. Come on in," he called out, thinking it was Eustratios.

"Are you Kimon of Sinope?" a voice asked.

Kimon looked up to see three men in uniform standing at the door. "I am," said Kimon, rising to his feet.

"The inspector general asks to see you. Please come with us."

Kimon hesitated. "The inspector general? Of the province?"

The officer nodded.

"Right now? What for?" asked Kimon.

"We have been told only to find you and bring you in for questioning," said the officer. "Will you come?"

"Certainly," said Kimon.

He grabbed his cloak and followed the men out the door. It occurred to Kimon to let Eustratios know where he was going, but he decided in an instant to say nothing of Eustratios unless asked.

The men led him through the busy, crowded streets to the city basilica, which was abuzz with servants, guards, officials, and citizens. Kimon was shown to a small receiving room enclosed with sliding doors, just off the right aisle of the basilica. "Wait here," said his escort, drawing the doors closed.

The room was empty and unadorned. The floor was made of terra cotta tiles and the walls were unpainted plaster. The only light came from a small, glass-pane window high upon the wall opposite the doors. With no place to sit, Kimon remained where he was, standing in the center of the room, facing the doors to await the inquisitor, wondering what would happen next.

Through the doors he heard the constant stamp of booted feet, with a word or two exchanged among the guards. "We have the Sinopean named Kimon. He's in here," said one.

"What about the other one?" said another voice.

"He wasn't there. We're still looking for him."

A reply was obscured by the noise in the hall. Kimon braced himself for confrontation, expecting the doors to slide open at any moment, but instead, the footsteps trailed off and nothing happened. He listened and waited, as the room began to lighten.

With time to spare, Kimon began formulating his defense against the expected challenge. Time passed and Kimon's attention drifted to the cracks in the plaster walls and the dead flies littering the floor. Still more time passed, and Kimon began to wonder whether he had been forgotten. Tired of waiting, he wanted to pound on the door and demand to be either seen or released, but his impatience could not overcome his timidity.

Outside the room, the building had quieted down. It was only about an hour after noon, but the workday was almost over. The place was clearing out. Surely they haven't forgotten me, thought Kimon.

The sudden rattle of the door startled him. Here again was the officer. "Please follow me," he said. Kimon followed him out of the room and across the now empty nave to another room near the back of the basilica. At the door, the officer stood aside and waved Kimon in, then waited at the open door. This room also was empty, but better lit, cleaner, and colorfully painted.

A moment later, the officer at the door entered and said, "The lieutenant governor will see you now."

"The lieutenant governor?" said Kimon. "What happened to the inspector general?"

The officer shrugged, then showed Kimon to an office one door down, richly decorated, with crimson curtains dressing a floor-length window and high double doors opening out onto a railed porch. A very large man in a finely embroidered dalmatic was standing in the center of the room, in front of a gilded curule chair, on which rested a blue velvet cushion with golden tassels.

"Welcome," said the man with a cordial grin. He was very large indeed, several inches taller than Kimon and perhaps a hundred pounds heavier, with thick, hairy hands and forearms and round, fat face. His upper and lower lips were clean-shaven, but his beard grew in neat curls beneath his chin and up both cheeks, uniting with the carefully clipped curls that covered his head.

"I am Pius Sempronius Rogatianus, the lieutenant governor of Cappadocia," he said. "And you are Kimon of Sinope?"

"That's right," said Kimon. "Kimon, son of the decurion Aristoboulos of Sinope."

Off to one side, a clerk applied his stylus to the wax of his tablet, writing quickly.

"Yes, yes, I've heard of your father," said Rogatianus. "Quite a wealthy man, is he not? Ships and whatnot, as I remember. What brings you to Neocaesarea?"

"Personal business," said Kimon.

"Really?" said Rogatianus. "Perhaps I can be of some assistance. What kind of business is it?"

"I'm looking for someone," Kimon answered. "Actually, several members of our household, who might have come this way."

"Is that so? Well, surely we can help with that. Have you tried the police?"

"I've checked the records and found nothing," said Kimon. "At this point, I'm afraid I've come in vain. I was just about to give up and go home."

"What a shame. I'm told you have asked around among some of the locals who were suspected of being Christians," said Rogatianus. "Are those whom you seek also Christian?"

"I have no way of knowing," said Kimon. "They would have to answer for themselves."

"But you have some reason to believe that they are, or you would not have sought them among the locals of that kind."

"It is possible that they are," said Kimon.

"It's such a tragedy what has happened in recent years. So unfortunate that so many people would be forced to flee their homes for fear of the law. We know quite a few have passed through our province on their way to Armenia. Have you looked there?"

"Not yet," said Kimon.

"You might try there next," said Rogatianus. "To tell you the truth, I can't say there are many Christians left in these parts. We're so close to the frontier, you know. I can provide you with an escort if you like, all the way to the frontier."

"Thanks, but, as I said, I'm inclined now to give up and go home for awhile."

"Are you sure I can't help? If I knew the names, I could at least make certain they do not appear in our records."

"I'd rather not say. I hope you understand."

"I do indeed. But at least allow me to provide you with an escort home."

"Oh, I don't think that will be necessary."

"No, no, I insist," said Rogatianus. "See that Master Kimon is provided a troop of cavalry to accompany him on his way home."

"Yes, your excellency," said the officer.

Rogatianus turned to Kimon and said, "If you are staying the night, I'd be please to have you as a guest for dinner."

"Thanks again, but I'd like to get an early start tomorrow."

"As you wish," said Rogatianus. "May the gods go with you, Kimon. And please give my regards to your father. I certainly hope to meet him someday."

Kimon left the room, followed by the officer.

Rogatianus watched Kimon cross the nave and leave the building. Then he turned to his clerk and said, "Tell my steward to come and see me."

The clerk bowed and hurried off.

When the steward appeared, Rogatianus was out on the porch, staring off into the distance. "Yes, excellency?" said the steward.

Rogatianus turned slowly. "Bring the girl to me this evening," he said.

"Yes, excellency."

"Privately."

"Yes, excellency. . . . Will that be all, excellency?"

"That's all. Oh, wait, one more thing."

"Yes, excellency?"

"Clean her up beforehand."

"Yes, excellency."

# XXV

The lieutenant governor's mansion in town was unremarkable from the outside. Strong, high walls without a single window on the surrounding streets. An unmarked door in the rear for servants and deliveries, and front door barely more impressive, distinguished only by a lintel of white marble carved with the face of a wild-eyed satyr, panting lasciviously, its long, pointed tongue stretching toward the street.

Makrina shuddered when she saw it in her hurried transit from the closed carriage to the darkened house. The firm, fat hands of Rogatianus's housekeeper took her swiftly through the vestibule and atrium, then down a covered colonnade bordering a small courtyard. In the midst of the courtyard, Makrina spied a bronze statue of a drunken Hercules, its erect phallus clearly visible in the dim light of the evening.

At the other end of the colonnade was a large room opening out onto the courtyard. A long, low serving table lay just inside the open doorway. Behind the table was a dining couch. "Wait here," said the housekeeper, leaving Makrina in the center of the room while she lit the lamps, one at each end of the table and two more in the courtyard. No sooner had the second light appeared in the courtyard than Makrina heard the front door slam shut. Then there was silence. The housekeeper was gone.

The sky above the courtyard was not yet as dark as the shadows in the house. Makrina pulled her palla tightly across her chest. The evening was cool and the silk gown given to her after her bath was too sheer to keep her warm. At first she had refused to wear it, until the housekeeper provided the light-weight cotton palla also. Even then she felt shamefully underdressed.

The table was already set with a small but varied feast. Whoever had set it had not expected to return to serve successive courses. It was all right there: candied apples, a roasted duck, stewed oysters and asparagus, pickled eggs, assorted nuts and plums. A pot of wine sat at one end, already mixed as far as Makrina could tell by stirring it slowly and savoring its aroma. She had not eaten at all that day and had not tasted such delicacies for ages. How long? She could not even recall. Years certainly, but how many?

She had intended to wait, but time passed and the sky grew darker, yielding the light to the lamps. Still the house was silent. At last she could stand it no longer. She sat down upon the couch and began to pick at the duck with a small knife. *Dear God, how good it tasted!* She filled a cup with wine and took several long sips, closing her eyes as she swallowed and sighing with pleasure afterward. Then she tried the apples.

"How are they?"

Makrina jumped and turned, spilling her cup of wine all over her gown and the couch. "Mercy!" she cried in panic.

Rogatianus laughed aloud, while Makrina wiped up the wine with her palla and struggled to control herself. Her fright and her fears and the laughter and the mess were suddenly too much for her, and she broke into tears.

"Now, now," said Rogatianus, settling next to her on the couch. "No harm done. A little wine, that's all. No harm at all."

He patted her back with his heavy hand, then attempted to press her head to his shoulder, but Makrina pulled away and sat up straight and stiff. Fear overcame frustration and her tears ceased. "Why did you bring me here?" she demanded.

"Why?" he said. "Why, for dinner. Why else?"

"Why dinner? Why here? Why now?"

"Why, why, why," Rogatianus laughed. "Just like a little child, a dear little child."

He reached out to touch her cheek, but she turned away and covered her head with her palla.

"Really, Makrina. Why are you so frightened? You have nothing to fear from me. Relax. Enjoy the evening. It's all for you."

"Why? What do you want?" she asked.

"To make amends," Rogatianus answered. "It has been a long time since our first interview. I didn't believe you then. Your story seemed so improbable. A rich young girl living like a goat in the mountains, lost among the pitiful peasants. It strains credulity even now. But I must confess I now have reason to reconsider your claims."

"What do you mean? What are you saying?"

Rogatianus rose to his feet and ambled slowly around the end of the dinning couch, speaking as he walked. "Through a few discreet inquiries, I have confirmed that a certain high-born girl from Sinope did disappear sometime ago, a girl named Makrina, liable for some offense, although that part is not entirely clear."

He sat down on the far side of the couch and leaned back on one arm. "What happened to her is still a mystery, but it appears the facts of the case, though limited, certainly fit your story, which inspires in me the unsettling suspicion—that the girl wasting away in my custody is actually the daughter of a decurion, not the insane and immoral waif she first appeared."

Makrina turned to face him. "You know then," she said. "You know that I am telling the truth."

"It would appear so," said Rogatianus, with a grin. "Of course there is still the question of the offense, and then also the question of jurisdiction, but no need to discuss that now. Tonight I must make up for my lack of hospitality."

He turned and filled their cups with wine. "Here," he said, handing her a cup. "Let us drink to your changed fortunes. Go on. Drink."

Makrina drank, but the wine that had seemed so delicious moments before, she now hardly noticed and could barely swallow. Her eyes filled again with tears. She tried to dry them with her palla before they fell, but it was no use.

"What's this?" said Rogatianus, taking the cup from her trembling hand. "No need to cry now."

"I just want to go home," Makrina sobbed.

"I know you do, and you will before long. As soon as I can settle a few legal issues. You'll be home before you know it."

She wiped her eyes and nose and regained her composure.

"Better now?" he asked. Makrina nodded uncertainly. "Here, try this," he said, handing her a slice of dried bread topped with a sliver of sauteed snail. Makrina took the treat into her hand and held it thoughtlessly. Then she reached instead for her cup of wine.

"Let me help you," he said, handing her the cup. "Drink up."

She drank again, much more this time, then caught her breath. Rogatianus chewed his food and watched her with delight, leaning back on one elbow, his legs stretched out on the couch. She tried to smile when she handed back her empty cup. "Good," he said, his mouth full of food. "Nothing like a little wine to cheer the heart."

He refilled her cup and gave it back to her.

"Thank you," she said weakly.

"My pleasure," said Rogatianus. He patted the cushion beside him and said, "Lie down, relax, have something to eat." Then he turned back to the table of food. "I make it a rule never to drink on an empty stomach. You should, too."

He worked for a while with a knife, carving strips of meat from the roast and filling a small dinner plate with servings of the various dishes. When the plate was full, he set it on the table in front of Makrina's place and waved for her to join him. "Come, eat, before it turns cold," he said. Then he went back to carving himself another helping.

Slowly, warily, Makrina lay down on the couch and began picking at her plate of food. The candied apples were especially good and reminded her of home.

"So tell me," said Rogatianus, between chews, "what could such a sweet, young, beautiful girl like you possibly do to make it necessary for you to flee?"

Makrina hesitated. "I —"

"No, wait. Don't tell me. Let me guess." He paused for a moment, looking up at the ceiling while holding the duck's leg he was eating straight up in the air. Then he looked at her with wide eyes. "Murder," he whispered.

"No," said Makrina with a scowl.

Rogatianus laughed. "Of course not. What, then?"

"I —"

"No, no. Don't tell me." Again he looked up at the ceiling. "I know—attempted murder."

"No."

"Inciting a riot."

"No."

"Rape—no, sorry, wrong sex. Alienation of affection!"

"No."

"Breach of promise?"

"No."

"Well, it couldn't have been anything as ordinary as theft."

"No, it wasn't," said Makrina.

"Then how about—assault and battery?"

Makrina held her peace.

"Slander?"

"You should know," she said.

"How so?"

"Through your inquiries."

"Yes, well, as I said, that part was unclear. Some nonsense having to do with the governor's wife."

"Lieutenant governor's wife," said Makrina.

"Really?" said Rogatianus. "Dear old Politta. How interesting."

"You know her?"

"Do I ever! But don't worry. I'm sure she deserved it." He tossed the bare leg bone onto the table. "So let's see," he said, counting on his greasy fingers. "That's assault, and no doubt battery, and also slander, and then disrespect for the dignity of official persons. Anything else?"

Makrina felt suddenly light-headed. The wine was having its effect.

"Hardly seems enough to leave home over," said Rogatianus.

"There was something else," said Makrina, trying hard to control her tongue. "I was a Christian. I mean I *am* a Christian. I mean, they found out I was a Christian, and . . . and . . ."

"And you hadn't sacrificed?" said Rogatianus.

Makrina shook her head.

"I see. Well, that is very serious, very serious indeed."

Rogatianus reached for his cup and made himself more comfortable.

"You know, Makrina," he said, "you were extraordinarily lucky to fall into my hands. That half-civilized centurion Valerius wanted to take you all the way to Melitene to stand trial right away, while the governor was making his rounds. You should have seen his face when I ordered him to leave you here for the governor's return. He was furious. You'd have thought he had a personal interest in you. Well, I can understand that, a young, beautiful girl all alone, outside the law's protection and entirely at his mercy. You were his trophy. I suppose he wanted to show you off."

He paused and took a sip of wine.

"It could have been even worse," he said. "He could have kept you as his slave or mistress and not even mentioned you to me or anybody. What a shame that would have been, to have your fine, firm body despoiled by one so low and uncouth. Horrible to even think of! Then again the conscientious fool could have taken you all the way to trial, only to see your sweetness wasted on even lower sorts. The governor, you see, is none too fond of Christians and might have sent you off for a tour of duty in the local brothel to make you change your mind."

Makrina stared down at her half-finished meal.

"But it was not to be," Rogatianus continued. "The Fates have appointed me to save you from both the brothel and the brigand, and from all other punishments you might have endured for you crimes. Unlike the governor, I'm a kind-hearted and understanding man, inclined toward mercy, especially when the accused is one so young as yourself. With my help, you'll be on your way home in no time at all, cleared of every charge, freed from every threat, without a care in the world. Your hard times will have come to an end, and you will owe it all to me."

"I suppose I should thank you," said Makrina, without looking up.

"Well," said Rogatianus, "courtesy would require it."

He reached out and touched her chin, turning her face toward him. "Such a stunning beauty," he whispered. "Your hardships seem to have done you no harm at all."

He admired her face a moment longer in the lamplight before turning to set his cup down on the table. Makrina looked away. Then she felt his hand on her buttocks.

"No, please. Please don't do this. I beg you," she said.

"You want to go home, don't you? You're almost there."

"Please don't. I beg you."

"Such a fine round rump."

Makrina tried to roll away, but her gown was caught beneath him, and before she could free it, he had rolled almost on top of her. She was trapped! A huge, hairy leg lay across her thighs, pinning her to the cushion, while his heavy hand ranged across her backside. He pressed his chest against her shoulder and lowered his mouth to the nape of her neck.

"Stop! Please! Stop!" she cried.

She squirmed fiercely and tried to push him away, but somehow she managed only to roll onto her back as he rolled on top of her. His great belly squeezed the breath from her body. She gasped for air as he pinned her arms to the sides and forced his legs between hers. With his teeth, he pulled apart the ties at the shoulder of her gown, exposing a breast.

"Stop! Stop please! Please don't do this! Please don't!"

He stopped suddenly and looked down on her with a toying grin. She felt the hot blow of his breath upon her bare chest and the press of his loins against hers. When he did not move, she looked up into his eyes.

"Have mercy on me, please!" she pleaded. "I'll pay you anything after I return home if you let me go now. Please, I promise. Have mercy on me."

Rogatianus chuckled. "This doesn't have to be a struggle," he said. "You want to go home; I want you to go home, too. Just imagine yourself home already. You do want to go home, don't you? It would be such a shame to have to send you back to jail to stand trial."

Makrina stared up at him in horror.

"Relax. Relax," he said. "One night of pleasure and you'll be on your way home tomorrow. I promise."

She was speechless, but in her head her soul was screaming: *What can I do? What can I do? Dear God! What can I do?*

Rogatianus waited without moving. Then he saw her eyes close and felt her body relax. "Think of home," he said. "You're almost there."

He let go of her left arm and reached down with his right hand to raise her gown. To her own surprise, Makrina found herself lifting her hips to let him pull the gown up around her waist. He then let go of her other arm and rose to his knees to expose himself.

Makrina clenched her teeth, keeping her eyes tightly shut. When she felt him tug at her loincloth, she trembled and stretched her arms out for something to hold on to. When the cloth came free, she began to whimper. Her hands in panic knocked a bowl and spoon onto the tiled floor. Then she felt his hand between her legs and his mouth upon her breast.

"No, no, dear God!" she sobbed. Her right hand gripped the edge of the table while her left hand closed upon a handle—a knife handle. Makrina gasped and opened her eyes. "NO!" she screamed bringing the knife down upon Rogatianus's neck. "NO! NO! NO!" she screamed again, each time stabbing the knife wildly into his neck and shoulder.

Rogatianus pulled away and sat back on his heels, clutching his neck with his hand. "What have you done? What have you done?" he cried. Blood covered his hand and soaked his tunic. He tried to climb off the couch, but the loss of blood made him swoon. He fell forward onto Makrina's stomach. "Gods! Gods! Save me!" he muttered.

Makrina looked down upon the bleeding hulk and screamed. For a moment she could do nothing more. Then she threw away the knife and tried to push Rogatianus off of her, screaming all the while. At last Rogatianus rolled away, tumbling onto the floor beside the couch. Makrina heard him gurgle and looked to see if he was dead. Dead or not, her panic would not let her wait.

She climbed off the other side of the couch, then noticed that her hands and gown were covered in blood. She screamed again and looked about to find her palla. Wrapping her arms and body in the palla, she ran out of the room and down the colonnade the way she had come. The bolt on the front door stopped her for one terrified moment, and then the door was open and she was off, running down the street and sobbing as she went.

The city was dark and silent until Makrina's sudden passing stirred the dogs in the neighborhood. From behind their walls, they began to bark and howl. One beast chained in an alley leaped at her as she passed. She shrieked and dodged and kept running.

She had no idea where she was or where she was going. All she understood was the need to get away, and it was easier to run downhill than uphill. She ran and ran through the narrow streets, turning always in the direction of down, until at last she came upon the river. A paved walkway paralleled the river, separated from it by a low wall. She followed the walkway until she came upon an opening in the wall, with steps leading down to the water. At the bottom of the steps was a landing where women gathered by day to wash their clothes.

Makrina stumbled down the steps in the darkness, then collapsed at the edge of the landing, out of breath and weeping. As the dogs quieted down, Makrina removed her palla and the thin, simple sandals they had given her to wear that day. Then she knelt beside the water and tried as best she could to wash the blood from her arms and gown. The smell of blood made her sick. To keep from vomiting, she leaned her head back and breathed deeply.

"Why, God?" she cried, looking up at the stars. "Why me? After all I've been through? After all this time? I only want to go home. Is that too much? Haven't I suffered enough? I would have died for you. I would have, you know that. But now . . . now I've killed a man. Please, Father. Please forgive me. Please. Help me, Lord. Help me. Show me the way."

"Who is that?" a man called from the far side of the river. "Who's down there? Answer me."

The watchman raised a lantern above the wall and peered down toward the landing, but in the darkness Makrina could see him better than he could see her. She gathered her palla and her sandals and started back for the steps, then noticed a narrow footpath between the water and the wall. She stole along the path in silence, ignoring repeated calls from the watchman. After a while he gave up and disappeared.

After half a mile or so, the path led Makrina to an archway under a stone bridge. The wall stopped at the bridge. On the other side was an earthen bank covered with tall grass. Makrina settled wearily on the grass using her palla as a pillow. Before long, she was asleep.

She awoke the next morning before dawn, to the cock's crow and the cooing of doves nesting in the stonework along the river. For a long while, she lay motionless in the grass, pretending to herself that she was dead. She felt dead. Dead to hope. Dead to faith. Dead to innocence.

She was still dead at first light, when she heard the watchman on the bridge above greet his relief.

"Did you hear the noise last night?" said one.

"You mean the dogs?" said the other.

"You'll never believe what happened."

"What?"

"Rogatianus was murdered."

"No! The lieutenant governor?"

"Yes. Pius Sempronius himself. In his own home, with his own dinner knife."

"By whom?"

"Some girl he plucked from prison for the usual."

"You don't say."

"I always thought it would be a jealous husband, but they're quite sure it's the girl. She claims the name of Makrina. Vicious little bitch, apparently. Severed his jugular. Bled like a butchered pig. Couldn't have done it without getting a lot on herself, so if you see a woman in red, sound the alarm."

The other man laughed and they walked away.

Makrina looked at herself. Blood still stained her gown and her arms. For most of the day she hid under the bridge, rubbing her arms and clothes with dirt to hide the blood and washing it out in the river, all the while wondering what she would have to do to survive.

# XXVI

It was a long silent journey for Kimon, back west through Amasia, then north to Phazemon and finally Amisos, accompanied all the way by Rogatianus's cavalry. At Amisos, finally free of his unwelcome escort, Kimon sought out his father's resident agent and heard from him the news from home—Simon, the son of Bardas, had been found in Cherson, across the Euxine Sea, and was returning to Sinope to aid in the search.

After a long day's sail, Kimon and Eustratios were again in Sinope, impatiently awaiting Simon's arrival from across the sea. Simon landed in Sinope two days later, bearing documentation from the independent city of Cherson, obtained by Aristoboulos, identifying Simon as a Chersonese diplomat. Thus equipped, Simon could travel anywhere in the Roman world without fear of persecution.

The day after his arrival, the three young men departed Sinope on horseback, heading south by the main road, which Kimon and Eustratios had taken months earlier. The first day brought them to the seedy caravansary in the valley of the river Amnias. They stayed the night and left the next morning under a cold, gray sky that made good its threat of rain before they had gone a mile. It rained all day and was still raining when they stopped outside the large timber house, just short of the village of Kargamon on the river Halys. In their initial search, Kargamon had been overlooked, lying as it did at the edge of Bithynia-Pontus, in an area many assumed within the boundaries of Galatia or Cappadocia.

Simon stayed in the rain with the horses as a precaution, his face hidden inside the hood of his cloak, while Kimon and Eustratios found shelter under the house's simple portico. Their first knock went unanswered, so they knocked again, louder this time. At last, the door creaked open just wide enough for them to see the face of the woman behind it. "What do you want?" she asked without smiling.

"Health to you, madam," said Kimon, sounding to Eustratios oddly pleasant considering their discomfort and the woman's unwelcome. "We're looking for the pensioner Gerasimos. Is he at home?"

"He's not here. He doesn't live here anymore," said the woman.

"Oh?" said Kimon, less surprised than he sounded. "Would you happen to know where he does live now?"

"I have no idea. He's gone for good, that's all I know. You'll have to look elsewhere," said the woman, about to close the door.

"Where else, madam?" said Kimon, quickly. "Perhaps there is someone else in town with whom we might inquire?"

"Ask the curator in the village. Good day." The door closed before them and was immediately bolted.

Kimon and Eustratios looked at each other. "Must be the weather," said Eustratios.

"Yes," said Kimon. "Her monthly weather."

They turned and trudged through the mud back up to the road where Simon awaited. "I know that woman," said Simon. "She was Gerasimos's housemaid."

"Lucky man," said Kimon. "She belongs to someone else now."

They headed on into the village and looked for the curator at the local imperial post station at the intersection of the main roads, the north-south road from Sinope to Claudiopolis and the east-west road from Nicomedia to Amisos. The clerk on duty referred them to an inn several doors down from the station.

Leaving Simon at the station to tend the horses, Kimon and Eustratios repaired to the inn. The first floor of the inn was one large, smokey, stone room with wooden benches and a few stools arranged about two open hearths at opposite ends. One hearth was cold; the seats about it, empty. The other was alive with an inviting blaze, but the men about it were less inviting. They paused a moment from their conversation to inspect the strangers, dripping water by the door.

From the back of the room, the innkeeper emerged, wiping his hands with a rag and greeting his guests with an inquiring expression but without a word.

"Two rooms for the night," said Kimon.

The innkeeper nodded. "Two silver each," he said.

Kimon nodded, and Eustratios dug into his purse for the rent.

"And warm wine for two," said Kimon.

The innkeeper nodded again. "Another eight," he said. Eustratios counted out the total and handed it to the innkeeper, who tucked it into a pocket in his leather apron and then exited through the door from which he had emerged. The travelers had just hung their wet cloaks on the pegs by the door when the innkeeper returned with the wine, served in tin cups with short, flat handles stamped with the Greek letter omega. Kimon recalled the inn's name—The Last Stop.

They took the wine and moved closer to the men by the fire.

"We're looking for the pensioner Gerasimos," Kimon announced. "We were told the curator might know his whereabouts."

A stout man with a fat face and small, squinched features stood up. "I'm curator of this town," he said with an air of authority. "Who are you?"

"I am Kimon, son of the decurion Aristoboulos of Sinope."

The barest sign of recognition flashed in the curator's eyes before he resumed his interrogation. "Why would you want Gerasimos?"

"He owes me money," said Kimon.

The curator chuckled and waved to his companions, still seated by the fire. "Well, join the crowd. He owes us all," he said. His companions nodded slowly. "Not that it matters. He's gone for good."

"Where to?"

"Ask Apollo," the curator answered with a shrug. "No one here knows. He's disappeared and we don't expect him back."

"Do you know where he might be found?"

"It's no use. He's gone."

"You don't have any idea what happened to him?"

"I said he's gone. That should be enough for you."

When Kimon hesitated, Eustratios spoke up. "Well, my lord," he said, "if he really has gone for good, then all that remains is for the courts to divide his assets among his many creditors."

The curator's face changed expressions as Eustratios's meaning sank in.

"They say," he said, "— they say he went east, toward Phazemon."

Kimon looked at him skeptically.

"You might as well know," the curator continued, "he was suspected of harboring fugitives, Christians to be exact, so he ran away over a year ago to escape the law. You might still track him down. Check with the authorities in Phazemon. They were alerted to his escape and were expecting him. That's all I know. I swear it."

Kimon nodded slowly. "That's help enough—for now," he said.

They left the next morning for Phazemon, arriving late the following day after passing through a succession of villages even smaller than Kargamon. Phazemon was a city about the size of Sinope, but on the day they arrived it seemed to have doubled in size, with its marketplace full of vendors, its inns full of travelers, and its taverns full of drunks. They learned why from the town clerk: the governor of Cappadocia was expected to arrive in a few days for the annual assizes.

The clerk barely had time to talk to the Sinopeans. "I've so much to do to prepare," he explained, passing through the crowded corridor of the civic basilica. "I don't recall that anyone of that name has come to our attention recently. If you can wait a week, I can have my assistants conduct a proper check of the records. Right now I'm afraid we can't manage it."

Before Kimon could respond, the clerk called out to a man in uniform named Proclus, who was just about to disappear into one of the many offices lining the walls of the basilica.

"Ever hear of a man from Kargamon named Gerasimos, wanted for harboring fugitives?" the clerk asked. "He supposedly fled there last year about this time, headed our way."

Proclus arched an eyebrow. "There was one at the village," he said.

The clerk's face went blank. "Are you sure?" he said.

Proclus nodded. "It was one of the names reported," he said.

The clerk turned to Kimon with the same blank face, paused, and then said, "There was a village between Kargamon and here where many Christians were apprehended last March by a squadron of the provincial militia—not our own police, you understand." He paused again before continuing. "The squadron commander reported taking many of those apprehended to stand trial in Neocaesarea. There was a Gerasimos on the list."

"May we see the list?" asked Kimon.

"We don't have it," answered Proclus. "I was only shown the list by the squadron commander."

"But we've been to Neocaesarea and there's no mention in the records there of Gerasimos or anyone else that we're looking for."

"Who else are you looking for?"

"A young woman named Makrina, my sister," answered Kimon.

The clerk looked at Proclus, who shook his head. "I don't recall that name on the list."

"What about Charita, Gerasimos's wife?" asked Simon.

"Charita, maybe," said Proclus. "I can't be sure."

"What about Gregorios and Ioanna and Salome?" asked Kimon, recalling the names from Makrina's letters.

"I only saw the list once," said Proclus, "and I remember Gerasimos because his name was at the top and the squadron commander was, for some reason, proud to have captured him. If there's no record of them in Neocaesarea, you might try elsewhere. The squadron commander might have missed the governor in Neocaesarea and taken them on to Sebastea or Melitene."

"You might try the village," the clerk suggested. "Someone there might know—that is, if there's anyone left."

"Anyone left?"

"There were rumors," said the clerk, "but there are always rumors. Try the village first, and let us know what you find."

They found the village with the help of a guide, a nervous fellow who begged for his fee as soon as the village was in sight and left as soon as he got it, when all they could see was a confused cluster of roofless stone walls surrounded by a crude but intact picket fence. The gate through the fence was open, and the way through it was crowded with fresh mountain grass, well watered by the spring thaw and the recent rains.

Kimon and his companions filed singly through the gate on horseback, looking and listening for signs of habitation. All about them lay charred shells of houses, better homes now for field mice and rabbits.

They stopped when they came to the edge of a clearing, ringed with ruins and sprouting weeds. Kimon took a deep breath and shouted, "HULLO!" A pair of crows fluttered suddenly from amid the ruins and winged their escape. Otherwise, there was nothing.

Kimon waited until he was sure, then kicked his horse up and loped off down a path leading west through the ruins. Eustratios followed him at a trot, but only as far as the edge of the clearing, where he pulled his horse up to the wall of a ruined cottage and peered inside.

Simon, meanwhile, scanning the periphery of the clearing, noticed a round, whitish stone, about the size of a loaf of bread, lying in the dirt near the walls of what appeared to have been a large house. He walked his mount closer to the stone and was almost on top of it before he realized that the stone had teeth, and had once had eyes.

Surprised and alarmed, Simon dropped down from his horse and squatted over his find, poking at it with his finger and rolling it over for a thorough inspection. Its underside was soiled by contact with the ground, but otherwise the bone was clean and free of vermin, evidence that it had lain there a long time. Nearby lay other bones in the same condition, though some bore the marks of gnawing.

Leaving his horse where it stood, Simon followed the trail of bones to the entrance of the ruined house. The double wooden doors of the house had been scarred by fire and then breeched by scavenging beasts, despite having been reinforced on the outside with boards. When Simon yanked away the reinforcing boards, the charred doors fell open on their own.

Stepping onto the stone threshold, Simon beheld a gruesome sight. Beneath the heap of charred roof timbers, from one wall to the next, lay a carpet of bones, some blackened by fire, some buried in ash, some crowded in corners, others trapped beneath fallen timbers. At his feet lay at least a dozen skulls and within a few paces were dozens more. Simon gasped in horror, quickly made the sign of the cross, then turned and called for Eustratios.

Eustratios trotted across the clearing, past the scattered skeleton he did not notice, and straight up before the doorway, where he jumped down and joined Simon on the threshold. "Good Lord!" he cried, staring in at the destruction and crossing himself. "God Almighty!"

"How many do you think there are?" asked Simon.

"God knows," said Eustratios. "A hundred or more. Perhaps the whole village!"

"Were they *all* Christians?" wondered Simon.

"They must have been," said Eustratios. "And this must have been their kirk."

Simon nodded and then again made the sign of the cross. Eustratios did likewise.

They stood amazed by the spectacle of death, until the sound of hoof-beats behind them drew their attention. Kimon reappeared, loping across the clearing toward them. "What is it?" he asked, pulling his horse up and dismounting.

Eustratios looked at him with wide eyes. "It's—it's—"

Before he could answer, Kimon stepped in between them and saw for himself. "Great gods!" he cried, recoiling in horror and pulling the edge of his cloak to his nose.

"There must be over a hundred," said Eustratios. "They might have come here to pray when the soldiers appeared."

"Lot of good it did them," Kimon muttered.

The three men stood there next to each other, staring at the bones and ashes, saying nothing until Kimon suddenly shook his head and backed away. "Is this all that's left?" he said. "Another dead end? Another grave? Another pit of death?" Simon and Eustratios looked at him uncertainly, and Kimon, not wanting to face them, turned and walked away.

When Eustratios caught up with him, he was tightening the cinch on his saddle, just for something to do.

"So where do we go from here, Eustratios?" said Kimon without looking up. It was less a question than a challenge.

Eustratios shrugged. "To Sebastea or Melitene, to check the records there," he answered.

"Of course. On to the next town in search of more victims, to read of their glorious resistance to the powers that be."

"It's all we can do."

Kimon turned on him. "What's the use? What are we likely to find? Anything more than Makrina's name on some list proving she's been butchered by soldiers in the woods or burned at the stake after a proper trial?"

"We don't know that," said Eustratios.

"All we lack is proof," said Kimon angrily. "Every lead we follow ends in death! Isn't that proof enough?"

He pointed to the house. "Everyone here died, and if Makrina was with them, she died here too! We could go on to Sebastea or all the way Melitene and find no mention of her in the records there because she died right here, in this tiny little town, unknown even to the gods!"

Kimon grabbed the reins of his horse and pulled it along after him. "Damn them! Damn them all!" he swore as he started away.

Again Eustratios followed after him, but only as far as the scattering of bones that had first drawn Simon's attention. Kneeling down, he began gathering the bones into the skirt of his tunic.

Kimon glanced back. "What in the name of Zeus are you doing?" he exclaimed.

"Just thought I'd bury them with the others," said Eustratios. "I can't just leave them lying about like rubbish."

"But they *are* rubbish. Worse than rubbish, they're unclean," said Kimon. "How can you stand to touch them?"

Eustratios shrugged. "They are the bones of a brother," he said. "Death has no more power over them. It's just not our way—to leave them lying about."

Kimon shook his head and walked away.

Eustratios collected the remaining bones and carried them back to the ruined building, where Simon had begun clearing away some of the debris from the doorway. A proper tomb would need a better barrier. Eustratios deposited the bones in a clear corner.

"What do you suppose we do with them?" he asked Simon. "We can't bury them all."

Simon thought for a moment, then glanced about at the tall, mountain fir trees rising above the ruined walls of the village. "Pine boughs," he said. The pair immediately set about clipping branches from nearby trees and arranging them carefully to cover the common grave.

Across the clearing, Kimon found a seat upon a pile of rubble, where he sat with his head in his hands. Under the blaze of a mountain sun, the frustrations and regrets of the past many months bubbled up into his consciousness at an ever increasing pitch. He was angry—at the emperors for their murderous vanities, at the bureaucracy for its self-serving obedience, and at the general populace for its complacency and pettiness. He was angry at the Christians, too, for their mulish faith and morbid defiance, and he was especially angry at his sister Makrina for her reckless piety.

But most of all he was angry at himself—for his failure to find her, for his waning will to continue looking, for the weakness he had shown when in the orbit of Marcellinus, and for the shameful dissipation into which he had slipped just as Makrina's ordeal had turned deadly. After years of schooling and inquiry, he still could neither quiet his doubts nor muster the will to choose a central truth in which to believe. His failure confounded his attempts to understand the suffering he saw. Who was to blame for all the bloodshed? Did Christians deserve to die for breaking the law? Had they earned their own end? Or were they right to resist and blameless for the bloodshed?

Across the clearing, a melody arose, a sad, solemn song for the departed, from Eustratios, the former server:

*With the Saints give rest, O Christ,*
*To the souls of thy servants,*
*Where sickness and sorrow are no more,*
*Neither sighing, but life everlasting!*

Kimon listened for a moment, then stopped his ears with his hands. "No more, no more," he moaned, his head bowed, his eyes closed.

His words could not have been heard for more than a few feet, but nevertheless the singing did stop. Kimon looked up to see Eustratios walking his way.

"We found this, sir," he said, holding out his hand.

In his palm lay a golden ring, in weight and workmanship far richer than any poor peasant could afford. Kimon took the ring and examined it. Engraved on its face were twin columns separated by a capital C, surmounted by a tiny eagle. It was the signet of the House of Canio.

"This was Makrina's," said Kimon. "She was here."

"Are you sure?" said Eustratios.

Kimon nodded and stood up. "Show me . . . show me where you found it," he said.

Eustratios led him back to the doorway and pointed to a pile of bones over which Simon was standing. "Right over there," he said. "

Kimon covered his nose again with his cloak. Then he felt suddenly faint. He reached for the doorpost to steady himself.

Eustratios saw him pale and stepped forward just in time to catch him as he slid to the ground. "Are you all right?" he asked.

Kimon closed his eyes and bowed his head. "I'll be all right," he said breathing heavily.

"I'll get you some water," said Eustratios.

Kimon kept his head down, his eyes closed, and his fingers curled around Makrina's ring. When Eustratios returned with the water, Kimon refused it. "Leave me be," he said, without opening his eyes.

"Are you sure you're all right?" said Eustratios.

"Yes, yes, I'll be all right. Leave me be," said Kimon, with a weary nod.

Eustratios left the skin of water lying against Kimon's leg and returned reluctantly to Simon. After some hushed consultation between them, Eustratios fetched a saddlebag to collect the pile of bones from where the ring was found.

Kimon waited in the dusty doorway, his eyes closed, his head now leaning back against the doorpost. His grip on the ring had relaxed, and he seemed almost asleep to Eustratios, who was forced to step over him on his way out with the saddlebag.

Just as he did so, Kimon looked up to see the shadow of the saddlebag pass across his face. It was an ill omen. Kimon scrambled to his feet and backed away from the scene in fear. He had not been asleep, and he knew what was in the bag. He hurried off across the clearing to where he had left his horse and settled again on the rock pile to wait.

Simon and Eustratios finished covering the remains of the dead with pine boughs, then paused to chant a few brief prayers for the dead before filling in the doorway with the largest stones they could find. When all was finished, they led their horses across the clearing to join Kimon, who was ready and waiting on the path leading out the way they had come. Without a word they started back for Phazemon.

They arrived in Phazemon near dusk, with just enough daylight left for Eustratios and Simon to put away the horses and catch a quick meal at the inn. Kimon did not join them, but retired early to his room.

The next morning at sunrise he was nowhere to be found. Simon and Eustratios prepared the horses for the journey home, expecting Kimon to return at any time, but when he had not appeared by the third hour they set out to look for him.

Finding him was not as hard as they first expected. Every shop, every tavern was closed on account of the annual assizes. The entire town had turned out at the city basilica to see the trials. The hardest part was picking Kimon out amidst the crowd. The basilica was packed, with no room to move about freely.

The governor sat in the judge's seat on a low dais at the apse end of the basilica. Various other officials stood behind on the dais, which was flanked by soldiers. The area immediately in front of the dais was railed off for use by the parties addressing the court in each case. The rest of the nave and the basilica's side aisles were filled to capacity with people, many of them simply spectators.

Kimon stood near the apse end, against a column separating the nave from the aisle. Simon and Eustratios could not have been farther off when they spotted him, and reaching him seemed next to impossible with the court in session. The governor had already dispensed of the few criminal cases brought before him and opened the docket of civil suits, in which it seemed everyone in Phazemon had an interest.

The first involved a woman of high rank by the name of Julitta, who stood before the dais with her advocate, a young man with a weak voice that grew ever weaker as he read a lengthy petition alleging an extraordinary theft by several of Julitta's neighbors. The woman, it was claimed, had been widowed early in life and left with an immense estate comprising thousands of acres of land for tilling and grazing, large herds of cattle and flocks of sheep, hundreds of slaves, and scores of storehouses, granaries, and other works. Inexperienced in management and innocent of the ways of the world, she had left the care of her estate to trusted others, while she tended to private charities, for which she was well known in those parts. Over the years, however, other landowners in the region, seeing her estate neglected, encroached upon her holdings, seizing herds, assuming grazing rights, and appropriating land and slaves and facilities for their own. When her loss could no longer be missed, and an investigation uncovered the complicity of her chief overseer, Julitta was forced to file suit lest the little that she had left fall into the hands of others also.

"Wherefore," concluded her advocate, "with due respect and worship, we do beseech and implore your excellency to restore unto the esteemed Lady Julitta all properties and privileges of which she has been deprived by the unlawful predation of others."

The governor, a grave man with blunt features, honored in his middle age with a wreath of gray hair around his bald pate, listened patiently while the petition was read and paused pensively afterward to consider the issue. "You want full restitution?" he asked the advocate in a conversational voice, barely heard throughout the hall.

"With due respect and worship," said the advocate, with a nod.

"So say you, lady?" said the governor, louder so that all could hear.

"I do," said the woman, with a reverent bow of her covered head.

"You have a list of particulars?" the governor asked the advocate.

"We do, your excellency," answered the advocate, handing a scroll to the bailiff, who passed the scroll to the governor, who untied and unrolled it partially. A man in uniform stepped forward and leaned over the governor's shoulder to view the scroll.

After a moment of study and a private conference between the governor and his assistant, the governor cleared his voice and looked up at the advocate. "This will take some time to examine," he said. "I propose to turn the matter over to my inspector general. Will that suit you?"

"Yes, your excellency," replied the advocate.

"And what of the advocates for the defendants? Are they present?" asked the governor.

"We are, your excellency," answered a man in the nave near the railing. A guard quickly moved a section of railing to let the man and two of his colleagues into the open area. The lead advocate was tall and well-dressed, with a pointed face, accentuated by a hairline that receded high on two sides but left a wavy crest flowing backwards from his forehead.

"Have you any objection to turning the matter over to the inspector general for examination?" asked the governor.

"We do, your excellency," said the man with the pointed face, "on the grounds that the plaintiff has no standing before the law, and so cannot bring suit for any cause, on account of her neglect of the imperial edict requiring all citizens to offer sacrifice."

A murmur of surprise and excitement ran through the audience. The governor raised his eyebrows, making no attempt to hide his own surprise. "Is this true, Lady—what was it—Julitta?" he inquired.

"It is true," said the esteemed matron, taking a deep breath and holding high her chin.

"Why so?" said the governor.

"I am a Christian and cannot sacrifice."

"You're quite sure of that, aren't you?" said the governor.

"I am."

"Well, we'll see how sure. Bring us fire and incense!"

The audience murmured louder while the governor conferred with his assistants. Soon there were soldierly shouts of "Make way! Make way!" A bronze altar, with coals already smoldering in the dish, was carried in and deposited in the open area. A clerk stood by it with a tray of incense. The bailiff pounded the dais with his staff, and the audience quieted down. The governor waited for silence before speaking.

"Here now, lady, is your opportunity to prove your loyalty and further your case," said the governor. "Whatever reasons you might have had for not sacrificing, whatever error you might have fallen into, all this is forgiven if you will now sacrifice. Please do so quickly, so that we may proceed."

The clerk offered the woman incense, but the woman shook her head. "I will not sacrifice," she said.

"Lady Julitta," said the governor, "may I remind you that much more is at stake than your petition. The law requires you to sacrifice. No rank is exempt. No person may refuse for any reason. To refuse is proof of disloyalty. The act itself is treasonous, and, as you must know, treason is a capital offense. If you refuse, lady, neither the frailty of your sex nor the dignity of your rank will protect you. You must sacrifice, or be prepared to lose everything."

Breathing deeply, the Lady Julitta closed her eyes and shook her upraised head, all the while pulling tightly the folds of her mantle.

"You may take my life as well as my possessions," she declared aloud. "I will lose my body before my mouth will utter any impiety against God my Creator!"

"Oh, nonsense," said the governor. "We're only asking that you do what I assume everyone else in this building has done already. Why is that so difficult? Why don't you just do it so we can all get back to business? Why make so much trouble?"

"I cannot act against conscience."

"Your conscience has nothing to do with this. You cannot defy the powers that be and not expect punishment. The laws of the empire must be obeyed. What you have shown here is outright defiance of the order upon which our peace and prosperity depends. You act against us all by refusing to go along with us."

"I will not sacrifice."

"Reason with her, counselor," said the governor to Julitta's advocate. "See if *you* can save her life."

Julitta's timid advocate turned to his client and attempted an appeal, but all the while she stared at the ceiling of the basilica, emphatically shaking her head. The advocate looked up at the governor and shrugged his shoulders to show his helplessness. The governor signaled to the bailiff to quiet the crowd, and the bailiff obeyed by pounding the dais.

"One last time, lady. Sacrifice and all is forgiven. Your case will go forward without prejudice. Justice will be done," said the governor.

"I will not sacrifice," replied Julitta.

"You force me to be severe in my judgment. Sacrifice or accept your fate!"

Julitta again shook her head and declared aloud, "I am a handmaid of Christ! I will not sacrifice!"

The crowd's reaction was loud and confused. Friends and relatives shouted, "Sacrifice! Sacrifice!" Others shouted, "Beat her! Burn her! Take her away!" The bailiff pounded fiercely to restore order, while the governor conferred again with his assistants. Finally, he stood and raised his arms for silence, then resumed his judge's seat when the crowd had quieted.

"I cannot allow this brazen defiance of the common good to go unpunished," he said. "What example would it set for people—to see laws flouted, the government defied, the public itself dishonored, and its shared values despised? I therefore sentence the Lady Julitta to die by fire at noon tomorrow."

There were groans and wails from her friends and relatives in the audience, but Julitta herself showed no emotion.

"Nevertheless," continued the governor, raising his voice over the noise, "if she relents and submits herself to our just and merciful rule, and offers the sacrifice required by law, I will rescind her sentence and restore her fully to the community. Let it never be said that our law is not merciful."

This addendum to the sentence left the audience mumbling uncertainly for a moment, and then another voice was heard above all.

"Your laws are unjust and so is your sentence!" shouted Kimon, standing now forward of the column, for all to see.

The hall was suddenly silent.

"Who said that?" demanded the governor.

"I said it, and I will say it again: Your laws are unjust and so is your sentence."

A guard was already moving in his direction when the governor ordered Kimon brought forward. The guard grabbed Kimon's tunic at the neck and pulled him down, then locked his arm around Kimon's neck, stopping his breathing. Thus subdued, Kimon was hauled before the dais and then thrown loose. The bailiff pounded the dais for order.

"Who are you?" asked the governor.

Still catching his breath, Kimon was slow to respond. A guard kicked him in the back with the toe of his boot. "Name, fool, and watch what you say!" the guard ordered.

Kimon looked up at the governor and answered, "I am Kimon of Sinope."

"Well, then, Kimon of Sinope," said the governor, "have you anything to say for yourself before I sentence you, too, to die?"

"For what crime, your excellency?" asked Kimon.

"For treason, of course."

"I have done nothing treasonous but have always obeyed the laws of the empire."

"For refusing to sacrifice."

"I have sacrificed many times to many gods, and I will sacrifice now if it suits you."

The clerk still holding the dish of incense started to offer some to Kimon, but the governor waved him away. "Then you are not a Christian?" said the governor.

"I am not."

"Why then do you protest the punishment of Christians? Who are they to you?"

"They are my countrymen, my fellow Romans, my brothers—and my sisters," said Kimon. "They do not deserve to die, and I will not be party to their murder. I will not remain silent while the innocent are made victims. I will not join this deceit, passing crime off as justice."

"This *is* justice! This is the law!" said the governor.

"It is a murderous law made by murderous men for murderous purposes."

"Enough of this!" declared the governor. "I have argued too long already with this foolish woman and do not care to argue further with you, Kimon of Sinope. Whatever cause you have to be so bothered by these proceedings is cause enough to sentence you here and now. For slanders against the imperial dignity, I sentence you to the mines. Perhaps before you die there you will learn to behave in public. Take him away."

The guard pushed Kimon off toward a side exit, ahead of the Lady Julitta, who stared at him in amazement.

# XXVII

Vitalis was pleasantly surprised when Marcus returned from Sinope to Byzantium with Eugenia in tow, and when Marcus informed him in private that she would accompany them all the way home, he could scarce concealed his delight. "How the gods have smiled on us!" he declared, with an impish grin. "Keep your hands off her," warned Marcus. "Keep your eyes off her, too."

But Vitalis, though loyal and obedient, could no more keep his eyes off Eugenia than he could keep his heart from beating. She was young and beautiful and innocent enough to be friendly to strangers, especially handsome young troopers. A few more years with her mother and she would have learned to take special care around men, to cover herself more completely, to avoid their gaze and discourage their interest. She thought she was just being polite, but her politeness only excited the interest of Vitalis, who often found himself obliged to look after her needs.

Still, during the long journey west from Byzantium, nothing like a conversation passed between them, partly on account of the watchfulness of Marcus and Nonna, her chaperon, and partly because Vitalis knew no Greek and Eugenia's Latin was not what it should have been. (Her sister had been a much better student in Latin, but then, Makrina had had more encouragement.) A few shy glances, a handful of friendly words, and an occasional smile were all they had shared before their arrival in Mogontiacum.

There Marcus found it prudent to leave his new charge, while he and Vitalis went forward to find the army of Constantine, which was back in the province of Belgica in pursuit of the Franks again. Eugenia was not pleased and pleaded with Marcus to take her with him. Mogontiacum was a dreary garrison town with gloomy gray skies and foreign-looking faces. The apartment was cramped and dim and not up to feminine standards. Crescens, the chamberlain, frightened her, and she was afraid of the other servants, too. Only Titus, the secretary, spoke Greek, and he seemed oddly aloof, as if *he* were afraid of *her.*

When Marcus steadfastly refused to take her along, Eugenia tried a tantrum and then tears, which won her the support of Vitalis. "Why not take her to Treveris and leave her at the palace?" he said to Marcus, the sounds of sobbing coming from the next room.

"No," replied Marcus. "The army is not in Treveris, and it's not on the way. She will do as she is told."

"She's not a soldier, sir," said Vitalis.

"No, she's not," said Marcus. "She's a woman, and barely that. Still a child, really. All the more reason why she must not win on this."

Eugenia did not win. Neither did she persist in her protest. When Marcus and Vitalis left early the next morning, she saw them off with a cheery smile and a penitent peck on Marcus's cheek. Vitalis did not understand.

Two weeks later, the Franks had been again subdued, and Vitalis returned to Mogontiacum with a detachment of lancers to escort Eugenia and Nonna to Treveris. The next day they were back on the road to Treveris, several hours from Mogontiacum, when Vitalis at last found his opportunity to converse with his young charge.

It was after noon. Eugenia and Nonna were riding in a covered carriage, lined with heavy cushions to soften the road. Vitalis and Titus were on horseback behind the carriage. It was a beautiful day in October, and the flaps of carriage's canopy were rolled high. Vitalis noticed that Nonna had nodded off to sleep, so he moved up alongside the carriage.

"Is she asleep?" he asked with an innocent smile.

Eugenia nodded and smiled back.

"It's a long ride, but the road is smooth," he said.

Eugenia nodded again. "How long?" she asked in uncertain, oddly accented Latin.

"How long before we reach Treveris?" said Vitalis. "Two days. We'll be there tomorrow afternoon."

"*Saturni dies*," said Eugenia, with some satisfaction.

"That's right. Saturn's day," said Vitalis. "Don't worry. It's a safe trip. It wasn't always so. A few years back the Franks were on the loose through here, but the legions put a stop to that. I was with the XXII Primigenia then, headquartered back at Mogon. We didn't spend much time in garrison that year. Most every night was under the stars, out here in the fields. We moved so often I thought we'd wear out our boots—"

"And Marcus?" Eugenia asked.

"Marcus? Oh, he was with the cavalry then. They had it easy compared to us—they had horses to ride. Anyway, all the marching paid off. We caught the savages unawares and slaughtered them by the thousands."

"Slaughtered?" said Eugenia.

"By the thousands," said Vitalis. "Later on the cavalry rounded up what was left. That was Marcus's doing. He made quite a name for himself then."

"Did Marcus slaughtered, too?" Eugenia asked imperfectly.

Vitalis smiled and said, "He didn't need to. He just forced them to surrender—the wives and children and all. We had already taken care of their warriors."

Eugenia said something in Greek and quickly crossed herself. Vitalis appeared not to notice. "You'll like Treveris," he said. "It's a pleasant town—not too crowded, a lot of nice stone buildings, beautiful gardens, a big arena, a fair-size circus—even a theater."

"But where will we live?"

"In town, near the palace, I imagine," said Vitalis.

"Palace?" said Eugenia.

"Near it," said Vitalis. "Lord Canio has been promoted. He's now commander of the Protectors, and he'll need to be near the emperor at all times. You might not see him much from here on out. It's a very demanding job. He'll be always on duty."

Eugenia nodded and said, "Yes," causing Vitalis to wonder how much she had understood of what he had said.

Then suddenly, Eugenia looked at him and smiled and looked away again, then settled back into the cushions of the carriage. Vitalis gazed at her admiringly for a moment, then dropped back behind the carriage when Nonna awoke from her nap.

To his own surprise, Marcus had indeed been promoted to commander of the Protectors. The old commanders of the Companions who had served Constantius for so many years were all retiring, and Constantine's aides were taking their place. Marcus took command of the Protectors, Bassianus took command of the Shieldmen, and Ablabius took command of the Lancers. But instead of taking up residence near the palace, Marcus found himself obliged to stay actually in the palace, in special quarters near the emperor's own chambers.

By the time Vitalis arrived with Eugenia, arrangements had been made for Eugenia to stay in the women's wing of the palace as a lady-in-waiting to the dowager empress Theodora, Constantius's second wife, who was just a year older than Marcus and five years younger than her step-son Constantine. Nonna was to live among the serving women at the palace, but Vitalis was assigned to the barracks for junior officers outside the palace grounds, so that in the months that followed he saw even less of Eugenia than she saw of Marcus.

Eugenia's first day at the palace began as a lonely one. The chief steward, an efficient eunuch, showed her to her quarters—a fair-size dressing room with an attached sleeping cubicle—then immediately took Nonna off on an instructional tour of the palace, leaving the Lady Eugenia alone with a silent squad of serving girls busily making up her rooms. They cleaned and swept without direction. They replaced the linens and the carpets, they polished the lamps and the furniture, and they filled the washbasin with fresh water. When the stewards arrived with Eugenia's trunks, the girls unpacked her entire wardrobe without question or comment.

Only when they were preparing to leave did one of the girls speak.

"Incense, lady?" asked the oldest among them, holding a match. Eugenia nodded obligingly, without even thinking. The girl struck the match against the flint and lit the lump of charcoal, sprinkled with tiny golden globules, in the handheld censor on a small table. The rest waited until the coal was surely lit, and then very quickly they all departed, bowing once to Eugenia before backing out of the room.

The room was suddenly quiet, but Eugenia could hear noises outside, faint and distant. Peering outside her chambers she saw many other servants scurrying about here and there, like ants in an anthill, each intent upon her own business, none paying her the least attention.

Back inside her dressing room, she heard voices through the walls. These, too, she assumed, were servants, before catching a few muffled phrases: "I can't believe she doesn't see it herself. Everyone else does." "You'd have to be blind not to. How long do you suppose before someone tells her?" "Who knows? It won't be me. She wouldn't believe me anyway." Eugenia sat down on edge of a chair and listened a while longer, until the voices faded.

She had never felt more alone in her life. She had never known stranger surroundings. She had never sensed herself so far from friends or family. And yet what had she to fear, with Marcus as her guardian? Marcus was strong and sure. He was powerful. He was close to the emperor. He would protect her. Had he not brought her to live in the most hospitable place on earth, next to her own home? The palace was beautiful. The servants were obedient and efficient. And she was not entirely alone: Nonna was there with her, somewhere now in the palace.

Eugenia suppressed an urge to cry and abruptly arose and set about examining her quarters and arranging things the way she wanted them. An hour later Nonna returned alone with endless instructions and insights: Don't enter the imperial suite unless bidden. Don't venture outside the palace unescorted. Stay out of the servants' quarters altogether. Don't interfere with the servants when they are attending to their regular duties. If you need help, see the chief steward or one of his female assistants. Food and drink are available in the ladies' triclinium between the first and third hours for breakfast and between the sixth and ninth hour for lunch. Dinner is served in the main dining hall at the eleventh hour in the summer and at the second hour of night in the winter. Attendance is optional, except when specially requested by the emperor or empress, who may or may not attend (usually not). At all other times, private meals in one of the smaller tricliniums are available upon prior request.

*How could she not have written them down?* thought Eugenia, reviewing the list in her mind while preparing for her bath. She followed Nonna nervously down the corridor to the ladies' bath, expecting to encounter at last another guest of the palace, but the bath was empty and quiet, except for the trickle of running water from a central fountain. Eugenia was both relieved and disappointed. *Where are the other women? What are they all up to?* she wondered. The longer she went without meeting anyone, the more she dreaded her first encounter.

After her bath, Eugenia ventured alone into the palace gardens. The palace was strangely quiet when she strolled out of her chambers in her favorite felt dalmatic, bright blue in color. In addition to her pale pink palla, a separate embroidered collar protected her neck and shoulders from the northern air. Confident of her appearance, Eugenia was prepared to meet anyone, except the first person she actually encountered, who sprang at her from behind a hedge, armed and aggressive.

"Stop in the name of the Augustus!" cried a little round-faced boy in Latin, brandishing a wooden sword in a most threatening manner. "Stop, I say! Caesar commands you to stop!"

When a startled Eugenia stepped back, the boy lunged at her, striking her fiercely on the thigh. "Ouch!" she cried, backing into the hedge.

The boy circled about her, menacingly. "I've got you now!" he cried. "You'll never get away! You're my prisoner and I'm taking you back as a trophy of war!"

"Hannibalianus!" shouted a heavy woman with a booming voice. "Stop that this instant! Give me that sword." With a sudden sweep of her fat arm, the woman disarmed the fearsome lad, who now looked about to cry. "How many times have I told you: Leave other people alone! This is the second time today and the third time this week you've made a nuisance of yourself. Do you want another thrashing?"

"That's enough, Brunilda," said another voice.

From the direction of the palace came another woman, beautiful, finely dressed, and quite sure of herself. The boy ran to her immediately, throwing his arms around her legs and burying his face in her ends of her palla.

"Yes, my lady," said Brunilda, instantly assuming a submissive demeanor.

"I was only playing," cried the child.

"Your are excused, Brunilda," said the woman.

"Yes, my lady," said Brunilda, bowing deeply and backing away.

"I was only playing," the child repeated.

"Yes, but you play too roughly for young ladies," said his mother. "Now run along and try to stay out of trouble."

The boy wiped his eyes one last time on his mother's purple palla and then ran off farther into the garden. The woman turned to Eugenia. "He didn't hurt you, did he?" she asked in slightly accented Greek.

"No," Eugenia answered, also in Greek. "I was just so surprised, I didn't know what to do. I've never been a trophy of war before."

The older woman smiled. "His last trophy was the milkmaid's cat," she said. "You must be Lord Canio's ward. I was told you were coming. What is your name?"

"Eugenia, the daughter of Aristoboulos. And yours?"

The woman thought for a moment, then answered simply, "Theodora."

In an instant, Eugenia realized her error. "Oh, my lady, please pardon me," she said with a low bow. "I should have known. I'm just so new here, and—and I've never met an empress before, either."

"Never mind," said the empress kindly. "It is a pleasure to meet you. Please have a seat."

They sat down on a marble bench opposite a bed of geraniums.

"I was surprised to hear you speak Greek," said Eugenia. "Are you also from the East?"

"Yes. My mother was from Syria, and my father was the praetorian prefect in the East, but he divorced my mother when I was very young, and she later married the emperor Maximian. So most of my life I have been in the West. I married the emperor Constantius thirteen years ago, when I was about your age, and I've been in Treveris ever since."

"It's a beautiful place," said Eugenia, politely.

"Pleasant enough," said the empress. "But cold in the winter, and often cloudy any time of year. Where are you from?"

"Sinope, on the Euxine Sea. Also cold in the winter. Sometimes even in the summer. And also often cloudy at any time."

"Then you should feel right at home here. Why have you come west?"

Eugenia hesitated before answering. "For safety," she said.

"Safety?"

"My lady, I am a Christian, or almost a Christian. I haven't been baptized yet, but my parents were afraid for me, so they asked Marcus to take me with him, because it's safer here."

"It is safer," said Theodora. "So is Canio also a Christian?"

"Oh, no, lady. I wish he were. Then he would have married my sister Makrina, and she'd be here instead of—wherever she is."

"You don't know where she is?"

"No," said Eugenia sadly. "For a while she was in the mountains somewhere, but we've lost touch with her."

"So your sister is a Christian and is hiding somewhere in the mountains of Asia, and Canio, because he still loves her, has brought you here for your protection?"

"Yes, my lady."

"Touching," said Theodora. "Eugenia, be careful to whom you mention these things. It is safer here for Christians, but not everyone would like it to be. You took a chance in telling me, and I thank you for your honesty and candor, but others might think differently. And then, of course, policies can change, for better or for worse."

A young girl approached them from the direction of the palace.

"Pardon me, Mamma, but the chamberlain is waiting for you," said the girl in Latin.

"Tell him I'll be with him in a moment," said Theodora. As the girl turned to go, her mother said, "Anastasia, I'd like you to meet the Lady Eugenia, who has come all the way from Asia to live with us for awhile."

"Asia!" said the girl. "I've always wanted to go to Asia. Sounds like such a pretty place."

Theodora turned to Eugenia. "Perhaps you can help my daughters with their Greek while you're here," she said.

"I would be my honor," said Eugenia. "They might also be able to help me with my Latin."

"That would be my honor," said the girl cheerily, before bowing again to take her leave.

Watching her go, Eugenia said, "Anastasia is a Christian name."

"Yes, it is," said the empress. "My mother was a Christian for awhile when I was little, and that's why my father divorced her. I was not raised a Christian, but I still remember some of what I learned as a child. And I liked the name Anastasia. . . . Come. Let me show you what an empress does with her days."

Constantine's court did not stay long at Treveris. As expected, very soon after his assumption of the purple, the twenty-one-year-old Maxentius, son of the retired emperor Maximian, convinced the Senate in Rome and the city's venerable Praetorian Guard to declare him the rightful Augustus of the West. Then, to protect himself against Severus, Maxentius invited his father out of retirement to lure the legions under Severus over to the side of the son and father in Rome. Next Maxentius, without his father's advice, persuaded the legions in Hispania, which had been under Constantius, to also switch sides, which left Constantine in control of just Britain and Gaul.

With the strategic situation thus greatly changed, Constantine moved his court south to Arelate on the river Rhodanus in the south of Gaul. The dowager empress Theodora and her six children moved with it, depositing her eldest son, twelve-year-old Dalmatius, along the way at the cadet school in Augustodunum. Constantine barely knew Theodora before becoming emperor, having been already in the service of Diocletian in the East when his father divorced his mother to marry the sixteen-year-old Theodora at Arelate in the West. For years he had privately resented the younger woman's displacement of his mother, but now as a widower and as a new emperor still needing to strengthen his claim upon the imperial dignity, he welcomed the widowed empress both for the dignity she added to his court and for her judicious management of the imperial household.

For her part, Theodora was relieved to find her step-son so much like her late husband as well as grateful for the favor he showed her and her children, but she was also mindful of her own inevitable displacement at court by a new empress who would bear the new emperor children of his own. She did not care to contemplate the candidates and discouraged the women at court from speculating on the matter, but her restraint in court matters showed that she saw herself as only interim mistress of the palace. The court's move south was enough to keep her busy for a while, in addition to the upbringing of her children and the education of Eugenia, whom Theodora adopted as one of her own.

Theodora's favor put Eugenia in good stead at court. All of the women wanted to be her friend, and she innocently welcomed them as friends, unaware of her own prestige. Some were also thinking of her as a possible mate for the young men at court, and once they were all comfortably settled into the spacious palace at Arelate, the introductions began—to Tertius, Deputy Marshal of the Palace and nephew of Livia, wife of Pertacus, commander of the Companions; to Gnaeus, a tribune of the Lancers and protégé of Ablabius; to Marcus, an assistant quaestor; and to another Marcus who was an aide to some general Eugenia could not remember.

Canio himself could not keep track of her acquaintances. He did not mean to neglect her, but his own duties were very demanding, and she could hardly have been in better hands, which is why he was surprised and embarrassed when the empress Theodora pulled him aside one day for a word in private.

"I am delighted to have her at court, and we are all blessed by her presence," she said, "but she is still very young, with a lot to learn about palace life. You are the closest to kin she has here. You can't be her father, but you must be to her at least an older brother. She needs a man to watch over her and to pay her a man's attention. If you don't, she may throw herself too easily at the first man who does."

That was all Marcus needed to hear. From then on, he made time for Eugenia whenever he could, dining with her privately or socially two or three times a week, taking an interest in her studies, and introducing her to men and women he trusted. He also consulted Lucius Caesonius, Constantine's Master of Offices, on the other men she was meeting. The only man to cause Marcus concern was his colleague Bassianus, Constantine's former aide, now commander of the Shieldmen. Eugenia seemed especially taken with the handsome and charming officer, which was understandable. Caesonius had nothing against him, except that several other ladies at court (some young, some old) also had their eye on the young bachelor. Marcus had nothing against Bassianus that he dared mention to Caesonius, but there was something about him that Marcus didn't like, and the thought of Bassianus and Eugenia together bothered him.

One day when Eugenia suggested Bassianus as a dinner guest, Marcus demurred.

"But I really like him," she protested.

"That's what I'm afraid of," said Marcus, without thinking.

Eugenia looked perplexed. "That I really like him, or that I really like *him?*" she asked.

Marcus didn't want to say anything against a colleague that might get around the palace, so he chose what he thought was the easier answer. "That you really like him," he said.

Eugenia was miffed. "So are you going to object to everyone I really like?" she said.

"No, of course, not," he replied.

"Then why not Bassianus?" she demanded.

"Well . . . I just don't want you throwing yourself at the first man who flatters you."

"I'm not throwing myself at anyone. Where did you get that idea?"

Marcus didn't know what to say.

"You're just jealous," said Eugenia. "You don't like me seeing other men."

"Jealous? Why would I be jealous? You and I are not betrothed."

"Then what concern is it of yours whom I see or like?"

"Eugenia, your father entrusted you to me. I'm your guardian, like it or not."

"And so you're going to lock me up for safe-keeping?"

"No! Honestly, I only want what's best for you."

"Then why can't I see Bassianus?"

"I didn't say you couldn't see him."

"But clearly you don't want me to."

At that point, Marcus gave up. "No, I don't want you to see him," he said. Then, as carefully as he could, he explained to her his concerns, both about Bassianus and about saying anything against a colleague at court. "I'm sorry if it seems I don't trust you to keep a confidence, Genia, but I'm trusting you now, and I really do only want what's best for you."

Eugenia was mollified, and even touched by his concern. She was even more touched by his last words on the subject. "It's true it's not all about Bassianus," he said shyly. "You're so beautiful and charming, part of me doesn't want to give you away."

Not long after arriving at Arelate, the empress invited a Christian over-seer to come for a stay at the palace. His name was Hosius, and he was overseer of Corduba in southern Hispania. The previous year, he had made a name for himself presiding over a regional council of overseers at Elvira. Comforted by Constantine's magnanimity and sensing his openness to examining the political relevance of the Christian religion, Theodora had obtained his approval to bring in Hosius for consultation. Scheduled discussions with the emperor were only part of the purpose of the visit. The other parts were to demonstrate to Constantine and his court what responsible Christians were really like and to signal to the Christian populace that the new emperor was open to hearing and perhaps addressing their concerns.

Hosius was provided a room to use as a chapel and allowed to conduct his usual services. Theodora was often in attendance, as was Eugenia and many other women at court. Few men came on their own, but several came with their wives from time to time, as work permitted. Marcus came more often than most men, but not as often as most women. He had already decided to become a Christian to marry Makrina, but he had not fully worked through his philosophical reservations and he was only then getting to know the Christian way of worship and the character of Christian fellowship. It helped that Hosius reminded him of the elderly Arcadius, who had nursed him to health after the murder of Alexander in the mountains. They were both Spaniards and spoke with the same quaint accent.

It also helped that he was seeing Christianity as it would be among those of his own rank and sophistication. Makrina had turned his head and made him look hard at the religion. Arcadius in the mountains and Briccus at Mogontiacum had shown him how men—thoughtful, educated, even manly men—could be Christian. But Marcus still tended to think of Christianity as a faith for the low-born and the provincial. The high-born Hosius and the empress Theodora altered his imagination, enabling him to imagine himself and even many of his friends in Rome, in the army, and at the palace as Christians.

The inevitable marriage was announced in February, much sooner than anyone anticipated: Constantine would marry Fausta, Theodora's eighteen-year-old step-sister by her mother, Eutropia, and her step-father, the formerly retired emperor Maximian. Maximian and Maxentius in Rome had offered Fausta to Constantine as part of an alliance against Galerius. Constantine had declined the alliance but did agree to not join Galerius in an alliance against Maximian and Maxentius. His marriage to Fausta sealed the deal.

Theodora was the first to be informed of the match, and indeed Constantine had consulted her on the possibility months earlier. She had not seen Fausta since her marriage to Constantius, when Fausta was just five, but who could be safer from Theodora's standpoint than her mother's daughter? Any apprehension she felt at the prospect was dispelled by

Constantine's sincerely expressed desire for her to stay on at the palace. She and her children were still his family, he said—her sons and daughters, still imperial princes and princesses. Fausta would need someone to school her in the duties of an empress. Besides, he said, he enjoyed her presence and valued her influence upon others.

Fausta's journey north from Rome to Arelate, with her father and mother, would take three weeks with the necessary stops along the way for the old emperor to grace the people of northern Italy with his presence and thereby build support for the new regime in Rome. The court at Arelate had barely a month to prepare for the imperial wedding. The first and most obvious preparation was the departure of Hosius. He had suffered imprisonment and torture under Maximian in the first year of the persecution, and both he and Theodora thought it best that he not be there when Maximian arrived. Other preparations were more pleasant, and the entire court was in a festive mood, the women especially.

Then, the day before Fausta's arrival, a letter arrived for Marcus from Aristoboulos in Sinope. He was in the habit of reviewing all correspondence first thing each morning, before the daily staff meeting with Gratianus, the praetorian prefect, but Titus, his secretary, brought him this letter as soon as it arrived, interrupting his brief noonday nap.

Marcus sat up on his cot to read the letter. A moment later he stood up suddenly and walked toward the window, still reading. He was a long while reading, and then a long while staring out the window after he had finished reading. Titus waited silently at the door. At last, Marcus turned and stared for a moment at the floor between them. "Send for Eugenia," he said without looking up.

Eugenia arrived a quarter of an hour later, meeting Marcus holding the letter in his antechamber. He didn't often send for her, which made her wonder. "What is it?" she asked

"It's a letter from your father," he said. "Kimon has been arrested and sentenced to the mines."

"Oh, no," said Eugenia, taking the letter from his hand.

"There's more, Eugenia. Makrina is dead."

Eugenia looked up at him in horror. "No," she said. "She can't be." Then she started reading. "My God! My God!" she sobbed as she read. "Oh, my God!"

When she finished reading, she threw her arms around Marcus and wept aloud, shaking with grief. "I'm sorry," he said, holding her tightly. "I'm so sorry."

"Makrina! Kimon! Oh, my God!" she cried. A moment later, she released him and said, "I must go home. My parents need me."

Marcus only looked at her and sighed.

"I must go home and look for Kimon," she said.

Reason began to reassert itself over feeling in Marcus. "Eugenia," he said. "It's still not safe, and there's very little you can do that your father is not already doing."

"I must go," she insisted. "Mamma needs me, and I want to go home, Marcus—right away."

Marcus shrugged sadly.

"I must tell the empress," said Eugenia before rushing off. "Maybe she can help."

Busy as she was, Theodora grieved with Eugenia for the better part of an hour, telling her to pray for her parents and Kimon and Makrina, and to pray also for God's guidance for a long while before deciding what to do. Afterward, she expressed her condolences to Marcus, telling him how much she admired his faithfulness to Makrina and advising him to stay close to Eugenia through the wedding week. She also informed Constantine of the news and with his permission arranged with Sergius Gratianus, Constantine's new praetorian prefect, to have others take over some of Marcus's duties for the time being.

At the same time, Theodora insisted that both Marcus and Eugenia participate in the wedding festivities, against their inclination to retreat entirely. Changes were made to have Marcus escort Eugenia to the major events, both to provide each other with compassionate company and to avoid burdening others with their grief.

Marcus was later grateful for Theodora's hand in things. At the magnificent wedding banquet, he found himself gazing often at Eugenia and noticing much about her for the first time. In her grief, the usually light-hearted Eugenia assumed a graver demeanor, which reminded Marcus of Makrina. Their accents were also similar. Eugenia said and did many little things the way he had seen Makrina say and do. Even her face testified to their close kinship: same ears, same mouth, similar eyes and eyebrows.

Eugenia caught him staring at her sadly more than once, and almost guessed what he was thinking. The second time, she squeezed his hand tightly and said, "Thank you, Marcus. Thank you for everything." He smiled and nodded.

When the wedding week of was over, Eugenia announced to him that she had decided to return home. "When?" was all he said.

"As soon as it can be arranged," she answered.

Marcus looked away without speaking, and expecting that he did not approve, Eugenia launched into her reasons for leaving. But to her surprise Marcus merely listened, then said, "Very well then."

The rest of that day as well as the next, as she prepared her departure,

Marcus seemed to avoid her, and when at last she found him on the third day, he was impatient with her and unhelpful. Surprised and hurt, she sought out Theodora. "Why is he suddenly so cold to me?" she asked.

"I think he's in love with you," the empress answered.

"In love with me?"

"Yes," said Theodora. "He's in love with you, but he hasn't yet admitted it to himself. He couldn't admit it before now because he thought he still loved Makrina. Now he can't admit it because he thinks he's losing you, and he's already begun preparing for another loss."

"That's it?" Eugenia wondered aloud.

"I'm almost sure of it. Remember, Eugenia, he has no other family. He has no brothers or sisters. His father and mother are dead, and now the woman he had pledged to marry is also dead. You are all he has left, and he dreads losing you."

"Then why doesn't he beg me to stay?"

Theodora shrugged. "Men don't like to beg," she said, "and besides, he can't beg you to stay without giving you a good reason to stay, and he doesn't have a good, compelling reason besides marriage."

"Then why doesn't he ask me to marry him?"

"Would you if he did?"

"Of course I would, now that Makrina . . . " Eugenia stopped and made the sign of the cross, then said, "I've always loved Marcus, ever since I was a little girl. I've even often dreamed of marrying him."

"I doubt that he knows that. He probably expects that you would refuse him and also think less of him for betraying Makrina by turning so suddenly from her to you."

"It *is* rather sudden," said Eugenia.

"Not really," said Theodora. "He hasn't known Makrina for a very long time. He has only remembered her, and remembering her has only gotten harder and harder for him. I expect he has to work at it. I'm sure there have been days if not weeks in which he hasn't thought of her at all. But he has thought of you often, and quite fondly from what I can see."

The empress leaned forward and took Eugenia's hand. "Listen to me, Eugenia," she said. "I understand your desire to return home, but you must consider the needs of others. Your parents have lost a daughter and may also have lost a son. You may be all *they* have left as well, and they need to know that you are safe. You will not be safe in the East as a Christian, and so running home now makes little sense. You should stay here, and if you ask me, you should marry Marcus. If you go, he will marry someone else very soon. He has waited a long time to marry, and now he's finally free to do so. If you leave him now, he will make himself forget you *and* your sister *and* your brother by marrying someone else as soon as possible."

"Do you really think so?" said Eugenia.

"The only other possible consequence of your leaving would be even worse. He could be so discouraged by losing you and your sister that it ruins him. I wouldn't expect that of Marcus, but then one never knows for sure."

"Lord have mercy," said Eugenia.

"Stay, child. It's the only thing that makes sense for anyone, and I know God will bless you for it."

Eugenia went to see Marcus immediately to tell him she had changed her mind, but Vitalis said he had gone for a ride alone and was not expected back that afternoon. She stopped by his quarters later, hoping to catch him before dinner, but no one had seen him yet. He wasn't at dinner either, or in his quarters after dinner.

Not knowing what else to do, Eugenia went back to her rooms to prepare for bed. It was already dark, so she lit a candle. Then she burned some incense before kneeling down before the wooden cross on the wall above her bedside table. On the table lay a small book of psalms Marcus had given her when they moved to Arelate. Behind the book, leaning against the wall, was the icon she had found in his apartment in Mogontiacum, which Makrina had given him four years earlier and which Eugenia herself had delivered to Marcus on the quay the day he left Sinope. She looked at the icon and then at the cross, then crossed herself and raised her arms to pray.

She started with her usual invocation: "O heavenly King, the Comforter, the Spirit of Truth, . . . let my prayer arise in Thy sight as incense, and let the lifting up of my hands be an evening sacrifice. . . ." But soon her mind jumped ahead to the pleas of her heart—for her mother and father, for Kimon, for Makrina, that the Lord would give her rest and have mercy on her soul, and then for Marcus, that he return safely, that he be comforted by his knowledge of Christ and by her own continued presence, and that he find happiness with her as his wife. "O Lord, please," she said aloud, "I promise to always love him and serve him as long as I live, if that be your will. Only show me. Show Marcus. And have mercy on us both."

A sudden noise cut her short, the sound of many men cheering somewhere outside. Curious, Eugenia wrapped herself in her palla and left her rooms. "What's going on?" she asked one of the serving women in the corridor.

"Night sports," said the woman, shaking her head.

Eugenia found her way outside, onto the stone porch overlooking the parade ground. The field was lit from one end to the other by torches, and a line of men were gathered along the edge. Beyond them, Eugenia heard the hoof-beats of a single horse galloping over firm ground. Then suddenly the men cheered as the horse seemed to pass in front of them.

Intrigued, she left the porch and hurried over to the line of men, all of them officers. They didn't notice her at first, in the dark and with their attention on the field, but her feminine scent betrayed her. "Here, my lady," said a centurion, welcoming her forward for a better view. "There he is. Can you see him?" he said, pointing off across the field. Eugenia peered into the darkness and saw a man on horseback circling the field.

"I see him," she said excitedly.

"Now watch and see if he makes it."

The rider came around at a canter, then kicked his horse into a gallop at the end of the field. In the middle of the field was a blazing torch planted in the earth. The rider bore down upon the torch at full tilt while lowering himself from the saddle in an attempt to snatch the torch off the ground. The first time he failed, and the men groaned with disappointment.

"Who is that? Brocchus?" asked one of the officers. "He can do better than that."

"Give him another chance," said another.

"Here he comes again."

Again the rider loped around through the darkness to the end of the field, and again he kicked his horse to a gallop, hanging dangerously from the saddle, inches above the lethal pounding of his horse's hooves. But this time his hand found its hold, and he snatched up the torch and raised it high above his head as he passed. The men cheered, and so did Eugenia. "*Io, Brocche!*" she shouted in Latin, clapping her hands and jumping up and down. The men around her laughed at her girlish display of enthusiasm.

A moment later, Marcus came up behind her. "What are you doing here?" he asked.

"Looking for you," she said. "I've been looking for you all day, to tell you I've decided to stay. That is, if you want me to. Do you want me to, Marcus?"

Marcus's lips turned slowly upward into a smile and then a grin. "Yes," he said. "I want you to stay. I want you to very much."

Eugenia's face lit up, and she threw her arms around his neck and kissed him passionately.

"What's this?" said an officer nearby.

"*Io, Canio,*" said another.

The men about the kissing couple laughed again and repeated the cheer together: "*Io, Canio!*"

# XXVIII

A month after the imperial wedding, the overseer Hosius returned to Arelate, not to the palace itself, but to a villa nearby, provided by Theodora. There he resumed his ministry to the Christians and seekers at court, while his former persecutor, the old emperor Maximian, was still in residence at the palace. There also Marcus took his first step toward admission to the Assembly.

"You know, Lord Canio," said Hosius, "the fellowship you seek to enter is no ordinary association of persons. It is not a banquet club or secret lodge of supposedly enlightened initiates such as one finds among the Greeks. It is a community of souls united in a most profound way, committed to living as one body, bearing each other's burdens, enduring each other's faults, confessing our sins one to another in all humility, whatever one's rank or station. Are you quite sure this is what you want?"

"I am," answered Marcus.

"The Assembly has its own order and structure, with overseers and elders exercising authority over their flocks as fathers over their families. To be brought under instruction into the order of catechumens, in preparation for full admission to the Assembly, you must be willing to submit yourself to the discipline of the Assembly and its ordained ministers. Are you prepared to do so?"

"I am," answered Marcus.

"Very well then," said Hosius. "We may proceed with our prayers."

The overseer and his tiny flock of distinguished persons began their prayers with a series of petitions with the accustomed refrains. To the left stood the women, the empress herself, her daughters, several others, and Eugenia. To the right stood Marcus himself, his secretary Titus, and Theodora's youngest son, Hannibalianus, who insisted on standing with the men. According to Christian custom, the women all covered their heads with the pallas, but the men were all bare-headed, a departure from the Roman practice of men also covering their heads when they prayed.

At one point, Hosius turned to Marcus and called on him to publicly renounce Satan in all his works and all his pomp.

"I renounce Satan in all his works and all his pomp," Marcus declared.

"Have you renounced Satan?" asked Hosius.

"I have renounced Satan," Marcus answered.

Hosius turned again to the east and prayed for the Father to send down the Holy Spirit upon the catechumen Marcus, that he may receive the light of wisdom and be accounted worthy of the mysteries of Christ.

Eugenia beamed with joy at Marcus, who kept his eyes fixed obediently on Hosius. Marcus was deadly serious and did not wish to distract the attention of the others by glancing back at Eugenia. They were already betrothed, with the wedding scheduled for September, four months from then. His induction as a catechumen was a necessary prerequisite, as it cleared away all impediments to their marriage, since Eugenia herself was still a catechumen, having been prevented from baptism by the persecution at home. Marcus accepted the requirement without reservation. Indeed, it had been a part of his decision all along, since that first kiss on the parade ground.

The Empress Theodora planned the wedding, decided on the guests, sent the invitations, and paid most of the bills. She also watched over the young, nervous bride in the final days, before Eugenia's mother arrived, barely a week before the wedding. Eugenia's father was still in Asia working for Kimon's release and could not come.

The reunion of mother and daughter was sad and joyous at the same time, for more reasons than Eugenia's impending marriage. "Who could have known?" wondered the tearful Hilaria shortly after seeing Marcus again for the first time in years. "Who could have known things would end up this way? You and Eugenia married, and Makrina and Kimon . . ."

Marcus did not know what to say or how to comfort either woman. He left them with each other most of the time. In fact, he had no choice. He was already busy with the planning of another campaign up north against the pestilent Franks, which he knew would cut short his time with Eugenia after the wedding.

The ceremony planned by Theodora omitted the Roman reading of entrails as an augury of the couples' fortune. It was instead a bloodless affair, baptized by Christian prayers, though otherwise thoroughly, consciously Roman.

Eugenia rose earlier than usual on her wedding day and spent the first hour alone in prayer. She had never been as diligent as Makrina about such things, but under Theodora's influence she was trying harder. The occasion, of course, provided its own reasons.

After sun-up, she went to greet her mother. They sat together on a sofa in her mother's chambers, talking quietly between themselves while shooing away officious servants intent upon their chores.

"I've missed you dearly these last few years," said Hilaria. "I wanted so much to be with you, to teach you all that you need to know to take your place as wife and lady. There are so many things I wish we had time for. Is there anything I need to tell you before tonight? Anything you can't already imagine?"

Eugenia blushed. "Will it hurt?" she asked.

"A little at first," said her mother. "But less so later, and in time the plea-sure will increase. But let tonight's pain be a reminder to you, that marriage is never without pain. Men are different, you know. They have different needs, different desires. You can't expect him to want what you want, or even to know what you want. You'll want to talk when talking's the last thing on his mind. You'll annoy him, and he'll annoy you. You'll do things to please him and he won't notice. He'll want to please you, but odds are he won't know how. You'll have to teach him."

"But Marcus knows me well already, and I know he loves me," said Eugenia.

"Marcus is a thoughtful and gentle man," said Hilaria, with a motherly nod of the head, "but he is a man nevertheless, and it's a foolish woman who expects her man to think as she does. Out of such foolishness come fights, when you decide that you've been wronged and all you want to do is hurt him to get even, to make him feel your pain. But he will never really feel your pain, Eugenia. He can only feel his own, and men are pained in different ways. There are things you must never say to him, Eugenia. You must never belittle him, especially in front of others. You must never speak of divorce. Above all, Eugenia, you must never, ever disparage his manhood. Strong as he is, you can destroy him by doing so, and destroy his love for you as well."

"But I could never hurt Marcus that way," said Eugenia.

Hilaria laughed. "I hope you are right, but anger sometimes over-whelms us," she said. "Just remember, there must be limits even to your fighting. If you feel hurt, it's far more effective with men to show him your hurt with your tears, than to try to show him how it feels by hurting him. Tears can work wonders, Eugenia, even when they are not real. Believe me. He won't know the difference."

Afterwards, Hilaria and Eugenia went to pay their respects to Theodora and the new empress Fausta, Constantine's wife. Then it was off to the baths, where Eugenia received the added attention of Theodora's attendants, who massaged and perfumed her body and dressed her long dark hair, oiling it and combing it and then arranging it in the latest style, a high pile with added pads of someone else's hair of like color, imported from India, tied together with white ribbons to form a conical tower three hands high.

Back in her chambers, Eugenia donned the traditional white tunic woven in the ancient way, all of one piece. She tied a rope of silk around her waist, securing it with a square "knot of Hercules," symbolizing the strength of her chastity. Around her neck she wore a golden collar, a gift from Theodora, and on the ring finger of her right hand, the gold engagement ring Marcus gave her at their betrothal. Her slippers and the palla draped over her tunic were saffron. Over everything, she wore a sheer veil of flaming orange that covered her eyes and nose and fell to the ground behind her. The veil was held in place by a wreath of myrtle and orange blossom around her head.

Marcus rose early that day, too. First he went alone on a ride through the countryside on horseback. Then he returned to the palace to go hawking with Ablabius, commander of the Lancers.

"This is a fine sport for a wedding day," said Ablabius. "Care to wager the male against the female? Your tiercel hawk against my little falcon-gentle?"

"A hundred 'd' on my tiercel," answered Marcus.

"I'll take it," said Ablabius.

Not far away a partridge alighted from its perch in a mulberry tree and winged its way unsuspectingly across the field. "That's you tonight," said Ablabius, nodding toward the partridge before siccing his falcon-gentle on it. The falcon raced after the partridge, but the latter found sudden shelter in a juniper bush.

"I shall not be so shy," said Marcus. "This is me tonight." He sent his tiercel off after a covey of quail rising in the distance. The hawk climbed speedily above the flock, then fell upon its prey savagely and successfully, feathers fluttering to the ground.

"Well," said Ablabius, "I hope you leave more of your prey than your hawk has."

"She'll survive," said Marcus, "even if not entirely intact." Ablabius laughed loudly.

Back at the palace, Marcus worked off his nervous energy playing handball before taking an early bath and submitting to a massage. Then he put on his bright white dress tunic with golden medallions embroidered on the shoulders, back and chest. The matching trousers sported medallions on the thighs. Around his waist he wore his belt of office, a deep-blue silk sash trimmed with gold. White leather boots protected his feet, with red leather bindings that reached nearly to his knees. His cloak was crimson and was held in place by a large bejeweled brooch.

The wedding party arrived first at the large reception room Theodora had chosen. It had an apse toward the east and a high ceiling lined with small windows of multi-colored glass. The walls were hung with white and green bunting, the colors of purity and fruitfulness.

The guests began arriving about the ninth hour, according to the palace's water-clock. They milled about the room, greeting the bride and groom and one another in hushed tones, waiting patiently for the guests of honor.

A page boy entered, ringing a little bell and announcing, "Half past nine. Half past nine." A moment later, a herald stepped into the doorway and declared in a loud voice, "Lords and Ladies, the Empress Theodora." The crowd parted as Theodora entered the room in her imperial robes, trimmed in silver, two attendants carrying her train. She moved to the apse end with stately grace, nodding with reserve to the guests, who bowed their heads. She paused briefly to greet Marcus and Eugenia.

Once in place, Theodora nodded to Hosius, who stepped to the fore, bowed to the empress, then bowed to the guests and said, "Peace be unto all."

"And with thy spirit," answered Titus, in his role as reader and chanter.

"Let us pray to the Lord," said Hosius.

"Lord have mercy," said Titus.

Hosius prayed and when he was finished, Titus added the amen and sang a hymn. Then he chanted a reading from the Apostle Paul's epistle to the Ephesians about the duties of husbands and wives. Next, Hosius himself chanted a passage from the Gospel according to the Apostle John, telling of the wedding feast at Cana, where Jesus turned water into wine. Afterward, he spoke briefly of the mystery of marriage and how the institution had been blessed by Christ's attendance at Cana and the miracle he performed there.

"Therefore," he said, "those who deny marriage to the young sin against God in despising what God himself has called good. For marriage was given unto man as a great mercy, that the man and the woman would find some comfort in their fallen states, and learn humility and love through their physical and spiritual union."

When he had finished, he stepped aside. Marcus and Eugenia turned to face each other, and in the center of the room, surrounded by their guests, the bride declared the traditional Roman marriage vow: "Where you are Gaius, I am Gaia."

Marcus lifted the orange veil from Eugenia's face, and they kissed. The guests all shouted, "*Feliciter! Feliciter!*" Happily! Happily!

The party adjourned to the banquet hall, where they enjoyed a modest meal, in keeping with Theodora's Christian sensibilities. There was plenty to eat and drink, but no salacious songs or jests, common at other weddings. There was one such jest, actually, by Ablabius, but Theodora made plain her disapproval, and no one dared to offend her afterward.

The highlight of the banquet was an appearance by the emperor Constantine, who offered his congratulations to the bride and groom and allowed them to kiss the hem of his purple mantle. The guests all stood at his entrance and waited until he had departed to resume their feast. He did not stay long. His wife, the empress Fausta, did not accompany him, as she was in her fifth month with child and would not appear in public.

A while later, Marcus's patron and former commander, Sergius Gratianus, the praetorian prefect, came over to offer his own congratulations.

"What was that I heard in the service about wives submitting themselves to their husbands?" he said with a grin. "Maybe there's something of value in this religion of yours after all."

Marcus laughed. "It has its attractions," he replied.

The feast lasted until dusk, when coaches appeared to carry the wedding party to a villa in the country, which the emperor had offered to Marcus for the occasion. The first coach carried the traditional flute players and torchbearers. The second bore the bride and groom. Three coaches after that carried all those who wished to go along.

Eugenia thanked Theodora profusely and parted tearfully with her mother. Marcus endured parting shots from his fellow officers, out of range of the empress. Once on their way and away from the palace, the accompanying guests joined in singing the very songs Theodora had prohibited.

At the villa, three young pages scattered walnuts on the pavement. There were no children around to pick them up, but their rattle was a familiar part of the event. The nuts symbolized the groom's childhood playthings, cast aside upon the arrival of his bride. The pages then led Eugenia inside, one holding a torch of tightly twisted hawthorn twigs, the other two leading her by the hand.

The threshold of the house was spread with a white cloth. Evergreen bows dressed the doorway. Marcus had gone ahead, and when Eugenia reached the door, he lifted her into his arms and carried across the threshold, reenacting the ancient abduction of the Sabine women by his Roman forebears. The guests, who had remained in their coaches, shouted their farewells and sweet-dreams, which went unanswered.

Three bridesmaids followed the couple inside. Theodora's daughter Anastasia carried the distaff; her older sister Constantia, the spindle, emblems of the bride's domestic duties. Olympia, the wife of Ablabius, carried a pitcher of water. Once inside, Olympia passed the pitcher to Marcus, who then handed it to Eugenia, who handed it off to a page. Then Marcus took the hawthorn torch and handed it to Eugenia, who passed it back to the page who had carried it in. The ritual showed the groom entrusting his bride with his hearth and home.

Constantia and Anastasia then shooed the page boys outside, while Olympia led Eugenia to the nuptial bed, then set about lighting the lamps and scented candles in the room. "Dreams of gold," she said in parting. Marcus waited in the atrium until Olympia returned. "Be gentle," she said with a grin as she breezed by him on her way out.

Marcus found Eugenia right where Olympia had left her. He paused and looked down on her for a moment before approaching the bed. She looked up at him smiling and then burst into laughter. Marcus laughed, too.

Marcus couldn't keep his eyes open afterward. He was spent completely and needed time to recover. A blessed rest overtook him, a contentment he had never known before—satisfaction without guilt, pleasure without remorse, love without loneliness. Always before, the act had torn him apart inside. Body and soul had warred against each other, straining toward opposite ends, the one panting after strange flesh, the other censuring his weakness and bemoaning his defeat. This time, for the first time, both soul and body had moved in harmony to merge his being with that of another. Two bodies became one flesh, their spirits united in faith and love, in joy and thankfulness. It was not good that the man should be alone, so God created the woman, and in their sacred union Marcus found a moment's peace from all his struggles, physical and spiritual.

But Eugenia wanted to talk.

"It was a beautiful day, wasn't it?" she said, lying his arms. "Everything was perfect, the ceremony, the rooms, the food. The food! Oh, wasn't it delicious? I should have eaten more. I hardly had a bite. Everyone behaved themselves, too, despite the best wine in the world. Such a perfect day. I don't want it to end. Talk to me, Marcus."

"You talk, I'll listen," he mumbled without opening his eyes.

"I'm so glad Mamma was there to see it. It would have been such a shame if she hadn't. Isn't it amazing how Olympia has changed? I used to think she was such a witch. Was I wrong?"

Marcus didn't answer.

"Oh, Marcus, don't fall asleep. When you do, the day is over, and I don't want it to be over."

He didn't move. Eugenia looked at him hopefully, but saw that it was no use. She looked around the room and noticed two new trunks against the wall. Wrapping herself in her palla, she climbed out of bed and went to inspect the trunks. In the first lay a note from her mother, on top of a stack of folded clothes. In the second were more clothes and a note from Theodora, with best wishes and prayers.

"Oh, Marcus, look at this," she said aloud. He didn't answer. She rummaged through the trunk from Theodora, pulling an item at a time out to examine it, sometimes holding them up against her naked body to see how they would look on her. "Beautiful," she said to herself, spreading a silken shawl across her curves to admire it.

She looked over at Marcus, still asleep. He looked so handsome and peaceful lying there with just the counterpane to cover him. She dropped the shawl and returned to the bed. Slipping under the counterpane, she snuggled up against him once more and soon joined him in blissful slumber.

✠　✠　✠

It was snowing the next morning, in another part of the world—ankle-deep by dawn in the city. A beggar huddled against a wall under a low-hanging eave for warmth and shelter. A tattered mantle covered the bowed head, the shivering shoulders, even the outstretched hand. The mantle failed to cover only the feet, which were wrapped in rags.

Two men came by. "Come on, let's go for drink," said one.

"Not me, I'm headed home to bed," said the other.

"Oh, come on, celebrate with me. I'm not often so lucky, or so generous. Did you see the face on old Gabinus when he rolled out those snake-eyes? Hah! Worth all my winnings just to see the old bastard lose. Sure you won't come with me?"

"I've had enough already."

"Look, I'm offering to let you drink my money away. If you don't drink it, I might as well give it to this beggar here."

The man held out a small purse, too high for the beggar to grasp.

"Give him a little anyway. Who knows? Maybe it's Hermes or Zeus under there."

"You know you're right. They do that kind of thing, don't they? Masquerade as beggars to see who'll have pity on a poor soul. Can't say I've ever seen them."

"You've never had the pity."

"Quite right, never have. Of course, tonight's been something special. The gods have favored me, and to show my gratitude, maybe I should favor this poor beggar, be his god for a day."

"Go ahead. I'm watching."

"Unless, of course, you'd care for a drink."

"Nope."

"Oh, well, it's only my change purse. Here." He dropped the purse into the beggar's hand.

"Thank you, sir!" said the beggar.

The man look down with surprise. "What?" he said. "That's no beggar's voice. Who's under there?" He bent over and tried to lift the beggar's hood, but the beggar cowered out of reach. "Come on," said the man.

"Please let me be," said the beggar.

"I only want to see your face," he said.

On his second attempt, the man took hold of the hood and stripped it off the beggar's head. She froze in fear, staring up at him. Her long dark hair was tangled and matted. The creases in her face were lined with dirt. Green mucus trailed from her nostrils. Even so, her natural beauty shone through—the round cheeks, the full lips, the little red nose, the wide, frightened, olive eyes.

"Who are you?" he asked.

The young woman didn't move or answer.

"What's your name?"

Still no answer.

"Come on, I know you're not dumb!"

"Let her be," said his companion.

"Let her be? A face like this could do a lot more than beg. Make a lot more money, too!"

"Please leave me alone," pleaded the woman. "I'll give you back your money. Just leave me alone."

"Ah, forget the money. Keep it. Just tell us who you are and what you're doing?"

The woman shook her head and began to edge away.

"Where are you from? How did you end up like this?"

"She's frightened, Aulus. Let her go."

"Are you whole? Can you walk? Let me have a look at you," said Aulus, reaching down again to take hold of her mantle.

She shook him off and scrambled to her feet and starting running.

"There's you answer," his companion laughed.

"Wait!" Aulus cried after her. "I only want a look! We could help! We could help!"

She didn't stop and soon disappeared into the falling snow.

# XXIX

The first thing they did to Kimon after taking him into custody was cauterize the Achilles tendon of his right foot, just enough to making running away, or even walking away, temporarily impossible. Then they carted him off south to Cilica in a cage with half a dozen other convicts. The route took them first through Amasia on the Iris River, then on to Cappadocian Caesarea, across the Anatolian plateau, and through the gap in the Taurus Mountains called the Cilician Gates, just north of Tarsus.

Turning off the main road, they journeyed for another 20 or 30 miles into a narrow valley choked with the fumes of a iron smelter. Past the smelter they came upon a large camp of crude log houses, surrounded by a palisade. The cart halted at the palisade's open gate, and a guard ordered every man out. "Come on, come on, unless you're dead already," he said in Latin, beating impatiently on the sides of the cart with a rod of hard wood.

Kimon rose stiff and weak and climbed uneasily over the side of the cart, then hobbled over to join the others.

"That means you," said the guard, poking the last man in the back over the side of the cart. The man appeared to move but only tumbled over, eyes open. "What this?" said the guard. He poked the man a few more times, without result, then said, "By Jove, he is dead already. Take him down to the furnace. If he isn't alive by then, throw him in."

The cart wheeled about and headed back down the road to the smelter. The guard turned back to the prisoners, sitting by the side of the road. "Anyone know his name?" he asked. No one answered. "No matter," he said, turning away again.

"Please, sir, may we have some water?" asked a thin young man with blond hair and rotten teeth.

"No water. Not now," replied the guard with barely a glance at the inquirer. Then, as if the thought had just occurred to him, he walked to the opposite side of the gate where a water barrel sat in the shade of the wall and ladled himself a drink.

Kimon looked out over the surrounding hills lying dry and hot in the afternoon sun. There was not a tree in sight for miles. It seemed that every last one had gone to build the camp or feed the furnace at the smelter. The latter more likely, thought Kimon.

It wasn't long before another guard showed up to take charge of the new arrivals. They were herded through the gate in single file and taken first to the camp barber, who sat each man down, one by one, on a stool in the open yard. There they received the convict's tonsure, losing the hair from their heads in a rough and artless cut.

Next came the dispensary, where they were stripped and examined in cursory fashion by the camp physician, who sent them back out with their clothes on, where an orderly recorded their names, hometowns, and occupations. He was less than impressed when Kimon volunteered that he could read and write excellent Greek and Latin.

"Not needed," said the orderly. "The edicts against the Christians have given us plenty of men who can read and write. Now, if you were a smith or a tanner, we could use you. Otherwise, it's to the mines."

Afterward, they were loaded onto an ox cart, which carried them off through the quiet camp, out the back way, then up and around the side of a barren hill. The view on the other side was astounding. Below them lay a vast pit, a mile or more from rim to rim. Its dusty sides were terraced, and all about at various levels there were men working, slowly like dying ants, digging at the earth with picks, pounding the exposed rock with sledgehammers, and loading chunks of iron ore into ox carts. Every so often there was a crack of a whip and a voice raised in anger. Otherwise, the scene was eerily quiet, despite the incessant impact of hammer and pick.

The cart wound down around the sides of the pit, stopping here and there to discharge its passengers. "You. Off," a guard shouted at Kimon.

Kimon climbed down as quickly as he could and was handed a heavy sledgehammer. "Get to work," said the guard, pointing to an outcropping of ore where a man with a hammer was already at work, while a second man loaded a nearby cart.

Kimon hobbled over and started pounding away. It was mid-afternoon, and the air in the pit was still and hot. In no time at all, he had worked up a fierce sweat. His clothes were already hopelessly soiled from his journey. There was no point in sparing them, but the warmth of his woolen dalmatic soon became unbearable, so he took it off, laid it aside, and continued working in his cotton undertunic.

"Hurry it up, man. You're falling behind."

Kimon picked up the pace of his pounding.

"Faster, Fortunatus. You're not dead yet."

Kimon glanced over his shoulder and saw that the guard had been speaking to the man loading ore.

"Come on, come on," said the guard, snapping his flail at the unfortunate Fortunatus. "Pick it up."

The man folded to escape the flail, then collapsed on the ground. "Get up," ordered the guard, kicking him with his boot. "Get up, I said!"

The man cringed where he lay, as the guard struck him again and again with his flail.

Kimon had stopped pounding and stepped forward, about to intervene.

"Don't or you'll be dead before he is," said the other man, still hammering away.

He was a young man with a dark bushy beard, wearing a short workman's tunic, which left his right shoulder bare. His head was covered with a rag tied in back. His exposed skin was deeply tanned by the sun, and he wielded his hammer with power and purpose. "Name's Drusus," he said between strokes.

Kimon turned back to his work. "Kimon," he said, letting his hammer fall with a whack. The guard gave up on Fortunatus and moved off.

"Where from?" asked Drusus. Whack!

"Sinope," answered Kimon. "And you?" Whack!

"Emesa, in Syria." Whack!

"Long way from home." Whack!

"Aren't we all." Whack!

"How long here?" Whack!

"Sixteen months." Whack!

"What about him?" Whack!

"Six years, maybe seven." Whack! "I don't think he remembers anymore." Whack! "Not that it matters." Whack! "He'll be gone before long."

"What do you mean?" Whack!

"Look at him. He's half dead now." Whack! "I'd wager a week." Whack!

"How can you tell?" Whack!

"You can tell." Whack! "A man stops laughing." Whack! "He stops smiling." Whack! "He stops talking." Whack! ! "He stops working." Whack! "Before long he stops eating." Whack! "Then one day he stops breathing." Whack!

"You've seen it before?" Whack!

"Many times." Whack! "They just give up and decide to die." Whack! "The worst part is"—Whack!—"they make it look easy." Whack!

"How long does it take?" Whack!

"Depends." Whack! "Sometimes months, sometimes years." Whack! "They say you're here for 15 years." Whack! "Most don't make it past ten." Whack!

"Does anyone survive?" Whack!

"Yes." Whack!

"Who?" Whack!

"The ones who escape." Whack!

"Save your breath," ordered the guard. "Just work."

They worked another hour before a bell signaled the end of the day. The prisoners loaded their tools onto carts, took turns at the water barrels, then started the long, silent procession up out of the mine and all the way back to camp. Their beards were grown long and wild, though the hair on their heads was uniformly short. Some wore headbands, while others tied rags over their bare pates. Most wore the remnants of the clothes they arrived in, but many were left with nothing but a ragged loincloth. None but the new arrivals bothered with sandals, their feet having grown thick and broad over time.

Once back in camp, the men moved obediently into a line for their supper, in the open square at the center of the camp. Kimon craned his neck to see where the line led. At first he could see only guards, visible by their spears, but as the line moved forward he saw a cart full of bread loaves and several stacks of wooden bowls.

The closer they moved, the more the men relaxed, speaking, waving, smiling wearily to one another. Guards kept the line moving in an orderly fashion. One by one the prisoners grabbed a bowl from the stacks on the ground and shook them upside down to empty them of dirt. An attendant filled each bowl with a thin, green soup. It wasn't much to look at, but it smelled at least edible. A second attendant dropped a large chunk of bread into each bowl before the men limped off on their own.

Kimon followed Drusus to the high ground at the edge of the square, where they settled on the hard, bare earth outside a cabin. Other men joined them, last of all Fortunatus. They ate first, sopping up the soup with the bread until both were consumed. Then they licked the bowls with greatest care, more thoroughly than dogs would lick a plate.

"This is Kimon," said Drusus to the others. Then he pointed each out: "Ursulus, Eusebios, Thomas, Heraclios, Antonius, Fortunatus."

Each man waved or nodded in his turn, except Fortunatus, who did not respond.

"Ursulus is here for extortion, Eusebios for swindling, Thomas is a Christian, Heraclios is a thief."

"I was framed," said Heraclios.

"You were caught," said Drusus. "Antonius—what are you here for, Antonius?"

"Destruction of public property, but I was framed, too."

"Sure you were," said Drusus. "Fortunatus is here for embezzling. Isn't that right, Fortunatus?"

Fortunatus groaned but did not deny it.

"Drusus is here for inciting a riot," said Ursulus.

"That's right, and I was not framed," said Drusus.

"What about you?" asked Ursulus.

Kimon looked around at the other men. "It's a long story," he said.

"It always is," said Ursulus.

Kimon hesitated, then said, "I denounced the governor of Cappadocia in public."

"What for?" asked Ursulus.

"For sentencing a woman to death unjustly."

"What did she do?"

"She refused to sacrifice."

"Oh, so you're a Christian?"

"No, I'm not," said Kimon.

"Was she some relative of yours?"

"No. I never met her."

"What? You never met her, you're not a Christian—what business was it of yours?"

"The sentence was a crime. I felt compelled to say so."

"Hah! You felt compelled to say so," said Ursulus, shaking his head.

"Every sentence is a crime," said Drusus. "Every judge is just as guilty as the men they convict."

"But only a fool would tell them so to their faces, in public no less," said Ursulus.

"Leave off him, Ursulus. He only did what we all wanted to," said Heraclios.

"Foolishness," said Ursulus before getting up and limping off.

"Let me see your hands," said Drusus.

Kimon held them out. His palms were already red and tender.

"Better wrap them tomorrow or you'll lose all the skin," said Drusus. "The first week is always the worst, especially if you're not use to labor. What did you do before this?"

"Not much of anything," said Kimon. "I worked for a while in the civil service, but that's all."

"Educated?"

"Yes."

"Well off?"

"Yes."

"Family?"

"Father and mother and sister. No wife or children."

"That's good," said Drusus. "The worst off here are the men with wives and children. They have lost too much, and it drives them mad. Fortunatus had a family. Isn't that right, Fortunatus?"

Fortunatus did not reply.

The first week was the hardest, the first full day especially. They were awakened by the clanging of metal upon metal an hour before sunrise. To the goading of guards, the prisoners stumbled down to a man-made stream that ran through the camp. The lower end was used as a latrine. The upper end was for drinking. In between was a stretch for washing. The prisoners made their way in the dark from one end to the other, then climbed aboard ox carts in the camp square.

They worked from dawn until about the tenth hour, with only occasional breaks for water and a half-hour rest at noon. They returned to camp again by foot in the early evening, after ten hours of hard labor. Kimon was exhausted and sore. His hands blistered and peeled. His neck, arms, and legs were sunburned. After supper, he could do no more than lie immobile on his pallet inside the cabin. He was too tired to even talk.

As bad as he felt at the end of the day, his darkest hours were before sunup, when the dread of another day of hardship made him feel the most like dying. Even after his body toughened to the debilitating routine, that first dark hour before sunup remained a time of near despair. He wasn't alone in suffering so. He noticed it in the others also. Men cheerful the night before walked about before dawn like souls condemned to Hades, tortured shadows of men without hope. The sun seemed their savior. Their spirits rose with it, and faded with it as well.

One morning, Fortunatus did not get up. The others pleaded with him, but he refused. "Go without me," he said, without lifting his head from his pallet.

"Can he do that? Can he refuse to work?" Kimon asked Drusus on their way to the latrine.

"Sure he can," said Drusus. "He just can't eat the days he doesn't work."

He was still where they had left him when they returned again that evening. Thomas saved him a piece of bread, but he wouldn't eat it. The others tried to talk with him, but he wouldn't speak and turned his face to the wall.

"Maybe he's just sick," Kimon suggested.

Drusus shook his head. "He's not sick. He just doesn't care anymore," he said.

The next morning, Fortunatus again did not get up. "Are you awake?" asked Thomas. "Can you hear me?"

Fortunatus lifted a hand in acknowledgment.

"You've got to get up," said Thomas. "You can't go without food. You've got to keep working."

"No," said Fortunatus, weakly. "No."

"You can't give up, Fortunatus. You've got to keep trying."

"Leave him be and let him die," said Ursulus. "He's suffered long enough. What's he got to live for, anyway?"

Thomas didn't answer.

"He's right," said Drusus. "Let him be."

They let him be, and that evening when they returned he was indeed dead. Drusus and Thomas hauled his body out into the street. "This is as far as I'm going," said Drusus.

"But how will I get him to the cemetery?" said Thomas.

"That's your problem," said Drusus. "Stay with him here and the guards will bring a cart to take him away for burning. Anything else is a waste of strength."

"I'll help," said Kimon.

Drusus looked askance at him. "Suit yourself," he said.

Kimon and Thomas dragged the dead man down toward the latrine, where there was a plot of land set aside for burials. "Sometimes the family comes to claim the body," said Thomas. "But Fortunatus's family gave up on him long ago."

Guards lent them shovels. Kimon took the first turn digging the grave, while Thomas rested. "How many men have you buried?" Kimon asked.

Thomas thought for a moment. "This makes seven, I think."

"Many Christians?"

"Only one. The first one. My brother Timotheos. He fell asleep in the Lord the first winter we were here. God rest his soul." Thomas made the sign of the cross.

"Your Christian brother?"

"My natural brother, too," said Thomas. "We were sent here together for refusing to sacrifice."

Kimon paused a moment and looked at Thomas, then continued digging.

"So why did you speak out against the governor?" Thomas asked.

"The sentence was unjust," answered Kimon.

"Yes, but why did you speak out, if you didn't know her and aren't a Christian?"

"You sound like Ursulus," said Kimon.

"I don't mean to," said Thomas. "But you see my brother ended up here because he spoke out at my trial, and I have always wondered why he did so. He wasn't on trial himself and could have escaped. Instead, he stepped forward and announced that he, too, was a Christian and would not sacrifice."

"Was that wrong?"

"I don't know in his case," said Thomas. "He had not been called to bear witness, yet he sought it anyway, against the instructions of the Assembly. We are told not to volunteer. The truth is I was angry with him for doing so. I didn't want him to suffer and die, and for a long time, I blamed him for having some selfish motive for his act, his own anger and impatience at what was happening to me or his disappointment that he wasn't the one called."

"Someone needs to stand up and speak out against injustice."

"Yes, but it's rare that men speak out when given the opportunity, and more common that some men seek the opportunity to speak out. Why do they do so? Is it righteousness in the face of evil, or anger that things are not as we would want them?"

"Now you really do sound like Ursulus," said Kimon.

"Sorry," said Thomas. "I can't judge you or my brother. I know in my own life there are many times I don't know what the right thing to do is, and all I can do is the best I can and beg the Lord's mercy."

Kimon stopped digging and wiped his face on the shoulder of his tunic. He was out of breath and panting heavily.

"My sister was a Christian," he said. "She was killed by soldiers in the mountains. . . . I had just found her bones before seeing the woman condemned to die, and I was angry. . . . Was I a fool to speak out? Yes. . . . Should someone have spoken out? Yes. . . . I was wrong, but I spoke the truth. As you Christians say, Lord have mercy."

Days later, Drusus pulled Kimon aside after supper. "Do you want to get out of here?" he asked Kimon in private.

"Of course," said Kimon.

"I know a way out," said Drusus. "Do you want to come with me?"

"An escape? I don't know."

"We are not alone," said Drusus, putting his arms around Kimon's shoulder. "There are others involved—on the outside. We'll go out the back way, through the mine itself. There'll be horses waiting for us not far away, and a guide to a place where we can hide and rest."

"But how will you get past the guards in camp?"

"That's the easy part," said Drusus. "There's a section of the wall behind the stables that's hidden from view, and a ladder in the stables to use in scaling the wall. They'll never see us."

"Are you sure?"

"We've tested it—gone out and in without being seen. The challenge is getting away through the mine fast enough to be faraway by morning. That's where you need outside help, but it's all arranged now."

"What will you do once you're out?"

"I'm heading for the coast, to hop a boat over to Cherson. We'll be safe there, out of the reach of Roman law."

"How do you know the Chersonese won't just hand you back over to the Romans?"

"That's why I want you to come. I need you, Kimon. You have contacts in Cherson, through your father. He can send help, even visit you there. You might even dare a return to Sinope."

"I don't know," said Kimon. "It's dangerous, and it's certain death if you fail."

"You have better chances here? You want to escape like Fortunatus?"

"I just don't know," said Kimon.

"It's our only hope, Kimon," said Drusus, tugging on Kimon's shoulder. "It's the hope of freedom. Cherson is outside the empire. We can live again as free men there."

"Yes, but, Drusus, it's a dependency of the empire. They would never let you live there freely, not for long anyway."

"But we are slaves here, and we will die slave here unless we escape. Come with me, Kimon. We can do it."

"I have to think about it," said Kimon.

"You have three days. Three days until the new moon. That's when we leave. And don't tell anyone."

"I'll let you know."

Kimon was still thinking about it the next evening when Thomas invited him to a Christian worship service. Kimon was shocked. "They let you do that? They send you to the mines for being Christians, but let you worship as Christians while you're here?"

"We're no threat to them here," said Thomas. "As far as the government's concerned, we're all dead men anyway. Besides, I think they know the faith keeps us alive, and in line."

Several hundred Christian convicts packed the old barn they were allowed to use. The setting lacked the usual adornments, which Kimon had seen in Sinope. The barn smelled of dirty bodies instead of incense. There were no special vestments for the leaders and singers, no painted scenes from Christian scriptures, not even a table for use as an altar, just a few benches up front for the overseers and elders and torches in the place of candles and lamps.

Yet all that the setting lacked in sight and smell, it made up for in sound. In the very middle of the barn was a handful of men chanting a series of hymns and psalms. One man among them stood out. His voice was manly and clear, and he sang with strength and power, verse after verse, psalm after psalm, relegating the other singers to the occasional refrain and accompaniment. All the while his eyes were closed, his bare head was tilted back, his hands were resting on the shoulders of other men on each side. There were no texts to sing from, and he never consulted the others. He sang solely from memory.

"That's the reader John," said Thomas. "He's been blind since birth and has memorized all of the psalms and services."

Kimon marveled at the feat, but he was moved even more when the whole assembly of men joined in singing. It seemed the building would fall down upon them, so powerful were the many male voices raised in song. Kimon had never heard anything quite like it, and in his weak and humbled state, its power made him tremble.

In time, one of the men at the front of the assembly rose to offer a series of petitions: "For the peace from above, for the salvation of our souls, let us pray to the Lord." The assembly punctuated each petition by singing *Kyrie eleison*—"Lord have mercy."

After the petitions there were more hymns, then more petitions, and then an old man up front rose and greeted the assembly, saying, "Peace be unto all." The men answered, saying, "And with thy spirit." The assembly fell silent.

The old man paused and lifted his eyes toward the rafters, then made the sign of the cross. Many in the barn did likewise.

"Brethren," the man began, speaking slowly and with some difficulty, "As many of you know, I was born a slave and remained a slave until my twenty-fifth year, when I was manumitted by my master upon his falling asleep, God rest his soul. I was a slave and now I am free. Even here today, in this place, I am free. We are all free. For once we were slaves to sin, but when we believed on the Lord Jesus Christ and were washed with the waters of baptism, our sins were forgiven and the chains that held us in bondage were broken. We put off the old man, the slave of sin, and put on the new man, clothed in righteousness, adopted sons of God, by the great grace of God. Amen."

"Amen," said those present.

The old man paused again before continuing: "In yet another way am I now free. When I still served my earthly master, my life was simple. I did as I was told. My days were decided for me. I was not blamed for being what I was or faulted for not being more. I was not responsible for my own condition; my master was, for the Lord does not hold the sheep responsible for their shearing, but the shepherd, and God will judge the master and not the servant for the servant's condition. We then who now live as slaves are freed of many cares for which others will be judged. Our responsibilities are limited, our judgment therefore light. We live simply. We work, we pray, we love one another, we give thanks. This is all that is expected of us and also all that is necessary for our salvation."

The old man touched his fingers to his lips pensively, then held up three fingers, trembling with age.

"There is yet a third way are we free," he said. "When we were in the world, we were often too much of the world. Who among us can say he did not often go to worship more mindful of this world than the next? How many things demanded our attention? How many things stole our thoughts away from our prayers? How many things distracted us from our hope and glory? I speak not of material possessions, but there were those also. And many among us perhaps went to worship like the unbelievers, with a mind to paying the occasional honor to God, in the expectation that God would in return bless us for it, not in the next life, but in this one here. But how many of us, even while avoiding the distraction of pleasure and ease and fortune, were consumed by matters that seemed then of great importance, that seem now not to matter at all? The rivalries, the contentions, the disputes over who and what and how and why, even in our own assemblies. Especially in our own assemblies. Here and now we are free of them. Here and now we are nearly free of this world and all its deceptions. Here and now, by the grace of God, we stand at the edge of this life, before the gates of the next, granted to see things in truer perspective, what matters and what doesn't, so as to prepare ourselves to meet our King, the great High Priest and Judge over all. This is a great mercy for which we should be thankful. Let us use this freedom wisely and well, that we may not only confess our faith, but bear witness to it unto the very end. Amen."

There were a few more hymns and prayers before the meeting broke up. Thomas offered to introduce Kimon to some of the overseers and elders, but Kimon declined. "It's late," he said, "and I've already too much to think about. Perhaps another night."

The next day, while hammering away in the mines, Kimon told Drusus of his decision to stay. He expected Drusus to plead with him to come, but Drusus responded coolly. The rest of the day they barely spoke. In the evening, Kimon did not see Drusus until the sun had set and Drusus returned to the cabin to sleep. He waited up to see if Drusus wanted to talk, but Drusus instead avoided him.

The next morning, Drusus was gone. The others did not notice at first, in the darkness before dawn. They were already in the cart, on their way to the mine, with the sky slowly lightening, when Ursulus looked around. "Where is Drusus?" he asked. The others looked around also. "You know," said Ursulus to Kimon.

Kimon stared back at him without speaking.

"He won't get far," said Ursulus.

"How do you know?" asked Thomas.

"They never do," he answered.

The day passed with no sign of alarm, then the evening also. The whole camp was talking. It wasn't just Drusus. There were others missing as well. Still, the guards appeared not to know.

"Maybe they made it," said Antonius the next morning on the way to the mine.

"It's too early," said Ursulus. "Another day or so. They'll find them."

That evening, they had just sat down with their bowls on the ground outside their cabin when a squad of guards raced into camp on horseback, dragging behind them the bodies of the escapees. They cut the corpses loose in the dusty square, then rode off. The stunned prisoners stared silently at the remains. There was little left. Flesh and bone together had been torn from the bloody trunks, leaving only the arms and heads intact. They must have been dragged for miles.

Kimon got up and limped slowly over to the bodies. There among them was Drusus.

"Can't say he didn't get what he wanted," said Ursulus from behind.

"What's that?" said Kimon.

"Freedom," said Ursulus. "There it is." He laughed aloud and then walked away.

# XXX

"He's dying, I tell you," said the aged augustus Maximian. "You could see it in his face. White as in death, he was. Then at other times twisted in agony. At times you could tell it was all he could do to keep from crying out in pain. No condition at all to be deciding matters of state. You can't trust a man in that kind of pain. They don't think straight. Yet there he was laying out his great scheme to save the empire, putting forth Licinius, another of his drinking partners, as his successor, just the way he chose Severus, that old fool. Daia was his pick, too, and look how he's turned out. Galerius himself doesn't trust him. That's why he wanted to promote Licinius."

"What was Diocletian's opinion?" asked Constantine.

Maximian—Fausta's father and Theodora's stepfather—gulped his wine from a great silver goblet. After meeting his former colleagues, Diocletian and Galerius, in conference at Carnuntum on the Danuvius, he returned not to the court of his son Maxentius in Rome, but to the court of his son-in-law Constantine at Arelate. Maxentius had infuriated his father by continuing to rule on his own from Rome as if his father were still retired. He had even murdered Severus, his former rival as Augustus of the West, whom Maximian had taken captive with a promise of safety.

"Diocletian deferred to Galerius as always," Maximian said in disgust. "He's been away from everything too long and relies on Galerius to do his thinking. He said to me—he said to me, 'If you could just see the cabbages in my garden that I planted with my own hands, how great and large they've grown, you'd never think to ask me to resume the purple.' He said that, I swear! Sometimes I think he's lost his mind. And yet there he was lending his approval to another of Galerius's supposed solutions."

He gulped again from the goblet.

"I explained things to him over and over again. I told him the only way to fix things is for me to return to the purple as augustus in the West, with you as my caesar, and have Galerius remain as Augustus of the East and keep Daia as his caesar. It's the only way to preserve the system that Diocletian himself designed."

"How did he respond?"

"He said I was too old! Can you believe it? Here is Galerius dying before our very eyes, and Diocletian says I'm unfit to rule because I'm too old. He forgets I'm not as old as he is. I'm as fit as ever and just the man to put things aright. Nobody else can do it. *You* can't deal with Maxentius alone. Neither can Galerius. He's already tried and humiliated himself. But you and I together could put down both my ingrate son in Rome *and* that upstart

Domitius Alexander in Africa. Then all would be right in the Roman world and Galerius could go on and die. I'd take over as Augustus in the East and make you the Augustus here. You could pick your own successor as caesar, and Daia would just have to live with it."

He took another gulp before going on.

"Instead, per Galerius's plan, Licinius gets bumped up from legate to augustus, without ever serving as anyone's caesar or even commanding more than one legion. You get demoted to caesar, and Daia is passed over and remains just a caesar. How do you like that?"

"They can have the title of augustus, as long as they leave me my legions," said Constantine. "Licinius is no fool, and someone with a level head needs to keep Daia in check."

"But you still have Maxentius to worry about. How will you deal with him?"

Constantine sipped his wine slowly. "That's something to think about," he said.

"I can help you," said Maximian, "just as I helped him. My old legions are just waiting for an opportunity to change horses. With your support, I know I can win them away from Maxentius. He's played the perfect scoundrel in Rome, soliciting bribes for official favors, seducing the wives of the city's leading men. I'm ashamed to say he's my son, and I'll throttle him myself when he's defeated, on account of the way he's treated me. If we move fast, we can catch him unprepared. Once he's out of the way, I can deal with the rebellion in Africa myself."

"I've other business in the north to tend to at the moment," said Constantine. "I've already put it off too long."

"The Franks can wait, Constantine. Think of Rome! Rome is what matters. She's calling us, son. She's our destiny!"

Eugenia conceived and was well along when Marcus went north with Constantine to deal with the Franks. It was not a difficult campaign, but it did take time to secure the frontier and repair its defenses.

They had been gone three months when a report reached the court at Arelate that Constantine was dead, killed in an ambush by the Franks. The praetorian prefect, Gratianus, suspended judgment and sent for confirmation, but the old emperor Maximian cast all doubt aside and immediately asserted his right to rule in Constantine's stead.

"These are perilous times," he told Gratianus and Theodora. "We cannot wait for new dangers to arise. The legions must have an emperor, or they will choose one of their own, and the last thing the empire needs is another rebel."

That same day Maximian sent messengers to the legions in southern

Gaul, notifying them of his succession and promising a bonus in silver to every soldier in the ranks to ensure their allegiance. He also ordered the manufacture of his image on cloth and in bronze, to be distributed as soon as they were ready throughout the realm.

The urgency with which he took charge caused more alarm in the palace than the report of Constantine's death. Fausta was in tears. She had delivered her first child, a daughter named Constantina, a few months before and was inclined to trust her own father in her husband's absence. Her distress made the misfortune more real than it might have seemed otherwise to many at court, including Eugenia. Without assurance to the contrary, Eugenia began to fear that Marcus, too, had perished. Would he not have been with the emperor at the fateful moment? Whether he was or wasn't, the death of the emperor meant that her husband had failed in his sacred duty.

The sadness, uncertainty, and shame might have overwhelmed both women, had Theodora not shown great calm and taken care to see them both comforted. "This is far too convenient for the ambitions of others. It would surprise me greatly if the report is true," she told Eugenia in private. Hilaria, who had prolonged her visit, also was suspicious, but kept her thoughts to herself.

Constantine learned of his own death at camp near Colonia. "Gratianus wants to know if I'm dead," he said, handing the confidential dispatch to Caesonius, Master of Offices. "Strange, but I don't feel dead."

"Shall we ask for the physician's opinion before responding?" said Caesonius.

"Maximian is the one who ought to be examined. What do you think he's up to? Is he just misinformed? Perhaps too eager to believe rumors that suit him?"

"Maybe he has reason to believe you should be dead, by now at least, according to plan."

"Maybe," said Constantine. "He couldn't possibly expect to get far with the rumor if I were still alive. Get Canio. He needs to hear this."

When Caesonius's own sources soon confirmed Maximian's actions, Constantine dispatched his own messengers to the legions in all of Gaul, warning them of the rumor and advising them that he was still very much in command. To Gratianus, he sent a confidential assurance of his safety, directing the prefect to inform his wife of the fact but not to confront her father with it. Play along, Constantine told him, and see to the safety of the empress.

Marcus, meanwhile, had assembled a small force of cavalry, including his own mounted Protectors, the Lancers of the imperial guard, and two squadrons borrowed from nearby legions. Thus accompanied, Constantine set out at once, driving south for eight days to Lugudunum on the Rhodanus River. It might have taken him another week to reach Arelate by land, but in Lugudunum Constantine commandeered everything afloat—every barge, boat, ferry, and raft able to carry men and horses downstream. In two days, the whole force was in Arelate, rested and ready.

Even so, they missed Maximian, who had departed in haste earlier that same day, fleeing east to the port of Massilia with his personal guard of 200 men and Constantine's treasury in his wagons. He tried to force his daughter Fausta to flee with him, grabbing her by the arm and pulling her toward the door, but she resisted so fiercely that he gave up and left without her.

Constantine paused only long enough at the palace to consult with Gratianus and comfort Fausta. Then he pressed on to Massilia, where he found the city gates locked and the walls guarded. When the gates did not open for his troopers, Constantine galloped forward, followed by Marcus and Caesonius. In his purple cloak and tunic, gilded armor, and white horse, he was easily recognizable. No-one could have mistaken him for anyone but an emperor.

"Open the gates!" he ordered impatiently.

"Who says so?" a voice on the wall shouted back.

Constantine looked up and saw Maximian himself, dressed for battle in his own fine armor and purple vestments. "I say so," he replied.

"You're supposed to be dead!" shouted Maximian.

"Sorry to disappoint you, but I am still very much alive," answered Constantine.

"I only did what was necessary," declared Maximian. "The palace was in chaos, the legions were restless. If I hadn't taken charge, there might have been civil war."

Constantine looked incredulously at Caesonius. Then he shouted back, "I thank you for your efforts, which are now no longer needed."

"Some thanks, coming after me with men and horses, as if I were some border bandit."

"You've taken my treasure and my town. Can the Franks do worse?"

"I've taken them only to protect myself from your jealousy and rage!"

"You would buy my pardon with my own purse?"

"I don't need your pardon, Constantine. I've done nothing wrong, only what was needed under the circumstances. Besides, you'd have no treasure at all if it wasn't for me. Neither you nor your father would have worn the purple if I hadn't first brought order to these parts."

"Haven't I treated you well? Honored you as an augustus? Welcomed you as family into my own household? Is this any way to repay me?"

"So you think I'm an ingrate like Maxentius. You forget all I've done for you. I've given you my good advice. I've shown you the way. I told you

the Franks would wait. I urged you to move on Rome. I offered you a way
to restore the empire, but you wouldn't listen. All my years of experience,
you brushed off like dandruff! You're the ingrate, Constantine! *You* spoiled
the peace. *You* destroyed the lawful succession worked out between me and
Diocletian. Who could blame Maxentius for doing the same in Rome? At
least he can boast a legitimate birth. Theodora's sons have more right to rule
than you do, you bastard!"

"Watch your tongue, old man!"

"Old man? Old man?! How's this for an old man?!" The old man seized
a spear from a guard and hurled it down at Constantine, who reeled away
upon his horse, colliding with Marcus's as he did so.

"He's mad, my lord," said Marcus, as they withdrew to a safer distance.

"I can see that, Canio. Tell me how to get him down!" said Constantine.

"I'm not coming down," shouted Maximian. "And you're not getting in.
So you go ahead and pitch your tent. You can't take the city with horse
alone, and it will be a long time before you're ready to try the walls. You
don't have any sappers or siege engines. And before you can bring them up,
I'll be long gone. You can't close the harbor. You lose, Constantine."

Maximian kept talking, adding insult to insult, but down below the
city gates were slowly and silently opening. Constantine pretended not to
notice, while Marcus casually turned his horse about and walked it over to
the squadron commander.

"I've got your gold," said Maximian. "See how long you last without
it. Your men won't fight if you can't pay them. You know that, or at least
you should. You've never really been tried as a commander. Never fought a
pitched battle, have you, Constantine? Just a few of skirmishes against puny
people like the Franks and the Picts."

A man in fine civilian attire appeared in the open gate, sank to his
knees, and bowed his head to the ground in Constantine's direction, then
made a welcoming gesture, all without interrupting Maximian's tirade. The
squadron commander gave the order to move.

"How's your mother, boy?" yelled Maximian. "Cleaned any inns lately?"
He laughed as loud as he could, then saw the column of horse charging
toward the wall. A look of horror appeared on his face as the column disappeared through the open gate below him. Then anger overcame his horror.
"Who opened the gate?!" he screamed in vain over the side of the wall. "Who
opened the gate?!" He disappeared from sight, but they could still hear him
screaming: "Who opened the gate?! Who opened the gate?!"

Constantine took his ease outside the city for several hours while his
emissaries negotiated Maximian's surrender. The terms were generous.
Maximian was to give up the purple for good, but would return to the palace to live as an honored member of the imperial family. The official version

of events, which Constantine would see published, would blame everything on an erroneous report and a misunderstanding. The next day Maximian returned under guard to Arelate, a crushed if not quite humbled man.

In time, the court of Constantine settled uncertainly into a tense but tranquil routine. Maximian kept to his apartments, except to visit his daughters and grandchildren. Constantine was busy with civil affairs, revising the system of taxation, amending the legal code to ease the lot of slaves, and expending public funds for the building of schools and other works.

    While the emperor toiled away in the palace, Marcus was very nearly idle, which left him without a convenient excuse for absenting himself when the time came for Eugenia to deliver. It wasn't a day to go hawking.

    He was sitting alone in a reception room outside the women's wing of the palace when Theodora's youngest son, Hannibalianus, wandered in. He was now six, having come into the world just four year's before the death of his father, the Augustus Constantius. "Have you seen my mamma?" he asked.

    Marcus smiled. "She's busy, little prince. Is there anything I can do for you?"

    "You can play with me," said the boy, hopefully. "Please, Lord Canio. I don't have anyone to play with, and I'm bored. Please play with me."

    Marcus knew he could not refuse. "As long as we play right here," he said. "So what shall it be? Knuckle-bones?"

    "Mamma won't let me play knuckle-bones," said the boy. "She says they're of the devil."

    "Does she? Well, we'll have to respect that. How about nuts?"

    "But I haven't got any nuts."

    "No nuts? That's a problem," said Marcus.

    "I know!" said the boy. "Let's play who-am-I? I'll start and you guess."

    "As you wish, my lord," said Marcus.

    Hannibalianus thought for a moment, then struck a pose, flexing his arm muscles and sticking out his flat little chest. With an expression of grim determination, he pretended to perform various feats of strength.

    The answer was obvious, thought Marcus. "Hercules!" he declared.

    The boy frowned. "No," he said. "Samson!"

    "Oh," said Marcus.

    "How about this one?" said the boy. He reached down and pretended to pick something up off the floor. Next he swung his arm around in a circle several times before stopping suddenly and making a single loud *cluck* with his tongue. Then he slapped one hand down upon the other. "Who am I?" he asked.

    Marcus was clueless. "Achilles?" he ventured.

"David!" said the boy. "Don't you know anything?"

Marcus shrugged.

"One more try, and this one's easy," said the little prince. He made an evil face and stomped around the room, pumping his fists up and down in the air.

Marcus thought through all that he knew of the Christian scriptures. "Herod?" he guessed.

"No, Canio. It's Grandfather! Can't you see?" He stomped around the room again. "See?" he said.

Marcus chuckled. "I see," he said, "but you mustn't mock your grandfather."

"Why not?" asked the boy.

There was a sudden cry of pain from the women's wing. Marcus stood up.

"Who's that?" asked Hannibalianus.

There was a second cry, more anguished than the first.

"We must go and help her," cried the boy, dashing out of the room.

"Wait," Marcus called, to no avail. Hannibalianus had disappeared.

For a while there was nothing. Then came another round of cries. They had just ceased when Marcus heard voices in the corridor. "Why can't I stay and watch?" asked Hannibalianus.

"It's not the place for little boys," said his mother, the empress Theodora. "Run along and play now, and don't disturb us."

She stopped in the door of the reception room to see her son off. Then she turned to Marcus. "She's having a very difficult time," she said stoically. "The midwives are doing all they can, but pray for her, Marcus. Pray for her and the baby."

Marcus nodded, and Theodora left to return to the scene. Since his betrothal to Eugenia, Marcus had attended many Christian services. He had stood for prayers led by other men, bowing his head when they did, singing the Lord-have-mercies and the amens and the alleluias with the others. But he had never prayed alone or led Eugenia in prayer. He knew he would have to someday, but he didn't know how to begin. It hardly seemed the right thing to do just because he knew he should. But now he needed prayer—Eugenia needed prayer—and, proud as he was, Marcus was not above begging God to save her.

It felt strange to kneel there in the reception room, where someone might see him—a man, a soldier, an officer of the emperor, kneeling before no one—but he did it anyway. And he made the sign of the cross in the eastern way, as Eugenia had taught him to do, touching his forehead, chest, and shoulders right to left with his thumb and first two fingers. He had crossed himself before when he knew that other Christians expected to see him do it, but this was the first time he crossed himself sincerely to mark the submission of his own body and soul to the Christian God.

Then he raised his hands and lifted up his eyes, and whispered the prayer of his heart: "O Lord Jesus Christ, Son of God, have mercy on me, a sinner. Have mercy on me and on my wife Eugenia and on our child. Preserve and protect us, and deliver us from this danger. Forgive our sins and save our souls, O gracious Lord. . . ." Before long he had slipped into familiar phrases from Christian worship, borrowed here and there from things he had heard many times but never put together in his own mind. ". . . Let Thy mercy be on us, O Lord, even as we have set our hope on Thee. Blessed art Thou, O Lord, teach me Thy statutes. Blessed art Thou, O Master, make me to understand Thy commandments. Blessed art Thou, O Holy One, enlighten me with Thy precepts—"

Then suddenly the words stopped, and Marcus was moved to fold himself forward until his forehead touched the floor. "O Lord, my God! My God!" he cried. "Spare the lives of my wife and our child. Have mercy on them and on me. Forgive me for my sins. Christ God, have mercy on us all!"

Moments later, he was interrupted by a maidservant sent to lead him down the hall to the birthing room. Theodora met him in the hallway outside. "Don't stay long," she said with the slightest trace of a smile. "There was some tearing but she should recover quickly."

Marcus found Eugenia lying with her eyes closed on a couch, covered with a blanket and surrounded by her mother Hilaria and several attendants. He knelt beside her and took her hand. At his touch, she opened her eyes and looked up at him, weary and sad.

"Oh Marcus," she said. "I'm sorry."

"Sorry?" he said.

"She's sorry it's a girl," said her mother Hilaria happily. "A healthy baby girl."

Marcus laughed nervously. "How did you know I wanted a girl?" he said.

Eugenia smiled and closed her eyes. "I love you," she whispered. He kissed her cheek.

"That's enough for now," said the midwife. "She needs to rest and we must watch for bleeding."

He kissed Eugenia's hand and then rose to go. Theodora met him again at the door.

"You are greatly blessed, Marcus," she said, smiling plainly now.

He answered, "More than you know, my Lady."

Eugenia did recover quickly, and the baby thrived. They named her Aemilia Theodora Macrina, spelled in the Latin way, and began calling her Macrina. The next few months were the happiest Marcus had ever known. His duties

were light and his delights were many—his wife, his child, their few fond
friends, and their powerful patrons. For all these, Marcus was sincerely
grateful. Humbling himself in prayer had opened his heart and changed
his outlook on life. His doubts about the Christian faith melted away in the
warmth of fellowship and in the knowledge that he had at last found a good
God, a loving God, a God who works wonders.

The whole court seemed happy through the autumn and early winter, even Maximian, who was even seen to smile in Constantine's presence
during the Saturnalia. The Empress Fausta made sure it was a gay affair,
decorating the palace with the colors blue, green, and gold and arranging
an elaborate banquet at which everyone, including the emperor, appeared
in costume. The table was set with finely wrought silverware, and when the
banquet was over, the guests were invited to take their knives and spoons
with them, along with the small felt bag of gold nuts. Such were the traditional gifts of the season. Marcus surprised Hannibalianus with a bag of
hand-carved marble nuts. He even sat down on the floor to teach the boy
the game.

Then one day in early January, Constantine summoned Marcus to his
study. When Marcus arrived, the emperor dismissed his secretary. "Do you
trust your men?" the emperor asked Marcus when they were alone.

"Certainly," said Marcus.

"With your life?"

"Of course."

"With mine?"

"Yes, of course, my lord. Is something wrong?"

"The Empress Fausta has informed me that her dear deranged father intends to kill me and has asked for her help in doing so. His plan is absurdly
simple, which makes me wonder if there's not more to it. She is to dismiss
the guards from outside my bedroom while I'm in it and leave the door unlocked. He then will slip in and do the deed himself."

"That's it? That's all?"

"You tell me, Canio. Anything more would have to involve
your Protectors."

Marcus almost laughed. "Not possible, my lord," he said. "To side with
Maximian against you they'd have to be madder than he is, and I know
they're not. I pick the guards here in the palace myself."

"I'm sure you are right. But let's take precautions. I want to catch him
in the act."

That evening the guards were posted as usual in the great hall outside
the emperor's suite, but not as usual in the antechamber outside his bedroom. An elderly eunuch was made to lie down in the emperor's comfortable,

canopied, curtained bed. "Don't fall asleep," the emperor warned the eunuch. "Your life depends on it."

The lamps were extinguished in the bedroom, and the door was left unlocked. Constantine and Marcus hid with a squad of Protectors in a room off the great hall. When all was ready, Fausta went and told her father.

As the hours passed, Constantine and Marcus played chess. Marcus made sure to lose, an easy task. Afterwards, the emperor dozed on a cot in the corner, while Marcus paced the floor. He had noticed this before about Constantine, that however tense the situation was, the emperor was always able to sleep peacefully.

After another hour, Marcus sat down against the wall with his Protectors. They, too, nodded off now and then, but Marcus discovered he could easily stay awake by watching others nod off. He made it a game, and before long some of his men were playing as well.

Well after midnight, they heard Maximian's voice in the hall outside. "I've had the strangest dream, an omen really, a premonition, and I must share it with the emperor at once," he told the guards.

The guards had been instructed to let him pass, which they would not have done normally. The old man hurried through the hall, through the antechamber, and into the emperor's bedroom.

A moment later, Maximian cried out in a loud voice, "Constantine is dead!" But when he emerged in triumph from the bedroom, there stood Constantine in the torchlight, with Marcus at his side and a squad of soldiers behind him.

Maximian froze, his eyes wide, his mouth agape—"speechless as Marpesian flint," as Marcus later told Eugenia—and holding the dagger, still dripping the eunuch's blood. Constantine regarded him impassively. "Take him," he ordered.

The guards quickly surrounded and disarmed the villain, forcing him to kneel and bow before the emperor while they bound his hands behind his back. A soldier's boot kept him doubled over, while their spears prevented him from lifting his head.

"You have one choice left in life, Maximian: how to die," said Constantine.

The soldiers took him away to his own quarters, where the ex-augustus hanged himself before dawn. Constantine ordered an elaborate funeral, befitting an emperor. The body was not burned according to Roman custom, but embalmed and bedecked and entrusted to a lead casket, then entombed inside a marble sarcophagus, where it remained in Arelate for many, many years.

# XXXI

A child's face peered through the iron bars into the dank and dim basement cell. It was a large room filled to capacity, mostly with vagrants rounded up to rid the streets of beggars during a visit by the praetorian prefect of the East. The cell smelled of urine and feces, sickness and corruption. The detainees sat or lay chained by the feet, men on one side, women on the other. In the corner, an old woman with straggly gray hair babbled endlessly, with occasional shrieks to protest some real or imagined evil. A man near the stairs groaned for water. Another coughed almost constantly.

Makrina coughed, too, sitting against the wall with her knees drawn up and her head and arms resting on them. She stared blankly at the floor, her mind idle, her soul worn thin, her will weakened by the daily struggle to survive, but for the moment at rest. Hope had died in the wasted lives around her. Would it die with her? she wondered.

She reached down and drew a fish in the dirt on the floor, then quickly rubbed it out. She drew instead the Chi-Rho, and then erased that. Then she drew a simple cross. The child at the window watched to see if she would erase it, too, but she let it be. The child ran off.

He returned within the hour, accompanied by a woman. Makrina heard their voices and saw him point in her direction. "Are you sure?" she heard the woman say. "Yes, I'm sure," said the boy. "See for yourself." The woman peered down into the cell. Makrina peered back suspiciously, covering her face with her mantle when she coughed. Then she remembered the cross in the dirt and hastily rubbed it out. When she looked again at the window, the boy and woman were gone.

A while later, the door at the top of the stairs opened and the jailer stepped in. "Which one?" he asked from the top step. The woman from the window stood in the doorway and pointed to Makrina.

"The young one. What's her name?" asked the woman.

The jailer checked his tablet. "Let's see. Says her name is—Salome, a vagrant, picked up for begging. You want her?"

The woman nodded. "How much?" she asked.

"Fifty denarii," said the jailer.

"Twenty-five," the woman countered.

The jailer sighed impatiently. "Twenty-five then."

The woman dug into her purse, counted out 25 denarii, and gave it to the jailer, who counted it again as he descended the stairs. He picked his way through the sprawling bodies, and then bent over and unlocked

Makrina's shackles. "That's it. You're free," he said, "as long as you stay with her. If we catch you on your own again, you'll be right back here."

The jailer started back toward the stairs, then looked back. "You're free, I said. Get up. Get out of here."

Makrina got up, found her way to the stairs, and followed the jailer up.

The woman was waiting for her in the street, but the boy was nowhere to be seen. She was in her thirties and modestly dressed, with sharp, lean features and dark, piercing eyes, quite a beauty at one time. "Follow me," she said, without any introduction.

Makrina followed her down the street, around the corner, past several alleys before turning into the doorway of a small, private bath. A large, homely woman carrying a stack of towels saw them enter. "Stop right there," said the woman, blocking the way. "I run a clean establishment, Afra, with no place for trash like that."

"This is a bath, isn't it? That's all she needs."

"With clothes like that, why waste money on a bath?"

"I'll take care of her clothes if you let her bathe. I'll pay twice the rate."

Makrina coughed into her mantle.

"She's sick. Take her away," ordered the woman.

"Four times the rate," said Afra.

"Six."

"All right, six then." Afra handed the woman twelve denarii.

The woman led them down a narrow corridor to an open pool, no more than twelve feet across. Around the pool were several booths, all without doors and all also empty. Inside each booth was a stool, a wash basin, and a large pitcher. "In there first," said the proprietress, pointing to one of the booths. Makrina stepped inside. "Off, off, before somebody sees what a mess I've let in. Just throw them over there."

The proprietress left while Makrina disrobed, casting her clothes into the corner as directed. Afra gathered them up and then excused herself. "I'll be back later. Delia will take care of you," she said.

Delia returned with tray of accessories: sponge, strigil, scrub brush, wash rag, and comb. "Great gods, look at you," she said in disgust. "I suppose next she'll want to bring her dog in." She filled the basin with water from the pitcher, then handed Makrina the sponge. "There you go," she said.

The water was cold and clean at first, but not for long. Delia returned three times to empty it, returning with fresh water. "Keep scrubbing," she said each time.

Afra reappeared with a bundle of clean clothes. "How is she?" she asked Delia. For the first time, Makrina saw Afra smile.

"You'll have to cut her hair. It's full of lice," said Delia. "Let me see your hands," she said to Makrina. Makrina held them out. The nails were jagged and broken, with dirt embedded underneath. "Use the brush and do what you can."

Makrina sat down naked on the stool and worked on her nails, while Afra applied a pair of shears unsparingly to her hair. The shears were hinged at one end and required both hands to operate.

"So your name is Salome," said Afra.

Makrina did not answer.

"You can speak, can't you?"

"Yes," said Makrina.

"Where are you from?" Afra asked.

Again Makrina did not answer.

"My little friend said he saw you drawing things in the dust. Forbidden things. Are you a Christian?"

Still no answer.

Afra bent over and whispered into Makrina's ear, "I am."

Makrina stopped working on her nails, but said nothing.

Afra waited for a response. When none came, she said, "Christian or not, you are welcome with me, as long as you behave yourself. It would be nice, though, to hear your voice."

"I don't know what to believe anymore," said Makrina. "I thought I was a Christian, but now I just feel lost."

"I'm not surprised," said Afra. "All alone in that miserable place. How did you end up like that?"

"I can't say," said Makrina.

"You can't because you don't know or because you don't dare?"

Makrina thought for a moment. "Both," she answered.

"I understand," said Afra. "Forget that I asked. It doesn't matter, not with me anyway. I'm hardly one to hear confessions. It's a shame about your hair, but it will grow back. Faith can grow back, too, Salome."

When Afra was finished, Makrina was nearly bald. Only a razor could have gotten closer, but there was no need for that. Afra plugged Makrina's ears with wax to keep the lice out, then gave her scalp a good scrub with the brush. Only then was she fit for a dip in the pool. The water was cool, even cold on her bare head, but Makrina didn't mind.

Afterwards, Afra provided her with a scented oil for her body, then helped her dress in the clothes she had brought. They were neither stylish nor new, but they were clean and in good repair, and Makrina was glad to have them. Delia looked at her critically. "Why she bothers, I'll never know," she said before walking off.

They left the bath and stepped out into the street. Makrina kept her palla pulled low over her head to hide her baldness. "We'll have to hurry,"

Afra said, taking Makrina's other hand. "The shops are about to close and I hadn't planned two for supper."

They stopped first at the baker for two loaves of bread, one a day old already; then the grocer for pine kernels and green peppercorns; and finally the butcher for a cut of lamb. While waiting for the lamb, Afra noticed Makrina staring wide-eyed at the pastries in the shop next door. They left with two small, fried wheat-cakes, dipped in honey and topped with ground pistachios.

Afra's apartment was not far away, above a cobbler's shop, now closed for the day. Afra unlocked the door at the top of the stairs and welcomed Makrina inside. "One more thing," she said. "Wait here. I'll be right back."

The apartment was one long room lit by an open window looking out over the street. A bed lay against one wall, directly opposite a wardrobe. At the back of the room, near the door, was a cupboard and a large chest. The walls were bare. The floor was covered with wool rugs. There were no chairs, just two pillowed stools by the window beside a covered brazier.

Makrina had not moved from the door when Afra returned with a vented metal pail carrying hot coals for the brazier. "Sit here," she said, taking off her palla and pointing to the stool closest to the bed. Makrina sat down without uncovering her head, while Afra added the hot coals to the brazier. "Use this to keep the coals alive," she said, handing Makrina a fan of woven straw.

Then Afra opened her cupboard, took out a shallow pan, a small jug of white wine, a slate shingle, and a paring knife. First she poured wine into the pan, then crumbled the day-old loaf of bread into the wine, pushing down on the crumbs to soak up all the liquid. Next she minced the lamb on the slate, right there on the floor beside the brazier. Then she scraped the meat into the pan, sprinkled the pan with pine nuts and peppercorns, and added a pinch of ground pepper and a splash of a familiar fish sauce called *liquamen*, used in the place of salt. With her bare hands, she kneaded the soggy bread and minced meat together with the seasoning to form four small patties.

After wiping her hands with a rag, Afra poured a sweet sauce of boiled must (unfermented wine) over each patty, then set the pan upon the brazier. The pan began to sizzle immediately. Makrina kept working the fan, now to blow the smoke out the window. Every once and awhile she would turn her head and cough into her palla.

Afra settled on the other stool and tended the patties to ensure they cooked thoroughly. The pan gave forth an enticing aroma that sharpened Makrina's hunger. She could hardly wait until they were done.

At last, Afra lifted the pan from the brazier and set it down on the slate she had used as a cutting board. Then she covered the brazier with its lid to snuff out the coals before they burned away to ash. Next she spread a white cloth between herself and Makrina and placed the fresh loaf of bread in the middle of the cloth. Last of all she took an earthen jug from the cupboard and poured two cups half full of dark red wine, then added a little water from the pitcher nearby.

Kneeling beside the bread, she looked up at Makrina and smiled. "Come," she said, offering Makrina her hand. "Let us pray."

*No! Let's eat! Now!* thought Makrina. But she knelt anyway and bowed her head. Afra covered hers with her palla, then raised her hands and her eyes toward heaven. Her prayer was a familiar one—for daily bread, for forgiveness of sins, for deliverance from evil, and for the Kingdom to come. Makrina swallowed hard when she heard it. At the amen, Afra made the sign of the cross. Makrina did so also, slowly, painfully.

They sat on the floor upon pillows and ate with their fingers, dipping pieces of bread into the pan and using their knives to divide the patties into bite-size chunks. Makrina ate quickly without saying a word. Afra watched her and ate slowly, refilling Makrina's cup and urging her to finish what was left in the pan. When it was all gone, she unwrapped the cakes, gave one to Makrina, and left the other with the bread between them. Makrina wolfed hers down quickly, with barely time to taste it.

Then her eyes fell on the cake remaining. "You eat it," said Afra. "I've eaten too much already."

Afterwards, they sat on their stools looking down at the street below. It was still light and the street was filled with people out for an evening stroll, visiting their neighbors, savoring the comforting smells of the dinner hour.

"How long has it been since you left home?" Afra asked.

Makrina stared absently out the window. "I can't remember," she said. "Years. Four or five. Maybe more."

"Can you go back?"

Makrina shook her head slowly.

"Why not?"

"I have disgraced my family."

"Do they not want you back?"

"They would, I am sure. But if I went back, it would only disgrace them more."

"How is that possible?" asked Afra.

Makrina did not answer.

"I ran away from home when I was younger than you," said Afra. "I disgraced my family, and after years on my own, I felt as you do—that I could not go back. So I stayed away until it was too late, until those who had loved me had died. Now I know I was wrong. I should have gone back, however painful it might have been. And it would have been very painful."

Makrina looked annoyed. "What could you have done that was so bad?" she said sharply.

Afra was stung. She blinked and flared her nostrils as she drew a deep breath. Then she leaned out of the window, looking past Makrina and down the street. "I was one of them," she said.

Makrina followed her gaze. A few doors down there was a house with several women loitering at the door. They were slightly dressed, with bare heads and arms and only the sheerest fabrics covering their curves. Their faces and necks were powdered white, but their cheeks and lips were painted red, and their eyes were outlined in blue and black. They lounged about like lizards, watching the men passing by, calling out to invite them in, taunting those who refused and groping indecently the ones within reach.

Makrina turned around and looked at Afra.

"What could you have done that was worse?" said Afra.

"I'm sorry," said Makrina, her eyes now on the floor between them.

"I forgive you," said Afra. "Please forgive me for prying. I only want to help. I know how hard it is for a young girl on the streets, and I have all this money. Oh, I know it doesn't show, not in this little place. I've saved it all instead of spending it. I tried to give it to the Assembly here, but they wouldn't take it because of how I earned it. So I try to use it to help others."

"Why me? Why not them?" Makrina asked, glancing back at the women down the street.

"I can't help them," said Afra. "They're as blind as I was then. They know I'm here. They know who I am. They know how I now live. But it's easy for them to dismiss me. 'She's made her pile and now she's set,' they say. That's what they all want—to make it all now and escape responsibility for the rest of their lives. They all plan to quit someday. No one forces them to work now. They do it because it gives them hope for a better life later. It makes sense, if this life is all you believe in, and if you can bear the pain of believing that all you are worth as a woman is a few silver coins."

Makrina stared down at the street. "How did you know I wasn't also one of them?" she asked.

"If you had been one of them, you would not have been arrested for begging," said Afra. "Look at them. Can you imagine any of them in that jail cell, in the condition you were in? I don't know what you've done, Salome, but I know what you haven't done. You haven't given up. You haven't lost all hope. You haven't given yourself over to your sins. If you had, you would have earned your ease and freedom on your back, as they do . . . as I did."

Afra leaned forward and took Makrina's hand. "You know the Parable of the Prodigal, don't you?" she said. "How the son was taken back by his father? You may feel lost, but you still know the way. It's the right way, Salome, and you must return to it. You are not lost, and you are no longer alone. I can help if you let me."

Makrina nodded, unable to speak. The sun had set, cloaking the apartment in darkness. Afra rose and set about preparing for bed, casting the remains of their meal out the window, putting away the wine and the utensils, never bothering to light a lamp. On the floor where they had eaten, she laid out a make-shift mattress of quilts. "I'll sleep here tonight. You can have the bed," she said.

Last of all she said her prayers, kneeling upon the quilts, bowing repeatedly, and signing herself. Makrina knelt beside her, silent and still, until the end, when she mumbled an amen after Afra's.

Cool night air flowed through the open window, cleansing the air in Afra's apartment but waking in the sleeping Makrina a cold, violent memory. It was all there again in her dream—the village, the soldiers, the giant, poor Gregorios's cracked skull, the gallant Gerasimos pleading with the wicked centurion. *Where is the ring? Who has the ring? My Greek is better than yours. I speak Latin as well: Velisne audire? Wait, please! My father has money, all the money you could want. Please let them go! Please! Ad ecclesiam, tum incende, tum incende. No! Wait! Salome! Ioanna! Wait! Da veniam! Da veniam!* "Da veniam! Da veniam! Ioanna! SALOME!!!!"

Afra threw off her covers and jumped up onto the bed, catching Makrina in her arms just as she sat up and screamed. "It's all right! It's all right! It's just a dream. You're safe now. It's all over. I'm here. I'm here." Makrina fought against her at first, then awoke and remembered where she was. With the recollection came a wave of wails and tears. "They died! They all died, and I couldn't help them! I tried but I couldn't! I just couldn't!"

"It's over. It's long past. It's not your fault."

"I tried to help them! I pleaded! I begged for mercy! I offered them money —"

"You did what you could. It's over. It's all over. You're safe now. You're safe. No one blames you."

Afra held her tightly with both arms, rocking her gently. Makrina rested her shorn head on Afra's shoulder, sobbing and shivering. In time her sobbing subsided and Afra laid her back down to sleep. "Stay with me, please," Makrina pleaded. "I'm so afraid. I don't want to be alone."

Afra curled up next to her on the bed, and they passed the night together, safe and warm in each other's arms.

The next morning they sat on the bed and Makrina told Afra about the village, then about her flight from Sinope and her life at home. She did not at first tell her everything, but the more she said, the less she could conceal.

Said Afra, "I can see why you left, Salome, but what keeps you from going home? After all this time, who would still hold the insult against you?"

"I still have not sacrificed."

"That's as much of a danger here as it is there. At least at home, you have your family to protect you."

"I don't have the money."

"But I have the money. I'll give you all you need."

"There is something else," said Makrina, "something very bad. I have committed a terrible crime, Afra. I have killed a man. Not just any man. I killed the lieutenant governor."

Afra gasped. "That was you?" she asked.

Makrina nodded.

"Oh, Salome!"

"My name is not Salome," said Makrina. "Salome died in the village. She was my very dear friend. My name is Makrina. The police know my name. They know I killed the lieutenant governor. That's why I took Salome's name. That's why I can't go back."

"I see," said Afra.

"The police must also know my father's name and who he is. Rogatianus did. If I went back, I would still have to answer for my crime. My father and mother would have to bear the shame and pain of seeing me tried and punished. They would lose me all over again, and everyone would know why. I can't do that to them. I can't bear to see how much pain I've caused them, how I've ruined their lives."

"You haven't ruined their lives."

"I have! I have, Afra. They were happy. We were all happy, my parents, my brother and sister. I was happy. I was to be married to a good man, a man I loved, a man who loved me. My parents were so pleased. Everything was as it should be. And then I . . . I was so foolish and headstrong . . . and then so angry! I ruined everything, my life and theirs."

Makrina wiped her eyes and nose with the sleeve of her tunic. "I can't go back," she said. "I can't bear to."

"You didn't ruin anyone's life," said Afra. "You may have sinned, you may have caused others harm, but you didn't ruin their lives. The only life you can ruin is your own, and you can only do that by throwing it away, and you haven't done that yet."

"But things were all right and now, because of me, they're all wrong!"

"Things were never all right. If that's what you mean by ruin, then all our lives were ruined a long time ago, when the first man turned away from God and sin and death entered the world. Nothing's been all right since. We were all born without grace, outside the presence of God. We were all ruined from the start, Makrina, all doomed to suffer and die."

"But I've destroyed their happiness."

"The worst off, Makrina, are those who are happy. They don't know they are doomed, so they don't seek their own salvation. It hurts us sometimes to disturb them in their happiness, but what is happiness anyway? For many, it's just blindness. They don't see their own sin. They don't see how sick and frail they are. They don't see far enough ahead to know how they'll end up, so they don't prepare. We don't want to disturb them in their happiness now, but sooner or later something will, and then where will they be? Without hope, without mercy, without love, for all eternity."

Makrina turned away. "It's so hard to always look to the next life," she said. "Sometimes I'm not sure I truly believe in it."

"I have to believe in it," said Afra. "After the way I've lived this one, the next one's my only hope."

It was market day, so they spent most of the morning at the market, coming away with a basket full of victuals: figs, dates, mushrooms, asparagus, cheese, eggs, and oysters, dug up from the river bed. Makrina could not wait to sample the dried figs. They were so plump and tender. The vendor stacked them one on top of the other to form tall columns of figs, pressed round like wheels.

After the market, they went again to the bath, which surprised Makrina at first. She had forgotten what it was like to bathe every day, and hardly thought she needed one.

The afternoon was spent preparing dinner, an elaborate little feast of half a dozen dishes. After dinner, Afra sent much of the meal home with Linos, her little spy. They passed the evening sitting by the window again, talking of their childhoods, until the sunset and they settled into their beds.

They hadn't been asleep long when they were awakened by a loud, male voice in the street, calling, "Afra! Afra!"

Makrina sat up in her bed. "Who's that?" she whispered.

"Afra!"

Afra got up and went to the open window. "Who's there?" she called down.

"There you are. It's me, Vegetius, your very own *miles gloriosus*, back from the wars."

"Go away," said Afra.

"Ah, come on, Afra. Don't you remember me? I know it's been awhile. Three, four years maybe."

Makrina got out of bed and sat down on the stool by the window.

"Stay back. Don't let him see you," Afra whispered.

"Don't you remember, Afra?" cried Vegetius.

"I remember," she answered.

"What do you say? Can I come up?"

"It's late. Go away."

"But I've come all this way, thinking of you the whole time, all the memories. We had some good times, didn't we, Afra?"

"Your drunk, Vegetius."

"I'm not drunk. Besides, you never turned me away drunk before."

"Hey, hero," said a woman's voice down below. "Why waste your time with her? I've got what you need."

"I like Afra," said Vegetius. "Afra and I go back a long way. Don't we, Afra?"

"Afra goes back a long way with everybody. There are younger fillies in the stable."

"I want Afra. Did you hear that, Afra? How's that for loyalty?"

The woman laughed. "She won't have you, hero. She's out of the business."

"What? Is that true, Afra?"

Afra didn't answer.

"She's turned pious, hero. She's a Christian now. Won't have a thing to do with you."

"A Christian? Afra?"

"Just ask her."

"Afra! Afra! Are you a Christian?"

Afra hesitated, not wanting to respond at all, yet feeling that she should. She leaned toward the window and shouted down, "Yes, I am. Now will you please go away?"

"See? I told you."

"A Christian," said Vegetius, scratching the back of his neck. "Fates be damned."

"Come along with me, soldier. I'll take care of you." Makrina saw her tug on his arm. "A little while with me and you won't even remember her name."

"Some other time," said Vegetius.

"No, now, hero. I need you now." The woman pressed up against him, but he shook her off with a groan and walked off.

"Thank God," said Afra. They both went back to bed.

The next morning before it was light, Afra sent Makrina off on an errand. "Go to the bakery across town," she said. "You know the one? Ask anyone there for the widow Berenice. When you find her, give her these."

She handed Makrina a small leather purse full of coins.

"She'll want you to stay and visit, and you shouldn't refuse her. The visit means more to her than the money. Oh, and take this key in case I'm not here when you return."

Makrina was preparing to leave when Afra said suddenly, "Did you see where I kept the coins? Here, under the chest. There's a false bottom that leaves room underneath, where they can't be seen. You have to move the chest to find them. If you look around, you might find other hiding places as well."

Then when Makrina was almost out the door, Afra pulled her back and kissed her forehead. "God go with you, Makrina," she said with a firm embrace.

Makrina did as she was told, finding the bakery and the widow without trouble. Berenice was a very old woman with a hunched back and a hooked nose, but also bright eyes and friendly, toothless grin. She couldn't hear half of what Makrina said, and Makrina couldn't understand half of the widow's mumbles, but the visit lasted over an hour anyway.

When Makrina returned to the apartment about noon, Afra was not there. Makrina waited patiently for most of the afternoon, watching the bustle in the street below, thinking over her life of late.

When at about the tenth hour Afra had still not returned, Makrina began to worry and to wonder. *What's happened to her? Where has she gone? Why did she show me where she hid her money?*

She had started pacing the floor when little Linos called for her from the street below. "Afra sent me," he said. "She's in jail, right where you were."

Makrina grabbed her cloak and hurried off with Linos leading the way. At the same barred window where she had first seen both him and Afra, they crouched down and peered inside. Afra looked up and smiled. "Be well, Salome," she said for all to hear.

"What are you doing in there?" Makrina asked through the bars.

"They came to make me sacrifice after you left. I refused, so here I am."

"What should I do?"

"You should go home, Salome, home to your parents. There's nothing to hold you here, and you have the means now to travel."

"But what will happen to you?"

"What will happen to me is God's will. My race is finished, almost at least. I can last until the end, but I will not keep running, and I will not hide any longer. I will win my crown."

"But Afra!"

"I'm ready, Salome. I'm at peace. I have longed for this for the past several years. I have led many, many men astray in my life. Now God has given me a chance to show some men the way of salvation. I will not disappoint Him."

"You knew they were coming, didn't you? That's why you sent me off this morning, so I wouldn't be arrested also."

"I thought they might come," said Afra. "I hoped they wouldn't, but now I'm relieved they did. It's almost over for me, Salome, but it's not over for you. You must still go home. Promise me you will."

"Afra!"

"Promise me."

Makrina wiped away a tear. "I promise," she said.

"Go soon, Salome. Go tomorrow. I don't want you to see me finish. I want to know that you are on your way home. Promise me you won't stay."

"I can't leave you now, Afra."

"You can't stay, Salome. This is not your time. Your time will come, but this is not it."

Her words were calm and clear and spoken with such sureness that Makrina recognized in them an authority beyond Afra's own. This was a prophecy. This was of God.

"Go tomorrow, Salome. Promise me you will."

"I will, Afra. I promise."

"You have been a blessing to me, Salome."

"And you to me, Afra. I owe you so much already. Will you plead to God for me?"

"I will, Salome."

"Is there any way I can thank you for all you've done?"

"You have thanked me with your promise."


At Afra's trial, the judge, a man named Cajus, invited her to sacrifice or endure a painful punishment. Afra replied that she had committed enough sin in her life and would not add another to her long list.

"From what I understand, you are a prostitute," said Cajus, "so what is there to keep you from sacrificing. You can't possibly be a Christian."

"My Lord Jesus Christ said that he had come down from heaven to save sinners such as me," said Afra. "The Gospels even tells us a prostitute bathed his feet with her tears and had her sins forgiven."

"Surely you've lost any chance of Christ forgiving you. You haven't even any proof that you are a Christian, except your saying so now."

"I do not deserve to be called a Christian as you so rightly point out. But the mercy of God has allowed me the honor of the name."

"How do you know that he has shown you such mercy?"

"I know that I have not been cast off by God because I am being allowed now to confess his glorious name, through which I believe that I shall receive pardon for all my sins."

"Nonsense," said Cajus. "What do your sins matter? Better to obey the emperors, for safety's sake."

"My safety is Christ," said Afra, "who promised paradise to the thief who confessed him on the cross."

"Sacrifice or in the presence of your lovers, who have dealt with you in filth, I will order you beaten."

"I am not ashamed of anything except my sins," said Afra.

"Sacrifice to the gods!" ordered Cajus, then he groaned with exasperation. "I have already demeaned myself enough with this argument. If you will not sacrifice, I will have you executed."

"This is what I desire if I am worthy, so that I may come to eternal rest."

"Sacrifice, or you will be tortured and then burned alive."

Afra was unmoved. She answered calmly and confidently, "The body with which I have sinned will accept the torments, but I will not stain my soul with the sacrifices of the devil."

Not wishing to waste another breath on the matter, Cajus wrote out his sentence on a piece of paper and handed it to the bailiff, who read it aloud to the court: "Afra, public prostitute, who has professed herself a Christian and that she does not wish to offer sacrifice, is to be burned alive."

That same day, Afra was led to an island in the river that flowed through the city. There the soldiers stripped her and tied her to a stake. As the fire grew at her feet, Afra lifted up her eyes toward the heavens and prayed aloud, thanking God for her deliverance. The flames rose about her, lapping at her bare flesh, but in their midst a brighter light shone forth from her face. All who beheld it were first amazed and then afraid. They covered their eyes and turned away. Some called on Afra's God to spare them. Then, in an instant, she was gone.

# XXXII

The augustus Galerius was indeed dying, as the unfortunate Maximian had suspected. A fistular ulcer had opened up in his nether parts and slowly eaten its way through his bloated bowels, leaving the augustus a debilitated wretch, too weak to work, too gripped with pain to take pleasure in anything. Worst of all, the disease left him unable to control the daily flow of filth from his corrupted core, forcing him to change his apparel five or six times a day and filling his apartments with a most disgusting stench that lingered long after he had left them.

The physicians at court were powerless to arrest the ulcer's advance. Some paid for their failure with their lives. Others diagnosed the disease as a supernatural affliction, beyond their area of expertise. His wife, the empress Prisca, blamed a curse by the Christians, taking revenge upon her husband's body for his part in their eight-year persecution. Desperate for relief, Galerius himself assumed such a belief, and in the eighteenth year of his reign moved to end the persecution with an edict of pardon and grudging tolerance. The emperors Constantine and Licinius joined him in sponsoring the new law. The emperor Maximinus Daia, ruling over Syria and Egypt, declined to endorse it. The usurper Maxentius, holding sway over Italy and Africa, was not consulted. The edict declared:

> The Princeps Caesar Galerius Valerius Maximianus, Undefeated Augustus, Pontifex Maximus, Germanicus Maximus, Egyptiacus Maximus, Thebaicus Maximus, Sarmaticus Maximus five times, Persicus Maximus twice, Carpicus Maximus six times, Armeniacus Maximus, Medicus Maximus, Adiabenicus Maximus, Holder of the Tribunician Authority for the twentieth time, Imperator for the nineteenth, Consul for the eighth, Father of the Fatherland, Proconsul; the Princeps Caesar Flavius Valerius Constantinus, Blessed, Lucky, Undefeated Augustus, Pontifex Maximus, Holder of the Tribunician Authority, Imperator for the fifth time, Consul, Father of the Fatherland, Proconsul; and the Princeps Caesar Valerius Licinianus Licinius, Blessed, Lucky, Undefeated Augustus, Pontifex Maximus, Holder of the Tribunician Authority for the fourth time, Imperator for the third, Consul, Father of the Fatherland, Proconsul—to the people of their several provinces, greeting.

*Among the steps that we have taken for the advantage
and benefit of the commonwealth, we have desired hitherto
that every deficiency should be made good, in accordance
with the established law and public order of Rome; and
we made provision for this—that the Christians who had
abandoned the convictions of their own forefathers should
return to sound ideas. For through some perverse reasoning
such arrogance and folly had seized and possessed them that
they refused to follow the path trodden by earlier generations
(and perhaps blazed long ago by their own ancestors), and
made their own laws to suit their own ideas and individual
tastes and observed these; and held various meetings in
various places.*

*Consequently, when we issued an order to the effect
that they were to go back to the practices established by the
ancients, many of them found themselves in great danger,
and many were proceeded against and punished with death
in many forms. Most of them indeed persisted in the same
folly, and we saw that they were neither paying to the gods
in heaven the worship that is their due nor giving any honor
to the god of the Christians. So in view of our benevolence
and the established custom by which we invariably grant
pardon to all men, we have thought proper in this matter
also to extend our clemency most gladly, so that Christians
may again exist and rebuild the houses in which they used to
meet, on conditions that they do nothing contrary to public
order. Therefore, in view of this our clemency, they are in
duty bound to beseech their own god for our salvation, and
that of the commonwealth and of themselves, in order that in
every way the State may be preserved in health and they may
be able to live free from anxiety in their own homes.*

Galerius signed the edict on the last day of April in the city of Serdica,
Moesia, while en route to his birthplace at nearby Romulania. Five days
later he was dead.

The new law survived him, however, and was published throughout
Asia Minor and Europe, save Italy. At once the jails were opened and the
prisoners released. Great crowds gathered in cities and towns to celebrate
their long forbidden rites. The mines delivered up their near dead. Faithful
fugitives hiding in the hinterlands emerged into the light and started home.
The highways were crowded with long lines of jubilant refugees, singing as

they went, blessing everyone they passed, giving thanks for the generosity of strangers inspired by their joy.

Makrina was among the first to return, just as she had left, in the back of an oxcart, still dressed in the plain, simple clothes that Afra had given her, her shamefully short hair hidden beneath her palla. Rumbling along the main street into Sinope, through the gates and past the garrison, she was overwhelmed with an aching nostalgia. How pleasant this dreary little city seemed on this spring day, with its soot-choked chambers forcibly ventilated by the strong, cool sea-breeze!

Makrina looked about eagerly for people who might recognize her. One or two looked at her curiously, but none seemed to know for certain who she was. Neither did Makrina recognize them. She stopped the cart midway through town, thanked the driver, and climbed down, taking her little bundle of things with her. Her father's townhouse was not far, just down this alley and then that one. She found it easily and knocked on the door.

After a moment's wait, the door opened. "Yes?" said a young maidservant whom Makrina did not know.

Makrina was taken aback. She expected to be recognized at her own home and suddenly doubted where she was. Could things have changed so much? Could her memory have failed her? Could her house have passed already into other hands? Should she have written ahead to announce her coming?

"Can I help you?" said the girl.

Makrina fumbled for what to say. "I—Is this the house of Aristoboulos?"

"It is. Whom do you wish to see?"

"The Lady Hilaria."

"And you are?"

Makrina blinked. "Her daughter, Makrina," she answered.

The maid looked puzzled, but welcomed her into the vestibule and closed the door. "Wait here," she said as she left the room.

Makrina did not wait, but wandered slowly into the atrium and then the tablinum, looking all around. Everything was the same. Everything was as she remembered it—the walls, the tiles, the couches, even the carpets.

Her mother found her in the tablinum, just off the garden. "KRINA!" she cried rushing to her daughter with arms outstretched. "My Makrina!"

"Mamma!" cried Makrina.

They were both at once in tears and in each other's arms. "Dear Krina!" sobbed Hilaria. "Oh, where have you been? What has happened to you? What has happened to your hair? Oh my dear!"

"I had to cut it," Makrina answered through her tears.

"Oh, but you're home! You're home! And that's all that matters. Are you well?"

"I think so," said Makrina.

"Let me look at you," said Hilaria, studying Makrina's tear-streaked but smiling face. "Still beautiful. Still so beautiful." Hilaria succumbed again to tears and hugged her daughter tightly. "I can't believe it! To have you back! It's too much to have hoped for."

"Is Pappa home?" asked Makrina.

Hilaria shook her head. "He's gone to get Kimon."

"Where's Kimon?"

"Oh Kimon, poor Kimon. He was sent to the mines in Cilicia, but he should have been released by now, thank God. We thought you were dead, Makrina. Kimon found your ring in the mountains, among all those bones."

"My ring?"

"The one Marcus gave you."

"My ring. Kimon found it? But how did he end up in the mines?"

Hilaria shook her head. "I don't know," she said, "but he thought you were dead and he was angry and said things he shouldn't have to some official. He will have to explain it to us all when he returns. What a blessing! To have you both back at once!"

Kallista, Chione's mother, appeared in the tablinum. "Welcome home, Makrina," she said.

"Lady Kallista!" cried Makrina, moving from her mother's arms to Kallista's. "Chione? Is she here?" She looked around hopefully.

"No," said Kallista, wiping away her own tears. "She's in Cherson, but she'll be back for a visit soon. She's married now, with two little ones of her own."

"Chione, married? And a mother?" Makrina turned again to her mother. "What about Eugenia? Is she here?"

"No, dear," said her mother. "Eugenia—lives in the West now."

"Married?" Makrina wondered.

"Yes," said Hilaria, her smile suddenly fading. "She married Marcus."

"Marcus who?"

"Aemilius Canio," said Hilaria.

"My Marcus?" said Makrina.

Her mother nodded. "We all thought you were dead, Makrina. He waited for you for years. We'd sent Eugenia west with him for her safety. Then when Kimon found your ring and—"

"He waited?" said Makrina.

Hilaria nodded again. "He begged us to find you. Pappa and Kimon looked everywhere. They hired others to look also. All they found was the ring." She shook her head. "They were married just last year."

"Last year? He waited that long?" said Makrina. "Last year?" she muttered to herself. She looked at her mother, then at Kallista, then around the room. *Last year?* she wondered. *Where was I last year? Last year? Last . . . . .*

"Oh, dear!" cried Hilaria, seeing Makrina's eyes roll back into her head, just before she slumped into her mother's arms.

Makrina woke with a start, grabbing in panic at anything within reach before opening her eyes to find her mother by her side. "Mamma," she sighed with relief.

She was lying on a couch in the tablinum, attended by her mother, Chione's mother, and several servants. "It's all right, you're home now," said her mother.

"What happened?" Makrina asked, sitting up.

"You fainted," said her mother. "Probably weak from traveling. Have you eaten today? We've brought you water and wine and some pastries. You remember Vassa. And Nonna?"

Vassa smiled and bowed as best she could, holding the tray of pastries. "Be well, my lady," she said.

"Welcome back, little one," said Nonna.

Makrina's face brightened. "It's so good to see you both again," she said.

"This is Eulalia, who met you at the door."

Eulalia bowed and said, "Be well."

"Be well," said Makrina. She sat up slowly, and Hilaria sat down next to her, handing her a cup of water and wine. Makrina took a sip, then lowered the cup to her lap. Vassa offered her a pastry, which she took but did not eat.

"Nonna has also been away for awhile," said Hilaria. "She went west with Eugenia and has only just returned."

"Your little sister is all grown up now and doesn't need me anymore," said Nonna, with mock dismay. "She has made you an aunt, Makrina."

"Oh?"

"A baby girl, born last fall," said her mother. "They named her Makrina."

"They did?"

"Aemilia Theodora Makrina ," said her mother. "Theodora for the empress Theodora, widow of the emperor Constantius. Eugenia and Marcus live at the court of the emperor Constantine, Constantius's son."

"Theodora follows the Christian religion and has taken a special interest in Eugenia," said Nonna. "She even planned and paid for their wedding. They were married in the palace at Arelate in southern Gaul. The king himself attended. It was so beautiful."

"It was indeed," said Hilaria.

"You were there?"

"Oh, yes," said Hilaria. "Your father wasn't. He was still trying to arrange Kimon's release at the time. I arrived just in time for the wedding and stayed until the baby was born. Theodora's a wonderful woman. They are very fortunate to have her as their patron."

"How is Chione?" Makrina asked.

Kallista sat down beside her, more than pleased to tell about her own daughter. "She married the son of a Chersonese senator, a very wealthy man and a Christian, too. They live in a villa high on a hill overlooking the sea. It's very different there, you know, much dryer and not as green, but a pleasant place. I'm sure she'll want you to visit soon."

"But she's coming here, you said."

Kallista nodded. "Within the week, and bringing her two little babes, two boys, Lauros and Euplios."

"Euplios?"

Kallista nodded. "After my own Euplios, whose memory is always with us," she said.

"How is your husband, Posidonios? I was always fond of him," said Makrina.

Kallista laughed. "He was fond of you, too, and I was sometimes jealous. He is fine. Your father saved us from losing everything under the edicts. We have much to be thankful for."

"We all have," said Hilaria. "I still can't believe that you're here again with us. We've missed you so much. When Kimon returns, my joy will be complete."

Hilaria wiped a sudden tear from her eyes and then recovered. The servants retreated from the room, leaving the three women on the couch.

"How is Kimon, Mamma? Are you sure he's all right?" asked Makrina.

"He was, the last we heard, just a month ago," said Hilaria. "Your father had won his freedom, but can you believe he turned it down? He wouldn't leave that awful place, even to spare his poor mother grief. Said he'd found something there he couldn't find elsewhere. I think he has joined your faith, Makrina."

"Kimon?"

"Yes, I believe so," said Hilaria. "I'm not surprised. You know your brother. Your father surprised me more."

"Pappa?"

"Not a Christian," said Hilaria, "but when Kimon wouldn't leave the mines, your father said he hadn't expected him to and was actually proud that he wouldn't, even after all the trouble it was to win his freedom. That, I don't understand. I think perhaps he was so frustrated with the imperial bureaucracy that he took some satisfaction in seeing it defied. Things are much different in the West under Constantine."

"It's a shame he doesn't rule all the empire," said Kallista.

"Someday perhaps he shall," said Hilaria. "I was very favorably impressed by him. Marcus thinks very highly of him, too. He has done very well for himself under Constantine, even without Theodora's help. He's the commander of the imperial guards, personally responsible for the emperor's safety. As a wedding present, Constantine gave Marcus an estate on the coast, near Massalia."

Hilaria noticed Makrina staring off into the distance, still holding her cup and her uneaten pastry in her lap. She looked much older than her years. Her face and neck had already lost the softness of youth. Her features had hardened. Her eyes appeared somewhat sunken. She coughed suddenly, unable to cover her mouth in time.

Hilaria raised her hand and caressed the little that was left of her daughter's hair. Makrina looked at her and smiled briefly, then looked away.

"I had better go," said Kallista, rising from the couch. "It's a great joy to have you back, Makrina. You are a blessing to us all. Chione will be thrilled to see you again."

She bent down and kissed Makrina on her forehead, then said her farewells and went her way.

"You should see the house, Makrina. It will do you good to feel at home," said Hilaria.

"Yes, it will," replied Makrina.

They toured the house for an hour or more, arm in arm, with many smiles between them, as well as an occasional tear. Very little had changed. Her bedroom was much as she had left it, except for the loss of her clothes chests, which had been sent to her in the mountains.

"We'll have to find you something pretty and festive to wear," said her mother gleefully.

The tour ended in their private bath, a small but beautifully tiled pool at the back of the house, with a little window overlooking the bay. Makrina could remember lounging in the warm pool for what seemed like hours in the past, but this time she didn't think to stay any longer than necessary. One difference she did notice was how wide and rough her feet looked upon the painted tiles. They were once so dainty that she could feel the texture of the tiles' painted surface. Now she could feel almost nothing.

Her mother brought her warm towels and new clothes, all made of silk and some borrowed from Demetra, the mayor's young wife. The uppermost garment was a peach-colored colobium, a loose-fitting, ankle-length tunic with short sleeves and creamy green stripes down both sides. Over it, Hilaria draped one of her own pallas of soft Ankyra wool, just the right weight for the cool spring evening.

After the bath came an early dinner in the triclinium. It had been a long time since Makrina had reclined to eat, and at first it seemed to her somehow indecent to do so. She couldn't say why, but sitting seemed more appropriate, if less relaxed. Perhaps because it was less relaxed.

Hilaria noticed that her dinner manners had slipped. Makrina ate quickly and ravenously, more out of habit than hunger. Hilaria let it pass on the first day, but later she felt compelled to advise Makrina to slow down and take greater care with her food.

After dinner, they sat on the upstairs balcony, waiting for the sun to set over the hills to the west. Makrina told her mother of her travails, just as she had told Afra a few weeks before, with significant omissions. They talked late into the night, long after the sunset, just the two of them, sitting in the dark over the harbor. There were many questions Hilaria wanted to ask, and many that she did ask. There was one question she did not dare ask, and Makrina did not volunteer its answer.

That night Makrina lay down in her own bed for the first time in seven years. It seemed, however, as strange a place as any other, the shell of her former life in a world no longer hers.

Chione arrived by boat from Cherson two days later and rushed over to see Makrina as soon as she heard the news. They met with hugs and tears and kisses, then quickly departed together for Chione's parents' house to show off her two little boys. Hilaria joined them later, and they stayed the whole day, including dinner. It was the happiest day Makrina had known in many, many years. Her mother even saw her laugh for the first time since her return.

But Hilaria also noticed the contrast between the two close friends sitting together, arm in arm, babies playing at their feet. Chione's hair was long and lustrous; Makrina's was unevenly and unnaturally short. Chione looked healthy, youthful, and gay; Makrina seemed weary of life and somehow sad, even amid the mirth, and was bothered by a persistent cough.

Makrina was at Chione's again the following afternoon when her mother sent word that her father was back, but without Kimon. "All I know is that he left with the other Christians and was nowhere to be found," Aristoboulos told Hilaria. Makrina hurried home at once and found him waiting at the door for her, already wiping his weary, teary eyes. She had never seen him weep.

Choked with emotion, he hardly said a word more than her name, as he held her tightly and kissed her head. "Dear Krina, dear Krina," he whispered.

Her father had changed, Makrina noticed. He looked much older, a little shorter, and not as strong as he always had. The years of worry and work had taken their toll. She had planned to tell him everything, knowing he would understand and would need to know to be prepared, but when she saw how diminished he was she changed her mind to spare him the burden. Neither her father nor her mother seemed to know anything about her crime, and it was easier on everyone to leave it that way.

It was a season for tearful greetings. Other fugitives were returning daily to Sinope. Many came by boat from across the sea, including the reader Andreas and his wife Theodoulia, with her mother Elena and their several children. Simon, the son of Bardas, returned again from Cherson, but only for a visit, for like Chione, he had already made a life for his family in their new land.

Theodoros, the former city clerk, walked in from the hills, where he had hid alone, surprisingly close to the city. He was a curious sight for those who saw him striding triumphantly into town, a little, bald man with a long, fierce beard beginning to grey, wielding in his right hand a heavy oaken staff a foot taller than he was.

The lapsed who had remained in town greeted the returnees with honor and repentance, while those who had held fast generously pardoned their weaker brethren. Both were joyed, above all, to see that the other had survived. Together, the congregation of Christians in Sinope quickly swelled to a size exceeding its strength before the persecution. For a while, at least, no one stayed away from the now permitted public services or neglected the feasts, fasts, and vigils.

Makrina attended services often with Chione, but whereas Chione stood with the mothers of infants in a side aisle of the rented basilica, Makrina kept to the back with the visitors and those under discipline. Friends often urged her to join the young women closer to the front, but she always declined. People began to wonder, and then to talk. Everyone had heard Makrina's story. Chione enjoyed telling it. But the story did not explain Makrina's reserve. Confessors like Makrina, having suffered for the faith and not denied it, held a place of honor in the Assembly. Why, people wondered, did Makrina not take it? And what kept her from the cup? Why did she not partake of the Thanksgiving?

"You're a champion, Makrina. A saint. An example for us all," Chione told her.

"I don't feel like a champion or a saint, Chione. I feel like a sinner, and I know I am one. If I've learned anything from my years away, it's how far I fall short. I'm not worthy, Chione, and never have been."

Weeks passed without word from Kimon. Aristoboulos was worried and restless. There was nothing he could do. While Kimon was in the mines, Aristoboulos had kept busy working for his release. Now he was completely helpless, and it caused him great impatience.

Hilaria never doubted that Kimon would return. Hadn't Makrina? But Hilaria was concerned for her husband and tried her best to comfort him. The only sure way was to keep Makrina close by his side. Even if they didn't speak, the presence of the other seemed to soothe them both.

One evening before the springtime sunset, while all three were lingering in the triclinium after dinner, Hilaria said, "Remember when you used to sing to us, Makrina? You used to love to sing? Why did you ever stop?"

Makrina shrugged her shoulders. "I grew up, I guess," she said.

"I used to sing to your father when we were first married, before Kimon was born. Don't you remember, Aristo?"

Aristoboulos grunted distractedly.

"I wonder if I still can," said Hilaria. "Eulalia, bring me my lyre," she ordered.

Eulalia delivered the lyre to her mistress, who tested each string for proper tuning before attempting a song. When satisfied, she struck a melancholy chord, then joined to it her voice:

> *A vine that grows on barren ground*
> *Never rises nor bears cluster.*
> *Untilled by caring hands, it dies,*
> *Its dry leaves lose their luster.*
>
> *But marry the vine to a sturdy elm,*
> *It bears its full sweet treasure.*
> *So then a maiden married as well*
> *Bears life in love and pleasure.*

She paused in her performance and turned to her husband, who smiled at last. "Catullus," he said.

"You do remember," said Hilaria, quite pleased. She struck another chord, then stopped. "How does it go?" she asked.

"A flower blooms in a secret plot," said Makrina.

"That's right," said Hilaria. "Why don't you try it, Makrina?"

"Oh, no, Mamma. It's been so long," Makrina protested.

"Go ahead. You can't have forgotten how to sing. We'd love to hear you," said her mother, handing her daughter the lyre.

Makrina cradled the lyre in her lap and struck the same melancholy chord. She sang hesitantly, in a voice less confident than her mother's:

> *A flower blooms in a secret plot,*
> *Many fair youths do desire it,*
> *But when its blossom fades with age,*
> *No boy or girl can love it.*

*So then a maid untouched and dear,*
*By time her beauty wasted,*
*No boy will then enjoy her charms,*
*No girl can call her blessed.*

She stopped and looked at her mother and then her father. "I can't remember anymore," she said.

She handed the lyre back to Hilaria, who sat down next to her, just in time to catch her daughter's first tear. Makrina hid her face on her mother's shoulder and wept quietly. "My poor, poor dear," said Hilaria, holding her daughter in her arms. "My poor dear Makrina."

There was a knock at the front door. Aristoboulos sat up at once.

"It's Master Kimon!" cried Eulalia from the vestibule.

Aristoboulos hurried off, with Hilaria and Makrina behind him. Kimon met his father in the tablinum. "Pappa! Kimon!" they exclaimed at once, clasping each other in arms. "Kimon, my son! Where have you been?"

"Kimon!" cried Hilaria.

"Mamma!" cried Kimon, putting an arm around her and receiving her kiss.

"Where have you been? We've been so worried," said his mother.

Kimon was bronzed and gaunt, but his clothes at least were clean and in repair, although hardly fancy. His head was balder than Makrina's, and his beard was thick and long and graying already. "I stopped for a bath," he said. "You wouldn't have wanted me home without one, would you have?"

"But all these weeks! Where were you?" said his mother.

"It's a long walk from Cilicia, Mamma," said Kimon.

"I could have spared you the walk if you had waited for me," said Aristoboulos.

"I'm sorry, Pappa. I was with friends and wasn't thinking. Please forgive me," said Kimon.

"With friends, of course," said his father.

"Of course," said his mother, hugging him tightly.

Kimon looked up and glanced at Makrina, without at first recognizing her. Then he looked again. *Who is this?* he thought, studying her hair and her features in the waning light. *Can it be? No!*

Makrina smiled. "Don't you know me, Kimon? Brother?" she said.

Kimon's mouth fell open. "My God," he gasped. "Is it really you?"

Makrina nodded and held out her arms. "Welcome back," she said.

They embraced and kissed and wiped each other's tears. Then they felt each other's shorn pates playfully and laughed despite themselves. "We're twins, you and I," said Kimon. "Twins in the faith."

Makrina, still crying, said, "But can you ever forgive me, for all the trouble I've caused you, Kimon?"

"Forgive you for what, Makrina? For showing me the way?" said Kimon. "Forgive me for not following you sooner. I might have spared us both a lot of pain if I had."

"Oh, Kimon, I love you," said Makrina, hugging him tightly. Then she turned to her parents, taking each by the hand. "Mamma, Pappa," she said, kneeling before them. "Please forgive me. Please forgive me for everything."

They were both too choked to reply at first. "We," her father began with difficulty, "We forgive you, Makrina."

"We love you," said her mother. "Please forgive us."

Makrina kissed their hands and held them to her cheek. "I do," she said. "I do."

# XXXIII

"What did he say?" asked Vitalis.

Marcus threw his map case down on his desk. "In a word—no," he answered.

"Did he give you a reason?"

"The usual ones, the ones I can't argue against, even if I could argue with him. I'm doing a superb job. He's lucky to have me. The empresses like me and trust me. I'm such a fixture in the palace it wouldn't be the same without me. There's no one to take my place, no one he would trust as much. I suppose it could all be true, but I'm sure he has other reasons."

"Such as?"

"Such as—he doesn't want to move against Maxentius next spring with legion commanders who haven't proven their mettle as legion commanders, and he won't take a chance with me."

"What makes you think that?"

Marcus shrugged. "It makes sense. It's what I would do if I were the emperor. He did say that he thought I could serve him better commanding cavalry than commanding infantry. I don't know where he got that idea. Probably from Gratianus."

Marcus poured himself a cup of water and drank it down. "So that's that, at least for now," he said. "I know you're as anxious to get back to troops as I am, Vitalis. I won't keep you any longer. You need the experience."

"Are you sure, sir? If you need me here, I'd gladly stay. I owe it to you."

"Of course I need you, but you're not staying. The legions need talent and you need time with troops. There's an opening for a tribune with VIII Augusta at Lugudunum. If you want it, it's yours."

"I'll take it."

"Think about it for a few days. You might find something else, although the VIII Augusta should put you in the thick of things next spring."

"I'll think about. Thank you, sir, for everything."

With a nod from his lord, Vitalis saluted and left.

He was no sooner out the door than the Lady Canio burst in, beaming with joy, her little babe riding on one arm. "Marcus!" she cried, holding up a piece of parchment. "She's alive! She's alive! Makrina is alive! It was all a mistake! She didn't die after all! She's alive!"

"Macrina?" he said, glancing confusedly at the smiling tot.

"My sister Makrina!" cried Eugenia. "She's alive and she's home now!"

"Alive?" said Marcus. "But how? What about the ring?"

"She had lent it to a friend!—Oh dear, a friend who died," said Eugenia, crossing herself quickly. "But Makrina survived and now she's home! It's all here in Mamma's letter. Look, Makrina even adds her own greeting! Oh, oh, I can't wait to see her again!"

Marcus took the letter and began to read, finding his seat at his desk, while his young wife whirled around the room ecstatically and the baby squealed with delight. "She lives! She lives! Praise God, your auntie lives! Oh, we must go tell Theodora. Come, little Krina. Oh, what will we call you now, now that your Auntie Makrina still lives? Let's go tell the empress."

Eugenia departed as suddenly as she had come, leaving Marcus alone with the letter. He read it slowly, barely able to concentrate and hardly believing his eyes. There, midway down the page, were several lines of fond, familiar script, which Marcus could not help but recognize:

> *Peace, joy, and love to my dear sister Eugenia and my beloved brother Marcus, from your devoted sister Makrina. I thank you both for your faithfulness to me while you believed that I still lived, and I pray that you may know only joy together in our Lord Jesus Christ. May God the Father bless you and keep you, and your little one, until the day of our reunion. Amen.*

He read her words over and over again. He ran his fingertips tenderly along the lines, knowing that her hand had touched the same surface. He even held the letter to his nose briefly, hoping to catch her scent. Then he sighed heavily and whispered aloud, trembling, "My God, how can this be? How can this have happened?"

Marcus had not thought of Makrina in years. Even before hearing that she was dead, he had shut her out of his mind. It was the only way he could get by, with everything else that his life had demanded. He had not quite given up on the dream of seeing her again, but as time passed other dreams had developed, offering greater hope of fulfillment. Eugenia had slowly stolen away his thoughts. Then, after hearing that Makrina was dead, Marcus had laid all his dreams of her to rest.

Now the grave was open, and the memories poured forth from it with surprising freshness and life. Marcus was overwhelmed. Dazed by recollection, he was unable to think of anything but Makrina. He sat for more than an hour, barely moving, turning the images in his mind around and around, studying their depth, their dearness, and their danger.

When Eugenia returned to rejoice some more in his presence, Marcus struggled to hide his distraction, forcing a smile and a laugh. Why should he not rejoice? he wondered. A woman he still loved was found alive and well. Still loved? Did he still love her? But how? How could he still love her?

That evening they were dining in the palace with several other high-ranking officers and their wives. Eugenia told them the whole story—Makrina's jilting of Marcus, her flight to the mountains, the news of her death, and then her sudden reappearance.

When she had finished, Bassianus, commander of the Shieldmen, asked the obvious question: "Does this mean that Marcus married the wrong sister?"

Olympia, the wife of Ablabius, was horrified. "What an awful thing to say," she huffed.

Eugenia was surprised and embarrassed, but Marcus tried to treat the jest lightly. "It all happened a very long time ago," he said.

Later as he was walking his young wife back to her rooms, she asked him bluntly, "You don't really wish you had waited for Makrina, do you?"

Marcus laughed, perhaps a little too easily. "God meant me to marry you. That's how it happened, and I have no regrets," he said.

Eugenia was pleased. "That's what I needed to hear," she said. Then she kissed him passionately on the lips. She might have invited him in for the night, but she was already six months pregnant and it was not thought proper. The kiss would have to do.

Marcus strolled back to his own rooms relieved and amused. It was certainly a shock, he thought, to find that Makrina was still alive, but nothing much to worry about. He loved Eugenia deeply and could hardly complain about their life together. She was a devoted wife, a loving mother, a beautiful and charming presence in the palace, who only added to his esteem among the men and women at court. He was proud to have her as his wife, even if she wasn't the shrewdest of women, even if her slowness did cause occasional embarrassment. That was just part of her charm.

The next day he went about his duties as if nothing had changed. More than once the memory of Makrina crept back into his thoughts, but he did not let it stay. He managed that way for several more days, relying upon his mental discipline to keep himself from slipping.

Then one morning he awoke in distress. He had dreamed he was making love to his wife. He was sure it was Eugenia at first, but he was just as sure later that it was Makrina. It was Makrina's lips he kissed, Makrina's breasts he caressed, Makrina's smooth white thighs that welcomed him. Marcus was ashamed but also enthralled by the experience, which seemed all too real even after he awoke. Makrina's naked image haunted him all day, but instead of steering his mind clear of it, he dwelt upon it longingly.

The next night he did not wait for the dream to return on its own. Instead, he lay awake alone in his bed, imaging what it would have been like to make love to Makrina. He knew it was wrong, but it was such a delicious delusion he could not resist. Perhaps, he reasoned, if he just satisfied the fantasy it would go away.

It did not go away. It grew. It flourished in his imagination. It made him question the way things had happened. He had come so close. He had waited so long. One more year and he would have had her. He would have waited one more year if Kimon had not found her ring and assumed that she had died. "Kimon, you idiot!" Marcus swore late at night, alone in his room after too much wine. "How could you make such a mistake? How could you be so stupid?" He did not just blame Kimon; he blamed himself. His own faithlessness had cost him Makrina. If only he had been more patient and less prideful!

A week after hearing the news about Makrina, Marcus was still bedeviled by such thoughts. He kept expecting them to fade away, but they only worsened. He did his best to hide them from Eugenia, but they had cast her in a different light. All her faults appeared before him—her flightiness, her vanity, her lack of discipline, her selfish demands on his attention. He had known about them all along, but they had never annoyed him as much as now. *When will this woman leave me alone? Can't she see I have work to do? Does she not have enough to keep her busy? Has she never thought of reading a book?*

His frustrations came perilously close to coming out just once, in a fight between them, the worst fight they had ever had.

Titus, Marcus's secretary, had asked to return to Mogontiacum for good. Marcus could not refuse him. Titus had been a faithful servant, but he had felt more and more out of place after Marcus married Eugenia.

In Titus's absence, Eugenia conceived an ambition to take over management of the household finances. It was a sudden enthusiasm, which she saw as confirming her new status as the Lady Canio. Marcus was not sure she was up to the task, but she pleaded with him so persistently that he finally gave her what she wanted.

Eager to prove herself, she combed the accounts, questioning every expenditure. One day she came to him with the balance book in hand. "What's this?" she asked, in the strange, unfeminine, officious tone she now assumed whenever speaking of their estate. "Fifteen hundred denarii per month to Pollentia? Who's Pollentia?"

"She was my housekeeper in Mogontiacum," Marcus answered, already on edge.

"Your housekeeper? I don't remember anyone named Pollentia in Mogontiacum."

"She left before you arrived."

"Why are we still paying her then?"

"She needs the money."

"I don't understand," said Eugenia. "If she needs the money, why did she leave your employ, and why can't she work for someone else?"

"I had to let her go, and to make it easier on her I offered to continue paying part of her salary."

"Fifteen hundred denarii a month? Marcus, you couldn't have been paying her more than that as a housekeeper."

"I give her more now because I can afford to."

"But this is far too much. It's enough for three housekeepers to live on, and she's not doing anything to earn it. I'll have to cut it back. If she's well employed now, we need to cut her off."

"No," said Marcus sternly. "Leave it as it is."

"But why?"

"Because I said so."

Eugenia's eyes widened and her face turned red. She pressed her lips together and drew in a deep breath, then expelled it. "I—You —" She was flustered. "This is not right," she said. "It's a waste of money. It's—irresponsible."

"We can afford it."

"That's not the point," said Eugenia. "This is no way to spend money. She's being way overpaid for doing nothing. Nothing, Marcus. I say we should cut it back."

"I said no," said Marcus.

"Who's doing the books now, you or me? They are *my* responsibility, and I say we should cut it back."

"It stays the same."

"I'm cutting it back."

"No, you're not. If you won't do as I say, I'll find somebody else to keep the books."

"You just don't think I can do it, do you? You don't think I'm smart enough. Here I've found something wrong, and you just don't want to admit it."

"I'm letting you keep the books. I'm letting you keep them as long as you do what I say."

"What *you* say! Always what *you* say! You just don't trust me."

"I thought I could trust you, but now I'm not so sure."

"What do you mean by that?"

"If you won't do as I say, how can I trust you?"

"How can I trust *you*?! Who was this Pollentia anyway? Was she your mistress?!"

Marcus snatched the account book out of Eugenia's hand. "Is that what this is all about?" he said. "Do you think I'm just paying her off to keep her away?"

"Are you?"

"No! She was my housekeeper!"

"At fifteen hundred a month?"

"I've had enough," said Marcus, starting for the door. "I have work to do. I'll be at the barracks."

Eugenia started after him, entering the long corridor outside his office. "Wait! I'm not finished!" she cried.

"I am!" he declared, striding down the marble hallway without looking back. Servants ducked quickly out of sight. The guards in the hallway stood stone-faced and still.

Eugenia hurried by his side, struggling to keep up. "You wouldn't treat Makrina this way! Oh, no. Makrina was smart. Makrina could figure. As if I can't. Do you wish you had married her now, Marcus? Do you? If you had, at least, you wouldn't have little Eugenia to embarrass you at court, would you? That's what this is all about! You wish you had married Makrina! Isn't it, Marcus? Isn't it?!"

Marcus stopped suddenly, grabbed Eugenia by the arm, and flung her to the floor at the feet of a surprised guard. "Take her to her quarters!" Marcus bellowed.

The guard tried to help her stand, but she fought him off. "Don't touch me!" she screamed, starting off again after Marcus. Before she had gone three paces, he stopped again and turned, blocking her way.

"Go now to your quarters or I will have him carry you!" he ordered.

"You wouldn't dare!" she hissed.

Marcus laid a hand on her chest and shoved her backward, into the arms of the guard. "Take her!" he yelled.

The reluctant guard grabbed her around the waist while two more rushed to assist him at Marcus's direction. "Put me down!" Eugenia cried. "Put me down, I'm pregnant! Tell them to put me down, Marcus! Tell them, Marcus! Marcus! *MARCUS!*"

The next day Marcus received a dreadful summons—from the Empress Theodora. "See me immediately," said the handwritten note.

He found the empress on a porch of the palace overlooking the city and the river, shielding herself from the morning sun with a gayly painted parasol imported from the Far East. Olympia and Theodora's daughters, Constantia and Anastasia, were with her, but she sent them away when Marcus appeared. "Health to you, my lady," he said in greeting.

"Health to you, Canio," she answered coldly. "How was your night?" she asked.

Marcus hesitated. "Restless," he answered.

"Good," she said. "Your young wife slept not at all, although I believe by now she has succumbed to fatigue. Pray that the babe is not endangered. Did you forget that she is with child?"

"No, my lady."

"Then what possessed you to behave so cruelly?"

He tried to think of an answer. "I . . ."

"Don't bother," said Theodora. "I have no intention of adjudicating disputes between all of the little girls and boys at court. I do have other interests, however. How you manage your finances is your business, Canio, but if I were you I would find someone else to look after them. Eugenia is much too young and inexperienced. She might make such a mess of things you'd never straighten them out. You should know that."

"Yes, my lady."

"How you manage your wife is another matter. This is the imperial palace, the seat of all government, the summit of all earthly dignity—and you have disturbed everyone in it with your childish little squabble. As a Christian, Canio, you are duty bound to love your wife, as she is duty bound to obey you. Whatever disagreements that may occur must be handled peacefully, and lovingly on your part. That does not mean giving her always what she wants. She is still just a girl, not even twenty. Don't spoil her. Be firm. But, for God's sake, Canio, being firm shouldn't require armed assistance. I will not stand for having ladies-in-waiting manhandled by palace guards. It was shameful and an affront to all decency, especially in her condition. It must never happen again."

"Yes, my lady."

"One more matter. I know about her sister. I know you were once in love with her sister and waited many years to marry her. I do not know whether your feelings for her sister played any part in this, but hear me now, Canio: If you hurt Eugenia, if you break her heart, I will ruin you. Do you hear me?"

"Yes, my lady."

"I will ruin you. Your career will be over. You will be finished. You will disappear. Is that understood?"

"Yes, my lady."

Theodora looked away, off down the river. "Go now, but promise me an end to this discord, and seal it with your kiss," she said, raising the silver hem of her purple palla.

Marcus pressed the hem to his lips. "I promise," he said.

Marcus did not return to duty that day. Instead, he brooded an hour or more in his quarters, trying to figure a way out of his melancholy. What could rid him of his regret? Who could drive this phantom female out of his heart? He called it Makrina, but he was not sure now that it was really her. It had been years—eight years—since he had actually seen her. Was it

Makrina or Sulpicia that his mind imagined? Whom was he dreaming of? What was he seeing?

Later that afternoon, he went to see Hosius and confessed everything to him—the dream, the fantasies, the anger, and the regret.

"I would never have believed it possible," he told the overseer. "She had been so long out of my mind, I thought I was free of her memory. But when I heard that she was alive, it was as if I had opened a box and found in it the same young girl I left so long ago, perfectly preserved, just waiting for me to find her."

"Is she still that same young girl you knew, after all these years?" Hosius asked.

"Is she?" said Marcus, not understanding.

"Is the real woman, the woman living now at home in Sinope? Is she the same young girl after all that has happened, to her, to you, to the world?"

"I doubt it," Marcus answered.

Hosius nodded. "Your fond memories will be with you always, and I am not surprised by their revival, considering the circumstances. The memories themselves are nothing to fear, but from what you have told me, your fantasies and dreams have gone well beyond what you actually knew of her. Is that not so?"

"That is so. I never knew her intimately."

"Do not confuse the woman you knew with what your mind has made from her. Your imagination is the servant of your desires. It has made her into someone else, someone she is not now and never was, someone to satisfy a longing within you, a longing no mortal woman can ever fully satisfy, not even your dear Eugenia. It is a longing for the unfallen Eve, the perfect and utterly faithful, utterly desirable mate. This is what all men and women seek in their mate and often think they have found, at least for a while, until they learn better. All they ever find in the fallen world are approximations, husbands and wives who may perhaps come close but in many ways fall short of the glory that God intended for the man and the woman. Don't be ashamed of the longing, Marcus; it's part of being a man. But don't be fooled into thinking the longing can be satisfied. It never can completely. And don't let it spoil the joy you *can* find in Eugenia."

"It seems already to have done so," said Marcus.

"That need not be the case," said Hosius. "What haunts you now is not a memory. It is a deceit. It is a phantom, at least partly of your own creation, but, I would guess, also the work of the Evil One or one of his many minions, who has caught you unaware and taken advantage of your longing to sow discontent and discord."

"A demon?"

"Perhaps. The devil is a ravening lion, seeking whom he may devour. The easiest are the unwary."

"What am I to do?"

"Fast and pray. Confess your sins and ask God to forgive them. And open your eyes, Marcus, to the truth of who you are as a servant of God. If God had intended you to marry the sister, you would have married the sister. Instead, He sent the sister to bring you to Eugenia. What is more, He sent the sister to bring you to Christ, at least to start you along the way. The sister was the forerunner, like the Prophet John, a voice crying in the wilderness. The wilderness was your heart, Marcus, which has since opened unto the Lord. Eugenia, too, has had a part in this, for it was she who walked willingly into that wilderness and watered the seeds of faith. This, the sister could not do. Only Eugenia could, and only then because God had appointed her to that task. She is your wife, your flesh and bone, your very own body."

Marcus smiled. "I love her dearly," he said.

"Of course you do," said Hosius. "You have already made your confession. Let us pray now."

Marcus knelt while Hosius stood and placed his hands on Marcus's bowed head. He prayed briefly on Marcus's behalf. Then he raised Marcus to his feet and said, "Go in peace, and know that God has forgiven you."

Marcus left Hosius feeling as if he had just awaken from a nightmare. By the grace of God, the spell was broken. He knew it at once. His regrets were gone. The phantom female had fled, freeing his imagination from its seductive grip. He saw Makrina now through the light of faith, as a dear though distant sister in Christ, a fellow soldier and sufferer, a joint heir to the promise of salvation.

He found Eugenia in her apartment, nursing their child in the company of a maidservant. Her eyes were swollen and weary. Her hair was out of place. Her clothes were wrinkled from the day before. The baby at her breast, whom they had already started calling Theodora instead of Macrina, was still suckling but seemed nearly asleep.

"I've come to ask your forgiveness," he said.

Eugenia's expression changed from apprehension to surprise. She broke the baby's hold on her breast and handed the child to the maidservant, who laid the baby down to sleep in a crib nearby. Eugenia stood up and straightened her clothes. The maidservant left the room.

"I'm sorry about the guards," Marcus began. "I shouldn't have treated you that way. I was angry and I shouldn't have been."

"I forgive you," said Eugenia weakly.

"I also owe you an explanation for the money," he said. "Pollentia was indeed my housekeeper, and she still cares for another woman who was also once a servant of mine—a slave girl, a Frank taken in battle before I brought you west, even before my father died. I took advantage of the girl, and she conceived and bore a daughter. The money is for them."

Eugenia's expression hardened.

"I was so ashamed, I didn't know how to tell you, Genia," said Marcus. "It was a long time ago. I was not the man I am now. I have never seen the child, and the mother has since married a soldier. Pollentia just makes sure they have all they need."

"You were never married?"

"No, of course not."

"You didn't love her?"

"No," said Marcus, shaking his head. "I never loved her. That's part of the shame of it. . . . I have only ever really loved Makrina—and now you."

Marcus could see Eugenia's eyes begin to glisten. "Do you love me as much as you loved Makrina," she said.

"More so, Genia," he said. "So much more so. I know you. I didn't really know Makrina. You are my wife, the only woman God meant for me. I know that now."

Eugenia tearfully lifted her arms and wrapped them around Marcus's neck. "Oh, Marcus," she sobbed, pressing her head against his chest and holding him tightly. "I love you, too. Please forgive me, for everything I said. I didn't mean any of it. I'm so sorry."

"I forgive you," he said, kissing her hair.

"I should never have asked to keep the books. Theodora made me promise to give them back."

"She made me promise never to break your heart."

"You would never do that," said Eugenia without looking up.

"No, I will never do that," said Marcus. "You are my very body, Genia. Bone of my bone, flesh of my flesh. Where you are Eve, I am Adam."

Eugenia looked up at him and smiled. "Where you are Adam, I am Eve," she said.

They kissed and held each other a while longer. Then when Marcus started to leave, Eugenia held him back.

"Make love to me, Marcus. Right now. Please?"

# XXXIV

The Emperor Maximinus Daia was prepared for Galerius's death. When the news arrived at his capital, Antioch in Syria, he moved swiftly with six legions through Cilicia, Cappadocia, and Galatia, arriving in Nicomedia in just two weeks. The legions throughout Asia Minor, formerly under Galerius's control, quickly swore allegiance to Daia. With Egypt, Palestine, Syria, and northern Mesopotamia also in his possession, Daia now controlled half of the empire's wealth.

Licinius, whom Galerius had intended to take over as the senior augustus, was now at a disadvantage. The provinces under his control in the mountains north of Greece were the poorest in the empire, able to support barely half as many legions as were under Daia's command. Licinius had no choice but to concede Asia Minor to Daia. In exchange for recognizing the waterway of Propontis as the border between them, Licinius received from Daia a promise of regular shipments of grain from Egypt, the empire's breadbasket.

To lessen his dependence on Daia, whom he did not trust, Licinius allied himself with Constantine against Maxentius, who still controlled Italy and Africa. To seal the alliance, Constantine promised his half-sister, Theodora's eldest daughter Constantia, in marriage to Licinius. Then, after easily and bloodlessly bringing Spain back under his authority, Constantine was ready for his march on Rome.

The maneuvering of emperors made little difference in Sinope. Daia's assumption of authority over Asia Minor at first raised fears among the Christians of renewed persecution. He had been severe in enforcing the persecution and had refused to join Galerius, Licinius, and Constantine in the edict ending it, but after settling himself in Nicomedia, he issued instructions through Sabinus, his praetorian prefect, directing local officials to abide by the new edict.

In Sinope, the most pressing matters were closer to home. The joy of reunion had given way to a difficult readjustment between the faithful and the lapsed. The fiercest contention arose over the question of who should succeed the executed overseer, the martyr Archelaos. The elder Philippos had been acting in his stead since the persecution began. He himself had never sacrificed, having escaped on account of his confusion with the reader Philippos, but he was faulted by the faithful for having gone along with the surrender of the Gospel books. The lapsed, however, were comfortable with his headship and saw no reason to replace him.

The chief critic of Philippos and principal candidate of the faithful was

Theodoros, Kimon's friend and former city clerk. Always intense but once shy and studious, he had returned from his trials with a fire for the faith and now boldly proclaimed the need for repentance and reform. He had many supporters among the faithful, and even some among the lapsed, including the lapsed server Eustratios, who had assisted Kimon in his search for Makrina. But Theodoros frightened many of the lapsed and was strongly opposed by Posidonios, Chione's father, who was generally viewed as the leader of the party of Philippos.

The reader Andreas, who had suffered as much as most, was put forward as a compromise candidate, a confessor whom nobody feared, but Andreas had a wife and children and declined in favor of Theodoros. No other alternatives could be found.

There were angry debates outside the new basilica, which was paid for largely by the lapsed. Both parties came together for the accustomed worship, but relations between them were strained and the essential unity of spirit was sorely lacking.

The conflict came to a head when Philippos tried to discipline Theodoulia, Andreas's wife, for her part in a factious argument that broke out among the women over responsibilities for the September feast in honor of Phokas, who was martyred under the Emperor Trajan, two centuries earlier. The outraged Theodoros complained to Philippos in private. When Philippos stood his ground, Theodoros called for a public protest, a silent but sensational demonstration of disunity. When the time came for the sharing of the bread and wine in the weekly Thanksgiving, the party of the faithful held back and refused to take part in the Thanksgiving.

The congregation was scandalized. There were calls for counter-protests and expulsions from the Assembly, which provoked threats to form another congregation of only the faithful and the truly repentant.

"This can't go on," Posidonios told Kimon. "The situation will only worsen if no solution is found. Once the congregation is divided with two overseers in one town, it will be impossible to heal the divide. The longer the division lasts, the more reason each congregation will have to ignore the other. Reunion for both sides would mean giving up too much."

"I agree, I agree," said Kimon sadly. "But what can we do?"

"We must reach a compromise on an overseer, someone both sides can support," said the reader Andreas, whom Posidonios had brought along to represent the other side.

"Yes, but who?" said Kimon.

"Whom would you pick, as an alternative?" Posidonios asked Kimon.

"I don't have an alternative. I like Theodoros, although I can see why others don't. I like Philippos, but I think a compromise candidate must come from among the faithful. But who is there?"

"There is you," said Posidonios.

Kimon laughed out loud. "You must be joking," he said.

"I am entirely serious," said Posidonios with a friendly smile.

"No, you can't be," said Kimon, still chuckling.

"You're the best educated man in Sinope, fully qualified intellectually for the office. You have friends in both camps. You've stayed out of the fight. You are liked and respected, even admired, not just within the Assembly, but around town. And you are unmarried."

"And never to be married if made the overseer. You are asking quite a lot," said Kimon.

"The situation requires it," said Posidonios. "This is a tragedy in more ways than one. It's a tragedy for the Assembly as a whole, but it's also tragedy for each of us individually. We will all suffer from the division. And it's a tragedy for the faith. What kind of witness is it to the rest of the town, if after all we've been through, we can't make peace among ourselves? Truly the situation deserves a sacrifice."

"But Theodoros is my friend. How can I oppose him? I've already taken one job from Theodoros. How can I edge him out of another, one that he wants so dearly?"

"We would count on you as his friend to persuade him to accept you," said Andreas. "I'll do all that I can to bring the others around."

"But I don't know how to be an overseer," said Kimon. "I've only been a Christian for a little over a year. I don't know the services. I wouldn't know where to stand or what to say. And I can't sing."

"Sure you can," said Andreas. "I've heard you. And you don't have to know everything. You'll never be alone in the worship. The rest of us will be right there next to you to show you what to do."

"Your duties will be mostly teaching and counseling, administration and discipline," said Posidonios. "It's nothing you can't manage."

"Isn't this rather irregular, picking someone so new in the faith, almost an outsider?"

"It's not unheard of," said Posidonios.

"From what I've seen elsewhere, I'd say it's not uncommon," said Andreas. "Anyway, it's God who really does the picking. Sometimes he picks an outsider, like the Apostle Paul."

"It's a calling, Kimon. It's not something that a man sets his sights on and schemes to achieve. It's something that comes to him when God sends it. God is calling you now. We're just delivering the message."

"I'm not worthy," said Kimon.

"You are worthy," said Posidonios.

"Yes, you are," said Andreas.

With eyes wide with amazement, Kimon took a deep breath and exhaled. "I'll have to think about it, and pray about it," he said.

"Of course," said Posidonios. "Just don't take too long."

Kimon tried to pray about it, but at first his thoughts kept intruding. Immediately his mind began to imagine himself sitting in the teacher's chair expounding the faith, standing up in front of the congregation to offer the peace greeting, presiding over baptisms and anointings and the ordinations of elders and servers. He couldn't but laugh at what he imagined. Still, the idea flattered him—until he mentioned it to Makrina.

She, too, laughed out loud. "You? My brother as overseer? Ha!"

He had not seen her so amused since his return. Makrina had always been serious-minded, but lately she seemed also much subdued, without the passionate enthusiasm of her youth. Once so active within the Assembly, she was now just there. She rarely spoke to anyone after worship and never joined the other women in their kirk chores or public charities. She spent her time instead at home, reading and praying, and painting again. She especially enjoyed painting scenes from the Gospels. She and Kimon often read aloud to each other and discussed the faith and had grown quite close since their reunion. But her lighthearted reaction to the idea reminded him of the way she used to be and now seldom was. She laughed so heartily it stirred her cough.

"It's a silly idea, isn't it?" he said, sitting down next to her.

"I didn't say that," said Makrina, recovering her voice. "In fact, I had the same idea myself a few days ago. Of course, I didn't take it seriously, but apparently it's not such a silly idea after all, or the others wouldn't have thought of it, and then proposed it."

"*You* thought of me as a possible overseer?"

"Oh, yes. You're a learned man and a sincere believer. You're thoughtful and kind. I think we'd be blessed to have you."

"You tempt me to pride," he said.

"I wouldn't want to do that," she said. "You still have a lot to learn, you know, and you're not the wisest man on earth. But you sincerely desire the truth and have your mind set on the right things, I think. You know what this means, though, don't you? It means bearing everyone else's burdens for the rest of your life. You will be dragged into every argument and laded with every care, earthly or otherwise. You'll have to put up with people at their worst, when they're proud and angry and offended or afraid, when they've sinned and don't want to admit it or make amends. Then there's all the administrative and sacramental duties you'll have to oversee. Kimon, you'll actually have to work for a living, every day for the rest of your life."

"I'd rather go back to the mines," he said.

Makrina laughed again. "No more sitting around at ease with me, reading and talking. Instead, you'll be listening always, to everyone's problems and complaints and confessions and requests, day after day after day. It won't be fun. I don't envy you."

"Maybe I'm not up to it."

"Who is, Kimon? Anyone who would actually want such an office would be insane."

"Theodoros wants it."

Makrina's smile faded suddenly.

"Why not him?" Kimon asked.

"No. Not Theodoros," she answered.

"Why not?"

"I shouldn't say. I'm no one to judge."

"You already have," said Kimon. "Just tell me why."

Makrina sighed. "It's that," she began, "as overseer, you have an opportunity, and a responsibility also, to help people move from this world to the next. Some people, even some very wise and pious and faithful people are too consumed with this world to be able to do that. They take everything that happens here and now so seriously that they lose sight of their own end."

"I see what you mean," said Kimon.

Makrina put her arm around him and leaned her head against his.

"I hate to urge this on you," she said. "It's a terrible burden. It will hurt me to see you troubled with it. I will miss seeing you marry and raise children. But you really are the best choice under the circumstances, perhaps the only hope for unity and peace, at least in my poor understanding of things."

Kimon fasted and prayed and studied the Scriptures for three days, but the issue was already settled for him by Makrina. Everything else only confirmed his resignation. He dreaded the work and did not feel worthy of the honor, but he couldn't say no without putting his own interests ahead of the whole Assembly's.

He told his father first of his decision. To his surprise, Aristoboulos took it well.

"Posidonios has already spoken to me on your behalf," he said. "It wasn't necessary. I realized long ago, Kimon, that you would never follow me in business. When you were in the mines, I even promised your God that if I won your freedom I would give you up to him. He seems to have remembered my promise."

Posidonios was relieved and grateful. The support of the lapsed was assured, he said, and Andreas had already brought several key members of the faithful aboard. After Kimon agreed, Andreas and two others went to see Theodoros to sound him out. The meeting was not encouraging.

"He's just a babe in the faith, a mere seedling!" Theodoros declared. "What does he know of the Scriptures or the ways of the Apostles? He has no formal training in the faith. He barely knows the accustomed responses of the worship!"

"He's your friend and follower, a man without guile, like Nathaniel, an Israelite indeed," said Andreas. "He's one of us. He shares our concerns, but he is also acceptable to the others."

"He is not qualified!"

"He's like Paul when he was chosen."

"Our Lord Himself chose Paul! Who chose Kimon? Whom has Kimon seen along the road? This is all Posidonios's doing! He wants Kimon as his puppet!"

From then on, Theodoros began to criticize Kimon publicly, referring to him derisively as "the neophyte"—the newly planted one. His attacks had exactly the opposite effect, however, as many of the faithful were already inclined in Kimon's direction. Posidonios was sure they had enough support to elect Kimon already, without Theodoros, but for the sake of unity and peace Kimon himself went to see his angry friend.

"I didn't ask for this," he explained. "I wanted you to be my overseer, but there doesn't seem to be any other way to bring everyone together."

"Who says everyone belongs together, Kimon? What separated us to begin with? Was it not the persecution? We all had the same choice. Some chose to sacrifice, while others risked death, and now we talk of bringing the two together as if they were of one spirit!"

"Can't they still be of one spirit?"

"Not without repentance, and there has been very little of that. I know these people, Kimon. They are not like the confessors you met in the mines. There are many who call themselves Christians who are barely believers at all. They come once a week to pay their respects to God, to make their meager sacrifice of a little time and a little money, and then they go home to live their lives like unbelievers. When the persecution came, when the Cross of Christ was offered to them, they melted away. Now that the persecution's gone, they are back again, talking unity and peace, rather than pleading for mercy."

"But there must be mercy. The strong must bear the weak," said Kimon.

"And what happens when the persecution returns, as it surely will someday, Lord have mercy. What standard will we have set for the Assembly? That denying Christ is no bar to re-admission?"

"Peter himself denied Christ and was forgiven."

"That was *before* he received the Holy Spirit, Kimon. Surely you can see the difference. These people were baptized with the same Spirit, but they cast it off when it was convenient for them to do so. Now they want it back.

Really, Kimon. I'm disappointed in you. I would expect you to be more discerning of such things. Mark my words—persecution will return, and it will return to cleanse the Assembly once again of the unrepentant and the pretenders!"

They argued for over an hour, but it was no use. Kimon left feeling drained and discouraged, and not entirely sure he had made the right decision. Against Theodoros, he felt quite keenly his own lack of learning and experience. How could he dare to imagine himself as overseer when there was so much he didn't know?

Makrina, however, was never more certain. "Don't let that man talk you out of it," she warned him, when he confided his flagging spirits to her. He was sprawled across a couch in the tablinum, and she was standing over him, straight and stiff, fists clenched at her side.

"Theodoros is wrong. You are the best candidate, Kimon, and you are our only hope. Whatever plan God has for Theodoros, it is not as overseer here in Sinope. Everyone is already behind you. The whole Assembly is counting on you, and you had better not back out. Do you hear me?"

Kimon looked up at her and laughed.

"Why are you laughing?" she asked.

"Because I haven't seen you like this in years," he said. "You really are my sister, the one I missed for so long."

Kimon wanted more time to win Theodoros over. At first, Posidonios agreed, but when Makrina told him of her concern for Kimon's resolve, he made other plans.

The very next Lord's Day, after the Thanksgiving, the elder Philippos paused before the dismissal to announce that a successor to Archelaos had been found, "and his name is Kimon, son of Aristoboulos."

Kimon himself was quite surprised, but he was not the only one. Theodoros was there also, standing a few feet in front of Kimon, up front and to the right, with the other earnest men of God. At the mention of Kimon's name, he looked around and glared at Kimon, who shook his head and shrugged to show his innocence.

Then Theodoros addressed Philippos for all to hear. "I must protest," he declared. "This is most irregular. No election has been scheduled, and no time has been allowed to examine this candidate. What right have you to name him now?"

"He has the favor of the people," said Philippos. "They are decided."

"The candidate has not been examined. How can the people have made their choice?"

"But, Theodoros, we all know Kimon. We have known him for years.

We know his family. We know how he suffered on our behalf even before he joined our Assembly."

"He is worthy," declared Posidonios, standing not far behind Kimon, with the married men.

"Truly he is worthy," said Andreas.

"Worthy," said another. "Amen," someone added.

Philippos turned again to Theodoros. "Do you say that he is not?" he asked.

Theodoros turned to Kimon. "I say ask Kimon. Are you worthy of this office, Kimon?"

Kimon looked around surprised and embarrassed. "No. I am not worthy," he answered.

"Not worthy, he says," repeated Theodoros.

"His humility makes him worthy," said someone.

"Amen. Amen," said the others. "Truly he is worthy. Worthy!" they shouted. "Axios! Axios!"

"He is too young!" Theodoros protested. "He is too new in the faith! He has no formal training and little practical experience! He is still a mere neophyte!"

"Axios! Axios!" some of the men shouted. Even some of the women spoke up, declaring Kimon worthy. Their high-pitched voices sounded strangely out of place. They were not allowed to speak in the Lord's house, except to give the customary responses of the worship. Makrina, for her part, kept silent.

"Axios! Axios!" the men declared, until Philippos raised his hands for quiet and said, "We have heard that he is worthy. Are there others who would say he is not?"

The hall was silent. Theodoros looked to his left and then to his right. His friends and supporters bowed their heads and held their tongues. "Eustratios?" he asked.

Eustratios, the former server, looked at Theodoros sadly and shook his head. "I cannot say it," he answered.

The little man with the great graying beard threw up his hands. "God save us!" he cried to the heavens. Then he turned and headed for the door. The men stood aside to let him pass, but no one said a word until he was gone.

Philippos watched Theodoros leave, then sighed aloud, made the sign of the cross, and said, "Alleluia." Laughter rippled through the hall before the return of quiet. Philippos waved Kimon to the fore and presented him to the people.

"How say we all now?" he asked.

"Worthy!" the congregation declared, with one mind and one voice.

"Worthy it is," said Philippos. "Let us pray."

For the next few weeks, Kimon prepared for his investiture as if for his own funeral. He kept close to Philippos's side, learning all he could of the duties of overseers and elders. Many hours a day, he practiced chanting with Andreas and the other readers. In the evenings, there were prayers at the Lord's house and the procession of persons, male and female, seeking guidance and consolation.

Then, in September, for the feast of the martyr Phokas, the overseers of Amisos and Kerasos arrived in Sinope, transported by boat at Aristoboulos's expense. In the midst of the Thanksgiving service, Kimon knelt before the Gospel book while the overseers laid their hands upon his bowed head and called upon the Holy Spirit to prepare and equip him and guide him in serving his flock. Afterward, they hung a long, embroidered stole upon his neck and placed the shepherd's staff in his hand. He served the rest of the ceremony by their side, as one of them.

For that one day, Makrina stood up front, with the younger virgins. She would have seen everything, but for the stream of tears that impaired her vision. Toward the end of the service, Kimon happened to glance her way and see her teary eyes and trembling smile. He smiled, too, and then tried unsuccessfully to hold back his own tears. They glistened upon his cheeks in the candlelight.

Kimon became Makrina's sole service to the Assembly. She waited upon him whenever he was at home, bringing him food and drink, fetching his books, arranging his pillows. It wasn't much really, as he was rarely at home, and when he was he was always preoccupied with some matter and never demanding.

Most evenings before bed, she would read to him while he relaxed upon a couch in the gynaeceum, which had become his study. One evening, she had just finished and was leaving when he called her back. "Makrina?" he said.

"Yes?"

"Who put you under discipline?"

"What do you mean?" she asked.

"I've noticed you haven't joined in the Thanksgiving for many weeks. Has someone barred you from doing so?"

"No one," she answered.

"No one? Then why do you not partake?"

"I have sins I have not confessed," she said. "I've been too ashamed. I've meant to confess them to you, but you've been so busy. I didn't want to burden you."

"I'm never too busy for you, Makrina, and it pains me to see you burdened. Share them with me and we'll bear them together."

"Very well then," she said. Makrina returned to the couch and sat down by his side. She thought for a moment, then said, "I have broken the commandments."

"Which ones?" he asked.

"All of them," she answered.

"All of them?" asked Kimon incredulously.

"Almost all of them," she said. "I have not worshipped other gods, but I have felt so estranged from God that I hardly felt I knew Him, and I have wondered what God I really do worship."

"Which commandments do you think you have broken?"

"I have not kept the Sabbath. I did not pray or fast for days or weeks at a time when I was in Neocaesarea. I have not honored God the way I should have."

"Who has?" said Kimon. "Who has prayed enough or fasted enough or honored God the way we should?"

"That doesn't matter, Kimon. What matters is that I haven't, and so I have sinned," said Makrina. "I have also stolen things. I stole a cloak once from a woman washing clothes in the river, and I stole food on many occasions. I stole vegetables from a garden at night, when no one would see me, and I stole apples and figs off the trees whenever I could."

"You needed to eat. You were destitute."

"I stole, Kimon. I took things because I did not trust that God would provide for my needs, because I told myself I had to have them right then, that instant. But it was never true. I could have lived without the figs or the apples or the cloak. Even if I had died without them, at least I would have died with a clear conscience. Where would we be if we taught children that it is permissible to steal when they feel a need? Where, Kimon?"

"It is wrong. You are right," said Kimon.

"And I lied, too. I lied about who I was. I lied to protect myself, to escape punishment for my crimes, and to avoid having to bear witness when I might have suffered for it."

"Makrina, God understands why —"

"He understands that I have sinned! Don't tell me I haven't, Kimon. That's why I have not confessed to Philippos or anyone else. They would only have made excuses for me, and I don't want excuses. I want forgiveness. I want to be whole. I expected that you would understand, but maybe I was wrong. After all, it took me many years to understand my own sins."

Kimon nodded his head sadly. "I understand," he said. "You have sinned."

"I'm not finished," said Makrina. "I have coveted many things. I have envied others for their good fortune and easy lives. I have even sinned in this way against my own sister. I have coveted her husband. I have coveted her life with him at the palace, the life I thought should have been mine, and I have resented her secretly for having taken it from me."

"She didn't know, Makrina. None of us knew. They wouldn't have married if they had even suspected you might still be alive."

"I know, Kimon. I know," said Makrina. "I can't hold it against them, and I no longer do. But for a while it was very painful for me, and when I thought of how close I came to her happiness, I would cry out at night in grief and anger, and I would blame you for not finding me and I would blame Mamma and Pappa for sending her with him. You see, I have not even honored my father and mother."

Makrina turned away and bit her lip.

"Does it still hurt?" asked Kimon.

"A little," she answered, "but less now. I try not to think of them, to avoid the pain, and the temptation."

"Temptation?"

Makrina nodded. "I have . . . I have excited my desire for Marcus and imagined him as my husband and lover."

"You have committed adultery in your heart," said Kimon.

Makrina nodded again.

"Lord have mercy," he said.

"One more sin," said Makrina. "I have murdered a man."

"In your heart," said Kimon.

"In my heart many times, but only once in the flesh," said Makrina.

"In the flesh? Are you serious? You have killed a man?"

"I stabbed him to death," said Makrina. "He bled upon my hands and clothes. It was horrible, Kimon."

"What happened?"

"He tried to rape me. He promised to send me home if I let him. I couldn't bear it. God forgive me, I just couldn't bear it."

"He promised to send you home? Who was he?"

"He was someone very important, the lieutenant governor of Cappadocia, a man named Rogatianus."

"Rogatianus? I know him! I met him in Neocaesarea when I was looking for you!"

"You met him? He knew you?"

"Yes! Yes!"

"That's why he believed my story! He just said he found out who I was. I had told him everything, and he said he had confirmed it."

"He didn't tell me anything!"

"They knew I killed him. They knew me by name. That's why I didn't come home. I thought everyone knew, and I was so ashamed and afraid. But

no one knew, Kimon. No one knew. And if I had come home right away . . .
if I had come home . . ."

Tears rolled down her cheeks. She shook her head and closed her eyes
and tried not to cry.

Kimon pulled her close and kissed her head. "You have suffered
enough," he whispered. "You have confessed everything. You have repented.
God will forgive you, and He will reward you with a new life, a life without
tears, without sorrow, a life everlasting."

The next day a letter arrived from Marcus announcing that Eugenia had giv-
en birth to a healthy boy, whom they had named Alexander, after Marcus's
aide. All was well, and Eugenia was already planning to return home to visit
as soon as she was able.

The same evening, Aristoboulos brought other news to the family. "We
have a new governor," he told them at dinner. "It's Marcellinus."

# XXXV

Philodemos was the first person from Sinope to see Marcellinus since the latter's departure for Egypt years earlier. With all the other mayors of the province, he had journeyed to Nicomedia to pay homage to the new governor.

"He's hardly changed at all," Philodemos told Aristoboulos upon his return. "Still as handsome and gracious and self-assured, although the years may have added a certain gravity to his demeanor. He asked about you and was pleased when I told him you were well. He asked about Makrina also, and he seemed especially pleased to hear that she was home and unmarried."

"Isn't he by now?"

"He didn't mention it, but you know he never talks much of his private life," said Philodemos. "Of course, I couldn't resist asking his assistant—you remember, that fellow Libanius. Apparently he is married, although his wife has yet to join him in Nicomedia. It seems she prefers Antioch."

"What a shame," said Aristoboulos. "I suppose it was too much to hope for."

"Perhaps not," said Philodemos. "Something tells me it's not a happy marriage. At least that's my guess."

Within the week a letter arrived from Nicomedia for Makrina. It was a very personal letter, shorn of the usual formalities of office:

> *Gaius Valerius Marcellinus sends to Makrina, daughter of Aristoboulos, his fondest greetings. The news that you are again safe at home has given me great joy. I have thought of you often and worried for your welfare. And more than once, Macrina cara, I have felt the pangs of conscience for my part in your hasty departure and exile. I hope you can forgive me. I pray that you will. Please write soon that I may know your heart indeed harbors for me no hatred. My heart holds only the dearest memories of you. Greet you father, mother, and brother for me. I look forward to the day when I may see you again. Until that day, may God keep you in his graces.*

"I don't like this," Makrina told Kimon. "He's married, and yet he writes as if he is not."

"Perhaps he wishes that he were not," said Kimon.

"Of course."

"Or perhaps he wishes to ignore that he is."

"Indeed."

"Or perhaps he won't be for long and he's thinking ahead."

"That, too."

"But then again, Makrina, it is possible to read this letter innocently, as simply an appeal for forgiveness and reconciliation. He even speaks of God as one who believes."

"He speaks as he knows I would like him to speak, Kimon. He knows the right words. He knows how to pluck at my heart to make it sing for him, or bleed for him."

"You may be right," said Kimon. "I made the mistake years ago of urging you to accept him. I don't want to do that again. Still, Makrina, I must say, it's been a long time. Can we be so sure he hasn't changed? I have. Marcus has. Why not Marcellinus?"

"Not Gaius," said Makrina.

"How can you be so sure?" Kimon asked.

Makrina suddenly turned aside to cough repeatedly into her palla.

"Anyway," said Kimon, "you shouldn't read too much into his letter. If he intends more, he will make it known eventually."

"I don't need this now. I don't want this now," said Makrina.

"All the more reason to treat it innocently," said Kimon. "You owe him a letter at the very least, to forgive him. Have you forgiven him?"

"I thought I had. Now I'm not so sure," she said. "The truth is, I never really blamed him for what he did to me. . . . I deserved it."

Makrina struggled for days to write a response. She was tempted at times to be insultingly brief, to discourage anything further. But the more she thought about him, the more she wanted to know. Where had he been all this time? Whom had he married? What did he think now of her Christian faith, now that the persecution had lifted?

Thinking of him also stirred her affections. She, too, wanted forgiveness and would have valued his friendship and fondness, after the way in which their lives had once been intertwined. But she was afraid to think too much of him and imagine again what could not be, and she certainly did not wish to give him reason to think more of her.

With Kimon's help, she finally settled on a brief reply, kind and cordial without risking or encouraging too much:

> *Makrina, daughter of Aristoboulos, to Gaius Valerius*
> *Marcellinus, Governor of Bithynia and Pontus, greetings. I*
> *am flattered by your continued concern and care in writing,*
> *and touched that you would ask my forgiveness. I have long*
> *since forgiven you and need now to ask that you forgive me*
> *for those faults of mine that contributed in no small way to*
> *the unhappy events of long ago. Praise God that they are*

*past. I continue to pray for your salvation and hope that*
*this reconciliation will bring you closer to our Lord Jesus*
*Christ. May God grant you and your wife many happy*
*years together.*

The letter was sent by boat and presumed to have been received within the week. Makrina was relieved when there was no immediate response, but when months passed without a response, her relief turned to disappointment. Hearing from Marcellinus had troubled her, but it had also thrilled her, and she missed the thrill, despite her conscious attempts to discount it.

Aristoboulos never regained his strength after the stressful years of separation from his son and daughters. Before the winter's end, he was stricken with fever and died. All of Sinope mourned his loss and turned out for the funeral. On a cold, gray, and damp day, the shipbuilder's body was borne from the house to the forum in a skiff draped in black cloth, carried upon the shoulders of his senior shipwrights. A band of mournful horns and melancholy flutes led the procession, followed by the skiff and then a dozen or so hired mourners loudly weeping and wailing their way through the city. Kimon had wanted to dispense with both the band and the mourners, in favor of the Christian custom of singing resurrectional hymns, but his mother insisted upon more familiar funerary forms. At least the body was not burned but interred intact in the family mausoleum, in the necropolis outside the city walls. Outside the mausoleum, Kimon led the Christians present in prayers and hymns.

Kimon took his father's death as a personal failure. "I thought we had more time," he complained to Makrina. "I should have made more of an effort to win him over. Here I am, the local overseer, and I can't even save my own father."

"You can't save anyone, Kimon," she told him. "Christ does the saving, and the Holy Spirit wins them over."

"But we could have done more," he countered.

"Yes, we could have," she said, "and God will judge us for that. But if He is just and loving, would He punish Pappa for our failure? Of course not."

"Is it too late for Pappa? Do you think it would make any difference to pray for his soul?"

Makrina shook her head. "I don't know," she answered, "but somehow that doesn't seem to matter. What matters for us is that we make our requests known to God, with thanksgiving and supplication, which we are commanded to do. Surely we can't be wrong to wish God to have mercy on his soul. But if we wish it and don't ask for it, aren't we hiding our hearts from God?"

Marcellinus made his first visit to Sinope as governor two weeks after Aristoboulos's death. It was an official visit, announced in advance throughout the region. There was business during the day and the usual series of honorary banquets each night, each with a different host, beginning with Philodemos the mayor.

Posidonios had offered to host a banquet, but Libanius, acting as Marcellinus's advance man, had declined. There were political considerations. Though the administration of the Emperor Maximinus Daia now tolerated the Christians, it was not favorably disposed toward them. On the contrary, the emperor actively encouraged a revival of the ancient cults, organizing their priests along the lines of the Christian clergy and requiring priests to wear distinctive white robes at all times. He had also funded publication of works attacking the Christian faith, including a book entitled *The Memoranda of Pilate*, written by one Theoteknos but purporting to be the memoirs of the former procurator of Judaea.

Under such conditions, a governor, especially one who shared the same capital with the imperial court, could hardly consort freely and openly with prominent Christians. Instead, he allowed Posidonios to pay him a brief, discreet visit at the house of Philodemos.

"He was his old self," Posidonios reported later to Kimon, "and he sends you his greeting, along with regrets that he is not able to meet with you personally, for obvious reasons."

Still mourning their recent loss, Makrina and her mother stayed at home during the visit, declining Philodemos's invitation to dinner on the governor's last night in town. Hilaria had urged her daughter to go without her.

"It will do you good just to get out for the evening, and you can't but enjoy seeing him again," she said. "He would certainly enjoy seeing you. You wouldn't have been invited if he had not given permission. He might even have asked for you."

Makrina held fast. "I want to see him, Mamma, but what good would it serve? I have more to lose than to gain," she said.

She did want to see him and knew that she would have jumped at the chance, had her father's death not forced her to see her life as from the grave. Her rational mind, beholding her own earthly end and heavenly goal, told her to steer clear of him. Even so, she wrestled that afternoon with the temptation of regret, struggling to pray it away in her room, on her knees.

From her room, Makrina did not hear the knock on the front door, neither the greetings exchanged in the atrium, nor the brief conversation in the tablinum, but she thought she heard her mother call her name. She rose and went to the railing overlooking the courtyard. "Mamma?" she answered.

"There's someone here to see you," said her mother, smiling brightly down below.

Makrina gasped, then backed away from the railing, afraid to be seen. She ducked quickly into her room and grabbed a hand mirror. "Dear God," she whispered, looking at her plain, sickly face. Her brown hair had grown back, but it was still unstylishly short, too short yet to braid or tie back or fix in any other fashion. She held it out of her eyes with a simple wooden headband stretching from ear to ear.

She put the mirror down and looked over her plain, off-white dalmatic and olive-green palla. "So be it," she said, making the sign of the cross. She raised her hands in a quick plea for help and mercy, then took a deep breath and started slowly from her room and down the stairs.

Marcellinus was waiting for her in the courtyard, smiling as he watched her descend the stairs. He was modestly dressed for a governor, in a long-sleeve, knee-length, green wool tunic with detachable white cuffs tied around his wrists. His deep blue cloak was handsomely cut and trimmed with a broad gold band. He wore dark blue trousers and crimson felt slippers. A black leather belt with a gold buckle girded his waist.

If he was at all surprised or dismayed by her appearance, he did not show it. But then, he wouldn't have, she thought. He was never that candid.

"This is a welcome surprise," she said, stopping an arm's length away. Sometimes Makrina was not so candid, either. "It's good to see you again, Gaius."

"It's a wonder seeing you, Makrina," he said. He stepped closer and kissed her cheek. Then he took her hand and pressed it between his. "Please pardon my interruption," he said. "When I heard you would not be at dinner tonight, I couldn't resist stopping by, even if unannounced."

"No pardon necessary. I'm glad you did," she said. "You are leaving tomorrow, I hear."

"Yes, unfortunately. It amazes me how much I've come to like this little town. My first day back, I thought I'd die of nostalgia. I might have, if I had missed seeing you."

He gazed admiringly into her eyes with a steady smile. Makrina half expected him to melt her heart there and then. She had feared that he would. But, strangely, it didn't happen.

"You are married," she said, smiling back at him.

Marcellinus dropped his eyes but not his smile. Then he sighed and turned and led her slowly into the courtyard. "Yes, I am married," he admitted.

"And who, may I ask, is the lucky woman?"

He sighed again and answered, "Clea."

"Clea?" she wondered.

"The niece of Sossianos Hierocles, the former governor."

Makrina laughed aloud, modestly covering her mouth with her hand when she did so. "I'm sorry, Gaius. I . . . I don't know what to say. I would never have guessed."

"She really was his niece," he said.

"Oh, of course," said Makrina. Then she laughed again, despite herself.

He let go of her hand and stepped away, still smiling but now with embarrassment.

"And how is the—uh—illustrious Hierocles?" she asked.

"He died six months after our wedding, quite unexpectedly," said Marcellinus.

"Oh, dear, I'm sorry to hear that," she said, just barely managing not to laugh again. Coughing helped her avoid it. "And where is Clea now?" Makrina asked.

"Antioch," he answered. "She won't leave there until it warms up. I assume she'll join me in Nicomedia this summer, but I have no way of knowing."

"That sounds like Clea," she said. "Any children?"

"No, thank God," he said. "Not that I don't like them, but we're hardly a family as it is. Children would only turn the farce into a tragedy."

His smiled faded and he looked away.

"I truly am sorry to hear that," said Makrina. "I wouldn't have wanted it for you, even after all that has happened."

"There is always the possibility of divorce, although there are complicating factors," he said.

Makrina shook her head. "Please, Gaius, let's not talk of this," she said.

"You're right," he said, "as you so often are. We've so little time, and I'd rather talk of you. How have you been, truly, all these years?"

She smiled sadly. "Not well," she said. "Hardly a happier topic of conversation. I lived like a peasant in the mountains. Saw my hosts—whom I had come to love—slaughtered for their faith. Begged on the streets of Neocaesarea. Lost my hair to lice. While I was gone, my little sister married the only—other man I ever loved."

"Who was that?"

"Aemilius Canio."

"Oh, yes. Marcus. Where are they now?"

"Where else? At the court of Constantine. Marcus commands the palace guards."

"The Protectors?"

"That's right."

"He's done well for himself, better than I expected."

"And I have a little niece named after me. You see, they all thought I was dead."

They looked at each other for a moment without speaking. Then Marcellinus said, "I suppose now I should ask for your forgiveness all over again. I had no idea you had suffered so much. I'm sorry, Makrina. I wish I hadn't handled things the way I did."

"It wasn't all your fault, and it wasn't all bad, either. I learned some things about myself, about faith, about life, about God. And I have been blessed to return and see my brother become not only a believer, but an overseer."

"I always knew he'd go far, as soon as he settled upon a direction. How is he?"

"Very well. You know he spent a few years in the mines and walks with a permanent limp now, but otherwise he has never been better. You should go see him. He'd love to see you."

"I would very much enjoy seeing him, but I'm afraid I can't," said Marcellinus. "Politics. I hope you understand."

"I do, but then again I don't," said Makrina. "You know the faith, and sometimes you talk like one of us. Why are you not a Christian, Gaius?"

"If I were at the court of Constantine, I probably would be. But I am at another court, and that is not an option."

"Which is more important, the court or the truth?"

Marcellinus stared at her with a look of hopelessness. Then he turned away. "I've stayed long enough for a married man. I'd better go," he said. "Thank you for taking the time to see me, Makrina. You still mean a lot to me, married or not."

Makrina pulled upon his cloak and kissed his cheek. "Farewell, Gaius," she said. "And may God go with you."

He nodded and smiled. "Farewell, Makrina," he said. "Keep me in your prayers."

He started back without her toward the tablinum.

"Gaius?" she called after him.

He stopped and turned. "Yes?"

"Write when you can. Will you?"

"I will," he said. "Gladly."

Makrina waited until she heard the front door slam shut. Then she bowed her head, there in the courtyard. "Lord," she said aloud, "why did I say that?"

# XXXVI

Winter prevented Eugenia from leaving Arelate until the spring, but in the spring it was Marcus who was leaving and not Eugenia. War had intervened, and Constantine himself would lead his legions into northern Italy.

Marcus was to accompany him. On their last night together, Eugenia did not leave his bed for her own, as she usually did. She had surprised him with a private dinner waiting for him in his chambers when he was finally free of his duties, later than usual. He was tired and still preoccupied with preparations for the march, but he seemed to welcome the chance to relax. He smiled often and listened quietly, gazing fondly at his wife throughout the meal. Eugenia was cheered by his attentiveness and affection. After a last, leisurely cup of wine, they made love right there, on the dining couch. It was already very late, and the servants had long since retired.

After going to bed, they lay awake in the darkness sharing confidences while waiting for sleep to come. "I'm afraid for us, Marcus," Eugenia confessed, her head resting in the crook of his arm, her long, dark, perfumed hair lying loose upon his shoulder and pillow. "I'm afraid the happiness we've known for so long is about to end. What if we lose the war?"

"We won't lose," answered Marcus soothingly.

"Are you sure? They say Maxentius has more men and horses."

"They're not all in northern Italy. . . . Besides, Maxentius is no match for Constantine. We will win, I promise you."

Eugenia was not satisfied. She did not trust Constantine as Marcus did. Marcus trusted the emperor more than he trusted himself. Not that he couldn't see Constantine's faults. Once when Marcus shared with his wife his frustration with his emperor, Eugenia joined him in his criticism. It was a natural expression of her sympathy for her husband. But Marcus responded quite unexpectedly. He turned on her coldly and snapped at her to keep silent. From then on, he never spoke against the emperor to her again. He was not alone in his loyalty. She had seen it in many other men at court. It was not just an allegiance but a devotion, even a kind of love, born perhaps of some secret need within them. They seemed to yearn for a leader the way women yearn for a man. Why? "What makes you believe in him so?" she asked.

"Who? The emperor? Because he's a good man and a good general. He's reasonable. He's intelligent. He's fair. He's prudent and cautious, and yet also decisive and bold. He values those under him and treats them with respect."

"But what if he's wrong?"

"He's not wrong. He's right. We can beat Maxentius."

"But he's not always right."

"No one is, but even when he's wrong, he intends what is right and good. He truly believes in just rule. You can see that in his reforms of the legal code and in his public works. Sure, he lords it over us. He keeps us at a distance. But, in a way, he serves us as much as we serve him. He's like a good father. The empire is his household."

Eugenia turned the idea over in her head, the emperor as father.

"Are you afraid of him?" Marcus asked.

"I don't know," she answered. "I don't know him as well as you do. The Scriptures say, 'Put not your trust in princes, in sons of men, in whom there is no salvation.'"

"Where does it say that?"

"Somewhere, one of the Psalms, I think. I've heard it sung at prayers. Titus used to sing it."

"He talks to Hosius," said Marcus.

"He does?"

"Sometimes he even talks to me."

Eugenia lifted her head and looked at Marcus, though in the shadows she could barely see him. "About the faith?" she asked.

"More than once, in fact. I've been afraid to say too much for fear of getting it wrong, and he hasn't probed deeply. It could be just idle curiosity, but he seems interested, at least intellectually."

"Do you think there's a chance he could come to believe?" Eugenia asked.

Marcus thought for a moment. "He has to believe in something, in some source of his own authority. His own father meant a lot to him. That's why he has worshipped the Sol Invictus, just as his father did. But I think the idea of God as Father appeals to him. It's possible for the man, Constantine, to believe. I'm just not sure it's possible for the emperor, the Augustus, to become Christian."

"I suppose it's too much to expect," Eugenia sighed, laying her head again on his shoulder.

"Too much to expect, but not too much to pray for," said Marcus.

"My only prayer right now is to have you back safely," Eugenia answered. "We've had it so easy compared to others, compared to Makrina and Kimon, compared to just about anybody. Maybe it's our turn to suffer. . . . Marcus?"

"Don't worry. God is with us. Now go to sleep."

☦    ☦    ☦

Fausta's older brother Maxentius had held sway in Rome for nearly six years by skillfully bribing key members of the Senate and army. He had led a dissolute young life in Rome until Constantine's succession spurred his own ambitions. That same year, the emperor Galerius proposed to end Rome's exemption from taxation and to disband the Praetorian Guard. Maxentius, then just 21, promised to spare both and to restore Rome to its greatness if the Senate and the Guard supported his bid for power. As emperor, he made sure the Guard was well paid and kept the people of Rome satisfied with circuses, games, public works, food subsidies, and other benefits.

To pay for everything, Maxentius made a habit of confiscating landed estates from their lawful owners under one pretext or another. He also openly solicited large gifts from the City's leading citizens. The burden thus fell randomly upon a disfavored few, and because most members of the upper classes were unaffected, no one dared dissent from the practice, much less organize opposition to the regime. The trend was worrisome, however, and the source of much gossip throughout the empire.

There were rumors, also, of another kind of tax levied upon well-to-do Romans. More than one had been obliged to lend their wives to the emperor for the night. One Sophronia, the wife of the city prefect, was even reported to have stabbed herself to death, rather than submit to that indignity. These and other injustices had created an uncertain order, outwardly stable but inwardly anxious. Noble Romans yearned for honest rule. Many looked to the north—to Constantine—for relief.

After the emperor Licinius's engagement to Theodora's eldest daughter Constantia, Constantine's half-sister, the emperor of the East, Maximinus Daia, proposed an alliance between himself and Maxentius. With Daia supporting Maxentius, Licinius would need to keep his legions closer to Asia than to Italy and was thus prevented from joining Constantine in an attack upon Maxentius. Constantine would have to go it alone with just 16 legions—90,000 foot and 8,000 horse—compared to Maxentius's 30 legions, including 18,000 horse.

But Constantine knew Maxentius to be a timid and inexperienced warrior. Twice before when threatened, Maxentius had remained with the bulk of his forces at Rome, relying upon the city's defenses and provisions to outlast his opponents. Thus, Constantine figured he could count on meeting piecemeal resistance in northern Italy, which, if destroyed, would produce better odds against Maxentius's main force at Rome.

In April, as soon as weather permitted, Constantine sent one legion into Rhaetia as a feint on the alpine passes north of Mediolanum. This succeeded in drawing off Maxentius's forces east of Mediolanum, allowing Constantine to march his main force unopposed from Brigantio to Segusio, a mountain town guarding the entrance into northern Italy, east of the pass through the mountains.

They forced the pass on a cold, clear night in May. The emperor and his staff watched the march from the steps of the small guard house at the pass's crest, where the road turned down the other side. The soldiers tramped by within ten paces of their emperor, but no one noticed him in the dark. All eyes alternated between the road beneath their feet and the sky in the north, where a strange red glow undulated eerily. "I've seen it in Britain, but never this far south," said Gratianus.

Constantine nodded thoughtfully. "What are we to make of this omen?" he wondered.

No one answered at first. "It's the ghosts of your father's legions, marching to our aid," Bassianus ventured confidently.

Constantine looked at Bassianus out of the corner of his eye, as he often did. "You think so?" he said with a slight smile. Then he turned to Marcus. "What would you say, Christian?"

Marcus was taken aback. No one had ever addressed him by that name. He glanced up at the glow to avoid looking the emperor in the eye. "Angels, my lord," he answered. "An army of them, assembling for battle."

The emperor's smile widened into a grin. "But the soldiers would more likely believe ghosts, Canio," he said. Marcus shrugged his shoulders and smiled sheepishly. The emperor then turned to Bassianus and said, "Perhaps the soldiers need to be told what to believe, eh, Bassianus? Go ahead, tell them."

"Gladly, my lord," Bassianus answered. The handsome young officer stepped up to the column of marching men. Pointing to the sky, he declared loudly, "It's the ghosts of the divine Constantius and his victorious legions, marching to our aid."

"Truly, truly," answered the soldiers. "Hail, Constantine," one called. "Hail, victor!" shouted another. "Hail! Hail!" the rest responded.

The word was quickly spread and the soldiers took heart in knowing they were not alone.

Segusio's small garrison held out for several days against constant bombardment from Constantine's catapults. When the walls had been breeched, the city gates were set afire and burned through. The town was then taken by storm, its garrison fleeing more than fighting. Constantine entered Segusio as liberator, having forbidden his troops from looting or abusing the town.

Next came Augusta Taurinorum situated amid the foothills of the Alps, aside the great Padus River. Here the liberator met a small force of heavily armored calvary, about 300, arrayed for battle before the city walls. Both horse and rider were completely covered with a combination of plate and scale armor. The riders were armed with heavy, steel-tipped lances streaming with red and yellow pennons. Commanders called them *cataphractarii*, as they were know in the East, but the common soldiers called them *clibanarii*, after an iron pot for baking bread in camp. They were an awesome and unfamiliar sight in the West. Constantine had seen such troops in the East among the Persians. Marcus had seen them, too. Most others of all ranks had only heard tell of their thunder, but they were not unprepared. Caesonius's spies had warned of their existence well in advance, and Constantine made sure his troops were trained to meet the threat.

When the cataphracts charged into the formation of infantry drawn up before them, the formation, on order, opened up to clear the way, then suddenly closed again from both sides upon the column of cataphracts, bringing the charge to a halt and leaving the knights no room to maneuver. The unfortunate cataphracts struggled to bring their lances to bear, while Constantine's infantry broke the lower legs of the horses with iron-bound clubs. Fallen riders and horses created greater obstacles to maneuver, creating panic among the cataphracts, who retreated as best they could, leaving half their number.

The iron pots suffered a final defeat at the city gates, which were locked against them, their commander having failed to leave a detachment of loyal troops inside. They were thus forced to flee across the Padus River, and disappeared down the road to the east.

Constantine's kind treatment of Segusio paid off. Taurinorum welcomed him as liberator, as then did Mediolanum, where his father Constantius had been cloaked in the purple nineteen years earlier by his father-in-law Maximianus. The former capital of the West celebrated Constantine's arrival with a public festival. He stayed ten days to allow his troops time to rest while his staff collected intelligence on enemy forces in the area.

Ruricius Pompeianus, Maxentius's lieutenant in the north, was busy assembling his forces at Verona, a hundred miles east of Mediolanum. To slow Constantine's advance, Pompeianus sent a large force of cataphracts and regular cavalry to bar the way at Brixia. There again in June, the cataphracts charged into a trap, with the same disastrous results. Watching the collision from afar, Constantine turned to Gratianus and Marcus and said, "Once was a marvel. Twice is a tragedy." The remaining cavalry fought valiantly but were forced to yield, laying the road open for Constantine's march on Verona.

The river Astesis bounded Verona on three sides. A swift current, steep river bank, and improved fortifications made a direct assault across the river impossible. To isolate the city, Constantine moved swiftly upon a ford several miles upstream. His cavalry was already across when they were attacked by Pompeianus, but Pompeianus had learned too late of the crossing and underestimated the size of the force already across. In fierce fighting his forces suffered heavy casualties and were thrown back in disorder.

Pompeianus himself sought refuge inside the city, but much of his army was forced east toward Patavium.

Within hours Constantine's catapults began pounding the city's walls, while the emperor watched from his tent at the crest of a treeless hill overlooking the town. Pompeianus knew his only hope was to rally his scattered forces outside the city to break the siege. That night, under the cover of darkness, he slipped away in a small skiff, disguised as a humble peasant. He reappeared the next afternoon, leading a column of reinforcements arriving from Aquileia, soon joined by the survivors of the previous day's battle.

Constantine was not surprised by Pompeianus's return, but he was still not prepared to fend off a major counterattack. The main body of his army was still strung out along the route of advance. Most had yet to cross the river. Others were already laying siege around the city. When the size of the threat became known, Constantine gathered what forces he could and threw them against the approaching column to slow its advance while he hurriedly repositioned his available forces.

Everyone was in motion. The emperor himself was constantly in the saddle, racing from unit to unit to spur them on. A guard of thirty Protectors chased after him, accompanied by his trumpeter and his vexillary, who carried the emperor's personal standard—a square banner of purple and gold, bearing the image of the emperor beneath the gilded sunburst of the Sol Invictus. Time and again they returned to the command tent, where Gratianus was collecting intelligence reports and mapping out the situation.

The emperor had just left the tent again for another check on his forces already in action, traveling down the road toward Patavium, when he noticed a squadron of light horse standing at ease amidst the trees topping a nearby ridge. "What are they waiting for?" the emperor wondered aloud. Then, without warning, he changed course, leaving the paved road and cantering up the grassy hillside toward the ridge.

Marcus followed right behind him, looking back once to make sure his Protectors followed as well. Their orderly procession became an untidy stream of black horses, white uniforms, and silver armor.

They were halfway up the hillside, within two hundred paces of the squadron in the trees, when Marcus finally recognized with horror the elbow-length scale armor of the squadron's troopers. "My lord!" he cried. "They are enemy!"

Constantine immediately pulled back on his reins, as Marcus came alongside and grabbed the bridle of his master's horse. Without stopping he forced the beast to turn around, with the emperor looking back over his shoulder to see for himself. Marcus looked back, too, just in time to see the riders in the trees start down after them. "Sound distress!" he shouted to the trumpeter. Turning back down the hill with the others, the trumpeter raised his yard-long brass horn to his lips and sent up a rarely heard but easily recognized alarm: the emperor was in danger.

A mile away, Gratianus looked up from his terrain model, drawn in the ground outside the emperor's tent. "Great gods," he muttered, staring off down the dirt road the emperor had taken just moments before.

That instant Ablabius galloped up. "Where is he?" he asked. The alarm sounded again in the distance.

Gratianus pointed down the road and ordered, "There, man! After him!" Ablabius turned in the saddle and waved to his ensign to follow. Then he galloped off down the road, taking a squadron of Lancers with him.

The emperor's party was on the road again, racing back the way they had come, with the enemy squadron in pursuit. Up ahead another body of horse, a dozen or so strong, emerged from a ditch beside the road and started toward them. Marcus eyed them warily, wanting to believe they were friendly. They were not. The trumpeter's distress call had drawn the attention of an enemy patrol.

Marcus was looking for a way to escape when Constantine drew his sword and raised it high. "Drive them!" he shouted over the pounding of horses' hooves. Marcus saw the Protectors in the lead raise their shields and lift their lances overhead, preparing to meet the enemy head on.

There was no time or room to maneuver before the two small forces met under the shade of a giant oak tree, growing out of the embankment at the road's edge. The initial collision threw one Protector and two enemy troopers off their mounts. Marcus's own mount trampled and nearly tripped over one of the downed troopers. He had tried to stay close to the emperor, but in the upset he suddenly found himself fighting for his life, hacking away at the oval shield of an enemy trooper with his long cavalry sword. He was, he thought, just about to bring the poor fellow down, when one of Marcus's men thrust his lance up under the trooper's cheek guard, piercing his neck. The trooper fell instantly, and Marcus turned away at once, with no thought other than the safety of the emperor.

Constantine himself was likewise engaged in a furious attack upon an unfortunate trooper, now separated from the rest of his patrol by the Protectors' greater numbers. Beneath each great blow from the emperor's sword, the trooper could only cower behind his shield until it broke in two and fell apart. The next blow sundered his shoulder, another severed his arm, another his neck. The victim slumped from his saddle and fell to the ground in a bloody heap.

By then the road ahead was clear, but the enemy squadron was nearly on them. "Come, my lord," Marcus called to Constantine. The emperor glanced once at the approaching threat, then turned and galloped off with Marcus. A rear guard of Protectors followed close behind.

A hundred paces down the road, Ablabius appeared at last with his Lancers. At first sight, the enemy squadron pulled up short and turned back. "Make way! Make way!" Ablabius ordered. The Lancers moved aside to receive the emperor's guard, which passed between them in a single file. Ablabius greeted Constantine with a salute and "Hail, Augustus." The emperor gave a slight wave of the hand and passed on without a word. His face was flush with excitement, his expression grim. The sleeve of his tunic on his sword arm was spattered with bright red blood.

Marcus, following behind him, also said nothing, but looked at Ablabius with wide eyes of relief. Back at the command tent, the emperor first noticed the wound that Marcus himself had missed—a grazed right calf that looked worse than it was. Marcus had it washed and bound quickly so it wouldn't keep him from the emperor's side.

The fighting continued throughout the day, but despite his brush with death Constantine refused to withdraw to the safety of the far side of the river or remain in any one place for very long. Instead, he ranged among his units in the fight, waving his bloody sword and urging them on in the name of the Unconquered Sun.

By late afternoon, word arrived that Ruricius Pompeianus had died in the fighting. The bulk of his forces had been destroyed or dispersed. The surviving units switched sides, accepting Constantine's offer of amnesty. Verona opened its gates to Constantine and was spared. Within days, northern Italy was Constantine's to command, and nothing remained between him and Rome but a few small garrisons.

✠     ✠     ✠

Holding tight to her towel and her cup of wine, Politta dipped a cautious foot into the private bath. "Too hot," she said, drawing back.

"Just the way I like it," said Clea, breaking the pool's surface with a flick of her toes. Stepping back, she suddenly stripped off her towel and struck a pose, spreading her arms out wide and daintily dangling her towel from one hand while holding her cup in the other. Gray light from the ceiling vents settled softly on her naked form. "How's this for thirty?" she asked.

Her hostess laughed. "Thirty? I would never have guessed. How do you stay so young?"

"It's a secret," said Clea, dropping her towel and stepping down into the bath.

"Oh, tell me," said Politta, laying aside her own wrap and edging carefully into the steaming water. "I'm no threat to you. I've ten more years to carry around."

"Well," said Clea, immersed to her neck but still holding her cup above water, "I break all the rules. I sleep late, I eat what I like, I do as I please, and I never worry over anything."

"You don't starve yourself like the rest of us?"

"Do I look starved? No, of course not. Starving only makes one look older. I prefer the plumpness of youth."

"What about sports?"

"No sports. They only harden the body."

"No sports? None at all?"

"One sport, if you count men. I make sure never to go long without one."

"Clea, I'm appalled," said Politta, smiling.

Clea laughed. "I knew you would be, you more than anyone," she said. "That's the real secret. If you want to stay young, you must act young, and what do young girls do but flirt and flit from one boy to the next?"

"Until they fall in love."

"Oh, I never do that. That ruins everything. It's when you fall in love that you start to worry, and then you start eating too much, and then you have to starve yourself or purge your stomach or punish your body with exercise. All of which adds years to your face and figure. No, no, I never fall in love."

"You should have warned me of that years ago."

"How is Titus Statilius?"

"Bored. As bored with me as I am with him. I should have stayed with Hippolytus. He wasn't nearly so boring, and there was never any wonder whom he was sleeping with."

"You should never have gotten involved with someone you could marry," said Clea. "I pursue only men so far above me or below me that the very thought of marriage would make us both laugh. That way there's no danger of falling in love and no question what the game is about."

"Which is it now, above or below?"

"Above, at the moment."

"You don't say. How far above?"

"Far enough."

"Oh, don't be so cryptic. Who is it? What's his name?"

"He has many names," said Clea coyly. "Galerius. Valerius. Jovius."

"Jovius? You can't mean . . ."

"Maximinus Daia."

"You're not serious."

"Caesar and Augustus."

"Nonsense."

"Pontifex Maximus."

"Enough nonsense," Politta protested, giving Clea a playful shove that caused her to spill her wine into the bath.

Clea laughed. "Oops," she said.

"You're joking, aren't you?" said Politta.

"No, I'm not."

"Swear that you're not, by the Fates."

Clea shook her head and smiled. "I swear that I'm not, by the Fates, by the Graces, by all the gods."

A salacious grin spread across Politta's face as she settled closer to her friend. "Then tell me about it. How far along are you?"

"Well along, but not quite there."

"But you've only been in town a week."

"It didn't begin here, silly. We had eyes on each other in Antioch."

"You don't say. And how do you know he's still interested?"

"He's still interested. He's already invited me to a banquet at the palace next week."

"But you know what he did to poor Valeria, the Emperor Galerius's young widow. She was still in her mourning clothes and Daia was begging her to marry him."

"And I'm grateful to her for refusing him. What a truly decent thing for her to do. She's out of the way now."

"Yes, and living in poverty in Syria, they say."

"So they say."

"They also say Daia's dangerous, for many other reasons, Clea."

"I'm not trying to marry him, Politta. I'm just having a little fun, however far it goes. When it stops being fun, I'll stop seeing him. I'll disappear and never bother him again. I'll just pick some handsome young—I don't know—porter perhaps, and play with him for awhile."

"Why, you little tart. And how long do you expect Gaius to put up with you?"

"Gaius? What does he matter? He's only my husband. I give him what he wants whenever he wants it, which isn't often, and I don't care what he does with himself. It's a perfect marriage, if you ask me. He's always trying to please the emperor anyway. How can he object if I do likewise? We're a team, you see. I'm an asset to his career. Why do you think he married me?"

"You mean he wasn't madly in love with you?"

"Don't be silly. If Gaius had married for love he would have married that young thing from Sinope."

"Oh, yes. That conceited little snot. What was her name?"

"Makrina."

"Yes, that's right. Whatever happened to her?"

"Hid out in the mountains until it was safe to come home."

"Is that so? And where is she now?"

Clea swallowed a sip of wine. "Back at home. Still unmarried," she answered.

"Serves her right," said Politta. "But how do you know all this?"

"Gaius has seen her."

"No! He's seen her? And he's told you?"

"No. He has seen her and he has *not* told me, but someone else has. I have my spies, you know."

"Oh. So you don't care what he does, but you spy on him anyway."

"I'm not a fool, Politta. I don't care whom he sleeps with. That doesn't mean I trust him in all other matters."

"So is he sleeping with the snot from Sinope?"

"I wish he were!" Clea laughed. "It might settle him down. He's been so edgy lately. I'm sure she's at least partly the reason, but no, he's not sleeping with her. They write letters instead."

"Really?"

Clea nodded.

"Are you sure they're not sleeping together?"

"Absolutely. You should read her letters."

"You have?"

"A few," Clea answered. "They're sickening. All about that religion of hers. She apparently thinks she can talk him into becoming a Christian."

"Can she?"

"Not likely. Gaius isn't one to throw everything he's accomplished away so easily. On the other hand, he just might be fool enough to let her bother him. That's why I watch him."

"What about his letters to her?"

"Those I haven't seen."

"It doesn't sound good to me," said Politta. "After all the trouble she caused years ago, I wouldn't be surprised if she found a new way to interfere."

Clea nodded pensively.

Politta splashed at the water with her free hand. "You know," she said, "if it hadn't been for her I could have had my fling with Statilius and still stayed married to Hippolytus. What an embarrassment that family caused me! What a mess they made of things. I'd give anything to put that girl in her place once and for all."

Clea set her cup on the edge of the pool, then slid entirely under water for a moment. When she came up, she cleared the water away from her face and said, "You might yet have that chance."

# XXXVII

After routing Pompeianus, Constantine proceeded slowly southward along the Via Aemilia to the Temple of Fortune on the Adriatic Sea, then followed the Via Flaminius through the Apennines and all the way to Rome, at least as far as the Milvian Bridge over the Tiber River. The entire route was unopposed. This lack of resistance made Constantine suspect a trap. Why else would his enemy have left the mountain passes unguarded? The narrow defiles through the mountains made it virtually impossible to maneuver on foot or horse. A handful of men, properly positioned and protected, could have held off an army for days if not weeks in the mountains. And if they were eventually overcome, as they would undoubtably be, they could at least buy time with their lives for their city and their emperor. But where were they?

Certainly Maxentius was no soldier. When his army collapsed in the north, he had set his hopes on a siege and planned accordingly, hoarding provisions, strengthening the city's garrison, and improving the city's defenses, at Italy's expense. When the army of Constantine arrived outside Rome in late September, the hills around about were already stripped bare of timber, forcing the besiegers to spend much of their time foraging for fuel and food farther out into the countryside.

Inside the city, Maxentius had about 12,000 men—ten cohorts of Praetorian Guards and two cohorts of urban augmentees, plus a few wings of Moorish and Numidian light cavalry. It was all that he had left in Italy. Africa held thousands more of his troops, but although it was still within Maxentius's realm it was no longer under his effective control. All summer long shipments of grain from African ports had been plagued with delays, frustrating Maxentius's preparations. The African legions also were slow to respond to his urgent summons, raising questions about their loyalty.

Yet for the sake of the city's morale, Maxentius did not delay celebration of the fifth anniversary of his accession to the purple. The day itself fell on the 28th of October. The celebration began on the 26th, with a parade of Praetorians, splendidly attired in their white, blue, and red tunics and their brightly polished silver-plated helmets with feather plumes. The tips of their spears and their oval shields also were trimmed in silver. The shields were colorfully painted with the insignia of their cohort and maniple. They marched in column to steady drumbeats, accompanied by the blare of trumpets and tubas. A succession of standards identified the units by their totems, animals real and mythical, topped with the image of their augustus, Maxentius. Dragon-headed streamers fluttered gayly down the Vicus

Patricius from the Castra Praetoria to the Flavian Amphitheater, then into the Roman Forum and down the Via Sacra, before turning through the imperial fora and heading back toward the camp.

The crowds cheered without restraint, happy to be relieved of their worries of the siege, if just for a while. They packed the side streets and the fora throughout the parade, and when it was over they moved as one great mass toward the Circus Maximus, filling it to capacity for the celebratory races.

The crowds cheered as well when the emperor appeared upon the imperial pulvinar to start the races, in the company of his chief military advisors and his ever-present bodyguards. It was a rare public appearance. There had been threats upon his life, and since the food riots of the previous year he had taken the precaution of shifting his residence from one private mansion to another, while still maintaining his palace on the Quirinal Hill.

Maxentius dressed for the occasion in a snow-white toga trimmed in purple and gold, wearing the red leather shoes of the ancient patricians. He was still just 26 years of age. In face and form, he resembled no one so much as his sister Fausta, Constantine's wife. Both had inherited their mother Eutropia's elegance, but whereas this contributed to Fausta's beauty, it worked against Maxentius's manliness. He was boyishly handsome, in a way that women find darling but men find effeminate. The veteran commanders and guards surrounding him on the pulvinar effected an unflattering contrast with their young pleasure-seeking caesar.

The first race finished without incident, to the apparent satisfaction of the crowd. But while they waited for the second race to begin, a loud voice somewhere near the pulvinar was heard to shout, "Are you afraid to fight Constantine in the open?" The stunned young emperor looked around. The challenge was so loud and clear that he thought for a moment that it had come from one of his own officers. The officers themselves looked around. Then they heard the voice again: "Are you a coward hiding behind the city walls?"

Maxentius twisted in his seat. "Who said that?" he snapped. The officers and guards searched the crowds to the right of the pulvinar. "Who said it?" an officer inquired of the guards. The guards looked down at the tiered seats of spectators and shook their heads. In the sea of people it was impossible to tell.

The Praetorian Prefect Aradius Rufinus leaned over the marble balustrade. "Who said that?" he asked. The men and women below looked up. "Said what?" one asked. Aradius grimaced, then turned back to his superior and shrugged his shoulders.

"Are you a coward?" the voice called, this time from the opposite side of the pulvinar.

Maxentius crinkled his racing program in one hand and pounded the arm of his chair with the other. "Who said that?! I demand to know!"

The officers moved to the opposite balustrade and stared down threateningly. "A pest, my lord," said the consul, Rufius Volusianus. "Probably drunk."

"Drunk or not, I want him arrested!" Maxentius ordered.

"Are you a coward?" asked a voice on the right. "Are you a coward?" asked another on the left. "Are you a coward?" asked a third. "A coward? Are you a coward?"

The frustrated officers and guards looked left and right, but the calls were coming from farther off in all directions. "Are you a coward?" the voices called. "*Esne ignavus? Esne ignavus? Esne ignavus?*" After the fourth or fifth repetition, it seemed that everyone in every part of the circus, except those nearest the pulvinar, was chanting in unison, "*Esne ignavus? Esne ignavus? Esne ignavus? Esne ignavus? Esne ignavus?*"

Enraged, Maxentius threw his racing program over the side of the pulvinar into the crowd and then stormed out of the circus. His officers and guards followed quickly behind him, chased away by the continuing chant, "*Esne ignavus? Esne ignavus? Esne ignavus? Esne ignavus? Esne ignavus?*"

The chant echoed distantly in the great hall of the old Palace of Augustus on the Palatine Hill, through which Maxentius passed after leaving the circus. "Ingrates!" he screamed. "Ingrates! Fat and greedy ingrates! Who saved them from Severus? Who held out against Galerius? Who has kept them fed for these past five years? If it hadn't been for me, they would have all starved! Africa would have eaten its own grain and sent Rome its chaff! Who do they think put down the rebellion? Who? Who?!"

"You, my lord," answered Volusianus, who had actually led the expedition to Africa.

"That's right! I did it!" Maxentius declared, beating his chest with his fist. "I made the plans! I gave the orders! I did it! And they call me coward!" Red with rage, the young emperor wheeled about and on impulse wrested a spear from the nearest guard and hurled it through the empty hall. The spear clattered to the floor at the far end of the hall, chased after by its owner.

Maxentius turned back to the others. "It wasn't my fault Pompeianus lost everything up north," he said. "I gave him all he needed, and he squandered it all. If only they knew how much I've planned for this siege, the preparations I've made. If only they knew what we're up against, they'd thank me for keeping out that usurping bastard out there. But what do they know of military matters? What does the mob know of anything? War to them is an afternoon at the amphitheater. The gods know I've given them enough of the games. They should thank me for that, too, and for the races.

Instead, they expect me to just ride out, slay the beast, and save the city, so they can go back to their boring little lives. If only it were that easy! If only it were just a matter of courage and daring!"

Maxentius sighed and looked away.

"But my lord," said Aradius, the praetorian prefect, "it can still be done."

Maxentius looked at him with surprise and dread. "What do you mean? What can be done?"

"We can defeat Constantine outside the walls, with a lightening stroke when he least expects it," Aradius answered. "Constantine's troops are spread out around the city. If we can catch him by surprise, we can defeat him before he can concentrate his forces. We know where he has his headquarters. If we attack him there with full force, we can capture or kill him. His legions then will have no choice but to switch sides."

Maxentius looked at Volusianus. "Why haven't you suggested this before?" he asked.

"We've talked about it between us, but we can't agree, my lord," Volusianus answered. "The risks are too high. Constantine outnumbers us two to one. Even a surprise attack would not be easy, and it breaks all the rules of war. Giving up a strong defensive position to hazard a battle on open ground against a superior foe? It's almost foolhardy."

"So foolhardy Constantine will never expect it," countered Aradius.

"What else would you suggest, Volusianus?" asked Maxentius.

"We should wait, at least a few more months."

"Will they wait?" Maxentius asked, pointing toward the circus. "One month and they're already tired and restless. Three more and they'll go to Constantine on their knees, begging him to take the city."

"We've no need to wait," said Aradius. "Waiting will only weaken us. We can end this now with a stunning victory that will not only rescue Rome but deliver half the empire into your hands. "

"When would you attack?" Maxentius asked.

"There is no better time than now, during the celebration, when he least expects a move so bold and decisive."

"I cannot agree to this," said Volusianus.

"You've had your chance, Volusianus," said Maxentius. "I listened to you and you've left me surrounded by my enemy. Now it's Aradius's turn. If the gods approve, of course. Let's ask them."

The walls around Rome, built by the emperor Aurelian some sixty years before, were now crowned with wooden parapets, hastily erected after the defeat of Pompeianus at Verona. Jutting out over the walls, they provided overhead protection for the defenders and made storming the walls more difficult. Beyond the walls along likely avenues of approach, the defenders

had erected a series of earthworks festooned with pickets. Both were plainly visible from Constantine's headquarters atop the ridge line north of the
Milvian Bridge across the Tiber River.

The bridge and the city seemed a world away to Marcus, standing on
the slope below the headquarters, gazing down on the bridge and city in the
late October light. The ancient stone bridge itself was blocked by barricades,
and a pontoon bridge had been constructed alongside, no doubt rigged for
easy destruction if necessary. Timber towers stood at the far end of both
bridges, providing archers an easy shot at anything on them.

"Not how you remember her, eh, Canio?"

Marcus turned, surprised and embarrassed to be caught at a pensive
moment by the emperor himself. "No, my lord," he answered. "I never imagined her dressed for battle. Never thought she'd need defending."

"And certainly never expected she'd need defending against you,"
Constantine added.

Marcus smiled and nodded, and turned again toward the city. Since the
incident at Verona, Constantine had treated Marcus with greater familiari-
ty. He was more talkative and at times surprisingly garrulous, throwing out
ideas and aspersions without his usual caution. It was an odd insight into
a man Marcus thought supremely serious and circumspect. Constantine
seem to need someone to relax against, someone to lean upon while he vented his brain, and for some reason he had picked Marcus. Marcus was still
adjusting to the change and not quite sure of his new role.

"Years ago," he said, "after my father's death, I stood on that very bridge,
looking back at those same silent walls. It was early morning and the city
was still asleep. I was leaving Rome for the last time, I thought, and Rome
didn't care, didn't even notice, and wouldn't have troubled herself if she had."
He glanced at Constantine. "Rome turned her back on me long before I
turned my back on her," he said.

"Now's your chance to chastize her for her infidelity," said the emperor.

Marcus shrugged. "It doesn't matter," he said. "I no longer feel the need.
There was a time when I would have wanted nothing more than to glory in
her praise, to sit in judgment at her courts, take my place in the Senate, and
serve my turn as priest in her temples. Now I no longer need Rome, not her
fame, not her wealth, not her glory, not even her gods."

Constantine stared silently at the city for a moment. Then he turned
to Marcus and said, "I had a dream last night, Canio." He reached over
and lifted Marcus's sword from its scabbard, then squatted down. In the
dirt at their feet, he drew a line, parting the earth with one long, verti-
cal stroke. Then he added a small loop at the top and to the right of the
line. Next he drew two long lines crossing each other and the first line,
forming an X over a P.

Marcus's eyes widened in amazement. Constantine wiped the sword blade on a patch of grass and stood up. "This is a Christian symbol, isn't it?" he said.

"Yes, my lord. It's the monogram of Christ, a Greek abbreviation of the name *Christos*."

Constantine nodded. "In my dream, an angel in gleaming white robes held out to me a golden orb topped with this symbol. Then he said to me, 'In this sign, you shall conquer.'" He looked up at the city. "Conquer Rome in the name of Christ?" he said. "And then what, Canio? Build a new Rome, for a new God?"

Marcus was stunned. Before he could think of what to say, Gratianus hailed Constantine from behind. Bassianus was with him, and so was Caesonius, who was out of breath and holding his helmet under his arm, after a hurried return to camp on horseback.

"It worked," said Caesonius, panting heavily. "He's coming out . . . tomorrow . . . before dawn." He pointed to the bridge down below. "Right across the bridge, in full strength. . . . They're not holding anything back. . . . They mean the attack to be decisive. . . . Their objective is right here, this very spot, and you yourself, my lord."

"He's a bigger fool than we thought," said Bassianus.

"He doesn't know we know," said Gratianus. "If we didn't know, he might succeed."

"Who's leading the attack?" Constantine asked.

"Aradius," Caesonius answered. "Although Maxentius has indicated he might do so himself."

"If he can get up his courage," said Gratianus.

"There's one interesting complication," said Caesonius. "Volusianus says Maxentius has taken auguries, all favorable to the attack. He's also had the senators consult the Sibylline Books."

"Sibylline Books?" said Bassianus.

Marcus cleared his throat and spoke up. "The recorded prophecies of the Sibyl of Cumae, a sorceress and fortuneteller," he said. "The books are ancient, going back several centuries, well before the Caesars."

Caesonius nodded. "The answer the senators came back with was, 'Tomorrow, the enemy of Rome shall perish.'"

Constantine showed no reaction at first. Then he smiled slowly. "The enemy of Rome," he said. "Who is more the enemy of Rome, Maxentius or me?"

The officers also smiled and looked at each other.

"Of course," said Caesonius, "Maxentius believes that you are and has taken courage from the prophecy. He has also spread the word about the prophecy among the Praetorians and encouraged them to believe as he does."

"And do they?" Constantine asked.

"Apparently so," Caesonius answered. "At least as far as Volusianus can tell."

Constantine turned to Marcus quizzically.

"They're Romans, my lord," said Marcus. "More Roman than we are. They believe in the city—its gods, its prophecies, its fate."

"We're all Romans, however we understand the prophecy," said Bassianus. "What difference should it make to us or to our soldiers? Fortune still smiles on us, whatever the books say."

"We have time to prepare," said Gratianus. "By dawn tomorrow, our whole army can be here, along this ridge, waiting. We will have the element of surprise, not Maxentius. The odds are still very much in our favor."

Constantine glanced over his shoulder at the city. "Sometimes odds are not enough," he said at last. "Sometimes spirit matters more."

He handed Marcus his sword. "Have your soldiers mark their shields with this," he said, glancing at the ground. "If they ask what it means, tell them—I had a dream that in this sign we shall conquer. That's all they'll need to know."

The soldiers—all of them—marked their shields as commanded, using charred sticks taken from their campfires. The officers, including Constantine, painted the monogram on their helmets. The troops were also informed of the Sibylline prophecy and given to understand that Maxentius was the enemy of Rome who was to perish on the morrow.

After nightfall, the legions stationed about Rome quietly left their positions and moved with utmost stealth to the ridge north of the Milvian Bridge, leaving behind a small watch to mind the campfires so that their movement was not noticed. By midnight, six legions—some 24,000 men—were ranged along the reverse slope of the ridge line, their flanks guarded by eight wings of cavalry. The soldiers slept as best they could when dressed for battle, stretched out under their heavy military cloaks, their helmets on their heads, their lances in their arms, their shields at their sides.

Well before cockcrow, they were quietly roused from their sleep and moved into place along the crest of the ridge, where they sat down in formation to await the dawn. The soldiers dozed in the dark for what seemed like only minutes before the first cock crew and the distant chatter of waking birds was heard. Or was it birds?

Before first light, the centurions and their lieutenants walked along the lines kicking the hobnailed soles of each man's boots to make sure he was awake. Slowly, very slowly, the gloom gave way. The order was given to stand ready. Beyond the abandoned campfires on the forward slope, the bridges at last became barely visible. At that very moment, black columns of cavalry clattered over both bridges and thundered up the empty slope, riders whooping fearsomely in the twilight.

Soldiers in the front line cohorts braced themselves for the assault, while interspersed companies of archers drew their bows, but instead of pressing forward the enemy columns turned left and right to secure the flanks for their advancing infantry. Cohort after cohort double-timed across the bridges and formed up on the other side, barely pausing before resuming their forward movement up the slope.

"How many is that?" Constantine asked, from his new position on the right flank of his own lines, where he had positioned the bulk of his cavalry. On his head he wore a gleaming silver cavalry helm, with a rigid peak jutting out over the brow and a golden crest rising from back to front and trailing a mane of scarlet horsehair. The monogram of Christ appeared in purple paint on both sides of the helm.

"Six so far," answered Gratianus. "It looks like another three or four yet to cross. Too many for a diversion. Too many for a simple raid."

"Let's just hope he commits them all," said Constantine. "If we hit him too hard too soon, he may pull back and call it off."

The expanding line of attacking Praetorians continued its march up the hill, driving for the center of Constantine's line, where his headquarters had been the day before. They were still a hundred paces off when Constantine's archers let loose a volley that fell with deadly result within the ranks of their foe. Immediately, the Praetorians raised a wild cheer and ran forward, ignoring a second flurry of missiles.

The front ranks of both forces clashed against each other with an awful roar, first hurling their light-weight, iron-tipped javelins over the heads of their enemy, then closing on them with shield and sword. The battlefield resounded with cries and clatter from wooden shields being pounded together and fiercely poked with swords and lances. The initial engagement lasted half an hour before the circular brass horns sounded retreat and the lead companies of Praetorians withdrew in good order to allow others to take their turn. Above the hills to the east, the sun had just begun to rise.

The broad slope north of the Tiber was covered with orderly masses of armed men, some falling back, many marching forward, others standing in reserve. Each was identified by its standard, bearing the unit's mystical totems and honorary medallions. Dragon streamers fluttered in the early morning breeze, while the banners identifying the Praetorian cohorts hung stiffly from the crossbars of their staffs.

"I count ten cohorts on our side of the river," Gratianus informed Constantine. "He's holding at least two more in reserve, which doesn't leave him much else. This is everything he has."

Constantine nodded. "Let him continue his attack upon the center before bringing the legions up in full strength," he said. "We don't want to scare him off before folding his flanks. If we do, they might get away. Signal to Bassianus to begin his attack."

At the other end of the field, Bassianus was waiting with the heavy cavalry, anchoring the left flank of Constantine's line against the river. After giving the order for Bassianus to move, Constantine rode off to tell Ablabius to begin his attack on the right flank, against the Moorish cavalry and urban cohorts to their front.

The first echelon of cavalry started off to the sound of trumpets, dragons snapping in the wind, a thousand hooves pounding the ground. The dark-skinned Moors responded with a charge of their own, filling the air with an unearthly wail of battle. The collision of beasts and bodies was heard across the field. Frightened horses neighed in distress, while men cheered or fell silently into the murderous stampede. The Moors fought fiercely, devilishly, but their light armor and small horses were no match for the heavily armed and armored steads of Constantine. A second wing of Moors started off to relieve the first, which broke free and fled away down river to regroup.

The scene was repeated with the attack of the second echelon of cavalry upon the remaining Moors, which the emperor watched with interest, barely able to keep himself from riding down to join the fight. When the Moors again fell back, Constantine ordered the third echelon to charge two cohorts of infantry guarding Maxentius's left flank, then returned to his original position, where Gratianus was monitoring the rest of the battle.

"The center's holding. No danger there," Gratianus reported. "But Bassianus seems hung up. After a single charge, he's fallen back. It's hard to tell why."

Constantine peered out across the battlefield to his left flank, where Bassianus should have been closing in on Maxentius's right. By now, the sun had risen in full above the hills to the east, beaming brightly into the emperor's eyes as he strained to see for himself what was happening. He tried to block the sun out with his hand, but it was no use. "All I can see is that he's not moving," he reported. Then he looked around at the other officers present. "Canio!" he called. "Go see what's keeping Bassianus. If he isn't moving by the time you get there, take over and keep attacking. And hurry!"

"Yes, my lord!" Marcus answered. He galloped off at once, exhilarated to be at last in motion. It had been hard, very hard, once again watching all the action without joining in. Now was his chance to get into the fight. He rode at full tilt along the reverse slope of the ridge, between the ready ranks of cohorts in reserve, deftly dodging the errant officer or orderly who happened in his way. Carinus, his new aide, could not keep up and fell behind for safety's sake.

When Marcus reached the far flank, the wings of cavalry were still idle, and Bassianus was nowhere to be seen. Almost immediately Marcus spied a familiar face on a passing horseman. "Terentius!" he called. The young officer turned in his saddle and then rode to meet Marcus.

"Canio? Is that you?" It was Julius Terentius, whom Marcus had not seen since his service with the XXII Primigenia. He stared at Marcus in amazement.

"Where's Bassianus?" Marcus asked.

Terentius shook his head. "He was thrown from his horse in the first charge and knocked cold. We've just pulled him back to safety."

"Who's taken over?"

"No one," Terentius answered with unfeigned annoyance. "The other wing leaders can't agree on who has seniority. They've sent to Gratianus for a ruling."

"What?!" said Marcus. Then he shook his head. "Don't answer. There isn't time. I'm in charge," he said. "Follow me."

Marcus found the two other cavalry prefects just before an advance by the enemy's Numidian cavalry. An attack might have landed a heavy blow upon the line, if Marcus had not been there to coordinate the response. On Marcus's order, Terentius led his wing down along the river bank and then up behind the enemy's formation, striking hard at the Numidians' follow-on echelon before the lead echelon made contact. The maneuver spoiled the momentum for the attack and forced the Numidians to wheel to their right to avoid being cut in two. When they did that, Marcus sent a second wing against their front, just as Terentius was breaking off his assault and retiring the way he had come.

The double blow had pushed the enemy cavalry off of their line of attack, leaving a cohort of urban augmentees unprotected on its flank as it engaged the legion in defense. When he was sure that Terentius had safely broken contact, Marcus sent his third wing against the flank of the urban cohort, causing it to crumple and then withdraw.

"Look, my lord," said Gratianus, pointing to the broken cohort, falling back from the far end of the line. The sun was now high enough in the sky for a clear view of the entire battlefield.

"Is that Canio?" asked Constantine.

"Who else?" said Gratianus. "You didn't think he'd let you down, did you?"

The emperor smiled. "Just tell him to keep it up. Before long, we'll fold the flanks in toward the center, and then drive the Praetorians into the river."

At that instant, a chorus of trumpets sounded in the distance. Two more cohorts of Praetorians started across the bridges at the bottom of the slope. Behind them a cavalcade of officers, aides, and bodyguards was riding out from the city. When they reached the bridge, the Praetorians moved aside to let them pass.

"Is this Aradius?" Gratianus wondered aloud.

"No," said Constantine uncertainly. "I think it's Maxentius. Isn't that his standard?"

Among the cavalcade's many dragon streamers were several standards, but the first in line was a broad purple square with gilded fringe, hanging from a crossbar. In the center of the square was a golden medallion bearing the image of Maxentius, surrounded by a golden wreath. Atop the standard's staff was a golden she-wolf standing above the letters S.P.Q.R., for *Senatus Populusque Romanus*—the Roman Senate and People.

Constantine looked back at his own standard, very similar in design, but instead of the she-wolf and the ancient initials, it bore a sunburst and a plaque with the words *Sol Invictus*—the Unconquered Sun. He stared at it for a long moment, until Gratianus took note. "What is it?" he asked.

Constantine turned his attention back to the battle. "Just a thought," he said. "For later. After we win. If we win."

With fresh reinforcements, the Praetorians regrouped and marched again upon their foe, anchored along the ridge line since before dawn. Seven times they attacked, and seven times they were forced to fall back. The Praetorians fought valiantly, but most of them had been at it for several hours without relief. Constantine's legions had the luxury of rotating their cohorts on and off the front line, thanks to their significant advantage in numbers. The legions stood firm and were prepared to hold their positions all day if necessary.

It wasn't necessary. By mid-morning, Constantine's mounted attacks upon Maxentius's flanks had all but destroyed the latter's cavalry along with two urban cohorts and two Praetorian cohorts. The remaining Praetorians were forced to withdraw toward the river, to form a smaller semi-circular line protecting their route of escape across the bridges. The legions at last left their positions along the ridge line and descended the slope in good order to keep the retreating Praetorians under constant pressure. The tide had turned. The Praetorian Guards were now fighting not for Maxentius, but for their very lives.

Maxentius himself rode back and forth behind his shrinking line, frantically urging the Praetorians on. He was unmistakable in his gilded muscle cuirass and antique Attic helmet. He was always careful in dress, and on this occasion his attire matched the classic form of Roman generals from the earliest days.

"Hold fast! Hold fast!" he cried, waving his bejewelled sword in the air. "The gods have spoken through the words of the prophetess: 'Today, the enemy of Rome shall perish.' Hold fast and it shall be fulfilled. Hold fast!"

No less frantically, Aradius worked to rally the weary remnants of the shattered cohorts and cavalry wings, which had fallen back on the bridges and begun to flee across the river. Aradius blocked their way with Maxentius's own bodyguard, giving orders that only the wounded could cross. Then he gathered up as many of the able-bodied as would follow and led them back into the fight.

Before long, however, a great press of the wounded and the frightened had gathered before the bridges. The guards held them back with violence, striking anyone who tried to cross with their swords and spears. Aradius returned again to rally the rabble, but a sudden shower of enemy arrows spread panic among the disheartened herd. It surged forward, man upon man, trampling the guards at the bridges and many others unfortunate enough to have lost their footing. Aradius cried in vain at the edge of the crowd, "Rally! Rally!" But his words were lost amid the screams and shouts of the dying and fleeing. "Rally! Rally!" he pleaded, tears streaming down his dusty cheeks. At last he gave up, and after wiping his eyes with his cloak, he turned his back on the bridges and ran off to die on the line.

Just then the emperor Maxentius, gazing with horror upon the fleeing masses, was seized with panic. He was trapped! The crowded little circle of doomed and bloody men was steadily closing in around him and he had no place to go. The bridges were clogged. Clogged with cowards, to his mind. Cowards who had abandoned him. And how was it that they should survive and he should perish? "I must get through!" he said to himself. "I must get through!"

Maxentius kicked at his horse and charged into the mass of men. "Make way! Make way!" he cried. "Let me through! I am the emperor! Let me through!" Many were trampled beneath his hooves, but he hardly noticed. "Make way! Make way, I say!"

"Make way! Do you hear?! Make way for the emperor!" cried a lowly guardsman, his left eye blinded by a drying trickle of blood from his forehead.

Maxentius persisted, shouting angrily at those around him. "Make way! Make way, I say!" He forced his way at last onto the pontoon bridge and started across, not content to go with the flow, but anxious instead to hasten his crossing. "Make way! Let me through! Let me through!" More than one poor soldier found himself suddenly face down on the planks laid over the row of boats that made up the bridge. One stumbled and fell into the water, saving himself by clinging to the prow of the nearest boat. Armored as they were, there was no question of who could swim. None of them could.

Maxentius was half way across, still goading his clumsy horse impatiently along when the planking below their feet creaked ominously. "Mithras, Mithras," murmured a horseless Moor, helping a wounded comrade along.

"Make way! Make way! Let me through!" ordered Maxentius. The planking creaked again, and then there was a loud popping sound as the wood gave way. "Save us!" cried the Moor as he and several others disappeared into the gaping hole between two boats. Men about the hole scrambled for a surer footing, cursing and jostling each other as they did so. A young recruit without thinking reached up and grabbed the bridle of Maxentius's horse, as something to hold onto. "Watch out, you! Watch out! Let go! Let go!" Maxentius commanded. He jerked on the reins to make the horse pull free, but with the man holding on to save his life, the horse strained against the weight, then lost its balance when the recruit did let go. The horse reared suddenly and stumbled backward, stepping blindly with one hind leg over the edge of the planking. In an instant, both horse and rider hit the water with a great splash, out of which emerged only the desperate beast, churning the river furiously to save itself.

Aradius and the remaining Praetorians fought on for hours, unaware of Maxentius's fate. They asked no quarter and so received none. The unrelenting legions of Constantine gave them no chance to disengage and withdraw across the bridge. Pinned against the river, the Praetorian cohorts were destroyed in place. By the mid-afternoon, it was all over. The proud Praetorian Guard, established by the first Augustus three centuries earlier, had met its end.

Sure of his victory, Constantine waited where he was while his soldiers cleared the bloody field, burned the dead, and rested. Aradius had fallen in battle. Maxentius's bloated body washed up downstream and was found the next morning in a clump of reeds. It was covered with mud and bore the marks of his horse's hooves.

The day after the battle, Constantine's army readied itself for the triumphal entry, polishing their helmets and spears with pig's fat and proudly re-marking their bruised shields with the magical monogram that had given them victory. The army entered Rome later that day, not from the north across the Milvian Bridge, but from the west, through the Aurelian Gate on the Janiculum Hill, not far from the domus Canio. Ablabius's Lancers lead the way, clearing the streets for Constantine himself, who was followed by Marcus's Protectors, who were followed by a legionary on foot carrying Maxentius's head at the point of a lance. The crowds cheered Constantine as victor and deliverer. They jeered and insulted his vanquished opponent.

The parade continued toward the Forum Romanum, where the people expected that Constantine would climb the sacred Capitoline Hill and enter the Temple of Jupiter, to offer a sacrifice to the great god in the city's holiest shrine. He did not do so.

# XXXVIII

The augustus, Maximinus Daia, reclined on a couch in the tablinum of his private chambers, leaning with one elbow upon a tasseled bolster, before a blazing fire in the hearth. His forehead was bare of hair on both sides. The once black growth still covering his crown was now half gray. He was just shy of 50 but thin and hard beneath his deep blue dalmatic with long, billowing sleeves. Silk stockings kept his legs from the November chill, while felt slippers protected his feet.

"So? What do you think?" he asked his guest, a sly smile cracking the grim lines that scarred his face. His voice was deep and threatening, even when he meant to sound pleasant.

Clea reclined upon the opposite couch, a crimson palla about her shoulders, a quilted coverlet draped over her legs, covered also by her long woolen robe. Her hair was parted perfectly in the middle and tightly tied behind her head, except for the tiny ringlets that formed a fringe about her powdered face.

"I see the potential," she answered coyly. "It's an ambitious project. Even with all the money in the treasury, you need a vision, a strategy, a scheme for bringing all of your aims together."

"That's why I sent for you," said the emperor. "No one in Nicomedia is better known for vision than you. The scheme you devised for Sabinus's house in Antioch was brilliant. The Muses must inspire you."

"It will take time, also."

"All the time you need. I won't be bothered. In fact, I should rather like having you around—that is, if your husband can spare you."

"He lives to serve you, my lord."

"Of course, he does. And I value his service greatly. Who knows where he will end up, with a wife as charming and capable as you by his side?"

"I should blush. You are too kind, my lord."

The augustus gazed at her admiringly. "You say that so sweetly," he said. "My lord?"

"There. You said it again."

"My lord," she said. "My lord, my lord, my lord."

The chamberlain entered quietly and bowed low before the augustus. "Please forgive the intrusion, my lord, but his Excellency, the Praetorian Prefect, begs a word with you in private, most immediately."

Daia didn't take his eyes off Clea or change his expression. "Send him in. I'll see him here," he said.

The chamberlain departed, and Sabinus, Daia's praetorian prefect, entered. He was a tall man of middle age, with a broad, square, and fleshy face. If he was surprised to see Clea, he didn't show it. He bowed beside the emperor's couch. "Health to you, my lord," he said in a rasping voice.

Clea giggled, and Daia smiled at her. "What is it, Sabinus?" he said, looking up.

"News from Italy. Maxentius is dead, and Constantine has taken Rome."

The smile disappeared from Daia's face. "How is this possible? What happened to the siege? Rome should have held out for months."

"Maxentius tried to break the siege with an attack on Constantine's center. The attack failed, and Maxentius was killed in the fight. The Praetorian Guard was destroyed completely."

Daia stared up at Sabinus in disbelief, then suddenly got up from his couch. "You know this with certainty?" he asked.

Sabinus nodded. "It is confirmed by all our agents," he said. "They tell a curious story. Maxentius rode into battle believing that the Sybil had fore-told his victory, but Constantine appealed to the god of the Christians and had his soldiers mark their shields with a Christian symbol. After the bat-tle, he ordered the symbol mounted atop his imperial standards."

"What symbol? What does it look like?"

"A Chi and a Rho together, one upon the other, representing the name Christ."

"I never want to see it," said Daia, staring into the fire. "I'll outlaw it. I'll try anyone for treason for displaying it openly, and the penalty shall be death by fire. See that it's done."

"As you wish, my lord," said Sabinus. "There is one final detail of signif-icance, my lord. The Senate has named Constantine 'Augustus Maximus,' but more importantly, it has elected both Constantine and Licinius as con-suls for the coming term."

"So they're in this together?"

"It would appear so," said Sabinus.

Daia began to pace the floor between the couches. "We must make plans," he said. "We've no time to lose. Summon the praetorium. Have them come at once to my chambers. And Peucetius, the finance minister, too."

"Yes, my lord."

Clea sat up to go.

"Damn that idiot Maxentius! He could have held out for months! How could he have been so stupid?" Daia continued pacing, his eyes on the floor. "We must move at once, before Constantine can recover, before Licinius can concentrate his forces. How many legions does he have in Thrace, do you know? What about Pannonia?"

He was still pacing, still peppering Sabinus with questions when Clea slipped unnoticed from the room.

It was still light when Clea arrived home to find Marcellinus waiting in her chambers. "Where have you been?" he asked somberly.

"At the palace," she answered. "Don't worry. I was only there to discuss decorating with Daia. He wants his chambers renovated with a lady's touch and has asked for my advice."

"Where was the empress?"

Clea sighed with annoyance. "Oh, Gaius, I don't know where she was. Picking parsley on the porch perhaps. What does it matter? If you are concerned that I might embarrass you, don't be. You'll only embarrass yourself by behaving like a jealous husband. Daia trusts you and he likes me, and I don't see how either of us would gain anything by spurning his attentions, especially at present. Have you heard the news from Italy? Maxentius is dead and Constantine now rules Rome, with Licinius as his ally. Do you know what this means?"

Marcellinus shrugged his shoulders. "War, most likely," he said.

"Of course," said Clea. "Daia's meeting right now with his generals to plan it. And do you know what war means? Opportunity, Gaius. There's lots to do and Daia will need plenty of good men to do it all. Men like you, Gaius. Think of it. With Maxentius gone, Daia is outnumbered. He'll need to elevate one of his generals to caesar, and the new caesar will need his own praetorian prefect, and who do you think the leading candidate for that honor is?"

Clea reached up and squeezed Marcellinus's cheeks gently.

"You, my darling husband," she said through a sudden smile. She let go and whirled about with a laugh.

"How do you know this?" he asked.

"How do I know this? How do I know anything, Gaius? By befriending the right people. Here you are, worrying over who has his hands between my legs, and all I've ever brought you is advantage. You should thank me. You should thank your stars for having married me."

Marcellinus just looked at her.

Clea smiled again and slithered up close, almost touching him. "We're two of a kind, you and I," she cooed. "We know what we want, and we know how to get it. We're a team, Gaius. You do your part, I do mine."

She backed off suddenly and turned away, pacing slowly through the room's fading light as she spoke. "Your part, Gaius, is to do your duty, serving those above you with absolute loyalty." She stopped and faced him. "You're good at that, aren't you, Gaius? Always loyal, always obedient. Except when it comes to a certain little vixen in a certain little seaport."

"What do you mean?" he asked.

"You know what I mean. I mean the letters, the gifts, the visits, the special legal consideration you've given the girl and her family."

His face reddened. "Why should you care?" he said. "Who are you to object?"

Clea huffed dismissively. "You think I'm jealous?" she said. "You think I'm worried you're sleeping with her? If you were, it would be easier to explain. But you're not, are you? No, of course not. She's a good little Christian, and you're—you're—I don't know what you are, and *that* worries me. These are dangerous times for Christians here, Gaius, and for anyone in the East who befriends them."

"Clea, that's nonsense," he said. "You exaggerate the danger because you hate them so much. You hate her!"

"Do I exaggerate?" said Clea. "Your king's enemy, Constantine, has befriended them and even adopted some magic symbol of theirs for his standard. He thinks it gave him victory over Maxentius. I heard it from Sabinus at the palace. Daia has already ordered the symbol outlawed, and things will only get worse with war. With Constantine on their side, we can only expect Christians to be on his, right? And after Daia's setback against the Christian king of Armenia last year, he hardly needs another reason to hate them, on top of the plague in Antioch, which some blame on Christians, and the poor grain harvest in Egypt. Hardly pleasant prospects, I'd say, for your fond friend's family. Hardly pleasant prospects for us if your 'friendship' becomes known. Tell me, Gaius, what do you think Daia's reaction would be to hearing that your friend's sister is married to Constantine's chief bodyguard?"

"You wouldn't dare."

Clea marched toward him. "No, I wouldn't," she declared to his face. "I don't have any interest in seeing you ruined, Gaius. I only want you to succeed, which is why I'm concerned that if *I* can find out such things, others can. And there are others, Gaius. Other eyes, other ears, other tattle-tale tongues. And other candidates for promotion. How long do you think it will be before it all comes out about you and this—this traitor? How long, Gaius? With a war on? You must cut her off now. You must end it. Not another letter. No gifts. No favors. No visits. Stay out of Sinope for awhile, for your own sake, to save your skin and your career."

He opened his mouth to speak, but before he could, Clea pressed herself against him, grabbing his wrists and leaning into his loins so hard he almost lost his balance.

"Gaius, you are so smart, so able, so charming and lucky. You could be the next praetorian prefect, ruling over a quarter of the empire. Who knows? Maybe half the empire, if all comes out well. Don't throw it away because of this foolish infatuation. You can't have her. You know you can't.

You can't have her and everything else you've worked for. You've worked so long and hard. I've worked with you, Gaius, and you can always have me."

She guided his hands across her body. "I am still your wife," she whispered, brushing her lips against his. "No man is more welcome here than you. No man is more wanted by me."

✠    ✠    ✠

Their litters were waiting outside the Domus Canio in Rome when Marcus and Felix returned through the atrium. "Are you sure you don't want it?" Felix asked, his voice echoing through the empty house. He had gained a little weight around the waist since Marcus had last seen him. It showed also around his neck.

"It's a steal at a million and a half," he said. "Needs a little work, but won't empty your purse. For all it's meant to you over the years, I wouldn't blink if you offered three million. You can't buy more memories, Marcus, for a price so low."

"You can't buy memories at any price, Felix," Marcus replied, stopping beside the barren lararium in the vestibule. "I don't have three million or even one million at the moment, and I'm not sure I'd buy the place even if I did. I can't imagine living here again for any length of time, and it's too big for just a place to stay when in town."

"But it's home. It bears your name and your father's name. It's your father's house."

Marcus looked around him at the spidery walls and dusty floors. "In my father's house there are many mansions—but this isn't one of them," he said.

Felix looked at him quizzically but was distracted by Calvina and Eugenia entering the atrium. Calvina, too, had gained weight, and on her it was more obvious. "There they are," she said. "Finished so soon? Surely you haven't seen it all yet. We've still another wing to explore."

"I've seen it all before," said Marcus.

"Well then? Is it a sale?"

Felix sighed and shook his head. "I'm afraid not, my dear," he said.

"Not?" said Calvina. "But Marcus, it's such an opportunity. You don't dare pass it up."

Marcus shrugged his shoulders. "I just can't see it, Calvina."

"Is it the money? Perhaps we can arrange a loan."

"It's not just the money," said Marcus. "I just can't see us having much time to actually live here."

"What a pity," said Calvina with a frown. "It would have been so nice to have you back at home, Marcus, and now with your charming wife and delightful children."

Felix turned to Marcus and said, "You know I'll never hear the end of this. She'll blame me for everything."

"I'm sure he did all he could," said Eugenia to Calvina.

"I know he did, dear. I'm just so sorry to see you go. When do you leave?"

"I leave tomorrow for Ostia," said Eugenia.

"How long will it take you to reach Sinope?"

"My guess is two to four weeks," answered Marcus, "depending upon the weather."

"And God's blessing," Eugenia added.

Marcus smiled and nodded.

"What about you, Marcus?"

"I leave for Mediolanum the day after tomorrow. The wedding of Licinius and Constantia is set for mid-February, but Licinius will be arriving early to discuss matters with Constantine."

"It's a shame you'll miss the wedding," Calvina said to Eugenia. "I'm sure it will be quite a spectacle."

Eugenia nodded her regret, and for a moment no one spoke.

"Shall we go?" said Felix at last. They started slowly toward the door, where a caretaker waited with the keys. Marcus and Felix led the way. "What's to come out of this meeting in Mediolanum?" Felix asked.

"Oh," Marcus pondered, deciding how much to say, "better understanding, for one thing. Soothed tensions. And very likely a new policy with regard to religion."

"Really?"

"Constantine is inclined toward allowing complete freedom, for Christians as well as everyone else, but he wants to bring Licinius around to the same position before acting upon it."

"Just freedom, or favor for Christians?"

"From Constantine, I expect both," said Marcus. "He's already promised the palace of Lateranus, where we're staying now, to Miltiades, the local overseer. He wants him to use it as an official residence."

They stopped just outside the front door while the women continued toward the waiting litters. "For a little gold, he could have had the domus Canio," said Felix, looking up at the family emblem above the doorway.

Marcus looked up also at the emblem. "The Lateran belongs to his wife, Fausta. It's already his to give," he said.

Felix laid his hand on Marcus's shoulder. "Sorry you won't be staying," he said. "I feel I was just beginning to get to know you again. So much as has changed, Marcus, you most of all."

Marcus nodded, and they embraced, briefly but warmly.

"I'll tell you someone else who's changed, although not the same way," said Felix, speaking so the women wouldn't hear.

"Who?" Marcus asked.

"Aelia Sulpicia."

Marcus cocked an eyebrow as Felix explained.

"Of course, old Ulpius died and Sulpicia remarried, this time to an advocate from Carthago. Not a bad fellow, and at first I pitied him, but as it turns out they both seem quite content. She doesn't get around the way she used to. I even hear she's having children. I suppose it's age."

Marcus chuckled. "Whatever it is, I'm glad to hear it," he said.

"Shall I give her your greeting?"

"Please don't," said Marcus. "Let's just leave her alone for now."

"As you wish."

Calvina called over, "You're not changing your mind, are you, Marcus?"

"No, no," answered Felix. "You're not, are you?" he said to Marcus, as they started toward the women.

"I'm not," said Marcus.

Calvina turned to Eugenia for a parting kiss and embrace. "It was such a joy meeting you," she said. "I felt so sorry for Marcus after his father died. He seemed so lonely. It's good to see him happily married."

She then turned to kiss and hug Marcus. "Take care of her," she said to him. "Don't tempt the Fates—or rather, don't tempt God."

"Fare well, Marcus," said Felix. "And good luck."

"Fare well, Felix. May God bless you and keep you until we meet again."

Marcus helped Eugenia into their litter and then took his seat next to her. The porters shouldered their load and started off, accompanied by a squad of guards on foot.

"Are you sure you don't want the house?" Eugenia asked, rubbing Marcus's hand between her own.

"I'm sure," he said. "It's sad letting it go, but it would be sadder trying to hold on to it."

✠     ✠     ✠

Andreas, the former reader promoted to elder by Kimon, had just returned from Amasia, where he had represented Kimon at a meeting with the local overseer, named Basileos. The purpose of the meeting was to discuss a proposed council of overseers from all of Asia Minor, to meet in Ankyra the following year. Basileos had drawn up a list of canons on discipline within the Assembly and requested comment from the other overseers in the neighborhood of Amasia. Andreas presented the list to Kimon in his father's study, which Kimon had made his own. A fire crackled in the hearth, its smoke curling slowly toward a vent in the ceiling.

The elder Philippos was also present, so Kimon had Andreas read each canon aloud for them all to consider.

"Canon I: As for elders who sacrificed to idols, without having endured torture but only the threat of torture, and afterwards recovered their senses, it seems meet and right to allow them the honor to sit in the seats of their order, but not to offer the Gifts, or to preach, or to perform ever after any other function pertaining to the office of elder."

"Sounds reasonable," said Kimon. "Philippos?"

"No objection."

"Next then."

"Canon II: As for servers who likewise sacrificed to idols, and afterwards recovered their senses, it seems meet and right to allow them the honor to sit in the seats of their order, but not to offer the bread or the cup, or to preach ever after, except in such cases as their overseer should be convinced of their humility and wish to give them something further."

"'Except in such cases' . . . I think that leaves me enough room to make use of Eustratios," said Kimon.

"Where would we be without him?" said Philippos.

"Read the next one."

"Canon III: As for those who fled but were caught, or who were betrayed by friends, who had property taken away from them or were cast in jail or endured torture and were torn in pieces, and yet cried out all the while that they were Christians, and yet had incense forced into their hands or accepted food out of necessity, all the while professing their faith and mourning their participation in unholy things, they are without sin and are not to be excluded from communion."

"Most generous, I'd say. Any objections?"

The elders shook their head, and Kimon nodded for Andreas to proceed.

"Canon IV: As for those who sacrificed under duress or ate at supper with idols, they should do a year as listeners and two years as kneelers, then to be admitted to the communion of prayers only for two years before receiving the Thanksgiving."

Kimon shrugged and so did Philippos. "That's five years total," said Andreas, thinking to himself. Then he, too, shrugged and continued reading.

"Canon V: As for those who have sacrificed a second and a third time under duress, let them kneel for a space of four years, then commune in prayer for two years, and in the seventh year receive the Thanksgiving."

"Just six years," said Kimon.

"You think more might be appropriate?" asked Philippos.

"Comparatively perhaps, but six is a long time as it is. Go on."

"Canon VI: As for those who have apostatized and even revolted and compelled brethren to apostatize, let them listen for three years, kneel for six, commune in prayer for one year, and afterwards receive the Thanksgiving."

"Ten years total," said Philippos.

"That's more like it," said Kimon with a grin. The elders chuckled.

"Canon VII: As for those who have sacrificed before baptism, and thereafter were baptized, it seems right to allow them to be promoted to orders, as having undergone a bath of purification."

Kimon nodded. "Of course," he said.

"Canon VIII: As for girls who have been engaged or betrothed, and thereafter have been seized by other men, it has seemed best that they be given back to the men to whom they were previously betrothed, even though they have suffered violence at the hands of the former."

"Violence?"

"I'm sure he means rape," said Andreas.

"Oh, yes. Well . . . of course."

"Canon IX: As for those elders or servers who abstain from eating meat, even refusing to eat vegetables cooked with meat, not for the sake of disciplining the body but because they loathe or abhor meat, let them be dismissed from the orders."

"Amen," said Philippos.

Kimon laughed aloud. "Next," he said.

"Canon X: As for those who have entered into sexual union with irrational animals —"

"Lord! Don't tell me we have any of those in our midst, do we?" said Kimon.

"Not that I know of," said Philippos.

"None that I know," said Andreas.

"God forbid," said Kimon. "Perhaps it's a problem peculiar to Amasia. So what does Basileos recommend for these 'irrationalizers'?"

Andreas scanned the list. "It varies by age and whether or not the sinner is married," he said. "Fifteen years kneeling and five more in prayer if they are under twenty years of age. Twenty-five years of kneeling and five years in prayer if married."

"A stern sentence but I almost think it's not enough," said Kimon.

"The Law says death, for both man and beast, or woman and beast," said Philippos, with a smile of embarrassment.

Kimon looked up at the ceiling. "Forgive us for even mentioning it," he said. "Go on."

"Canon XI: If the wife of anyone be involved in adultery, or any man commit adultery, she or he must complete one year with the weepers, two with the listeners, three with the kneelers, and one standing at prayer only before receiving the Thanksgiving."

"How many was that?" Kimon asked.

"One, two, three, one—seven in all."

Kimon shrugged. "Next."

"Canon XII: As for women who become prostitutes and kill their babies, and who make it their business to concoct potions to cause abortions, ten years under discipline, by degrees."

Andreas looked up from his parchments and said, "He notes here that the old rule has been to bar them from the Thanksgiving for life, but he believes leniency may provide a better incentive for such women to reform."

"I should hope so. Philippos?"

"I suppose it might. No objection."

"Canon XIII: As for willful murderers, let them kneel continually and receive the Thanksgiving only at the end of their lives."

Andreas paused for Kimon's comment, but Kimon seemed caught by the thought. Andreas waited a moment longer, still without a response, so he continued.

"Canon XIV: As for involuntary manslaughter, five years discipline by degrees." He looked up and added, "That, too, is a change from seven years according to the old rule."

"Just five?" said Philippos. "Compared to life for willful murder?"

Kimon took a deep breath. "I suppose it would depend on the circumstances," he said. "What's next?"

"Lastly, Canon XV: As for those who have practiced divination or sorcery, according to the superstitions of unbelievers, five years by degrees. Three kneeling and two in prayer."

"Any objections?"

The elders shook their heads.

"I suppose I should consider my own list, with any sins peculiar to Sinope," said Kimon. "If you know of anything out of the ordinary, pass it on."

Philippos chuckled.

Someone knocked at the door. Andreas opened it to find a surprised Makrina. "I'm sorry," she said. "I didn't know you were meeting."

"We were just finishing," said Kimon. "Come in. Sit down."

The two elders paid their respects to Makrina and then departed, closing the double-doors behind them. Makrina sat down in the chair vacated by Philippos.

"What is it?" Kimon asked.

Makrina opened her mouth to speak, then suddenly closed it again. "Nothing, really. I just wanted to talk," she said.

Kimon smiled and waited.

"I haven't heard from Gaius since October," she said. "He doesn't usually wait this long to write. I can't help but wonder whether something's wrong, whether something has happened to him."

"We would have heard if anything had happened to him, anything serious. Maybe he's just too busy. Not enough light in the days, perhaps."

"It can't be that," she said. "He's always been busy, but never too busy to write. And if he has suddenly lost interest, you'd never suspect it from his last few letters. They were quite cordial. Too cordial, in fact. They made me afraid he was falling in love with me again. He's married, you know. Now I'm afraid he has stopped writing because his wife has found out, or because he has caught himself and decided to give up on me."

Kimon nodded thoughtfully. "That would explain things," he said.

"Oh, Kimon, I feel so guilty. I should have left him alone."

"But he came to you."

"I should have turned him away! I certainly shouldn't have asked him to write, and then kept writing him back, so promptly and so warmly. I only encouraged him, and now God knows what trouble I've caused. I knew better. I knew I shouldn't have encouraged his attentions, but I told myself I was doing it for him, that by writing I could show him the way of faith. I wrote to him as an acquaintance, an old friend, and then the letters grew more intimate and I convinced myself we were like brother and sister, sharing confidences the way you and I do. But that was just foolishness on my part. We were never just friends, and we certainly weren't brother and sister. He's a man and I'm a woman. He's handsome and charming and lonely, and I'm—I'm a little lonely, too."

"Makrina," said Kimon, patting her on the knee.

"I suppose I shouldn't pretend to be so concerned about the trouble I've caused Gaius," she said. "My greater pain is the trouble I've caused myself. I really liked receiving his letters, Kimon. I liked sharing my thoughts with him. I liked thinking of him. I liked knowing that he was thinking of me. Now it hurts me that he hasn't written. . . . I've tried to discipline myself to give up the things of this world, to prepare myself for what's coming. Gaius stands for everything, for all that might have been, all the world's comforts, all the joys I've missed. I know it can never be, but the faintest hope still tempts me. It's just a fantasy, I know, but a very pleasing fantasy, a fantasy of life without the Cross of Christ, without death itself."

She turned her head and stared into the fire. Kimon saw its golden glow illumine her sunken eyes and hollow cheeks. He wanted to console her, but not with false hopes.

# XXXIX

"Thirteen legions!" the emperor Licinius exclaimed, his words echoing in the high-ceilinged hall. "Seventy thousand men, nine hundred horse, on my side of the Bosporus, right outside Byzantium! Who's holding back the Persians, or are they in on this, too?"

Constantine smiled. "Obviously we've underestimated Daia's daring," he said.

"Couldn't he at least have waited until after the wedding before stabbing me in the back? Couldn't he have given me at least a week to get to know my new wife properly before calling me out to play?"

"Respect for marriage was never high in his esteem."

"You don't say. Well, well, well. I hate to bed your sister and run, but circumstances have overcome me. If I don't leave now, he'll be sauntering into Sirmium before I'm out of Italy."

"What's there to slow him down?"

"A few garrisons along the way. Who knows how long they'll hold out, or whether he'll even bother with them? If he's smart, he'll thrust himself forward fast and hard, drive deep into Pannonia, and penetrate all the way to Sirmium as fast as he can. If he does that, it won't just be your sister who gets violated this winter. He won't meet any real resistance until he gets as far as Naissus, and that won't be enough to stop him. Maybe 14,000 troops. I've another 11,000 in Moesia, and 40,000 more in northern Pannonia, but they'll never get there in time. My only real hope is to meet him as far south as possible and keep him busy until I can bring everything together. I'd be grateful for anything you can spare, but they'd have to be ready and they'd have to be fast."

"I have three wings of cavalry wintering here—over 2,000 horsemen waiting for the spring before heading back up north."

"You don't say? That might just do. I'll trade Constantia's dowry for them."

Constantine chuckled. "It's a deal, but I want them back, and I don't want them parceled out. You'll have to keep them together as a single unit."

"Fair enough," said Licinius. "I'll even let you name your own commander."

Constantine thought for a moment, before a name popped into his head. "Canio," he said.

"Canio?" said Licinius.

"Aemilius Canio. He commanded my left flank at the Bridge, and I know him well. My father liked him. I'm sure you will, too. He's a good man. A Christian, even."

"You don't say. Maybe he can say some special prayer to give us victory."

"Maybe he can."

✠    ✠    ✠

The whole house heard them return from the park. "We're back!" Eugenia announced in the vestibule, as soon as they were inside the door.

"So did you buy it?" Makrina asked, continuing the conversation while setting little Alexander down on his feet. He toddled off happily.

"Of course," Eugenia answered with a guilty grin. "I couldn't resist. It's so beautiful. And I don't think Marcus will ever notice how much I spent."

Nonna reached out for little Theodora's hood. "Here, little one," she said. "Off with it."

"Where's Dolly?" the little girl asked.

Eugenia bent over and patted her daughter's head. "I don't know, dear. Would you like some hot cider?"

"Yes! Yes!" the girl exclaimed.

Eugenia straightened up. "We have some, don't we?"

"I'm sure we do, lady," said Vassa. "Although it may need to be heated. I'll see to it."

The young maidservant Eulalia helped everyone off with their heavy winter cloaks, returning them to the pegs on the wall, from which they kept falling.

"Where is everyone?" Makrina asked.

"In the study, lady," Eulalia answered. "Posidonios stopped by for a visit."

"Oh?"

Makrina hurried over to the study and slid open the doors without knocking. Kimon, Posidonios, and her mother Hilaria looked up at her and stared. Makrina had not looked so well in years. She was wearing the fine bright clothes Eugenia had brought her from Rome and had allowed her sister to dress her hair and fix her face. The joy of having her sister back and her delight with the children had raised her spirits and rallied her health. But the others greeted her somberly.

"What is it? What's wrong?" she asked.

Posidonios stood up from his chair by the hearth, just as Eugenia joined Makrina in the doorway. "Come in, both of you. And close the door," he said, waiting until they had done so. "I have been asked by the governor, Marcellinus, to deliver a message. The emperors Constantine and Licinius have issued joint instructions from Mediolanum providing complete freedom of worship to everyone in the empire, Christians specifically. But with the emperors Licinius and Daia now at war, we Christians here in the East have all fallen under the suspicion of disloyalty toward Daia. Marcellinus expects very soon that he must order the arrest of leading Christians. He fears that sterner measures may follow, and so he strongly urges both you, Makrina, and Kimon to seek safety elsewhere."

"Where would we go?" Makrina asked.

"I'm not going anywhere," said Kimon. "I will not leave my flock to the wolves."

"Then I'm not going, either," said Makrina.

"It's better that you go," said Hilaria.

"But why would they bother with me?" said Makrina.

"Marcellinus wants you safe," said Posidonios.

Makrina shook her head. "I've fled before," she said. "I won't do it again, especially if it's just to spare Gaius trouble."

"*I* want you to go, Makrina," said Kimon. "*I* want you safe."

"So do I," said her mother. "It won't be like last time, Krina. You can stay with Chione in Cherson."

"Of course," said Posidonios, "you can't get there until the weather clears, and so you'll need to stay somewhere else first. But you won't be going alone. Eugenia will have to go with you."

"Me? But why?"

"You are the wife of a member of Constantine's court. You are a potential hostage. You are in greater danger than Makrina. Marcellinus didn't mention you in his message to me because he doesn't know you are here, but if he did, I'm sure he would want you gone."

"But he does know, or he soon shall," said Makrina. "I told him so in a letter."

Posidonios looked at her with concern. "When did you send your letter?" he asked.

"Three days ago."

"How did you send it?"

"Official mail. It goes first to Libanius in Amastris, then on to Nicomedia. Why?"

"Marcellinus suspects that someone's reading his mail. Eugenia's presence could now be known."

The room fell silent. From elsewhere in the house, little Alexander was calling for his mother.

Posidonios turned to Eugenia. "It's not safe to stay," he said. "You must leave this house now."

"But where can I go?" she asked.

"I'll show you where. It's better if no one knows. I'll wait here while you pack. Just a few things now. You can send for the rest later."

"I'll help you," said Makrina. "Me, too," said Hilaria.

The women hurried out and headed for the stairs to the bedrooms, leaving Kimon and Posidonios in the study.

"Mamma!" Alexander called out, spying Eugenia in the curtained walkway beside the courtyard.

"Oh Lord, I haven't time!" she moaned.

"Don't worry," said Makrina. She stooped and snatched up her nephew. "What a happy little boy," she said. "Your Mamma is busy. Come and play with me."

"Thanks," said Eugenia disappearing up the stairs.

Makrina whirled the child around in the tablinum, again and again until the boy squealed with delight. "You like that, don't you," she cooed. "Yes, you do. What a happy boy you are."

"There he is," said Nonna, entering from the kitchen. "Didn't care for the cider, did you?"

"I've got him now, Nonna. He's all right," said Makrina.

"Are you sure he's no trouble?"

"Trouble? This little fellow. No! You're no trouble. I'll take care of him."

Nonna returned to the kitchen as Makrina continued bouncing Alexander around the tablinum. "No trouble at all," she said. "You're a happy boy. Your pappa is a prince and your mamma is a beauty. What a blessed little boy you are!"

Before long there was a knock at the front door. Eulalia rushed from the kitchen to answer it. Makrina heard a man's voice in the atrium. A moment later, Eulalia appeared again. "Who is it?" Makrina asked.

"It's the new curator," Eulalia answered. "He says his name is Florianus. There are two men with him—soldiers."

Makrina stood suddenly still. "Did they say who they're here to see?" she asked.

"No, lady. Shall I tell your mother?"

"No," said Makrina. "No. I'll see them. Come with me."

Still holding Alexander, Makrina returned with Eulalia to the atrium where she found three men in military cloaks, trousers, and boots. Two also wore bronze helmets with broad rear flanges to protect the back of the neck.

"Pappa!" cried Alexander, pointing to the helmets.

Makrina smiled. "Health to you," she said. "Whom are you here to see?"

"Forgive the intrusion, lady," said the man without a helmet. "My name is Florianus. I am the curator of Sinope. I'm here to see a Lady Canio, the wife of Aemilius Canio, who serves the court of Constantine."

"Here to see her, or to arrest her?" Makrina asked calmly.

Florianus's eyebrows rose in surprise. "I have orders to take her into custody," he said.

"Very well then," said Makrina. "Here I am."

Makrina turned and passed Alexander to Eulalia, fixing her glare upon her surprised servant's eyes.

"You are the Lady Canio?" Florianus asked.

"Don't I look like the Lady Canio? Bring me my cloak," she said to Eulalia. The girl fetched her cloak from the vestibule and helped her into it. "Tell the others where I've gone. But don't alarm them, do you understand?"

"Yes, lady," said Eulalia.

Suddenly Alexander lunged toward Makrina, almost falling from Eulalia's arms. Makrina helped to catch him. "Oh, it's all right, little one. Your Mamma will be back soon," she cooed, patting him on the back.

The boy started to cry. "Mamma! Mamma!" Eulalia struggled to hold on to him.

"Please, let us go," Makrina said to the soldiers. "The sooner, the better."

"Mamma!"

"As you wish," Florianus said. "This way."

"Mamma!"

Eulalia closed the door behind them.

✠   ✠   ✠

"Poor Libanius!" Clea declared to Politta in the latter's apartment in Nicomedia. "He works so hard, and he was so careful, too. He didn't even tell Gaius he had her in custody until Gaius had had a chance to order her arrest himself, after reading Makrina's letter. Gaius, of course, was negligent as usual when it comes to that family, so a few days later Libanius simply announced to Gaius that he had captured the Lady Canio after receiving an anonymous tip. But the poor fellow had to trust those imbeciles in Sinope to actually get the girl, and they arrested the wrong one!"

Clea doubled over with laughter, nearly falling off the couch.

"Careful, dear Clea," said Politta, patting her confidante on the back. "Don't hurt yourself."

Slowly Clea regained her composure and settled back against the couch cushions. "I swear, the place must just breed stupidity," she said.

"Yes, like no place else," said Politta.

"Just imagine the look on Libanius's face when he walked into the cell and saw Makrina sitting there. Libanius knows Makrina, but I'll bet his first thought was, 'My stars, how much alike they look!'"

She laughed loudly again, slapping the couch with her hand.

"But what happened to the real Lady Canio?" Politta asked.

"Oh, by the time Libanius realized the mistake, she was long gone, across the sea somewhere, well out of reach. Her sister's still in jail, of course, for having abetted the escape."

"Poor soul."

"Who? Makrina?"

"No, Libanius," said Politta. "He must have felt so foolish, telling everyone he has the Lady Canio, and then having to tell them all that, no, he has her sister."

"Oh, everyone in the palace knows him now, having all had a good laugh at his expense."

"But not Gaius, I'll bet."

"No, not Gaius," said Clea.

"How did he react?"

"Cool as polished marble when he heard the first report," said Clea. "And then appropriately angry when he heard the second. After all, he's the one who actually had to deliver the embarrassing news to the praetorian prefect. Of course, he had other reasons to be angry, but he doesn't dare come down too hard on Libanius for fear of it all coming out."

"Poor Gaius."

"Please, spare me," said Clea. "Gaius has only himself to blame, and he doesn't need anyone's pity. He's playing too many games at once, and he knows he can't win with every throw of the die."

"You make him sound so cold and calculating."

"He is," said Clea. "He took a calculated risk in not putting the whole family under house arrest as soon as the war broke out. I'm sure he thought of it, but he elected not to do it because he's keeping his options open. What if Daia loses the war? Having friends at the court of Constantine could save his career."

Politta sat up suddenly. "That's his 'game'?" she asked.

"It could be," said Clea. "It makes sense, doesn't it?"

"You don't think he really loves Makrina?"

"Loves her?" Clea thought for a moment. "Is he foolishly, stupidly sick with desire for her as a woman? No. Is he drawn to her because she fits along a certain course he might choose to take, should circumstances permit or perhaps require? Yes. In that way, he does love her. But enough about Gaius."

Clea drew her legs up onto the couch and made herself more comfortable. "I've told you my news. Now you tell me yours. You said you had something I shouldn't wait to hear, something shamefully interesting."

Politta smiled slyly. "Well," she said, "your news is certainly hard to top, but this just might do it. Do you remember me telling you about an acquaintance of mine named Rogatianus? Actually, he was a little more than a mere acquaintance, if you know what I mean. He was lieutenant governor of Cappadocia, and then one morning they found him dead, stabbed to death in his own home in Neocaesarea, by some girl he was no doubt trying to seduce, who then disappeared into the night, never to be seen again."

"Oh, yes," said Clea. "'Butchered like a pig,' I think you said."

"At least that's how it was described to me," said Politta. "Well, by a most amazing coincidence the girl who is supposed to have butchered the pig proudly claimed the name of—Makrina."

Clea's pretty little mouth fell open. "No-o-o-o," she said. "It isn't possible."

"Why not?" said Politta. "Where was our little Makrina at the time? Hiding in the mountains, right? A fugitive from justice. We know for sure she wasn't at home in Sinope, which means she could have been in Neocaesarea."

"Makrina's a common name," said Clea.

"Indeed, it is," said Politta. "I'm not saying she did it, but she might have done it, which makes it worth looking into, at the very least."

"How did you hear of this?"

"The governor of Cappadocia at the time is also an acquaintance of mine—just an acquaintance, mind you—and I happened to see him again just yesterday here in Nicomedia. I'll introduce you to him, if you like."

"How much more does he know?"

"Not much, but I'm sure there's somebody in Neocaesarea who remembers something. It was such an embarrassment at the time they hushed it up. Nowadays, I expect people would be more willing to talk."

"I don't know," said Clea, gnawing pensively on a fingernail. "Gaius has been such a good boy lately. I'd hate to provoke him. It might be a little much to ask him to put the woman he loves to death." She giggled at the thought.

"But he doesn't really love her," said Politta. "You said so yourself. He's just keeping her as an alternative to you, should the situation require a—switch in sympathies."

Clea stared at her friend without speaking. She did not like having her vulnerabilities pointed out.

Politta sensed her discomfort but would not let up. She leaned close to Clea and said, "This may be your chance to eliminate his alternative once and for all."

Clea frowned and turned away. "Who is this ex-governor?" she asked. "Perhaps I should meet him."

# XL

It was already mid April when Marcus at last linked up with the army of the emperor Licinius at Hadrianopolis in Thrace. With his 2,000 horsemen, Marcus had just completed a coordinated reconnaissance-in-force south of Hadrianopolis, as far as the port of Herakleia on the Propontis, to which Daia was laying siege. It had taken Daia eleven days to capture Byzantium and two months to secure the rest of the ports on the northern shore of the Propontis, excepting Herakleia. Why he had bothered was a vexing question.

"Is he stupid?" Licinius wondered aloud, while a weary Marcus stretched his legs and removed his riding gauntlets. Of all the emperors Marcus had met, Licinius was the least imperial. In the field at least, he was just another general, although undoubtedly the one in charge. He hadn't even waited for Marcus to dismount before calling for a report.

"What did he think I would do with two free months to prepare? Just wait for him in Sirmium? Does he think *I'm* stupid?"

"Maybe he's trusting his numbers," said Valentinian, Licinius's praetorian prefect. "He knows he has us two or three to one. Odds would say he's safe."

"If he's relying on the odds, he's a fool," said Licinius. "This isn't dice."

"Maybe he doesn't intend a permanent invasion or victory. Maybe he's just trying to win concessions," offered Mestrianus, Licinius's master of horse, who had, at present, fewer horses to master than Marcus.

"With 70,000 men? Why go through all the trouble? And why the long sieges? Why not just rape the countryside and retire? It doesn't make sense. You're sure this is no trap?" he said to Marcus.

"I didn't see any evidence of it," Marcus answered. "We met very few patrols and no serious threats. The better part of his force was encamped around Herakleia, unused and ill-ordered, just waiting. They're spread out over a distance of thirty miles, and for most of the day half their number are away foraging. If it's a trap, it's quite convincingly disguised."

Licinius rubbed the stubble on his face. He had cut his beard for his wedding to Constantia, but he was already letting it grow back. "He's an incompetent fool," he said. "If we move fast, we can catch him off guard, before he has a chance to concentrate his forces. We'll have better odds then. And if they're as disorganized as you say, a sharp blow might send them flying, like robins from a roost."

He turned to Valentinian and said, "Plan a route to put us just east of Herakleia, between Daia and his base in Byzantium. That will give him another reason to panic. If he does, we'll destroy him."

✠     ✠     ✠

Across the Propontis, Libanius stood still and silent in a quiet chamber of the palace in Nicomedia, while Marcellinus paced the floor before him, airing his concerns with uncharacteristic candor.

"Something is not right," Marcellinus said. "You can see it in their faces every time they tell us of a new town taken. They put on a good show— these military men—trotting out the numbers of men and ships and horses captured, the stores of grain, the heads of cattle. I half expected some young officer to volunteer a count of apples seized."

Libanius chuckled politely.

"You can tell," Marcellinus continued. "For all their boasting, you can tell they're embarrassed that it's all they have to show for two months' work. Am I wrong, Libanius? Do my eyes deceive me? Do my ears?"

Libanius shook his head. "No, your excellency. I would trust them before my own," he said.

"I could be wrong," said Marcellinus. "I'm not a soldier, Libanius. I wouldn't think of telling them how to do their job, but I'd be very surprised if there isn't another army out there, growing stronger every day it's left unmolested. And it seems to me that *that* is what they should be talking about, and not about these piddling little ports!"

An orderly entered sheepishly. "Your pardon, my lord," he said, bowing low.

"What is it?" asked Marcellinus with annoyance.

"Your wife, my lord, the Lady Clea is here to see you, in private, most urgently, she said."

"Most urgently," Marcellinus repeated. "Very well. Send her in. Go on, Libanius. Tomorrow," he said.

Libanius nodded a silent greeting to Clea on his way out. She smiled in return and waited until he was gone before turning on her husband. "I hear that you have released the Sinopean from jail," she said, smiling no longer.

Marcellinus eyed her warily. "She's under house arrest now," he said. "She can await her trial as well at home."

"What if she flees?"

"There are guards to stop her."

"What if she eludes them?"

Marcellinus shrugged. "What if she does? Isn't that what you want, to have her gone?"

"She's fled before and then come back. She could do both again."

"She won't flee, Clea. She won't leave her mother and brother."

"And how do you know she won't?"

"She has given me her word."

"Her word? You have communicated with her?"

"Yes. I have," replied Marcellinus.

"You swore to me you wouldn't write to her!"

"That was before she was arrested."

"What difference should that make? Her arrest is only another reason not to have anything to do with her. Can't you see that?"

Marcellinus shook his head impatiently. "What do you want, Clea? Do you want me to throw her in jail again? Do you want to see her suffer?"

"I want you to do your duty, Gaius. I want you to do what is expected of you as governor. She has committed a crime. She has given aid to the enemy in time of war. She should be convicted and punished, not sent home to her mother."

"She was only protecting her sister," he replied, regretting his words as soon as he said them.

"Listen to you!" Clea exclaimed. "You are justifying her actions! You are taking her part! Whose side are you on, Gaius? Tell me, whose side are you on?!"

"Lower your voice," he warned. "Everyone in the palace will hear you."

Clea marched up to him and glared into his face. "Whose side are you on?" she demanded in an angry half-whisper. "Would you rather be serving Licinius, or perhaps Constantine? That certainly would make your little friend happy, wouldn't it?"

Marcellinus rolled his eyes and turned away, but she followed him. "Use your head, Gaius," she told him. "You are not serving Constantine, are you? You are not in Rome or Mediolanum or wherever else he has his court these days. You are in Nicomedia, serving the augustus Maximinus Daia, and everything you have, you owe to him. Everything, Gaius. And it can all be taken away at a whim if you displease him!"

"If I displease him? If I displease him?! And how shall my treatment of Makrina displease him? Daia doesn't care about Makrina. Daia doesn't even know that she exists. And if he knew, he wouldn't care even then. He has other things to worry about at the moment, Clea, in case you haven't noticed. There is a war on."

"That's why she should be in jail, Gaius! She's a traitor, she's the enemy, she's on the other side!"

Marcellinus moved away again, retreating to the other side of the room. "This is absurd!" he declared. "This is irrational!"

"Irrational? Who is being irrational? Who's showing mercy for the enemy of his emperor, with a war on and the outcome still in doubt?"

"You're just jealous, so you want to see her suffer. And you want *me* to make her suffer!"

"I have every right to be jealous, Gaius. I am your wife!"

"My wife!" he cried, throwing his hands in the air and turning about. "My wife, indeed! Then, please, good wife, please do me the honor of not sleeping with my coachman."

Clea's eyes flashed wide with rage. She closed on him swiftly and swung her open palm into his clean-shaven cheek. "I haven't heard any complaints from you all these years!" she screamed. "Strange that you should begin just now to care about your honor!"

Marcellinus clenched his teeth and his fists. Tears of anger watered his eyes. He wanted so much to hit her back—*to knock her busy little body to the floor!*—but he didn't dare, for fear of what she might then do to retaliate.

Clea withdrew anyway, out of reach. "I am your wife, Gaius, like it or not, and I have every intentions of remaining you wife. I don't want you changing wives as you change horses—because you suddenly decide that another one will take you where you want to go."

"What are you talking about?" he said.

"You know what I'm talking about. You're worried about the war. You are worried it might not go so well for Daia, in which case it might help to have connections to Constantine. That's where the girl comes in."

"Is that what you think? That she's just a fresh horse for me to ride away on?"

"Isn't she?!"

"No!"

"Then what is she, Gaius? Is she the love of your life? Are you so foolish-ly infatuated with her that you would jeopardize your career to please her? You're a little old for such foolishness, aren't you? Isn't it a little late to decide you really should have married somebody else, or picked a different court to serve? To tell the truth, I find it difficult to believe you'd be that stupid, you of all men. So what is it, Gaius? What do you see in her? You're never slept with her, so it's not her body. What is it, then? Why do you still care for her after all these years?"

Marcellinus didn't answer. Instead he snatched his cloak from a nearby chair and threw it around his shoulders as he headed for the door.

"Where do you think you are going?" she asked.

He stopped abruptly and looked back at her. "To Hades, dear lady," he said. "I'll see you there later."

Clea was gone when Marcellinus returned to his office an hour later, having walked off his anger along the way to and from the city harbor. It was not yet the ninth hour, but the palace was already nearly empty, the fresh spring day having provided a good excuse for most offices to knock off early.

Marcellinus, however, did not want to go home, or to the baths. He was never one to socialize at the baths anyway, and there was work to do. There was always work to do. It could wait until morning, but it might also help him get his mind off Clea and Makrina. Sending away his secretary and orderly, he settled down at his desk and began working through a stack of reports.

Another hour passed. He paused a moment and poured himself a cup of water from the pitcher on the side table. His mind turned back to Clea. Would she be home when he returned that afternoon, or would he find her out with friends, perhaps out for the evening? Any other day it would not have mattered, so accustomed had he grown to her comings and goings. But today he felt they needed to settle something, to reach an understanding or at least declare a truce between them. He was surprised by her anger and apparent jealousy, and he feared what she might do if she were not appeased.

He was again at his desk half an hour later when an orderly appeared to deliver a large leather pouch, the kind that advocates carried to court when pleading their cases. A paper note was tucked into the pouch's leather binding. The note said, "See to this immediately." A scribbled S at the end of the sentence identified the sender as Sabinus, the praetorian prefect.

Marcellinus untied the binding, opened the flap, and removed from the pouch a sheaf of papers. The top piece was a charge sheet, recognizable by its familiar form. Scanning the sheet, he noticed first the seal of charging official, the governor of Cappadocia; then the crime, murder; and then the accused—Makrina, daughter of Aristoboulos, of Sinope.

His heart stopped. His face paled. His eyes alone remained in motion, hurrying over the page again and again to be sure of what they saw. The victim's name was there also: P. Sempronius Rogatianus, no one Marcellinus recognized although he was identified as the lieutenant governor of Cappadocia at the time, years earlier, before the death of the emperor Galerius.

Beneath the charge sheet were half a dozen depositions, from the inspector general of the province, a chief of police, and several servants of various kinds. Marcellinus shuffled quickly through them, reading enough to cause him alarm. They were quite detailed and vividly set down, sometime soon after the crime, it seemed. The crime itself seemed real enough, but how could the killer have been Makrina? Her name appeared in at least two of the depositions, with one alleging her home as Sinope. But if this much was known at the time of the crime, why had the investigation not identified her sooner?

It was all too neat a bundle, and too coincidental in its appearance, for

Marcellinus not to suspect Clea's involvement. He stuffed everything back into the pouch and headed off in haste to the prefect's office, intending to tell Sabinus everything. He was romantically involved with a girl named Makrina. She was an old friend, a woman he had almost married. His wife was jealous and angry and all too eager to believe and allege that the two Makrinas—his friend and the killer—were one in the same. But they can't be. They just can't be. He knew his wife and he knew Makrina, and he could only believe that his wife was willfully mistaken.

Sabinus, he was sure, would understand. It would be humiliating to admit his affections for Makrina, and he expected severe censure and perhaps mild punishment, possibly an order to end the affair, but he was willing to take that chance. He was a man and subject to the same passions as all real men, including Sabinus himself, who would surely understand and forgive Marcellinus's indiscretion if he forthrightly confessed it and begged for mercy.

But Sabinus was not in his office, having left that afternoon to join the emperor, still besieging Herakleia on the other side of the Propontis. He would not return for several days. Marcellinus was beside himself. Should he wait for Sabinus to return? Should he hurry after him and risk his annoyance at having to deal with such a personal matter with so many other more important matters at hand? Sabinus expected immediate action. What could Marcellinus do in the meantime?

One thing came to mind. In the prefect's antechamber, he wrote out a quick letter to the curator Florianus in Sinope, instructing him to take Makrina back into custody. An orderly delivered the letter to the imperial post riders, headquartered in the palace, and within the hour the letter was on its way.

Too distressed to work, too restless to ride in his litter to his house up the hill from the palace, Marcellinus walked home on foot. Clea and Politta surprised him in the atrium, resting at ease in lounge chairs. Clea, stone-faced, looked up at him and said coldly, "Greetings, Gaius. What's new?"

Politta stifled a nervous titter.

Marcellinus stared back at his wife. "This is your doing," he said to her. "The charges. The depositions."

"I had something to do with it, but very little," she replied.

"You fixed things to incriminate Makrina."

"Now, Gaius, do you really think I would frame someone for murder just to avoid losing you? You flatter yourself. I've only taken the initiative to make her identity known, as any good and loyal citizen should."

"I don't believe you."

"It's all true, Gaius," said Politta. "I discovered it myself, quite by accident. Makrina did it. She killed the man and fled."

Politta was smiling at first, but Marcellinus's grim gaze made her quail and look away.

"Don't look so sad, Gaius," said Clea. "It doesn't have to be the end for her. Considering the circumstances, I'm sure Sabinus would be satisfied if she merely renounced her Christian faith and offered a sacrifice to the Caesars."

"She will never do that," said Marcellinus.

"No, I don't expect she will," said Clea. "But then, you never know. If she's capable of murder, perhaps she's also capable of apostasy. You will allow her the option, won't you? You might very well be able to talk her into it. You know how persuasive you can be. Give it a try, Gaius. Maybe she'll do it for your sake. And if she doesn't, well, that's her choice, her god over you. . . . That's the difference between us, Gaius. I want you; she doesn't."

He stared at her without speaking.

"You forced me to do this, Gaius. I might have withheld the information for your sake, but you wouldn't leave her alone. I couldn't just stand by and let you ruin your life and mine over her, now could I? It's for the best, Gaius. Someday you will thank me for it, someday after your promotion to praetorian prefect. Go on, Gaius. Hurry to Sinope. Do what you can. Talk to her. Plead with her. Sleep with her if it helps. Your have my blessing. Can I help you pack?"

Marcellinus didn't answer.

"What's the matter, Gaius? Cat got your tongue?"

Politta tried unsuccessfully to stifle a laugh, covering her mouth with her hand. Clea smiled and chuckled. It was all the encouragement Politta needed. She laughed out loud. Clea joined her, eyeing Marcellinus with derision. He turned in silence and walked away.

✠ ✠ ✠

Marcus was in the saddle, on the march, when the courier caught up to him on horseback. "Lord Canio?"

"Yes?"

"A dispatch from Mediolanum."

The courier passed Marcus a leather pouch and rode off. Marcus broke the wax seal on the pouch and opened it.

"Orders?" asked Terentius, riding alongside Marcus.

"Actually, it's a letter from my wife. She's in Cherson, or was when this was written. It's over a month old."

"Cherson? That's good then. She's safe."

"Yes, but her sister has been jailed in Sinope for helping her escape."

"Her sister? The one you almost married?"

Marcus looked up from the letter. "You remember that much?"

"How could I forget? She held more of your attention than the army did in those days."

"That's true," said Marcus. "She did."

# XLI

The emperor Maximinus Daia took Herakleia the last week in April and was allowing his soldiers time to enjoy their spoils when he learned of Licinius's presence near Selymbria, on the coast between Herakleia and Byzantium. Daia ordered his army east toward Selymbria, but his vanguard made it only as far as the first post station, 18 miles outside Herakleia. The way was blocked by the 30,000 men of Licinius's six legions, encamped about the second post station, another 18 miles down the road, near a place known locally as the Serene Fields.

Licinius offered to parley with Daia, as he had after Galerius's death, but Daia refused him. "They say he has already promised Jupiter he will eradicate the Christians if he wins in battle," said Valentinian, Licinius's praetorian prefect.

"You don't say," said Licinius. "Daia always was a superstitious sot."

Later that day, Licinius summoned Marcus to his tent. When Marcus reported, the emperor put an arm around Marcus's shoulder and led him away from the others in attendance, to speak to him privately. "Constantine told me before I left that you have a special Christian prayer for victory," said Licinius.

"He did?" said Marcus, alarmed at first, until he saw the grin on Licinius's face.

"Write one out for me," said Licinius. "Not too long and not too fancy. And not too Christian, either. Something the troops can say on their own."

"As you wish."

"Bring it to me before supper, and don't let anyone else know of it. Understood?"

"Perfectly, my lord."

Marcus returned to his tent and wrote out a brief prayer, borrowing words from Christian worship. He later passed it to Licinius as a folded note. The emperor smiled and said thanks without reading it.

The next morning, Terentius returned from the day's first officers' call.

"Here's a strange one," Terentius said, showing Marcus a small wooden placard, the kind used to disseminate the password through the ranks each night. "The emperor wants us to teach this to our troopers and have them recite it before we go into battle."

Marcus examined the placard and found his prayer, or something similar:

*Supreme God, we beseech Thee,*
*Holy God, we beseech Thee,*
*Unto Thee we commend all right,*
*Unto Thee we commend our safety,*
*Unto Thee we commend our empire,*
*By Thee we live,*
*By Thee we gain victory and happiness,*
*Supreme Holy God, hear our prayers.*
*To Thee we stretch forth our arms.*
*Hear us, Holy Supreme God.*

Not quite what Marcus had written, but close enough. "Did they say where they got this?" he asked.

"They did, but I'm not sure I believe them," said Terentius. "According to Valentinian, the emperor came out of his tent this morning claiming that a messenger from God appeared to him in the night and taught him this prayer. The first thing the emperor did, even before heading to the latrine, was to dictate the prayer from memory to his secretary."

"That explains it," said Marcus.

"Explains what?" said Terentius. "You're not saying you believe them, are you?"

Marcus smiled. "Not the part about it being night," he said.

☩    ☩    ☩

Marcellinus left his armed escort outside in the alley and waited alone in the atrium while Eulalia went to announce his presence. He was weary from his hurried journey to Sinope, but too anxious to stand still or sit down. The girl returned a moment later with her mistress, Hilaria. "Makrina's not here. She's in jail—again," she said without a word of greeting.

"I'm not here to see Makrina," said Marcellinus. "I'm here to see Kimon. Would you please send for him?"

"He's in the study," said Hilaria coolly. "You know the way."

Marcellinus hesitated, then started off alone for the study, cutting through the open courtyard on the way. The doors of the study were open, as were the doors to the study's balcony. Kimon was sitting upon a tall stool before a large writing desk, angled so as to make the most of the light from the balcony doors. He looked up when Marcellinus appeared. A broad grin stretched across his face, baring long white teeth behind a full black beard just beginning to gray. He turned in his seat and said, "Welcome, Gaius. Or, I should say, your excellency."

Marcellinus had not seen Kimon in years and the sight of him brought back many memories. He pursed his lips to suppress a smile. "Greetings, Kimon," he said with restraint.

"If you are looking for Makrina —"

"I know where Makrina is. I'm here to see you."

"Well, then, come in," said Kimon. "Sit down. Would you like some refreshment?"

"No, thank you."

"You look tired. Surely some wine. Bring us some wine, Eulalia."

Marcellinus turned just in time to see the girl hurry off to the kitchen.

"Have a seat," said Kimon, reaching for a walking stick leaning up against the desk. He rose and took a few uneasy steps toward a couch nearby. "Please, sit down."

"I haven't come to visit, Kimon," said Marcellinus, not moving from where he stood. "I've come to find out what you know about this case involving Makrina."

Kimon stopped before reaching the couch and leaned upon his stick. "Are you sure it involves her?"

Marcellinus exhaled impatiently. "Please, Kimon. No coyness. Just tell me what you know."

"I'm afraid I can't help you, Gaius."

"Why not? Do you think I came here to crucify her? I came here to save her life if possible, but I can't unless I know what you know."

"I am her confessor, Gaius. What I have heard from her is between her and God, and God has forgiven her."

"So what if he has?" said Marcellinus. "The law has not, Kimon, and I am sworn to enforce it. Unless I can disprove the allegation or find sufficient cause for mercy, she is doomed."

"She is in your hands, Gaius."

"My hands? My hands are tied, Kimon! I have no power of my own. I have only the authority vested in me by the Augustus, and with that comes the burden of executing his will, which, in this case, could require her death. I can only act within allowances, and I am being watched. My own fate is at stake. I cannot show her undue mercy. If there is any reason why she should not suffer the full penalty for this crime, I must know it now. If there is a case to be made in her defense, it must be very well made to save us both. I can't wait until the trial to find out what it is. I must know now, Kimon, if you want me to save her."

Eulalia appeared again at the door holding a tray with a small pot of mixed wine and two drinking bowls. Kimon motioned for her to set it down on a low serving table next to the couch.

When she had gone, he said to Marcellinus, "Talk to Makrina. She will tell you everything."

"Everything?"

"More than I would let her, if I were her advocate. Not because she trusts you, Gaius, but for your own sake."

"What do you mean?"

Kimon shook his head. "I'll let her explain."

Marcellinus sighed and moved about anxiously, while Kimon reached for a drinking bowl.

"Why didn't you both flee?" said Marcellinus. "I warned you of the danger. I risked my own safety to do so. If you both had fled, none of this would have happened. I wouldn't be here now and she wouldn't be in jail. And who knows how things would have turned out later, with this war on?"

Kimon handed him a bowl of wine. "She wouldn't go," he said.

Marcellinus took a quick gulp and said, "You should have made her."

Kimon chuckled. "I would have, Gaius, but she outsmarted me. She outsmarted us all by getting herself arrested in Eugenia's stead. After that, I'm afraid we had lost our chance."

"I sent her home, didn't I? I made it easy for you. You could have escaped and taken her with you."

"We would have broken the law."

"Damn the law, Kimon!"

"I don't understand, Gaius. You come here to enforce the law, yet you fault me for not breaking it."

"I wish you had! It's too late now. Everything is . . . You didn't want to flee, did you?"

"No, I didn't."

"Why not?"

Kimon shrugged. "It didn't seem necessary—or right, I should say. I have responsibilities now, Gaius, just as you have. I know that must be hard for you to believe about me, considering how I was years ago. But my responsibilities require me to set an example for others, to show them the way to live."

"The way to live? What example are you setting for them by staying? An example of courage? Of defiance?"

"Of patience," said Kimon. "Of a willingness to suffer joyfully the pains of this life in hope of the next."

"And what about Makrina? Is she, too, setting an example?"

"She is, but that's not why she stayed," said Kimon. "She has her own reasons for staying. I wanted her to go, Gaius. I would have made her go, but she wanted to stay. God apparently wanted her to stay also. That's at least how it happened."

"But can God want her to die?!"

There was pain in Marcellinus's eyes. Pain and anger. Kimon saw it, and it saddened him. "God desires not the death of the sinner, but that he should turn and live," he said softly. "But because we live in sin, we must die to sin before we can be raised in newness of life."

"I know that, Kimon. I've heard it all before. But sometimes it seems to me that you Christians seek death as if it were good. Is that it? Is death good?"

"No, Gaius. Death is never good," said Kimon. "God did not make man to die, but man died when he turned away from God. God is the source of all life, and we die when we hide ourselves from him, just as plants die when they are hidden from the sun."

"But we all die, don't we, Kimon? Whether we seek God or not, we all die."

"We all die," said Kimon. "God forbid that we should never die and live forever in sin and suffering."

"Then death is good," said Marcellinus grimly. "We need it. We deserve it."

Kimon shrugged and sighed. "Gaius," he said, "We will all die, but for those who believe, death has lost its sting. Christ has trampled down the power of death by his own death. He has shattered the gates of hell. Death can claim us, but it cannot keep us. We have been redeemed."

"Yes, yes, and there are other cults that promise redemption and a life after death. But yours requires death itself, and sometimes for the pettiest reasons. Makrina can save her life by sacrificing to the Caesars. That's all that's required. Everything would be forgiven. I can guarantee it. She doesn't have to deny Christ. She just has to offer a pinch of incense to the emperor to prove her loyalty. That's it. That's all."

"She will not do that."

"I know she won't, but that's all that's required. Why it's too much is beyond me. That, of all your teachings, I don't understand. I don't understand why she should have to throw this life away to earn the next one."

"She doesn't earn the next one," said Kimon. "It's a gift from God."

"I know the promise, Kimon. Tell me something I don't know."

"It's not just the promise, Gaius. It's not just the hope of another life or a better life as a reward for good behavior in this one. It's the knowledge of what life really is. Life is the love of God, which can only be enjoyed in his presence. Life is communion with God, uniting ourselves to God, accepting the gift of his life humbly and gratefully, giving thanks back to him for the love he has given us. That is true worship. That is true life. This life you and I know now is but a feeble remnant of the life first given to Adam, a fading pulse in a dying body. We are all dying, Gaius. Makrina is dying, but by keeping the faith she is also passing from the death of this life into a truer and eternal life in Christ."

Kimon sat down on the couch at last and said, "This is a hard saying, Gaius, and even among baptized Christians, there are many who still see life as you do, as the world does. To them, this is the life that matters. The next life is the end of life, a reward for a life that is over. They don't yet see where this life leads. They don't see how wrong it is, how insane it is, how different it would be if man had not sinned. They still somehow believe that things can be set right in this world, if only people were good, if only everyone believed in Christ and became a Christian."

"If only Constantine were king," said Marcellinus.

Kimon nodded. "It would be a blessing to be governed by him. He is, from what I hear, a good ruler, as good as one can expect, though not as good as one might wish. Constantine cannot make men honest or good. He cannot rid us of our sins. No man can, except Christ, our true king, and his kingdom is not of this world. In this world, even under Constantine, there will always be avarice, envy, lust, pride, sloth, and therefore injustice and dishonesty, poverty and suffering, despair and death.

"Years ago, Gaius, you tempted me to believe that things could be put right in this world, with just the right reforms, the right laws, the right men in charge. I tried to believe you, but I gave up when I saw that even if *I* were king, the world would not be healed or made whole. My own failings told me it would never work. That's why it's so hard to tell people how sick this world is, because they can't understand how sick the world is until they see how sick they are themselves. And the people who believe the strongest that things can be put right in this world are the sickest because they are the most blind to their own sins. Only when we see how sinful we are, how sick in our souls we are, can we begin to understand how feeble this life is. Makrina understands. Makrina is ready for the next life, for real life. That's why she didn't flee. Go and see her, Gaius. Talk to her. You will see, too."

Night had fallen in Sinope. In her cell in the garrison, Makrina had said her prayers and lain down in the darkness to sleep, covered by the woolen blanket and upon the woolen sleeping rug her mother had brought her, her head resting upon a pillow of cotton. The room was large enough for ten prisoners, but Makrina had it all to herself. It was as clean and dry as one might expect for a cell, and though not entirely free of vermin. Makrina found it quite tolerable. She had known worse.

Cool night air settled in through a single barred window ten feet above the floor. Makrina slept a few feet away from the wall, where she could see the stars through the window on a clear night, and where she would stay dry when it rained. This night was clear and quiet, and sleep came easily to her.

She woke at the sound of the door creaking open. A flicker of lamplight floated in with a visitor. Makrina sat up. Peering past the tender flame, she smiled. "Welcome, Gaius," she said.

Marcellinus stopped in the middle of the stone steps leading down into the cell, holding an oil lamp in his hand. "Health, Makrina," he replied.

"I heard you had arrived, but I didn't expect to see you until tomorrow."

"I would have come even sooner, but . . . there were people to see."

"I understand," said Makrina.

He waved the lamp around to one side, surveying the empty cell. "My apologies for the accommodations," he said. "I hope you are not too uncomfortable."

"I have learned to be content in many things," Makrina answered.

Marcellinus sat down where he stood, on the steps, setting the lamp down beside him. Makrina pulled her blanket about her and waited for him to speak. He took his time. "So here we are," he said at last, "after all these years."

"Where we might have ended up the first time, if you hadn't forced me to flee," said Makrina. "You should have arrested me then and made me sacrifice."

"I couldn't do that, Makrina. I couldn't bear to see you suffer like the others."

"You misjudged me, Gaius. I would not have held out like the others. I would have given in."

"No," he said. "You were fierce in your beliefs. You had faith. You would have faced the beasts."

"It was anger in me, and pride, especially pride. Not faith, and certainly not love. Faced with losing everything in the arena, I would have sacrificed. I know that now. I did not know that then. I had my chance to endure the worst a few years later. Instead, again, I chose to escape. I sinned to do so."

"Did you kill him?" Marcellinus asked.

"I killed him," Makrina answered.

"But you didn't mean to," he said. "You didn't plan to. He forced you to."

"I meant to kill him. I wanted to kill him. And afterwards for quite a while, I was glad that I had killed him. I sinned, Gaius. I killed a man to save myself pain and shame. That's how I know now I would have sacrificed, if you had forced me to, when you had the chance."

Marcellinus drew a deep breath and then released it in a trembling sigh. He swallowed hard to clear his throat. "I loved you then," he said. "I know you don't believe me, but I did."

"I believe you did," she answered, "in your own way, as much as you could."

"Did you never love me?" he asked.

Makrina looked away for her words. "I was charmed by you. I was flattered by your attention. I enjoyed your company."

"But you didn't really love me."

"No, Gaius. I'm sorry. I don't think I did," she said. "I might have, Gaius, if things had been different, if we had not been divided by faith and events. I very well might have. And if I had married you, I expect I would have been content to live with you, as much as circumstances allowed."

Marcellinus smiled at her sadly and said, "If we had married, I might have joined you in your faith."

"Perhaps you would have. That would have made me very happy."

"I never forgot you," he said. "I never stopped believing that you were the kind of girl I should have married. I'm not sure why. In a way, it was your pride that attracted me. You thought so much of yourself, I was inspired to think very highly of you also. I always imagined myself marrying the most desirable woman in the empire—the richest, the smartest, the strongest, the most beautiful."

"I was none of those," said Makrina.

"I thought you were," said Marcellinus. "For a long time, I thought you were. But, never meeting another like you, I eventually married someone who was indeed rich and smart and strong and beautiful—but ruthless. And also faithless. And that lack has left me cold."

"Yes, I can tell," said Makrina.

Marcellinus bowed his head and rubbed his forehead slowly with the fingertips of one hand. "I've never spoken of this to anyone, but I've been such a boy about some things. I wanted truly to help restore the empire, to see justice done, to see the government strengthened and the people served. I expected that others wanted such things, too. It was easier to believe that under Diocletian. There was so much talk of restoration, reform, service. I saw myself as part of that. I imagined myself doing great things for the empire. If I had to do some things I didn't like or thought wrong, well, I convinced myself that such things were necessary if I wanted ever to do greater things."

"Did you ever do greater things?"

Marcellinus shook his head. "I served myself very well. I succeeded best at my own success. The greater things were always beyond my abilities. Yet I still must do things I know are wrong, things I wouldn't do if I were a free man, if I weren't concerned with keeping my place in the world."

He smiled suddenly. "Strangely," he said, "it was Clea who showed me how self-serving I had become. She encouraged me in it, without any of my schoolboy excuses for going along with this or that policy. More and more I find that people are more like her than me. They have no illusions. They're in it for themselves. I might have ended up just like them, but I couldn't help but contrast the encouragement I got from Clea with the censure I know I would have heard from you. You've been my conscience all these years. That's why I still feel drawn to you, why I can't stop wondering what I would be now if I had married you."

"It's not too late, Gaius."

"Not too late? For us?"

"For you," Makrina answered. "You can start anew. You can still be saved. The Grace of God can make you whole, Gaius. You can be born again as that young boy who believed in doing good and great things. It's not too late. It's never too late. You must believe that."

He threw his hands up helplessly and sighed. "I would have to give up everything—my office, my honors, my fortune, my whole life, all that I am."

"Not everything. Not all that you are. You would salvage your conscience and save your soul. And God willing, you might start anew, in the West where Christians are welcome. You could go home to Rome, or to the court of Constantine. Marcus would help you. I know he would. You could build a new life."

"A new life. A life with you?" he asked.

"Oh, no, Gaius. I can't go with you."

"Even if I confessed your faith and accepted your God?"

"Oh, Gaius, no. I can't. I can't, Gaius. I would, but I can't. I'm dying, Gaius."

"We're all dying," he said. "Kimon explained it to me this afternoon."

"No, I mean I'm dying physically. I'm very sick. I'm too weak now to even stand to greet you."

Marcellinus stood up and started down the steps to her.

"Don't, please," said Makrina. "Stay back. There is nothing you can do."

He stopped and strained his eyes to see her better in the lamplight. "What is it? Is it this cell?" he asked.

"No, no. It's not the cell. I've been sick for a long time, since before returning home. I was sick when you saw me last. I just didn't know how sick. Now I am much worse, and I don't expect to live much longer. Please, stay back. I wouldn't want to harm you."

Marcellinus covered his nose and mouth with his hand. "My God," he said. "Why didn't you tell me?"

"I don't know," Makrina answered. "I didn't want to worry you. It wasn't your concern."

"But it is my concern. I would have wanted to know."

"It can't be helped, except through prayer. Will you pray for me, Gaius? Will you pray to the one true God for me?"

"I will, Makrina. For you, I will."

"Thank you, Gaius. It strengthens me to know that. Now please go. I'm tired and must rest. Good night, Gaius. Sleep well. May God go with you."

"Makrina . . ." He paused and stared, then sighed finally. "Good night," he said. "And farewell."

# XLII

Licinius would have preferred to confront Daia on the first of May, the anniversary of Daia's accession as emperor, just as Constantine had confronted Maxentius on the latter's anniversary. But Licinius could not allow Daia more time to assemble his forces for battle. On the morning of the last day of April, the two armies marched into position on opposite sides of the battlefield. Daia's men beat their shields with their spears and gave their usual threatening cheers, but Licinius's men did something never seen before.

Once in position, they laid their shields on the ground and knelt down upon them. Then they removed their helmets and bowed their heads, resting their spears on their shoulders. With one great and solemn voice, they recited in unison the prayer to the Supreme God delivered to them the day before. Licinius himself knelt and repeated the prayer, as did all of his officers at every level and with every unit, without exception.

The soldiers of Daia were amazed and unnerved. What was this strange oath? They had heard of Constantine's appeal to the Christian God before his victory over Maxentius. Was the same magic on the side of Licinius?

Licinius's men were emboldened by their appeal, believing then that God was on their side. They donned their helmets and took up their shields and very soon advanced upon their enemy in a new and winning spirit.

The result was never in doubt. From the first, Licinius's men gained the upper hand, driving their opponents from the field in panic. Many hundreds were slaughtered before they could escape. Thousands more fled in disarray. All was chaos and lamentation in Daia's camp. The forlorn emperor himself threw off his purple robe and fled the field in the guise of a servant, riding without respite until he had reached the nearest village on the coast, where he commandeered a humble fishing boat to carry him across the Propontis and back to Nicomedia.

Abandoned by their commander, Daia's legions, most of which had never joined the battle, switched sides and swore their allegiance to Licinius, who received them with magnanimity. By noon, the battle was over. Licinius's cause was secure. Marcus took his leave of the emperor, then turned his command over to Terentius, instructing him to take them on to Byzantium for provisioning. "Wait for me there. I'll be back in a fortnight," he said.

"But where are you going?" Terentius asked.

"To Sinope first and then Cherson, for my wife and family."

✠   ✠   ✠

Libanius arrived in Sinope just as Licinius's men were bowing their heads in prayer three hundred miles away. "Good news, your excellency," he announced. "Daia has taken Herakleia."

Marcellinus was unmoved. "What about Licinius?" he asked.

"They're certain now he has only six legions with him. Hardly a match for our thirteen. This could be the end of Licinius."

Marcellinus nodded.

"You should have heard them all at the palace," Libanius continued, "suddenly full of confidence, boasting of their great strategic victory. They were right all along, they say. It was all in the plan and so forth, as if luck were never needed."

Libanius's amusement faded when he saw that it wasn't shared. He assumed a more serious demeanor.

"A victory over Licinius will give us half the empire, the better half at that," he said. "Constantine will sue for peace. There is talk already of Daia appointing a caesar of his own to take Licinius's place. His star is still rising, your excellency, and ours with his."

"So it would seem," said Marcellinus.

Libanius waited for him to say more, but Marcellinus only turned away and stared out the open window, looking out over the bay.

"Your excellency," said Libanius, "the victim's family has arrived with me from Nicomedia."

"His family?" said Marcellinus, turning back around.

"His widow," said Libanius, "as well as a brother and a sister. The brother is the imperial procurator for inheritance taxes in the diocese of Asiana. The sister is married to the governor of Cyprus. The Lady Clea arranged for them to come. She accompanied them."

"My wife?" said Marcellinus, with eyes no longer lifeless, but hard and cold.

"Yes, your excellency."

"And the Lady Politta? Is she here, too?"

"Yes, your excellency."

"Of course," said Marcellinus sarcastically. "I should have expected them. And you should have warned me!"

"I'm sorry, your excellency. I didn't have a chance. I didn't know they would be sailing with us until they were aboard."

"Is there anyone else I should know about? Any official auditors or agents of affairs?"

"No, your excellency."

Marcellinus glared at Libanius skeptically.

"None, my lord," said Libanius, shaking his head. "Just the family of the victim, Lady Clea, and Lady Politta. That's all."

"That's all?" said Marcellinus. "That's enough," he added, answering his own question.

He turned away again and drew a deep breath, then exhaled at once and bowed his head.

"They have asked when they might expect a hearing," said Libanius.

Marcellinus looked up sadly. "Why keep them waiting?" he said with a shrug. "We have the main witnesses. Clea has seen to that, also. Tell them—this afternoon."

They met about the ninth hour in a reception room off the nave of the city basilica. The double doors were closed and guards were posted both inside and out, to keep the curious at bay. The witnesses were already there, waiting nervously in the corner, when the relatives of Rogatianus arrived, accompanied by Clea and Politta and ushered to their seats by Libanius. Marcellinus himself had avoided them all afternoon, and they were not pleased.

"I hope this can be settled swiftly," said the brother, Sempronius something, to Libanius. "I have many important matters to tend to at the palace, and with the war on I can't afford an extended absence."

"To my mind, the sooner we depart this depressing place the better," said the sister, an aging beauty who had brought along her adolescent son, a ungainly and ungraceful lad who knew at least enough to keep his mouth shut.

The victim's widow was almost as taciturn, but the most impatient. Her only words for Libanius were, "Condemn her and let us go."

Against the outer wall of the empty room, between open windows, lay a small dais, draped in crimson cloth for the occasion. In the center of the dais sat the curule chair, a simple wooden seat with a low back and short arms. Behind the chair stood a gilt standard from which hung a banner bearing the likeness of the Emperor Maximinus Daia. To the right of the dais stood a smoldering tripod, censing the room with the sweet aroma of roses. To the left stood the new curator, Florianus.

A moment later Libanius returned behind Marcellinus, who ascended the dais and took his seat as judge. The guards then opened the doors and pushed back the crowd that had gathered outside.

Makrina entered in a chair with handles, carried by her own servants. She was covered head to toe by a heavy woolen cloak of greenish gray, which hid even her face to everyone, even Marcellinus, who was sitting directly in front of her. The servants set her down, removed the handles from her chair, and departed. Her mother Hilaria stood beside her, along with Philodemos the mayor, whom Marcellinus had pressed to plead for Makrina, in the place of her brother, who was under house arrest.

Libanius leaned toward Florianus and whispered, "Can she stand?"

"The accused will stand," Florianus announced, to Libanius's dismay.

"She cannot stand," said Hilaria defiantly.

"It's all right, Mamma. I'll stand," said Makrina, before raising herself uneasily from her seat. As she stood up, the hood of her cloak slipped back upon her head. Politta gasped audibly. The relatives of Rogatianus stared in horror at the young woman they had come to see punished. Her hair was streaked with gray. Her cheeks were empty and ashen. Her eyes seemed shrunken in their sockets. Skin barely covered bone on her chin and cheeks and forehead, giving her a ghastly look of death and danger. The sister and widow of the victim covered their noses and mouths with their pallas.

Marcellinus saw what he could not see the night before, but showed no surprise. At the first sign of a smile appearing on Makrina's pale lips, he looked away. "Charges," he said almost inaudibly to Florianus.

There were three listed on the parchment in Florianus's hand: murder of a senior officer of the emperor, escaping official custody, and aiding the escape of a person wanted by imperial authorities. Florianus read them aloud with supporting details, as the clerk, standing beside him, hurriedly copied down his words on a wax tablet, in Latin shorthand.

When Florianus had finished, Marcellinus turned toward the several witnesses, most of them from Rogatianus's household, still standing in the corner. "Do the witnesses stand by their statements delivered to the court?" he asked.

One by one, they each answered. "Yes, excellency."

Then Marcellinus turned to Philodemos. "Has the accused anything to say in her defense?" he asked.

Philodemos shook his head and answered, "No, your excellency."

"No?" said Hilaria to Philodemos.

The mayor shrugged his shoulders and deferred to Makrina.

"No, Mamma," she said.

"Nothing, Makrina?" said Hilaria, incredulously. "Nothing about the vile man who forced himself on you?!"

"Excellency!" cried the brother, Sempronius.

"Surely something should be said," declared Hilaria. "He got what he deserved and nothing less."

"Slander, your excellency! This is a vicious slander!"

"It is the truth, your excellency! The man tried to rape her. She merely defended herself. He got what he deserved!"

"Your excellency, I must protest! My brother is not on trial here and cannot defend himself, on account of this woman's indisputably criminal act."

"These are the facts of the case. They must be heard!" said Hilaria.

"Who has alleged them?" Sempronius demanded.

"Makrina has," Hilaria answered.

"We have not heard her."

"I have," said Hilaria.

"We have not."

"Silence!" ordered Marcellinus. All eyes turned to him, except Makrina's. She had closed hers and bowed her head.

Marcellinus turned to the witnesses in the corner. "Is there anyone who will support this allegation against the victim, Pius Sempronius Rogatianus, with a claim of fact?" he asked.

The witnesses looked at each other and shook their heads.

"The allegation then rests upon the claim of the accused," said Marcellinus.

"Pardon, please, your excellency, but the accused herself has not made the allegation," said Sempronius.

Marcellinus turned to him coldly and said, "Would you wish her to?"

"I merely mean that we —"

"I know what you mean," snapped Marcellinus, turning away from him. "Lady Hilaria, we must hear it from the accused herself, if she will speak."

Makrina hadn't moved. Her head was still down; her eyes, still closed.

"Go on, Makrina. Tell him," said her mother, grasping her arm.

Philodemos leaned close and said, "If you would speak, now is the time."

"Tell him, Makrina. Tell him now," said Hilaria.

Makrina slowly shook her head.

"Please, Makrina. You must speak! You must speak to save yourself!"

Makrina looked up at her mother. "I will not justify my actions," she said.

"But the truth must be known. Otherwise, what will people believe?"

"They will believe what they want to believe, what their friends and family believe. It is always so. I cannot change it. It does not matter."

"Makrina!" said Hilaria. "Your very life is at stake! You must show cause for mercy to avoid the worst!"

A light shone suddenly in Makrina's eyes. She smiled and touched her mother's cheek with one hand.

"The worst, Mamma?" she said. "What can they take from me that I would not gladly give? This body? This tired, sick body? Who would want it? Who would want it now? Not even I. They cannot harm me, Mamma. They cannot keep me from what I most desire. They cannot make me live here in sin any longer than God wills. What they can do to shorten my days can only be a blessing to me. I am so tired, Mamma. So tired of this life."

Hilaria's eyes filled with tears. "Oh, Makrina, my dear Makrina," she cried, pressing her cheek to her daughter's and hugging her tightly, repeating her name again and again as they wept together.

Politta blinked repeatedly and touched the edge of her palla to one eye, glancing at Clea to see if she noticed. Clea appeared unaffected and was still watching Marcellinus, who waited for mother and daughter to recover before clearing his throat to speak. "Our most merciful Augustus Maximinus," he said softly, "allows that the accused be forgiven for all crimes committed if she will but honor him with a sacrifice, thus declaring her love for and loyalty to his divine genius, the protector of the empire and benefactor of our lives. Will the accused please do so?"

An orderly with a dish of incense stepped forward and stood beside the smoldering tripod.

Makrina looked up at the image of the emperor hanging over Marcellinus's head. "I am a Christian," she said with a smile. "I have one lord and king, Jesus Christ, the Son of God, who rose from the dead and sits at the right hand of the Father. Him alone will I worship, with the Father and the Holy Spirit—never a sinful, mortal man such as our Caesar."

She then leveled her gaze at Marcellinus and said, still smiling, "I will not sacrifice."

Marcellinus stared back at her without moving, as if transfixed by her gaze. She would not sacrifice. He knew it. There was no point in arguing or pleading with her. She would sooner die and she meant him to face that fact.

He lowered his eyes to the floor between them. For a while longer, he did not move. Makrina and all the others stood by in silence, waiting for him to speak. Libanius looked at him quizzically. Clea's gaze on him hardened. Politta saw her clench her teeth and tighten the grip upon her folded fan, until her knuckles turned white.

At last, Marcellinus turned to Libanius, without raising his eyes. "A tablet," he said, holding out his hand, his voice breaking.

Libanius and Florianus looked about until the clerk offered them his own, on which the trial was recorded. Libanius handed it to Marcellinus, who took its wooden stylus and quickly scratched several lines of text into the wax. Then he handed it back to Libanius. "Read it," he rasped.

Libanius scanned the words once with his eyes, then read it aloud, substituting whole words for the customary abbreviations: "I, Gaius Valerius Marcellinus, governor of Bithynia and Pontus, judge the accused, Makrina, daughter of Aristoboulos of Sinope, guilty of all charges. As the accused has refused to sacrifice or plead for mercy, the sentence —"

Libanius stopped suddenly and looked up at Makrina and then Marcellinus, who had bowed his head.

"The sentence," Libanius said again, "is death—as the accused herself desires."

Hilaria lowered her head to her daughter's shoulder and wept. Makrina enclosed her mother in her arms, but kept her gaze fixed on Marcellinus.

Once again, she smiled, though he didn't see her. "Thank you, Gaius," she said. "Thank you."

# XLIII

Fair winds followed Marcus from the fishing village outside Herakleia on the Propontis. The small boat he commandeered slipped easily eastward, past Byzantium, through the Bosporus of Thrace, to another Herakleia— Herakleia Pontica—where they put in briefly to take on food and water. They set sail again in less than an hour, edging along the mountainous coast of Paphlagonia, past the tiny ports of Tium, Amastris, Kromna, Kytorus, and then Ionopolis, home of the snake-god Glykon.

On the third day after the battle, they came upon the slender neck of land tethering the dead volcano to the mainland. They sailed right beneath the walls of the city, so close Marcus could have swum ashore in the time it took to say his evening prayers. The maneuver around the volcano and into the harbor of Sinope, on the south side of the isthmus, took another long hour, too long for Marcus.

It was the third of May, and the same breeze that had blessed their journey now bathed the town with cool, sweet mountain air, scented with pine and cherry. The sights and smells of the little town overwhelmed Marcus with memories more physical than mental. He leaped ashore before the boat was secured, leaving his aide Carinus to unload their things and deal with the customs agents.

No one challenged the uniformed stranger hurrying alone from the busy harbor, but everyone who saw him sensed that he knew where he was going. Marcus thought he knew, too, but before long he was lost in the rabbit warren of quiet, shaded alleys running oddly among the private homes on the city's harbor side. Was it this way or that? Up hill or down? After several wrong turns, he gave up and looked about for someone to ask, but the many curious eyes that had followed his every step were now nowhere to be seen. "Lord have mercy," he muttered to himself, making the sign of the Cross.

Immediately a woman's face appeared in an open, upstairs window across the way. "Whom are you looking for?" she asked cautiously.

Marcus greeted her with an embarrassed grin. "I'm looking for the house of Aristoboulos," he answered. "I know it's around here somewhere, but I've been away a long time. Do you know where it is?"

The woman smiled and nodded, and then disappeared inside. A moment later a dark-haired boy, about ten, emerged from her house and joined Marcus in the street. "Stephanos will show you," said the woman, standing again at the window. "Go on, Stephanos."

Marcus bowed toward the woman. "Thank you," he said.

"Thank God," she replied, and then she was gone.

The boy grinned and waved his hand. "This way," he said confidently.

Stephanos strode proudly through the alleys with his soldier in tow, pleased to be seen by his neighbors and friends. They walked up and then down and once to the left. Then it all made sense. "This is it," said Marcus, feeling suddenly foolish for having been so close and so lost.

He paid the boy for his trouble with two solid silver coins, each worth 25 denarii. "One for you and one for your mother."

"Thank you and thank you," he said, bowing low.

Marcus watched him disappear down the alley, then turned and knocked. The great bronze knocker was worn smooth by much use, except around the edges, which were covered with a patina of bright green.

Before long, Marcus heard the bolt being drawn. Then the door creaked open. "Health, Nonna," he said cheerfully.

"My Lord!" the gray-haired Nonna cried in astonishment. She turned about and announced, "It's Marcus," then opened wide the door and welcomed him in. "Oh, oh, I mean, Lord Canio," she said, looking flustered. She hesitated a moment longer and then on impulse embraced him suddenly and briefly, giving him a quick peck on the cheek. "Forgive me," she said.

Marcus laughed. "Of course," he replied.

The first face to appear in the atrium was a little girl, round and white like her mother's, with dark, wavy hair parted in the middle and pinned on both sides. She peered shyly around the corner from the tablinum, waiting until her father saw her and called her name, "Theodora!"

"Tata!" the girl screamed, running to his arms. Marcus scooped her up and kissed her pudgy cheeks, once, twice, three times. The girl giggled with delight. "It's my tata, Nonnie," she squealed in Latin.

"And where did you come from?" Marcus asked his daughter.

Nonna answered for her. "From Cherson, just yesterday," she said. "You're just in time."

"It seems so," said Marcus, carrying Theodora into the tablinum, where they met Vassa holding the eighteen-month-old Alexander. "Pappa!" cried the delighted boy, throwing his arms out.

Marcus laughed and took the boy into his other arm. "So it's Pappa, is it? Not Tata?"

"Pappa!" said the boy.

"He speaks more Greek than Latin now," said Nonna.

"I'm not surprised," said Marcus, kissing his son on his cheeks and continuing toward the courtyard.

"It *is* you!" cried Eugenia, hurrying across the courtyard. "I can't believe it. What a surprise!" They hugged and kissed as best they could before passing the children off to Nonna and Vassa. Then they hugged and kissed again.

"How did you get here? What about the war?" said Eugenia

"It's as good as over, at least for us," said Marcus. "Daia is out. Licinius has beaten him, with a little help from me."

"But—But Daia was winning, wasn't he?"

"He was never winning," said Marcus. "He was only wasting his time. Believe me, I've come straight from the battlefield. Daia is finished. His legions have abandoned him, as he abandoned them."

"Welcome, Marcus," said Hilaria.

Marcus looked up. "Health to you, Hilaria," he said, taking her hand and kissing her cheek without letting go of Eugenia. "It's good to see you. You're well, I hope?"

Hilaria shrugged.

Marcus looked around and asked, "And where are Makrina and Kimon?"

At the edge of the courtyard he saw a bearded man, simply but completely dressed, leaning on a walking stick. Marcus stopped and stared. The grin was unmistakable, though the graying whiskers nearly concealed it. "Kimon?" said Marcus, letting go of his wife.

"Welcome back, once again, Marcus."

"Kimon!"

Kimon stood his ground as Marcus clapped him to his breast with a hardy slap on the back. Joy overwhelmed them and moved them both to tears. They dried their eyes on each other's cloak, before ending their embrace.

"Look at you," said Marcus, tugging with both hands on Kimon's whiskers and marveling at his humble attire. "A philosopher after all."

"Less a philosopher than you," said Kimon, shaking his head and wiping his eyes once more.

Marcus shook his head. "I was never a philosopher, Kimon. I was always just a soldier, though it took me years to admit it."

"Not just a soldier, Marcus. A good soldier, a Christian soldier, and a good Christian husband and father, too, from all I can tell."

They embraced again amid fresh tears, which quite embarrassed them when the women and children joined them. Marcus turned away to wipe his eyes, then turned back when he had recovered. "Where is Makrina?" he asked. "Is she here? Is she well?"

Eugenia and Hilaria both lowered their eyes. Marcus saw their dismay. "Is she?" he repeated.

Eugenia touched her husband's arm and looked at him as if to speak, but then she shook her head and turned to Kimon.

Kimon placed a hand on Marcus's shoulder. "Makrina's here," he said, "but she is not well. She's dying, Marcus."

Marcus looked each of them in the eye and saw the same sadness. "Dying?" he said. "Of what?"

"Only God knows," said Kimon. "She's been sick for a long while and is wasting away. Whatever it is, it hasn't threatened anyone else."

"I must see her. Where is she?"

Kimon nodded toward the double doors to the study, from which they had all just come.

As Marcus neared the doors, he heard the voice of a young woman reading aloud from the Psalms of David. He recognized the words, having heard them many times in the public worship:

> Purge me with hyssop and I shall be clean,
> Wash me and I shall be whiter than snow.
> Make me to hear joy and gladness,
> That the bones which thou hast broken may rejoice.

He opened the doors slowly. It was Eulalia, the servant girl, sitting on a stool by the window. She paused and looked up as he entered.

Makrina lay on the couch nearby, covered with blankets. Her eyes were closed, and she seemed asleep. It had been so long since Marcus had seen her, and she was so changed now that he wasn't sure he recognized her.

"Is that you, Marcus?" she said weakly and without opening her eyes.

The sound of her voice made him tremble. "Yes," he answered, barely able to speak. He fell to his knees beside the couch, taking her pale hand in his and kissing it gently.

Kimon nodded to Eulalia to resume reading, and she began again, in a lower voice, where she had left off:

> Hide thy face from my sins,
> And blot out all mine iniquities.
> Create in me a clean heart, O God,
> And renew a right spirit within me.

Makrina opened her eyes and smiled at Marcus. "I knew you would come," she said. "I saw you. You were in a little fishing boat. You looked so worried. I wanted to comfort you, to tell you not to worry. I asked God to let me comfort you, but a voice spoke to me, like the voice of angel, assuring me that we would soon be together again. And here we are."

Marcus nodded, unable to speak, wiping his eyes with the sleeve of his tunic.

"When I saw you on the boat, you were praying. What were you praying for?" she asked.

He swallowed hard to relax his throat. "To find you safe," he said.

"I am safe, Marcus. Safe at last from the temptations of this world. I have finished my race."

"She has won her crown,"said Kimon.

"Not yet, Kimon," said Makrina. "Gaius couldn't do it. I knew he couldn't. He couldn't kill me, so he tricked them. He sentenced me to die, but he did not say how. They thought he was putting me to death when he was just letting me go."

"Gaius? I don't understand," said Marcus.

"Valerius Marcellinus. Don't you remember? You knew him in Rome."

"Governor of the province," said Kimon. "He was here a few days ago for Makrina's trial. It's all over now. Makrina confessed her faith bravely."

She closed her eyes. "Help him, Marcus. Help Gaius, if you can. He is not far from believing, but he has much to lose, much to give up in this world."

She opened her eyes again. "You now have much to lose, too, Marcus. Don't let it tie you to this life. There is freedom in poverty. That's a lesson I could only learn by losing you, Marcus. Not when I turned you away so many years ago—for that I did pridefully, not knowing what I was doing, not knowing what it would mean—but when I came back to find you married to Eugenia. Only then did I understand my loss."

"I waited for you, Makrina. I waited for years."

"I know you did, Marcus. I thank you for it. For your patience, God gave you Eugenia. You saved her, and I thank you for that. Take care of her, Marcus. Love her and show her the way of faith."

"I will," said Marcus. Eugenia patted his shoulder from behind.

"Mamma?"

"I'm here, Makrina," said Hilaria.

"Don't wait too long, as Pappa did. I want to see you in the next life. Don't give up on her, Kimon."

"I won't, Makrina. I won't," he said.

"Eugenia?"

"Yes, Makrina?"

Makrina smiled at her. "You have been greatly blessed. Take care of Marcus. Serve him faithfully and honor him as your head. And don't let life in the palace turn your eyes from the Cross. Your time will come. I'm only going on ahead of you. I shall see you again before long. Remember Christ when you remember me."

"I will," said Eugenia. Her voice was barely audible.

"Where are your children?" Makrina asked.

Theodora and Alexander were brought in. Makrina squeezed their little hands and told them to obey their parents. Then she thanked Nonna

and Vassa and finally Eulalia for their service and also asked their forgiveness, urging them to believe in Christ and accept his baptism.

"I'm tired now. I'm so tired. Kiss me, Kimon, and let me hear the Word
of God as I depart."

Kimon kissed Makrina's forehead, then took up the Gospel of John
and began to read of the resurrection of Lazarus, chanting from the words
of the Lord as he would in the public worship. One by one, they took their
leave with kisses and tears. Kimon kept reading:

> Verily, verily, I say unto you, except a corn of wheat fall into
> the ground and die, it abideth alone; but if it die, it bringeth
> forth much fruit. He that loveth his life shall lose it; and he
> that hateth his life in this world shall keep it unto life eternal.

Hearing these words, Makrina, the handmaiden of God, closed her
eyes and fell asleep in the Lord.

THE END

CPSIA information can be obtained at www.ICGtesting.com
Printed in the USA
LVOW12s1036260514

387280LV00022B/1617/P